ANA

LOUISVILLE

OHIO RIVER

GREEN R.

B

ELIZABETH?

GREENVILLE

MUNFORDVILLE

KENTUCKY

SCALE OF MILES   20

GLASGOW
BOWLING GREEN

PKINSVILLE

LOUISVILLE & NASHVILLE R.R.

CLARKSVILLE

ALMYRA

GALLATIN

CUMBERLAND RIVER

EDGE-FIELD

LEBANON

THE HERMITAGE

TENNESSEE

NASHVILLE

ANTIOCH

BRENTWOOD

LAVERGNE

SMYRNA

MURFREESBORO

SPARTA

KINGSTON

HOLLOW TREE GAP

WOOD

MILL CR.

FRANKLIN

HARPER'S

TRIUNE

STONE R.

WOODBURY

HILLSBOROUGH

THOMPSON STA.

COLLEGE GROVE

NASVILLE & CHATTANOOGA R.R.

SPRING HILL

RUTHERFORD CR.

McMINNVILLE

CHAPEL HILL

COLUMBIA

TENNESSEE RIVER

PHILADELPHIA

EASANT

SHELBYVILLE

MANCHESTER

ATHENS

FOUCHÉ SPRINGS

LEWISBURG

ALTAMONT

HILLSBOROUGH

CHARLESTO

LE

AMPBELLSVILLE

LYNNVILLE

TULLAHOMA

PELHAM

TRACY CITY

CEBURG

MULBERRY

BYRD'S MILL

HARRISON

CLEVELAND

RICHLAND CR.

PULASKI
FAYETTEVILLE

ELK R.

COWAN

CHATTANOOGA

JASPER

KINGS HILL

ELKTON

COWAN PASS

REED'S BR.

RINGGOLD

SUGAR R.

BRIDGEPORT

ROSSVILLE

TUNNEL HILL
THEOFORD FORD

SULFUR SPR CR.

STEVENSON

SNODGRASS HILL

CHICKAMAUGA

DALTON
CRAWFISH SPRING

RENCE

MEMPHIS & CHARLESTON R.R.

LOOKOUT MT.

LAFAYETTE

NBRIDGE

ATHENS

McDONALD'S STA.

CAPERTON'S FERRY

McLEMORE'S COVE

LEE AND GORDON'S MILL

RTLAND

HUNTSVILLE

ALPINE

CHATTOOGA

WESTERN & ATLANTIC R.R.

BIA

DECATUR

TENNESSEE

RIVER

SUMMERVILLE

MOULTON

SOMERVILLE

GUNTERSVILLE

ROME

KINGSTON

DAYS GAP

SAND MT.

GAYLESVILLE

CEDAR BLUFF

LAWRENCE

ABAMA

BROOKVILLE

BLACK CR.

BLOUNT'S PLANTATION

MULBERRY FORK

BLOUNTSVILLE

TURKEYTOWN

GADSDEN

ATLANTA

JASPER

GEORGIA

FIGHTIN' WITH FORREST

a novel
by

CHARLES GORDON YEAGER

PELICAN PUBLISHING COMPANY
GRETNA 1995

First published by
Dixie Publishing Company, 1987

Pelican Publishing Company Edition, 1988
Second printing, 1995

ISBN 0-88289-728-4

Library of Congress
Card Catalog Number
87-071837

Manufactured in the United States of America
Published by Pelican Publishing Company, Inc.
1101 Monroe Street, Gretna, Louisiana 70053

"War means fightin', an' fightin' means killin'."
—Nathan Bedford Forrest
Lieutenant General, CSA

"I doubt if any commander since the days of the lion-hearted Richard killed as many enemies with his own hands as Forrest."
—Richard Taylor
Lieutenant General, CSA

"Forrest's capacity for war seemed only to be limited by the opportunities for its display."
—Pierre G. T. Beauregard
General, CSA

PREFACE

First, let me say that I am not a writer in the classic sense; I am just a man trying to tell a story. This book lacks clever metaphors, beautiful or witty similes, and glowing descriptions of the grandeur of sunsets or the varied colors of autumn. Neither will there be found in it references to mythology, poetry, or quotations from the works of philosophers or erudite men. It is a story told with few embellishments, written in the simplest, plainest language I could muster. If called upon to identify the literary style, I should probably classify it as modern business letter.

How and why the book has been written require explanation. A few years ago, one of my granddaughters gave me a copy of *The Wartime Papers of R. E. Lee* which I found myself studying rather than only reading. The book kindled a long dormant interest in the Civil War. Most of my reading at first centered around the Army of Northern Virginia, in which my grandfather served for almost four years as a private soldier in the Alabama Eleventh infantry. I ran across a few brief but highly complimentary references to Lieutenant General Nathan Bedford Forrest, who fought in what was known as the West. These caused me to read one of his several biographies, and this amazing man captured my attention to the point that I read everything I could find about him. With this interest in Forrest came a compulsion to retell his story; for although he was a popular and dashing hero to the people of the South during the Civil War and for many years afterward, awareness of him has diminished since the turn of the century to the point that he is relatively unknown today. I hope this book will change that.

Just before the war ended, Forrest suffered the only military defeat in which he commanded all of the Confederate forces engaged; and this occurred in the defense of Selma, Alabama, a small industrial city twenty-eight miles southeast of my home town, Marion. After cutting his way through the troops of Major General James H. Wilson, which had him backed up against the Alabama River at Selma, it was to

Marion that Forrest went to reassemble his scattered forces and lick his wounds. This is a story of two young men from the vicinity of Marion who served with him. It is about their lives, their families, their loves, their conflicts, and their own experiences in the war, all intertwined with Forrest's military exploits.

Born in the backwoods of a poor, pioneer family, and without the benefit of formal education, Forrest fought his way up and prospered as a trader in cattle, horses, merchandise, slaves, and real estate. He then became a successful planter in Mississippi; and when the Civil War came, he volunteered as a private but was subsequently commissioned and rose to the rank of lieutenant general. General Wolseley, Commander-in-Chief of the British army and a student of the Civil War, wrote of him: "Forrest had no knowledge of military science nor military history to teach him how he should act, what objective he should aim at, and what plans he should make to secure it. He was entirely ignorant of what the generals in previous wars had done under similar circumstances. What he lacked in book lore was, to a great extent, compensated for by the soundness of his judgment upon all occasions, and by his power of thinking and reasoning with great rapidity under fire, and under all circumstances of surrounding peril or of great mental or bodily fatigue. Panic found no resting-place in that calm brain of his, and no danger, no risk appalled that dauntless spirit. Inspired with true military instincts, he was verily nature's soldier."

General Joseph E. Johnston, CSA, named Forrest as the greatest soldier of the war; and Major General William Tecumseh Sherman, USA, called him "That devil Forrest" and once said that they must get Forrest if it cost 10,000 men and bankrupted the United States treasury. Following the war, he said: "After all, I think Forrest was the most remarkable man our Civil War produced on either side. To my mind he was uneducated, while Jackson and Sheridan and other brilliant leaders were soldiers by profession. He had never read a military book in his life, knew nothing about tactics, could not even drill a company, but he had a genius for strategy which was original, and to me incomprehensible. There was no theory or art of war by which I could calculate with any degree of certainty what Forrest was up to. He seemed always to know what I was doing or intended to do, while I am free to confess, I could never tell or form any satisfactory idea of what he was trying to accomplish."

Forrest had an undying devotion to the cause of the Confederacy to which he subordinated his fortune, his personal ambition, and his life. He looked for and demanded the same dedication from others. Every soldier under him knew that he was expected to fight to the death if necessary; and he knew, also, that Forrest had no respect nor mercy for a coward. It was the general's order to his officers to shoot any man who wouldn't fight, and he emphasized this by his own actions.

In battle Forrest was an aggressive fighter who took the initiative whenever possible. He soon learned that the excitement of an advance inspired his men and gave them courage as they charged together screaming the Rebel yell, while standing still in the open waiting for a charge could steal the grit from the staunchest of men. He was always at the front and close enough for the naked eye to see what his opponents were doing. As the opposing lines were closing, he took his place at the skirmish line, almost always on his horse, and moved from point to point in the battle wherever the line was hardest pressed.

His method of warfare was a dangerous business. He was wounded six times, and his uniform was often riddled by bullets. Twenty-nine horses were shot from under him; and in close hand-to-hand combat, he is known to have taken down at least thirty of the enemy.

Early in the war, Forrest realized that men on horseback were at a decided disadvantage in combat with soldiers on foot. Mounted men could not fire as accurately, nor were they able to reload their guns as quickly as men on the ground. A trooper sitting on a horse made a good target, while the man on foot could take advantage of all possible cover and means to steady his aim. The cavalry leader adopted the infantry method of fighting, using his horses primarily for rapidly transporting his troops. There have been claims that the German Panzer units during World War II adopted their tactics from him; and there is a man in Baldwyn, Mississippi, who alleges that he met in the 1930's a German named Rommel who came to visit the Brice's Cross Roads battlefield. Forrest also learned that the saber was not the most effective weapon at close quarters and discarded that weapon for his men. His troopers were armed with six-shooter pistols, most of them carrying two and some as many as four, for close work. They also carried rifles for more distant fighting.

Forrest employed artillery as aggressively as he fought. Instead of placing his guns in a strategic, well guarded position removed, for safety of the weapons, from the immediate fighting area, he used them almost like shotguns, taking them right up to the enemy lines and firing their double shot canister at short range. According to Colonel D. C. Kelley, this was considered madness by the ordinary commander; but the splendid results Forrest attained justified the risk. He loved his guns, and one of his favorite places during a battle was with the artillery.

Use of the flank movement occurred to Forrest in the first action in which he was engaged, although it is doubtful that he then knew the military terminology for such a maneuver. This became his stock in trade; and his tactics were to throw out skirmishers, dismounted, who would engage the enemy from the front and hold their attention. He used these troops in such a way as to keep the enemy in constant expectation of an attack. Meanwhile, having picked out a portion of his men, he would send them, under cover of timber or high ground, to gain the rear and flank of the opposing forces. The moment he saw any alarm or confusion in the enemy ranks, or as soon as firing from the flanking column was heard, he would charge in front with every available soldier. He did not weaken his fighting strength by holding a part of his men in reserve.

If the enemy wavered or retreated, Forrest was relentless in pursuit. Like "Stonewall" Jackson, he firmly believed that a retreating enemy, if hit quickly and hard, could easily be turned into a routed enemy. Troops put to rout are out of control and disorganized, often throwing away their weapons in order to run faster. They can be easily killed or captured with little risk to the pursuers, and Forrest always pushed hard after them.

One of Forrest's favorite maxims was, "War means fightin', an' fightin' means killin'." I first used this as the title of this book, but later shortened it, and then shortened it again to *Fightin' with Forrest*. He knew that campaigns could not be conducted or battles fought without casualties, but he could not tolerate the unnecessary or useless loss of his men. When they went down, he wanted some purpose or military gain from it.

The duty of a commanding officer is to so direct, control, and influence the soldiers who must do the fighting that he can get the most out of them. I think no commander on either side in the Civil War got more fighting, marching, or work out of the men under him than did Forrest, not even "Stonewall" Jackson with his "foot cavalry." He accomplished this because he never asked them to do anything he would not do himself; and whatever their lot, he shared it.

With the men he led, strict discipline was not exercised; yet under the influence of one who inspired the timid with courage and the brave with the spirit of emulation, they always fought like trained veterans. The battle at Brice's Cross Roads is an example of what men can do under such leadership. From ten in the morning until almost five in the afternoon, almost without cessation of firing, Forrest's men stood up in the blazing summer heat against twice their number of Federal troops, thoroughly well armed and equipped, and finally drove them from the field in wild disorder.

What kind of person was this fighter? He has been described as a kindly man whose eyes would often fill with tears unashamedly as he talked with his wounded after a battle, but he was also capable of unremorsefully shooting one of his men for running from the enemy. He was a good conversationalist with a soft, pleasant voice; and his eyes twinkled when he spoke. He had a good sense of humor, but was a highly moral man who was offended by a smutty story. Obscene and vulgar words were not a part of his normal conversation. He was grave and dignified, except in anger; then, he was terrible to behold. He had a violent temper, and in paroxysms of rage or the excitement of a fight, he was a different man. His naturally sallow complexion changed completely; the capillaries became so greatly engorged with blood that the skin of his face took on a scarlet hue. The blood vessels of his eyes had the same congestion, giving him an expression of savageness which could not be misunderstood. Everything suggestive of kindly feeling or tenderness vanished. His soft voice became harsh, husky, and metallic in tone and loud enough to be heard above the roar of battle. At such times, his language was often profane and abusive, especially when angry; yet in moments of rage or excitement, his perception became more acute. Nothing seemed to escape his glance, and each emergency or change in the situation was met with promptness and nearly always with success. He was deeply devoted to both his wife and his mother; and a word from either, even when his temper was at the highest, would bring him quickly under control.

An attempt has been made to keep the events as historically accurate as possible. There are times, however, where I have knowingly digressed from the facts; and such a deviation has usually occurred when I have substituted a fictional character for an actual person in a particular situation. In these instances, credit has been given to the real persons by numbered references to ''Notes and Comments'' appearing at the end of the book, according to chapter.

Having spent three and a half years in the U. S. Navy during World War II, I am aware that men thrown together in wholly male units develop the foul habit of using rough, vulgar, and profane language. I do not believe this is needed to give a story realism or that sex and off-color stories are required to attract readers. I hope I have not erred in judgment, for this work contains only mild expletives, used for emphasis, and only a few slightly off-color stories, one of which was included solely to show a facet of Forrest's character.

To give the story realism, Southern dialects have been used; and I make this plural because the dialects differ among people. Even the individual is not consistent in the way he talks. He may know the correct way to express himself, and at times will do so; but more often than not he will resort to his careless or lazy way of speaking. I overdid this at first, and it made tedious reading; so I removed a great part of it from the manuscript. Many of the anecdotes and events involving Forrest personally have been related by educated men who quoted the general as they, themselves, would have spoken. I have changed this and have him speak as I believe he would have expressed himself. He was an uneducated man who butchered English grammar and often used the backwoods, pioneer vernacular of his youth; yet he was very effective in communicating what he wished to say both orally and in writing. Forrest has been quoted as saying, "To get there first with the most." He has also been quoted, "To git there fustess with the mostess." I do not believe he said either. From what I know of his background and life, he probably said, "Tuh git theah fust with thuh mos'"; but this is difficult to read, especially if there is a lot of it; so I have greatly modified the dialects throughout the book.

I have made another change in the manuscript—for the benefit of the average reader, I have removed material, including details of some of the battles and raids, from the story itself and placed this in the "Notes and Comments," where it is still available for the true Civil War buff.

Now let me turn to a more important matter, the acknowledgment of where credits are due. John Allen Wyeth is regarded as one of the most accurate and thorough of those who have written about Forrest. His biography, *The Life of General Nathan Bedford Forrest*, published by Harper and Brothers (now Harper & Row, Publishers, Inc.), has been my principal source of information for Forrest's military exploits and for material and anecdotes establishing the man's character, as it has been for others; but I have referred frequently to *The Campaigns of Lieut.-General N. B. Forrest and of Forrest's Cavalry* by General Thomas Jordan and John B. Pryor, *General Forrest* by Captain J. Harvey Mathes, and *Personal Recollections and Experiences in the Confederate Army by an Old Johnnie* by Captain James Dinkins. I have tried to stay with Wyeth's accounts of events as much as possible, but have often turned to other sources for details or more logical recordings of particular incidents; however, I am much indebted to Wyeth, who spent many years of research and study in amassing the material from which I have been able to draw so freely.

In my effort to portray the historical events accurately and in detail, my research has not been limited to the volumes mentioned; but it has included visits to battlefields and many writings of the battles and campaigns covered in this work and of the weapons and equipment used during the war. From this I have learned one thing about written history—it is not exact. There are too many factors such as loyalties, prejudices, egotism, protection of reputations, or just plain error or lack of information which give variations in the recording of any happening.

I have endeavored to make this novel unbiased; and in presenting Forrest, I have done so objectively, showing both his good and bad traits. The events and statistics are as accurate as I could determine them, so the reader can draw his own conclusions as to the man's character and of his ability as a soldier and leader of men.

On the endleafs at the front and back of the book, for ready reference, are maps which contain nearly all of the places mentioned in the work. The one at the front covers the area from Louisville, Kentucky, southward, and the one at the back covers the area northward from Cahawba, Alabama. The covered areas overlap, so most places of interest to the reader can be found on either map.

The early setting of the story is in and near the Black Belt section of Alabama. This belt extends eastward from the state of Mississippi across the lower central portion of Alabama to a point just beyond Montgomery. Approximately fifty miles in width, it is made up primarily of fertile, clayey, limy soils. Generally it is flat in nature with many open, unforested areas; and because of this, the local people know it as the prairies. The rich soils of the Black Belt make it highly productive in the raising of corn and cotton, especially cotton. By the middle of the nineteenth century it has become the locale for large plantations owned by slaveholders who have prospered here. The town of Marion lies just above the northern rim of the belt in central Alabama. A few miles south of the town are the rich prairies inhabited in 1853 mostly by planter families and their slaves. To the north is the hill country. Here much of the soil is made up principally of red clay, and is only as fertile as the layer of topsoil above it. In places this is rather thin. This hilly country is highly forested and has been settled mainly by small farmers. Few of them own slaves, so the farms are usually modest enterprises where the farmers and their families perform most of the labor. They make a living through hard work, thriftiness, and self-sufficiency; but few acquire wealth in these hills.

At this time, Marion is a quiet little town of 1,300 white people and 3,000 slaves and is the county seat of Perry County in which it is centrally located. It lies five miles west of the Cahaba River (once spelled Cahawba) which originates in the area of small mountains northeast of Elyton (now known as Birmingham) and flows southward to join the Alabama River about eight miles southwest of Selma. At that river junction lies Cahawba, the first official capitol of Alabama. Although there had been previous meetings of state officials at Huntsville, Alabama, Cahawba was selected as the seat of the new state's government because of its central location. Marion and Cahawba are connected by a railroad which, at Marion Junction, fourteen miles south of Marion, crosses the main line running between Selma and Vicksburg, Mississippi. Nineteen miles west of Marion is Greensboro, the county seat of Hale County. Twenty miles north is the village of Brent; and less than two miles beyond that, across the Cahaba River, is Centreville, the county seat of Bibb County. To the southeast, twenty-eight miles away, is the small industrial city of Selma, the county seat of Dallas County.

Marion has become an educational center for the state. The Marion Female Seminary, established in 1836, provides education for girls and young ladies mostly at the primary and secondary levels, with a few college courses. Judson Female Institute, founded in 1839 by Milo P. Jewett with the assistance of General E. D. King, a prairie planter, is one of the first institutions in the United States to educate young ladies principally at the college level. Howard College, founded in 1842, provides education at both secondary and college levels for young men. Although Judson Female Institute is only fourteen years old and Howard College just eleven, the schools have become well enough known to attract students from as far away as the adjoining states.

Now, at last, we are ready to get on with the story.

DEDICATION

This book is affectionately dedicated to my Sara, who, to me, is, and always will be, the epitome of the lovely, gracious, Southern lady.

APPRECIATION

It is not possible to mention all who have helped and encouraged me in writing this book, but I do especially want to thank the following: my cousin, Thomas B. Yeager, for the historical material about Marion, Alabama; Patricia "Pat" Carr and my cousin, Pierce Bruce, for reviewing and screening the first draft of the manuscript; Carter Perkins for his encouraging comments at the time I was about ready "to throw in the towel"; my "Ol' Buddy," J. Arthur "Jake" Turner, Jr., for his candid and helpful suggestions; Donna Sarber for her patience and understanding in the final preparation of the manuscript for typesetting; Caroline Raboy, "Chuck" and Helen King, and Marcia Scott for proofreading it; those employees at Rose Printing Company who did everything possible to help a neophyte writer publish his work; and my wife, Sara, for putting up with me during the period, almost five years, that I worked on this project.

Cally wants to thank my golfing and gin-playing friends at "Silver Lake" for some of his stories and to explain that he dared not repeat others, although they were equally as good, or better.

CONTENTS

Chapter 1

The Beginning of a Friendship

In Central Alabama, the road from Marion to Selma runs eastward; and about three-quarters of a mile after crossing the Cahaba River, it turns sharply to the south for two miles before turning again eastward to Perryville, where it joins the road from Centreville to Selma. At the first turn a smaller, less travelled road leads eastward to Plantersville. The home of John Randolph Rushton and his family lies at the junction of these two roads.[1] The house sits about a hundred yards east of the main road and a slightly greater distance south of the smaller road. It faces west, and a white board fence runs for about six hundred feet along the side of each road. On a post by the gate for the driveway leading to the house is a sign reading, ''PRAIRIE'S EDGE.'' This is an apt name, for the plantation lies at the very northern edge of the Black Belt; in fact, some of the Rushton holdings extend into the hill country north of the Plantersville road.

The house is large; but it is not the pretentious, columned mansion so often associated with the Southern plantation of this period. The original house was a two-storied, rectangular building with a veranda at both levels running fully across its fifty-five-foot front. It was built of rough-sawed wood, painted white; and the upper porch and its roof are supported by square, solid, wooden posts about ten inches thick. To the original structure has been added a single-storied brick wing on both the north and south sides. The house is shaded by three large water oaks, in a line and equally spaced, across its front. The drive leading from the gate passes between rows of large pecan trees before it circles the center oak in front of the house.

At about four o'clock one Saturday afternoon in July 1853, John Rushton was sitting in a wheeled chair near the south end of the lower veranda in a spot well shaded by one of the oaks. He is a man of only thirty-five years, but his graying hair and lined face make him look older. Around the south end of the house, mounted on a small but beautifully conformed roan mare, rode a young boy. In his right hand and under his arm, he possessively clutched a large and very unusual gun, an English made Whitworth rifle.[2] It is a heavy gun, too much so for a boy his size, but it is one of the best available and had been his father's gift when he celebrated his twelfth birthday the previous day. Pulling his horse up near where his father was sitting, the boy said, "She's a real beaut, Daddy."

"I hope you are ready for this, Randy—I don't like your going out alone with no more training and instruction than you've had with that gun."

"May Jason go with me?"

"No. How about Golan?"

"I'll be all right by myself," Randy replied, nudging the mare with his heels.

As the horse moved off, the father said, "Be careful, Son, and remember what I told you about the gun."

"Don't worry, I'll remember."

Once through the gate, he turned right, and then turned right again when he reached the road at the corner of the fence. After travelling about half a mile, he came to another small road leading northeastward into the hills. Taking this road, he continued another mile until he came to a grove of oak, black gum, and hickory on his right. Here he turned off the road and moved about an eighth of a mile into the trees before he stopped, got down from his horse, and tied her to a tree.

From a leather box on a belt around his waist he took a short false muzzle with four pins at one end and attached it to the end of the rifle barrel by fitting the pins into holes which had been drilled to receive them. He next took from the box a hexagonal cartridge enclosed in light cardboard with a small slip of paper at one end. Barely inserting this end of the cartridge into the muzzle extension, he removed the slip of paper, freeing the powder, some of which trickled down the hexagonal bore of the barrel. He then brought out a metal bullet starter which was placed over the barrel extension; and with a sharp blow with the heel of his hand against a plunger, he drove the bullet with the remaining powder and an oiled wad into the barrel. Extracting the ramrod from its place beneath the barrel, the boy rammed the charge and bullet home. He removed the muzzle extension, returned the ramrod to its holder, inserted a percussion cap in the nipple of the gun, and now had his weapon ready for firing.

Slowly and carefully he moved to the edge of a circular clearing about a hundred yards in diameter. Staying back in the shadows, he took position by the trunk of a tree and waited. He knew that it wouldn't be long—he had been here twice before watching them, and each time the deer had come out of the opposite wood into the open area about this hour. After no more than fifteen minutes, he spotted a slight movement in the trees across the clearing and felt a thrill of excitement which only a hunter knows as he anxiously peered into the wood in front of him. He watched as they slowly emerged—first a doe, then a young deer which had lost its fawn spots, another doe followed by her offspring, and finally a buck with a beautiful spread of antlers. Looking nervously all around them, the deer moved cautiously out into the open and began to graze, glancing up frequently to scan the surrounding area.

Randy still did not stir, standing fixedly beside the tree. It was not until the buck turned its side to him that he moved. Slowly he raised the gun and brought the butt to his shoulder. He held the barrel against the trunk of the tree for support, carefully cocked the gun, and, taking aim, pulled the trigger. In his excitement, however, he failed to squeeze the trigger slowly as his father had shown him; and the jerky movement of his hand was enough to pull the none too steady rifle off target.

The explosion of the gun and the sound of the bullet passing by and on into the trees behind them startled the deer. The buck whirled and, with a leap, started back to the wood from which he had come. From off to his right, Randy heard a second shot; the buck jerked in midair and tumbled headlong to the ground where he struggled briefly and then lay still.

Randy rushed out into the open, gun in hand; and over to his right, back in the shadow of the trees, he saw a youth in homespun clothes rapidly reloading a gun.

"What a shot! What a beautiful shot!" he cried. "Come on—let's see if he's dead."

"Load your gun fust," a firm voice commanded.

Randy stopped without question and quickly began reloading his rifle. The other boy, his gun now ready to fire, came from the shadows to join him and quietly watched with curious interest the loading of the unusual gun until it was completed and the ramrod replaced.

Finished with his task, Randy looked closely for the first time at the other boy. Beneath a straw hat, rather long, light brown hair outlined a tanned face with sharp, well defined features. He was barefooted; and, without shoes, he was still almost six inches taller than Randy, who was above normal height for a boy his age. He was dressed in a recently made homespun shirt, and his pants were of the same fabric but had obviously seen many washings. The pants showed two right angle tears which had been neatly darned, and the boy had just about outgrown the trousers as the bottoms of the legs were at least six inches above his feet.

They were held up by homemade suspenders which crossed in the back. He wore a belt, but it was only to carry the sheath for a Bowie knife which seemed out of proportion to its owner. It was the youth's eyes, however, which quickly caught the observer's attention. Blue in color, they seemed to be piercing and unlikely to miss much falling within their range; yet they had a softness to them as though they belonged to a person who would laugh quickly and often. Randy was certain the boy was older than he, but just how much he was not sure—there was an appearance of strength and maturity about him which belied his youthful face.

Thrusting out his right hand, he said, "I'm Randy Rushton. I live over on the main road."

Hesitantly, the taller boy took the hand; but when he did, it was with a firm and friendly grip. "I know who you be. I've seen you before with your pa over't Marion. I'm Francis McCord, but ever'body calls me Buck. We live up the road a piece, about halfa mile. Let's take a look at the deer."

As they went toward the fallen animal, Randy noticed Buck was carrying his gun pointing downward with the left hand under the barrel and the right hand close to the trigger with the thumb resting on the hammer ready to cock it. He did the same.

Buck spoke again. "Didn' aim to sound bossy back there, but Pa always says don't never go to no downed critter 'thout bein' ready to shoot. Never know what you might find."

"That sounds like good advice."

"Believe it."

As they approached the deer, Buck moved to the left so that he came up to the animal from its back and rear. Seeing no sign of life, he firmly shook the animal with his foot. Randy, who had hung back as an observer, made mental note of the care Buck had taken to insure he would be clear of the animal's antlers and hooves in case it made a sudden move.

"Well, I guess he's dead all right. We gotta bleed an' gut 'im, but fust we gotta hang 'im. Don't s'pose you gotta rope on your hoss?"

"No, I don't."

"Well, let's git to work"; and with that, Buck found a small tree from which he cut a stick about an inch thick. Piercing a hole between the bone and large tendon, just above the hock of each of the deer's hind legs, he pushed the stick through them. Looking over at Randy, he said, "I gen'ally puts this just above the hoofs, but this is a big one; an' without a rope, we'll have trouble raisin' 'im high enough."

His next step was to find a large tree limb with a "Y" which would be at the right height for hanging the animal. He located one in a nearby oak and said to Randy, "You git one end of the stick, an' I'll git t'other."

After they dragged the animal beneath the "Y," Buck said, "We've gotta lift this booger an' hang 'im by layin' this stick across the forks of that 'Y.' Let me git my end fust—then I'll help with yours."

It was a struggle, but they finally had the deer hanging. Buck got out his knife and cut the animal's jugular vein, stepping back to avoid the flowing blood. When the deer's throat was cut, Randy, who had been quietly watching, made a slight, involuntary sound and paled considerably at the sight of the blood; but it was the disemboweling which really got to him. When Buck slit open the animal's abdominal area and began cleaning out the cavity, Randy felt the blood drain from his head; and a feeling of nausea and dizziness swept over him. He would have toppled over had he not leaned against a nearby tree.

Buck happened to turn and see this reaction. Grinning, he asked, "Y'all right?"

"Yes, sure."

"Wanta do this?"

Swallowing with considerable difficulty, Randy replied, "No thanks; you're doing fine—just fine."

"Why don'tcha go git your hoss while I finish up here?" Buck asked in sympathy for the other's feelings. Randy, grateful for the suggestion, left at once; but he took his time in getting back with the mare. By then he had fairly well recovered, and the deer had been cleaned out. Trying to stay clear of the viscera on the ground and avoid looking at it, he helped Buck lower the deer and then brought his horse over to the carcass.

"We'll lay 'im 'cross the back of your hoss, an' you hold 'im there while I git some vines to tie 'im so he won't fall off."

Buck disappeared into the trees, returning shortly with some wild grape vines which he used to fasten the deer's legs underneath the horse's belly. "He's got a real good rack, an' the head'll make a nice mountin' if you stuff it. There's a fella named Smalley who's good at it. He lives over by Jug Miller."

"Wait a minute! This isn't my deer—you're the one who killed it."

"But I shot 'im for you. When you missed, I knowed you wouldn' git another shot, so I dropped 'im for you."

"I can't take your deer!"

"Well, I can't take 'im. Pa don't believe in shootin' nothin' that ain't doin' no harm or ain't needed for food. Now this deer wasn't botherin' nobody; an' we don't need 'im for eatin', 'cause Pa just killed one yestiddy. He wouldn' like it if I come home with another'n.''

"Why don't we share it?"

"I'd ruther not."

"Well, Daddy does love venison, and we don't have it very often since he doesn't hunt anymore; but I really don't feel right about taking your deer."

"Forgit it. I'm just sorry you missed 'im."

"Well, it's getting late; and I had better get going," Randy said. He retrieved his gun and climbed into the saddle. He looked down at Buck to say goodbye but realized he didn't want to leave—there seemed to be something drawing him to the other boy.

"I appreciate the deer," he continued, "but most of all, thank you for your help. If I had killed it, I wouldn't have known what to do with him." Pausing briefly, he impulsively added, "I'd sure like to have you for a friend."

This last remark caught Buck by surprise; but he, too, felt an unseen bond pulling him toward the smaller boy. After a moment's hesitation, he replied, "Me, too."

"Maybe we could go hunting together, or something," Randy said eagerly.

"My pa's a great believer in work. I've got reg'lar chores 'most ever' day, an' then I help Pa a lot; but I gen'ally has ever' Saturday evenin' an' ever' Sunday after church meetin' an' dinner for myself, to do as I please."

Randy had no difficulty in understanding that Buck meant he had Saturday and Sunday afternoons free; most of the people he knew referred to afternoon as "evening," and everyone had "dinner" in the middle of the day. He jumped at the opening, "How about next Saturday, right after dinner? We could meet at this place."

"I'll be here."

The rider had moved off a short distance when Buck called, "Hey, Randy!" Without reining in his horse, Randy turned in the saddle and looked back.

A grinning Buck said, "Don't forget to skin that critter before you eat 'im."

"Maybe I should skin you instead."

"Don't think you got the stomach for it," Buck responded; and both boys laughing, with a final wave, headed for home.

Buck was happy and in good spirits as he came out of the wood onto the road within sight of his home. He remembered his gun was loaded, and he had to clean it. Picking out a small twig at the top of a tree, he took careful aim, fired at it, and was pleased to see the twig fall. Smiling happily, he turned toward home again.

The house was not large like that of the Rushtons; neither was it a small one, but a fine home according to the standards of the hill people with whom Buck's family associated. Built only eight years before upon the insistence of his mother, who wanted something better than a dog-run log cabin, it was square in shape, of one story, with a roof which came to a point over the center of the house and sloped down to the four sides. There was a porch across the front covered by a shed-type roof. The house, painted white, sat back about fifty feet from the road; and there was a picket fence enclosing the front yard, which was actually his mother's flower garden. There was no grass in the yard—his mother wouldn't tolerate it; but it was filled with bushes which flowered in season, various plants she had rooted from cuttings, and many flowers which she grew each year from seed carefully selected and saved from the best blossoms of the previous year. Both the house and the flower garden were well kept.

Buck came to the house whistling, trying to imitate, with some success, a mocking bird singing in a nearby tree. As he passed through the front door, he entered a twelve-foot-wide center hall which ran from the front to the back of the house. The rear section of the hall served as the dining room. In the front portion, there were several chairs and a washstand, complete with bowl, pitcher, and towels. This section of the hall served as the family sitting area when the weather was not cold enough to require a fire. To the right of the hall at the front was a bedroom; and the kitchen was at the back; separated from the bedroom by a large pantry which was entered from the kitchen. The bedroom on this side was for company; but it was seldom used, and it held his mother's spinning wheel and a small loom with their accessories. It was here that she made the homespun which served so many purposes for the family. On the left of the hall were two bedrooms separated by a large closet which could be entered from either of them. The front bedroom was larger than the other and was that of his parents. It had a large fireplace and served as the sitting room when the weather required a fire. Buck had the smaller bedroom on this side. There was a porch across the back like the one in front, except one end of it had been enclosed to make a storeroom.

"I'm home," Buck called and headed for the storeroom for the patches and oil needed to clean his rifle. As he passed through the sitting area, his mother answered, "I'm in the kitchen."

Buck got the items needed and went to the kitchen. He started to sit down in one of the several chairs there; but his mother, who was at the table in the center of the room finishing up the canning of some beans he had gathered from the vegetable garden that morning, interrupted with, "Just a minute, Young Man; I ain't had no hug today."

"Aw, Ma," he protested, but he went willingly to her outstretched arms and held her tightly. She was tall for a woman, almost seven inches above five feet. She was somewhat heavy, having a large frame and appearing to be slightly plump; but she was not fat. She looked like what she was, a strong person who would thrive on hard work. Like Buck's, her eyes were blue; but they lacked the piercing quality of his. Her facial features were somewhat on the coarse side; but her full lips, like her eyes, would be quick to smile. She was not a beautiful woman, nor was she homely; anyone looking at her would know this was a good woman, for great strength of character showed in her face. What no one knew except her husband, and to some extent Buck, was that she was an excellent manager with very good judgment in business matters. Her husband's success in acquiring land, farm stock, and other assets was due in great part to the sage advice and suggestions she had given him.

Buck liked it in his mother's arms and hoped he would never grow too old or too big for it. His thoughts were interrupted by the sound of footsteps on the back porch and a voice at the door saying, "Can I git in on some of that?"

Buck released his mother and, looking at his father standing in the door with a bucket of milk in his hand, asked with a grin, "You wanta hug me or her?"

"Not you by a long shot, Young Fellow." He walked over to the table where he placed the milk pail and then kissed his wife gently on the forehead and gave her a friendly squeeze. He stood six feet three inches tall, and weighed approximately two hundred twenty pounds. Wide-shouldered and muscular, he did not appear to have an ounce of fat on him. He was an exceptionally large man at a time when the average man was rather small, but this open display of affection did not seem out of character for him. One look at his piercing gray eyes left no doubt where Buck had acquired that quality, to a lesser degree, in his. Except for a large mustache, he was clean shaven; his facial features were sharp and well defined. He was a handsome man in a rugged way; and despite his eyes, he appeared to be a kindly and gentle person.

Buck picked up his gun to clean it, but his father interposed, "I'll do that; go ahead an' git your chores."

Handing him the gun, Buck looked at the woodbox by the stove and saw it was full. He smiled at his father, said, "Mucha 'blige" and headed for the barn to water and feed the stock.

When he returned, the gun was no longer in sight; so Buck knew it had been cleaned, loaded, and returned to the gunrack over the back door of the dining room. His father was seated at the end of the kitchen table; his mother was busy at the stove. He took a chair at the side of the table and noticed the beans had been cleared from it and put away.

The father looked at his son and said, "Thought I heared shots from two guns a while ago."

"What makes you think there was two guns?"

"Well, the shots was too close together for one gun; an' the second gun was heavy'n the fust."

"I guess I learned you pretty good."

"The onliest thing you ever learnt me, Young'n, was to hold tight to my purse when you go to town with me."

"I think I overdone it."

They all laughed. "He got you that time, Cory," Buck's mother said. She enjoyed this banter between her menfolk.

"Le'me tell y'all about them shots," and with that Buck went into a detailed account of his meeting with Randy at the clearing.

When he finished his lengthy story, with occasional interruptions by his parents with questions, his mother said, "That Randy, he seems like a right nice boy. I don't think you oughta josh 'im about him bein' squeamish over the sight of blood. When I was a youngster, it usta bother me a heap to see an animal gutted. Fact is, I ain't so fond of it now."

"You never was much help killin' hogs," her husband said. They both laughed. Buck didn't know why; maybe something had happened once that was funny to them. They often laughed at things which didn't seem funny to him at all, but he didn't mind—they were entitled to their secrets.

Again his mother commented, "If you're goin' to be friends with that Rushton boy, I think you oughta bring 'im over here so's your folks can git to know 'im an' he can know us."

"Yes'm."

"If you wanta, when you see 'im next Saturd'y, ask 'im to come have dinner with us Sunday."

"Can I, Ma, can I? I'd like that."

"I'll fix somethin' special for y'all. But right now, you better wash up for supper." Buck got up and started for his room; but before he got to the dining room door, his mother added, "An' wash them dirty feet!"

As she watched him pass through the dining area toward his own room, she felt an emotional surge of love for, and pride in, this stripling boy. This was followed by a feeling of sadness as she recalled that he was all she had to show for the pain of four birthings. One had lived only a few weeks, and the other two had died soon after birth—blue babies, the doctor had called them. Shaking off this dark mood, she said, "I've got to finish that boy's britches—he's done outgrowed another pair."

Randy approached his home in an elated mood. As he passed through the gate and made his way up the driveway, he noticed his father was still on the veranda; but he had moved his wheeled chair closer to the door where the late afternoon shade from another of the water oaks now covered the area. The father could see there was something behind the saddle; but Randy was halfway from the gate before he was able to identify it as a deer. As soon as he did, he called, "Mother! Ellen! Come here, if you can!"

A young girl just under eleven years of age appeared promptly on the porch, soon followed by a woman in her mid-thirties. They went to the edge of the porch and waited for the horse and rider to reach them. All three stared in disbelief at the deer lying across the horse's back. Randy drew rein in front of them and with a big smile said, "Is there anybody here who can skin a deer?"

"I can't believe it—I just can't believe you killed a deer the first time you went hunting!" his mother said in amazement.

"I'm real proud of you, Son," his father said. "I know what it means to get your first deer—or any deer, for that matter. Take him on around back and get Golan to take care of it for you. Then come right back; we're anxious to hear all about this."

"He's got a fine set of antlers, Daddy; may I have the head stuffed and mounted? I understand there's a man over near Jug Miller's place who does this."

"I don't see why not; your mother can probably find a place to hang it."

"I'm not so sure," she responded. Looking at Randy, she continued, "It may wind up in your room."

"That's all right with me; that's where I want it," he replied. "If you hear a shot, I'll just be unloading my gun," and he moved off to the rear of the house.

Dismounting in the back yard, he held the horse's reins and emptied the gun into the air. Golan, a large negro man in his early forties, immediately appeared from his nearby workshop; and Randy turned the deer over to him with instructions to preserve the head and antlers for mounting and to treat the skin so that it could be used for a floor rug. A sullen negro boy of fifteen years came from the kitchen, which was in a separate building behind the main house, and took the reins from Randy.

"What do you think of the deer, Jason?" Randy asked in a friendly but excited way. Without replying, Jason moved off toward the stables leading the horse. Obviously chagrined, Randy watched him go.

"Don't pay no 'tention to dat boy, Massa Randy; he ain't got the manners of a billy goat," Golan said.

At a loss for words, Randy made no response and dejectedly made his way back to the front veranda where he found his parents and sister, all now seated in a semicircle facing an empty chair obviously meant for him. His gloom quickly vanished; and leaning his gun against the house, the young boy took his seat. He began excitedly to relate his afternoon experiences, except there was no mention made of his reaction to the bleeding and cleaning of the deer. When he came to the end of his story, he relaxed, sank back in his chair, and concluded, "So you see, I can't take credit for the deer."

"That was a very generous thing for the young man to do," commented his father.

His mother turned to her husband and asked, "This boy, would he be the son of that Mr. McCord with whom you have been trading horses for mules?"

"I'm sure he is; he has a boy a little older than Randy."

"These are ignorant hill folks. I'm not sure they are the kind of people with whom we want our children to associate."

A dejected Randy was about to reply when his father spoke up impatiently, "These are not ignorant people. They may lack academic education, but they know more about the everyday things essential to survival than you or I will ever know. It was from the McCords that I first learned about rotating crops and the value of planting peanuts to improve the soil. McCord is well versed in the basics of animal husbandry and raises the finest mules in this part of the country. You wouldn't believe the quality of the horses he is now producing; they are equal to ours. I firmly believe that if he, or his father who originally settled on their place, had used slaves, Cory McCord would be one of the wealthiest planters in this county today. As it is, he hasn't done badly. His father started many years ago with a hundred and sixty acres. They have bought any land adjoining them which came up for sale. McCord recently purchased another quarter section, and I believe his total holdings must be about a section and a half—more than half as much as the fifteen hundred acres we have at Prairie's Edge. I don't know of a more honest man or one with higher principles; his word is his bond, and he is respected by all who know him."

"How can he farm all of that land without slaves?" his wife asked.

"He doesn't. He believes that at least half of the land should be left in the natural state for wood, lumber, and 'God's critters an' varmi'ts,' as he calls them. Also, he leaves half of his arable land fallow each year. His father had a free negro sharecropper on the place, a man named James. Mr. McCord helped him buy his own place farther back in the hills, but now three of that negro's sons, with their families, are sharecropping with Cory McCord."

Carolyn Rushton remained silent. She knew better than to contend with her husband about something upon which he took such a strong position; besides, she had no rebuttal for the facts he presented; but really, a hill boy? She still was not certain of the position she should take—time will decide, she reasoned, time will decide.

Randy was relieved by his father's strong defense of the McCords, but he was puzzled about a man who bought land but not negroes. He asked, "Why doesn't Mr. McCord have slaves?"

"He, like his father before him, believes a man should not own another man."

Randy's sister Ellen, who up to this time had said nothing, hastily interposed with obvious anxiety, "Is he an ab'litioner?"

"Ab-o-li-tion-ist," corrected her mother.

"Ab-o-li-tion-ist," repeated Ellen slowly.

"No, Ellen, he isn't. He believes that owning slaves is a question of conscience which each person must settle for himself."

"Well, I'm certainly glad of that! I'd hate to have an ab-o-li-tion-ist living so close to us!" Ellen replied with relief.

Appearing to be talking to himself more than to the others, John Rushton continued, "It takes a man with a great deal of integrity to stand on a principle which is so contrary to his economic well being and progress. I'm not sure that deep down I do not agree with their position. Perhaps, if I had their integrity, I should do the same."

"Tush! That is a lot of nonsense, John Rushton!" emotionally responded his wife; and she continued with equal feeling, "There is not a master in this state, or the whole South, for that matter, who is kinder to, or better looks after the welfare of his people than you. And as for integrity, I know of no man who can hold a candle to you in that respect. I don't like to hear you talk this way."

Reaching over and patting his wife's hand, which was gripping rather firmly the arm of her rocker, John said with a gentle smile, "Sorry, Honey, didn't mean to upset you. I'm not about to free our slaves."

Jason suddenly and quietly came out of the house onto the porch, "Rose say supper'll be ready in fifteen minits," he said; and he turned and went back inside. John wondered how much of the conversation Jason may have heard and what effect, if any, it might have on the disgruntled slave.

"Well, I'd better get cleaned up for supper," Randy said; and retrieving his rifle, he went inside. His room was upstairs at the back and on the right side of the original building. As he washed up and changed clothes for supper, his thoughts dwelled on the conversation which had taken place on the porch. He had difficulty in understanding his mother at times. He loved her and knew she loved him, though she seldom openly showed affection to him or his sister. She was not very tolerant of the shortcomings of others, especially those who weren't members of the family. To her family she was unquestionably dedicated and loyal, wanting only the best and what was right for them; but she was a perfectionist who found it difficult to settle for anything which did not come up to her own high standards.

It was his fervent hope that she would not place a barrier in the way of his budding friendship with Buck. He was sure he could count on his father for support; his father was different, a very understanding man who judged another by his worth as a person rather than by his social position or the value of his worldly goods. It was good to have someone like this on his side.

Randy gave his hair a final brush, donned his coat, and went downstairs to join his family for supper.

Chapter II

Blood Brothers

Both boys had looked forward eagerly to their next meeting. Randy was pleased that his mother had offered no further objection and suspected that the matter may have been settled privately between his parents. When the long week finally passed, Buck was the first to reach the clearing.

This time he came by horse and, upon arrival, stayed back in the shade of the trees waiting. He was dressed as before, except his pants weren't as old or as short as the other ones, which his mother had retired to the rag bag. When he spotted Randy, he moved out to meet him.

"Howdy!" he called.

"Hello, there!" came the response.

Their horses drew together and stopped. "Whatcha wanta do?" Buck asked.

"I was hoping you would help me with my marksmanship; I missed that deer, you know. Before I forget, my parents told me to thank you for the deer and tell you how much they enjoyed it. I think Daddy ate it twice a day for about four days."

"They was welcome," Buck replied somewhat awkwardly; and then continued, "that is a queer gun of yours. What kind is it?"

"It's a Whitworth—made in England. Daddy gave it to me for my birthday last week, so I haven't had much practice with it. He claims it's one of the most accurate guns made, but you can't prove it by me. It has a telescopic sight, but Daddy said that it will be a while before I'm ready for that." He handed the gun to Buck for examination.

"This is some gun! Never seen nothin' like it."

"It shoots a six sided bullet. The bore doesn't go straight in; it turns as it goes down the barrel. Daddy says this makes the bullet spin and fly more accurately and farther."

Returning the gun, Buck said, "It's kinda heavy. Till you grow some more, you better rest it on somethin' when you aim it."

14

"I know, but Daddy says I'll grow to it in time. What kind of gun do you have?"

"It's a Model 1841 that's been rifled. Some calls it the Mississippi rifle. Let's go over to the river. There's a gravel bar on t'other side that's got a good bank to shoot into. It's a good place to go swimmin', too."

"Sounds all right to me," Randy replied without conviction. He wasn't sure about the swimming; he had never been swimming and didn't know how. He was glad his mother wasn't here; she would have put a stop to his going.

Together they moved off through the wood to the road. Reaching that, they went at a trot to the main road and then straight ahead toward the river. Randy was impressed with the fine and easy gait of the buckskin gelding the other boy was riding. The horse looked as if it may have come from the Rushton stables. As they moved along the road, they passed the rich bottom land on the left, a part of Prairie's Edge, where the green corn was already higher than Buck's head. About a quarter of a mile from the river, Randy challenged, "Race you, on the count of three, to this end of the bridge."

"You're on!" came Buck's eager reply as he brought the head of his horse even with that of Randy's roan.

"One—two—THREE!" Randy counted; and at the last count, both boys put heels to their horses and raced for the bridge, urging their mounts with shouts and by vigorous prodding with their feet. To Randy's surprise, it wasn't much of a race; the larger horse reached the bridge three lengths in front of his mare. They slowed to a trot and continued across the bridge.

As he drew alongside Buck, Randy said, "I can't believe you beat me like that; I know my horse is smaller, but she's fast for a short distance. I've run her against some pretty good horses, and she's always held her own. Did y'all raise him, or is he one your father got from Daddy?"

"We raised 'im. He's out of a mare Pa got over't Plantersville that was bred with a stud he got from your pa. Don't think there's a hoss in this county that can outrun 'im, not even Pa's stallion."

"I can believe that. What's his name?"

"Skin. What's yours?"

"Roana."

They had reached the far end of the bridge, and Buck led the way down a narrow trail from the causeway to the lower bottom land. He then turned back to the east, passed through a wild plum thicket, and came out on a gravel bar which ran for a considerable distance along the edge of the river. About a half mile to the south, the river made a rather sharp turn to the left; and there was a bank about eight feet high which the river at flood stage had cut out over a period of years.

"Let's start at a hundred yards." Buck said and moved off southward to the bank. Dismounting, he found several pieces of broken tree limbs which he placed against the bank for targets. Telling Randy to bring the horses, he stepped off a hundred yards and marked the distance with another piece of limb which he drove into the ground as a stake. The boys then watered the horses at the river and led them to the shade of some nearby trees where they were unsaddled and tethered.

Buck began the instruction as his father had taught him, with explanations of ballistics, holding the gun, sighting, breathing techniques, and squeezing the trigger. He followed this with dry firing; but Randy soon tired of this as he was anxious to shoot the gun. They began to alternate actual firing with dry firing, and Buck was well pleased with the progress his friend was making; but he called a halt to the practice when he noticed that Randy seemed to be feeling tenderness in his shoulder from the kick of the gun.

"Let's go swimmin'," he said.

"I don't know how to swim; I've never tried."

"Ain't nothin' to it. I ain't never seen no critter that couldn't swim—even a little ol' kitten, if it falls in the water, can swim. Come on, this gravel bar slopes off kinda gradual, an' we'll stay outa the deep water."

Randy's first experience in the water was surprising; he showed absolutely no fear and took to the water as if born to it. He was so much at home in it that Buck had to caution him several times to stay close to the bar lest he be caught in the river current. For more than an hour they swam and frolicked in the river.

"I'm kinda hungry," Buck said. "Ma fixed some ham an' biscuits—they're in the saddlebags."

"I'm glad she did. I could eat a horse."

"Don't eat mine. I ain't sure that little mare of yours can carry two."

After dressing and eating, they found a sandy spot and stretched out on their backs watching the clouds drifting by. At first there was little conversation, but occasionally one would ask the other if he could make out an image he thought he could see in a cloud formation.

"Tell me about your family, Buck. Do you have any brothers or sisters?"

"Naw, I'm the onliest one livin'. Ma had three more, but they all died when little bitty babies. They was what they call blue babies—nobody knows what causes it."

"Tell me about your folks."

"Ma comes from North Perry—area knowed as Morgan Springs.

She's got a heap of relatives up there, but we don't see 'em very of'n. She was a Russell—her pa was Andrew Russell, one of the fust settlers in that area.[1] On Pa's side, his pa come here from South Ca'lina when Pa was a little boy an' built the log house where I was borned. Aaron James, one of our sharecroppers, lives in it now. Pa's gran'pa fit with Francis Marion durin' the Revolutionary War. That's how come I be named Francis. Never thought of it before; but I bet Marion was named for him, just like me. I'm glad they don't call me Francis; I don't like the name. Buck's a lot better.''

"Does your father have relatives in this area?''

"Pa had just one brother who lived; all the other chillun, I think there was fo', died from a fever when they was young'uns.''

"Does he live around here?''

"Him an' Pa went to Texas when it looked like Mexico was gonna fight the Texans. Ma calls it Pa's 'fool trip'; Pa come back, but his brother stayed out there. We don't know if'n he's still livin'. Pa ain't never heared from 'im.''

"Your mother, what is she like?''

"Ma? Well, she's kinda big, but she ain't fat; no sir, she ain't fat at all. She works hard, an' she cooks real good; but she's a demon on dirt—never seen nobody who hates dirt like her, always washin' an' cleanin' somethin'. She laughs a lot, an' she gits a kick outa me an' Pa kiddin' one another. I think she kinda hates to see me grow up—she makes me hug 'er at least on'st ever' day; but I like it, an' I hope I never git too big for it.''

"And your father?''

"Pa? Well, he's somethin' else. I guess he's about the smartest man in these parts. He knows more about the woods an' God's critters an' varmi'ts than any man I ever seen. Anything he does, he's the best, be it shoot'n a gun, plowin', readin' sign, choppin' wood, fixin' somethin', or anything—he's the best. An' strong! Pa can lift an' tote things that other folks can't git offa the ground. He farms good, too. He farms diff'rent from most folks; an' he makes good crops, even when the weather don't hold too good. But about the best thing he does is breedin' animals. He raises real fine mules, an' now with the hosses he's been gittin' from your pa an' from over near Plantersville, he's raisin' some good saddle hosses. If Pa's got a fault, I guess it's bein' kinda close with his money. He don't b'lieve in buyin' nothin' that we can raise or make ourselves, an' he don't b'lieve in payin' for nothin' he buys if'n he can swap somethin' for it. He's some kinda trader, too. Don't never swap pocket knives with him! Now, I don't mean Pa ain't honest an' fair in his tradin'; he just knows what he's doin'. They ain't a more honester

man in this whole country than my pa; an' he's a good pa, too. Ever'
Wednesday evenin', an' sometimes all day Wednesday, he sets aside for
me. He calls it my schoolin'. We do things together—huntin', fishin',
swimmin', trackin', makin' things, farmin'—he's a good teacher.
Sometimes we just go out in the woods, an' he learns me about critters
an' varmi'ts an' trees an' plants an' such. I've learnt a lot from Pa. Man,
you sure got me to talkin'; you ain't told me nothin' about your folks."

Randy laughed. "I was beginning to wonder if you would talk all
day. As for my family, my mother came from South Carolina. Her
father is dead, but her mother is still living. She has brothers and sisters,
all living in South Carolina; but we don't see them very often. Mother is
pretty strict on my sister and me about our manners, the way we talk,
neatness, getting our lessons, doing the right thing at the proper time,
and all that stuff. We have quite a few slaves, and Mother doesn't have
to do much herself; but she stays busy telling others what to do. She
helps my father a lot; he's crippled. A horse fell with him about three
years ago and crushed both knees. He gets about the house in a chair
with wheels on it, and he still keeps a pretty tight rein on running the
plantation. We have over a hundred people, as Daddy wants them
called—he doesn't like to hear them referred to as slaves. He has an
overseer, Mr. Pring, who supervises the farming and the people; but he
and Daddy don't always agree on things, especially about handling the
people. Mr. Pring thinks Daddy is too easy on them. Daddy has a two-
wheeled cart that Golan, our carpenter and handyman, built for him. He
drives that around the plantation and keeps an eye on what's going on.
When I'm not in school, I usually drive him; he's teaching me how to
run the place."

The mention of school caught Buck's attention. "What kinda school
do you go to?" he asked.

"We have a school at home. It's held Mondays through Fridays,
except during July and August when it's so hot. We have a teacher,
Miss Childers from Richmond, Virginia. Daddy calls her an old maid;
she also helps him with his accounts and letter writing."

"Who all goes to the school?"

"Just me, my sister Ellen, and Sally Beaumont, the daughter of one
of our neighbors, who lives at the plantation, Cahaba, which joins ours.
Miss Childers also teaches the girls music and what mother calls 'The
graces.' Mother says that I could use a little of that, but Daddy says,
'No'."

"I ain't had much learnin' from books. Ma learnt me to read an'
write. I ain't so good at readin', but I read the *Good Book* to Ma an' Pa

ever' night after supper. Ma learnt me to cipher, too; she says I'm good at it.''

''You've never gone to school?''

''Naw.'' Embarrassed, he changed the subject. ''You got any brothers or sisters 'sides Ellen?''

''No, Ellen and I are the only ones. We don't have any relatives in the area either. My father was an only child, and both of his parents are dead. They came here many years ago, when Daddy was a boy, and started Prairie's Edge.''

''You ever have a good clos't friend?''

''I don't know whether you would call him a close friend, but I think of him as one. His name is Jason; he's one of our people. His father is our carpenter and handyman, and his mother is one of the house servants. Jason's about three years older than I, and when we were small we played together. As we grew up, he more or less looked after me since he was quite a bit older. We played together, rode together, got into trouble together; and I think he sometimes took punishment which should have been mine or which at least we should have shared. I'm not sure that it didn't hurt more to see him take the blame for things than if I had taken it myself. I thought a lot of Jason, and still do.''

''What happened?''

''About three months ago, Jason and I got into a disagreement about something and wound up in a tugging match. He lost his temper and hit me. He had done it before when I was smaller but not in the last few years. Someone saw it, I don't know who, and told his father. Golan reported it to Daddy. Daddy didn't order any punishment but told Golan he thought it best that he handle it. Daddy doesn't believe in whipping our people, but Golan took a strap to Jason and whipped him something awful.''

Randy found it difficult to continue, but went on with the story. ''Mother thought Jason should be sold, but Daddy said he wasn't going to sell a fifteen-year-old boy away from his parents and that he would not sell two faithful people like Golan and his wife, Beulah. Jason never had any work assigned to him except to look after me; and everyone felt this had to come to an end, so Jason is now learning to be a house servant. I heard Daddy say that if he had to sell Jason when he got older, he wanted him trained so he could go into a good position rather than having to go to the fields. I'm afraid, though, it isn't working out.''

''Why ain't it?''

''Jason has become surly and does nothing unless he is specifically told to. Mother says that no one would ever want him for a house servant. It's probably only a question of time until he's sent to the fields."

"Have you talked to 'im?"

"I've tried. He listens, but I can't seem to get through to him."

"Too bad."

"Did you ever have a friend?"

"Naw, not a real one."

"I guess real friends are hard to come by. By the way, you never said how old you are."

"Thirteen; was thirteen in May." Looking at the sun, he added, "We'd better git our butts home."

They saddled their horses, got their guns, and were soon back on the road. When they reached the junction near Randy's house, Buck said, "My folks think they oughta know you, an' you them. Ma said I could ask you to come eat Sunday dinner with us tomorrow. Can you come?"

"I don't see why not. If my folks have other plans, I'll get word to you tonight. What time?"

"We usually git home from church meetin' about one. Ma won't have dinner ready before two. How's about one-thirty?"

"That's fine."

"Our house's about a quarter of a mile up above where we come out of the grove today. It's on the left, with a picket fence; you can't miss it. Bring your gun; I think Pa'd like to see it."

"I'll be there"; and with that, they parted.

At supper that night, Randy told his parents of his invitation to have dinner with the McCords. "I'm not sure I like this," his mother said. "I don't know anything about those people. There's no telling what they may serve or how clean they will be in preparing the food."

"There's nothing to worry about, Honey," her husband said. "I ate dinner with them once, got caught in a hard rain over there one day last year. Mrs. McCord sets an excellent table, and her house is as clean as you would ever hope to find."

That seemed to settle it. Randy breathed a sigh of relief, but he couldn't help wondering what he would be eating.

Randy got up as usual the following morning. He was concerned as to what he should wear to the McCords' house that day. He would be dressed in a suit and wearing a cravat when he got home from church, but he was afraid he would be over-dressed in these clothes. Buck would be going to church, too; but Randy wasn't sure how he would be dressed. He knew what his mother would say, so he went to his father for advice.

"They will probably attend the Methodist Church up in the hills. I doubt Buck will be wearing a cravat, and I'm pretty sure he won't wear a coat in this hot weather. I think a good pair of pants and a shirt would be sufficient, but not any of your newer ones."

"Buck asked me to bring my gun; he thinks his father would like to see it."

"I'm sure he would. He's quite a marksman—the best I've ever known. Take along the telescopic sight; I doubt he's ever seen one."

Before the family left for church, Randy had asked Golan to have his horse waiting for him. When they returned home, he wasted no time in changing clothes and heading for the back yard where the little mare was hitched. He met his mother in the hall.

"You aren't going like that, I hope. You are a guest for dinner, you know."

"I was planning to; I don't want to appear as a fancy dandy. I'm sure they won't be all dressed up, especially Buck."

"What in the world are you doing with that gun? I hope you aren't going hunting on Sunday?"

"No, mother," he replied. "I'm just going to show it to Mr. McCord."

"Well, be off with you; you don't want to be late," she said, obviously unhappy about his going.

With that, Randy escaped out the back door and lost no time in getting on his way. As he approached the McCord house, however, he began to lose a little of his eagerness and enthusiasm. How would he fit in with the McCords, who were from a background so entirely different from his own? If not accepted by Buck's parents, how would this affect his being friends with Buck? He would soon have the answers to these doubting questions.

Buck had no such misgivings. In his own environment he was comfortably at ease. He felt only excitement over Randy's visit and his parents' interest in meeting his new friend. He took a seat on the front porch where he could watch the clay road in the direction Randy would appear. He was still dressed in his Sunday clothes which consisted of an almost new shirt and a new pair of pants his mother had just made. He was also wearing shoes but not by choice—they were killing his feet. He got a new pair every fall, and they were expected to last until the following year; but during the last six months he had grown so much that the shoes were now much too small for him. He had started to take them off when he got home from church, but his mother told him to keep them on until after dinner. He hadn't let her know how much they hurt; maybe he should talk to her about it. She might get Pa to let him have a new pair now. A boy on a small roan came in sight from around the bend in the road, and Buck lost all thought of shoes. He went to the front gate and waited. When Randy rode up, he directed him to the rear of the house and opened and closed the wide gate to the back yard for him. Randy dismounted, and they unsaddled the horse and turned her loose in the pasture just beyond the barn. Randy saw several fine horses already there, including Buck's gelding.

He also saw across the pasture, which was only about two hundred yards wide at this point, a small lake which looked as if it had been created by damming up a creek. He wasn't sure; for if a dam existed, it was hidden from view by a barn-like building with a large shed roof along one side which covered an open area. He followed Buck, who led the way onto the back porch and through the kitchen door. Buck's mother was busy at the table, but she wiped her hands on her apron and extended the right one as the boys came in.

"Ma, this here's Randy."

"Hello, Mrs. McCord," Randy said as he took the outstretched hand and shook it.

"I'm right proud to make your acquaintance, Randy; Buck has told us so much aboucha. We been lookin' for'ard to you comin'. Buck, you take 'im on in the sittin' room, an' let 'im meet Pa when he comes out. There's some fresh water if Randy wants a drink or to freshen up."

The two boys went into the front hall, and Buck motioned to the washbowl and pitcher on the washstand. Randy wasn't thirsty, and he didn't think his hands were dirty; but he washed them in case Buck's mother expected it. As he was hanging up the towel, a door opened behind him. Turning, he saw one of the largest men he had ever seen.

"I'm Buck's Pa," the big man said, offering a large hand with long fingers.

"I'm Randy," the boy replied, extending his own hand, which was engulfed in the firm but gentle clasp of the other.

"Proud to meetcha; we're right pleased you could come."

"He brung his gun, Pa; I asked 'im to so's you could see it," Buck said excitedly. He left, and soon returned with the rifle and the unmounted telescopic sight. He handed the gun to his father.

"I'll swear," McCord said. "A six-sided bore. Never seen one of these before. You got one of the bullets?" he asked, looking at Randy.

"Yessir," Randy replied, bringing one from his pocket and handing it to McCord, who examined both the gun and cartridge carefully.

"This is a fine made gun; never seen better. Don't happen to know where your Pa got it, do you?"

"I'm not sure. It was made in England, and I think Daddy has had it for some time. He says it's one of the most accurate guns made, also one of the longest ranged. The bullet isn't as large as most rifles, though; it's only .45 caliber."

"What's that you got, Buck?"

"It's a telescopic sight that goes with the rifle," Randy answered for him. "I've never had it on the gun. Daddy doesn't think I'm ready for it yet. He says the gun has such a long range that this kind of sight is needed to see the target clearly."

"I've heared of these, but this is the fust I've seen."

"You can try it out, if you would like, Mr. McCord."

"May take you up on that sometime, Randy; I'd like to see just how accurate it is."

Sadie, who had been busy placing bowls and platters of food on the dining room table, interrupted the conversation. "Dinner's ready," she said, "if y'all can put down that gun long enough to eat."

"We're comin'," Cory replied. "It's been a long time since breakfast." He leaned the gun against the wall, and the three of them joined Sadie at the table.

"Randy, you set right there on the left next to the end, an' Buck'll set next to you." They all took their places.

"We'll hold hands whil'st Pa says the blessin'." This was a new experience for Randy as he took the hand of Buck on his left, that of Mr. McCord on his right, and bowed his head.

Cory McCord spoke in a strong but respectful voice, "Lord, we thank you for all your blessin's; an' ask that you bless this food an' Buck's friend who's come to share it with us. Amen."

Randy raised his head and looked closely at the table. There was no cloth on it, and it was set with four plain, white, inexpensive plates. On the left of each was a napkin wrapped around a knife, fork, and spoon; on the right a glass. The table was laden with food. There were ham, venison, fried chicken, butter beans, peas, green beans, corn, gravy, biscuits, and cornbread. There were smaller dishes containing butter, jam, jelly, pickles, and relishes. All qualms about what might be served quickly vanished. His father was right; Mrs. McCord set a good table.

Once the food had been passed around, each dish to the guest first, and the glasses filled with either sweetmilk or buttermilk, conversation became sparse; and full attention was given by the diners to the food in front of them. There were not the separate courses as served in his own home, nor the conversation which always went with every meal; but Randy was hungry, and today he could do without the conversation and the leisurely dining. As soon as he finished one food on his plate, he was immediately offered a second helping, most of which he declined. After several refusals, Buck's father asked, "What's the matter, don't you like my wife's cookin'?"

Taken by surprise, Randy stammered, "Why no—I mean yes—what I mean is, I like her cooking very much; it's just that I took so much the first time that I really can't eat more."

Buck laughed at Randy's discomfort; Cory smiled; and Sadie said impatiently, "Cory McCord, you orta be shot for pullin' somethin' like that on Randy the fust time he eats with us! He'll think we ain't got no manners at all. Don't pay 'im no mind, Randy; he's always a-teasin' folks."

Randy laughed, relieved that it was only a joke. He appreciated the humor of it but wondered how something like this would go over in his own home. "You really had me going for a minute, Mr. McCord. I didn't know what to say; I thought you were dead serious."

"Just wanted to see how you'd take a little kiddin'; you might find a lot of it around here."

"Did I do all right?"

"Just fine; you done just fine," Cory said with a friendly smile.

Randy was pleased. He liked these people, and they seemed to like him. He would fit in with them.

When the meal was over, Buck started to help his mother clear the table; but she told him that she would do it today, so he and Randy went out to the back porch where they sat and talked. It was about half past three when Buck said, "Let's go swimmin'."

"It's a long way to the river."

"Naw, in the pond."

They crossed the pasture to the pond and the nearby structures. Randy looked over the area with interest. A dam had been thrown across a creek which had backed up into a large pond. On the near side of the dam was a millrace over which was turning an undershot water wheel about ten feet high. To the side of the wheel were attached twelve free-swinging buckets which scooped up water at the bottom of the wheel, carried it to the top where they were tilted, spilling their contents into a trough that carried the water to a nearby vegetable garden and fruit orchard which had been graded so the water would run down between the rows of planted vegetables and between the trees. Observing his friend's interest, Buck said, "It's kinda dry, an' the garden an' trees need water. When they git enough, we take the buckets off. They're fixed to go on an' off easy.''

It wasn't just the irrigation system which drew Randy's attention. There was a shaft from the center of the wheel which extended to the open area underneath the roof. With wheels and belts, now idling, power could be supplied to a sawmill and a large table saw. There was another belt which could furnish power to equipment in the enclosed barn-like building. Without being asked, Buck volunteered, ''That one powers the grist mill for meal an' grits an' the flour mill. It can also power Pa's lathe an' drill in there. It don't power more'n one thing atta time, though.''

''Your father built all of this?''

''Yeah, with that forge,'' pointing to one under a corner of the shed, ''an' the other tools, he can build 'most anything.''

''I can believe that.''

It didn't take long to shed their clothes and get ready for the water. As they approached the side of the pond, Buck said, ''Watch out for snakes.''

''Snakes!''

''Yeah. They won't bother you unless you git too close or you bothers them.''

Buck carefully examined the edge of the pond and the water. ''Don't seem to be none about today.''

He waded into the pond with Randy following closely behind and nervously scanning the water. ''When we git to swimmin' an' splashin' around, any snakes close by'll take off up or down the creek. We'll go over t'other side; it's deeper, an' the grape vine's over there.''

The boys spent over an hour swimming and dropping from the vine on which they would swing out over the water. Randy was in his element, needing only time before he would become a good and strong swimmer.

While they were dressing, Randy asked his friend,''How did you get the name, 'Buck'?''

''When I was a little un, Pa started callin' me 'Buckskin' on accounta my hair was the color of a buckskin hoss. It's changed an' ain't that color no more; but the name stuck an' it got shortened to 'Buck.' When my geldin' was foaled two years ago an' Pa seen he was gonna be a buckskin, he said that was gonna be my hoss, an' he gelded 'im so's he would'n be so hard to handle. I was already named 'Buck,' so I called 'im 'Skin'.''

Looking over at his horse grazing alongside Randy's mare, Buck said, ''Watch this,'' and gave a shrill whistle. Skin's head came up; the horse looked in the direction from which the whistle had come, spotted

Buck, and trotted over to him.

"Hey, that's something! Do you think we could train my horse to do that?"

"We can try. You can do a lot with a hoss an' a little nibblin's an' a lot of patience."

It was time for Randy to go, so they caught his mare, which had followed Skin over to them, and started back toward the house. Randy said, "Mother would like for you to have dinner with us Saturday. Think you can make it?"

Hesitating, Buck replied, "I don't know. You think it'll be all right?"

Realizing the probable cause of his friend's concern, Randy said, "I'm sure it will. Maybe there are a couple of things I ought to tell you. We do serve a little differently; we have our dinner in courses. We start with soup; and when that is finished, they take the dishes away; then they serve the next course, and so on. Also, there will be a lot of silverware at each plate. Don't worry about which piece to use; just watch mother, and do as she does. We eat at a rather leisurely pace, too; there's a lot of talking going on during the meal."

"Sounds kinda skerry."

"You'll be all right; just watch Mother. Come over about half past eleven. We eat at twelve."

By this time they had reached the house. After saddling his horse, Randy sought out Mrs. McCord and found her in the kitchen. "Thank you for the wonderful dinner; I have enjoyed being with y'all today."

"We was glad to have you an' want you to come back real soon, but won't you stay an' take supper with us before you go?"

"No thank you. I'd better be getting on home; they're expecting me, but I'll be back."

Picking up a small basket containing several jars, she said, "Here's some blackberry jam an' plum jelly your folks might like."

"I'm sure they will; and thank you again, Mrs. McCord, for everything." Randy said and extended his hand.

"It ain't no han'shake I want," she said; and ignoring his hand, she reached out and pulled a startled boy into her strong arms. Unconsciously his arms went around her, and he found himself returning the embrace. He could understand why Buck liked this; he did, too.

When she released him, he said. "That was better."

At supper that night, Buck told his parents about Randy's invitation. "I don't know, Son," his father said, dubious of his going, "them folks is different from us. You might feel out of place over there.''

"Folks is the same all over, Cory," Sadie said. "Some does things different; but deep down, it don't make no never mind whether they lives in log cabins or mansions. That Randy's a good boy, an' he must come from some mighty good folks.''

"If'n I go," interjected Buck, "can I have my new shoes now? My feets growed so much, I done outgrowed mine; an' they just kills me.''

"Why didn' you say so before? I know what it's like for your feet to hurt. When mine hurt, I hurt all over. Cory, I want you to take this young'un to town this week an' git 'im some shoes that fits.''

"He's shot up like a Jimson weed, all right," Cory replied; and looking under the table at Buck's feet, he added, "an' if there wasn't so much turned down for feet, ain't no tellin' how tall he'd be.''

Buck laughed—not so much from his father's trite joke as over the fact that any objection to his going seemed to have disappeared.

Tuesday morning Buck and his father started for Marion to get the shoes. When they reached the junction with the main road, Cory drew rein and said, "Wait here a few minutes, Buck; I wanta talk to Mr. Rushton—won't take long.''

"Can't I go, Pa?''

"Not this time. I'll be right back; just wait here.''

Leaving Buck wondering what this was all about, Cory turned toward the Rushton home; and he rode up to the veranda where John Rushton was sitting, bringing his horse to a stop in front of him.

"Hello, Cory. Good to see you. Won't you get down and have a seat?''

"Howdy, John. No thanks—this ain't a social visit, an' Buck's waitin' down at the forks. What I got to say won't take but a minute.''

John sat back and waited. "Your boy et dinner with us Sunday. He's a fine boy—does y'all right proud.''

"Thank you, Cory.''

"My boy's comin' over here Saturday.''

"I know.''

"I don't want him hurt none.''

"He won't be.''

"Can I count on that?''

"You've got my word.''

Cory thought about that a moment before he replied, "Guess that's good enough." He turned his horse and went down the driveway to the road. John watched the large man go, straight and erect in the saddle. A feeling of sadness and disappointment came over him—disappointment with himself. Cory had given him the chance to say that being hurt wasn't always a one-sided thing, but he had missed the opportunity. Why do we always know so well what to say when the chance to say it has passed?

After supper that evening, John sat relaxed in his chair, not asleep but not altogether awake, either. He still controlled his thoughts which turned to his meeting that day with Cory. In his mind he could picture Cory sitting erect, his body almost motionless, as he rode down the driveway on the trotting horse. Cory had always been such a good horseman. Suddenly John was wide awake. It wasn't just the rider; it as the horse, too! Anyone would have looked good on a horse with a gait that smooth. He surely would like to breed the new mares he had just bought to that stallion. He had heard that Cory never had any of his animals standing at stud and wondered if he would sell the horse. He had to have the service of that stallion.

Promptly at eleven-thirty Saturday morning, Buck rode up in front of the Rushton home; and this time it was Randy who was waiting on the porch. Buck was wearing the same clothes he had worn Sunday; but they were freshly laundered, neatly ironed, and fitted him well. Both his straw hat and shoes were new. Randy came off the porch to meet him, and they went together around to the rear of the house. Randy called Jason who came out of the kitchen and indifferently ambled over to them.

"Jason, this is my friend, Buck McCord. He's going to have dinner with us. Please take care of his horse."

"Howdy, Jason," Buck said in a friendly tone of voice.

Jason did not reply, but stood silently glaring at Buck. Resentfully he took the reins Randy impatiently thrust into his hand and led the horse off to the stables. As the two boys went toward the back door, Randy said, "See what I mean?"

"I see you got a problem, all right." In a low voice he inquired, "When I meet your Ma, do I shake hands with 'er?"

"Only if she offers you hers. Come on, they're all waiting to meet you."

When they entered the sitting room, Buck first saw Randy's father in his special chair; he appeared to be a kindly and gentle person, and the boy knew at once he would like him. His wife, sitting on his right, looked to be several years younger than he. Her face was somewhat stern but not severe. There was a quality in her eyes that had a softening effect, but her aristocratic mien made Buck feel uncomfortable; and he was not sure how he would get along with her. On the other side of Mr.

Rushton was a thin-faced, rather grim-looking woman who seemed to be quite a bit older than Randy's parents. Buck knew she must be the teacher. As he looked to her left, his heart suddenly seemed to leap into his throat; for there was the prettiest girl he had ever seen. Her black hair was in two braids which had been doubled up and tied with blue ribbons, yet it still reached to her shoulders. She was wearing a bright blue dress almost the exact color of the ribbons. Her brown eyes and pretty little mouth were smiling in a friendly way.

"My folks," Randy announced, bringing Buck back to the moment at hand. "First, my mother."

"It's nice to meet you, Buck," Carolyn Rushton said, smiling; but she did not offer her hand.

"Glad to make your acquaintance," Buck replied self-consciously.

"My father."

"Good to see you, Buck. You look a lot like your father." He thrust out his hand.

"Howdy do," Buck replied as he walked over and shook hands.

"Miss Childers, our teacher," Randy said.

"It is a pleasure to meet you, young sir."

Buck had never been "sirred" before. "Howdy," he replied.

"And last and least, my pesty little sister, Ellen."

"Randy! That is no way to introduce your sister!" his mother admonished.

"Hello, Buck," Ellen said with a pleasant smile as she rose and extended her hand.

"Howdy, Miss Ellen," Buck replied, clumsily taking the small, dainty hand. The firmness of her grip, however, surprised him.

"Sit over here," Randy said; and both boys sat down.

Carolyn Rushton opened the conversation by asking Buck to thank his mother for the jelly and jam and commenting on how good it was and how much they were enjoying it. Buck had little to say; when brought into the conversation through questions directed to him, he answered as briefly as possible. During a lull, Ellen, who had not spoken since the introduction, suddenly asked, "Did you really shoot that deer while he was in the middle of a leap?"

"It wasn't much of a shot. I was restin' my gun against a tree."

"Randy said you taught him to swim," she continued. "I wish I could swim."

"Ellen!" her mother exclaimed.

Buck had been on the verge of offering to teach her when Mrs. Rushton's firm voice brought him to the reality of the situation. Blushing at the thought, he replied, "Wasn't much to teach. He took to the water like a duck.''

Jason came to the door, still wearing his sullen expression, and announced, ''Dinner is ready.''

Carolyn rose, ''Shall we go?'' she said, and led the way. Randy went to his father; and following Mis Childers and Ellen, he guided his chair out of the room, closely followed by Buck who was trying to assist but was getting in the way more than he was helping.

When they entered the dining room, Buck almost panicked; he had never seen anything like this. It was a large room with a table long enough to seat a dozen people easily and covered in a spotlessly white cloth. There were six places set at the far end of it. At each were a dinner plate, a smaller plate, a crystal goblet filled with ice water, a napkin, and more silver flatware than he believed would ever be needed. Mrs. Rushton was directing the seating.

Randy saw the consternation expressed on Buck's face and placing his hand on his friend's arm, whispered, ''Don't worry; just watch Mother.''

Randy pushed his father's chair to the end of the table and then held his mother's chair, assisting her as she sat down. Seeing this, Buck, with considerably less grace, did the same for Miss Childers. He wanted to assist Ellen, but she was already seated by the time he had finished helping the teacher. He then took the seat between them, directly across from Randy who was on his mother's right. They were served by a tall, neatly dressed negro whom the Rushtons addressed as Samuel. By watching Mrs. Rushton carefully, Buck made it through the meal with no serious blunder; but when it was over, he had no recollection of what he had eaten. As in the sitting room, he had little to say unless specifically drawn into the conversation. When they finished dessert, John Rushton said, ''Randy, why don't you take me to the office, and then show Buck the horses.''

Randy helped his father from the room with Buck following. As they reached the hall leading to the south wing of the house where the office was located, Buck remembered his mother's instructions to be sure to tell Mrs. Rushton he had enjoyed his dinner. Excusing himself, he retraced his steps toward the dining room; but before he reached the door to that room, he stopped when he heard Ellen say, ''He surely is handsome, but he talks so funny.''

Another voice muttered, ''He don' talk no better'n a nigger. He ain't nothin' but white trash.''

''Jason, I'll not have you speak of a guest in this house in that manner,'' Mrs. Rushton's voice, sharp in anger, came to him. ''I've had all of your impudence I am going to take! Samuel, go tell Mr.

Rushton I shall be in to see him in a few moments.''

Buck beat a hasty retreat around the corner and down the hall which Randy and Mr. Rushton had taken. He met Randy coming out of the office, and the two of them continued on down the hall and out a side door.

John was at his desk talking with Samuel when Carolyn came in. ''Mr. Rushton, I want to talk with you!'' she said in a voice showing her anger.

He knew she was terribly upset, for it was only at such times that she addressed him this way. ''Looks like something is bothering you, Honey.''

''There certainly is! That impudent Jason just made a very disparaging remark about Randy's friend. I have had enough of his impertinence. I don't care what you do with him, but I will not have Jason in my house any longer!''

''I'm sorry. I don't blame you for being mad; you've been right about him all along. I should have done something sooner; I've known for some time that Jason would never make a house servant, and I shouldn't have put you through this.'' Turning to Samuel, he said, ''Tell Jason to get Mr. Pring. I want to talk with the two of them together.'' Samuel left to comply with the instructions.

''While we are talking, there is another matter I wish to discuss with you. This boy, Buck—did you see the way he stared at me during the entire meal?''

John laughed. ''Don't you know why? He was watching you to do exactly as you, so he wouldn't commit a social error. You should be flattered.''

''This is no laughing matter, John; and what you have said only supports my own view. Buck is socially untrained, poorly dressed; and even Jason says he talks like one of them. He called him white trash. The boy is not a suitable companion for our son.''

''Sit down, Carolyn!'' John brusquely ordered. ''I'm going to tell you something, something I've never told anyone before.''

Astonished by the commanding tone of his voice which was entirely new to her, Carolyn promptly took a seat and sat quietly waiting.

''When I was about Randy's age, not long after my family moved to Prairie's Edge, I also met a young boy in the woods one day. He was two years older than I and the most remarkable person I had ever known. He could do almost anything to perfection—ride, shoot, swim, trail an animal—you name it, he was good at it. He knew the forests and the creatures of the forest. He was smart, too, being particularly adept at anything mechanical. He could make or improvise almost anything needed. His honesty and morals were above question, but he was a backwoods boy—his clothes were rough; he had no formal education; and his grammar and diction were atrocious. I knew he wouldn't meet the approval of my snobbish parents, so I never mentioned him to them. We met frequently, and I went often to his home where I was always welcomed. I looked up to that boy and loved him as a friend more than any person I've ever known. See this little scar on my wrist? He has one like it. In an Indian ritual not long after we became friends, we cut our wrists, mixed our blood, and took an oath to be blood brothers forever.'' John paused for a moment, and then continued:

"Well, it wasn't forever; just two short years, or until my parents found out about him and insisted I bring him to Prairie's Edge so they could meet him. He, like Buck, made a bad impression socially; and they couldn't see his good qualities for those superficial things that have so little basic value. I was ordered not to see him again; and despite my pleading, I couldn't change their minds.'' His voice broke as he added, "And I lost the best friend I ever had.''

John waited a few moments to get control of himself and then went on, "I broke an oath we had taken together. I know it was a childish thing, but it was done in all seriousness and was meaningful to each of us. I never forgave my parents for what they did to me and never felt the same toward them after that; but worse, I've never forgiven myself for not standing up to them. I was almost fifteen years old at the time and mature enough to make the decision for myself. I am not going to do to my son what my parents did to me, nor will I let you. I don't give a damn if that boy sits at our table barefooted and eats with a Bowie knife, he is going to be made to feel he is wanted at Prairie's Edge as long as he is Randy's friend!''

Carolyn was stunned. She had never seen her husband so emotional or so adamant before. He had always taken things so calmly; she recalled the stoical way in which he had accepted the fact that he would never walk again. Then she realized the deep hurt he had suffered and continued to carry with him all these years; and there awakened in her a feeling of compassion and love for this man, whom she had always thought so invulnerable, such as she had never known before. The cool, controlled facade behind which she lived melted; and with tear-filled eyes she went quickly to her husband, knelt by his chair, and put her arms around him. "Oh, John, I knew something had come between you and your parents, but I didn't know what it was. I have been so terribly foolish; how can you ever forgive me?''

He answered by gently extricating his left arm which she had pinned to his side; and placing both arms around her, he drew her close to him.

In silence, except for her soft crying, they clung together. They remained this way until her sobbing stopped. She then rose; and standing with her back to him, she took a small handkerchief from her pocket and carefully wiped the tears from her eyes and cheeks. Straightening her dress, she returned to her seat. Only then did she trust herself to speak.

"I didn't realize what I was doing to the boy, much less to our son," she said. "I promise you this, John, Buck will always be welcome in this house, not because Randy or you want it, but because I want it, too."

"Thank you, Carolyn."

"The boy, your friend, he was Mr. McCord, wasn't he?"

John answered by nodding his head.

Someone could be heard coming down the hall; and Mr. Pring, accompanied by Jason, came to the door. Carolyn looked at her husband; he seemed to be all right now, so she said, "Come in, Mr. Pring, I am just leaving." She stood, and left the room.

"Come in and sit down, Mr. Pring," John said. Pring waited for Carolyn to pass and then entered and took a seat. He was followed by Jason, who remained standing.

"I'm afraid our experiment with Jason hasn't been very successful. I would like for you to take him over. I want to give him one more chance, however; I want you to put him to working with the horses. He is good with them; and if he applies himself, he should be productive in the stables. If he does not work out there, go ahead and put him in the fields. I leave that decision to you." Looking at Jason, he asked, "You know why I'm doing this, don't you?"

"I knows; 'cause you's the massa an' I's the slave."

"No, Jason. That's not the reason; that is the authority. The reason is that you have not applied yourself, and you have displayed a disposition which makes you entirely unsuitable for work in the house. I hope you will show more industry and a better attitude in your work with the horses. If you don't, Mr. Pring has no choice other than sending you to the fields. It is up to you. Do you have anything you would like to say?"

Jason remained silent. To both of them, Rushton said, "That will be all."

"Wait for me in the back yard," Pring said to Jason. "I want to speak to Mr. Rushton."

When Jason left, Pring asked, "Can I express an opinion, Mr. Rushton?"

"You may always do that, Mr. Pring. I wouldn't want to lose the benefit of either your opinion or your knowledge."

"I think we're wasting time with that boy. I don't like the things I've been hearing about him."

"You're probably right, but I want him given another chance—and a fair chance, Mr. Pring. I have my reasons for this."

"He'll get the chance, and a fair one. I'll see to that."

"I'm sure he will."

The boys spent a couple of hours looking at the horses and the elaborate stables and fenced pastures. Afterward they saddled their horses, and Randy showed Buck around the plantation. It was well after five o'clock when they got back to the house.

"I better be gittin' home, but fust I've gotta say my goodbyes to your folks."

They went inside and found John still in his office. "Where's Mother? Buck wants to see her."

"I think she is in the butler's pantry. It's down the main hall, Buck, the small room just past the dining room. You go ahead; I'd like to speak to Randy a minute."

Buck found the room without difficulty. In it was a small desk where Mrs. Rushton was at work with her household records. Buck gently knocked on the open door. Mrs. Rushton looked up.

"Can I come in?"

"Why certainly, come in, Buck; and do sit down for a moment."

He took a seat in a chair by her desk. "I want to thank you for the good dinner an' all I et. It was good."

"Well, I'm glad you enjoyed it; but I'm a little concerned, Buck; I felt you may have been rather ill at ease at dinner today. I hope not."

"Yes'm, I guess I was, kinda."

"I don't want you ever to feel that way in this house, and I was at fault by not making you feel more at home. You are among friends here, friends who would understand if you didn't do something just right. Do you know what I am trying to say, Buck? I don't seem to be doing it very well."

"Yes'm, I think I understan'; an' thank you for sayin' what you just did."

"You will always be welcome here, and I want you to feel at ease and at home with us."

"Yes'm, but it might take a little time in doin'."

"We'll all be patient and try not to expect too much too soon; but we shan't give up trying, shall we?"

"No, ma'am." Feeling the conversation was over, Buck stood up to leave.

"Before you go, Buck, let me get your mother's basket." She picked up a small bell and rang it before continuing. "We slaughtered a cow yesterday, and I would appreciate it if you would take a piece of beef to your mother."

Samuel came in response to the bell, and he was sent for the basket and meat, returning shortly with them. Mrs. Rushton handed the basket containing a neatly wrapped package to Buck. Extending her hand, she said, "Goodbye, Buck. I hope we see you at Prairie's Edge again real soon."

"I'll be back," he said with a grin as he took the hand and shook it.

Buck left; and as she watched the boy go, Carolyn Rushton thought how stupid she had been not to see what was beneath his rough exterior. She was as much of a snob as John's parents. Thank goodness, John had straightened her out. He had been right again, as usual.

Buck returned to the office; but before he could take his leave, Mr. Rushton asked, "That stallion your father rides, did he raise him?"

"Yes sir."

"Do you have a full brother to him?"

"Not a stallion; just my geldin'. The stud was the colt, Thor, Pa got from you; an' the mare come from a man over by Plantersville. We still got the stud, but lost the mare last year in foalin'. The foal breeched."

"That's too bad; I was impressed with the smooth gait of the stallion. How many gaits does he have?"

"Just three. Pa don't go for them fancy gaits. Mine is just as good as the stallion, an' easier to handle."

"I'm sure he is. It's too bad you lost the mare; it's a blow to lose a dam like that."

Buck said goodbye to Mr. Rushton, who also urged him to feel free to visit them any time. He and Randy left by the side door leading to the yard where his horse had been tied. He was disappointed that Ellen was nowhere in sight; he had hoped to see her again. From the other wing of the house came the sound of someone playing a pianoforte. He felt sure it was Ellen; but he was too bashful to ask to see her, so he said to Randy, "Tell Miss Ellen I'm sorry I didn' git to see her ag'in, an' tell her goodbye for me."

"Sure," Randy said disinterestedly.

Buck looked at him. He had noticed his friend had said nothing during the conversation in the office. "Is somethin' wrong, Randy?" he asked.

"Daddy just told me they have given up on training Jason as a house servant. I knew it had to come. He is being assigned to the stables. If he doesn't work out there to Mr. Pring's satisfaction, he will go the the fields.''

"He'll be all right, Randy. I wouldn' worry none about him; I got a feelin' he's the kind that'll take care of hisself.''

"Maybe so; I don't know.''

In an effort to get his friend's mind on a more pleasant subject, Buck volunteered, ''Me an' your Ma had a nice talk together.''

"You did? What did she say?''

"She wants me to feel at home here. an' she wants me to come back soon.''

"She did?'' Randy said, his voice showing his surprise; this wasn't at all what he had expected.

After Buck left, Randy went back into the house. When he turned into the main hall heading for the stairs, he met his mother. On a sudden impulse, he went to her, wrapped his arms around her trim body, and squeezed her tightly. To his surprise, he felt her arms go around him; and she returned the embrace. They stood that way for a few seconds. Holding her son tightly, she asked, ''What brought this on?''

"I guess I just needed a hug.''

"So did I, Randy; so did I,'' she replied with a slight quiver in her voice. She had not felt so close to her son in such a long, long time.

The following afternoon the boys got together again and went to the river where Randy did a lot of dry firing under Buck's instruction. They also spent some time throwing the Bowie knife, Buck again the teacher. After a swim, they dressed and stretched out on the sandy spot to reflect upon and solve the problems of the world as they knew it.

"If I asked you for a favor, you wouldn' laugh, would you?'' Buck hesitantly inquired.

"Of course not.''

"Can you learn me to talk like you?''

Randy laughed. ''You said you wouldn' laugh,'' Buck complained.

"I wasn't laughing at you. I was laughing at the thought of Miss Childers' face if I told her I'm going to teach grammar and diction. Of course, I'll help you; but I don't know how good I'll be at it. Have you ever studied grammar?''

"What's that?''

"It's the way we put words together to say something. There are rules on how to do it.''

"Ain't never studied that.''

"Do you know what diction is?''

"Ain't studied that neither.''

"Diction is the way we say things, the way we pronounce words."

"There's my trouble!"

"It's a little more than that. Do you know what nouns and verbs are?"

"Don't believe I do."

"Well, nouns are words that mean things—that identify something, like tree or horse or river. Can you think of some nouns?"

Buck looked around as he slowly answered, "Bridge—gun—rock—foot—pants—saddle."

"That's good. Now a verb shows action; it tells what a noun does, like the word run. We say the horse runs. Can you think of some verbs?"

"Walk—ride—swim—shoot—talk—load."

"That's very good."

The instruction continued; but the farther it went, the more Randy realized his inadequacy as a teacher. At supper that night he turned to Miss Childers for assistance.

"Buck wants to improve his way of speaking, and he has asked my help," Randy said. "He can read, and I wondered if you have a grammar book we can use."

Miss Childers had been troubled by the hill boy's discomfort at dinner the previous day and was shocked at the way he talked. She was more than willing to help and replied, "I certainly do, and I'll be glad to give it to him. If there is any way I can be of further assistance, I should like to do it."

Randy's parents turned quickly and looked at each other. Each knew what the other was thinking.

Later that evening, John and Carolyn sent for Miss Childers. After she came in and was seated, John asked, "Miss Childers, are you really interested in helping Buck?"

"I most certainly am. There is something very appealing about that boy, and I have the impression that he has a very bright mind which should be trained academically."

"If it can be worked out, would you accept him as another student? He will be far behind the others and will require quite a bit of your time as well as a lot of patience."

"I should be most pleased to have him—he would be quite a challenge for me as a teacher, one which I should like to take on. Do you anticipate a problem in arranging it?"

"There could be. His father is a strong believer in the work ethic and may not consider time spent in school as being productive. He has himself done quite well without any formal education. Also, he is not a person to accept anything gratis from anyone—doesn't believe in 'being beholden,' as he puts it; but neither is he free with his purse strings. I'll have to talk with Buck's parents, but I want to be sure his mother is present when I do.''

The following morning, Randy was sent to the McCord farm to find out if it would be convenient for his father to come over that afternoon to see Buck's parents. It was, so the meeting was set for two o'clock. John let Randy drive the cart but instructed him to get Buck away from the house while he talked with Mr. and Mrs. McCord. When they approached the house, they could see Cory and Buck on the front porch. By the time the cart reached the gate, the McCords were outside it, waiting by the road.

"Howdy, John; howdy, Young Man," Cory said.

"Hello, Cory," John replied, offering his hand.

Cory took the hand, for the first time in many years, and shook it. "I can tote you in the house, or you can drive around back an' set in the cart while me an' Sadie set on the porch. You'll be in the shade there."

"I think it will be better in the back." Then to his son, "I'll drive, Randy; you and Buck take care of the gate. After you close it, y'all go swimming or something."

When John drove up by the back porch, Sadie and Cory were already there. After he exchanged greetings with Sadie, the McCords took seats in the porch rockers and waited for the visitor to begin the conversation.

"I'll come right away to the purpose of this visit," John said. "We have a teacher for our two children, a Miss Childers, who also teaches the daughter of one of our neighbors. She has indicated a willingness to take Buck as another student, if that is agreeable with you." He paused to give them time to consider what he had said.

"What brought this up?" Cory asked.

"Buck asked Randy to help him talk better, and Randy needed help to do it."

"What do your missus think of it?"

"It was her idea as much as mine; we seemed to have thought of it at the same time."

"An' when do this schoolin' take place?"

"The classes are held each morning from eight until noon and then from one until three, Mondays through Fridays. There are no classes during July and August."

"An' what might the cost be?"

"There would be little to you. I already pay Miss Childers, and she is willing to take Buck as an additional student during her regular school hours. There are really no additional expenses involved, except some books.''

"Could we have a little time to think on it?''

"All the time you need; classes don't start again until September. Do you have any further questions that I may answer for you?''

Cory looked at his wife; she shook her head; he replied, "I don't believe so."

"I think the boys went swimming. I would like to see the progress Randy is making, and I'd also like to take a look at that irrigation system you have down there. Can I get to the pond in the cart?''

"Why sure," Cory said. "I'll open the pasture gate an' go with you.''

Sadie spoke for the first time since their greeting, "Mr. Rushton, I wants you to know that whatever the decision be, we'll always be beholden for what you're offerin' to do for Buck."

"It would really be our pleasure to do it, Mrs. McCord. I hope you can see the way clear to letting him attend the classes; he's a mighty fine boy.''

"So's yours. When y'all come back, bring the boys. I'll fix some coffee, an' I got a fresh baked pecan pie that needs cuttin' awful bad.''

After John and his son left, Cory and Sadie returned to the chairs on the back porch. They sat and rocked in silence, each occupied with his own thoughts. "Whatcha think, Sadie?'' Cory finally asked.

"It's a Godsend, Cory; truly a Godsend! My prayers done been answered! My boy's gonna git some book learnin' at last.''

"We'll miss 'im on the farm.''

"I been thinkin' about somethin' for some time, ever since Aaron told you his boy Noah was gonna git married an' wanted to sharecrop on his own. I think it's time you quit farmin' yourself an' give full time to animal raisin'. There'd be a lot of money in it if you could do with cows what you done with mules an' horses. You could raise more of them, too.''

Cory could see the wisdom of these suggestions; Jobe's boy, Adam, would probably be taking a wife soon. By clearing more land for him, he would have the same crop return that he had now. He could certainly sell more horses and mules; there were people waiting to buy them; and milk cows—everybody had them, and people were always looking for better ones. "That makes sense, Sadie; I think I'll give it a try.''

At that moment, Cory caught sight of a negro man coming hurridly across the pasture toward the house; it was Abel James, one of his sharecroppers. Abel wasn't one to hurry, and Cory wondered what his problem could be. The negro came through the gate and on up to the edge of the porch.

"Have a seat, Abel, an' rest yourself; you ain't used to movin' that fast."

Abel laughed as he took off his hat and wiped the sweat from his brow with his hand. "Thankee, Mista Cory; don't mind if I do," he said and took a seat on the steps. He then continued, "Hot today; this's a good'n. We needs rain, though; cotton's doin' good, but corn's a-hurtin'. Hard to git weather what suits both."

"What's on your mind, Abel; know it's somethin' 'sides the weather."

"Yassuh, Mista Cory, it is. It's about my boy Seth. He done tuck up with one of Mr. Rushton's niggers, a gal name Samant'a. I didn' know nothin' about it till today, or I'da put a stop to it before it got this fur. A free nigger ain't got no business messin' aroun' with no slave gal. Now the fool boy wantsa marry 'er."

"Can you afford to buy 'er if Mr. Rushton'll sell?"

"Not by myself, but my brudders'll help; 'pend on how many bales she cost. I don't know why that fool boy couldna got 'im a free gal; there's a few of 'em aroun', an' they don't cost nobody nothin'."

"Love's like a fly, Abel; just soon light on manure as molasses. I'll talk to Mr. Rushton about it; gotta see 'im tomorrow on anotha matter. If need be, maybe I can help out with the loan of a bale or two."

The following morning, Cory went to Prairie's Edge. He found John in his office and after the exchange of greetings, he sat down. "Me an' Sadie thinks it would be good for Buck to git more book learnin', an' we 'preciate the kindly offer; but we can't accept without payin'—maybe in mules or somethin'."

"That's fine, Cory; I'm delighted. I think you are definitely doing what is best for Buck, and you will never regret it. As for payment, I prefer none; but we'll work out something which will be satisfactory to everyone."

"Now, there's anotha matter I need to talk to you about. One of my sharecroppers, Abel James, has a boy named Seth who's got it in his head to marry one of your darkies, a gal named Samantha. Could you see your way clear to sell 'er an' at what price? Abel will have a little cotton this fall, an' his brothers'll help out. If they can't make up enough, I'll loan 'em the rest."

"It's hard to believe Samantha is old enough to be taking a husband.

Mr. Pring tells me she is a hard worker; she'll make the boy a good wife. This brings to mind something I've been thinking about for some time. If you have no objection to telling, what kind of agreement do you have with your sharecroppers?''

"Don't mind tellin'. I furnish the land, a house, the outbuildings, a garden spot, the seeds, the mules, the plows an' other tools, 'an two milk cows. I guess that's about all, except I may hafta advance some money occasionally. They furnish the labor. When we settle up at the end of the year, the cost of the seed an' what it took to feed the animals comes off of the gross; an' we split the rest even.''

"Would you mind shutting the door, Cory? I don't want this to be overheard; and I would appreciate your not repeating it to anyone except your wife.''

After the door was closed, John went on, "Just between us, I don't think slavery will continue in this country for too many more years. If I don't see the end of it, I believe Randy certainly will. You, with your sharecropping, may have the alternative. I have been thinking about experimenting with it, but don't want to go blindly into something without knowing its profitability. We may have the solution here to several problems.'' He paused briefly and, getting no comment from Cory, continued:

"You know I have about a hundred acres north of the Plantersville road which adjoins your property. I'm not using the land, and most of it would have to be cleared for farming. If your sharecroppers will clear the best fifty acres of that land, I will free Samantha; and she and her husband can sharecrop it. I do not want to go into sharecropping openly at this time, so I would like for you to run it for me, but as if it were your own operation. We will let folks think you have leased the land from me. I shall reimburse you for the cost of everything you supply them, and the stock and equipment will be mine. Whatever profits are derived as the landowner's share can go to Miss Childers as extra compensation for teaching Buck. All I ask is that you run the operation as your own and that you keep accurate records so I can know exactly how profitable it is. If this proves to be as good as I anticipate, I shall set up some of my better people as sharecroppers on Prairie's Edge. In time, they should be able to buy their freedom.''

Cory sat silently through the discourse, but he was mentally digesting every word; and he liked what John was saying. "There'll be no trouble about records; Sadie keeps 'em, an' she's mighty good at cipherin'. I don't think I ever heared a deal that was so fair to all concerned. The Jameses should have no trouble gittin' the land cleared by next plantin' time. There may be some sellable timber; what about it?''

"They can use what they need to build a house, barn, outbuildings, and fences. Any left can be sold and the proceeds applied to what I owe you for supplying the new tenants.''

Cory stood up, saying, "John, let me shake your hand; not just for what you're doin' for Buck an' them two darkies, but for what you got in mind for the future.'' Going over to John's desk, he reached over it, took the waiting hand, and shook it firmly.

"Thank you, Cory; but you may be giving me more credit than due. I could be just looking for a way to save my own bacon.''

"Maybe, but I don't believe it.''

When Cory got home and told Sadie what had transpired at Prairie's Edge, she was ecstatic. "This is God's hand!'' she said. "He sometimes moves in mysterious ways, an' all these things ain't come together by themselves. This is God's doin's, an' praise the Lord for it! Praise the Lord!''

Both boys were excited over the news of Buck's going to school at Prairie's Edge and could hardly wait for classes to begin. Time seemed to drag for them except when they were together, and this was as frequently as possible. Cory appreciated the fact that John Rushton could not get out with his son to teach him the things he felt every boy should know, so he invited Randy to join him and Buck on the days they spent together; and he took as much interest in teaching Randy as he did his own son. He spent a lot of time on their marksmanship, cutting sign, and following trails. They hunted and fished together, sometimes camping out overnight. Cory took time in the woods to identify plants and animals and to explain the habits of the latter. He also taught them crafts and how to work with wood and leather. From deer skins he showed them how to make sheaths which could be secured to their saddles to hold their guns and how to make moccasins. He taught them ways to defend themselves against attack by knife, fist, or wrestling. There was little they missed in learning how to survive or to defend themselves.

One rainy day Cory said it was time they learned something about metals. Taking them down to the forge, he showed them how to make, temper, and sharpen a duplicate of Buck's Bowie knife. He then had them make a sheath and belt for it. When it was finished, Cory turned to Randy and asked, "You got a cent in your pocket?''

"Yessir.''

"I'll sell you the knife for a cent. Would give it to you, but they say it's bad luck to give a knife to a friend.''

"I don't want to lose you as a friend," Randy said. Paying the penny, he became the proud possessor of the knife. On their afternoons together, he and Buck spent almost as much time practicing with the knives as they did with their guns. They became highly proficient with both, and also as swimmers. It was at swimming that Randy really excelled, that coming as naturally to him as the other things came to Buck.

One day in the early part of August, Samuel, who also served as John Rushton's valet, came to Randy's room and told him that his father would like to see him right away. When Randy reached the door of the office, he saw his mother was also there. From their appearance, he judged that both of his parents were in a serious frame of mind and wondered what the meeting was about.

"Sit down, Randy," his father said. "We have something to discuss with you." Randy took a seat and waited apprehensively, not knowing what to expect.

"Your mother and I think it is time for you to take a look at the young negro men and select one to be your personal servant. We had expected Jason to be the one, but the incident involving the two of you has made that impossible."

Randy thought of Buck, and he knew that his independent friend would never understand his having a servant just to take care of him. "I don't want a personal servant," he said. "I'm doing fine with the help I get from Samuel and the women house servants."

"All young gentlemen of your station have a valet to serve them," his mother said; "and it is time to start training one for you."

"I don't want one!" Randy reponded.

"Your mother is right, Randy. Samuel has been with me since I was ten. I couldn't get along without him."

"I know you need him, Father; but I want to take care of myself. I don't know what I'd do with a valet hanging around me all of the time. I don't need one, and I don't want one!"

"If you feel so strongly against it, we shan't press the matter now," his mother said. "I am sure you will realize one of these days that you require someone to look after your personal needs, and you will regret not having trained anyone to do it."

"Maybe I shall, Mother; but I don't think so."

Carolyn looked at her son, and smiled. "I hope you never do," she said. She felt he was making a mistake, but she was proud of his independence and of his taking a firm stand against their trying to force on him something he did not want. Her boy was growing up and she liked the direction he was taking.

While waiting for school to start, Randy continued to coach Buck in grammar and diction; and with books supplied by Miss Childers, Buck was beginning to show a little progress. The boys were spending a lot of time together. Randy usually had dinner with the McCords on Wednesdays and Buck with the Rushtons on Saturdays. They sometimes spent the night together at one home or the other. Buck was feeling much more comfortable at Prairie's Edge, his timidity and uneasiness disappearing as he became more familiar with the people and surroundings there. The highlight of every visit to the Rushton home was seeing Ellen again, although he held her in such awe that he found it difficult to talk with her; but that wasn't necessary for him. He had placed her so high upon a pedestal that he was content just to see and be near her.

One afternoon as the boys lay on the sand by the river after a swim, Buck said to Randy, "You know, my Pa's got a scar on his right wrist. I asked 'im . . ."

"Him," Randy corrected.

"Him how he got it, an '. . ."

"And."

"And he said that when he was a young'un . . ."

"Young boy."

"A young boy, he had a real good friend; and they cut their wristes..."

"Wrists."

"Their wrists, and mixed their blood. Then they took an oath to be blood brothers. It's som'p'n . . ."

"Something."

"Something Indians do."

They lay quietly for a while, and some time passed before Randy broke the silence. "Buck, would you be my blood brother?" he asked.

"You'd hafta cut your . . ."

"Have to."

"Have to cut your wrist."

"Just a little would be enough, wouldn't it?"

"I think so, and I'd be real proud to, Randy." He took out his knife, wiped the blade on his trousers, and started to place the sharp edge to his wrist.

"Wait a minute!" Randy said. "Let's decide on the oath first."

They remained quiet, thinking. After a few moments, Randy

suggested, "How about, 'With the mixing of our blood, I take you to be my blood brother for as long as I live'?"

"Shouldn't it have something about swearing?"

"Of course. We can begin it with, 'I solemnly swear' and end it with, 'So help me, God'."

"That sounds good. Do we say it together?"

"Yes."

Buck placed the blade of the knife against his wrist, and carefully pressed it until a trickle of blood appeared. Randy, who was watching closely, blanched. Buck handed him the knife and said, "Don't cut too deep. There's a blood vessel in your wrist that'll bleed like a stuck pig."

Randy glanced quickly at him. He had lost all interest in correcting grammar. Gritting his teeth, he grimly pressed the blade slowly against his wrist and at the first sight of blood, hastily snatched it away. The boys then joined the two cuts and tightly pressed them together. Slowly they repeated the oath together.

"I'll always honor that oath," Randy said.

"Me, too," Buck replied.

Randy took a hankerchief from his pocket and tore it in half for bandages. They wrapped each other's wrist tightly, and the bleeding soon stopped. The bandages were removed before they left for home.

At supper that night, Ellen noticed Randy's cut when he reached for a piece of bread as he was served by Samuel. "Randy cut his wrist," she announced.

Carolyn quickly glanced at her son's wrist. "We don't discuss things like that at the table, Ellen," she said.

Carolyn looked at her husband and smiled. He returned the smile; and reaching under the table, John gently pressed her left arm, the lower part of which was resting atop the napkin in her lap. She knew he was saying, "Thank you for understanding." To her surprise, she was more than understanding; she was quite pleased that the two boys had committed themselves to a lasting friendship.

Chapter III

The Maturing Years

The long-awaited day for school to open finally arrived. Carolyn Rushton, anxious that things start well for Buck, had one of the servants watching for him so she and John could be on hand when he arrived. He rode up about ten minutes before eight o'clock and was warmly greeted by them. He wore homespun as usual; but he made a good appearance in his clean, freshly ironed, nicely fitting clothes and the new shoes.

It had been agreed that Buck would have dinner with the Rushtons on school days. At the suggestion of John, Carolyn had made a trip to Buck's home to extend this invitation. As John had expected, there was resistance to it on the part of Cory. Carolyn, as tactfully as she could, pointed out to Buck's parents that learning social graces was a vital part of a young person's education and that they were still teaching Randy and Ellen how they should behave at the table and in their association with others. With Sadie's help, Cory was persuaded to go along with it. Although he was considered a guest, as long as he attended school at Prairie's Edge, Buck frequently showed up with a quarter or half of venison, a wild turkey, quail, fresh fish from the pond, or assorted jars of jams, jellies, and relishes. This disturbed Carolyn, but John told her she would have to accept it just as Buck's parents had accepted his having dinner with them.

Shortly after Buck's arrival, a small buggy driven by a negro man drew up in front of the house; and a blond, blue-eyed girl got out. The buggy drove off, returning to Cahaba, the home of the Beaumonts, about a mile south of Prairie's Edge. Although seven months older than Ellen, Sally Beaumont was much the smaller of the two girls. She was quite pretty, and Buck noted the poised manner in which she greeted the Rushtons. Without waiting for an introduction, she turned to Buck, gave him a friendly smile, extended her small hand, and said, ''I'm Sally Beaumont. I'm glad to meet you at last. I've heard so much about you,

46

but we never seemed to be here at the same time. Guess we'll make up for it now.''

''An' I'm glad to make your acquaintance,'' Buck replied as he took the little hand. He knew he was going to like this girl, but it was a different kind of liking from that he had for Ellen.

Buck saw Sally's eyes light up as she looked past him toward the stairs. About that time Randy's cheerful voice was heard, ''Hello, Sally! Hi, Buck! Y'all ready for school?''

''I'm always ready for school. You know me, the eager student. Where's Ellen?'' came Sally's cheerful response.

''She should be here in a minute.''

''She's here already,'' Ellen replied from the direction of the stairway; and she immediately made her appearance. ''Hello, Sally, Buck!'' she said, ''Don't y'all know I'm never late? You're just early.''

Before Buck could respond to her greeting, Carolyn spoke up, ''You had better get to the classroom, or you will all be late.''

With the girls leading the way, the boys followed down the hall of the north wing to the classroom where Miss Childers was waiting; and Buck's formal education began. It couldn't have been under better circumstances—a teacher who was sympathetic and pleased to have him as a pupil and three fellow students, much farther advanced, all eager to help and to make him comfortable in his new surroundings. Despite these conditions, it was still a difficult period for him. He was far behind the others, both academically and in social development. Situations frequently arose where he was at a distinct disadvantage, such as the first time he was called upon to stand and answer a question about one of the lesson assignments for the day. He stood, ill at ease, and was haltingly attempting to explain something which he did not fully comprehend himself. Hoping to relieve some of his tension, Miss Childers in a sympathetic tone asked, ''Are you nervous, Buck?''

''Yes'm,'' came his response, ''I feel like a one-legged man in a butt kickin' contest.''

Both girls covered their faces with their hands and tried to control their giggles. Not so Randy; he laughed loudly.

''That will be enough,'' Miss Childers said to the laughing students; then in a conciliatory tone she addressed the befuddled boy, ''Buck, we should not refer to that part of the body in mixed company.''

''Yes'm. I'm sorry,'' he murmured contritely.

''It's all right; you didn't know.''

School brought many changes in the routine of Buck's life. He still had his chores to do—milk the cows in the morning, fill the wood boxes in the kitchen and bedroom, bring in water from the well, and feed and water the stock in the late afternoon. The time with Cory was changed from Wednesdays to Saturdays, with Randy usually joining them for dinner and the activities of the day. One Saturday Cory asked Randy to bring both his gun and sight when he next came over, and Randy showed up with them the following week. Cory attached the sight to the gun and said, "I wanta see just how good the gun is. We'll take it over to the river an' give it a try."

For use as targets, Cory carried with him two boards about twelve inches square on which he had stained in the center of each a circle four inches in diameter. At the gravel bar, he set the targets against the bank and stepped off a hundred yards. Setting the sight for that distance, he fired from the prone position and found the shot a little high and to the right. He fired again with the same results. Calibrating the sight, he fired again and found the shot to be on target. He next moved to 200 yards, and the gun was shooting slightly high. He recalibrated the sight until the gun shot true. Returning to 100 yards, he found it was still on target. Starting at 300 yards, he increased the range in increments of fifty yards, firing at least three rounds at each distance. The gun was very accurate up to 400 yards. At 600 yards he could not stay in the circle, but he hit the board consistently; however, at 700 yards, the radial deviation was great enough to cause him to miss the board about half the time. At 800 yards he could hit the board only one-fourth of the time.

Buck and Randy watched in awe this remarkable shooting. Cory was no less surprised himself; for with his own gun, an 1841 Mississippi rifle like Buck's, he could depend on consistently hitting a target the size of the board at only 200 yards. Cory made up his mind that, regardless of cost, he had to have one of these guns.

That night Randy told his father about the shooting he had witnessed that afternoon. It came as no surprise to John Rushton, but a thought occurred to him. He asked Randy, "What did Mr. McCord think of the gun?"

"He could hardly believe any gun could be so accurate."

"If you see him tomorrow, tell him I would like to discuss something with him, at his convenience, of course."

Two days later Cory came to Prairie's Edge. He found John in his office and noticed a Whitworth rifle standing in the corner. He wondered what Randy's gun was doing there. After exchanging greetings, he sat down.

"I appreciate your coming over," John said.

"No trouble. Wanted to give you a report anyhow. The Jameses have made good progress clearing the land. Soon's all the crops're in, they can give full time to it. Seth's pushin' 'em purty good; he's real anxious to get married.''

"Would you like for me to go ahead and free the girl?''

"Let 'em clear the land fust.''

"The reason I asked you to come over was to talk to you about the stallion you ride. Is he for sale?''

"Not that one. You may not want 'im, anyhow. He was sired by that colt, Thor, I got from you; an' he's much as half brother to some of yours.''

"I know, but I have some new mares I would like to breed to him; and I've got a proposition for you. See that rifle over there? Several years ago I was hunting deer over beyond Demopolis. One of the men on the hunt had a Whitworth. After seeing the gun, I had to have one. They aren't easy to get; so when I ordered mine, I also ordered one to give Randy when he got older. The guns were a long time coming, and I had my accident before they got here. That one has never been fired, and I'll never be able to use it. I have heard you don't stand your stallions and jacks at stud, but I hope you will make an exception. I'd like to trade the Whitworth for six stud services by your stallion.''

"Them's purty high fees just for a hoss to have a little fun.''

"I don't think you appreciate how much that horse is worth at stud. He and Buck's gelding have the smoothest trotting gait I've ever seen. Frankly, I think I'll be getting the better of the bargain.''

"I'm not convinced of it; but if that's what you want, it's fine with me. I was aimin' to git one of them guns, anyhow.''

By the time school closed at the end of the following June, Buck was a different boy. He had grown considerably during the year and was now almost six feet in height. Randy, too, had grown; but he probably would never exceed by much the five feet and ten inches his father had attained. The greatest changes in Buck, though, were in his manner of speaking and his development of confidence in the new environment into which he had plunged so suddenly.

Life had also gone well for Randy during this period, but in the middle of June he received some disheartening news from his father. Mr. Pring had reassigned Jason to the fields. When he first went to the stables, Jason had applied himself; for he did love horses and liked to be around them. However his good performance did not last. His discontent with being a slave began to resurface, and it showed in both his attitude and the quality of his work. When John told his son of Mr. Pring's decision, Randy could only say, "I knew it was coming. I talked with Jason and told him this would happen unless he changed his attitude, but he didn't seem to care. Will you sell him?''

''Not now; he's still too young. It may come to that; Mr. Pring says he is a born trouble maker. You know him better than anyone else; do you have any suggestions?''

''I know that deep down he is better than he appears on the surface. Maybe working in the fields will straighten him out. Don't sell him before he's eighteen, anyway.''

''If that's what you want.''

The year 1855 came and went. In the fall of 1856, after the crops were harvested and the cotton and surplus corn sold, Cory came to Prairie's Edge with the records and the landowner's share from Seth James' sharecropping.

''Looks like Miss Childers will get a nice bonus for teaching Buck this past year,'' John said.

''No more than she deserves for what she's done for him. I can't believe the change in the boy. I never thought a lot of book learnin' an' such was important, but I was wrong. 'Course, I know it wasn't all her doin's. A lot of the things he's learned was from you an' your missus.''

''He's a bright boy and learns quickly. We were glad to do what we could. As for the sharecropping, I'm pleased with the results of our little project; and starting with the next crop, I'm going to set up three families a year as sharecroppers. If things go right, I'll put into the program every willing family I believe is capable of making a go of it. I know all of them can't do it, and I'll continue to take care of those who can't or won't. I'm convinced that proceeds from farming will be as good through sharecropping as by doing it with slave labor I have to support. They will have more incentive to produce when they reap part of the benefits of their labor. Where any loss will occur will be in losing the value of their increase when they become free. Let's face it, Cory, the assets we planters have accumulated have been as much or more from the reproduction of slaves as from our agricultural pursuits.''

''Can't dispute that. Since you're now goin' into this open like, I guess it's time for you to take over Seth an' Samantha.''

''I would appreciate it if you would continue as is for a while. My hands may be full for a few years until everything is going the way I want it. This Seth thing is doing fine, so let's leave it alone for the time being.''

After Cory left, John sent for Mr. Pring and informed him of his decision. He carefully explained the sharecropping operation to him.

''How will I fit into this?''

"Almost like you do now. We shall build a house and necessary outbuildings for each family on the land they farm. These people will need someone to advise and guide them, almost as much as they require supervision now. You will probably find them to be more cooperative and better workers since they will get part of the profits. I want you to stay very close to what they are doing."

"I believe that this can work, Mr. Rushton; and it's a fine thing you are doing. Don't know how some of the other planters will take it, though."

"I'm not worried about that. If they have any foresight, they will get into it themselves."

"While I'm here, I want to talk to you about Jason. I hate to keep bothering you about him, but I'm afraid he is going to be serious trouble. I've heard he has been talking to some of the people about the injustice of slavery, saying no man has the right to own another. He's trying to get them stirred up. I know you won't let me put the strap to him, but he ought to be sold to someone who will."

"I hope it doesn't come to that," John replied. His mind went back to the remarks he had made on the veranda three years ago, and he knew where Jason had gotten some of his ideas.

Things had been going well on the McCord farm; Cory had followed Sadie's suggestion and was no longer farming himself. Two more of the James children had married and had become tenants on the farm, bringing the total to seven families, not including Seth and Samantha. Cory even loosened the strings of his purse and had been spending money freely. He had bought another jack, several young colts, and more mares. Already his production of mules had doubled; and by not selling any of his horses, he had greatly increased his breeding stock. He was also buying selected milk cows and bulls and was beginning to see results in the improved production of their increase. He had no ready market for the additional milk produced, so he placed the better cows with his tenants and sold the less productive ones they replaced. By doing this, he was still able to use the better producers for breeding purposes.

One day Buck happened to be in the room when Cory took a money box from its hiding place in the fireplace chimney. Cory opened it and showed the contents to his son. "What do you see?" he asked.

Buck couldn't fathom the point his father was trying to make, so he answered, "Money?"

"But what kinda money? You see, it's mostly gold. Neither me nor Pa believed in banks or paper money. Gold's the thing. When you sell somethin' always git gold if you can. If you can't git gold, then swap what you git for gold. No matter what, gold'll always be valuable. Now come with me; I think it's about time to show you somethin' else.''

Buck followed his father from the house and across the pasture to the blacksmithing area under the shed. Going to the anvil which was bolted to a section of a tree trunk about eighteen inches high, Cory pointed to a small slot type hole next to the rear edge of the anvil base. The slot was difficult to see on the dirty, rough wood; and Buck had never noticed it before.

"There's a hollow place under that anvil. Your gran'pa an' me has never kept more'n a thousan' dollars in the money box. If we got more'n that, we put it in the slot. Don't know how much is in there, but I expect it's consid'able. We ain't never took the anvil off to look."

"Does Ma know about this?"

"She does."

Three more years passed. John now had nine families in the sharecropping operation and would soon have four more, adding three new ones and taking over Seth James. He was pleased with the success thus far. As anticipated, those in the program were working harder. They were accumulating credit balances on the books, and some of the first brought into the new venture would soon be in position to start purchasing their freedom. This would be a slow process, however, as there would be several involved in each family. There had been an unexpected benefit from the program; a number of the people not yet selected were also working harder in order to prove their capability to be sharecroppers.

Randy was now riding a chestnut mare, one of the six Rushton horses sired by Cory's stallion. This horse had been named Chessy; and like Roana, had been trained to come to Randy's whistle. Roana had been passed to Ellen who loved to ride and was often seen on the little mare about and near the plantation.

In the early part of 1859, Buck said at supper one night that school at Prairie's Edge would come to an end in June. Both Cory and Sadie received the news in surprised silence before Cory asked, "Why?"

"Miss Childers feels that the others are now ready for college. Randy will go to Howard, and Ellen and Sally will attend Judson."

"I wasn't much for you goin' to school at Prairie's Edge; but I'm real proud of what it's done for you an' the man you've become, an' I'd like to see you go on. Will they take you at Howard?"

"They'll take me, but it may not be at the college level."

"Go over to Marion an' talk to 'em, an' start as high as you can."

Sadie, whose face had shown her disappointment over Buck's announcement, was now beaming. She reached over and placed her hand on that of her husband. "You're a good man, Cory McCord," she said. "God'll bless you for this."

"He's already done it," Cory replied.

It was a sad day for Buck when the last day of classes at Prairie's Edge arrived. He had continued to grow in stature as well as poise and now stood six feet and two inches tall. He was well built; and although he still dressed in homespun, his clothes were always neat, and he wore them with self-assurance. He was a handsome young man, as was Randy, the latter having reached the height of five feet and almost eleven inches.

Both Ellen and Sally had matured into beautiful young ladies. Ellen was almost five feet and four inches tall, while the diminutive Sally barely reached five feet. The vivacious personality of the latter more than made up for her lack of stature. A strong camaraderie had developed among the four young people during their years together, and this was apparent in the way they enjoyed each other's company. Although openly at ease around Ellen, inwardly Buck still stood in awe of her. To him she was the finest and most beautiful person in the world. The original attraction he felt when he first met her had grown in depth each year until now he was hopelessly in love with her; hopeless because he could not bring himself to believe she could ever return his love. Although he was ashamed of neither his background nor his parents, he felt there existed between his way of life and hers such a broad chasm that he could never expect her to cross it. Despite these misgivings, his love for her was so great that several times he had been on the verge of declaring it, but fear of rejection always stopped him. He felt certain that such a rebuff would bring an end to the seemingly platonic relationship they both enjoyed, and he could not bear the thought of losing that.

When the four students came from the classroom for the last time, they found John and Carolyn Rushton waiting on the veranda with Sally's parents, Edmond and Priscilla Beaumont. They were joined by Miss Childers. Refreshments had been prepared for a little party to celebrate the occasion. Carolyn was serving the punch; and as she handed a cup to Buck, she said, "I'm sorry your parents aren't with us today."

"They appreciated your invitation; but you know Ma, she's not much for leaving the house. There aren't many places she will go, besides church," Buck replied.

Buck had been the last one to be served, so Carolyn filled a cup for herself and said, "Today you young people are seeing the end of an important period in your lives, as will John and I. We shall miss having you around all week, especially at dinner. It won't be the same without you."

"Oh, you'll be welcoming the change," Sally said. "I can't imagine Mother putting up with what you have all these years."

"Nor I," Mrs. Beaumont confirmed; "you are truly a saint, Carolyn."

"While passing out compliments, let's not overlook the marvelous job Miss Childers has done," Carolyn said. "We can be pleased with our children's accomplishments."

"I had exceptional material with which to work," Miss Childers responded. "I am proud of all of them, especially Buck for what he has done in only six years. He had a long way to go when he came to us."

"Yes, about two miles," Randy spoke up; and this brought a laugh.

'I'll never forget his calling it 'pausing' a sentence," Sally said.

"That's the way he did it—one pause after another," Randy replied, bringing another laugh.

"Listen to the mathematical genius who still thinks eleven times twelve is a hundred and twenty-two," Buck retorted, referring to a boner Randy had pulled in class that morning.

"Touché! But the funniest thing you ever did was the remark you made about feeling like a one-legged man." The four young people laughed.

"Why did he say that?" Carolyn asked.

"I'll tell you later, Mother," Ellen said and then defensively added, "he was just terribly nervous at the time."

Smiling, Buck said, "I guess I did feel a little at a disadvantage."

"There's something I've been curious about," Sally said, changing the subject. Looking at Randy, she continued, "You and Buck both have a scar at the same place on your right arm; does this have any significance?"

"I'd like to know the answer to that, too," Ellen said, remembering the cut on Randy's wrist and her mother's strange reaction to it.

The young men looked at each other. "Shall we tell them?" Randy asked.

"It's all right with me," Buck replied.

"Not long after Buck and I became friends, we cut our wrists, mixed our blood, and took an oath to be blood brothers. It's an Indian custom."

"Why, that's one of the sweetest things I ever heard!" Sally exclaimed.

"And that's the way it's been ever since, and always shall be," Randy stated. Looking at Buck, he continued, "Right, Brother?"

"Right!" Buck responded, lifting his cup as in a toast.

With a half-smile he continued, "I'm not sure there was much blood mixed. I've seen more blood on Ma's finger when she pricked it with a needle than there was on Randy's wrist. I think I got short changed."

"What are you talking about? I bled so much, I stained the whole gravel bar."

"That's hard to believe," Ellen said, aware of her brother's aversion to the sight of blood.

"I'll prove it to you. The next time the river gets up, I'll take you over there and show you how red it runs when it gets up over the bar."

"I suppose the red clay country it passes through has nothing to do with it?"

"Absolutely not. That color comes from good old Rushton blood rushing on to sea!"

Everyone laughed. Then Sally, looking first at Ellen and then at Buck, inquired, "Does this make you blood brother and sister?"

Buck didn't like the question. He certainly didn't think of Ellen as a sister, and the last thing he wanted was for her to look upon him as a brother. To answer, "No", however, might be misunderstood, so he replied, "I'll leave that for Ellen to decide."

Ellen didn't care for the idea either; she said, "I'll have to think about that!"

Carolyn was following this conversation with interest. She watched her daughter and Buck very closely during these last exchanges and with a mother's intuition knew there was something between them she had not noticed before. Was this good; would she want her daughter to marry this young man in homespun? She wasn't sure; what would her life be like in his world? Perhaps they weren't aware of each other's feelings, and nothing would ever come of it. Like before, she reasoned, time will tell.

When Buck got home late that afternoon and released Skin into the pasture, he noticed a strange horse there. It had the conformation of a fine animal, but appeared somewhat jaded. When he took his tack to the harness room he saw on the floor a well worn saddle with a bedroll tied behind it. He went into the house and found his mother, as usual at that time of day, busy at the stove. His father was seated with another man at the kitchen table, and each had a cup of coffee before him. The stranger, whose age he found difficult to guess, was dressed in a soiled and dingy buckskin suit. He was lean and lithe, and looked as tough as a pine knot. His grizzled hair and beard both needed trimming.

"Buck, come shake hands with Cally Callaghan. Cally this here's my boy, Buck."

"If this is a boy, he's gonna be a lotta help to his ma when he grows up. Glad to know you, Buck," Cally said as he rose and shook Buck's hand vigorously.

"Pleased to meet you," Buck replied. After shaking Cally's hand, he went to his mother and gave her the expected hug. He looked at the woodbox which had been filled.

Cory saw the glance toward the box and said, "Thought you'd be kinda late today, so I took care of the stock, too. Come on an' have a seat."

"Mucha 'blige," Buck said, and sat down with them.

"Me an' Cally got acquainted when Tom an' me went to Texas. He's on his way to see his kin in Tennessee an' come by to bring word from Tom."

"How is he?" Buck asked, looking toward Cally.

"He's doin' just fine; got a big ranch southeast of San 'Tonio an's raisin' hosses an' cattle. He's married; got three gals an' two boys."

"Tom wants me to sell out an' join 'im out there, but I got too many irons in the fire to do it," Cory said.

"Y'all git washed up for supper," Sadie interrupted, as she began filling bowls and platters to carry to the table.

After supper, the three men retreated to the back porch. Before they sat down, Cally said, "Cory, I know you ain't a drinkin' man; but I've had a long tough trip an' could use a little nip. I couldn' find none in Marion when I come th'ough there. You wouldn' happen to have a little tucked away for snake bite or somethin'?"

"Sadie usually has a little hid away; I'll git it," Cory said. "You won't find none openly in Marion. They charges a thousand dollars for a license to sell it."

"That discourages honest trade," Cally replied.

Cory left, and he returned shortly with a glass and almost a full bottle which he handed to Cally. Pouring out a stiff drink, Cally tossed it down and poured another. This one he drank more slowly, sipping it. Properly fortified, he was now ready for conversation. He and Cory began reminiscing about their experiences in Texas, and Buck soon recognized Cally as a natural and humorous story teller. After completing one tale, he said to Buck, "Your pa was quite a man in them days.''

"Still is," Buck replied.

Looking at the big man sitting beside him, Cally said, "Don't doubt it a bit. I seen Cory in the dawgonedest fight I ever seen in my life. There was a young fellow, a big son-uv-a-gun, who come out to fight Mex'cans, but got there a little late. Well, this young fellow was full of vinegar, an' made the brag that he ain't never met the man he couldn' whup. Somebody told 'im he mustn'a never met Cory McCord an' pointed your pa out." Cally paused to take another sip and then continued:

"Well suh, that young fellow—wish I could rememba his name—you rememba it, Cory?" Cory shook his head; and Cally resumed the story, "Well, he challenged your pa to a fight to see who was the best man; but Cory never liked to fight just for fun an' wouldn' have no part of it. That fellow couldn' take 'No' for a answer an' kept proddin'. Cory didn' pay 'im no never mind till one day the fellow called 'im a liar about somethin' he said. That done it. I seen a heap of fights in my time but never one like that. He wasn't quite as tall as Cory, but he was heavier. That was before your pa got so fat."

"What do you mean, fat?" Cory said.

"Now, don't get testy, Cory. Anybody'd git fat on this easy livin' an' eatin' Sadie's cookin'." Cally looked at Buck and winked.

Cory laughed, refusing to take the bait any further; and Cally, satisfied with the reaction he had gotten, continued his story: "Both of 'em took a beatin' you wouldn' believe. I don't see how either one of 'em stood it. Cory finally whupped 'im; but not 'cause he was a better fighter, he just outlasted 'im."

"Wouldn' want to tangle with that wildcat ag'in," Cory said.

"He didn' ask for a rematch neither," Cally replied.

Sadie appeared and announced that the company room was ready and she had a tub filled with hot water for Cally to take a bath; but Cally would have no part of it. He said it might "spile" him. Bidding everyone goodnight, he carried the bottle with him as he went to the harness room for his bedroll and on into the barn.

Cally was in no hurry to leave. Cory was busy clearing more land for pasture. Some of the Jameses had been working for him; but the crops were now demanding most of their time, so Buck and Cally joined in the work. They were cutting down some good timber, and Cory was dragging the logs off to one side until he decided what was to be done with them.

A week had passed since Cally's arrival, and the three men were sitting on the back porch after supper. Cally had fetched the bottle and finished the little whiskey left in it, not much but enough to get him into a talkative mood.

"I was lookin' at the ir'gation thing you fixed up for the garden. That's purty good."

"Unless we get too much rain, we always have a good garden," Buck volunteered.

"I know a fellow out near San 'Tonio who ir'gated some of the richest land I ever seen. With all that water, you wouldn' believe the things he growed. He was braggin' to the sto'keeper where he traded about his 'taters. The sto'keeper told 'im if they was so fine, to bring 'im some; an' he'd see if he could sell 'em. This fellow, whose name was Higgins, asked 'im how many he could use, an' the sto'keeper said a hundred pounds. 'Stead of bein' happy about it, Higgins got real mad, sayin' that he wouldn' cut one of his taters for nobody!"

This brought a good laugh, and Cally picked up the empty whiskey bottle. "Where can I git some whiskey to pay Sadie back?"

"It ain't necessary, Cally."

"I know, but I wanta git some for myself, too."

"The closest is about two miles up the road. There's a man name Barlow who moved in there a coupla years ago with his two boys. I heared they come from up on Sand Mount'n. They make corn liquor. It's plain white; but folks who buy it says it's good, an' they call it Sand Mount'n white lightnin'. It ain't a legal still, 'cause they don't pay no taxes; but nobody ever bothers 'em."

The next day, following Cory's directions, Cally left for the Barlow place and returned a couple of hours later with Sadie's bottle filled and a gallon jug of his own. He said to Cory, "There was one of them James boys up there workin' at the still. He was one of them who helped us t'other day; I believe his name is David."

"That'd be Abel's boy. He's been havin' some trouble with 'im. I better talk to 'im about it."

The next day, Cory sent word to Abel that he wanted to see him. That night after supper, Abel showed up at the house; and when Cory told him about David's working at the still, Abel said, "Since that boy took to drinkin' he's give me one heap of trouble. I wouldn' give 'im nothin' to swap for liquor, so I guess he's workin' for it. I'll put a stop to it; you can 'pend on it. Don't know how there can be so much diff'rence in boys. Seth ain't never give me no trouble atall, 'cept marryin' that slave gal."

The following week, Buck rode over to Marion to check on his application for admission to Howard College and found he had been accepted at the college level. While talking with Dr. Henry Talbird, the president of Howard, he was told of plans which would require some additional building at the institution. Buck was too much Cory's son to miss a chance like this; and before leaving, he had an agreement to supply lumber in payment of his school expenses for the first year.

One night after supper, Abel again showed up at the house. This time he told Cory that the Barlows had been bringing David whiskey and were trying to get him to go back to work for them, and he was afraid David would do it. Cory told him not to worry; he would take care of the matter. The following morning, Cory rode up to the Barlow house. Before he dismounted, Sam Barlow appeared on the porch, followed by his two sons, Jethro and Caleb. Knowing Cory wasn't a customer, Sam Barlow asked, "You got bus'ness here?"

"You might say I have. One of my tenants, Abel James, is worried about his boy David. The boy's been drinkin' an' gittin' mixed up in somethin' that ain't exactly legal. Abel tells me y'all been carryin' liquor to 'im an' tryin' to git 'im to work at your still. I'd 'preciate it if you'd leave the boy be."

"He ain't no boy; he's a man an' old enough to make his own mind up."

"That may be but take a little advice; leave that boy alone!"

"We ain't takin' no advice an' no orders from you."

"Here's one order you better take. Stay off of my place. I don't want to see nor hear of any one of you ever settin' foot on my place ag'in." With that, Cory turned his horse and rode off. Behind him he heard Jethro ask:

"Want me to git your gun, Pa?"

"Let it be," Sam replied.

Two weeks went by; and Cory, with Buck and Cally, continued to clear the land. Randy sometimes appeared and pitched in. One day Abel showed up at the work site to see Cory.

"I hates to keep bother'n' you, Mista Cory, but dem Barlows been back to see David twice mo'. The fust time, they brung 'im liquor, an' tried to git 'im to work fur 'em. They say he is old enough to do as he please. I told that boy, as long's he stay in my house, he gonna do as I please; an' if he don't, I'll break 'is plate—I'll saw off his end of the table! The nex' time they come, they try to git 'im to leave home. I's 'fraid he gonna go."

"Guess this'll take more'n talk to settle," Cory said. "Let me think on it."

After supper that night, Cory got from Cally the directions to the

Barlow still. He went to his bedroom, and came back wearing moccasins and carrying a rifle. "I'll be back in a little while," he said as he started for the barn.

Buck followed him. "Let me go with you, Pa."

"There are some things done better alone," Cory replied. Buck knew it was no time to argue, so he said nothing else; but he helped his father saddle his horse.

Cory mounted the stallion with his rifle in his hand and placed it in the sheath tied to the saddle. "Hand me the ax," he said.

Buck got the ax and gave it to his father. He walked beside his horse to the wide gate and opened it for him. Cory rode off to the northeast on the clay road, leaving Buck standing by the gate. Buck was again at the gate, holding it open, when Cory returned almost three hours later. "Any trouble?" he asked.

"Nary a bit."

They unsaddled the horse, turned him loose in the pasture, put up the tack, and went to bed.

When the Barlows arrived at their still the following morning, they found it completely destroyed. The copper cooker and condenser coil had been hacked to pieces. The oak barrels of mash had been turned over, their contents spilled, and the barrels broken up. Sam Barlow looked at the devastation and hissed one word, "McCord!"

That same morning, a heavy, rugged buggy drove up in front of Prairie's Edge. A young boy of nine was at the reins. Beside him was a well dressed man with a neatly trimmed beard who appeared to be under forty. At the back of the vehicle were a leather portmanteau and a large black bag. John Rushton was sitting on the veranda and had watched them come up the driveway. When they stopped, he said, "Come have a seat."

"Thank you," the man replied. Taking the reins from the boy, he tied them loosely around the whip standing in its socket. He and the boy got down from the buggy and climbed the steps to the veranda. Approaching Rushton, he offered his hand and said, "I am Doctor Woolley from up in Bibb County; and this is my nephew, John Yeager. He makes his home with us since he lost his folks a few years ago."[1]

"Pleased to meet you, Dr. Woolley," John said, taking his hand. "I'm John Rushton. I've heard of you; understand you have a plantation south of Brent on the road to Marion."

"Yes; our local community is known as Elfers."

Looking at the boy, who was obviously curious about the chair with wheels, John extended his hand and said, "Hello, John. You've got a good name. That's mine, too, you know. I'll bet you would like to have some lemonade.''

"Yessir, I would," the boy replied, taking the hand but still looking at the chair.

Rushton pulled a cord which rang a bell inside the house. A young negro appeared and was told to bring some iced lemonade. He then turned to the doctor and asked, "To what are we indebted for this visit?"

"Actually, two reasons. I was in Selma to attend to some business and to meet with Dr. White on a medical matter. I took John along, because I thought he would enjoy the trip; but to be honest, I guess I just wanted a good driver. Anyway, I finished up with everything a day early and decided to come see you on a couple of matters. I would like to buy one of your fine horses, and the other matter is your sharecropping venture. Word of it has gotten around, and I'd like to know more about it."

"Do you have many slaves?"

"About eighty."

"Then you may be interested in the way I have gone into it." John gave a detailed account of how he had started the sharecropping on a gradual basis, how it worked, its profitability, and the prospect of the people to buy their freedom. Dr. Woolley listened carefully, and occasionally interjected a question.

When John had completed his explanation, Dr. Woolley said, "You may be going in the direction we all should take. I intend to consider this matter very carefully. Just between us, the end of slavery in this country may not be too far off, and the time to prepare for the change is now."

"I agree with you wholeheartedly, and that is the principal reason I have gone into this. If I can be of any further help, feel free to call upon me. Now, about the horse; I'm sorry to say I have none to sell at this time. I have already committed all except my breeding stock. There is a man nearby, however, Cory McCord, who is raising horses equally as good as mine. Why don't you stay the night here at Prairie's Edge, and go over this afternoon to see what he has for sale? We would be pleased to have you and your nephew, and you have a long drive to your home."

"That's a gracious offer, but I don't want to impose upon your hospitality."

"No imposition, Doctor. The pleasure will be ours. Besides, it will give me a chance to know my young namesake better."

After dinner, Dr. Woolley left his nephew at Prairie's Edge and set out alone for the McCord farm.

Shortly before noon, Cory, Buck, and Cally, with a two-mule team, had snatched a large stump from where it had been circled with a trench three feet deep. It had been a hard effort, with Cally handling the team and Cory and Buck prying with long heavy poles. It was a good time to knock off for dinner, so they unhitched the mules, retrieved their guns, and rode the mules back to the house, Cory on one and Buck and Cally on the other. The guns they always carried with them, because they would sometimes see game or stir up a rattlesnake. The stump with its large spreading root structure was left by the hole.

After dinner they had a few chores to do around the house and did not return right away. When they got ready to go back to their task, Cory decided they could do better pulling the large stumps with a four-mule team. Leaving Cally to catch and harness two more mules, he and Buck returned to the area being cleared. They began to hitch the two mules to the stump to drag it to the burn pile. Cory was securing the chains while Buck held the reins. Without warning, from the wood on the east side of the clearing came the crack of a rifle, closely followed by another. At the sound of the first, Buck saw his father knocked to the ground, and blood suddenly colored a large area of his left sleeve between the elbow and shoulder.

"Pa!" he called and moved toward him. That movement probably saved his life, for the bullet from the second shot only creased the side of his head, but it sent him sprawling.

He was momentarily stunned, but was quickly brought out of it by Cory's voice yelling, "Git to the hole!"

Buck moved quickly to his father and got him to his feet, with Cory yelling to his son to leave him alone and get to the hole. A third shot came as they scrambled around the base of the stump, and Buck saw one of the roots shattered by it. They dropped into the trench, and Buck looked at his father's wound which was bleeding profusely. With a handkerchief and a piece of root, he hastily improvised a tourniquet, and stopped the flow of blood. Buck was sure the upper arm bone, like the root, had been shattered.

The Barlows were still out there, apparently all three of them; and Buck looked at his and Cory's rifles leaning against an oak tree about thirty feet away. Beside them were the cartridge boxes. "I'm going for the guns, Pa. Keep this tourniquet tight, and stay down."

Keeping the stump between him and where he thought the Barlows would be, he crawled from the hole and ran zigzaggedly, not for the guns but for the cover of another large tree. A shot rang out as he neared the tree, but it went wide. It helped him to locate better the position of the Barlows. He moved to the right, darting from tree to tree, until he got to the one against which the guns were resting. He reached quickly around the trunk and grabbed one gun and then the other. In the same way he retrieved the cartridge boxes.

"Pa," he called softly, "you stay down. I'm going to circle to my left."

"Can you bring me a gun?"

"Think I can do better in the woods."

"All right, but be keerful; there's three of them."

Buck took off his shoes in order to move more quietly, and faded back into the shadows of the trees. Moving farther to the east in an arc, he came to a spot which commanded a view of the area he thought the Barlows would be trying to reach to get a shot into the hole behind the stump. He could hear them coming very slowly in an effort to be quiet. He crouched behind a tree waiting, his own gun cocked and in hand, the other nearby. He heard a slight sound to the left of where he had expected them to appear; and looking in that direction, he saw Caleb emerge from between two underbrush trees. He watched for another to show; he had two guns and wanted two of them, but he couldn't wait. Caleb slowly raised his gun, pointing it in the direction of the hole where Cory lay. Buck aimed for the left side of Caleb's chest and fired. Caleb fell, hardly uttering a sound. Buck was sure he was dead by the time he hit the ground, for he never moved.

"Paw! He got Caleb," Jethro yelled from a hidden position not far behind the man on the ground.

"Can you help 'im?"

"Naw, I think he's dead—he ain't moved a muscle."

"That musta been Buck. Be keerful. They say he's like a Injun in the woods. Move up closer an' see if you can spot 'im."

"I ain't gittin' no closer."

"Then shut up, an' let's git back to the mules."

"What about Caleb?"

"We'll git 'im later. The woods ain't no place to be with no Injun."

They could be heard retreating through the trees. Buck wanted to follow, but his father demanded his attention. He went to the hole and found Cory passed out. His eyes were shut; the tourniquet was loose; and the wound was beginning to bleed again. As he tightened the restraint, Cory opened his eyes.

"You all right?" Buck asked.

"Yeah, did you git one of 'em?"

"Caleb."

"Sorry it wasn't Sam."

"I've got to get you home."

"Not yet. To git out of them woods with their mules, they'll prob'ly go out the gate at the pasture corner over by the road. They think they'll be safe at that distance an'll be in the open for a little. You can git another'n with the Whitworth."

Buck looked across the pasture to the area Cory mentioned and said, "I figure about 550 yards."

"More like 650; but split the diff'ence, an' set the sight for 600. Don't try to be fancy; go for the middle of the body; an' try to git Sam."

There was a noise to the right; and Cally came into view, rifle in hand, riding a running mule which he was vigorously kicking in the sides. When he drew up to them, Buck said, "The Barlows shot Pa. Let's git him on a mule, and you take him to the house."

"I ain't goin' nowhere till you shoot," Cory said.

Buck set the sight on the Whitworth, rested the cocked gun on a large root, and waited. He had hardly taken position when they appeared at the pasture corner, two men riding mules, one of them leading a riderless animal. They were headed for the gate as Cory had predicted. Buck took a deep breath, exhaled part of it, and carefully aimed at the middle of the body of the stockier of the two men. Leading his target slightly as it moved across the clear area, he slowly squeezed the trigger. The gun recoiled against his shoulder, and Buck saw Sam fall from the saddle. The other rider dropped the reins of the mule he was leading and, frantically kicking the sides of the one he was riding, headed for the gate. He didn't bother to open it but dived from the back of his mount over the fence, leaving both animals in the pasture.

Buck was disappointed to see the man he had shot get up from the ground. In one hand he held the reins of his mule; and with the other, he clung to the saddle. He managed to keep the mule between him and Buck as the animal half dragged him to the gate. He eventually got the gate open, and escaped to the road. The other two riderless mules followed, and all of them disappeared to the northeast. Buck had reloaded the Whitworth hoping for another shot; but the Barlows did not give him one, so he again turned his attention to his father.

They got Cory home and stretched him out on the bed. Buck told Cally to saddle a horse and ride to Marion for a doctor. As Cally left the room, Buck directed his mother to get a basin of water and some bandages; and for the first time, he noticed her ashen face. She left and soon returned with the requested items. By then Buck had cut away his father's sleeve and was looking at the terrible wound the bullet and splintered bone had made. Placing himself between the injury and his mother to shield her from the sight of it, he took the bowl of water and the bandages and suggested that she wait outside.

"I'll stay; you might need me," she said grimly.

As he began cleansing the wound, a buggy drove up in front of the house. Sadie left to see who it was. In a few minutes she returned with a bearded man who was carrying a large black bag.

"God's done sunt a doctor," she announced with matter-of-fact conviction.

Buck was trying to fasten a compress he had placed over the wound. The stranger said, "I'm Doctor Woolley. Let me take a look."

He examined the wound carefully, probing it and feeling the surrounding area. "It will have to come off," the doctor said. "There is too much damage for it to heal properly, and the danger of sepsis or gangrene is too great."

"Ain't no other way?" Cory asked.

"Not to my knowledge. We've got a lot to learn about wounds like this."

"Do what you gotta do. You're the doctor."

The operation was performed on the table in the kitchen with Buck assisting. As they were moving Cory, Aaron James appeared, having heard of the shooting. Using the horse Cally had saddled, Aaron was dispatched for the sheriff.

Cory's arm was removed about six inches below the shoulder. By going that high, there was sufficient skin and tissue for a flap. Cory came through the operation very well. While it was in progress, Cally went to Sadie, who had been sent out of the room. She was sitting quietly at the dining room table; her eyes were shut, and her lips were moving without sound as she prayed silently.

"There's somethin' needs doin'. Better it be me than Buck. I may not be back; can you fix me up with grub to last fo' or five days?"

Asking no questions, Sadie got up and left the room. She returned soon with a bag filled with food. One of the lumps showing in it was in the shape of her emergency bottle of whiskey. "You're a good woman, Sadie," Cally said when he saw the bag.

"You got a coffee pot an' skillet?"

"In my bedroll."

"Here's a poke for corn. You know where the shelled corn's at. Need anything else?"

"Think you done took care of ever'thing."

When he had saddled his horse and had the two bags tied behind the saddle, Sadie came out of the house. Giving him her hand, she said, "Thank you, Cally. You're a true, good friend. We'll be beholden, an' there'll always be a place at our table for your plate, if you can come back."

"Thankee, Sadie; an' take care of that ol' hoss. They ain't no more like 'im.''

"I know. He'll be all right. God didn' send that doctor for nothin'.''

It was almost seven o'clock before Sheriff Robert West arrived from Marion. The operation was over, and Cory was sleeping from a large dose of laudanum. Dr. Woolley had returned to Prairie's Edge without mentioning the reason for coming to the McCord home. Sadie had cleaned the kitchen and was getting together something for Buck to eat. She had neither taste nor desire for food herself. Buck had taken his father's dismembered arm to the family grave yard where he had buried it. When he returned from this unpleasant chore, he found the sheriff talking with Sadie.

After greeting Buck, the sheriff asked for details of what happened. Buck carefully related the afternoon's series of events. When he finished, the sheriff inquired, "What brought this about?''

"I'm not sure. You'll have to ask Pa.''

"Where's this man Callaghan you mentioned?''

"I don't know,'' Buck replied. He hadn't thought about Cally. "I'll ask Ma.''

He went into the kitchen, and talked with his mother. Returning, he reported to the lawman, "She said he left to attend to something. He didn't say what, but he may not be back.''

"Uh uh,'' the sheriff responded. "I'd better get to the Barlow place.''

"I'll go with you,'' Buck replied, picking up his gun. When he got his horse and went to the front of the house, he found the sheriff already mounted and ready to go. From the southwest they could hear a horse coming at a gallop. They waited to see who it was, and Randy rode up. He was carrying his rifle.

Randy said, "I just heard from Dr. Woolley. I got here as fast as I could.''

"You know Sheriff West, don't you?''

"Sure,'' and the two men exchanged greetings.

"We're going to the Barlow place,'' Buck said. "There could be shooting.''

"Let's go,'' Randy replied.

The three men moved off up the road. When they passed the area where Sam Barlow was shot, Buck pointed it out to the Sheriff and got down and closed the open gate. When he remounted, the lawman asked him where he had been at the time of the shooting; and he pointed out the place to him.

Just before reaching the Barlow house, the road passed thorough a wooded area. About fifty yards from the clearing in which the house sat, the sheriff suggested that they tie their horses and proceed the rest of the way on foot. As they came into the open area, they saw the house, dark and quiet in the dusk of the late afternoon. No one was in sight. At the sheriff's suggestion, they spread out and approached the house cautiously.

Randy saw it first. From a large oak at the left edge of the clearing was hanging a man with a rope around his neck. It was Sam Barlow, swinging very slightly in the gentle evening breeze. They went to the body and cut it down. He appeared to have been dead for some time.

The sheriff hailed the house, identifying himself. No reply came back. Twice more he called and still no response. Again the trio spread out; and they moved slowly toward the house, alert for fear of a shot from the dark cabin in front of them. The house was reached without incident. Inside things were in disarray. There was a pool of blood in a chair and more on the floor beside it, but most of it had dried. Randy avoided looking at it.

Examination revealed someone had grabbed food and clothing in a hurry and left. Outside there were only two mules, both still saddled. One of the saddles was stained with blood. "Looks like Jethro took off like the devil was after him," Sheriff West said.

Glancing at the body lying beneath the tree, Buck replied, "Maybe he was."

Taking a closer look at the ground, they could see where the body had been dragged from the house to the tree. Other sign showed that a horse had been used to hoist Sam. The sheriff examined the body as well as he could in the light of the moon which had come up.

"That bullet did a lot of damage," he said. "It struck him above the hip joint, and I believe it splintered the pelvic bone. No telling what all it's done inside. He could have been dead when strung up. Guess no more than two men know and probably just one. Maybe the doctor can tell us."

"Now I know why he was hanging onto the saddle," Buck said.

They loaded the body across one of the mules and took the other one to carry Caleb. By the time they got back to the pasture gate, it was well after dark; but a bright moon provided fair visibility.

"Do you think you can find Caleb's body?" the lawman asked.

"Yes, but if we go in there tonight, we may destroy the sign."

"I ain't worried about that. It's the sign in this area where Sam was shot that I'm interested in. Nobody can hit a man from where you said you were."

Randy laughed. "Don't give him a shot at you from that distance. He used a Whitworth.''

"What range did you fire at?''

"I set the sight for 600 yards. I guessed it at 550; Pa figured 650. I split the difference. Pa was just about right. I shot low; I was aiming for the middle of the body.''

"I want to take a look at that gun when we get back to your house.''

Buck had no trouble locating the body, which they loaded across the spare mule. When they got back to the McCord house, the sheriff went inside, where he carefully examined the Whitworth and sight. He noted that the latter was still set for 600 yards. He shook his head in disbelief and handed the gun back to Buck. He then asked if any of them knew of any Barlow relatives in the area, and none of them had ever heard of any. Before leaving with the two bodies, the sheriff said he would be back the next day.

Cory spent a fair night, aided by two additional doses of laudanum. Dr. Woolley stopped by early the following morning on his way home. He changed the bandage on Cory's arm and seemed pleased with the appearance of the stub. He suggested that they get a doctor from Marion to take over, as he was too far away. Buck asked how he happened to be so convenient when needed, and he said that he came looking to buy a horse but would see them later about it. Buck got information from him of the kind of horse needed.

The sheriff arrived about nine o'clock, and went in to see Cory.

"How are you doing?'' he asked.

"Tol'ably, just tol'ably,'' Cory replied.

"Sorry about your arm, but it saved your body from the ball; and probably saved your life.''

"Hadn't thought of it that way; just lucky, I reckon.''

"What was this all about, Cory?''

"Fool judgment on my part.'' He then related the events leading up to the ambush.

"You shoulda come to me.''

"That ain't my way.''

"I know, dammit! But we got law here in this county now, and the days of you people settling things among yourselves have got to come to an end.''

"I can't argue with you on that. I coulda got my boy killed.''

"You damned near did. Have you seen that crease on his head?''

Sheriff West asked Buck to go with him to the scene of the shooting and to bring the Whitworth. They first went to the area where Cory was shot and Caleb had been killed. The sheriff carefully examined the ground, saying little but asking many questions. He picked out an oak tree at the edge of the wood from which the Barlows had emerged when Sam was shot.

"Let's see if that gun is as good as y'all say. See if you can hit the trunk about four feet off the ground. You got three shots."

Buck looked at the tree. He judged the trunk to be about eighteen inches in diameter and the distance about 600 yards. Checking the sight and then resting the gun on the root as before, he fired three carefully aimed shots.

"Now, let's take a look over that way," the lawman said.

When they got to the pasture corner, the sheriff headed for the tree. There were three newly made holes forming almost an equilateral triangle, the top of which was about four feet above the ground.

"If I hadn't seen it, I wouldn't believe it," was his only comment. He examined the surrounding area briefly and said to Buck, "Let's go to the Barlow place."

They found no indication that anyone had been there since the previous evening. There was a cow in pain from needing to be milked. Buck fed and milked her, pouring the milk into a trough in a pen holding two hogs. There were a few chickens, and he fed them some corn. There was also a goat, but the animal was grazing in a grassy area near a small stream and needed no attention.

"I'll get one of the neighbors to take care of the animals," the sheriff said. "Don't suppose you'd want to take them?"

"Not I, and don't give them to any of our tenants, either."

They went to the still which was located in a small hollow with a running brook. When the sheriff saw the wreckage, he couldn't help chuckling.

"Cory really did a job on it. Doubt I would have been as thorough."

They returned to the Barlow house, and the lawman said to Buck, "I'm going up the road to see the Smiths about taking care of the animals. We'll probably sell the mules to pay the burial expenses. You can go on home now. I wouldn't worry about this, Buck. It seems to be a case of self-defense. Even though you shot Sam after he had apparently quit the fight, you couldn't be sure he had. Besides, he was still on your property with a rifle; and he was an ambusher who would have tried it again at the first opportunity. The doctor ain't sure; but he thinks Sam died from the hanging, although he is of the opinion he most likely would have died from the wound. He lost a lot of blood and was tore up pretty bad inside. There could be an inquest, but I doubt the county lawyer will ask for it. One more thing, though, if Jethro shows up here again, you let me take care of it. Understand?''

"Yessir."

"Tell your folks I'll stop by on my way back to town."

"I'll tell Ma to expect you for dinner."

"That's what I had in mind."

After dinner the sheriff went in for a word with Cory before returning to Marion. He assured him there probably would be no action taken against Buck. He also told him about Buck's exhibition of shooting.

"He's a good shot, an' that's a fine gun. Don't think either's got a equal. I never admitted it to 'im, but Buck's better'n me."

"I can believe it. Until today, you were the best I ever saw."

Chapter IV

College

Under the diligent care of Dr. C. A. Woodruff of Marion, Cory's arm healed well, and rather quickly. By the end of August he was up and around and fairly active, but he found everyday living difficult for a busy man with only one arm. He was a resourceful person, however, and in time would learn to do for himself most of those things for which he now required assistance. Reliance upon others was difficult for this independent man to accept. There was much to be done—land to be cleared, logs to be hauled, lumber to be cut, new fences and stables to be built, and new pastures to be planted, besides the everyday work required on a stock farm. Cally was sorely missed, but Randy often showed up to give a hand wherever needed. The Jameses worked when they could spare time from their crops, but things needing to be done were piling up.

Buck had a decision to make, and it wasn't an easy one. He knew what it had to be, but he delayed announcing it as long as possible. At supper one night he told his parents he was going to postpone entering Howard College for a year. Sadie was disappointed, but she realized it was something he had to do. Cory accepted it without comment—the delay was an especially bitter pill for him as he knew the decision was forced by his inability to fulfill what he felt were his responsibilities.

Buck wasn't looking forward to breaking the news to the Rushtons. Randy's parents had taken such an interest in his education that Buck dreaded breaking the news to them; but worst of all, he hated to tell Randy, who had looked forward so eagerly to their going through college together. The Sunday following the announcement to his parents, Buck was having dinner with the Rushtons, as was Sally. While at the table, something was said about the coming school year, and Buck took the opportunity to bring up his change of plans. He said, "It doesn't look like I'll be able to make it to Howard this year. Until Pa has fully recovered and adapted to getting along with one arm, I don't see how I can go off and leave the folks. I should be able to make it next year all right.''

Up to this point the conversation at the table had been light and lively, but now a hushed gloom momentarily settled over the room. Carolyn broke the silence. ''I am so sorry to hear this, Buck. I certainly hope the setback is only temporary and that you will be able to continue your education.''

''I'm planning on it.''

''I hate to see our group broken up,'' Sally said. ''It won't be the same without you.''

Buck looked at Ellen. Her eyes met his with intense disappointment clearly showing on her face, and then she dropped her eyes and looked at her plate. ''It certainly won't,'' she said softly.

Randy sat in silence as though his whole world had suddenly crumbled around him. Could this mean the time had come when he and Buck would each take his separate path? He hoped not; but he feared that Buck's education, once interrupted, might never be resumed. Would his parents allow him to stay out for a year so he and Buck could start together? He dismissed the idea as immature; besides, his mother would never see any sense in it. Trying to hide his feelings, he said nonchalantly, ''If you don't go with me, who's going to look after you?''

''Hadn't thought of that; guess I'll have to fend for myself. You go ahead and blaze the trail; that will make it easier for me when I get there.''

John asked with concern, ''Is there anything I can do to help the situation so you can go ahead as you planned?''

''No sir, nothing I know of; but thank you, anyway. Pa is adjusting very well; and one of our tenants, Noah James, has a sixteen-year-old boy, Artie, who is going to work for us full time after the cotton is picked this year. He's pretty sharp and is good with animals. With training, he'll make a capable hand with the stock. There's no reason I shouldn't be able to make it next year.''

The following morning, Buck went to Marion to discuss his situation with Dr. Talbird at Howard. The latter was understanding and indicated there would be no question about his acceptance the following year; but the lumber was badly needed, and he would like to have it as scheduled, if possible. Buck assured him it would be delivered as agreed.

On his way home, he stopped at Prairie's Edge. Randy was driving his father about the plantation, so Buck set out to locate them. He found Mr. Rushton and Randy at the edge of a large field waiting for Mr.

Pring, who was riding toward them from a group of people working at the far side. Buck reached the cart first and, after exchanging greetings, waited with the Rushtons for the overseer. As Pring drew closer, they could see he was agitated about something.

"Jason knows he's going to be sold," Pring said excitedly. "Don't know how he found out, unless somebody overheard us talking. I'll never understand how these people know everything that goes on. I think we better put him in chains until the trader gets here tomorrow."

"Not until we turn him over."

"You're the boss, but he may run."

"We'll take that chance."

Pring shook his head in a gesture of disbelief and resignation. He finished his business with John and returned to the workers across the field. After he left, John turned to Buck and said, "I guess this calls for an explanation. Jason has been causing trouble. He is trying to incite some of our people to protest against slavery by shirking their work or running off. Some of the younger men are beginning to listen to him. He has been spending a lot of time at night with the son of one of your tenants, a young negro named David. I've heard David is a pretty sorry individual. Anyway, I decided to sell Jason under the condition that he be resold out of the area. A trader is coming by tomorrow; he is moving a group to Mississippi."

"You're right about David. He's given Abel a lot of problems; in fact, he's the one who brought about the trouble with the Barlows." Buck looked at the disconsolate Randy, and his heart went out to him. He wanted to say something but didn't know what might ease his friend's pain. He said, "He'll be all right."

"I'm not so sure," Randy replied.

"Don't blame your father; Jason forced it on him."

"I know."

"I've got to take a little trip tomorrow. It'll take all day. Come go with me."

"Go ahead, Randy," his father said. "It will be better if you aren't around."

"What time?" Randy asked.

"Be at my house about eight."

"I'll be there," he said indifferently.

When Randy arrived at the McCord home the following morning, Buck was waiting and ready to leave. There was a two-year-old filly with a halter and lead rope tied alongside Skin.

"Where are we going?" Randy wanted to know.

"To pay a debt—one to Dr. Woolley."

As he was getting on his horse, Buck saw Abel coming through the pasture in a great hurry. He waited for him.

"Mista Buck, is your pa home?" Abel asked, almost out of breath.

"He's in the house. What's the trouble?"

"My boy David, he runned off wif that wuthless nigger, Jason, 'scuse me, Mista Randy, of Mista Rushtons."

"When did this happen?"

"Last night, but I just found out about it. I was lookin' for David, an' my youngest gal, Rachel, say she woke up last night an' seed 'im leavin'; an' Jason was waitin' wif two hosses. She didn' think nothin' about it at the time, 'cause Jason's been there lotsa times before at night. But dis time, David took his things."

"This could be serious if he is helping a runaway slave."

"That boy been headed for trouble a long time."

Randy broke in, "Daddy didn't know about this when I left. Maybe I should go back and tell him, unless you can send word."

"Abel can go when he finishes talking with Pa; can't you, Abel?"

"Yassuh, be glad to. I'll take one of the mules, if you don't mind."

"Take your pick," Buck said. Then to Randy, "We'd better hit the road."

They left the house and rode in silence. Randy finally spoke, "Where will they go?"

"I've an idea that Jason has this well planned. They will probably head north to get into the underground railroad. There are quite a few people in northeast Alabama and eastern Tennessee and Kentucky who are strongly opposed to slavery. My guess is they will head in that direction. They took the horses to get out of the area fast. They will travel by night and will probably abandon the horses. They stand less chance of being caught on foot."

"I hope they make it."

Apparently they did. The horses were found just north of Elyton and were returned to Prairie's Edge, but the two negroes had disappeared.

On September 5, 1859, Randy, Ellen, and Sally left for Marion together as Howard College and Judson Female Institute were beginning their fall terms on the same day. Buck came to Prairie's Edge to see them off. He was standing on the veranda with John and Carolyn watching the carriage carrying Ellen and Sally as it went down the driveway toward the road. Randy was following on Chessy, and behind him was a wagon with their trunks and other baggage. A feeling of sadness and forlornness seemed to engulf him—never had he wanted anything so badly as he wanted to go with them. Ellen looked back and waved a small handkerchief. It did nothing to lift his spirits, so he raised his hand and responded only half-heartedly.

Carolyn was watching Buck, whose face showed his inner feelings. "They're not leaving forever; they'll be back."

"I know," he replied. "I just feel like it's forever."

Judson Female Institute is located on Bibb Street, two blocks south and two blocks east of the new Perry County courthouse which faces west on Washington Street. Randy accompanied Ellen and Sally there and stayed until they had registered and their trunks and other belongings were taken to their room. When he was satisfied they would be all right, he left them, returning to Washington Street where he turned south to Howard College.

At the administration office Randy learned he would have two roommates, Bill Williamson from the southern part of Perry County and Kevin Kelley from Huntsville in northern Alabama. He put his horse in the college stables and went to his quarters where he found the wagon waiting with his luggage. The driver carried his trunk and other gear to his room.

Both of his roommates had arrived ahead of him and were already settled in, but neither was there. It was a large room furnished with a single bed and a double decker. There were three small desks, each with a chair, and a lamp and three clothes presses. From things left on them, it was apparent that the two lower beds had been claimed, leaving the upper for the late comer. He began unpacking and was still putting his clothes away when two young men appeared at the door. One was rather thin with brown hair and hazel eyes. He was about an inch shorter than Randy. The other was even shorter and stocky, about five feet seven inches tall. He had dark brown hair and light brown eyes.

Noticing some of Randy's things on the upper bunk, the taller of the two newcomers said, "Wouldn't you know he would grab the best bed."

"Yeah, some folks don't give you a sporting chance," the other added.

"I don't mind if you don't," Randy responded; "besides the doctor said I'll be over my bed-wetting problem in another six months."

"You can have the lower bunk," the taller one quickly offered.

"Just kidding," Randy said. "I'll be fine up there. I'm John Randolph Rushton, Jr., better known as Randy." He offered his hand.

The taller man replied as he shook hands, "I'm Kevin Kelley from Huntsville, and this is Bill Williamson from around Uniontown."

"I'm from Perry County, too—not far across the Cahaba on the Perryville road," Randy said as he shook hand with Bill.

"I've heard of your family," Bill responded. "Your father's the one who raises the fine horses. We have one of them. That stallion is my father's pride and joy."

"It's good to know they are being recognized." Then looking at Kevin, he asked, "How did you happen to wind up away down here from Huntsville?"

"Love. Just plain love and infatuation," Kevin replied. "I went with my family to Warm Springs this summer and met the love of my life who is going to Judson. I prevailed upon my father to let me enroll at Howard, and here I am."

"If I may ask, who is this fetching young lady who fetched you so far?"

"Alice McKinley. Her folks have a plantation near Newbern."

"I've heard Daddy speak of that family. I have a sister and a neighbor at Judson. Maybe they'll get to be friends."

"It's about time for dinner," Bill interposed. "We'd better get to the dining room. After we eat, we sign up for classes."

"Bill was here last year; so if you want to know anything, ask him."

"Do we have classes all day Saturday?"

"Only until noon. Sundays are free, too, except we are required to attend morning church services. Since both Howard and Judson are Baptist schools, most students from these schools go to Siloam Baptist Church in town. We sit on one side of the church; and the Judson girls, as everybody calls them, sit on the other. There are several churches in town. You may go to the one of your choice, but you have to go."

"I told you," Kevin said; "he's a veritable fount of knowledge. Facts flow from him like lava from Mt. Etna."

With a grin, Bill motioned his head toward Kevin and said to Randy, "I hope diarrhea of the mouth isn't contagious."

They all laughed. Kevin replied, "I'll have to watch that banty rooster soldier-to-be; he's got the spurs of a fighting cock."

"What do you mean by 'soldier-to-be'?" Randy said.

"Bill's trying to get into West Point."

"Looks like I've got a good chance to make it next year," Bill said.

They left for the dining room; and as they walked across the campus, Randy knew he had been lucky in the draw of roommates, but this was little compensation for Buck's not being there.

It had been Randy's intention to go home the first weekend, but the men at Howard received an invitation from the young ladies of Judson to attend a tea at the school at four o'clock Saturday afternoon. He was going to send his regrets; but his roommates prevailed upon him to go, explaining that this tea was becoming an annual tradition which afforded the students of the two institutions an opportunity to become acquainted.

This first week passed quickly for everyone except Kevin, who grew more impatient each day to see Miss McKinley. At his urging, the three of them arrived at Judson promptly at four; and Randy was surprised to see several young men already there. They were received by the president of Judson, Dr. Noah K. Davis, Mrs. Davis, and the dean of women. After they passed through the receiving line, Kevin saw Alice and made a beeline for her. Randy spotted Ellen and Sally talking with two other young ladies. Sally saw him and waved.

"Come on, Bill. I'd like for you to meet my sister and her roommate."

As they crossed the room, Sally said something to the other girls, who turned to face them. Ellen smiled and waved, but Randy didn't see her—his eyes were glued to a vision of loveliness, a gorgeous strawberry blond who, with a coquettish smile, was watching them approach. When they reached the young ladies, Ellen said, "May I present my brother, Randy. Randy this is Beverly Watson," nodding toward the strawberry blond, "and Doris Smythe," looking at the other girl. "They have the room next to ours."

"I am pleased to meet you. May I present..."

Before Randy could introduce his friend, Beverly interrupted, "Why Ellen, you never told us you had such a handsome brother! I declare, I do believe you were trying to hide him from me!" Coyly she offered her hand, taking no notice at all of Bill and ignoring the introduction Randy was trying to make.

Randy, who had never shown interest in any girl, was speechless as he stood holding the small hand. He was brought back to awareness of the others by Sally, who said with a tinge of sarcasm, "What's the matter, Randy; the cat got your tongue?"

"Oh, er, hi, Sally," he stammered. "This is my roommate, Bill Williamson. Bill, my sister, Ellen; Miss Sally Beaumont, our neighbor and Ellen's roommate; Miss Beverly Watson; and Miss Doris Smythe."

The introductions were hardly acknowledged before Beverly said, "I declare, I'm just dying of thirst. Do let's go have a cup of tea, Randy." With that, she latched onto his arm and steered him away to a table on the other side of the room where one of the members of the senior class was pouring.

Sally watched the couple as they walked away. She was furious and was on the verge of making a comment about the forwardness of some people, but held her tongue. She had been in love with Randy for as long as she could remember. Although he had never indicated by word or action that he felt the same way about her, neither had he ever paid attention to any other girl; and she looked upon him as her beau, secure in the belief they would one day be married and unite the adjoining plantations of their families. This was her first encounter with a threat to her relationship with Randy. She didn't like it; but even worse, she was frightened by it.

Ellen had long ago sensed her friend's feeling for Randy and knew she must be distressed. Doris was unaware of Sally's being upset, but she was embarrassed by the brash conduct of her roommate and tried to turn the minds of the others to something else by asking Bill, "Don't you live near Uniontown?"

"Yes," he replied; "you're not from that area, are you?"

"No, but not too far away. Beverly and I both are from Marion Junction."

"We're practically neighbors," Bill replied. "I don't remember seeing any of you last year. Is this your first year at Judson?"

"Yes," they replied, almost in unison.

"I think you will like it here. Judson is growing rapidly, far more so than Howard."

"You were at Howard last year?" Ellen inquired.

"This is my second year." Looking at Randy and Beverly being served across the room, he asked, "May I get you ladies a cup of tea?"

"Only if you bring all of the cups at the same time; we want no favoritism shown, either all or none," Doris replied.

"I'll take that dare," Bill said and started for the table.

"Wait," Doris said. "We had better go with you. I believe you would have tried it."

"That was my intention, although it may not have been my best."

As they started toward the table, the young lady pouring finished serving Beverly and Randy. Beverly saw the others coming and said to him, "It's getting awfully crowded in here, and I can't bear crowds. They just smother little old me. Let's go out to the portico where I can breathe." Taking his left arm, she steered him by the receiving line and out the door. Randy was aware of the dean of women's disapproving look as they passed by her, but Beverly appeared not to have noticed it. On the large porch, she led the way to a corner where they could be to themselves.

"Is this your first year in college?" she asked.

"Yes."

"I declare, that's hard to believe, you looking so mature and all, and so courtly, too. I bet you live a very exciting life at Prairie's Edge. That is the name of your home, isn't it?"

"That's it, but it's a quiet life we lead. How did you know the name of my home?"

"Law, I must have heard Ellen mention it. I'm just crazy about your sister. I think she must be the sweetest girl in the whole world. I'd give anything to have a sister like her."

"I wouldn't say that she's the sweetest girl in the world, Beverly; I think you could give her a lot of competition for that honor."

"My goodness, Randy. How you carry on. I'll bet you are the biggest flirt in all Alabama and that you just steal all the girl's hearts and then leave them pining away."

"There's nothing could be farther from the truth; there is one heart I would like to steal, but I'm afraid I wouldn't have much of a chance."

"Fiddle-dee-dee, Randy. I don't believe there's any heart you couldn't steal if you set out to do it." Then she coyly added, "Especially mine."

"I hope you mean that."

"I never meant anything more," she replied, demurely dropping her eyes.

It happened that quickly; Randy had not just fallen in love, he was completely infatuated. He dreamed of Beverly; he talked about Beverly; he spent every possible moment with her. She became the center of his life. His original intention of going home almost every weekend was forgotten.

The young ladies at Judson were allowed to receive young men under closely chaperoned conditions only on Saturday evenings and Sunday afternoons. The intervening time was much too long for Randy, so he would sometimes arrange to meet Beverly in town after classes, making the meetings appear strictly by chance. It was on one of these occasions that he and Beverly came out of a confectionery shop and saw Buck driving a four-mule team pulling a wagon loaded with lumber. Seated beside him was one of the James negroes.

"Buck!" Randy called.

"Randy," he replied. "How are you doing? It's been a long time, Ol' Buddy." He quickly drew rein and brought the team to a halt, stopping the wagon in the street.

"Come on, Bev. I want you to meet Buck." Grasping her arm above the elbow, he steered her to the wagon. Buck handed the reins to the negro and leaped nimbly to the ground. He removed his straw hat with his right hand and moved it to his left, expecting to shake hands with the young lady.

"Bev, I would like to present my good friend Buck, Buck McCord. Buck, this is Miss Beverly Watson. She is one of Ellen's classmates."

"I heard Randy had become acquainted with a very beautiful young lady, and you certainly fit the description."

Beverly looked at this mule driver in work-worn homespun holding his sweat-stained hat and was appalled that this could be the friend whom Randy seemed to idolize. She made up her mind to bring an end to this friendship as quickly as possible. Her first impulse was to treat Buck coldly to indicate her disapproval, but she was not sure she had Randy sufficiently under her thumb to chance it. She forced a smile but did not offer her hand and said, "Thank you. I declare, I feel like I know you already as Randy has told me so much about you."

Despite the apparent friendliness, Buck had a feeling that it didn't ring true. He was afraid he had made a poor impression and thought it would be better to break off the meeting in hope of seeing her again under more favorable conditions. "I've got the street blocked; and this lumber has to be unloaded at Howard, so I'd better get moving."

"I'm sorry you've got to rush off," Randy said; "but Mother has invited Bev to spend midterm break at Prairie's Edge. Y'all will be able to get better acquainted then."

"I'll be looking forward to it," Buck said.

Beverly did not reply. Buck got back on the wagon and took the reins from the negro's hands. As he drove off, he heard Randy say, "I know you are going to like him when you know him better; everyone does."

Buck suspected that he was not alone in sensing Beverly's antipathy toward him.

From her correspondence, Beverly's parents, Charles and Margaret Watson, were aware of their daughter's having met Randy and of her seeing him regularly. They were quite pleased with the news. Although they did not know the Rushtons personally, they had heard enough about them to know that Randy would be a good catch. When Beverly's letter came requesting permission to spend the midterm break at Prairie's Edge, they lost no time in paying her a visit. Their interest was not the usual parental concern for a daughter but their desire to have her make a marriage which would be in their own interest. Things had not been going well for them for several years. They had not managed the plantation nor their personal affairs as they should and now found themselves mortgaged heavily and in danger of running out of further credit. Upon their arrival at Judson, Margaret lost no time in getting Beverly aside for a mother-daughter talk.

"About this young man, Randy; what kind of a person is he?"

"Quite nice, Mother; I'm sure you'll like him. He is very handsome and has excellent manners. He's been well brought up."

"You know it is very important to us that you make a proper marriage."

"I understand, Mother. I overheard Father say once that Mr. Rushton is probably the wealthiest planter in the area, even richer than either General King or his nephew."

"Beverly! That isn't what I mean."

"I know what you mean; as soon as I saw Randy, I knew he was the solution to our problem."

"How can you talk that way!"

"Don't try to pull the wool over my eyes, Mother. I know about our financial situation."

"It appears you do, Dear. Do you think he will propose marriage?"

"You underestimate me."

Margaret considered this for a moment before she replied, "I believe I have, at that. Perhaps we had better rejoin your father."

It was Wednesday, November 22, the beginning of the midterm break; and the Rushtons were anxiously awaiting the homecoming of their children and the arrival of their house guest. When they first learned of Randy's interest in the Watson girl, John had discussed with his wife some of the things he had heard about her parents. It was generally known that the family lived exceptionally well, travelled extensively, and that Charles Watson was inclined to be a heavy gambler. John had also learned from a friend in Selma, who was in a position to know, that Charles Watson had gone through his own inheritance and had just about gone through that of his wife, having mortgaged their holdings almost to the limit. They were reluctant to pass judgment on the young lady because of her parents, but they were anxious to see for themselves the kind of person who had so thoroughly captivated their son.

The carriage dispatched to Marion for the young people arrived at Prairie's Edge about half past two. This time Randy rode in the carriage beside Beverly; Chessy was tied to the rear. The sound of the vehicle in front of the house brought John and Carolyn to the veranda. Although Sally would be driven to her home, she got out with the others to speak to John and Carolyn. As they watched the foursome alight from the carriage and come to the porch, they were impressed by the beauty and poise of Beverly. Ellen ran ahead to embrace her parents and was waiting with them when the others came up the steps. Without greeting his parents himself, Randy, beaming and his voice showing considerable pride, said, "Mother, Daddy, this is Beverly; Bev, my parents."

"Hello, Beverly; welcome to Prairie's Edge," Carolyn said as she went to her guest with extended hand.

"Hello, Mrs. Rushton, Mr. Rushton," Beverly said, taking the proffered hand and curtsying. "I am so thrilled to be here! Randy has told me so much about you; but I can see he has been much, much too modest. I declare, I just love this place already and know I am going to have the most wonderful time of my whole life!"

Ellen almost burst out laughing; for standing behind Beverly and Randy, Sally grimaced as though gagging. Both Carolyn and John saw this; and John kept a straight face with difficulty, but Carolyn had no such problem. She was not at all amused, disapproving strongly of the unladylike behavior. "We have been looking forward to your coming," she said; "and I'm sure we shall get as much pleasure from your visit as you."

"I hate to interrupt this," Sally said; "but let me say hello and goodbye; I've got to be on my way." She went to Carolyn and embraced her, and then to John and gently kissed him on the cheek.

"Wish you could stay," John said.

"I'll see you before I go back," she replied as she started for the steps.

"Have dinner with us Saturday," Carolyn called. "Buck will be here."

"Thank you, I shall if the folks don't have other plans for me."

When the carriage drove off with Sally, the rest of them went inside the house. Beverly was shown to her room, and Ellen stayed to help her get settled. It wasn't long until Randy came by to see if she would like to see the plantation. Using his father's cart, the two of them spent the next two hours riding through the slave quarters, by the stables and pastures, and around the fields.

Buck had been invited for supper and showed up about five o'clock. Beverly was surprised to see him still dressed in the same type of homespun clothing, only this time they were newer and much cleaner. She was amazed at the way he fitted right into life at Prairie's Edge and how he was accepted almost like one of the family.

Supper that night left much to be desired by everyone except Beverly and Randy. The house guest monopolized the conversation; and by the time dinner was over, she knew the acreage of Prairie's Edge, the number of slaves the Rushtons owned, the number of breeding stock, and all about the sharecropping operation. She showed considerable surprise upon learning that the sharecroppers were being allowed to buy their freedom and didn't hesitate to let it be known that she thought this was a terrible mistake.

Later that night in their room, while Carolyn was preparing to retire, she said to John, who was already in bed, "I'm afraid I was a little disappointed in that girl."

"Not me; I was greatly disappointed. Did you ever see such a question box? You would have thought she was screening me for a loan. About the only things she didn't cover were my balance with the factor, whether I have any mortgages, and the stocks and bonds I own." He paused for a moment and then asked, "You don't suppose she already had that information, do you?"

"Of course not. Perhaps we are being unfair. We shouldn't jump to conclusions from the first impression."

"That wasn't my first impression. The first was when she greeted us this afternoon." John laughed. "Did you see Sally?"

"I most certainly did, and I didn't think her very funny."

"Well, I did. Kinda felt like throwing up, myself. I hope Randy doesn't go overboard for this girl."

"From the way he's behaving, he seems pretty badly smitten with her."

"I'm afraid so, but it's hard to believe someone like that could appeal to him, despite her beauty. I gave him credit for better judgment. I had always expected he would marry Sally. Now, there's a girl who is down to earth and got a head on her shoulders."

"I had always hoped that, too. Maybe it will happen yet. Randy has always been such a sensible boy; perhaps he is just going through a stage of growing up. My mother used to say that every boy had to go over Fool's Hill before he settles down."

"I'm afraid this is more like a mountain."

"Did you go over Fool's Hill, John?"

"No, I met you on the way up and came back down."

"What a sweet thing to say," Carolyn replied; and went to the bed and kissed him affectionately on the forehead.

With a twinkle in his eye and the slight trace of a smile, John said, "Tell me, Carolyn, you weren't coming down that hill from the other side, were you?"

"Why, John Rushton! How could you ever think such a thing!"

"Just wanted to know," he said with a chuckle.

At breakfast the following morning, Randy said he had mentioned to Buck that he wanted to see his parents before returning to college and Buck had invited him to bring Beverly over for dinner with them Friday. He had also included Ellen in the invitation, if she would come. Beverly wasn't enthusiastic about going but didn't know how to get out of it. Ellen was delighted. There had been very few occasions during the years she had known Buck that she had been given the opportunity to visit the McCords; besides, Buck would be there.

It was decided to go horseback as Beverly wanted to ride one of the Rushton horses. They arrived at the McCord home half an hour before noon and were met at the front gate by Buck, who led the way to the rear of the house. The girls waited while the horses were unsaddled and turned loose in the pasture. They then went inside where they met Sadie coming from the kitchen, wiping her hands on her apron as she prepared to greet her guests. Randy gave her a big hug, and she shook hands with Ellen, saying, "We don't git to see enough of you."

"It's always good to be here," Ellen replied.

"Miss Sadie, I would like to present my friend, Miss Beverly Watson," Randy said.[1]

"My, what a pretty thing you be. I'm glad to make your acquaintance," Sadie said as she offered her hand.

Beverly took the hand reluctantly, wondering what Sadie had just wiped from it; and properly replied, "Thank you. I am pleased to meet you, Mrs. McCord."

Down at the sawmill, the last piece of lumber had been cut from a log. Cory reached over to the lever controlling the belt and turned off the power. The two James negroes working with him knew it was time for dinner, and the three men began brushing sawdust from themselves. Cory was fully recovered now, but he required help in getting rid of the sawdust. Each of them then headed for his home and the noon meal.

Cory got to the house just as Beverly's introduction to Sadie was completed. His clothes were not entirely free of sawdust and were well worn. The left sleeve of his shirt had been cut off, exposing the nub of his left arm.

"Hi, Mr. Cory," Randy said, going to him and shaking hands.

"Howdy, Randy. Howdy do, Miss Ellen," Cory replied.

Randy turned to introduce Beverly and was alarmed to see her staring straight ahead with her eyes wide open and the color drained from her face. Fearing she was about to faint, he grasped her by both arms to steady her.

"What in the world is the matter?" he asked.

"I-I-I don't know," she stammered. "I suddenly became ill. Take me out to the porch. Please!"

With Ellen's assistance, he helped her to the front porch and got her seated in a rocker. Sadie and Buck followed. Cory knew he could be of no help, so he went to his room to clean up for dinner. Sadie suggested that Beverly would be better off lying down, but Beverly would have no part of that. After a few minutes, she seemed to be all right again. Much of her color had returned, but she was still a little shaky. She said to Sadie, "I'm so sorry, Mrs. McCord. I declare, I don't know what came over me. I must have had something this morning that disagreed with me. I think I had better go back to Prairie's Edge and rest."

"We're sorry to see you go, Miss Watson, an' you can lay down here; but you know best. Buck, hitch up the buggy; she ain't got no bus'ness ridin' no hoss."

Buck left for the barn and ten minutes later drove the buggy up in front of the house. Randy assisted Beverly to it; and after she got in, Buck said to his friend. "I'll get the horses to you and bring back the buggy."

"Thanks, but I'll send it back, and the driver can take care of the horses."

"No trouble; I'll do it." Turning to Ellen, he said, "You don't have to go, do you?"

Before she could answer, Randy spoke up, "Why don't you stay? Mrs. McCord has gone to a lot of trouble to prepare this dinner, and I hate for all of us to leave."

Ellen was elated over the suggestion, but she wasn't sure she should let the ailing Beverly go without her. She looked at their house guest and asked, "Will you be all right, Beverly?"

"La-di-da, I couldn't be in better hands than Randy's. Of course, I'll be all right, Honey. You just don't worry your pretty little head about me." She saw Cory come into the sitting area from his room and said to Randy, who had gotten into the buggy beside her, "I think we'd better go now." Randy clucked to the horse, and the buggy pulled away.

Cory came to the porch and watched the vehicle as it went down the road. To himself he said, "That is one puny gal! Hope Buck never gits one like her; she won't be worth a tinker's dam."

Dinner was a pleasant affair for everyone; the awkwardness created by Beverly's indisposition was quickly dissipated by the friendly and easy atmosphere in the McCord home. It was the first time Ellen had eaten with them, and she liked their custom of holding hands while grace was said. She was sitting to the left of Cory and to the right of

Buck, so she had the hand of only the latter to hold. The feeling of
Buck's strong but gentle clasp sent a warm glow through her. This was a
custom she would adopt in her own home someday.

After they finished eating, Ellen offered to help Sadie and was
allowed to clear the table. When this task was completed, Sadie would
let her do nothing more; so she joined Buck, who was impatiently
waiting on the porch.

"Would you like to see the place?" he asked.

"I'd love to."

They left the house and went to the pasture gate where Buck whistled
for Skin. To his surprise, Roana also responded. As the horses trotted to
them, Ellen was delighted and asked, "Can you teach me to whistle like
that?"

"I can try."

He showed her how to hold her tongue and purse her lips. She had
little success at first; but was determined to do it and kept trying, with
improvement, as they rode around the farm. Buck told her how Randy
had trained Roana with dried apples and suggested that she do the same,
so the horse would respond to her signal.

At Ellen's request, they went first to see the water wheel. The
sawmill where Cory had returned to work also intrigued her. She looked
at the millpond with its grapevine swing at the far side and thought how
much fun it would be to swim and to drop into the water from the vine.

Leaving the pond, they went to the new stables Cory was in the
process of building. Afterward, they rode out into the larger pastures to
see the horses, mules, and cows. When they came to one where the
northwest end had been recently cleared, Ellen thought that this must be
where the fight with the Barlows had occurred. She asked Buck,
"Where was your father shot?"

"In the arm."

Ellen laughed. "Silly goose," she said. "You know what I mean."

He pointed out the spot to her; and without saying anything, she
turned her horse in that direction and rode to it. He followed.

"Where were you, and where were they?"

Before she finished asking questions, the entire story had been drawn
from him. She looked toward the corner where Sam Barlow had been
shot and said, "It's hard to believe you could hit a man that far away.
Tell me, Buck, does it bother you that you killed a man and may have
killed another?"

"No. Maybe it should, but it doesn't. With Caleb, it was shoot him or
let him shoot Pa. When Pa first told me to shoot Sam as he was trying to
get to the gate, I wasn't sure it was the right thing to do; but it didn't take

me long to make up my mind. They had badly wounded Pa and had creased me in trying to kill us in a cowardly way. I knew Sam would try again if I didn't get him first. The next time he might have better luck. If I had it to do over, I would do the same thing.''

"A life is a precious thing; but under the circumstances, I don't think it would bother me either. I'm glad it doesn't you.''

Buck looked at Ellen, and the love he had hidden so long welled up in him as never before. He was on the verge of telling her how much she meant to him and of the years he had loved her; but, again, that terrible fear of rejection kept him from speaking. Little did he know how right was the time, nor how much Ellen would have liked to have heard those words.

"The other Barlow man, what was his name?''

"Jethro.''

"Have you heard anything about him?''

"No. Not a word. I check the Barlow place occasionally, and there's been no sign of his having come back.''

"Watch out for him; he could be dangerous.''

"He is. He won't fight in the open.'' Buck laughed. "You should have seen him dive over the fence. That was the last I saw of him. He didn't lift a finger to help his wounded father that I could see. The sheriff thinks he may have skedaddled before Cally got to the house, but he could have been hiding somewhere when Cally hanged Sam and left later.''

It was after four when they got back to the house. They found Sadie busy at her loom, and Ellen was fascinated by what she was doing. There were looms at Prairie's Edge, but she had never seen them work. Sadie took delight in explaining the whole spinning and weaving process to her. They came out of the room as Cory arrived. Ellen said to him, "I was glad to get a chance to see your water wheel with the buckets. I had read about them, but I'd never seen one. It's called a noria, you know. The Romans used them before Christ was born.''

"You don't say,'' Cory said, surprised. "I thought I made the fust one.''

Ellen laughed. "At least the first around here.''

Buck said to Ellen, "I'd better get you home before they send for you.''

"I've had such a good time that I hate to go.'' She held out her hand to Sadie and said, "Thank you for having me. Randy and Beverly don't know what they missed.''

"Like I told Randy once, it ain't no han'shake I wants,'' and she put her large arms around Ellen and hugged her tightly. "Ain't nothin' like a good hug.''

As Randy had done, Ellen automatically responded to the unexpected embrace and found that she, too, liked it. When Sadie released her, she said, ''That was a nice end to a wonderful day.''

The following morning, Ellen had breakfast with Randy and Beverly, her parents having eaten earlier. Beverly seemed fully recovered and was in her usual buoyant spirits. The previous day had been a disaster for her. She couldn't understand why Randy was so close to people who lived in such a modest house and who dressed and talked the way of Buck's parents. She had done a lot of thinking about it and had made up her mind to end as quickly as possible Randy's friendship with Buck. When she married him, she had no intention of having any of the McCords included among their friends and associates. Randy gave her the opening she wanted when he mentioned Buck's coming to Prairie's Edge that day.

''Randy, I do declare, I don't see what you have in common with those McCords. They just don't seem like your kind.''

''Don't judge them by outward appearances; they're fine people. Buck and I have been friends for a long time.''

''They're more than friends,'' Ellen interposed, ''they're blood brothers.''

''Blood brothers?'' Beverly questioned, in surprise. ''What do you mean?''

Randy answered, ''As boys, we took an oath to be blood brothers. It's an Indian custom. You cut your wrists and mix your blood. That makes you blood brothers.''

Beverly grimaced. ''What a ghastly thing to do.''

''It wasn't bad. It was just a small cut. See the scar,'' he said, showing her his inner wrist.

Beverly shuddered, and quickly turned her head. ''I don't want to see it! I can't stand the sight of scars and deformities and things like that. It was those awful people and the man with no arm that made me ill yesterday.''

Ellen's face flushed with anger. ''What do you mean, awful people!'' she said. ''The McCords are some of the finest people in this county. They may be backward in the way they talk and unpretentious in the way they live; but they are good, decent citizens, and we should have more like them!''

''Why, Ellen, how can you say something like that? Didn't Buck kill one man and shoot another?''

"Yes, he did, and he would have killed another one if he could. The dirty cowards tried to shoot him and his father from ambush. They needed killing. Don't you talk to me about Buck; he's the kindest, sweetest, and most gentle man I know!"

Realizing from Ellen's outburst and Randy's expression that she had made a serious blunder, Beverly attempted to get out of a bad situation as best she could. She said, "Why, Ellen Rushton! I do believe you are in love with that Buck McCord. I'm so sorry, Honey; I would never in all the world have said anything against him or his family if I had known that."

Still angry, Ellen blurted out, "Maybe I am in love with him; if I am, it's my own business!" Realizing what she had said, Ellen was horrified and embarrassed. Her face turned crimson, and she became very quiet, all the fight now gone from her.

"Well, I declare," Beverly said, smugly.

Randy couldn't believe the sudden eruption and turn of events. Because of his own aversion to the sight of blood, he could understand and empathize with Beverly's peculiar reaction to physical disfigurement; but he was astounded at his sister's admission that she was in love with Buck. Ellen and Buck? The thought had never occurred to him, but he liked it. Did Buck return that love? He must; he had always shown an interest in Ellen from the first time he met her. How about that—Buck for a brother-in-law! But what about Beverly? He had suspected she didn't care much for Buck, and she seemed to have confirmed this with the remarks about his family. And Ellen, she had never been very friendly with Beverly; but it was apparent that she actually disliked her. He would like to do something to heal this breach between them but wasn't sure how he should go about it. Perhaps time would do it for him. In the lull that came at the table, he said, "Let's forget about the McCords." Then to Beverly, "The folks decided to have a barbecue today and invited the Beaumonts and some other neighbors. Golan's been barbecuing the meat and cooking his famous gumbo all night. Wait'll you try his gumbo! There's no other like it around here. Golan came from the bayou country of Louisiana, and he puts something in it they use down there. Nobody knows what it is, and he won't tell."

"Oh, I can hardly wait! There's nothing in the whole entire world I like better than good gumbo," Beverly exclaimed. She was relieved with the change of subject and realized she would have to use discretion in anything concerning Buck.

"You should have told me. Because it takes so long to cook, Golan always makes a lot; and Mother has what is left over put up in jars. We nearly always have some on hand.''

Ellen sat quietly, completely subdued after her outburst. She was embarrassed by her admission that she was in love with Buck, something she had never fully admitted to herself; but she knew in her heart and mind that, now it had been said, it was true. But Buck, how did he feel about her? She thought of Sally's question on the last day of school. Did he look upon her as a sister? He had avoided answering Sally's question as had she. Maybe he didn't—she certainly hoped not.

When Sally arrived with her family, Ellen quickly steered her up to her room and told Sally about Beverly's getting ill at the McCord's home and what had occurred at the breakfast table that morning.

"I'm glad you told off Miss Gushy. Did she really almost faint from just the sight of Mr. McCord's arm?''

"That's what she said caused it. I've never been so embarrassed in all my life as I was when I admitted to being in love with Buck. I wanted to crawl under the table. Honestly, I didn't know it myself until it came out then.''

"Well, I did. I've known it for years.''

"How could you have known it?''

"Anybody who saw you around him would know it.''

"Like your being in love with Randy?''

"Who says so?''

"I do.''

Sally laughed. "I guess we know each other better than we know ourselves.''

"Getting back to Beverly,'' Ellen said, "what are we going to do about this delicate prairie flower?''

"She may be a flower to you, but she's a stinkweed in my rose garden! I've thought of a lot of things I'd like to do, but not one of them is legal.''

"I can't understand how Randy can be so blind, and I always looked up to him for his intelligence.''

"I can tell you one thing; the battle with that strawberry helfer isn't over.''

Chapter V

Secession

The year 1860 saw a steady deterioration of the political situation in the United States. The question of whether slavery should be extended into new states and territories was bitterly dividing the country. All efforts toward compromise were getting nowhere. Bitter debates and harsh words spoken in Congress inflamed rather than abated the ardor of the strong proponents on each side. Despite a solid front, things were not going well for the Southerners. When the Democratic Party convened in Charleston, South Carolina that spring and rejected a pro-slavery platform, the delegates from eight Southern states walked out of the convention.

The Democratic Party reconvened in June in Baltimore, and Stephen Douglas was nominated as their presidential candidate after another walk-out by the delegates from the South. The Southern Democrats held their own convention in Baltimore; and nominated John C. Breckenridge, a native of Kentucky and then Vice President of the United States, as their candidate to run on a pro-slavery platform. This division in the Democratic Party made almost certain the election of the Republican candidate, Abraham Lincoln, who had been nominated at their convention held in Chicago in May of that year. Although Lincoln represented himself as a moderate on the question of slavery, there was widespread opinion among those in political control in the South that his election would be the precursor to an end of that two-hundred-year-old institution in the United States.

It was in this unstable and uncertain period that Howard College began its fall term. Buck enrolled as planned. He was fortunate to be able to room with Randy and Kevin; Bill had gotten the appointment to West Point and had entered that academy. The young men at Howard followed very closely the political developments in the nation. They came mostly from slave-owning families and were strongly opinionated, some quite vocal, in their pro-slavery stand. There were a few like

Buck, whose families had no slaves, and some theological students who showed no opinion one way or the other on the slavery issue.

Randy found himself in the middle of the road. He respected the views of people like the McCords on slavery, and suspected his father was not a strong advocate of its continuation. He looked on it, however, as an economic necessity for the South; and realized the wealth and continued well being of many families, like his own, depended upon the asset value and reproduction of the slaves they owned. His father's venture into the sharecropping operation seemed to him to be a move in the right direction, and he was pleased that some of the Rushton people had already purchased their freedom. He saw nothing wrong in this as long as the slave owner was compensated for the lost asset and the slave was capable of supporting himself.

The election of Lincoln in November as President of the United States only added to the unrest and excitement already prevalent on the campus. With the Democratic Party vote split between Douglas and Breckenridge, Lincoln won a clear electoral college majority but only a plurality of the popular vote. A united opposition to the Republican candidate would probably have been successful.

There was wide discontent in the South where the political reins were in the hands of a few, most of whom were strong in their pro-slavery stand. On December 20, in a state convention, South Carolina voted to secede from the Union effective December 24, 1860. That state subsequently demanded the removal of all Federal troops from the Charleston area; this was ignored by President Buchanan.

Major Robert A. Anderson, in command of all forts in the Charleston harbor area, moved his small force of Federal troops into Fort Sumter, the most secure of the forts guarding the harbor. President Buchanan announced that Fort Sumter would be defended. President-elect Lincoln tried not to say anything which would inflame the situation, but he did reiterate his position that slavery should not be extended into the new states and territories.

Other Southern states began to take positive actions. Georgia state troops seized Fort Pulaski on the Savannah River on January 3, 1861. Two days later, Alabama forces took over Fort Morgan and Fort Gaines, which guarded the approaches to Mobile Bay. The following day, the Federal arsenal at Apalachicola was taken over by Florida state troops.

On January 9, the *Star of the West*, a merchant ship with 250 Federal troops aboard, attempted to reinforce Fort Sumter but turned back when fired upon by South Carolina forces. On the same day, Mississippi voted in convention to secede. Similar votes followed in Florida on the 10th, Alabama on the 11th, Georgia on the 19th, and Louisiana on the

26th of January. Texas was next by a vote in convention on February 1 which was ratified by popular vote on February 23.

Delegates from the seceded states, South Carolina, Georgia, Florida, Alabama, Mississippi, and Louisiana, met in Montgomery, Alabama. On the 8th of February, they enacted a provisional constitution of the Confederate States of America, almost identical with the United States Constitution. The following day they elected Jefferson Davis, a Mississippian and a former Secretary of War, as provisional president of the new republic. He was inaugurated in Montgomery on February 18, 1861.

Near the end of February, Randy had gone into town to meet Beverly at one of the confectionary shops. She failed to appear, but Doris Smythe showed up to bring word that Beverly had been assigned some additional work and would not be able to keep the appointment. On leaving the shop, Randy saw two young men, whom he judged to be farm boys in town for a lark, standing on the corner with rifles in their hands. They appeared to be drunk; and paying no further attention to them, he started across the street but stopped about half way to let an oncoming carriage pass.

Unexpectedly, the sound of a discharged gun came from behind him; and he saw the pair of carriage horses bolt in fright. As they started their stampede past him, he instinctively reached for the cheek strap of the bridle on the near horse with his left hand and the top of the hame with his right. Hanging on while being dragged up the street, he managed with the help of the negro driver to bring the frightened team to a halt just beyond the courthouse square. The horses had calmed down to the point that the driver could control them, so he turned his attention to a lone lady occupying the carriage; he was surprised to find that she was Mrs. Napoleon Lockett, the wife of a wealthy planter living in Marion and a friend of his mother. He could see that she was frightened and upset.

"Are you all right, Mrs. Lockett?" he inquired.

"Oh, it's you, Randy. Thank the Heavenly Father you were there. If you hadn't been, we would be half way to Old Town Creek by now."

Randy looked at her trembling hands and asked, "Would you like for me to see you home?"

"You are a dear boy; but I'm not going home just yet. I have a very important errand to attend to first. If it wouldn't inconvenience you, I should appreciate your going with me."

"No inconvenience at all," he replied and got into the carriage with her.

As they pulled off, she said, "As you know, Randy, we are very close to Governor Barry Moore, with two of our sons having married daughters of his. We've just gotten back from Montgomery where he invited us to attend the inauguration of President Davis. It seems that none of the submitted designs of a flag for our new republic have been found suitable; so I am on my way to see Mr. Nicola Marschall, who teaches art and music at the Female Seminary, about designing one. Do you know Mr. Marschall?"

"I don't believe I've had the pleasure."

"He is quite an artist. Came to this country from Prussia and has been teaching art and music at the Female Seminary for about ten years, except for two years he was absent on a visit home." The carriage stopped in front of the seminary, and she added, "I am still rather shaky; please come with me, Randy."

They found Mr. Marschall in his classroom studio with one of his pupils, Miss Mary E. Jones. After introductions were completed, Mrs. Lockett said, "As you know, Mr. Marschall, we have seceded from the Union, and our new Confederate government needs a flag. It must be one which can be recognized from a distance. Would you make up a design for it?"

"Of course, Mrs. Lockett. Do you have anything particular in mind?"

"Perhaps it shouldn't be too different from the United States flag."

"How many states are there in the Confederacy now?"

"Seven since Texas came in on the 24th, but I'm sure there will be more."

Picking up a large card, Marschall drew three designs. Each had two lateral red bars separated by a white one. On one design he placed in the upper left corner a blue field containing seven white stars in a circle. On the second he placed the blue field with the stars at the left of the white bar. The third had the blue field and stars in the center. When he finished, Mrs. Lockett, who had been standing by his side watching and occasionally making a suggestion, turned to Randy and asked, "Which do you like?"

"They're all good, but I like the first one best."

"So do I. Mr. Marschall, they also need a design for a uniform for the army. Do you have any ideas about this?"

"On my trip home, I was in Verona and saw a group of Austrian Army sharpshooters in gray uniforms which had green trimming. The green indicated their branch of the army, and their rank was shown by marks on the collars of the coats. I think that something along this line would be good."

"Could you draw the designs right away?"

He took a piece of paper and made several rough sketches of gray uniforms with different colors on the collar—buff for officers, yellow for cavalry, blue for infantry, and red for artillery.

"Those look very good," Mrs. Lockett said. "I'll take them along with the flag designs and see what happens."

On March 1, 1861, a flag of Nicola Marschall's design, the one with the field in the upper left corner, was raised over the capitol at Montgomery.[1] His design of the gray uniform was also adopted by the Confederacy.

On March 4, 1861, Lincoln was inaugurated as the sixteenth President of the United States. In his inaugural address, he repeated his position that he did not oppose the institution of slavery where it was already established and had no lawful right to interfere with it. He also said that the Union was perpetual, and it would defend itself. He left no doubt that he intended to carry out his Constitutional duties as he saw them to be.

The eyes of the nation were focused on Charleston harbor. Major Anderson had reported to Washington that he could not hold Fort Sumter without reinforcements. Lincoln announced his plans to supply and support the troops at that fort. His cabinet backed his decision by a vote of only three to two; Secretary of War Simon Cameron abstained from voting.

On April 8 the Federal cutter *Harriet Lane* left New York to relieve Fort Sumter. The next day two more ships followed her on the same mission.

General Pierre G. T. Beauregard, commanding the Southern forces around Charleston, was directed by the Confederate Secretary of War, Leroy Pope Walker, to require the evacuation of Fort Sumter. New demands made on Major Anderson to surrender the fort were rejected, although Anderson indicated he would be forced to surrender soon if not provisioned and reinforced.

Knowing help was on the way from New York, the Confederates notified Anderson they would attack in one hour. At 4:30 on the morning of April 12, the Confederate batteries opened fire on Fort Sumter. The fort surrendered on the afternoon of April 13, 1861.

When news of Fort Sumter reached Marion, Dr. Henry Talbird called a meeting of the Howard College students in the chapel. He pointed out to them that they had only a short time before the end of the current school year and urged that they finish the term before rushing off to enlist in any of the many state militia companies being formed or already in existence throughout the South.

As Buck, Randy, and Kevin left the meeting to return to their room, Randy asked, "What do y'all think we should do?"

"For the time being, nothing," Buck replied. "I certainly don't feel obligated to fight for slavery, but I do believe any state which joined the Union has the right to leave it. If the Federal government takes no action against us, I don't see where we have anything to fight about. I don't think the Confederacy is going to take any military action against any Federal installations or territory outside our boundaries."

"I agree," Kevin said. "Besides, since we've gotten this far into the term, I'd like to finish out the year before doing anything."

"Whatever we do, let's stick together," Randy proposed.

"I'm for that," Kevin replied.

"Me, too," Buck said.

Randy did not find Beverly quite so patient. Filled with romantic notions of war, she was fired up as much as the young hot-bloods at Howard. When Randy saw her the following Saturday evening, he found she was excited and ecstatic over the fall of Fort Sumter, far beyond anything he had expected.

"I declare," she said. "I do wish I were a man. I would be on my way right now to Charleston to join up with the gallant heroes who have shown those nasty Yankees that we will not let them stay in our country and are not afraid to do something about it."

"I'm not sure that firing on Fort Sumter was a smart thing to do," Randy said. "Maybe war would have come, anyway; but I'm certain this will bring it on."

"What are you going to do, Randy?"

"I don't know yet. Buck, Kevin, and I are waiting to see what develops. We would like to finish the school year, if possible, since the end is so near. We'll stick together in whatever we do."

"I do hope you will make up your mind soon. You don't know how proud I would be to see you in uniform. I just know you will be a captain, or maybe even a colonel."

"A private is more like it," he replied with a laugh. "I've had no military experience or training." Then he became very serious. "Beverly, you know how much I care for you; but we've never discussed marriage, because graduation from college seemed so far away. Things are changing now. If I go into the army, will you marry me before I leave?"

The unexpected proposal caught her completely by surprise. Her first reaction was one of elation; for after all, this had been her goal. She was on the verge of accepting, but doubts began to creep in. What if Randy were wounded and badly mutilated; she couldn't spend her life with a man like that. Also, if the war didn't end quickly and he had to be away for a long time, she would be tied down to an absent husband and limited in the social activities in which she could take part. She thought about the young man from Selma whom she had met this past summer. He had been so attentive to her, and he had come from a family which her father said was one of the wealthiest in that city. He was a lot more fun than Randy, who was really kind of stodgy and much too serious for a young man his age. She was not sure that life with him would be very glamorous or exciting; besides, it appeared doubtful she would be able to break up his friendship with Buck. This was not the time to commit herself to Randy.

"Oh Randy, I am so honored by your proposal, but do you think, with the war and all, we should do that now?"

Randy's proposal had come as much of a surprise to him as it had to Beverly. It was precipitous, and he knew Beverly was right. He could be disfigured, maimed, or even killed in a war; and it wouldn't be fair to her if this happened. "I guess you are right," he said. "This is something to be considered after the war, if there is one; but I want to know, will you wait for me?"

"Of course I shall, Randy. I'll be waiting for you to come back to me, as I know you will; and then we can begin our life together."

"I'll ask your father for your hand the first chance I get to see him."

Knowing an engagement would tie her down and obligate her almost as much as marriage, she stalled by saying, "I don't think that will be necessary, Randy. Let's keep this to ourselves. It will be our very own secret."

Puzzled by her response and somewhat dejected, he replied, "Well, if that's what you want."

The South didn't have long to wait to see how the chips had fallen. On April 15, Lincoln called for 75,000 volunteers to put down the insurrection in South Carolina. This brought reaction in Virginia where secession was voted in convention on April 17 and subsequently ratified by popular vote on May 23. After action by the convention, Virginia forces moved quickly on Harper's Ferry on April 18 and captured the arsenal there which the Federal troops had partially destroyed by fire before abandoning it. On April 19, Lincoln ordered the blockade of all Confederate ports. Arkansas voted to secede on May 6, followed by Tennessee on May 7. Tennessee's vote of May 7 was ratified by popular vote on June 8, despite strong Union support in eastern Tennessee. North Carolina seceded on May 21.

The Confederate Congress voted on May 20 to move the capitol to Richmond, Virginia; and four days later, Federal troops moved across the Potomac and occupied Alexandria, Virginia. The South had been invaded.

At Howard College commencement exercises on May 31, Dr. Henry Talbird announced he would raise an infantry company from Perry County; and immediately afterward, forty students and three professors volunteered for service in that unit.

When Randy, Buck, and Kevin returned to their room following the graduation exercise, they still had made no decision as to their future course.

"I think we should enlist in Dr. Talbird's company," Randy said. "We'll be with a lot of friends from college and from this area."

"The thought of going into an infantry company with all the marching that goes with it doesn't appeal to me," Kevin said; "but I'll go along with what y'all want to do. I've got a cousin, a minister, who is raising a company of cavalry in Huntsville; and he wants me to join up with him. I'm sure he can take all of us if you are interested. You will have to furnish your own horse and arms, though."

"What do you think, Randy?" Buck asked. "We've spent a lot of time in the saddle, and both of us know horses. I'd prefer a mounted unit, too."

"So would I. Slogging through rain, mud, and even snow doesn't appeal to me." Looking at Kevin, he continued, "Wire your cousin to see if he can take the three of us."

"I'll get it off right away and wait for an answer before leaving. If my cousin is available, I should have a reply by tomorrow. If y'all don't want to stay over until then, I can go out to Prairie's Edge to let you know after I hear from him."

"Let's stay over," Randy said. "We can send word to our folks by the wagon driver when he picks up the baggage. I'd like to get this settled before going home."

Kevin got the message off; and when they checked with the telegraph office at the railroad depot the following morning, they found the hoped for reply. Captain Kelley could take all three of them and wanted them to report as soon as possible with horses and arms.

After reading the message, Kevin handed it to Randy; he read it, and passed it on to Buck. Kevin waited until Buck finished it. "I can get the afternoon train," he said, "and should be in Huntsville tomorrow or the next day. When shall I tell him you'll be there?"

"It's at least four or five days by horse," Buck replied.

"I've got to see Bev before I go," Randy said. "We can be there in a week, don't you think, Buck?"

"Sure." Turning to Kevin, he added, "Tell your cousin we'll be there by the eighth, God willing and the creek don't rise."

Buck arrived home shortly after noon, and his parents were waiting to greet him when he rode up by the back porch. He had no sooner dismounted than his mother had him in her arms and said, "It's about time you was gittin' here. I ain't had no hug from you in a long, long time."

As he held her tightly, Buck replied, "I've sure missed yours. Nothing will ever take its place."

When she released him, Cory took his son's hand and said, "Things just ain't the same 'thout you around. Let's git this hoss took keer of, an' then there's a lot of ketchin' up to do."

"I'll fix you some'n t'eat," Sadie said and went into the house.

They rejoined her shortly in the kitchen where she was warming up food left over from dinner. She looked with beaming pride at her tall son; and as she turned back to the stove, she mumbled thanks to the Good Lord for giving him the opportunity for an education. The men sat down at the table; and she poured and brought two cups of coffee to them.

Buck was reluctant to break the pleasant spell of his homecoming but knew he had to tell his parents of his decision, and the sooner the better; so he said, "Randy and I are going into the Army."

Sadie turned and looked at him; the joy was gone from her face. "I knowed it was comin'," she said.

"Why?" Cory asked.

"Not for slavery. I don't believe in it any more than you; but I do believe we've got a right to leave the Union, and we've been invaded. Our country's got to be defended, and it's my duty as much as the next man's."

"That's good enough. I just wanted to be sure you was doin' it for the right reason. If they'd take a halfa man, I'd go with you."

"With one arm, you're still more of a man than most of us will ever be; but a war's no place for anyone with a handicap like that."

Sadie left the room without speaking. The men watched her go and wondered what it was all about. She returned soon carrying a stack of clothes which had been dyed with butternut hulls.

"There are two cotton outfits. I knowed you'd be goin', so I got 'em ready." She placed the stack of clothing on the table and turned back to her task at the stove. "I'll make some wool uns an' send 'em to you before it gits cold."

Buck casually examined the clothes. "Pa, how did you ever find me a ma like this?"

"'Twasn't easy—had to go back in the hills a far piece."

Sadie ignored her husband's response. "Seems there's always a war for a McCord. I don't wanta see you go, Buck; but I want less for you not to if you feel like you oughta."

"You gonna join up in Marion?" Cory asked. "I understand Porter King's raisin' a comp'ny."

"No. Kevin's cousin in Huntsville is forming a company of cavalry. Kevin is leaving today to join him. He contacted the cousin who said he can take Randy and me. We stayed over the extra day waiting for his reply. We must be in Huntsville next Saturday and have to furnish our own gun and horse. It's a five day ride, so we'll have to leave Tuesday."

"I want you to take the Whitworth," Cory said.

"Pa, I don't want to take your gun; besides, I probably can't get ammunition for it."

"Me an' John knowed it'd be needed, so we bought all we could find. We both got two new cases aside from what we already had. Y'all take keer of it, an' it'll last a long time. As for the gun, it's too heavy for a one-armed man. I been usin' my Mississippi rifle. You got more use for the Whitworth than me."

"Looks like y'all been two jumps ahead of me."

"We figured you'd feel bound to go," Sadie said, "We're just thankful you finished the year's schoolin' fust."

Buck saw the pained expression on his mother's face and went to her. He took her in his arms and held her tightly. Sadie buried her face in the hollow of her tall son's shoulder, and he could feel her body shake from the sobs she was trying so hard to control; and his own eyes filled, and tears began to trickle down his cheeks. Suddenly Cory was there beside them, placing his arm around his wife. As the three of them stood together, Buck said a silent prayer of thanks for having such understanding and loving parents.

Randy arrived at Prairie's Edge while his family was still at the dinner table. Carolyn recognized the sound of his footsteps when he came into the back hall and was almost at the door of the room when he got there. She embraced him; and when she released him, Ellen was standing by waiting her turn. He gave her an affectionate hug and a brotherly kiss on the cheek. He then went to his father and warmly shook hands.

"I don't know when I've had such a greeting, but I like it."

"We've missed you so terribly and are glad to see you again. I know you must be hungry, so sit down; and we'll have your place set. We hadn't expected you this soon." Carolyn picked up a small bell from the table and rang it.

Randy took a seat at his usual place and said, "Guess you're wondering why I stayed over another day at school."

"You might say that," John replied.

Samuel appeared, and Carolyn instructed him to set a place for Randy and to bring him some food.

"Buck, Kevin, and I have decided to go into the army together. Dr. Talbird is organizing an infantry company, and most of the Howard men and some of the professors are joining it. Kevin has a cousin in Huntsville who is organizing a cavalry company. Kevin telegraphed him yesterday to see if he could take the three of us. Buck and I waited for his answer. He can take us, so we are going to join up with him. We all prefer cavalry over infantry."

"I knew it had to be something like this," Carolyn said with resignation.

"Is this something you must do, or are you doing it because those around you are going into the army?" John asked.

"I believe it is my duty. It's certainly not something I want. I'm afraid I don't have the enthusiasm for war that some of the fellows have."

"I'm glad of that, but I'm pleased you want to do your part. I pray this will be a short affair and few will be lost or hurt in it."

"I don't feel very optimistic about that."

"Neither do I," John replied.

"I'm glad you will be with Buck," Ellen said.

Randy looked at her and smiled, "I'll take care of Buck."

Ellen returned the smile, "Or he you."

"You look after each other," Carolyn said firmly. She felt better about Randy's going since Buck would be with him.

"Does Beverly know?" Ellen asked.

"Not yet. We decided only yesterday and didn't know until this morning whether we would be accepted. I'm going to Marion Junction to see her tomorrow."

"When will y'all leave?" Carolyn asked.

"Tuesday. We have to furnish our own horses and arms, and it will take us about five days to get there by horseback."

"I'm not sure you wouldn't be better off signing up with a local company," John said. "You would know most of the men in it and would have a better chance of being elected an officer than you have in a company of strangers. I can understand, though, your preference to cavalry over infantry. I'd probably make the same choice.''

"Who is this cousin of Kevin?" Carolyn asked.

"His name is David C. Kelley. He's a minister."

"Well, I am certainly glad to hear that. I understand soldiers can sometimes be rather rough and crude. I hope he will be a good influence on all of you.''

"We may need it."

"I'm sure you will," John said.

"Most of the planters' sons are taking a servant with them to do the cooking and other menial chores around camp,'' Carolyn said. "You don't have a valet, but I want you to take one of our young people with you.''

"No thanks; I've learned to cook and take care of those things while camping with Buck and Mr. Cory.''

"I'm sure you have, but I'd feel much better knowing you have someone with you.''

"I'll have Buck; he's enough."

"You're a very stubborn young man," his mother said.

"And reared by a very persistent lady,'' Randy replied with a smile.

Monday afternoon Buck rode over to Prairie's Edge to finalize the plans for the trip. He found Randy in his room trying on uniforms which had been hurriedly made by the slaves under his mother's close directions. "Looks like you are ready to go," Buck said.

"I don't think I'll ever be ready to go; it's something I have to do. Do you think this world will ever see the time when all differences will be settled without war?''

"It hasn't so far. How did your folks take it?''

"Pretty well. They expected something like this."

"Mine, too; and Beverly?"

"She's elated. Sometimes I find it hard to understand her. She's got a lot of foolish ideas about war being glamorous. I don't see it that way. War is a rotten business, and I'm not looking forward to it; but a man's gotta do what he's gotta do.''

"I think most of us feel that way."

They sat down and prepared a list of the things needed to be taken with them. It was agreed that they would camp out at night instead of seeking lodging in order to prepare themselves for the life ahead. They decided each would take one case of ammunition for his gun and a pack mule. They would probably have to sell the mules after arrival in

Huntsville, but that should be no problem. The best route appeared by Montevallo and Elyton, so it was agreed Randy would be at Buck's house at seven o'clock the following morning. Buck left Randy to his uniforms and packing and sought out the rest of the Rushton family. When he reached the head of the stairs, he heard someone playing the pianoforte in the music room and knew it must be Ellen. He would see her parents first, and he found them together in the office. Carolyn looked up as he appeared at the door.

"Come in, Buck," she said.

"I just want to say goodbye to y'all before I leave. We are getting an early start in the morning, so I won't see you again."

Carolyn bit her trembling lower lip. After a moment, she said, "This is a sad time for us—to see our young men go off to war. I'm so thankful you and Randy will be together. You will both be in our prayers every day; and promise me, Buck, y'all will look after each other, won't you?"

"Of course we shall, but don't worry about us. We'll be all right."

"We're proud of you both," John said, "and know you will acquit yourselves well; but a word of caution, be careful and don't take unnecessary chances."

"That advice won't be hard to follow," Buck replied with a smile.

"God be with you," John said, offering his hand.

Buck took the hand in both of his and held it firmly for several seconds as he thought of how much he had grown to love and respect these people who had been so good to him for the past seven years. He released the hand and turned to Carolyn, who had gotten up and was standing nearby waiting. She ignored the hand he offered; and rising on the tips of her toes, she reached up and pulled Buck's face to hers and kissed him on the cheek. "Goodbye, Buck," she said. "Be sure to see Ellen before you go. She's in the music room with Sally."

"I was planning to," he said and left the room.

As they listened to his retreating footsteps, Carolyn said, "It was a fortunate day when he came into our lives. He has become like a second son to me." John smiled but said nothing.

Buck found Ellen and Sally playing a duet. When they saw him at the door, the music stopped as if on a signal.

"I'm sorry to interrupt," he said. "That was beautiful. You always play so well together."

"We've had a lot of practice," Sally replied. "I hope you haven't come to say goodbye."

"Afraid I have."

Sally stood up. "Y'all excuse me; I've got to see Miss Carolyn." She went to Buck and took his hand. "Goodbye, Buck. You and Randy will always be in my thoughts and prayers. Come back to us safe and sound."

"I intend to. We appreciate the thoughts and need the prayers." Ellen got up from the music bench. "Are you leaving now?"

"Yes."

"Where's your horse?"

"Out back."

"I'll walk there with you."

She took his arm, and together they went to the back yard where Skin was hitched, neither speaking; but each was keenly aware of the excitement created by the presence of the other. He untied the reins from the hitching post and laid them across the pommel of the saddle. He looked at Ellen and could see the sadness which appeared to be overwhelming her. This seemed to be the opportunity for which he had so long waited. If she was sad because of his leaving, he could declare his love to her, knowing it was returned.

"You look upset," he said.

"I am. I can't bear to see y'all go. I'm so worried about Randy. He doesn't have your fortitude, and there's the thing he has about the sight of blood. He's tried to hide it all these years, but I know it's there. Promise me, Buck, that you will look after him."

The excitement he felt drained away, leaving only a hollow, empty feeling. This wasn't at all what he hoped to hear. His spirits dashed, he tried to hide the way he felt as he replied, "Of course, I shall; but don't worry about Randy. There's more mettle in him than appears on the surface. Believe me, he'll be just fine."

He mounted his horse; and looking down at Ellen's upturned face, he forced a smile and said, "See you." He touched the brim of his hat as he nudged his horse and rode away.

As she walked back to the house, Ellen thought what a fool she had been. He had given her the perfect occasion to let him know she was sad because of his leaving, and she had muffed it by making him think it was only over her concern for Randy. She wouldn't miss the next opportunity that presented itself.

The first night on the road, Buck and Randy camped beside a stream near Montevallo. After eating and cleaning up, they sat by the campfire talking. The conversation gradually died down; and they sat quietly relaxed, each lost in his own thoughts. Randy finally broke the silence.

"Buck, you've done it; how does it feel to kill a man?"

"I guess it depends on the man. If he needed killing like Caleb, it didn't bother me at all. If I killed a good man accidentally or for little or no reason, then that would be different and an awful thing for me to live with.''

"I hope I can. It's not that I'm afraid of dying, if duty calls for it; it's just that I don't like the thought of taking the life of another person. Do you know what I mean?''

"I surely do. I imagine there are a lot of people in both armies who feel the same way; but in war, it's kill or be killed. Don't think of the enemy as someone you might know but as a killer who is trying to get you.''

"There's something else that bothers me—the sight of blood. You recall the time I first saw you clean a deer and almost fainted. I'd surely hate for something like that to happen in battle and cause me to fail to do my part. I don't think I could live with that kind of disgrace.''

"You'll be all right. You remember when we went to the Barlow house with the Sheriff? I told you there could be shooting; and you didn't hesitate a bit, just like you haven't hesitated to go in the army. As for the blood, you'll have to grit your teeth and do what has to be done. I'm not worried; you'll do your duty.''

"I hope so. But I'll tell you one thing; I'm glad you're with me. I think I can go through anything as long as you are there.''

"I feel the same way about you, Randy. We'll look after one another, right?''

"Right, Brother.''

Buck smiled. "We'd better get to bed; we've got a long ride tomorrow.'' As he got up to roll out his bed, he groaned and said, "Man, I've really gotten soft. I've got muscles aching that I had forgotten all about.''

Randy stood up; and he, too, groaned. "I see what you mean. We'll be stiff and sore tomorrow. Hope this wears off before we get to Huntsville.''

Chapter VI

Forrest

Buck and Randy arrived in Huntsville on the afternoon of June 8. Captain Kelley's headquarters were located without difficulty, and they found Kevin waiting for them. The complement of the company had not been filled; it numbered only seventy-three men but was increasing almost every day. Lacking adequate camping equipment, the volunteers from Huntsville were staying in their homes, and those not from the immediate area were quartered in homes of local people who took them in at no cost. Kevin had arranged for Buck and Randy to stay with his family.

They found their company commander to be a deeply religious man of strong character who was devoted to the cause of the South. He was well educated and a fluent speaker and appeared to be a man of good judgment as well as a natural leader. In addition to Kelley, there was another officer in the unit, Lieutenant Hambrick.[1] Kevin had already found his niche in the organization, serving as unofficial company clerk and courier.

The company drilled twice daily, but lack of equipment and supplies hindered its becoming an effective unit. In the middle of July, Kelley received orders to proceed to Memphis, Tennessee, to be enlisted in the Confederate army and to equip his command. With such camping gear as they could muster, the company marched as ordered.

There was no organized mess for the company. Each man was issued his allotted rations; and from necessity, groups of from five to ten men joined together to form small messes. Each group carried in a camp chest its frying pan, dutch oven, coffee boiler, spoons, plates, cups, and containers for lard, coffee, meal, salt pork, and flour. The men took turns at cooking and cleaning up after a meal. Their experience in camping out with Cory and the things he had taught them now stood Randy and Buck in good stead as they joined Kevin and five others in a mess.

Upon arrival in Memphis, they found several cavalry companies there for the same purpose, among them three others from Alabama. Those three companies had set up camp in the same area; and Kelley's command, now numbering ninety men, camped beside them. Supplies and equipment were sparse, and almost a month had passed with only mediocre results in obtaining what was needed.

Captain Kelley returned to camp one afternoon and, seeing Kevin, motioned for his cousin to follow him to his tent. "Go to the captains of the other Alabama companies and ask them to meet me here right away. Tell them it's very important."

Within a half an hour, the three captains, Bacot from southern Alabama, Trewhitt from Gadsden, and Milner from Marshall County, had arrived for the meeting.

"I've called y'all together, because we have a very important decision to make. I met today with Lieutenant Colonel Nathan Bedford Forrest, and he has offered us the opportunity to join his command. He is in the process of raising a battalion of cavalry; and at this time, he has in his unit the Boone Rangers under Captain Overton, Forrest's Rangers under Captain May, and a company of Texans under Captain Gould. Forrest seems to have the ability to get what he wants. I have been able to push my requisitions for supplies and equipment ahead of everybody else, except him. I understand he procured at his own expense considerable equipment, including saddles and pistols, in Kentucky and successfully brought them out of that state under difficult conditions. He gets things done. It might be a good thing to tie up with him."

"I don't know," one of the other captains said, "I heard he clawed his way up from a dirt poor family and has no formal education or military experience whatsoever. I also heard he is a former slave trader."[2]

"That's true, but he's quite a fighter," Trewhitt said. "If just half of what I've heard is so, he's the kind of man I'd want on my side in a fracas."

"What have you heard and how good is your source?" Kelley wanted to know.

"My father has a good friend who has been active politically and in civic affairs here in Memphis for many years. He knows Forrest quite well, having served as an alderman with him; but he has known of him before that. Forrest did come from a poor, pioneer family who settled in northern Mississippi after migrating from Bedford County, Tennessee, where he was born. He was under sixteen years of age when his father died and left him, the oldest male of eight children, the responsibility of taking care of a large family. Through hard work and good business judgment, he has done exceptionally well. He became a horse and cattle trader, then a partner with an uncle who was a merchant in Hernando, Mississippi, and later a trader in slaves and real estate. After making a fortune in these ventures, he gave them up to become a very successful planter in Coahoma County, Mississippi. He is married to a gracious lady from a fine family. When the war started, he volunteered as a private. My father's friend was one of the several prominent and responsible men who recommended to the governor of Tennessee that Forrest be made an officer. It was upon these recommendations that he was commissioned and authorized to raise a battalion of cavalry.''

"How did he get the reputation as a fighter?'' Milner asked.

"He earned it. Not long after his father died, a panther attacked his mother, clawing her rather badly. He was just a boy; but he set out alone at night with his dogs, and tracked the panther until it was treed. He waited until daylight and killed the animal. Then there was another incident about this time. A neighbor had an ox which kept breaking down the fences and getting into the Forrests' grain fields. The boy served notice on the man that he would kill the animal if he found it in one of their fields again. The neighbor disregarded his warning; and when Forrest found the ox in a field, he killed it. The man heard the shot and came running with his gun. By the time he reached the fence separating their properties, Forrest has his gun reloaded and was waiting. He told his neighbor that he didn't want to harm him; but if he climbed on the fence or made any attempt to use his gun, he would kill him. He cocked the gun and took a steady bead on his neighbor. The man left, and that ended the affair.'' After a pause, he continued:

"There was another incident in Hernando. The uncle, his partner in the mercantile business, became involved in a dispute with four members of a family of planters. The situation got so bad that the four men came to town to settle things in their own way with the uncle, an elderly man. When Forrest saw what was happening, he stepped to his uncle's side and told them he wasn't a party to the disagreement and didn't want to become involved; but he would not stand by while they attacked or maltreated his uncle. He had barely finished speaking when one of the men drew a pistol; and fired at him, missing. This was the signal for a fusillade, and his uncle was mortally wounded. Forrest drew a twin-barreled pistol and, firing deliberately, shot down two of the men. A bystander saw him helpless with an empty gun and ran to him and handed him a knife. With a face crimson with rage, eyes wild, and nostrils flared, he rushed the men still standing, wounding first one and then the other. They both fled and left town. All survivors of the fight were arrested. Forrest was released after making a statement, but the others were held for trial.''

"He sounds like a fighter," Milner said.

"He is," Trewhitt replied. "There was another incident of which our friend claims personal knowledge, if I'm not boring you with these tales.''

"Not at all," Kelley said.

"This has to do with his sense of justice and took place not long after Forrest came to Memphis to live. There was a man in Memphis at that time who killed another man with little provocation. The murderer was jailed, but the people were so indignant over the incident that a mob formed around the jail with the intention of hanging him. Forrest heard about it and hurried to the jail. By that time, the mob had gained entry into the building and had seized the prisoner. Forrest shouldered his way through the crowd and placed himself between the leaders and the man. He took a knife out of his pocket, opened it, and held it in his left hand above his head. I understand he is ambidextrous, but prefers his left hand in time of crisis. Anyway, he declared defiantly, in such a way that none who heard him or saw him doubted it, that he would kill the first man who laid a hand on the prisoner. He then addressed the mob and their leaders, appealing to their reasoning and better judgment, and convinced them by his own sincerity to let the law take its course.''

"He's brave enough, but seems rather impetuous," Bacot said. "What do you think, Kelley?"

"Let me think on it and pray about it," Kelley replied.

"I'll go along with whatever you decide," Bacot said.

"So will I," Milner added.

"I, too," Trewhitt said; "but I hope it's to join up with him. I'd like to serve with Forrest.''

"Y'all have breakfast here with me at six tomorrow. We can make our decision then.''

The following morning, Kelley announced that he believed Forrest was a natural leader who got things done, and he had decided it would be wise to become a part of his command. The other captains unanimously voiced their approval of the decision.

By the first week in October, Forrest had attracted eight companies to his battalion, designated A through H, with Kelley's becoming F Company. In addition to the four Alabama companies, the others included one from Memphis under Captain May, one from Texas under Captain Gould, and two from Kentucky under Captains Overton and

Logan.

It was the custom for the men to elect their officers. Forrest was elected lieutenant colonel; Kelley was chosen as major; Lieutenant Schuyler was appointed adjutant; J. P. Strange became sergeant major; and S. M. Van Wick took the position of battalion surgeon.

Lieutenant Hambrick was chosen to replace Kelley as captain of F Company, and Kevin was elected lieutenant to fill the vacancy created by the promotion.[3]

The battalion had a complement of approximately 650 men. Despite Forrest's efforts to equip them, by the time the organization of the battalion was completed, fully half of them had nothing better than shotguns which they had brought from home. Many of the men, however, including Buck and Randy, had been supplied with sabers and .36 caliber Colt Navy revolvers. These guns were single action, which required cocking before firing, used percussion caps, and had to be loaded with powder and ball similar to a muzzle loading rifle.

During the stay in Memphis, the troops usually drilled or had firearm or saber practice twice daily. Major Kelley was a strict disciplinarian and worked the men hard. Forrest fully supported practice with sabers and firearms; but he wasn't strongly in favor of drilling, feeling that it was hard on both men and horses. He was a meticulous man, however, attentive to the smallest details. He was especially concerned with the welfare of the men and the condition of their horses and equipment. He could easily overlook a blunder while drilling; but woe be it to him whom Forrest found to be lax in taking care of his mount or failing to look to the animal's needs. He was everywhere observing, examining, and correcting all of those things he considered important.

Because of their marksmanship skills, Buck and Randy were made instructors on the firing range. To conserve ammunition, this was principally dry firing with only occasional use of live ammunition to measure progress. It was on an improvised rifle range that they had their first personal meeting with Forrest. He showed up with Major Kelley and stood quietly watching the simulated firing.

"See you got privates teachin' shootin'," he said to Kelley.

"They're the best shots in the battalion," Kelley replied. "Both of them have very unusual guns; I've never seen any like them. The distance and accuracy they get is unbelievable."

"I'd like to see one."

Randy was the nearer of the two, so Kelley called, "Rushton! Get your rifle and bring it over here."

Randy got his gun and reported as ordered. This was his first opportunity to get a close look at his battalion commander. Before him was an erect, very broad shouldered, muscular man who stood six feet and two inches tall—a man of great physical strength and vitality. He had a neatly trimmed mustache and chin beard. His bushy black hair was full cut and slightly wavy. His broad, high forehead, the shaggy brow above piercing eyes, prominent cheek bones, and bold assertive nose told not only of his Gaelic origin, but also of the bulldog tenacity of the man. His uniform was neat and well fitted; it was evident that he took pride in his appearance. Randy thought he might be a kindly man who could also be severe and explosive. Coming to attention before the two officers, he held his gun in his left hand and saluted with his right. Kelley returned the salute smartly, Forrest indifferently.

"Colonel Forrest would like to see your gun," Kelley said.

Forrest took the gun handed him by Randy and examined it closely. "I never seen one like this," he said. "What kind is it?"

"It's called a Whitworth, sir. It's made in England."

"I don't see no rifling in it."

"That six-sided bore turns at the ratio of one full turn in twenty inches. It uses a six-sided, elongated bullet. The turn of the bore is twice that of normal rifling. This gives the bullet more spin, making it go farther and more accurately."

"How good is it?"

"I can hit a target the size of a man fairly consistently at 600 yards."

"Six hundred yards! That's hard to believe. The other man, he got a gun like this?"

"Yes, sir."

"Can he shoot good as you?"

"Better"

"I'd like to see that." Randy noticed as Forrest returned the gun to him that the piercing quality of his eyes had disappeared, and there was now a twinkle in them.

Kelley spoke up, "This range is too short. Would you like for them to find a suitable place and give you a demonstration tomorrow? I'd like to see it myself. I've never seen them shoot anywhere near that distance."

"I sure would."

"Take care of it, Rushton," Kelley said. Then to Forrest, "Would ten o'clock tomorrow morning suit you?"

"Just name the place."

The next morning, at a large open field bordered on one side by a dense wood, Buck and Randy set up two board targets approximately two feet wide and five feet high. They improvised 600 yards away two rests from which they could fire at a standing position. Colonel Forrest and Major Kelley rode up about ten o'clock and dismounted.

"Are you all set?" Kelley asked.

"Yes, sir," Randy replied.

Kelley said, "Colonel, you know Rushton; the other man is Private McCord."

"McCord, huh?" Forrest said, eyeing Buck closely. "Well, let's see some of that miracle shootin' I've heared about."

"I see you have two targets," Kelley said. "Each of you try six shots."

When the firing was completed, Forrest said, "Let's see how you done."

They mounted their horses and rode to the targets. Randy's target showed four hits scattered over it. Buck had six hits, all within a twenty inch circle.

"That's some kinda shootin'," the colonel said. Turning to Randy, he continued, "I thought you was braggin', but it ain't braggin' when you can back up your mouth."

The officers got on their horses; and as they rode off, the two privates heard Forrest say to Kelley, "Major, write a recommendation th'ough channels that some of them guns be bought by our gov'ment for sharpshooters. I'd like to have a company armed with them guns."

By the last week in October, the battalion, though poorly armed, was ready for duty. Lieutenant Colonel Forrest was ordered to proceed with his command to Dover, Tennessee, on the Cumberland River, and to report to Colonel A. Heiman, who was in command there and was beginning to throw up earthworks and fortify the position which afterward came to be known as Fort Donelson.

The battalion moved out of Memphis at dawn, and Forrest was mounted and waiting as they marched out of camp past him. His eagle eye was carefully observing every man and his mount as they rode by, and he was quick to call a rider's attention to anything he found amiss or did not like. When the last unit had passed, he then rode hastily forward through them to the head of the column. Randy and Buck did not know at the time, but this was to be a standard procedure for their commander; and if it was raining and he saw an uncovered cartridge box, the owner was fortunate to get by with only a reprimand.

From Dover, the new battalion was ordered to report to General Floyd Tilghman at Hopkinsville, Kentucky, and was placed in observation in the stretch of country between the Cumberland and Green Rivers. At that time, Kentucky, which had tried to remain neutral in the conflict, found itself invaded by both Confederate and Federal forces. Major

General Leonidas Polk, commanding the Confederates in western Tennessee, fearing that Kentucky would be occupied by Federal forces, moved quickly and seized the Mississippi River port of Columbus, Kentucky, and fortified it.[4] Brigadier General Ulysses S. Grant, commanding Federal forces at Cairo, Illinois, countered by crossing the Ohio River and occupying Paducah, Kentucky. Shortly afterward, Simon Buckner, who had been placed in command of the professed neutral Kentucky State Guard, formed a Confederate camp in Tennessee. He failed in an attempt to seize Louisville and fell back to Bowling Green, Kentucky.

General Albert Sidney Johnston, commanding the Confederate Western Department, with headquarters in Nashville, strengthened Polk's position at Columbus and concentrated a large force at Bowling Green under the command of General Hardee. He also had a force firmly planted at Cumberland Gap, the chief passage between eastern Kentucky and eastern Tennessee, under General Zollicoffer. Between Cumberland Gap and Columbus were fortified posts, the most important of which were Fort Henry on the Tennessee River and Fort Donelson on the Cumberland River. Hopkinsville was another of the strong points on this long thin line.

In November 1861, while his battalion, now reinforced with a small detachment of artillerists under Lieutenant Sullivan with a four-pounder gun, was encamped at Princeton, Kentucky, Forrest received information that the Federal Gunboat *Conestoga* of Admiral Foote's flotilla had steamed up the Cumberland to destroy a Confederate warehouse at Canton Landing. By a rapid march, Forrest had his entire command at the landing the following morning. Sullivan's small gun was masked, and the troops were concealed in the brush and timber and behind logs along the river bank near the expected point of landing. The commander of the *Conestoga* was too wily to be caught in this manner; stopping short of the landing by several hundred yards, he dropped anchor and threw some shells into the timber to be sure no lurking enemy took him unawares. On Forrest's orders, Sullivan replied with his four-pounder; but by the time he got off his second shot, the broadsides of the gunboat made his position untenable, and he had to withdraw his gun to a position of safety.

As the small gun and its crew moved to the rear, Forrest said to Major Kelley, "Git me them two fellows with the fancy guns."

Kelley dispatched a courier to Captain Hambrick of Company F directing that Buck and Randy report to him with their rifles. The courier had difficulty in locating Hambrick, so the sharpshooters didn't report as promptly as expected; and during the time, the gunboat continued to fire into the area. When they arrived, it was to find an impatient and vexed commander.

"When I send for you, I want you to come arunnin'."

Before either could reply, the courier said, "Colonel, I had trouble locating Captain Hambrick."

Somewhat mollified, Forrest said curtly, "Come with me," and led them, crawling the last twenty yards, to a spot where there was a clear view of the *Conestoga*.

"Can you make out anybody in the pilot house?" Forrest asked.

Looking through his telescopic sight and adjusting it, Buck said, "I see three men. One's a helmsman; one's an officer; and I'd guess the other to be a pilot."

"You got a good shot at 'em?"

"Yes, sir."

"Let's see how good you are playin' for keeps."

"Randy, you take the one with the braid on his cap, and I'll take the one who appears to be a pilot. We'll need to fire together. When I say 'ready,' start squeezing the trigger."

The rifles went off almost as one. Forrest was watching through field glasses and could see that both targets appeared to have been hit. As they disappeared from sight, so did the third man in the pilot house.

"You done it!" Forrest cried. "When you git reloaded, keep an eye on that pilot house. You may git another shot."

While they were reloading, Buck looked at Randy and said in a low voice so Forrest wouldn't hear, "That wasn't too bad."

"It wasn't too good, either. Took a lot of teeth gritting."

They didn't get a second shot. In a few minutes, the *Conestoga* lifted anchor and slowly backed down stream and out of sight around a bend.[5]

In bivouac that night, Forrest was in high spirits. It was not a great victory that had caused much damage to the enemy, but the mission of the *Conestoga* had been thwarted. The thing that pleased him was how his raw recruits had taken their baptism of fire; he liked their response to command and the eagerness they had shown for the fight.

The battalion returned to Hopkinsville, arriving there November 21, and was increased by the addition of two more companies, I from Huntsville under Captain C. C. Davis and J under Captain Charles McDonald, the latter unit being known as the McDonald Dragoons. This increased the complement of effectives to about 790 men.

On November 24, under orders from Brigadier Charles Clark, in whose district Forrest was stationed, he was directed to take some 300 men and make a reconnaissance in the direction of the Ohio River. With these troops he marched to Greenville where he was fortunate enough to capture some arms and equipment which had been collected by the Union forces. From there he proceeded to Caseyville on the Ohio River and on in the direction of Marion in Crittenden County. Approaching this village, Forrest was informed of the arrest of a prominent citizen who had been thrown into prison for being a "Southern sympathizer." On inquiry it was learned that two extreme Unionists had been the instigators of the arrest; Forrest decided to hold them as hostages for the safety of the imprisoned Southerner who, upon approach of the Confederate cavalry, had been taken away to a place of greater security.

One of the persons to be held was Jonathan Bells, and Forrest took personal command of the detachment assigned to take him into custody. Dr. Van Wick, the battalion surgeon, accompanied him and was riding at his side as they approached Bells' house. The surgeon was dressed in full uniform. Someone inside the house selected him for the target and, with deadly aim, sent a bullet through his heart. The man firing the shot ran out the rear door of the house and escaped into the wood behind it.

The death of his surgeon was a hard blow for Forrest. He was almost equally upset over the escape of the man who had killed Van Wick, and this brought about a decision which radically altered the lives of the two young men from Perry County. That night in camp, Forrest said to Major Kelley, "If one of them men with the Whitworth rifles had been along, we could probably have got that killer before he reached the woods. From now on, I want them two men from Company F detailed to me; an' they are to ride with me. When needed, I want 'em handy." With that order, Buck and Randy became an unofficial part of Forrest's staff.

The reconnaissance lasted for three weeks. During that time Forrest lost no opportunity to gather up hogs, cattle, horses, and other supplies to be driven south for the needs of the army. On the return trip to Hopkinsville, a squadron of Federal cavalry, estimated at about 400 in number, followed the Confederates for part of a day. Forrest turned on them and offered battle, but they showed no disposition to close with him.

Reporting on December 26 to General Clark with the supplies he had gathered, Forrest was ordered to make a tour of observation in the direction of Henderson, Kentucky. Taking a detail from Companies A, C, and D, he placed them under Lieutenant Crutcher and Captains May and Gould; additional details taken from Companies E, F, and G were placed under Major Kelley; and an independent detachment of twenty-five Kentuckians was placed under Captain Merriwether. On the morning of December 28, a company of forty Tennesseans under

Captain Starnes and Lieutenant McLemore overtook Forrest and volunteered to accompany him.

A few hours later, a scout reported a body of Federal cavalry, estimated at about 500 men, had crossed the road some eight miles distant and were moving in the direction of a small village called Sacramento. Forrest determined, if possible, to overtake and attack; the order to "move up" was given, and all pressed forward at a rapid gait.

One mile from Sacramento, Forrest came in sight of the rear guard of the Union cavalry which had halted, seemingly in doubt whether it was friend or foe behind them. Seizing a rifle from one of his men, Forrest fired a shot at the enemy. Their doubts satisfied, the Union troopers immediately disappeared in the direction of their main column.

Disregarding tactical formation, Forrest ordered his men to follow him but not to fire until they were within close range. As they galloped along the road, the enemy was soon sighted, deployed in line across and on either side of the road in a heavy grove. From this position, they opened fire on the Confederates at about 200 yards. Recognizing the danger of moving directly on them in column, Forrest for the first time put into execution the maneuver which he afterward practiced so frequently and with much success.

Posting his men on horseback in a position of least exposure, he threw forward a number of men dismounted as skirmishers, Buck and Randy among them because of their long-range guns. These men had orders to keep the attention of the enemy in front of them actively engaged. Forrest held a brief conference with his subordinate commanders; and his famous movement by the flank and rear, before the frontal attack, was inaugurated. Starnes took the left with thirty men, and Kelley took the right with sixty, all mounted and starting from a point which could not be seen by the enemy.

The dismounted troops in front, behind trees and logs and in fence corners, were firing away at the enemy and receiving volleys in return. When Kelley's column swung into view from the right, and Starnes threatened the other flank, Forrest, with saber in hand and eyes strained to catch the first suggestion of confusion in the Union line, saw when the moment had come.

In a way that showed the most intense excitement, Forrest shouted, "Charge! Charge!" and was off at full speed and well out in front of his men. His face was flushed till it looked like a painted warrior; and his eyes, usually mild in expression, glared like those of a panther about to spring upon its prey. With no semblance of formation, the mounted troopers in his squadron followed, trying desperately to catch up with their leader who, standing in his stirrups with saber in left hand, looked a foot taller than any of them. Threatened on both flanks, and assailed in such an aggressive fashion from the front, the Union cavalry, despite the gallant efforts of their officers to hold them to their position, broke and fled. For nearly a mile to and through the village, the fight was little more than a horse race. The best mounted of the Confederates, among whom were Forrest, Starnes, and Merriwether, soon began to overhaul the fleeing enemy, who either surrendered or went down at close range from saber thrust or pistol shot.

When Forrest charged with his contingent through his line of dismounted skirmishers, Randy yelled to Buck, "Let's go!" They ran for their mounts which were in custody of horseholders, quickly mounted, and set out to catch up with the disorganized charge of their fellow troopers.

Beyond Sacramento the Union officers had succeeded in rallying a squadron of the fleeing cavalry and turned on their pursuers in what developed into a bloody hand-to-hand combat. Before they reached the enemy, Buck and Randy, on their fast horses, had almost caught up with the leaders; and they were just behind Captain Merriwether when that officer's head suddenly seemed to explode as a Minie ball caught him in the brain. Blood and a part of the flying brain tissue splattered on Randy. As the captain fell dead from his saddle, Randy panicked. With a low cry, he wheeled his horse to the right into an open field.

Buck reacted instantaneously, wheeling with him; and as he came alongside Chessy, he grabbed the horse's bridle, and brought her to a stop. Looking at his ashen-faced friend, he said, "It's teeth-gritting time, Ol' Buddy."

Buck's calm and steady voice helped Randy regain control of himself. "Right," he grimly replied, and both men rushed to the fray.

Forrest was being assailed from all sides; but before they could bring him down, a quick thrust of his saber mortally wounded Captain Bacon. As Randy and Buck rode into the melee of fighting men, Randy saw another Union officer, Captain Davis, spurring his horse to attack Forrest on his blind side; and Randy brought his own fast moving Chessy between the two men. As he cut off Davis, the latter slashed at him with the saber blow intended for Forrest; but Randy managed to parry it with his own weapon.[6]

Chessy was moving too fast to stop quickly. By the time Randy got the mare turned around, Forrest had realized his danger and rushed Davis with such impetus that their horses collided, and riders and mounts fell in a heap. Davis struck the ground with such force that his shoulder was dislocated; being unable to continue the fight, he surrendered. Beyond the severe shock and several bruises, Forrest escaped injury.

In the meantime, Buck was having his own problems. He was attacked by two of the enemy at the same time, one on each side. He dispatched one with the thrust of his saber; but as he was withdrawing it from the enemy's body, the other antagonist made a sweeping downward blow at him with his own weapon. Fortunately Skin shied, and the blade missed; but it struck Buck's saber in front of the hilt with such force that it tore the weapon from his grasp, and his hand was numbed by the blow. Reaching for his pistol, Buck had difficulty with the deadened hand in unfastening and raising the flap of his holster. He spurred his horse, and Skin moved quickly out of range of another blow from the saber. By the time he had the horse turned to face the enemy again, he had gotten out his pistol and fired it point blank into the body of the charging Union trooper, knocking him from the saddle. He looked for another adversary, but Captain Davis had capitulated; and the fight had gone out of the remaining Union cavalrymen, who were raising their hands in surrender.

The pursuit and fight, which lasted about three hours, was called off. In addition to Captain Merriwether, Forrest lost one other killed and three wounded. The Union report showed one officer (Bacon) and eight troopers killed and forty men missing. Forrest had personally put down three of them.

Since their detail to Forrest, Buck and Randy had joined the mess of noncommissioned officers and couriers assigned directly to the battalion commander. While eating their evening meal in bivouac that night, a courier came to Buck and said Colonel Forrest wanted to see him. Buck went to the commanding officer's tent where he rapped gently on the front tent pole.

"Come in," a voice said gruffly.

Entering the tent, Buck saw Forrest sitting on a camp stool beside a field desk. His face was grim and severe as he glared at Buck. Finally he spoke, "I knowed a fellow named McCord once. You look a lot like 'im. As I recollect, he wasn't from Huntsville, but come from down in central Alabama."

"That's where I'm from," Buck said. "My father is Cory McCord."

"That's him. You ever hear 'im mention me?"

"No, sir."

"We was pretty busy out there today, but I wasn't too busy to see that friend of yours turn an' run an' you leave the fight to go after 'im."

"He came back, Colonel."

"What if he hadn'?"

This was something Buck hadn't considered. He thought the matter over carefully before responding. "Then I guess you would have lost two men today. Before I left home, I promised his sister and his mother I would look after him. I don't take lightly to giving my word, especially to ladies like them."

Forrest stared at him briefly before replying, "No, I guess you wouldn'."

"Randy's no coward, sir. We grew up together; I know him. We were in the skirmish line today and not a part of the charge. After you passed through us, it was Randy who said, 'Let's go!' and ran for his horse to join the charge without orders. He's had a problem all of his life with the sight of blood. He almost fainted the first time he saw me gut a deer. When Captain Merriwether was shot in the head today some of his blood and part of his brains splattered over Randy. I guess it was too much for him, and he momentarily panicked; but he came back, and he gave a good account of himself."

"I'm aware of that, but let's git one thing straight," Forrest said. "Rushton is his own man. I'll have no man in my command turning from a fight with the enemy. Regardless of what he does, you stay with the fight; or by all that's holy, I'll have you shot for desertin' in face of the enemy! Do I make myself clear?"

"Yessir."

"That's all. Tell Rushton I want to see him."

Buck got to the flap of the tent and stopped, turning to face Forrest. "Colonel," he said, "my ma is a very religious lady with a lot of faith. I've often heard her say that the Lord moves in mysterious ways."

"What are you drivin' at?"

"If Randy hadn't made that little detour in getting to the fight, the chances are he wouldn't have been in position to throw himself between you and Captain Davis' saber." As he turned and went out the tent, he added, "Good night, Colonel."

Forrest automatically responded, "Good night," but his mind wasn't on it.

Randy approached the Colonel's tent with trepidation. He felt deeply the shame of failing in his duty that day, and Buck had told him Forrest saw him turn away from the fight. Never had he dreaded facing anyone as he did his commander that night.

"Come in," a voice commanded impatiently at his gentle tap on the tent pole.

He entered, stood stiffly at attention, saluted, and said, "Private Rushton reporting as directed, sir."

"At ease," Forrest replied not bothering to return the salute. He continued, "There ain't much goes on around me without me knowin' about it. I seen you turn an' run from the fight today. If I didn' owe my life to you, I'd have you court-martialed an' shot for it."

"I've no excuse, sir. Captain Merriwether being killed like he was did something to me. I'd never seen anything like that before."

"If you can't take things like that, why did you join the army?"

"I felt it was my duty."

"Well, if you stay in this army, you're gonna see a lot more of what you seen today. War means fightin', an' fightin' means killin'!" Forrest paused; he liked that, so he repeated, "Just remember, war means fightin', an' fightin' means killin'."

"Yessir."

"I'll have no cowards or liver-bellies in my command! You ever turn tail to the enemy ag'in, I'll have you shot for a coward, if I don't do it myself fust. You understand?"

"Yessir."

"Before I change my mind an' have you shot anyway, git the hell outa here an' try to be a soldier your folks'd take some pride in!"

"Yessir; I will."

Randy left the tent and returned to the campfire. Buck had been anxiously awaiting his return, and when he saw his friend approaching, he went to meet him so they could talk privately. "How did it go?" he asked.

"Rough, but he gave me another chance."

"That's all you need."

"That's all I've got—one more chance," he said dejectedly; "but it's more than I deserve."

Chapter VII

Fort Donelson

Forrest remained in bivouac near Sacramento giving his men and their mounts two days' rest. Randy had been quiet, brooding over what had occurred at the fight. He seemed to prefer staying away from the other men and had nothing to say to anyone except Buck, and not much to him.

Randy noticed that Buck had acquired a second Colt Navy revolver and was working on the holsters. "Where did you get the other gun?" he asked.

"That fellow I shot yesterday willed it to me."

"That was nice of him, but aren't you supposed to turn it in to the quartermaster?"

"Maybe so; I don't know. Until someone tells me differently, I'm going to keep it."

"What are you doing to the holster?"

"Experimenting a little. When that Yankee knocked the saber out of my hand, I kinda lost enthusiasm for the weapon. I think I'll stick to revolvers, but I don't like these flaps on the holsters. I almost got killed while trying to get my gun out. I'm going to cut the flap off and use a leather thong to hold the gun in the holster. I'm trying to figure a way to get the thong loose in a hurry. I believe that by doubling it and securing one end over a button, I can tie a big knot in the thong near the button and free it with a brush of the hand. Also, I believe that by cutting a gap in the top side of the holster by the trigger, I can get my finger on the trigger while pulling out the gun."

Randy sat down and disinterestedly watched Buck as he worked. In a low voice he asked, "You hear any comments from the fellows about what happened yesterday?"

"Not a word."

"Do you think the others know about it?"

"Some may, but I wouldn't lose any sleep over it. You went back to the fight. Do your job, and this will blow over.''

"I'll do that and more."

"Don't get reckless. This business is dangerous enough without that."

"I've got to vindicate myself. Like Colonel Forrest said last night, war is fighting, and fighting is killing."

As the days went by, Buck continued to experiment and practice with the gun. He could be seen in spare moments drawing and firing it, usually without caps, by pointing the weapon rather than taking aim. As his proficiency increased, even he was surprised at the speed with which he could draw, cock the gun, and fire it. He found another short cut. Instead of cocking the gun with his right thumb, he could fire even more quickly by hitting the hammer with the lower edge of his left hand; and by the time he got the gun pointed at the target, all he had to do was pull the trigger. After working with this a while, he carried it a little further; by continuing to cock the pistol in this manner, he could get off subsequent shots faster. At first he would pull the gun off target in firing this way, but practice steadily improved his accuracy as well as his speed.

His work with the holster and practice with the gun attracted the attention of his fellow troopers. Many of them joshed him about it; but as his proficiency in drawing the gun and his accuracy in firing it improved, he began to have a number of imitators. Among them was Randy, whose concern over his own problem and how the other troopers might feel toward him had gradually disappeared. Even Forrest treated him as if nothing had happened and had not terminated his detail from company F.

When the reconnaissance ended, Forrest returned to Hopkinsville with his small force, arriving there in the early part of January 1862. For the remainder of that month and the first week in February, units from his command were sent on routine but uneventful patrols.

January produced a considerable change in the military situation in Kentucky. On the 7th of that month, Federal infantry under Colonel James A. Garfield struck a body of Confederates under the command of Humphrey Marshall near Prestonburg in eastern Kentucky and dispersed them. On the 18th at Beach Grove, near Mill Springs, Brigadier General George H. Thomas, in command of Federal forces, was engaged by Confederates under Zollicoffer. Thomas won the battle after a fierce contest in which Zollicoffer was slain. The defeated Southerners fled into northeastern Tennessee.

This broke the Confederate line Johnston had established across

Kentucky and northern Tennessee, leaving the right of it hanging in air. Facing Johnston were Major General Henry W. Halleck's Department of Missouri forces at Cairo and Paducah, under Brigadier General Ulysses S. Grant, and Major General Don Carlos Buell's Department of Ohio forces at Louisville under his direct command. Buell's forces alone totalled 114,000. Johnston had less than 65,000 men scattered from Columbus, on the Mississippi, across western Kentucky, northern Tennessee and central Kentucky.

Halleck ordered Grant to move against Fort Henry and Fort Donelson. Both of these forts were in Tennessee just south of the Kentucky border. Fort Henry guarded the Tennessee River; and Fort Donelson, only twelve miles to the east, at Dover, protected the Cumberland River. These rivers, both navigable and flowing northward into the Ohio River, provided natural routes into Tennessee, northern Alabama, and eastern Tennessee.

In the early part of February, Grant moved south on the Tennessee with 15,000 troops supported by seven gunboats under Admiral Foote. Fort Henry was his first objective. Brigadier General Tilghman was in command of just under 3,000 Confederates in and around that fort. Grant disembarked his troops downstream of his objective; and Foote moved on upstream and opened fire on Fort Henry on February 6, preliminary to a planned assault by land. The heavy fire from the gunboats so badly damaged the fort and disabled its guns that the fort surrendered to Foote before Grant invested it, but not before most of its garrison had escaped to Fort Donelson. Tilghman surrendered only ninety men in addition to himself and his staff.

Grant then began preparations to move on Fort Donelson. Foote moved his flotilla down the Tennessee to the Ohio and back up the Cumberland to support him. The struggle for this small citadel proved to be one of the decisive battles of the war, having a tremendous impact upon future events, both militarily and politically.

General Johnston began moving troops into Fort Donelson to reinforce it.[1] Among these was Forrest's command, which arrived on February 11. It was a dreary but rather mild winter day as the troopers marched inside the entrenchments around the fort and the small town of Dover. Fort Donelson could hardly be called a fort. It had adequate batteries to command the Cumberland River, and these had been placed northeast of Dover; but its defenses were little more than a series of shallow earthen entrenchments around the batteries and extending south of Dover.

Forrest reported to Brigadier General Gideon Pillow, who commanded the fort at that time, and was ordered to make a reconnaissance in the direction of Fort Henry. Leaving most of his troopers to set up camp, he moved out as directed with 300 men. About three miles west of Dover, scouts riding ahead of the column reported a detachment of Federal cavalry on the road moving in their direction. Attacking with the same ferocity that had carried the day for him at Sacramento, Forrest drove them back upon a heavy column of Federal infantry moving in the direction of Fort Donelson. Here he broke off the attack and returned to the fort to report the situation to General Pillow.

On the following morning, Forrest made another reconnaissance over the same route, this time with his entire force plus three companies of Kentucky cavalry and a battalion of mounted Tennesseans, a force of about 1,300 men over whom he had been placed in command as acting brigadier general. When the advance guard of the Federal force moving on Fort Donelson was encountered, Forrest dismounted a portion of his troops and, taking advantage of a favorably situated ridge, checked their advance. As additional Federal troops came up to their stalled vanguard, the firing became more intense.

Buck saw a group of Federal cavalry move off to the south and pointed them out to Forrest.

"Kelley!" Forrest called, and the major moved to his side.

Pointing to the moving cavalry column, Forrest said, "They're tryin' to turn our left. Take three companies, an' give 'em a go."

Taking the three nearest companies not on the firing line, Kelley led a dash into the enemy cavalry for close quarters work, and the Federal troopers quickly retired upon their infantry. By the time Kelley returned, the Federal troops in front of him had increased to the point that Forrest knew he was facing Grant's main force; and he immediately dispatched a courier to Fort Donelson with this information. Knowing he could not hold his position, he withdrew slowly toward Dover, skirmishing steadily until he was within the Confederate entrenchments again. Grant moved his army up and invested the town and fort with no further opposition.

Upon return to their encampment, Forrest's men were allowed to prepare a hot meal; once fed, they were put to work digging more entrenchments and fortifying them with logs. Buck and Randy were working with the enlisted men of Forrest's staff. One of them, Sergeant Carlis, said, "That was quite an army we run into today. Wonder how many men they got."

"More than we have," Buck replied; "and I hear they've got more on the way."

"Looks like General Floyd got here just in time with his division of

Virginians. Understand he's in command now, since he's senior to General Pillow.''

"Is that good or bad?''

"Don't know. We'll have to wait and see.''

On the following day, the 13th, Grant had most of his troops up and in position, Brigadier General John A. McClernand's division on the right and Brigadier General Charles F. Smith's on the left. The Confederates had Buckner's command on their right, Heiman's in the center, Pillow's on the left, and Forrest's on the extreme left.

Skirmishing resumed early that morning. At ten o'clock, the Federal troops under Smith made a vigorous attack upon a portion of Buckner's and Heiman's lines but were repulsed. An hour later, a portion of McClernand's division made a furious assault on a Confederate battery, and this was also repulsed with heavy loss to the assailants.

During the day, Forrest moved about constantly as he observed the movements of enemy troops. As usual, Buck and Randy were with him. In the course of these observations, they were often within range of Berge's Union sharpshooters who had concealed themselves in trees, behind rocks, stumps, and fences, or wherever they could find cover and fire on targets of opportunity within the Confederate lines. Spotting one of them in a tree and rather recklessly exposed, Forrest turned to Buck and said, "Let me have your gun.''

Buck handed him the gun; and Forrest set the sight, aimed carefully, and fired. The sniper tumbled headlong to the ground.[2] Forrest handed the gun back to Buck with a grin, and said "You ain't the only one who growed up in the woods. I knocked a panther out of a tree like that when I was no more'n a youngster.''

As night came on, the weather, which had been mild for the preceding days, suddenly turned bitterly cold, with alternating sleet and snow; and this continued for the next forty-eight hours

The following day, the 14th, Grant, having been reinforced by Brigadier General Lew Wallace's brigade from Fort Henry and other troops which had arrived via transports on the Cumberland, strengthened Smith's command by Wallace's brigade, placed Wallace in command of a division in the center, and extended McClernand's division farther to the right to cover the road to Charlotte. With his troops, now numbering 27,000, in position and the fort enveloped, he was ready to begin the attack.

Admiral Foote was ordered to move his gunboats up the Cumberland and to assault the fort's water batteries. Grant made no coordinated movement with his troops, thinking that Foote could bring about the same results he had achieved at Fort Henry. By neutralizing the water batteries, Foote would control the river; and surrounded by a superior force on land, the Confederates would be forced to surrender.

Foote opened fire at three o'clock that afternoon at a distance of one mile and kept closing the range. The water batteries replied, and the duel lasted for an hour and a half with unabated fury. Forrest rode with Major Kelley, Randy, and Buck along a small depression until it brought him to a position where he could see both the gunboats and the water batteries. While the attack was at its height, enemy shells exploding without cessation in and about the fort and Foote's gunboats pressing ever closer to their target, Forrest turned To Kelley excitedly and cried, "Parson! For God's sake pray; nothin' but God Almighty can save the fort!"

Kelley's silent prayers were answered, for Foote dared to press his gunboats too close, some within less than 400 yards; and the badly mauled water batteries rained havoc on them. Although the Confederates had only one long-range gun still in action, Foote was forced to withdraw, some of his boats unmanageable as they drifted downstream. Foote was wounded, and his gunboats never again became a factor in the siege.

While a blizzard raged outside that night, General Floyd called a council of war. He was badly outnumbered, but the commanding general greatly overestimated the enemy force, believing Grant to have 50,000 men. Convinced that they could not hold the fort with only 14,800 men under their command, the generals decided to attack the enemy's right and center, beat them back, and, if possible, destroy them. This would open an escape route in the direction of Nashville.

Their movements muffled by the high winds from the tail of the blizzard, the Confederate troops were massed on the left, leaving only a small regiment, the 30th Tennessee under Colonel Head, with 450 effectives to hold the entrenchments on their right.

At four o'clock on Saturday morning, February 15, 1862, the Confederates began to move out through the snow. Although still in overall command, Floyd placed Pillow in command of the attacking forces. Pillow personally commanded those on the left, and Buckner those in the center. A better time for the attack could not have been selected as Grant was not with his troops. He had left for a conference down-river with Foote on one of the latter's gunboats. Pillow hit McClernand's forces at dawn, just as the cold Federal troops were rising from their icy beds and shaking off the snow. The Southerners, many of whom had only shotguns or squirrel rifles, rushed in for close work; and the fighting was severe and deadly. They pressed the Federal lines hard but met steady resistance. With terrible carnage, the battle raged for two hours before the Confederates began to gain the upper hand. Oglesby's Illinois brigade was foremost in the Federal line and was badly mauled, losing 836 men.

Forrest, from his position on the extreme Confederate left, had worked his way to a point on the enemy's right flank and rear. When he saw the first break in Oglesby's ranks, he yelled, "Charge!" and, at the head of his men, rode into the wavering line. Randy and Buck were close by their commander's side, and Randy spurred his horse savagely. He was determined to make amends for his conduct at Sacramento; and with repeated urging, his fast horse was soon leading the assault as Randy recklessly hurled himself at the enemy. So desperate was his attack that Buck had difficulty staying with him. They were soon upon the enemy, firing their pistols at point blank range. With pressure from the front, the cavalry on their flank and rear, and their ammunition gone, the Yankees left the field, holding up their empty cartridge boxes to show why they could no longer stand their ground.

Forrest saw an enemy battery poorly protected and, without orders, led his troops in an assault against it. They rode down the gunners before they could escape, capturing six pieces of artillery. In the attack, Forrest's horse was shot; and that of his brother, Lieutenant Jeffrey Forrest, was killed and in falling injured its rider. Forrest was soon remounted on a sound horse, and General Pillow rode up at that time.

"Leave Gantt's battalion to guard our left, and move the rest of your troops to assist Buckner, who is advancing," Pillow said; and then pointing to a section of enemy artillery, he continued, "Those guns are doing considerable damage and annoying our advance. They must be silenced; Forrest must do it."

Looking at the guns strategically placed on a hill and well guarded by infantry, Forrest said, "They're well situated and protected. I'll need infantry help."

Pillow ordered up the nearest infantry, the 2nd Kentucky, better known as "Hanson's Orphans," to support him. With sabers drawn and bayonets fixed, the force moved out through undergrowth so thick that the infantry had no difficulty keeping up with the mounted troopers.

As he worked his way through the tangled brush, Buck had a strange sense of foreboding such as he had never experienced before. He had heard and read about people who had felt premonitions of disaster before a catastrophe and wondered if this could be one. Was death waiting for him ahead? Was he afraid? No, he could face whatever was in store for him; but suddenly the thought of never seeing Ellen again came to him with jarring reality, and anguish and a feeling of emptiness seemed to sweep over him.

He looked toward Randy, who was riding on his right. Randy was sitting easy in the saddle and letting Chessy pick her way through the underbrush. He seemed to sense Buck's eyes upon him, and he turned to meet his friend's gaze. As their eyes met, Randy smiled grimly. Buck nodded but said nothing and turned to look toward his commander.

Forrest, sitting tall and erect on his horse, his dark mustache and chin beard gray with frozen moisture from his breath, his lips compressed, face flushed, and eyes blazing with excitement from anticipation of the coming fight, instilled confidence and daring in all around him. Buck thought of his orders to his officers before they set out that morning, "Shoot any man who won't fight!" Regardless of what lay ahead, how could any man fail to fight when led by one such as this? His thoughts were arrested by the sight of a clearing ahead and, beyond that, the enemy guns on a hill heavily guarded by infantry. As they came to the edge of the trees and undergrowth, both cavalry and infantry paused without command, waiting for their commanders to size up the situation ahead before ordering them forward.

Colonel Hanson shouted to his men, "Hold your fire until at close quarters!" and then to the cavalry, "Come on you leather butts, let's take 'em!"; and he rushed into the clearing. Screaming the Rebel yell, the Confederates poured into the open area, meeting a deadly fire from the enemy. Again, Randy was in the forefront with Buck once more struggling to stay with him. Crowds of Confederates, men and horses, went down in the withering fire. Those following, screaming like demons, leaped over their fallen comrades and came on with enemy muskets blazing in their faces until is was hand-to-hand with a brave and determined foe. Under pressure of the desperate onslaught, however, it was soon over as the Yankees were forced to give way.

Forrest found himself again on foot and his clothing damaged from several bullet holes. His horse, bleeding from several wounds, had fallen beneath him. Randy quickly brought a riderless mount and turned to look for Buck. With a sinking feeling in the pit of his stomach, he realized his friend was nowhere in sight. Looking back across the clearing through which they had come, he saw Skin, head down, gently nudging a still body on the ground. Before he could turn to go to the fallen Buck, his commander's booming voice came to him. "Come on! Let's go git 'em!" Forrest yelled as he charged after the retreating enemy.

Randy sat his horse momentarily transfixed. Every instinct and feeling he had drew him to Buck, but he remembered Forrest's words that morning "Shoot any man who won't fight." After what had happened at Sacramento, he believed he would sign his own death warrant by turning back, but it wasn't fear of that as much as it was of the disgrace which would go with it. With a heavy heart he dispiritedly followed his commander.

Some distance in front of Buckner's forces, Forrest halted his men. Wanting to see for himself what was before him, he decided to take Randy and Buck and scout the area ahead. When he looked for them, he saw only Randy. "Where's McCord?" he asked.

"He's down in the clearing back yonder. With your permission, sir, I'd like to go back for him."

"You know where he's at?"

"Yessir. His horse was over him."

Forrest looked at the forlorn Randy, misery clearly written in every inch of the young man's face; and he knew what dedication to duty it had taken for him to leave his fallen friend to pursue the enemy. He started to say that he hoped he would find him to be all right but never got the words out, for over Randy's shoulder he saw Buck in a blood stained coat gingerly riding his buckskin horse toward them. "Don't think that'll be necessary; here he comes, now."

Randy wheeled his horse and quickly rode to meet Buck. "You all right?" he asked.

"Think so," Buck replied. "Caught a Minie ball along the ribs. It knocked me off my horse; and I must have hit my head on something when I fell, because I was out like a light."

"How about the wound?"

"The Minie hit the ribs and glanced off. Tore up my side pretty good and may have cracked a rib. Sore as hell, but I'm all right. It's about stopped bleeding."

"Thank God," Randy said. "Anything I can do for you?"

"Not a thing. I'll be all right."

Selecting two other men to accompany him, Forrest went forward to scout the area ahead. Pushing through some heavy undergrowth, they came unexpectedly upon a line of infantry and a battery of artillery which made themselves known with a volley of rifle fire. As they turned to escape, the battery opened up on them. A shell crashed through the body of Forrest's horse just behind the rider's leg, tearing the animal to pieces. Disentangling himself, Forrest ran on foot back to his men.

Here he again met General Pillow who gave him orders to use his men in collecting the captured artillery and small arms and in removing the Confederate wounded from the field.

At the same time, about two o'clock in the afternoon, General Pillow ordered Buckner to make a retrograde movement back into the Confederate lines at the fort. The left wing of the Confederate assault force was also ordered to retire. It did so slowly and was followed a short distance by McClernand's division which had been heavily reinforced.

About the time Buckner was retiring toward the center and right of the Confederate works, General Smith, commanding the Federal left wing, was ordered by Grant, who had just arrived on the field, to attack the entrenchments in his immediate front. Colonel John W. Head with his small force of only 450 men held his position with obstinacy. As soon as Buckner heard firing in his direction, he realized the danger and hurried reinforcements to him. Unfortunately they did not reach the scene in time to prevent Smith from forcing entry into one of the outer angles of the Confederate entrenchments, beyond which he was unable to advance. Smith made assault after assault, but Buckner was now on the scene with additional reinforcements and, taking command of the defense, successfully repelled the attacks until night put an end to them.

It was almost dark when Forrest led his command back to the entrenchments around Dover after completing the duty imposed by General Pillow.[3] Weary from the hard work of the day, made especially difficult by the cold, bitter wind and snow, the troopers were made as comfortable as conditions permitted and were soon asleep. Buck was treated by one of the doctors who found no broken ribs, only severely damaged cartilage and an ugly gash-type wound; neither was serious, but both were extremely painful. With a mild dose of laudanum, he was not long in getting to sleep in the hospital tent.

At eleven o'clock that night, General Floyd sent for Dr. J. W. Smith, a resident of Dover who was thoroughly familiar with the area around the besieged town. Floyd had received information that Grant had been heavily reinforced and that the enemy had returned to the positions they had occupied before the fight that day. Hoping to find a route to escape, he asked Dr. Smith to go with two men to ascertain whether the ford at Lick's Creek could be crossed on horseback. Upon returning, Dr. Smith found Floyd holding a conference with Generals Pillow and Buckner and Colonel Forrest. He reported to them that he had examined the creek carefully and found it high enough to come only to the saddle skirts of a horse.

Pillow thought they should attempt to move out immediately or try to cut their way through the enemy the following morning. Floyd's medical officer spoke up and voiced the opinion that taking the men through icy water in freezing weather would cause the death of more than half of them. Buckner opposed the withdrawal. He thought his present position could not be held but stated that the troops were too exhausted from the day's fight to make the march. He also said they had not been issued rations regularly for several days; their ammunition was nearly exhausted; and a sortie would result in a virtual massacre of the troops, more disheartening than a surrender.[4]

Forrest offered to cut a way through the enemy if the others would follow, but his suggestion was ignored. Discouraged with the course things were taking, he returned to his command and sent out two scouts to see if the enemy had returned to their original investment positions. When they came back and reported that they had seen only campfires but not men, Forrest relayed this to the generals, pointing out that the fires were probably old ones which had been fanned into flame by the high winds and then fed by the wounded who had not been removed from the battlefield. He pleaded for an escape or a try at it and guaranteed that the enemy cavalry would not bother the Confederate rear. He had little respect for the Federal horse he had seen up to this time.

His urgings were to no avail. The conference ended with a decision to surrender. Forrest protested that the army was neither whipped nor hemmed in and announced he would not surrender himself nor his men. He strode out of the room and aroused his sleeping troops. When they gathered about him, he explained the situation to them.

"So there you have it," he said. "I ain't surrenderin' to nobody. I'll take anybody what wants to go out with me, but I'm goin' if I have to go alone an' die in the try!"

Without question, the men silently began gathering their gear and getting their horses ready for what lay ahead on this miserably cold night. Randy went to the hospital tent where Buck was sleeping and awakened him.

"They're going to surrender the fort," he said.

"Surrender the fort after we whipped their butts today!" Buck said in astonishment. "I can't believe Forrest would surrender."

"He isn't. That's why I'm here. He's going out and will take anyone who wants to go with him. It's going to be a rough trip; it's cold as a well digger's rear end out there, and we'll have to ford a flooded creek crusted with ice. If you don't feel up to it, I'm staying with you."

Buck sat up with a groan and grabbed his throbbing side. "I'm going if it kills me. Get our horses and stuff together while I get ready. I'll see if I can talk that doctor out of some of that medicine he gave me. And don't overlook those two extra Navy Colts and saddle holsters I picked up after the fight."

"I won't," Randy said as he hurried out.

Within an hour, the troopers silently mounted their horses and rode out behind their commander. Not a man was lost, and not an enemy was encountered. The troopers and artillerymen were followed by a number of infantry. Approximately 1,500 went out with Forrest, and others escaped by different means or by following his route. There is little doubt that most of the Confederates at the fort could have escaped had the effort been made.[5]

Chapter VIII

Nashville to Shiloh

The night of the sixteenth found Forrest camped alongside a small stream sixteen miles from Fort Donelson on the Clarksville road. He had moved slowly in order to afford protection to the infantrymen who came out with him. The enemy cavalry, although little used in battle the previous day, had not followed, much to the regret of Forrest. In his present frame of mind he would have liked to have had "a go at 'em."

It had stopped snowing, and the stars shone brightly; but it was a bitterly cold night. After a meager but hot supper prepared from the sparse provisions they were able to bring with them, the men huddled dejectedly around large campfires trying to keep warm. Word was passed that their commander wanted to talk to them and to assemble informally. Forrest stood in front of his tent and watched his men silently gather. When he was satisfied they were all there, he spoke in a calm, clear, firm voice: "Today I seen some long faces in this outfit, an' I don't like it. You ain't got nothin' to be ashamed of. You fit well at Donelson an' done all that was asked of you. You ain't been whipped, an' you ain't gonna be whipped as long as you fight like you done yesterday; so don't look whipped. We ain't seen the last of the enemy, an' he damned well ain't seen the last of us. I don't want to see no more hang-dog looks around here. I'm proud of every man Jack of you who come out of Donelson with me. We got vedettes an' pickets out; an' nobody's gonna surprise us, so git a good night's rest. You've earned it!"

The men had assembled with hunched shoulders and sagging spirits; but by the time their commander finished speaking, they were standing erect and proud. Forrest turned toward his tent but whirled to face his men again. He said, "Before you go, let me hear one more time that yell you gave when we charged them batteries!" The men erupted into the Rebel yell which was to accompany countless Confederate charges before the war was over.[1] In the stillness of the cold, clear night, it reverberated from the nearby hills as they screamed it over and over again, each time with more spirit and enthusiasm. Finally, a smiling Forrest raised his hand, and it gradually died away.

"Thank you. We all needed that. Now git a good night's sleep; tomorrow's gonna be a long day."

As the troopers began to leave, Forrest spotted Buck and Randy at the front of the circle of men and motioned for them to come over. "How you feelin'?" he asked Buck. "You had us worried yesterday."

"All right. A little sore, but I'll make it."

"Where in the hell did you fellows git them hosses?" he asked.

"We raised them, or our fathers did," Randy replied.

"What breed are they?"

"Basically Kentucky saddlebred. That's what Father started with, but he's added other blood along the way as has McCord's father, who got his original stock from Daddy."

"I don't much cotton to bein' outrun when chargin' the enemy," Forrest said with the trace of a smile.

"I'm sorry, sir. I guess I was trying to prove something."

"Well, you done proved it. From now on, y'all just stay with me; don't try to take the lead." He smiled again as he added, "I wouldn' want folks to git the notion I ain't got the best hoss.

On Monday, February 17, the march was continued; and Forrest arrived with his troops in Nashville the following day. That city was in a state of panic and chaos. Buell's army was reported to be advancing upon it, and General Albert Sidney Johnston had pulled the Confederate army out of Murfreesborough. General Floyd was in command of the city. A vast amount of supplies had been left behind by Johnston with no provision for moving them out of the enemy's path. Mobs had begun looting government warehouses and stockpiles; everywhere there was confusion, and disorder was rampant throughout the city.

General Floyd turned over the command to Forrest, who, using force where necessary, quickly brought the city under control. Commandeering all available transport, he began moving supplies to the south by train and wagon. He was still in Nashville twenty-four hours after Buell's army arrived at Edgefield, located upon the opposite bank of the Cumberland. He left the city as the enemy entered it, but by then he had moved great quantities of supplies and materiel out of their reach. He marched to Murfreesborough where he reported to General Johnston on the twenty-third.

The following day, Forrest was ordered to Huntsville to rest his men and to recruit. On this march, Buck's wound, which had appeared to be healing satisfactorily, suddenly became inflamed. By the time he reached Huntsville, it was badly swollen and extremely painful; and he had a high fever. Forrest temporarily disbanded his command by giving them furloughs, to reassemble on March 10; but Buck was in no condition to make a trip home. Randy wouldn't leave him, so he volunteered to help with the recruiting.

Kevin again took Randy and Buck into his home and arranged for their family doctor to treat Buck. The doctor opened and drained the wound and applied an ointment which proved very effective. Buck was soon on the mend; and by the time the troopers reassembled, he had recovered and was again on duty. All of Forrest's men returned without exception, newly clad and ready for the rough campaigning ahead, many with fresh mounts to replace their jaded ones. The command was increased by a new company raised by Forrest's brother, Captain Jesse A. Forrest.

Forrest was ordered to move his command to Burnsville, Mississippi, not far from Corinth, and reached there on March 16. Here another company, raised in Fayette and Hardiman Counties in Tennessee and commanded by Captain C. H. Schuyler, was added to the command, which was now organized as a full regiment. Forrest was elected colonel; D.C. Kelley was promoted to lieutenant colonel; Private R.N. Balch was elected major; and J.P. Strange was made adjutant. At Burnsville, the regiment went into camp with daily drills and post and picket duty.

General Johnston was at Corinth where he had massed his army. About thirty miles to the northeast at Pittsburg Landing, Tennessee, on the Tennessee River, Ulysses S. Grant, who had been promoted to Major General, was encamped with 45,000 men, some of which were in the vicinity of a small church named Shiloh. It was reported that General Buell with a large portion of his army was enroute to join him.

Forrest was ordered to dispatch a scouting party to Marr's Landing, also on the Tennessee River, to watch Buell and report his actions. The movement of that army toward Grant was confirmed. The report caused Johnston to hurry forward his army in order to strike and crush Grant before Buell could reach him. The Confederate movement toward Pittsburg Landing, or Shiloh, as the battle also came to be known, began on April 2, 1862.

Forrest's regiment was attached to General John C. Breckenridge's division and marched with it as far as Monterey, Tennessee. At this point, Forrest was directed to advance along the south side of Lick Creek, throw out a picket line, and closely observe any movement of the enemy. On the night of April 4, his men were disposed on this part of the field so close to the Federal encampments that music from various bands along their lines could be heard.

Early on the morning of the 6th, heavy firing from the left and center of the Confederate line told the battle had begun. Sherman's division was camped around Shiloh church, that of Prentiss was to the east of him, and McClernand's was to the northwest. The first major encounter was between Shaver's Arkansas brigade and Peabody's brigade, the latter a part of Prentiss' division; and the battle spread westward as the remainder of Prentiss' division and that of Sherman were attacked vigorously and pushed back out of their camps. McClernand, Sherman, and Prentiss finally managed to stabilize a line of defense north of the campsites.

As soon as the sound of battle was heard, Forrest led his regiment across Lick Creek and sent a request to his commander-in-chief for instructions, but he received none. The firing grew heavier; and from the direction of the sound, it was evident that the Federals were being pushed back. About eleven o'clock, Forrest rode out ahead of his command toward the enemy and found they were giving away toward the river. He returned to his men and, waiting no longer for orders, marched toward the firing. Unable to find Breckenridge or any other commander to whom to report, he advanced at a gallop in the direction of the sound of the heaviest fighting. As they came up, they met the men of Cheatham's division, who had just been repulsed from an attack on Prentiss in a position which was to become known as "The Hornets' Nest" because of the vicious fighting at that point. Forrest passed ahead of Cheatham's men to an open field across which were planted two or more Federal batteries. Another was in a nearby peach orchard. One of the batteries opened up on his troopers. Seeing General Cheatham, Forrest rode to him.

"I'm Colonel Forrest. Will you give me orders to charge those guns? I can't let my men stay here under their fire; I'll have to move forward or back."

"I can't give you orders," Cheatham replied. "If you make the charge, it will be on your own responsibility."

Without hesitation, Forrest said, "Then I'll do it," and immediately ordered his command forward.

As they moved into the open field, they received a salvo from the battery, killing three men and four horses. The bugle sounded the charge; and the cavalry moved on the enemy at full gallop, screaming the Rebel yell. The battery did not have time for a second round as the troopers rode on and over the gunners. The guns to the right were protected by dense undergrowth and escaped the charge. The infantry came up and took possession of the guns, and the cavalry unit fell back behind them.

Shortly after this, Forrest received orders to move to where Prentiss was being pressed hard. Advancing rapidly, he arrived with his command to see the disorganization of that Union division. Again the bugle sounded the charge; and the regiment rode hard at the flying infantry, passing through their ranks, and cut them off by taking position between Prentiss's troops and the reserves at the river landing. Here Prentiss surrendered about 3,000 of Grant's army.

Keeping on the right flank of the infantry as it pushed on, Forrest came upon a battery planted in the last stand by the Federals on a ridge near Pittsburg Landing. Throwing forward his skirmishers, he advanced with them and discovered great confusion in the ranks of the enemy. He sent a courier to General Polk with this information and ventured the suggestion that a vigorous attack by the infantry would drive the Union army into the river.

At about two o'clock that afternoon, General Johnston received a wound in his right leg. Unknown to him, it had cut an artery; and blood poured from it into his high boot. Not realizing the seriousness of the wound, he did not have it attended to; and at about 2:30 that afternoon he fell from his horse unconscious and died shortly afterward. Command of the army passed to General P.G.T. Beauregard.

Forrest's advice for pressing the attack was not taken. The Federals had been pushed back to a new line of defense established at River Road, and the Confederates went into camp on the battlefields just taken.

During the night the enemy's gunboats kept up an almost constant shelling of the wood in which the Confederates were trying to sleep. Soon after dark, Forrest took Buck and Randy with him to the front. Creeping along the river bank, they reached a position where they could see lights from arriving steamers and could hear the commands and sounds of disembarking troops. Forrest hurried to pass this information to his superiors. He located General Chalmers, who was asleep in his tent, and had his orderly awaken him. Chalmers appeared and asked, "What do you want?"

"Where can I find the commander of the army?"

"I don't know. Why?"

"I've been down by the river close to the enemy. I could see the lights on the steamships an' hear the orders given in landin' troops. They're gittin' reinforcements by the thousands; an' if this army don't move an' attack 'em before daylight an' before other reinforcements git here, it'll be whipped like hell before ten o'clock tomorrow."

Forrest rode away, located the commander-in-chief, and told him
what he had heard and seen, and was told to go back to his regiment.[2]

This was Sunday, and all that night Buell's troops were landing. On
Monday morning, the Federals, with more than 25,000 fresh troops,
advanced full of fight and swept the Confederates away. Forrest was
protecting the Confederate right flank and was heavily engaged; and
when the order for retreat was issued, Breckenridge covered the
movement with Forrest between him and the enemy. That night, about
four and a half miles south of Pittsburg Landing, Forrest took part of his
command and moved toward Lick Creek to guard against an enemy
advance from that direction. The retreat toward Corinth was resumed
the next morning with Forrest covering the Confederate rear.

Near Monterey, Sherman advanced with two brigades of infantry
behind the Fourth Illinois cavalry under Colonel Dickey. Reaching the
fork of the road leading to Corinth, a part of his force, under General
Wood, was ordered on one road, while Sherman took the other,
accompanied by the cavalry. A half of a mile south of the forks was a
field, and beyond that was a clearing of fallen timber several hundred
yards wide. The Confederate camps could be seen beyond this point
about one-half to three-quarters of a mile. Sherman immediately pushed
forward a strong line of skirmishers and advanced in the direction of the
encampments.

Forrest was observing Sherman's approach and deployment. His
command had been augmented by 220 "Texas Rangers" under Major
Thomas Harrison, a company from Wirt Adams' regiment, and two
companies of Morgan's Kentucky cavalry; and he had them hidden
behind a wooded ridge which ran almost parallel to the road. He had
dismounted some of his men, and these were offering little resistance to
the advance of the Federal skirmishers, behind whom came the Union
cavalry, which was about two hundred yards in front of the infantry
brigade in line of battle. After passing through the fallen timber a short
distance, and while crossing a small stream, Dickey's cavalry was
thrown temporarily into confusion.

Waiting for this moment, Forrest yelled, "Charge!"; and with the
bugler sounding the call and the men shouting the Rebel yell, the
troopers, about 800 in all, rode right over the infantry skirmishers into
the enemy cavalry. Being in confusion when the assault was launched
against them, the Federal cavalry gave way in a wild stampede, running
roughshod over their comrades in Sherman's first line of infantry. These
troops panicked, threw down their guns, and also broke for the rear,
suffering considerable damage from the Confederate sabers and pistols.

As they approached the second line of Sherman's reserves, a brigade in line of battle, the Confederate troopers pulled up their horses; and, under the direction of their officers, made their way safely back to the rear. Unfortunately for Forrest, with Randy and Buck by his side, he had advanced too far; and the Union soldiers and a few cavalry rushed forward and attempted to capture or kill him. They fired at him from all sides, shouting, "Shoot that man!"

"Kill him!"

"Knock him off his horse!"

"Don't let them get away!"

So close were they that one infantryman pushed his musket almost against the colonel's side and discharged it, the ball entering just above the left hip. Forrest was barely able to maintain his seat; and to add to his peril, his horse was badly wounded in two places.

Buck and Randy were in the middle of the melee with infantrymen and a few cavalrymen pressing them on all sides. A cavalryman made a short backhanded slash at Randy's head with his saber. The blow was not hard, but it had sufficient force to cut off the lobe of his right ear and to open a four inch gash in his cheek. Randy turned his pistol on his adversary, fired into the middle of his body, and saw him crumble and fall from his horse. Blood was streaming down his face and neck, but Randy continued firing at the milling enemy about him and saw another go down. Buck was also firing as rapidly as possible and very effectively at this short range. He had emptied both guns he carried on his belt but fortunately had in saddle holsters two more which he had acquired at Fort Donelson. He got one of them out just as Forrest's badly wounded horse made a desperate leap in the direction from which they had come. Both Randy and Buck turned with him; and the three, with pistols blazing, cut their way through the men surrounding them and headed for safety. Chessy was hit by one of the numerous Minie balls flying about them as the enemy tried to bring them down; and Randy trailed the other two, his horse being slowed by the wound. The shot had caught Chessy in the right hind leg; and although moving with pain and difficulty, the mare was valiantly striving to respond to her rider's urging, but she was gradually losing ground to the other two horses.

Forrest was in the lead with Buck purposely placing himself between his commanding officer and the enemy. Randy brought up the rear, riding low in the saddle as he leaned over his horse's neck talking gently to the mare and encouraging her to keep going. He felt something smash into his back below the left shoulder; and he was suddenly falling, falling, falling; and then came a jolt, and blackness swept over him. When his body hit the ground, he rolled into a ditch beside the road; and there he lay, unconscious.

Buck had been so intent upon protecting his wounded commander that he did not turn to look back at Randy until they were out of normal rifle range. When he saw the riderless Chessy trailing them, he quickly pulled Skin to a halt. Forrest also stopped; and when he saw Chessy, he came back to Buck.

"Randy's down. I'm going back for him."

"Not now," Forrest said softly. "You wouldn' have a chance in range of all them rifles. If you want to help 'im, wait'll dark, it's almost here. I'd go with you, but I can't hardly stay on this horse."

They turned south again and proceeded at a walk. At the fallen timber, they were met by some of Forrest's men.

"You'll be taken care of now, Colonel. I'll wait here until dark. Let the pickets know I'll be coming in."

"All right. Friendship will be a good password. Do you want any help?"

"No, sir. I'll do better alone."

"I think so, too," Forrest said. He grimaced from pain as he started his badly wounded horse south again.

Chessy limped up about this time, and Buck caught and tied the mare to one of the trees. Examining her wound, he found it to be a clean one. The Minie ball had entered the leg below the rump and had come out at almost the same level. The wound was still bleeding, so he found some moss and packed each end of it. The injury did not appear to be serious, and he was certain that the horse would be all right with proper care. He sat down on the ground; and leaning back against one of the tree trunks, he began reloading his pistols while waiting for dark. It was only a few minutes in coming, but it seemed like an eternity to him.

He got up; and mounting Skin, he rode quietly, listening for every sound and peering intently into the dark. He passed numerous bodies but did not stop to examine them as he was certain Randy would not have gotten that far. When he reached the place where he and Forrest had first stopped, he halted and dismounted. He lifted the reins over Skin's head and dropped them to the ground, knowing the horse would stay there unless he signaled him. He listened for a moment but could hear nothing but the usual night noises, except from the north he could make out what he was certain was the distant marching of a large body of men moving away from him. He took off his boots, tied them together, and hung them over his horse's back.[3]

With eyes and ears straining, he moved slowly and quietly up the road. He soon came upon a body but found it to be that of a Yankee cavalryman. Then he found another, and another, and still another—all

Yankees. Ahead he saw a body in the middle of the road; and as he approached, there were more. He counted a total of seven and knew this was where they had been surrounded.

Sure now there were no enemy close by, he called Randy's name loudly but received no response. Knowing that, unless taken prisoner, Randy was behind him, he retraced his steps, pausing frequently to call and listen. He had gone about one hundred yards when a slight sound behind and to the left of him caught his attention. Returning in the direction from which the noise came, he noticed the ditch beside the road and saw a man lying face down in it. As soon as he could make him out clearly, he knew who it was; and he turned him over gently. Randy groaned from the movement and opened his eyes.

"Can you hear me?" Buck asked.

"Yes," he replied faintly. "I knew you would come, but I didn't want you to find me. I want to die, Buck; just leave me here."

"The hell I will! Let's get you out of this ditch. Can you stand up?"

"I don't think so; leave me here," he pleaded.

Buck slowly raised his friend to a sitting position and examined his wounds. The ugly cut on his cheek and the severed ear had stopped bleeding, but the one in the back was still oozing blood. The ball had struck near the bottom of the shoulder blade while he was leaning over his horse's neck. Striking that flat bone at an angle, it had glanced upward and passed out of the body at the shoulder. Randy had lost a lot of blood.

Buck whistled for Skin and shortly afterward heard the horse coming up the road. Randy asked, "Is Chessy all right?"

"Yes. She's wounded, but it doesn't seem to be serious."

"If I don't make it, I want you to have her."

"You'll make it. I'm going to get you in the saddle and ride behind to hold you on. It will be easier on you than lying across the back of the horse. I'll put your arm over my shoulder and lift you up. Help as much as you can until we get to the road. Then I'll need your help getting you on the horse."

"Just leave me here."

"Noway. I'm taking you back if I have to carry you on my shoulder."

Knowing he meant it, Randy elected to make things as easy for him as he could. "I'll do what I can," he said with resignation.

After he got Randy in the saddle, Buck climbed up behind him, and holding his friend's swaying body, moved slowly down the road. He retrieved Chessy at the fallen timber and continued on southward at a walk, trying to lessen the pain he knew Randy was enduring. He had travelled no more than a quarter of a mile when he saw motion at the side of the road ahead. He felt certain it was one of their vedettes; nevertheless, he proceeded cautiously. When he reached the area where he had detected the movement, a voice from his left commanded, "Halt right there! Don't make no sudden moves."

He pulled Skin to a stop, and from the trees on the left a mounted man emerged with a carbine pointed at him.

"You got a password?"

"Friendship."

The vedette turned his head and spat tobacco juice and then, looking at Buck holding the sagging Randy, replied, "That seems right enough. You'll run into the pickets about a quarter mile. They'll be lookin' for you. There's a hospital tent on the right about two hundred yards past the pickets."

"Mucha 'blige."

"Good luck."

He reached the hospital tent and turned Randy over to one of the surgeons. While they were attending to him, he obtained some medication from an orderly and treated Chessy's wound. He had just finished with this when the surgeon came out to see him.

"Your friend's wounds don't appear to be too serious, and he should recover from them all right, even though he's lost a lot of blood; but there seems to be another problem. I don't believe he wants to live."

"I was afraid of that. He's in love with a girl who's got a mental thing about scars and disfigurement. I don't think he wants to face her with part of an ear gone and the scar he'll have on his cheek."

"That's too bad. He seems like a fine young man. We'll do what we can for him as Colonel Forrest ordered. He'll be moved out of here tonight or tomorrow for a hospital somewhere. I don't know where it will be; I understand those around Corinth are all full."

"Did you treat Forrest?"

"Yes."

"How is he?"

"Pretty bad. The ball hit a bone above the hip and ranged upward. It went through the large muscle of the back and lodged against the spine. We were afraid to try to remove it at this time. I hope he pulls through."

"He'll make it. No single Minie ball's going to take that fireater out. And thank you, Doctor, for taking care of my friend."

"Had no choice. Forrest said he'd personally kick our butts if we didn't, and that man's got a big foot!"

Forrest's severe and painful wound did not entirely heal for several weeks, and he went to his home in Memphis to recover. During his absence, Lieutenant Colonel Kelley temporarily took over command of the regiment. Buck was unable to locate Randy for a week after leaving him at the hospital tent. The wounded had been scattered for many miles in provisional hospitals set up wherever facilities were available. The regiment was encamped near Corinth, and Buck had just finished his midday meal when Kevin came up with another lieutenant, a short stocky fellow whose uniform markings showed him to be an artilleryman.

"Buck, I don't believe you ever met Bill Williamson. Bill, this is Buck McCord."

The two men shook hands and exchanged greetings. Kevin continued, "Bill resigned from West Point when the war started and has been assigned to a river battery on a hill at Grenada guarding the Yalobusha River. It's kinda dull duty, and he came up here to try to get transferred to a field artillery unit. He's seen Randy."

"Where?" Buck asked.

"In Coffeeville. The home of a Mr. Caraguey was turned into a hospital. I went by to see one of my men who had been injured and was being treated there, and I ran into Randy. I hardly knew him. The doctor says there's no reason he shouldn't be healing, but Randy has no will to live; and they don't know how to treat that."

Buck turned to Kevin, "Is Colonel Kelley at headquarters?"

"He was a few minutes ago."

"Bill, it's nice to meet you, and good luck on your transfer. Now, if y'all will excuse me, I need to see the Colonel."

"We understand," Kevin said. "If there's anything we can do, let us know."

Buck found Lieutenant Colonel Kelley at the headquarters tent and explained the situation to him. "What do you want from me?" Kelley asked.

"A furlough for myself and authority to take Rushton home to recuperate. Maybe his family can snap him out of it."

"That's no problem; I'll have the papers drawn up right away. How will you get him there?"

"I'll move him to Okolona by wagon and from there by the cars to Selma."

Since most cars moving south were empty, Buck had no difficulty boarding one with Skin for Okolona. He left the train there and arrived in Coffeeville on April 19. Randy was in worse condition than he expected, despite the gloomy picture Bill had presented. His ear and cheek were healing without any problem, and a large black scab covered the cut on his face. The wound in his back was doing fairly well, but there was still a little infection present. Randy looked pale and emaciated. When he first saw Buck, he brightened up a bit; but this soon passed.

"How did you find me?" He wanted to know.

"Bill Williamson told us. I've come to take you home."

"I don't want to go home," Randy said determinedly.

"You've got no choice, Ol' Buddy. I have orders to take you home. You wouldn't want me to get shot for disobeying them, would you?"

Buck borrowed a wagon from the surgeon in charge of the hospital and arrived at Okolona two days later. He left the vehicle and Skin at a livery stable there and took the next train south. He arrived at Prairie's Edge in the late afternoon of April 22 in a buggy borrowed from one of John Rushton's friends in Selma. Randy was left with his parents, who were badly shaken over the condition of their son. Buck did not get to see Ellen, who was at Judson; so he stayed only a short time with the Rushtons, as he was anxious to get home.

Both Cory and Sadie came to the back porch to see who had driven into their back yard in the strange buggy. "Bless God, it's Buck!" Sadie cried and hurried down the steps to greet her son. She embraced him; and, while holding her, Buck extended his right hand to his father.

After supper they sat for a long time at the table talking. Cory and Sadie plied Buck with questions, and he was surprised at how much they knew about Forrest. The Colonel's conduct at Fort Donelson, Nashville, and Shiloh had received considerable publicity; and he was already a hero in this part of the country.

"He claims he knew you, Pa," Buck said.

Cory did not reply at once, carefully considering his response. It was brief, "I believe I did make his acquaintance."

Buck noticed his father hadn't mentioned it having been a pleasure as he normally would have done. He was curious but did not pursue the matter.

The following morning Buck returned to Prairie's Edge and found John Rushton with drawn face sitting alone on the veranda. His heart went out to the older man, for he knew how much Randy meant to him. As he came up on the porch, John pointed to a chair near his own; and Buck sat down.

"Something's wrong, Buck. What's the real problem?"

"I think it's the disfigurement and scar he will have. He's afraid Beverly won't have anything to do with him now, but I can't believe she would be like that.''

"Don't bet on it.''

Buck looked at him in surprise. "With your permission, I'd like to ride over to Marion to tell her and ask her to come see him.''

"You've got it, but you're wasting your time; I've heard she's been seeing a young man from Selma. Tell me, Buck, how did it happen?''

Buck first told him about Forrest and his way of fighting and how only he and Randy had horses which could keep up with the colonel in a charge. Then he told of the fight at the fallen timber and their ride into the Federal line. He ended with, "I don't know how any of us got out of it alive.''

"Forrest must be a holy terror. We could use more fighters like him.''

"There aren't any more like the colonel,'' Buck said, rising. "I'd better be on my way, but I'll speak to Randy before I go.''

"Don't tell him where you are going.''

"I won't.''

In the main hall he met Carolyn. For the first time since he had known her, he saw this strong, dignified lady lose her composure as she threw her arms around him and began to cry almost hysterically. He said nothing but held her gently and let her cry it out. When she regained control of herself, she said plaintively, "Oh, Buck, he looks so bad. He won't eat and has hardly anything to say. He just lies there and stares at the four walls. What are we going to do?''

"We are going to pray a lot; and you're going to nurse him back to health and make him realize he has a lot to live for.''

"Please try to convince him to take some nourishment. He's just wasting away up there.''

Buck went upstairs; and when he entered Randy's room, he found his friend lying on his side staring disinterestedly out the window. "How're you feeling today?'' he asked.

"So so.''

"I hear you're still not eating enough to keep a jaybird alive.''

"No appetite.''

"What's the matter; have you become so attached to half-raw salt pork that decent food doesn't suit you?''

"Could be.''

"Just came by to see how you're doing. Take care of yourself, and get some food in that belly of yours.''

Randy made no response, so Buck left. On his way downstairs, his thoughts turned to Ellen; and he became excited over the prospect of seeing her again. He found Carolyn on the porch with John and stopped to speak to them before leaving.

"We sent the carriage for Ellen this morning," Carolyn said. "She should be here soon. Won't you wait for her?"

"I've got to go into Marion," he replied. "If I don't meet her on the way, I'll go by Judson."

Buck left; and not far beyond the Cahaba, he met the Rushton carriage, the horses moving toward him at a brisk trot. He raised his hand, and the approaching vehicle stopped. He rode alongside it and saw that Sally was with Ellen.

"I knew it was you as soon as I saw you!" Ellen exclaimed.

"It's good to see you. How've y'all been?"

"Lonesome with y'all gone," Sally spoke up quickly.

Buck looked at Ellen; she met his gaze squarely with a smile. Then the smile faded. "I'm worried about Randy; Mother's note didn't sound good. Is he badly hurt?"

"Not too badly. I don't think the wounds themselves are the problem."

"What is it then?"

"Maybe you'd better talk to your folks. I think they understand."

"You've got me worried."

"Maybe there's nothing to worry about. Does Beverly know?"

"Only that he's been wounded. I asked her to come with me, but she said she couldn't."

"I've held you up long enough; I know you are anxious to get home. I've got to go into Marion and will see you later."

"I'm glad you brought him home," Sally said.

"He'll be better off here," Buck replied; and touching his heels to the horse, he started again toward Marion. Encouraged by Ellen's look and smile, he decided the time had come to let her know how he felt about her. He would stop by Prairie's Edge on the way home.

At Judson he had to wait a few minutes for Beverly to come out of a class. When she saw him, she came right over, making a great show of friendliness. "Why, Buck, what a pleasant surprise!" she said. "I declare, it's so good to see you. What ever brings you to Judson?"

"It's about Randy; I need to talk to you."

Buck could see a change come over her, and the gushy friendliness faded. "I heard he had been wounded," she said. "Nothing serious, I hope."

"I'm afraid it is. He took a pretty bad shot from a Minie ball, but that wound is doing all right; and he had a saber slash against the side of his face. That's healing, but it's creating a problem.''

Beverly became nervous. ''Why is that?''

''He lost the lower part of his right ear, and I'm afraid he will have a large scar across his cheek.''

Beverly shuddered and bit her lower lip. ''He should never have gone off to war,'' she said tartly. ''I tried to talk him out of it, but he just had to go.''

Buck knew it had not been this way, but he took no issue with what she said. ''He's convinced that everything will be over between you and him because of his disfigurement, and he doesn't want to get well. I can't believe you would let something like this come between you. Go see him, Beverly; show him how wrong he is.''

''I can't do that,'' she replied, turning her head slightly so she would not face him. ''Looking at scars or people with deformities does something to me. Don't you remember how I almost fainted when I saw your father with his arm off?''

''But those things can be overcome, if you try. Randy did it. The sight of blood had a similar effect on him. The first time he saw someone seriously wounded, he panicked; but he got control of himself and did what was expected of him. Now it doesn't bother him any more. You can overcome it, too, if you love him enough.''

''Well that's kinda changed, too. I've been seeing a young man from Selma.'' Then using attack for defense, she said angrily, ''I don't see where this is any of your business, anyway. I think you are sticking your nose into something that's none of your affair!''

Jolted by this sudden turn of events and disgusted with her callous attitude toward Randy, Buck was gripped by anger such as he had never experienced before. Speaking coldly and deliberately, he said, ''Don't tell me this isn't my business, not while my friend is dying because he was fool enough to fall in love with a two-timing hussy like you.''

''How dare you talk to me like that! My father would horsewhip you within an inch of your life if he knew about this!''

''I hope you tell him. If he comes looking for me, tell him to bring that dandy from Selma along. I'd like nothing better than to rearrange their faces so you'll faint every time you look at them!'' With that, he turned and strode off.

Buck was half way to the Cahaba before his anger cooled and reason returned. He was deeply ashamed for losing his temper and for his behavior toward Beverly. He had never talked to anyone like that before, and he was afraid that he had put the relationship between her and Randy beyond any hope of repair. He was not only disgusted with himself, his conscience was hurting; because he knew he had been wrong. Also, he couldn't help worrying about what Randy would think of him for the insulting remarks made to Beverly. He was in no mood to face any of the Rushtons, much less Ellen; so when he arrived at the road junction near her house, he continued on the road leading toward home.

The incident with Beverly nagged at him the rest of the day; he couldn't get it off his mind. That night, Sadie looked at her son and said, "There's somethin' bother'n you, Buck. Wanta talk about it?"

He started to say he'd rather not but thought better of it; so he related the events leading up to, and including, the confrontation with Beverly. When he finished he said, "There's no excuse for what I did. I'm ashamed of myself and hope Randy never hears about it; but I'm sure he will. Do you think it would do any good if I went back to Marion and apologized to her?"

"No. Let it be. I think Randy's lucky to be shed of 'er. She ain't very staunch to be foolin' around with som'uns else whilst he's off to war. She's a pretty cold-hearted critter not to go see 'im after him bein' away so long an' hurt like he is."

Cory, hoping to get his son's mind onto another subject, asked, "How long can you stay?"

"I've got to be back on the 3rd of May. Pa, Colonel Forrest lost his horse when we got into that mess where Randy was wounded. He knows horses and really took a liking to Skin and Chessy. Do you have a good one I can take him?"

"You mean as a gift?"

"Yessir."

"I s'pose so; but if he offers to pay, don't refuse it."

"All right, if that's what you want. If I take a horse back with me, I'd better figure on eight days to travel. I have to return a wagon to Coffeeville."

"About them pistols of yours; I notice you been messin' with the holsters."

"Yessir, I can draw and fire the guns faster."

"I'd like to see it."

Buck left the room, returning with the guns belted around his waist. He took them out, removed the caps, and returned the pistols to the holsters. He faced the front door. His right hand flashed to the gun on his right side, and it was snapped almost instantaneously at the door. It happened so fast the normal eye would have had difficulty detecting the movement, but not Cory's eye.

"You're on the right track, but there's a little awkwardness. The holster's too high; I seen one in Texas might do. I got a good piece of leather down at the shop. Let's see what we can do with it tomorrow. I think maybe you got another problem with them holsters."

"I do, keeping the powder dry. I have to put them in my saddlebags when it rains."

"They ain't much use in saddlebags. We'll see what we can do about that, too."

The next morning they went to work on new holsters. Cory directed while Buck did the cutting, punching, and sewing. The new belt fitted below the waist, and the holsters were part of it. They were so low that the pistol grips were about even with his hips. The grip of the right gun pointed to the rear, while that of the left pointed forward. The right hand could grasp each quickly. As Cory had surmised, Buck could draw either gun with a smoother, more fluid motion and a little faster. They then made an easily removable cover of lightweight leather which fitted over the top of each gun to protect it from rain.

That afternoon, one of the Rushton people came to the McCord home with an invitation for Buck to have supper at Prairie's Edge the following night.

He accepted, but with strong reservations about facing the Rushton family, not knowing what they may have heard about his meeting with Beverly. He arrived early for an opportunity to talk with John, whom he found alone in his office. Buck took the offered seat and asked, "Has Randy heard anything from Beverly?"

"I think so. Someone brought a note from Marion yesterday. I don't know what was in it; he didn't say."

"I think I really fouled things up," Buck said and related his conversation with Beverly. When he finished, he said, "I should have come by and told you sooner, but I was too embarrassed about what I said to her. Maybe something could have been done to straighten out the mess I made."

"I doubt it, but don't blame yourself; you were right about her. She isn't the girl for Randy, despite his feelings for her. She wasn't looking at him as much as she was at what he would inherit someday. I understand the young man from Selma is from a very wealthy family, so I suppose he is a better catch. His name is Gothrow; you may have heard it before—his father is involved in a number of businesses in Selma. The young man isn't in the army; it seems his family can't get along without him in their foundries and powder plants. I wish I had the courage to tell her off like you did. As much as I dislike the girl personally, I would have been forever in her debt had she come forward to stand by Randy now.''

Supper that night was far from a happy occasion; gloom seemed to have settled upon everyone from the room above. Right after dessert, Buck said he would have to go as he was leaving early the next morning to rejoin his regiment. John asked Samuel to have his horse brought to the front of the house, and Buck went upstairs to say good-bye to Randy. In the light of the lamps, Randy appeared even paler and thinner than before. As Buck looked at his friend, the startling realization came to him that this could be the last time he would see him alive. He took Randy's hand and said, ''Gotta leave in the morning, Ol' Buddy. Is there anything I can do for you before I go?''

''No,'' he replied. ''Just take good care of Chessy.''

''She'll be in first-rate shape when you get back. When shall I tell them to expect you?''

''Not very soon.''

''Well, don't get accustomed to this easy living. We need you up yonder. I know I do.''

''Good luck, Buck. I couldn't have asked for a better friend.'' Then he added, ''Or brother.''

''Me, too,'' Buck replied and quickly left the room so Randy wouldn't see the emotion welling up in him.

Buck slowly made his way downstairs and was told that his horse was out front. He bade good-bye to John and Carolyn; but before he could say anything to Ellen, she said, ''I'll walk to your horse with you.''

She took his arm as she had done before, and they left the house. Buck experienced the same thrill of excitement he had known the last time they walked together. Neither spoke until they reached the horse. He unfastened the reins; and holding them in his hand, he turned toward her. She reached out and gently placed her right hand on his arm and said, ''The last time, I asked you to look out for Randy; and thank you for doing that. This time I'm asking you to look out for yourse . . .''

She never finished the sentence; for Buck reached for her, and she was suddenly in his arms. As he pulled her soft body close to his, her arms went quickly around his neck; and she stood on tiptoe to reach his lips as he bowed his head to kiss her. They stood like one, clinging together, each lost in the ecstasy of the moment.

The kiss finally ended, but they still clung together; and he said softly in her ear, ''I've waited so long for this, so awfully, awfully long. I've loved you from the first time I saw you.''

''And I've loved you, too. Why didn't you ever tell me?''

"When I first met you, you were like a princess—so far beyond my reach. I couldn't bring myself to believe you could ever feel the same way about me, and I was afraid to tell you I love you for fear it would destroy the relationship we had."

"And I was afraid you would think me forward if I let on how I felt about you. What silly idiots we've been!"

"I can't believe this has really happened." Then he anxiously asked, "You will marry me, won't you?"

"Any time, any place."

"Let's go see your parents and get their consent before I leave."

John and Carolyn were in the sitting room. When the glowing couple appeared at the doorway, they knew what had happened and looked at each other and smiled.

Buck was the first to speak, "Ellen and I just discovered that we have loved each other for years." This wasn't exactly what he had intended to say. "What I mean is that I've loved her for years, and she didn't know it; and she's loved me, and I didn't know it."

"I don't know why not," John said. "I knew it. Didn't you, Carolyn?"

"Of course, I did."

Buck and Ellen looked at each other and laughed. Buck said, "I came back to ask for Ellen's hand. We would like to have your blessing before I go."

"You have it, Buck. We're glad you will officially become a part of this family. Congratulations to you both, and we wish the best for you," John replied.

"I think John has expressed my feelings, too," Carolyn added. "When will the wedding take place?"

"When I get my next furlough, I hope."

"Do you have any idea when that will be?"

"No, ma'am."

"Then we'll have to make plans on that basis."

After the young couple left to go outside, Carolyn went upstairs to tell Randy of the engagement in hope it would cheer him up.

Outside, Buck said a long good-bye to Ellen and reluctantly took his departure. He was so happy he felt as though he would explode from exhilaration, but he managed to control himself fairly well until he reached the road junction and turned onto the Plantersville road. Here he put spurs to his horse; and racing at a hard gallop, he let go with the Rebel yell over and over again.

Carolyn had just finished telling Randy about Ellen and Buck, news which he accepted with complete indifference. Before leaving the room she asked, "Can I get anything for you, Dear?"

"No, thanks."

Through the open windows there unexpectedly came the sound of a bloodcurdling yell. Startled, Carolyn cried, "My goodness! What in the world was that?"

Randy chuckled. "That, Mother, is the Rebel yell."

"What a frightening thing," she said with a shudder.

"You should hear it when hundreds or thousands of men yell it together as they charge."

"That could be awesome."

"It is. It demoralizes the enemy; but to us, it lifts our spirits like nothing else I've seen or heard. It makes us like one. We know we are not alone, and it seems to take all our fears away. We feel we can do anthing—surmount any obstacle. It has almost a magical effect on us."[4]

Carolyn looked at her son; he seemed to be revitalized. This was the first time since he came home that he had shown the least interest in anything. She walked over to the window where she could better hear the yell, which was growing fainter as the rider moved farther from the house. She was almost entranced by it. The spell was broken by her son, "Mother, I'm kinda hungry. You wouldn't happen to have some of Golan's gumbo put up, would you?"

"I certainly do!"

Again she heard the yell of the exuberant suitor, this time even more distant. As she happily crossed the room on her way downstairs, she asked herself, "How could that yell have had such a remarkable effect upon Randy when all else had failed? Does it really work like magic?"

Across the hall the Rebel yell rang out again, this time in the higher pitch of a feminine voice.

"My goodness gracious!" Carolyn exclaimed. "That was Ellen!"

From the bed came what would have been a hearty laugh but for the weakness of the occupant.

Buck reached Okolona on April 29, picked up his horse and the wagon, and continued on to Coffeeville to return the borrowed vehicle. He went in the front door of the provisional hospital; and as he started down the hall, a man in the first room on the right called to him, "Hey, horse soldier! You got a minute?"

"Sure," Buck replied and went into the room, which was occupied by several patients. The one calling was seated on a cot by the front window. He had a bandage around his head and another around his thigh.

"I saw you come in. Those are a couple of fine-looking horses. They belong to you?"

"Yes."

The man moved his hand, and Buck could see the sparkle of a ring on his finger. "You wouldn't want to sell one, would you?"

"Hadn't counted on it," he replied, still looking at the ring.

"I'd sure like to have one of them."

"Is that a diamond ring?"

"Sure is, the real thing."

"Could it be made into a ring for a lady?"

"Any good jeweler can do it. If you're thinking about a swap, forget it; this is a mighty fine ring. It's worth a lot more than a horse."

"And those are mighty fine horses. I don't know anything about diamonds; how can you tell it's genuine?"

"A real diamond will cut glass; a fake one won't." He removed the ring from his finger, leaned over toward the window, and scratched the letters "GPR" on one of the panes.

Buck touched the glass with his fingernail and was satisfied that the glass had been cut.

"Those your initials?" he asked.

"Yep. That's me, Greek P. Rice from over in Coahoma County." He offered his hand.[5]

Buck shook hands and said "I'm Buck McCord from Perry County, Alabama. I might be interested in a trade if you are, but not the buckskin."

"Like I said, this ring's worth a lot more than a horse; but I need one bad. The surgeon said I can go home tomorrow to recuperate, and I need transportation. Give me a hand, and let's take a look at that filly."

Rice examined the mare carefully as only a man very knowledgeable about horses would do. Buck put a saddle on her and rode the mare first at a walk and then at a trot. He then helped Rice in the saddle, and he tried her at a trot. As he dismounted he said, "This is really a fine animal, one fit for a general."

Buck smiled. "I know," he replied. "I think he'll make it."

Rice looked at him quizzically and said, "I thought you would be taking me in a swap, but now I'm not so sure."

"She's a good horse; came from our breeding stock. Any time both traders are satisfied, it's a good swap."

Rice took the ring off and handed it to Buck. "It's set in almost pure gold. It can be made into a fine ring for a fine lady." He smiled and added, "You can always tell her you loved her more than a good horse."

"More than a million of them."

"Where are you headed?"

"Corinth. My regiment's there."

"You wouldn't happen to be with Forrest?"

"Yes. You know him?"

"No, but I know of him. He owns a couple of plantations in Coahoma county. He's quite a man."

"Well, you can tell folks you are riding his horse."

"That right?"

"Yes. I was taking this one to him; but I just got engaged, and the ring seems more important."

Buck began to transfer the saddle to Skin. Rice asked, "You travelling alone?"

"Yes."

"Be careful. It's reported there are a lot of marauding deserters and no-accounts between here and Corinth."

On the afternoon of May 2, Buck was passing through a large wooded area a considerable distance southwest of Ripley. He had seen no houses or good water for some time, and both he and Skin needed a drink. The road passed through a clearing. On the left was a planted field of a few acres and on the right was a small cabin and a barn which had a horse lot adjacent to it. In front of the house was a well. He rode up to it and called to the house but received no response. He called twice more; and receiving no answer, he got down to draw a bucket of water. The door of the cabin swung open, and there appeared in it a young woman of no more than twenty years. In her hands was a shotgun pointed at the new arrival. A toddler came up to her and held onto her left leg.

"Git on your horse, an' keep ridin'," she said.

"I'm sorry, ma'am. I didn't think anyone was at home. I just wanted water for my horse and myself."

"That's what them others said—just wanted a drink of water. Now, git!"

"What others?" he asked.

"Them no-good deserters who took my onliest mule an' come at me to do me harm." Her chin began to quiver as she struggled to hold back her tears.

"Are you all right? They didn't hurt you, did they?"

She sniffed before replying, "I'm all right," she said gamely.

"I'm sorry I frightened you. I'm no deserter. I'm Private McCord with Forrest's cavalry regiment. I took a wounded friend to his home in Alabama, and I'm on my way back to join my regiment."

"Git your water, an' go."

He lowered the bucket; and when it was filled, he began to raise it. "How many men were here?" he asked.

"There was three, but just two left. The other'n's around the corner of the house. He ain't goin' nowhere but to hell."

Buck took a drink and set the bucket on the ground for Skin. While the gelding was drinking, he moved to his left where he could see beyond the corner of the house; and there was a body in dirty, ragged butternut lying on the ground. He turned to the woman and said, "If you've got a shovel, I'll bury that for you."

"It's in the barn. Bury the scoun'rel in the lot. The groun's softer, an' it's good enough for him. He'll fit real good in the manure there."

Buck dug a shallow grave and dragged the body to it. The woman came out of the house, still carrying the gun, and walked over to him. "Where's your man?" he asked.

"Off fightin' the war," she replied. Her chin began to quiver again, "I don't know what I'm gonna do. I got a crop to make, an' now I ain't got no mule an' me with two young'uns to feed. I know the Good Lord ain't gonna give me a bigger load than I can tote, but I do wish He didn' have such a good opinion of me."

"Maybe He's got a right to it," Buck said. He squatted down to roll the body into the grave but decided to go through the man's pockets first. He found no identification on him; but to his surprise, there was a small bag containing several gold and silver coins and over a hundred dollars in greenbacks and Confederate paper money. He offered the money to the woman, but she drew back in fright.

"I can't take that money!" she exclaimed.

"I don't see why not. We don't know who he is, and it would do no good to bury it with him. Take this money, and use it as you see fit. I don't know of anyone who has more right to it. You can consider it payment for the mule."

She took it in disbelief. In her entire life she had never seen that much money, much less at one time.

Before he left, Buck asked, "Which way did they go?"

"Same as you."

"How far ahead are they?"

She looked at the sun before replying, "About two hours."

"Were they armed?"

"Just knives. The cowards prob'ly th'owed their guns away when they run. My mule's got a white blaze an's dark blue. If you happen to find 'im, just head 'im for home an' slap 'im on the rump. He'll make it back."

Late that afternoon, in the shadows ahead, Buck thought he could make out a mounted man and another walking beside him; but they disappeared from view. He took the cover off his right pistol and proceeded cautiously but saw nothing except their tracks leading into the wood. About an hour later, he came to a small clearing on the left of the road. At the far edge of it was a little stream by which he made his camp and built a fire not far from a hickory tree. By this time it was dark. With some small branches, a blanket, his hat, and the saddle he put together what appeared from a distance to be a sleeping man, and propped up his rifle beside it where it could be seen. He went behind the hickory and sat down with his back to the tree. Here he waited, getting up only when necessary to feed the fire.

More than an hour passed before he heard the sound of either a mule or horse approaching from the southwest. The noise made by the animal stopped, and then he heard it again briefly. He knew they had probably seen his fire and had tied the animal by the road. He got up so he could see the ruse he had prepared. His alert ears picked up the sound of two men approaching cautiously, and he made them out as they came into the open area. They stopped and watched what appeared to be a sleeping man near the fire and then stealthily made their way across the clearing with their knives drawn. One was in a Confederate uniform; the other was dressed in blue. To his astonishment, Buck recognized the latter as Jethro Barlow when he came within the light of the fire. He waited until they were about five feet from their target, and he stepped out where he could be seen. "If you're looking for another lone woman to bother, you've made a mistake," he said coldly.

The men looked toward him in fright; but then they saw no gun in his hands. The one in butternut yelled, "Git 'im!"; and they both charged with upraised knives. So quickly that they never saw how it happened, they were facing a firing pistol. The first shot caught Jethro, and he went down; but he was up again quickly and ran for cover in the trees across the stream on his left. The second shot caught the man in butternut but did not stop him. Buck fired again, and he kept coming. The third shot was enough; the man fell face down in front of him. His hands frantically dug into the dirt, and then he lay still. Jethro was out of sight, but Buck could hear him thrashing through the underbrush as he ran away in a northeasterly direction.

Buck searched the dead man and found no identification on him, but he was carrying almost the exact amount of coins and paper money as the one he had buried at the cabin. He took the man's shirt off and bundled the money in it. He dragged the body off into the wood and then walked down the road until he found the blaze-faced mule tied to a tree.

He attached the shirt bundle to the saddle, untied the animal, turned him toward home, and slapped him smartly on the rump. The mule started off down the road at a jerky trot. As he watched the animal go, he thought perhaps his mother was right—God does sometimes seem to move in mighty mysterious ways.

Chapter IX

Corinth to Munfordville

Buck reached Corinth on May 3 and found things in a state of high excitement. Major General Halleck, who arrived at Pittsburg Landing from St. Louis after the battle of Shiloh, had taken personal command of the Federal troops there. He had delayed pursuing Beauregard and did not begin a concerted move against him until the last week in April, and it was not until May 3 that he reached the outer defenses of Corinth. Instead of vigorously attacking the outnumbered foe, he began building fortifications for a siege. This was continued for twenty-seven days with frequent interruptions by Confederate sorties from Corinth. By the time he was ready to launch an assault in force, Beauregard pulled out on the night of May 29-30, withdrawing to Tupelo, Mississippi.

Forrest had left his home in Memphis on April 29 to return to his command, but he made the effort too soon. His wound became infected and exceedingly painful. It reopened, and another operation was required to remove the ball. This confined him to bed for another two weeks, and it was not until the first week in June that he was able to take the field.

At Prairie's Edge, a miraculous change had taken place in Randy, both mentally and physically. He was once again alert and interested in what was going on around him; but best of all, his appetite had returned. His wounds were healing well; however, he was so debilitated that considerable time would be required for him to recover fully.

Ellen and Sally had returned to Judson on April 27, but they came home the following weekend. By then Randy had improved to the point that he was sitting up several hours each day. Sally stayed at Prairie's Edge as Ellen's guest; but during those few days she spent most of her time with Randy, reading to him, talking to him, and waiting upon him. She claimed to be doing this to "give Miss Carolyn a rest"; but this pretext fooled no one, and Randy's family wisely left the young couple to themselves.

When Sally returned with Ellen to Judson Sunday afternoon, Randy found a void in his life which made him aware, for the first time, how much he enjoyed the company of his diminutive, cheerful neighbor. She had promised to come back the following weekend, and he looked forward more each passing day to seeing her again. By the time she returned, he was ambulatory; but he still had little strength. Again they spent most of the weekend together; and when she left for school, he was thankful that it was for the final week of the term.

After Judson let out for the summer, Sally came faithfully to Prairie's Edge each afternoon and usually could be found with Randy. As he grew stronger and more active, they took walks and rode together. His wounds had healed, and the scabs from those on his face had disappeared; but across his right cheek was the long red welt of a scar which was marked along its edges where the surgeon had taken stitches. These smaller marks were fading and in time would disappear, but the scar would always be there.

One afternoon in the latter part of May, Randy and Sally rode over to the gravel bar by the river where he and Buck had spent so many hours together. They tied their horses and sat in a sandy spot with the warm sun on their backs as they watched the muddy waters of the Cahaba flow slowly by. Neither was very talkative, content with just being together.

"A penny for your thoughts," Sally said.

"I've been thinking it's about time for me to return to the regiment."

"Oh, Randy, do you have to go back now?"

"Afraid so. My furlough says it's for me to recuperate and, when able, to return to duty. I'm going to miss you, Sally, like I've never missed anyone before."

"And I'll miss you, too," she said sadly. "These days with you have been heavenly."

"Do you think you could spend the rest of your days with a fool like me?"

"All I ask is the chance."

He took her in his arms and kissed her, again and again. When he released her, they were both breathing heavily. Sally got to her feet and started brushing the dry sand from her dress. "I think it best we go now," she said.

"Maybe we had," he replied, as he stood up.

Neither had much to say as they began their ride back to Prairie's Edge. While crossing the bridge, Randy said, "I want to ask you something that's been worrying me, does my having part of my ear gone bother you?''

Sally looked at him with sparkling eyes, "Absolutely not," she said. "You know how people crop the ears of their stock to prove ownership—I'll just look at that ear and say to everybody, hands off! This one's mine!''

Randy laughed. "You're a nut," he said. "How about the scar; I'll have that the rest of my life, too?''

Sally grew serious; and she replied, "Buck told how you got that wound; and every time I look at the scar, I'll remember how you received it, and I'll be proud of you for it. Don't ever be ashamed of that scar; you should wear it with pride and dignity.''

"Hadn't thought of it that way; guess I could take some pride in it. Wish I could say the same for the one in the back; I'm glad it doesn't show," he said with a laugh. Then he added on a more serious note, "Have you thought about when you would like to get married?''

"It would be nice to have our wedding at the same time as Ellen and Buck, if we can.''

"That's a great idea! Buck can be my best man and I can be his.''

"Yes; and Ellen and I—one of us can be the maid of honor and the other the matron of honor.''

Randy laughed. Life with Sally wouldn't be dull.

On June 6 Randy arrived at Tupelo, not long after Forrest had returned to duty. He was warmly received by Buck, who had already heard of his engagement to Sally through a letter from Ellen. Randy had gained back most of the lost weight, and much of his vigor had returned. The ear didn't look bad, and the scar had lost much of its bright red color. His first interest was Chessy, and he satisfied himself that she was fully healed. He had hardly gotten back into the routine of camp life before he and Buck were summoned on June 11 to Forrest's tent. They found the colonel busy with a map at his field desk.

"I got some bad news," Forrest said. "I been ordered to Chattanooga to organize a brigade of cavalry. They won't let me take my regiment from here, but they are lettin' me take a few officers an' twenty men as an escort. I'd like to have both of you as part of the escort; but I ain't orderin' you, because you may want to stay with the regiment.''

Buck looked at Randy who nodded affirmatively. "We'd like to go with you, Colonel," he said.

Arriving in Chattanooga on June 19, it was Forrest's good fortune to find that the Eighth Texas cavalry, better known as Terry's Rangers, was to form a part of his small brigade. This unit had entered the service in the early months of the war and was made up of hardy rough riders from the cattle ranches of Texas, men who from their earliest days were accustomed to horses and the ready use of the gun and pistol.[1] Colonel John A. Wharton had commanded the regiment since the loss of its first commander in 1861. In addition, there were assigned to the brigade of acting Brigadier General Forrest the Second Georgia regiment of cavalry, under Colonel J. K. Lawton; the Second Georgia battalion, commanded by Colonel Morrison; and 100 mounted Kentuckians under Lieutenant Colonel Woodward.

Buck found in Chattanooga a competent jeweler who was operating a small shop in the center of town. He took the ring he had acquired in Coffeeville to him and had it made into a diamond solitaire for Ellen. There was enough gold in the man's heavy mounting to make a matching wedding band.

Forrest was told he was to make an incursion into middle Tennessee. This was preliminary to a plan formulated by Generals Beauregard and Braxton Bragg following the withdrawal of the Confederates from Corinth to Tupelo. The plan entailed Bragg's moving the army from the vicinity of Chattanooga into Tennessee and on into Kentucky in coordination with General E. Kirby Smith's making a simultaneous move into that state from the vicinity of Knoxville. The campaign was for the purpose of liberating and occupying Kentucky and for cutting Grant's and Buell's lines of supply from the Ohio River.

With his usual energy, Forrest applied himself to organizing and equipping his command. By July 6, he had his light brigade ready for its mission. During this period, he sent scouts into middle Tennessee and from them learned there were at Murfreesborough two regiments of infantry, the Ninth Michigan and the Third Minnesota; a portion of the Seventh Pennsylvania cavalry; and a battery of four guns. He picked Murfreesborough as his first objective.

On July 9, Forrest crossed his brigade over the Tennessee River and moved by two routes to McMinnville, Tennessee. There he received as accessions to his command four additional companies, bringing his force to 1,500 men. He left McMinnville; and, just before daylight on the 13th, his advance column reached the outskirts of Murfreesborough.

A company of Wharton's Texans was sent forward; and when challenged by a Federal outpost, replied, ''A company of the Seventh Pennsylvania cavalry marching to join our command at Murfreesborough.'' The Federal sentinels were not aware of the true identity of the troopers until they had been surrounded and covered by drawn pistols. The picket force was captured without a shot being fired.

From the pickets, Forrest learned that the Federal forces in Murfreesborough were divided. The Ninth Michigan and two companies of the Seventh Pennsylvania cavalry were encamped near each other at the edge of town. Two companies of the Eighth Kentucky cavalry, one company of the Ninth Michigan, and other small detachments were guarding the jail in which a large number of Confederates, mostly civilians, were being held. They were also guarding the inn where Brigadier General Thomas T. Crittenden, who had arrived there on the 12th, had made his headquarters. The Third Minnesota and Hewett's battery occupied a camp a mile and a half beyond the town.

Quickly forming his plan, Forrest divided his force into three sections. The Texans under Wharton were to attack the Michigan Ninth infantry and the nearby cavalry, capturing them if possible, but failing in that, holding them engaged until action against the other enemy forces had been completed. Colonel Morrison's battalion, divided into three squadrons under Forrest's personal leadership, would advance immediately into the center of town and assail the jail, courthouse, and the inn where General Crittenden was known to be. Colonel Lawton would take the remainder of the troopers through the town and throw them at the Third Minnesota and Hewett's battery to prevent their junction with the Federal forces being attacked in Murfreesborough.

At the command, "Charge!" Wharton's Texans rushed down the pike, the noise on the road and their wild yells rousing the Yankees from their beds. Before the Pennsylvania cavalry could get to their horses, the Texans were among them; and those not captured or killed, rushed over to the camp of the Ninth Michigan. The infantry commander, acting Brigadier General W. W. Duffield, called to his men to get their arms and stand their ground. By this time the Texans were upon them at close quarter, and Duffield was wounded by a pistol shot from Wharton. The Federals, now under Lieutenant Colonel John G. Parkhurst, rallied and poured a heavy fusillade into the Confederates, who were scattered throughout the camp. Wharton was badly wounded, and his regiment withdrew some 200 yards.

Parkhurst concentrated the Federal troops in a lot fenced with heavy cedar posts and, with wagons and hay, made a rather formidable stockade. Knowing a direct attack would result in heavy losses, Lieutenant Colonel Walker, who had taken over command of the Texans from the wounded Wharton, was satisfied to keep the enemy penned up until reinforcements came to him.

Forrest charged straight into the center of the town with his detachment. General Crittenden, his staff, and the provost guards were quickly captured at the inn. The squadron assigned to take the jail found it had been set afire by a Yankee soldier who, with the other troops at the jail, had run to the courthouse to join the garrison there. The occupants of the burning building were rescued with difficulty from their locked cells, some barely in time to be saved from the flames.

The Yankees in the courthouse were pouring volleys into all confederates who came within sight and range. Forrest organized an assault on that building and gained access to it with a hastily improvised battering ram. Hand-to-hand fighting took place inside the building; but it was of short duration, for the outnumbered Federals soon surrendered.

With the town under control, Forrest sent a portion of his troops to reinforce the Texans and moved with those not assigned to guard prisoners to the support of Lawton, who was to attack the second camp. Upon hearing the uproar in town, Colonel Lester, commanding the Federal forces composed of the Third Minnesota and Hewett's battery, had thrown his men in line of battle and started moving toward Murfreesborough. They had proceeded only bout 400 yards when they met Lawton and were checked. When Forrest arrived upon the scene, the troops were engaged at long range; but having artillery, the Yankees held the advantage.

Forrest led a detachment of troopers around the enemy's flank to a position where he could fall upon their camp from the rear. Lester had left about 100 men in charge of the camp. Rushed suddenly from an unexpected direction, the men there offered little resistance. As they were in the act of surrendering, one, showing more fight than the others, blazed away at Forrest from behind a wagon but missed from a distance of only thirty feet. He was immediately gunned down by the Confederate leader with his pistol.

Satisfied that the enemy forces under Lester could neither advance nor retreat, Forrest made a wide circle to where the Texans had penned down the forces under Parkhurst, arriving there about eleven o'clock in the morning. As part of his escort, Buck and Randy had ridden close to their commander all day. When Forrest saw the strength of the Federal position in the improvised stockade, he knew an assault on them would be costly; and he had no artillery to blast them into submission.

"Let's try a little brag an' bluff," he said; and then to his brother, Bill, "I want you to go in with a flag of truce. Tell 'em the rest has surrendered, an' I got my whole force; an' if they want to save their butts, they better surrender, or I'll kill ever' last one of 'em."

"You can't do that," Bill protested.

"I know it, an' you know it; but they don't know I won't do it!" Forrest said impatiently. He then looked at Randy who was sitting on his horse close by, "How about cleaning that up into polite talk."[2]

Randy thought it over for a moment before replying. He then started the message, "Your compatriots have all surrendered. I demand the surrender..."

"Make it unconditional surrender like that damned Grant done at Donelson!" Forrest interrupted.

"I demand the unconditional surrender of your force as prisoners of war, or I will put every man to the sword. This demand is made to prevent the effusion of blood."

"Effusion of blood! I like the sound of that, but it still ain't got the right pitch. Let 'em know I got the men to git the job done."

"We can change the last sentence to say that I have an overpowering force at my command, and this demand is made to prevent the effusion of blood."

"That's good! You got it, Bill?"

"Yes."

"Good. Take Rushton with you, just in case."

Colonel Duffield and Lieutenant Parkhurst had both been seriously wounded, and the forces under them had suffered eleven killed and eighty-six wounded. Believing his situation to be hopeless, Duffield surrendered his command at noon.

Leaving a sufficient number of troopers to guard the prisoners, Forrest hurried with the remainder to the other side of town where Lawton was holding in check the forces under Colonel Lester. A flag of truce was sent in to Lester with the following message:

"Murfreesborough, July, 1862.

"Colonel,—I must demand an unconditional surrender of your force as prisoners of war, or I will have every man put to the sword. You are aware of the overpowering force I have at my command, and this demand is made to prevent the effusion of blood. I am, Colonel, very respectfully, your obedient servant,

"N. B. FORREST

"To Colonel Lester   Brigadier General of Cavalry, CSA"

Upon receipt of the message, Colonel Lester asked permission to consult with Colonel Duffield. As Duffield was wounded, Lester was taken to him under escort. Finding that all of the other troops had surrendered, Lester immediately capitulated, turning over about 400 infantry and Captain John N. Hewett's Battery B, Kentucky light artillery, which included three six-pounder smooth bores and one ten-pounder Parrot gun.

Among the Confederate prisoners crowded into the county jail were two who were fortunate that Forrest had chosen this day to take Murfreesborough. One was a spy, under the name of James Paul; and the other was Captain William Richardson, who had fallen in with him by chance and was travelling with the spy when they were captured. They both had been condemned to death as spies and were to be executed at sunrise that morning.

At Forrest's request, Richardson identified the Yankee soldier who had tried to incinerate those confined in jail. Later, when the roll call was made of the prisoners, that guard's name was called; but no one answered. Forrest said, "Pass on; it's all right."

Immediately after the surrender of the last detachment, Forrest gathered the prisoners and captured property together and started in the direction of McMinnville, camping that night nine miles east of Murfreesborough. Before leaving he destroyed the depots containing all government supplies and materiel which could not be transported. Also destroyed were the railroad bridges in the immediate vicinity. He reached McMinnville on the night of the 14th. From here he sent the officer prisoners to Knoxville to be exchanged and paroled the privates and noncommissioned officers.

That night after supper, Randy and Buck sat by the campfire, and by its flickering light reread their last letters from home. As Randy folded one from Sally, he said, "I don't know how I could have been so blind to Sally and have fallen for someone like Beverly."

"When the heart dictates, the mind doesn't question why."

"It was a lucky day when I came to my senses. I think my folks were relieved when I broke up with Beverly."

"You better believe it," Buck replied; and then he asked, "You never mentioned it, but what did Beverly have to say about my conversation with her?"

"When?"

"The day after we got back home."

"You talked with Beverly?"

"I went to Marion to see her."

"You did? I didn't know that."

"Didn't she write you?"

"Yes, but I never opened it."

"Why?"

"I knew from Beverly's letters before Shiloh that things weren't the same between us, and I felt I was losing her. When I got cut up at the fallen timber, I was certain everything would be over for us. That was the reason I didn't care whether I lived or died—I couldn't face losing her. When the letter came to me at Prairie's Edge, I knew she must have learned about my wounds and was telling me it was all over. I didn't want to hear this, so I never read the letter.''

"Well, I'll be damned," Buck said.

Randy got up and went to his saddlebags. After rummaging around in one of them, he came up with a well-worn envelope addressed to him in Beverly's handwriting. He handed it to Buck. "See, it's never been opened. Read it if you want.''

Buck took the letter and examined it casually; then he returned it. "No thanks," he said.

Randy held the letter, undecided what to do with it. On impulse, he tossed it into the fire. They watched as the paper slowly caught fire and then burned brightly. They sat silently while the flames consumed it, leaving only curled ashes. "Now we'll never know what she said," Buck mused.

"It couldn't have been very important," Randy replied, "not now, anyway.''

Murfreesborough was an important station on the enemy line of supply, and several Federal forces were ordered from their bases to intercept and destroy the Confederate raiders.[3]

Forrest remained at McMinnville a few days resting his troops and their horses. From here he sent out many scouts who brought in information of the enemy movements, and he was fully aware of the conditions facing him. Despite his precarious situation, he refused to listen to suggestions made by some of his officers not to risk conflict with the Federal infantry forces rapidly being concentrated against him and to retire with his prisoners and captured property.

"I didn' come here to make a half of a job of it," he declared. "I'm goin' to have 'em all.''

Forrest swept northward in the direction of Lebanon and Nashville, raiding and burning as he went.[4] He then turned in the direction of Manchester, stopping southeast of Murfreesborough for a few days to rest his men and horses again. While in bivouac, he paroled recently captured prisoners; and Randy and Buck assisted the adjutant in this task. As they were winding up the job, a tired and bedraggled soldier in dirty butternut rode up on a rather jaded horse.

"I'm looking for Colonel Forrest," the newcomer declared. "I was told he's in this area.''

"You'll find him at his tent, the larger one over there," Randy said, gesturing toward Forrest's tent about fifty yards behind them.

"Thanks," the rider replied. "I'm from General Bragg's headquarters with dispatches. I've ridden my butt off tryin' to find y'all. You leave a good trail, but you don't stay no place very long."

"Can't afford to," Buck said. "The area's full of Yankees looking for us."

"I know; been dodgin' 'em."

"After you deliver your messages, come back and have supper with us. Doesn't look like you or your horse has been eating too well lately. We've got some corn for him."

"You can say that ag'in; the critter's in pretty bad shape. Thanks for the invite. We'll be right back," and he left for Forrest's tent.

The messenger returned in about ten minutes and brought the news that among the papers delivered to Forrest was the latter's promotion to brigadier general.

General Nelson had reached Tennessee and was constantly prodded by Buell to get Forrest. From Murfreesborough, Nelson wired him on the 24th that Forrest had escaped and had burned a bridge, killing three of the eighty men guarding it and capturing the rest. Despite the hot weather and hopelessness of his task, Nelson valiantly persisted in his efforts to catch up with the raider. Forrest was at Manchester on July 27, where he ran into a detachment of General W. Sooy Smith's cavalry, killing three and capturing fifteen of them. By the 30th, Nelson was ready to give up, telegraphing Buell: "With infantry in hot weather it is a hopeless task to chase Forrest's command mounted on race horses."

"Destroy him if you can," Buell came back.

From McMinnville, Nelson reported that three wagons had been cut off close to camp, a patrol fired upon with four men killed, and two sentries had been shot. He further reported that Forrest was at Sparta, Tennessee, and that he had sent a regiment of cavalry out to entice him. Forrest moved out of Sparta on August 15, swooped around his pursuers, and moved in the direction of Murfreesborough. Before reaching that town, now heavily regarrisoned with Union forces, he turned southward and then again toward McMinnville and followed a branch railroad leading there, tearing up the track and burning bridges. Buell dolefully dispatched to Miller at Nashville: "Our guards are gathered up by the enemy as easily as he would herd cattle. One resolute company properly stockaded could defy Forrest's whole force."

Fully informed of the various columns marching to corner him, and knowing that General Bragg had already crossed the Tennessee River with a heavy infantry force and was heading for Altamont as he began his planned thrust into Kentucky, Forrest decided to proceed to Altamont and await Bragg's advance guard there. Although he moved with his usual speed, he was unable to escape an additional body of Union troops under General McCook, who had headed him off and was occupying Altamont.

Forrest knew a brigade which had been rushed forward by General Thomas was close behind him, coming from the direction of Murfreesborough. There was but one route left for escape, and this he followed. Throwing his scouts well in advance, he had moved only a few miles when his vedettes came rushing back with the information that they had just encountered a considerable force of infantry not more than half a mile ahead which was advancing immediately upon him. Fortunately he received this information before the main body of his command had been discovered. He took to the brush with his entire force, successfully concealing them within half a mile of the route along which the Federal infantry was moving. The rear guard of the enemy had scarcely passed when he led his men back onto the road and resumed the march.

Forrest, however, was not yet out of danger. Being compelled to pass near McMinnville, now heavily garrisoned with Federal troops, it was his intention to make a detour around the town. When about eight miles from it, he turned from the main road onto a byway which was little travelled. Unfortunately he had not cleared the main road when a heavy column of Federal infantry came in sight. They deployed at once with artillery and small arms. Forrest offered no resistance, putting his men in rapid retreat. He, with half of his command which had cleared the main road, continued ahead at full speed. That portion which had been cut off turned back, scampered away in the opposite direction, and was soon out of danger. Cutting across the country, this group rejoined the main column before sundown.

On September 3, Forrest reached the advance guard of General Bragg's army at Sparta, bringing with him his "Pets" (the four pieces of artillery he had captured at Murfreesborough) and his entire command. At Sparta he received the good news that the four Alabama companies of his old regiment were to rejoin him and he would be allowed to keep a section (two guns) of the artillery he had captured. When he reported to General Bragg, he was directed to move forward in the line of advance of the Union army under General Buell, which was moving north toward Louisville, Kentucky, to contest Bragg's invasion of that state, and to harass and impede Buell's progress as much as possible. Forrest again moved toward Murfreesborough, and the Union forces remaining there retreated toward Nashville. Pressing after them, he crossed the Cumberland River a few miles from that city and was in almost constant conflict with the rear guard and flankers of Buell's army.

He put his section of artillery to good use in impeding Buell's advance. By pushing the guns in close proximity to the Federal infantry, they were compelled to deploy and advance upon him in battle line in order to drive him away. This was exactly what he wished to accomplish; for the more they formed in line of battle, the greater would be the delay in their march toward Louisville.

By September 8, Bragg's army had advanced into southern Kentucky, and on the 10th Forrest arrived at Glasgow with his cavalry. He was temporarily attached to the division of the Confederate army commanded by General Leonidas Polk; and under Polk's orders, he pushed his command beyond Munfordville on the Elizabethtown and Bardstown road. In this movement, Forrest threw himself between the Federals at Munfordville and their only avenue of escape and, with the rapid advance of the Confederate infantry, contributed to the capture of a brigade of Federal infantry which surrendered on September 17.

Forrest proceeded along the line of the Louisville and Nashville railroad, destroying bridges, capturing Federal outposts, and reporting ultimately at Bardstown to General Polk. Here he received a letter asking him to report immediately in person to Bragg's headquarters. On the last day of September, Bragg directed him to turn over the brigade, which he had organized and had thoroughly armed and equipped by captures from the enemy, to Colonel John A. Wharton and to proceed at once to establish headquarters at Murfreesborough and undertake the organization of a new brigade. After a convincing plea, he was allowed to take with him the four Alabama companies of the "Old Regiment" which had served him so well at Sacramento, Fort Donelson, and Shiloh.

It was a dejected Forrest who returned to his brigade after this session with Bragg. For the second time, a unit which he had organized, trained, equipped, and built into an effective fighting force had been taken from him and given to another. Now he was charged with doing it again.

This action by Bragg firmed up something that had been in the back of Forrest's mind since he had been made a General. He sent for Buck and Randy; and when they reported, he said, "I just got some more hard news. I'm to turn over my command to Colonel Wharton an' go down to Murfreesborough to recruit a new brigade. I'm bein' allowed to take the four Alabama companies with me; that's all, except my staff. There's goin' to be a lot of paper shufflin' and trainin' involved. I want both of you on my staff. There'll be a commission as lieutenant in it for you. Rushton, you'll be an assistant adjutant helpin' with the paperwork. We're gonna have a lot of new recruits, an' some prob'ly ain't never shot a gun. McCord, you'll be in charge of trainin' 'em with pistols an' rifles, but no sabers. I'm doin' away with that weapon except for officers. Pistols are better for close work. I guess we'll call you assistant ordnance officer. But on a march, or in a fight, I still want y'all close by me with them Whitworths.''

Chapter X

West Tennessee

No time was wasted by Forrest in setting up his headquarters and recruiting operation in Murfreesboro when he arrived there during the first week of October, 1862. Hiding the disappointment, and what he considered an indignity, in having his brigade taken from him, he applied himself to the task ahead.

He was now so well known as a dashing cavalry leader, and so popular with the people in the area, that he had little difficulty in gathering about him within six weeks a very formidable body of mounted men. Among them was James W. Starnes, who was the captain of the company of Tennesseeans which had voluntarily joined him in the scouting detail in Kentucky and had then fought so well at Sacramento in December, 1861. A new regiment, designated as the Fourth Tennessee Cavalry, was organized with Starnes as the commanding colonel. Two other regiments of Tennessee troops were organized at this time—the Eighth, under Colonel George G. Dibrell, of which Jeffrey E. Forrest, the youngest brother of the general, was elected major; and the Ninth under Colonel J. B. Biffle. These three regiments of Tennessee troops, with the Fourth Alabama cavalry under Colonel A. A. Russell, and one battery of artillery under Captain Freeman and Lieutenants John W. Morton and William W. Williamson, were organized into a brigade to which Forrest was assigned as commanding officer. Russell's Fourth Alabama regiment, to distinguish it from Roddy's Fourth Alabama, was made up of the four veteran companies Forrest brought with him from Kentucky and new recruits. Bill Williamson, the new artillery officer, had been brought into the organization upon the recommendations of Kevin and Randy.

Commissions for Randy and Buck as second lieutenants came through while at Murfreesboro, and they headed for a local tailor's shop to have new uniforms made. Fortunately the tailor had some gray woolen fabric on hand, and they each ordered two complete uniforms and two extra pairs of trousers, plus a heavy coat. As they left the tailor's shop, Buck said sadly, "You know, those will be the first clothes I ever had, other than shoes and hats, that Ma didn't make for me. I wish she could have made these—she would have been so proud to do it."

"Your mother sews very well—better than most tailors. I have always thought your clothes fit better than mine, except that first pair of pants I saw you in."

They both laughed. "That was an old pair, and I had shot up like a weed that year," Buck said.

"Those pants didn't shoot with you," Randy replied. "I'd better write Daddy for some money. I may not have enough to pay for the uniforms."

"I can let you have some if you need it."

Randy looked at his friend in surprise. "Did you win at seven up or something?"

"No. Pa and Ma made me a new sheath for my gun before I left home. They sewed twenty gold pieces in it which I've never touched."

"How about that! Here I've been travelling all this time with a wealthy man and didn't know it."

Forrest's brother, Captain William Forrest, upon instructions from the general, assembled a group of irregulars who served as scouts. These men, made up principally of daring, independent Tennesseeans, were well acquainted with their state. As they were not of the regular service, they drew no pay; they lived by foraging on the foe when they could, and on friends when they couldn't find the foe. They numbered about forty and were soon dubbed "The Forty Thieves" by the regular cavalrymen. They fought as well as they foraged; and as foragers, they had no equals.

After being commissioned, Buck and Randy became members of the mess of General Forrest and his staff. One night Captain McLemore, who had taken over the company formerly commanded by Colonel Starnes, was having supper with them. During the meal, he said to Forrest in a voice loud enough for the benefit of the others:

"I was over at your brother Bill's camp today, and that's quite a crew he's got. I don't know where he finds them. There was one old character, all dressed up in dirty buckskins, who told one of the funniest stories I ever heard. He said there was a very highfalutin lady who liked to go horseback riding every day. One day she rode up to the main street to cross it but wasn't able to get across because of a crowd watching a parade go by. She stopped her horse by them and waited for the parade to pass. All of a sudden, her horse broke wind. According to this character, it was a monstrous, noisy wind, so strong that it almost took off the hat of a man standing by the horse's rear. The man grabbed his hat and held on. The lady, from her lofty perch, said, 'My good man, I am so sorry. Please accept my apology.' The man looked up at her and said 'There wasn't any need for you to apologize, lady; I thought it was the horse!'"

The narrator started to laugh heartily and looked around the table to enjoy the reaction of the others to the story, but his mirth quickly faded when he realized no one else was laughing. He looked again at Forrest at the head of the table and knew he had committed a serious faux pas. The brigadier's face and neck had turned a fiery red, and he seemed to be having difficulty controlling himself. He stared at the storyteller a long time before he spoke; and when he did it was in a slow, cold, precise voice. "Captain, you are a guest at my table, so I'll try to say this in as nice a way as I can. I don't like smutty stories, especially one that disparages a lady. I'd thank you not to ever repeat another in my presence."

Captain McLemore was embarrassed but showed a lot of poise; he replied, "My apology, General. I didn't know your feelings about this. There was no intention to offend you and no disrespect meant to the fine ladies of our country. You may be assured that I will not repeat the error."

"Your apology is accepted," Forrest replied. Appreciating the young officer's grit and response, he added with a grin, "But there was no need to apologize, I thought it was the hoss, myself." This brought a roar of laughter from the tense officers around the table and put the guest at ease.

When the meal was over, Buck said to Randy, "Got time to go over to Bill's camp with me?"

"Wish I could, but I'm up to my butt in paper work and need to get at it. Don't suppose it's Cally, do you?"

"Probably not, but it sounds like him. I've got to be sure."

Bill's camp was close by; and as he came up to it, Buck saw the familiar back of a man in buckskins talking to a group assembled before him. Knowing Cally was probably in the middle of a story, he stopped short of the men and waited for him to finish. He heard Cally say, "Yessuh, that was one of the finest Chris'mas dinners I ever et. The table was loaded with food—pies an' cakes an' taters an' the biggest turkey you ever seen just stuffed full of popcorn dressin'."

"Popcorn dressin'!" one of the listeners said. "I ain't never heared of popcorn dressin'.''

"You never heared of popcorn dressin'? Why, the folks where I come from couldn't cook a turkey 'thout popcorn dressin'. They stuffs the turkey with popcorn dressin', sews it up tight, sticks it in the oven; an' they know it's done when the dressin' blows the tail offa the turkey.''

When the laughter died down, most of it directed toward the man who had taken the bait, Buck walked up behind Cally and said, "Well, look who's here. I thought they would have hanged you by now.''

Cally turned quickly at the sound of the familiar voice. "Well, I'll be danged!'' he said; "If it ain't Buck!'' He got up and shook hands, pumping with his usual vigor.

As they walked away from the crowd around the campfire, Cally asked, "How's Cory?''

"Just fine, Cally. He healed fast and has adjusted very well to the loss of the arm.''

"An' your ma?''

"She's fine, too. Works as hard as ever, but she thrives on it.''

"That Sadie's a good woman. If I'da found me one like her when I was young, mighta amounted to somthin' myself.''

"You're a pretty fine person as you are,'' Buck said. "We feel lucky to have you for a friend. How have you been? We wondered about you. Pa wrote Uncle Tom, but he said you hadn't gone back there; and he promised to let us know if you showed up. We didn't know where to reach you.''

"I been all right. Kinda lost heart in goin' back to Texas. Just been knockin' around here in Tennessee. Tried to git in the army, but nobody's int'rested in a ol' coot like me. Heared there was a man here who wasn't so pa'tic'la, so I come over an' jined up with Cap'n Bill. You didn' git in no trouble over what happened back home?''

"No. Killing Caleb was plain self-defense. It wasn't all that plain about Sam, but they weren't sure whether I killed him, or you.''

Cally laughed. "That's what I figured an' why I strung 'im up. He was about dead when I got there an' wouldna lasted much longer, but he was live enough for me to enjoy it. Never had much likin' for bushwhackers.''

"I'm afraid we're all bushwhackers now.''

"War's diff'rent. How's your friend Randy?''

"Fine. He was wounded at Shiloh, but he's all right now. He's here with me; we're both on Forrest's staff.''

"What happened to Jethro?''

"Was he at the Barlow place when you got there?''

"Didn' see hide nor hair of 'im, but all three mules was in the yard. I put 'em in the lot.''

"He must have taken off after you left. One of the mules was gone. He never came back, but I ran into him between Coffeeville and Ripley, Mississippi, not long ago. He was in a Yankee uniform and had been running with a couple of Confederate deserters. If he joined the Union army, he must have deserted, too. I had a little run-in with him and one of the butternuts. Put a bullet in him; but from the way he was tearing through the wood, I don't think he was very badly hurt.''

"Too bad you didn' git 'im. He'll be trouble long's he lives.''

General Joseph Wheeler had been promoted to the chief command of the cavalry in the department; and Forrest was ordered to march to Columbia in Murray County, preparatory to being sent to break up the enemy's communications and to make a diversion in the rear of Grant's army in northern Mississippi and West Tennessee. The brigade took position in Columbia in the first week of December, prior to its move into west Tennessee. It was poorly equipped. Many of the weapons issued to the men were old and not efficient. Dibrell's regiment alone had 400 flintlock muskets. Forrest made application to Bragg for proper guns and equipment, but the Confederacy was too hard up for weapons and other materiel to supply them. Arms or no arms, Bragg informed him that he was expected to march at a very early date and must prepare for his expedition.

Forrest appreciated fully the dangerous character of the work he was now called upon to do. He was to cross a large, wide, unfordable river, the fifth in size in the United States, without the help of a bridge. This river, the Tennessee, in its upward sweep from northern Alabama to the Ohio, flows nearly due north, cutting the state of Tennessee in two. Its western shore was picketed by the cavalry of a brave and vigilant army. The western part of the state had the Mississippi River as its western boundary. On the north were Kentucky and the Ohio River; to the south, from Memphis to Corinth, was stretched the mighty and effective army of Grant. Once in this territory west of the Tennessee, swarming with an enemy well armed and equipped, there could be no escape except by recrossing the river. The stream was well patrolled by a fleet of gunboats to prevent incursions from the east and, if one was made, to prevent the possibility of escape.

Forrest sent a crew of men to the Tennessee near Clifton to build flatboats to ferry the troops across the river. Having heard nothing from them, he had Bill send two of his scouts to Clifton to ascertain the status of the construction. On December 8, he asked Buck to go to Bill's camp to find out when he expected the scouts to return. Upon arriving at the

camp, Buck saw Cally talking to a group of about a dozen men who
were assembled in front of him in a semicircle. Bill wasn't at the camp;
but one of his men knew where he was and volunteered to go get him.
While waiting, Buck walked over toward the group of men. He stopped
short of them but close enough to hear what Cally was saying.

"I don't know about that statement of yours, Smithers, that Yankees
is pretty smart people. I've seed some in my day what didn' take no
prize, like the one who loved apple pie so. There was a lady who run a
little eatin' place who made real good apple pie; fact is, she got kinda
famous for her pie; 'cause folks begin to talk about it, an' the word got
spread around. Well, there was a Yankee fellow who lived in a town
about fifty miles away who was a fool about apple pie; an' when he
heared about her pie, he just had to have some. He got on his hoss an'
rode fifty miles to her town; an' when he got there, he went in her place,
an' asked for some apple pie; an' she brung 'im a piece. 'Not a piece,'
he said, 'a whole pie.' 'A whole pie?' she asked. 'A whole pie,' he said.
So she got 'im a whole pie an' started to cut it. 'You want it cut into fo'
pieces or six pieces?' she asked. 'Just cut it into fo' pieces,' the Yankee
said, 'I don't believe I can eat six pieces.'"

Buck laughed. Every army ought to have a Cally, he thought.

On December 10, Forrest received orders to move. He had been
advised his flatboats were ready; but he did not believe his troops were
adequately equipped, and he again appealed to his commander for guns
and ammunition. The answer came back that they were not available
and he must do the best he could and go on without them. The two
flatboats were concealed near Clifton in a slough behind an island at the
east side of the Tennessee River. Forrest arrived there on December 15,
1862, with his command of 2,100 men, and began crossing the river,
mostly at night. He placed long lines of sentries up and down the river to
warn of enemy boats in the area. When one was sighted, the flatboats,
which could carry only twenty-five men and their horses, were run in
behind the island. Despite their precautions, the crossing was detected
by a southbound boat which reported it to Major General W. T.
Sherman. Sherman forwarded the information on to Grant, who was
now at Oxford, Mississippi, with his suspicion that the movement was
designed to draw them back from their purpose of going to Vicksburg.

Forrest's first stratagem was to make the enemy believe his force was
large, and he carried a number of drums with him to create the
impression he was accompanied by infantry. He was successful in this,
and his presence west of the Tennessee created great excitement in the
Federal army commands and caused the immediate movement of many

of their troops.[1]

After crossing the river at Clifton, Forrest moved his troops toward Lexington, with Russell's Fourth Alabama in the vanguard. About five miles east of that town, he met a cavalry force of 773 Federals supported by a section of artillery, all under the command of Colonel Robert G. Ingersoll. The Federal cavalry was pushed back across Beech Creek; and in a flanking movement led by Captain Gurley of Russell's regiment, the two guns and their crews were captured, and the Federal cavalry was put to flight toward Jackson. In addition to 11 killed and 11 wounded, 147 Yankees were captured, including Colonel Ingersoll.[2] Seventy badly needed horses were also taken. On the part of the Confederates, the fighting was almost wholly done by Russell's regiment and a section of Freeman's guns. The Federal cavalry was pursued until it reached Jackson, which was well fortified and heavily garrisoned with troops under the command of Brigadier General Sullivan. Forrest sent the Eighth Tennessee under Colonel Dibrell to break the railroad north of Jackson; and Russell was dispatched with his Fourth Alabama and Cox with the Second Tennessee battalion of cavalry to the south to destroy bridges, culverts, and trestles on the two railroads leading from Jackson to Corinth and Bolivar. With the remainder of his troops, Forrest made a great show of assault on Jackson in order to hold the Federal troops there while the details accomplished their missions.

Dibrell left Jackson on the night of the 18th, and by daylight of the 19th, reached Carrol Station on the Mobile and Ohio Railroad in time to fire a volley at a passing train. He dismounted the troops, charged a stockade at the station, and captured it after a feeble resistance, taking over a hundred prisoners and a large amount of ammunition, stores, tents, and other military supplies. The stockade was burned, as were supplies which he could not take with him. He was able to arm adequately over a hundred of his men who had only flintlock muskets.

At Jackson, the Union forces were in their breastworks and anticipating a general assault. Leaving a small line of skirmishers to keep up the appearance of an attack, Forrest moved northward and encamped on the night of the 19th at Spring Creek. That night the ordnance officer sent Buck to where the artillery units were encamped to get information from Captain Freeman about the condition of his ammunition. Just after he left that camp enroute back to Forrest's headquarters, he came upon Lieutenant John Morton in a heated confrontation with a large, burly man dressed in worn civilian clothing. The latter had a rifle in his right hand and was carrying a slab of bacon in his left. As he rode up to them, Buck heard the large man say in an angry voice to Morton, who was both youthful in appearance and small of stature, "Ain't no pap-sucking, two-bit officer gonna call me a thief!"

Buck quickly got down from his horse and walked up to the side of the two men, who were facing each other with such intensity that neither paid any attention to him, each keeping his eyes on the other.

"I'm telling you for the last time, you'll return to camp with me, and we'll find out where that bacon came from; or I'll put a bullet in you right here!" Morton replied as he began to unfasten the flap of his holster.

"The hell you will!" the man cried. He dropped the bacon and grasped his rifle with both hands as he began to raise and point it toward the lieutenant.

He had hardly started the move before Buck's hand went quickly to his right pistol; but instead of firing, he smashed it into the side of the large man's head at the temple. The burly man's knees buckled, and his eyes rolled upward as he sank to the ground unconscious.

"Mucha 'blige," Morton said, finally getting his gun out.

"Who is he?"

"I'm not sure, but I think he's one of Bill Forrest's scouts. I saw him slipping out of camp with the bacon and headed him off here. He didn't cotton to the idea of returning with me. Is Bill in camp?"

"Yes, his outfit's camped near us."

By this time, several artillerymen, attracted by the commotion, had arrived upon the scene; and Morton said to them, "Take this man and that bacon back to camp and see if you can find out where he got it." Then to Buck, "If it won't inconvenience you, I would appreciate your stopping by Bill's camp and asking him to come over. I know his men don't draw rations from the commissary, and I'm glad to share with them when we have it and they are short; but I don't like this thieving."

"Neither do I. The fellows have always shared with them; I don't know why he would do it." By this time, the artillerymen had gotten the suspected thief back on his feet and started back to camp with him and the bacon.

"Thanks again, Buck," Morton said. "I don't think I would have gotten my gun out in time."

The following morning, Dibrell, Russell, and Cox rejoined Forrest at the camp, all having successfully completed their missions. Leaving Russell and the Fourth Alabama at Spring Creek to cover his rear, Forrest again moved rapidly to the north, taking prisoners and leaving destruction in his wake.³

Forrest went into camp on the night of the 24th and rested his men and horses on Christmas Day. Food was plentiful, and the men were fed well on this holy day. Late that afternoon, Cally appeared at headquarters looking for Buck. He found him with Randy and several other members of Forrest's staff.

His usual light, bantering attitude was lacking; and Cally was seriously concerned as he said to Buck, "Need to talk to you for a min'it." As they started away from the group, Cally turned to Randy and said, "Maybe you oughta hear this, too."

When the three of them were out of earshot of the others, Cally said to Buck, "The man you clobbered over't the artill'ry camp—he's one of the scouts. Scroggins is his name, an' he's one helluva mean, no-good cuss. He was stealin' the bacon—don't know why; we had plenty in camp, but he was. Cap'n Bill shoulda run 'im off, but he didn'—just bucked an' gagged 'im.⁴ Scroggins is plenty mad about the whole thing an's been makin' the brag that he's gonna git you an' Lieutenant Morton."

"You think he's serious?" Randy asked.

"Dead serious. I can take care of this pretty quick, if you want."

"No. We need every man we've got until we get back across the river; but thank you, anyway. Does Morton know about it?"

"Don't think so."

"I'll tell him, so he'll be on guard."

"Maybe you better ride close to 'im, Randy, an' keep a eye on his back. Don't think Scroggins got the guts to come at 'im face to face."

"I'll do that," Randy said.

"I appreciate your letting me know, Cally." The scout started to leave and Buck asked him, "Did you have a good meal today?"

"Real good—almost as good as turkey an' popcorn dressin'," Cally replied with a grin.

"Nothin's that good," Buck responded.

As Cally left, Randy said to Buck, "Popcorn dressing? Never heard of it."

"An old Tennessee hill folks' recipe. You'll have to ask Cally about it. He'll be glad to explain."

"Maybe I will. Mother might like to have the recipe."

Buck laughed. "I doubt it."

Early on the 26th, Forrest turned his column southward along the railroad leading from Union City to Dresden and McKenzie. The bridge over the North Fork of the Obion, on the branch line running to Paducah, was destroyed. Forrest had most of his command concentrated, and it now included a battalion of 430 men under Lieutenant Colonel T. A. Napier which had joined him.

Informed that a heavy column of infantry was moving in pursuit from Trenton to Dresden, Forrest dispatched Biffle toward Trenton with his regiment to prevent surprise from that quarter. Forrest reached Dresden late on the 26th, capturing the town and destroying the Federal supplies and the railroad in that area. The next day he moved on to McKenzie in the direction of Huntingdon and Lexington. Here he learned that two brigades were moving to intercept him on his return to the river crossing at Clifton.

All bridges across the Obion which lay immediately in front of him had been destroyed, and the crossings were well guarded by Union forces. Forrest learned, however, that there was a bridge on an unused country road which was so rotten and unsafe as to be considered impassable, and it had been overlooked by the enemy. He reached that bridge, located between McKenzie and McLemoresville, shortly after dark on the 27th. Forrest joined his tired men in cutting timbers and repairing the bridge and its supports. Far into the night, the men, egged on and energized by the enthusiasm of their leader, labored in a sleety drizzle repairing the causeway, which ran for a quarter of a mile across a miry bottom on each side of the bridge. When nothing else could be found, precious bags of coffee and flour, captured from the enemy, were used to fill holes in it. Half of the troopers and their horses were moved across with little difficulty, but not so the wagon train and artillery.

When the wagons, heavily loaded with supplies and ammunition, reached the muddy, slippery, and dangerous causeway, the driver of the first wagon, who saw what was ahead, pulled his team to a halt, stopping all of those behind him.

"What in the hell's the matter?" Forrest yelled. "Keep them wagons movin'!"

"General, this causeway an' bridge ain't safe. There's no way we can cross here."

"The hell we can't! Git your damned butt down from that wagon. I'll take it across!" Forrest yelled, his anger rising.

As the driver climbed down, Randy said, "I'll take the next one."

"And I'll take the next," Buck volunteered.

The three officers climbed onto the wagons; and with Forrest leading, the train started across the causeway and bridge. The heavily loaded wagons soon began to mire and slide in the soft mud, sometimes slipping precariously close to the edge of the causeway. Forrest called up twenty men to each wagon; and with their straining and pushing, the train was moved across the river with only two wagons slipping over the edge and overturning, both of them loaded with ammunition. With Forrest raging and turning the wet, moonless night even darker with his cursing, the men waded into the icy water and managed to get the wagons upright and back onto the causeway. Fifty men were assigned to each piece of artillery, and they were able to move them over safely. The last of the troopers then crossed, and it was well past dawn when Forrest followed them.

Scouts brought information that a brigade of Federal infantry under Colonel C. L. Dunham had crossed ahead of them at McLemoresville, coming from the direction of Trenton and moving toward Huntingdon, and that another brigade under Colonel Fuller was several miles west of McLemoresville following him. Generals J. C. Sullivan and I. N. Haynie were travelling with Fuller. Forrest was about midway between these two columns, and they could have overwhelmed him had they known of his position. In front and to the south, and in direct line with his route to escape back over the Tennessee, was General G. M. Dodge with two brigades made up of seven regiments, two batteries of light artillery, and Stewart's cavalry, plus another regiment and section of artillery which had joined him at Purdy. To retrace his steps northward would mean almost certain destruction, for there was a large Union force behind him at Columbus. Forrest's force numbered 2,000 men as Biffle's regiment was absent at this time. Both men and horses were now exhausted by the terrible strain of constant marching, fighting, and labor during the past two weeks in cold, inclement weather.

Forrest waited until the enemy had passed ahead of him, and then moved to McLemoresville where he went into camp and rested his men. He left there at ten o'clock the following morning, the 29th, and marched south toward Lexington on a rough, very hilly, and miry road. He camped that night about nine miles short of Lexington and about two miles north of Parker's Crossroad, where a road leading south from Huntingdon through Clarksburg joined the one on which he was moving.

He dispatched his brother Bill with his irregulars on the road to Huntingdon to observe the enemy, report his movements, and retard his progress southward as much as possible. Captain Forrest ran into a heavy enemy column near Clarksburg moving in the direction of the Confederate camp. He sent a courier to General Forrest with this information and tried to check the advance of the enemy, but with little success. He lost a few men but inflicted greater loss upon the Federals.

Because of the jaded condition of his men and horses, Forrest decided to chance a battle with the enemy the following morning in order to give them a much needed rest. He sent the courier back to his brother with orders to do all he could to check and delay the enemy and to keep headquarters informed of the situation. He dispatched Captain McLemore with three companies of the Fourth Tennessee to proceed via back roads to Clarksburg on the Huntingdon road to hold that approach in close observation and as a provision against additional enemy forces coming unannounced from that direction.

At four o'clock on the 30th, Forrest roused his men and soon had them moving toward the crossroad. Before reaching it, he received word from Captain Forrest that his irregulars had been pushed back until the enemy was now near the Confederate main body. Forrest threw his men into battle line; and about the same time, the enemy, numbering slightly more than 1,800 men under Colonel Dunham, appeared and formed to attack.

Forrest dismounted Dibrell's and Russell's regiments and pushed them forward as skirmishers with 150 mounted men on each flank and brought up his artillery to a favorable position. The Federal artillery, four pieces, had opened upon the Confederates with spirit. Forrest's guns responded vigorously, dismounting one of the enemy guns and killing several horses at the first fire. The others, with their infantry support, quickly retired to better cover back toward Parker's Crossroad. They were followed by yelling Confederates.

At the crossroad, the Federal forces were again formed, this time in two lines and facing north—a brigade of infantry, the three remaining guns in the battery of artillery, and a detachment of cavalry—a force slightly larger than Forrest had at hand. The Confederate leader again dismounted all of his men except approximately 100 on each flank. He disposed them in line of battle nearly parallel to and north of the enemy. His artillery was divided into three sections, one in the center and the other two on the flanks. The Confederate artillery opened the engagement in earnest, quickly driving the enemy under cover of a ridge in their rear. Forrest advanced his line of yelling Rebels; and after an hour of spirited fighting, drove the enemy back into a skirt of wood about a half of a mile south of the crossroad. There they held and, in turn, made a strong and well led attempt to regain the ridge from which they had been driven. When the Confederates reached the crown of the ridge, they found the enemy had advanced to within eighty yards of them; and they opened a withering fire upon the Yankees with all arms. The enemy was obliged to fall back, leaving their dead and wounded and two pieces of artillery which had been immobilized from the loss of their horses.

The Federals retired behind a strong fence in the wood, and Forrest concentrated his artillery upon them, silencing their one remaining cannon. About eleven o'clock, the Federals made a resolute forward movement to within sixty yards of the Confederate cannon but were repulsed with slaughter as Forrest's artillery enfiladed their battle line. As they retreated to their previous position, Colonel Napier, without orders from his commander, charged them with his battalion right up to the fence behind which they were posted; and he fell there, mortally wounded. His men retired with considerable loss from their valiant effort.

Forrest sent Russell around the enemy's left and Starnes around their right to take them in flank and reverse, and he repositioned his artillery to enfilade the enemy line. Observing that the Confederate line had been diminished, Dunham made another charge, which was met and stopped by grape and canister from the Confederate artillery. At the same time, Russell and Starnes had reached the Federal rear and captured Dunham's wagon and ammunition trains. Hemmed in from three sides, the Yankees retreated in disorder and stopped about a half or three quarters of a mile south of the crossroad, some having broken across the road into a cornfield. White flags began appearing all along the line of the Federal forces, and the firing on both sides immediately ceased. Suddenly Colonel Carroll of Forrest's staff, greatly excited, rode up to his commander.

"General," he said, "a heavy line of infantry is in our rear, and we are between two lines of battle. What shall we do?"

"We'll charge 'em both ways!" Forrest snapped. Having sent McLemore out on the road from Huntingdon to prevent such a surprise, Forrest could not believe the enemy had been able to come upon him unexpectedly. To satisfy himself the report was true, he galloped with Carroll to the indicated quarter, where he found Fuller's troops had arrived and were already in battle order. Forrest was within eighty yards of their line before he saw them. A Federal officer well in advance of his troops called to him, "Halt and surrender!"

"I've already surrendered!" Forrest replied. "I'll bring up my command an' surrender 'em properly." With that, he wheeled his horse and galloped to safety, Colonel Carroll following.

Forrest rejoined his troops and started them at double quick time to the south toward Lexington. Fuller, moving his men at the same pace, overran the horse holders of Cox and Napier; and the men of those commands were unable to get off the field. Cox and about 250 men were captured. When Fuller's men reached the ridge formerly held by the Confederates, their artillery poured a deadly fire into the Rebels. The horses of four caissons and two brass cannons were killed, and these guns and caissons had to be abandoned. Wheeling with his escort and about fifty of Dibrell's men, with Buck and Randy close by, Forrest charged the enemy guns. They dispersed the gunners and threw the infantry into such confusion that it gave the other Confederate troopers time to regain their horses.

As the contingent with Forrest rode upon the guns in this charge, Randy's horse stepped in a hole and went down, throwing him over her head. Fortunately neither rider nor mount was injured, but the others in the charge were well ahead of him. Among them was Scroggins, who was trailing Buck. When they had closed upon the artillery, Buck fired the last shot from his second belt gun. As he was returning it to the holster to get one from the saddle holsters, he heard a voice behind him and turned to see Scroggins "I been waitin' for this, Lieutenant; I coulda did it before, but I wanted you to know it was me."

Buck saw Scroggins raise his rifle to his shoulder, pointing it toward him. He spurred Skin in the hope the horse would carry him out of the line of fire and clawed at the saddle holster trying to get a loaded pistol. Rifles and pistols were firing all around him, but the report of one seemed to drown out all the rest. Buck expected the impact of a bullet but felt nothing. Then he saw the end of Scroggins' rifle sag; and suddenly the man's body jerked as a second shot rang out above the others. The big scout slowly rolled from his saddle. Behind him Buck saw Forrest with a smoking pistol in his hand and knew it was from him the two shots had come. Their eyes met; and with a quick nod to show his appreciation, Buck got his pistol from the holster and returned to the fight.

Calling off his men, Forrest galloped with them to the main body of his troops, capturing on the way three caissons pulled by frightened horses running toward the Confederate line. Colonel Starnes, realizing the situation from the noise of the renewed battle, fell upon Dunham's rear and kept him occupied while Forrest's troops moved out of the enemies' range. They kept on south to Lexington, arriving there on the night of December 31, 1862, bringing with them Dunham's wagon and ammunition trains.

The men and animals were fed and rested, and the wounded were cared for. Strangely, General Jeremiah C. Sullivan did not pursue.[5] Forrest was in a high state of rage and fury. He had always prided himself in the fact that he knew where the enemy forces were and that he could guess what their next move would be. The thing he tried to guard against by sending McLemore to Clarksburg to cover the road from Huntingdon had happened; Fuller had come unexpectedly onto the battlefield in his rear. From McLemore he had heard nothing, as though he and his squadron of three companies had disappeared from the face of the earth; yet, he knew Fuller could not have captured or killed all of them. The loss of Cox and Napier and their men was a military blow that was hard for him to accept, but the loss by capture of Major Strange, his adjutant and friend, was a personal tragedy. The anger seething within him was evinced by his sharp and profane tongue and lack of patience with those around him. As usual, when he was in one of these moods, even his close associates walked softly and tried to avoid him. He had no sooner arrived in Lexington than he sent for his brother, Bill. Upon the latter's reporting to him, he asked sharply, "You know anything about McLemore?"

"No. Haven't seen 'im."

"Didn' think you would. I sent 'im to Clarksburg, behind Dunham, to guard the road from Huntingdon. He let Fuller git by 'im an' come up on my rear without lettin' me know. I ain't seen hide nor hair of 'im since he left. I don't believe Fuller coulda got 'em all. I want you to send your best woods man, somebody who can move around in a country full of enemies, back to Clarksburg to find out what in the hell happened to him an' his men."

"I guess Callaghan would be the best for that."

"Git his butt on the way!"

Although the stay in Lexington was to be short, a temporary hospital was set up to get the wounded out of the cold, dismal weather. Satisfied that his men were fed and made as comfortable as possible under the conditions, Forrest, still fuming from the events at Parker's Crossroad, which had robbed him of an overwhelming victory over Dunham, made his way to the hospital to visit his wounded. As he went among them, shaking their hands, talking to them about their homes and their families, consoling them as well as he was able, the anger and venom inside him gradually diminished; and when he went into a room where the surgeons were amputating a man's leg, he stood and watched for a few minutes with tears coursing unashamedly down his cheeks and beard. Not wishing to see more of this, he turned quickly and went outside. There he ran into Buck and Randy.

"When I have to kill one of my men, I want to know why." he said to Buck testily. "Who was that today, an' what brought it on?"

"His name was Scroggins, one of Bill's scouts. Lieutenant Morton caught him stealing bacon from his camp; and when he confronted him,

Scroggins was going to shoot Morton. I happened by and hit Scroggins on the side of the head with my pistol. He swore to get both of us. I guess I was first.''

"The next time a man needs killin', do it yourself; don't leave the dirty work for somebody else!'' With that he walked away.

"Yessir,'' Buck said in a low voice, mostly to himself; for his commanding officer had no interest in his reply.

At two o'clock on the morning of January 1, 1863, Forrest roused his sleeping troopers and continued the march toward the Tennessee River at Clifton. At daylight another halt was made, and the men were given three hours' rest. During this time, the prisoners were paroled and released to make their way back to their units as best they could. Major Jeffrey Forrest was sent forward with a detachment to raise the flatboats and bring them to the west side of the river. At about half past nine, the entire command rapidly followed Major Forrest. Speed was necessary, because the general believed the numerically superior enemy force he had left at Parker's Crossroad would surely pursue him; and his scouts had brought information that General Dodge was moving to interpose his troops between the Confederate cavalry and the river.

He had marched for more than two miles when his advance guard brought word of a large body of enemy cavalry in the immediate front. The regiments of Dibrell, Starnes, and Biffle were hurried into line of battle and advanced until they came in sight of the enemy in battle array. The order to charge was given, and the Union cavalry was swept from the field.[6]

After the defeat of the Federal cavalry, Forrest left one regiment of his command to act as rear guard and placed with them a section of artillery under Lieutenant Bill Williamson.[7] He told him to fortify as best he could with rails, logs, and anything else at hand; and with the aid of the detachment of cavalry left with him, he was, if attacked, to fight to the last in order to give the remainder of the command time to cross the river.

Randy, sitting close by on Chessy while the order was given, said to Forrest, "With your permission, I'd like to stay with Williamson.''

"There may not be much future in it, but you can stay,'' Forrest replied.

Bill quickly threw his guns in line as directed. When they galloped up to the selected position and unlimbered, the horses and caissons were started to a safer place away from the guns. Forrest saw this and did not understand their rapid movement to the rear. Thinking the drivers were acting cowardly, he struck the one in the lead across the shoulder with the flat of his saber, at the same time yelling, "Turn them horses around, an' git back where you belong; or by God, I'll kill you!"

"General, I'm movin' accordin' to tactics," the man responded.

"No you ain't! I know how to fight, an' you can't run away with the ammunition chests!"

The artillerymen reluctantly returned the horses and caissons to the area of the guns.

Shortly after noon on January 1, the Confederates reached the Tennessee River. As luck would have it, the gunboats were not in sight. The first thing Forrest did was to hurry four of his guns across the river with the ammunition chests, the artillerists, and a few of his men. As soon as they were on the east shore, two guns were placed in position at the point of crossing; and one was sent upstream and the other downstream to keep off any craft which might be approaching from either direction. Scouts were sent up and down the river to warn of the threat of any gunboats. About two thousand men and horses, six pieces of artillery, and a train of wagons and captured stores were put across a river six hundred yards wide in the short period of ten hours.[8]

Forrest's men had had only one full night of undisturbed rest. Although he lost 500 men by capture, killed in action, or wounded, he killed, wounded, or captured 1,500 of the enemy. His men crossed the Tennessee with inadequate arms but re'..rned properly armed and with a surplus of modern and effective weapons. He also brought out many stores and supplies, including 1,800 badly needed blankets, thousands of rounds of small ammunition, and a great quantity of ammunition for his artillery. With volunteers added to his force along the way, he had more men after he crossed back over the river than he had at the start of his campaign; but most important, his force, which had been made up principally of raw recruits, became seasoned veterans in a very short space of time.

Chapter XI

Central Tennessee

After Forrest left Bragg in Kentucky and went to Murfreesborough to raise and organize his new brigade, the latter committed a serious tactical blunder by allowing Buell to get past him in the Federal army's dash for Louisville. In an inconclusive battle fought at Perryville, Kentucky, on October 8, 1862, in which only a part of each army was engaged, there was no clear victor; nevertheless, Bragg decided to abandon his campaign and withdrew southward. Buell failed to pursue diligently, and he was replaced by Major General William S. Rosecrans, who commanded the troops under General Grant which had earlier defeated in northern Mississippi the Confederate forces of Major General Sterling Price at Iuka and of Major General Earl Van Dorn at Corinth.

Bragg's retrograde movement continued southward to Murfreesborough. Here he stopped and with 37,000 men met Rosecrans, who had followed him with an army of 45,000. A desperate and bloody battle was fought by the banks of Stone River on December 31 at the same time Forrest was engaged at Parker's Crossroad. Bragg won the advantage on the first day, crushing Rosecrans' right; but the Federal center, under Major General George Thomas, held firm. Bragg failed to capitalize on his initial success, and the two armies were inactive as they faced each other the second day. Bragg attacked the following day but was repulsed with heavy losses from the Federal artillery. There was only sporadic fighting on January 3; and after dark, Bragg drew off in retreat to Tullahoma, thirty-six miles to the south. Both armies claimed victory; Rosecrans lose 13,000 men, while Bragg lost only 10,000; but the former held the contested ground. Rosecrans' army was so battered, however, that he could not pursue; and he was unable to resume the offensive for six months.

It was a tired and bedraggled force Forrest crossed to the west bank of the Tennessee on January 1, 1863, but their spirits were high. The success of the raid, and the way Forrest had brought them out after successfully avoiding a devastating defeat at Parker's Crossroad, gave the men of the new brigade full confidence in their commander. In turn, he looked with great pride upon these men, most of whom he now considered to be seasoned troopers despite their brief time in the army.

Leaving vedettes along the river and pickets farther to the east, Forrest moved his tired troops to a bivouac five miles away on the road to Mount Pleasant. Here he stayed two nights to give his men and their horses a rest. The first night, he sent word to the troops through their commanders of his appreciation for their good job and told them to get some well-earned rest. One of the new recruits asked a seasoned veteran, "You ain't going to sleep with the enemy on our tail, are you?"

"Course, I am," the veteran trooper responded, "Old Bedford said to."

Forrest moved his command leisurely to Mount Pleasant. Shortly after arrival there, Captain Bill Forrest, who had not seen his brother since the river crossing, came to Forrest's headquarters to make a report; and he ran into an unexpected confrontation.

"Do you know what happened to your man Scroggins?" the general asked.

"No. I haven't seen him since the fight at the crossroad. He must have been lost there; none of the men know what happened to him."

"Well, I know! I killed the son-of-a-buck; he was tryin' to kill McCord. Did you know he had tried earlier to kill Lieutenant Morton?"

"Yes, I knew that."

"What did you do about it?"

"He's not under the military code of conduct; and I thought about sending him away but decided against it, as I was afraid he'd go to the enemy and give information about us, so I had him bucked and gagged."

"Well, you didn' buck an' gag 'im long enough. Let me tell you, Bill; an' I don't aim to repeat this ag'in. Under military code or not, if one of your men ever tries to kill an officer, or even threatens to do it, I want that man shot. How you go about it is your business, but you take care of it. You gotta have control over them men, or they'll become no more'n a mob. Do you understand?"

"Yessir."

"That scum bottom of a Scroggins damned near killed one of the best men in this brigade."

On orders from Bragg, Forrest moved his command to Columbia where the men and horses found the rest they badly needed. While here, an inventory was made of the supplies and equipment captured in the raid, and among these was a regulation officer's sword of very fine steel which Forrest took for himself. He tested it by running his finger along its dull edge. Like all officers' swords, it was sharp only a small distance from the point. He had it ground to a razor's edge the entire length of the blade; he wanted an effective weapon in battle. To him war meant fighting, and fighting meant killing; and he intended to do his share.

At Columbia the brigade was joined by Captain McLemore with the three companies that had been missing since before the battle at Parker's Crossroad. When he reported to the general he was met with an unexpected blast.

"Where in the hell've you been?"

"When I got to Clarksburg, sir, I couldn't locate Captain Forrest to join up with him. I found that a large Federal column under Colonel Dunham had already passed through Clarksburg headed south, so I presumed that Captain Forrest had been pushed back by it toward Parker's Crossroad."

Before he could continue further, Forrest interrupted, "What do you mean, join up with Captain Forrest? Your orders were to git behind Dunham an' guard the road from Huntingdon to keep any more Yankees from comin' on my tail unexpectedly from that direction, which you didn't do. Fuller come down that road an' hit me from the rear an' damned near destroyed us after I had Dunham whipped good an' about to surrender!"

"General, I have written orders here which were given me by Major Strange," McLemore said, reaching into his coat pocket for them.

"Le'me see them orders," Forrest demanded.

McLemore handed a folded paper to the general, who opened it and read the document carefully. He then burst into a raging frenzy of profanity, ending with, "These ain't the orders I told Strange to give you!"

"They're the only ones I received."

Forrest glared at McLemore, but the spunky captain met his belligerent gaze without flinching. Forrest's hot anger quickly cooled, and he said rather calmly, "I s'pose so. Accordin' to this, you were to proceed by back roads to Clarksburg to join up with Captain Forrest to assist 'im in observin' an' delayin' the enemy.''

''Yessir.''

''Well, what happened?''

''I knew I couldn't join Captain Forrest by following Dunham on the road from Clarksburg to Parker's Crossroad, so I asked my men if any of them knew the area; and one of them claimed to be familiar with it. He said he knew a road which joined another that would take us around the enemy. We moved out quickly with him as a guide. He got us on the wrong road, and we went away from the crossroad instead of toward it. It was well past daylight before I discovered the error. By the time we got to the crossroad, you had quit the field; and a large infantry force was between us. We were northeast of you and tried to cut around the enemy to join up with you to the south but kept running into Yankee patrols. I thought the best thing to do was to save my command, so we headed back northeast and managed to cross the Tennessee near Perryville. We had no rations nor feed for the horses and had to forage for them. This slowed us up, and we rejoined you as soon as we learned where you were.''

''You done all right, Captain, specially in holdin' onto them orders. I'd hate to court-martial an' shoot an innocent officer,'' Forrest replied with the glimmer of a twinkle in his eyes.

''Not as much as I,'' McLemore responded with a nervous laugh.

A few days after arrival in Columbia, Buck asked Randy, ''Have you seen Cally or heard anything about him?''

''Not a word other than his being sent to find out what happened to McLemore.''

''I'd better check on him.''

Buck found Cally at the scout camp; the old scout was looking tired and even thinner than usual. ''Hadn't seen you so didn't know whether you made it back,'' Buck said.

''I made it, but there was times I had my doubts; I didn' git in till yestiddy. I went to Clarksburg lookin' for Cap'n McLemore. I picked up his trail an' followed 'im almost to the river but kept gittin' cut off by enemy patrols. They was ever'where. Soon's I knowed he was on this side, I crossed over myself. Had to swim the river with my hoss. Wouldn' recommend it for a reg'lar thing this time of the year.''

''Sounds like you had it kind of rough.''

''No rations for three days, an' Yankees ever'where I turned. I was afeared of makin' a fire till I got back on this side of the river an' damned near froze my butt off. I'm beginnin' to believe I'm a bit too old for this kinda work an' been thinkin' about givin' the whole thing up. Fact is, I ain't warm yet. Let's go over by the fire."

As they drew near the blazing campfire, one of the half dozen men sitting around it lifted up a jug and said, "How about a drink, Cally? You, too, Lieutenant, if you like."

"The lieutenant here ain't a drinkin' man, but can't say the same for myself. I never refused but one drink in my whole life, an' I didn' understan' the question then."

Cally took the jug and, lifting it up to his shoulder, took a big, long drink from it. Wiping the back of his left hand across his mouth, he said as he returned the jug to its owner, "That's mighty fine stuff, Turner. These ol' bones need somethin' to warm 'em up."

"Figured you might want a little nip; heared you had a bath t'other night," Turner said with a grin.

"The coldest I ever had!"

"When did you ever have one before?" another of the scouts asked.

"Let's see. When was the last time I swum a river? Musta been the summer of '59."

"I swear, Cally, you must be about the dirtiest man in the whole world," the scout replied.

Cally looked at him with a pained expression, "You know, Jim, you could hurt my feelin's with that kinda talk. You see, I just happen to know the dirtiest man in the world. Yessir, know 'im personal; an' I don't like bein' considered in the same breath with him. He was a Yankee who come out to Texas on his way to Californy, but he run out of money an took a job on the ranch where I worked. Me an' Skunky, that's what we called 'im, was out huntin' strays an' made camp by a creek one night. Settin' aroun' the fire after we et, I smelt the most gosh-awful stink I ever smelt in my life. It woulda peeled the paint off a privy. I looked at Skunky an asked 'im if he'd did somethin in his pants, an' he said that he was afraid he had; so I asked 'im why he didn' go to the creek an' clean hisself up. You wouldn' believe what that dirty Yankee said."

"What did he say?" Jim asked eagerly.

"He said, 'I ain't th'ough, yet.'"

While the men, most of whom had gathered after Cally began telling his story, were roaring with laughter, Buck looked at his gloating friend who was thoroughly enjoying their reaction; and he knew Cally would be around for a while—he would never leave such an appreciative audience.

The next day, Bill Williamson came to headquarters and sought out

Randy. "I've got a problem and need your help," he said.

Randy saw an artillery manual in his friend's hand and thought that he knew the problem. "Glad to, if I can," he replied.

"It's about the general's ordering the horses back to the area of the unlimbered guns. It's wrong to endanger the horses and caissons that way, but I believe the general will take drastic action if we move them to a position of safety in the future."

"Your manual covers this, doesn't it?"

"Yes, but I'm afraid he'll blow his top if I show it to him."

"He could, but I don't think so. He's more anxious than you that things be done right. Would you like for me to go with you?"

"I surely would."

They found Forrest in his tent. Randy knew it was a ticklish situation and approached the general as tactfully as he knew how. He said, "Lieutenant Williamson would like to explain to you the necessity of moving the artillery horses and caissons away from the guns when they are unlimbered for action." He waited anxiously for the general's reaction and response.

"I see," Forrest said. "Well, go ahead; I ain't got all day."

"Sir, as you know, artillery pieces become primary targets for both the enemy artillery and assault forces," Bill said, talking rapidly. "If the horses and extra ammunition are kept by the guns, we are in more danger of losing them. Loss of the horses would immobilize the guns, and loss of the ammunition would make them useless. I have marked the pertinent part of the artillery tactical manual covering this, if you would like to read it. Also, if you have time, I can give you a demonstration of how field guns are unlimbered and placed for action."

"I'll take time. Can you do it tomorrow morning?"

"Yes, sir."

"I'll be at your camp at seven o'clock, an' I'd like for you to leave the book with me. I'll fetch it back tomorrow."

Forrest watched the drill the following morning very closely. When it was over, he said to Bill, "Thank you, Lieutenant; that was a fine demonstration. Would it inconvenience you for me to keep this book a few more days?"

"No, sir. Lieutenant Morton has another."

"Good. Now I'd like to speak to the man I ordered to take the hosses back to the guns."

The artilleryman was brought to Forrest, who apologized for having rebuked him when he was properly performing his duty. Within a week the general had mastered the artillery manual; and from that time, he took a very personal interest in his artillery, often placing and sighting the guns himself.[1]

Near the end of January, Forrest received orders from Major General Joseph Wheeler, who had been promoted to be chief of cavalry, to take 800 men and proceed to the Cumberland River to interrupt the navigation of Federal boats on that stream. He was given discretion to choose the point where he thought the mission might best be accomplished and selected a position near Palmyra, not far from Fort Donelson, where he masked his guns, hid his men, and waited for any passing craft.

He was joined by General Wheeler, who brought with him a portion of Wharton's brigade. Wheeler concluded that the Federals must have learned of the ambush and that they would not send any boats on the river at that time. He thought Fort Donelson could be captured easily and decided to move against it.[2] Forrest was opposed to this course of action, feeling the results from an assault upon such a formidable position, one which could not be held permanently, would not justify the losses that would be incurred. He strongly urged that the undertaking be abandoned, but Wheeler could not be swayed from his decision. The premonition of disaster weighed so heavily upon Forrest that, on the morning of the engagement, he spoke to Major Charles W. Anderson and Dr. Ben Wood, the latter a surgeon assigned to his command.

He said, "I have a special request to make of you in regard to the proposed attack on Fort Donelson. I have protested ag'inst the move, but my protest has been disregarded. I intend to do my whole duty, an' I want my men to do the same. I have spoken to none but you on this subject, an' I do not wish that anyone should know of the objections I have made. I have this request to make. If I am killed in this fight, you will see that justice is done me by officially stating that I protested against the attack, an' that I am not willin' to be held responsible for any disaster that may result."

After the Federal forces captured Fort Donelson and the nearby town of Dover, they had built their defenses around the town more than around the fort. Wheeler believed that a simultaneous rush from two sides against those defenses would be successful. The town and Fort were garrisoned with 800 men of the Eighty-third Illinois infantry and formidable light and heavy artillery, all under the command of Colonel A. C. Harding.

The Eighth Texas (Terry's Rangers) of Wharton's brigade was sent out on the road toward Fort Henry, from which it was reported reinforcements for Dover, under Colonel Lowe, were coming. Forrest's troops and the remainder of Wharton's were dismounted for the assault, Forrest from the east and Wharton from the west and southwest. Under a flag of truce, a message was sent to the commander of the fort demanding immediate and unconditional surrender. The Federal commander declined to surrender his forces without an effort to defend his position. The Confederate artillery promptly opened upon the advance guns of the Federal field batteries, forcing them to retire to the vicinity of the fortifications.

Forrest, his men dismounted and waiting for the moment set for the coordinated attack, observed several companies of Federal troops marching at double quick time from the fort toward the river. They were moving to occupy a ravine a little beyond their central position, but Forrest thought they were attempting to escape. Without waiting for the scheduled attack, he mounted his men and charged what he thought was a fleeing enemy. These Federal troops opened on the Confederates and then ran back into their breastworks. There they joined the entrenched Federals and continued firing on Forrest's men. To their fire, the garrison added the discharge of several of their guns loaded with grape and canister. Horses and men went down in dreadful slaughter. Forrest's horse was hit and fell within a few steps of the guns. When his troops saw their commander go down, they thought he had been killed and retreated under the shower of grape and canister being rained upon them by the enemy artillery.

Forrest was not badly hurt. He disentangled himself from the dead horse and hastily beat a retreat from the withering fire, taking whatever cover he could find. Buck and Randy had been in the forefront of the charge and joined the other troopers in the withdrawal after Forrest fell. Buck looked back and saw his commander was alive and, in trying to escape the deadly fire, had taken cover behind a tree stump. Seizing the reins of a riderless horse, he raced to the dismounted Forrest; and when he saw that the latter was not seriously wounded, he tossed the reins of the extra horse to him. Before Buck could dismount to help him, Forrest yelled, "I can make it! Git the hell outa here!"

Buck needed no urging; he wheeled and galloped back to a point of safety. Forrest, using the horse as a shield, mounted it and was not far behind.

The discomfited troopers were again formed for assault, this time on foot; and simultaneously with the advance by Wharton's column, they rushed forward, Forrest again on horseback at the head of his detachment. The Federals were driven from the houses, which they had occupied as sharpshooters, and on all sides from the outer entrenchments. They took cover in the redoubts of the fort from which they again poured a severe fire into the Confederates. These pressed forward to the breastworks but were unable to gain a footing within the entrenchments. Forrest's horse was shot down, the second killed under him that day; and he was badly shaken in the fall. A number of his men were killed within a few feet of the breastworks, but none made it into them.

The troopers now took refuge in the nearby houses, from which the Federals had been driven. Again they saw Federal troops running toward the river; and, taking this as a charge on their held horses, they rushed back to protect their mounts.[3] The Federals, however, were only running to join other troops in rifle pits where their reserve ammunition was kept.

On the left, Wharton's command easily drove the Federals into their works, capturing a few prisoners and one twelve-pounder, brass, rifled cannon, which was brought from the field. The garrison was stubborn, holding off the Confederates until almost nightfall, at which time the Rebels had a secure position within ninety yards from the main rifle pits of the defenses. Before making a third assault, a conference was held; and it was found there was insufficient ammunition for another one. It was also learned that enemy reinforcements were arriving and had already fired upon the Confederate outposts. Decision was made to pull out; but before doing so, a detachment was sent to the river to destroy a boat loaded with supplies. As they retired, other details were sent to gather up all the wounded who could be carried away on horseback or in wagons and to bring off the captured gun and other property, among which was a large supply of blankets found in the Federal quarters. These were badly needed as the weather was extremely cold.

The Confederate troopers, worn out by the work of the day and dispirited by defeat, went into bivouac about four miles from Dover and shivered disconsolately through the freezing night.

Here in a roadside house, by the light of a log fire, Generals Wheeler, Wharton, and Forrest talked over the dismal failure of the day. Wheeler wrote his report admitting defeat without a word of criticism for either of his subordinates. Forrest, however, was in an uncontrollable mood; and his irritability was not lessened by the injury received when his horse fell, his fatigue, and the loss of one-fourth of his men killed, wounded, or captured.

General Wharton was sitting on one side of the fireplace opposite General Wheeler, who was dictating his report to one of his staff. Forrest was lying down on his waterproof coat in front of the fire, his head on a turned-down chair and his feet on the hearth. The noise of a horse arriving, followed by the voice of Major Anderson, brought

Forrest to his feet. He went outside and found his adjutant so nearly frozen that he had to help him from his horse and into the house. Without ceremony he went to the only bed in the room, jerked the cover from two officers occupying it, and brusquely ordered them to get out. He took off Anderson's boots, rolled him in a blanket, put him in the vacated bed, and returned to his place on the floor.

General Wharton said, "When the signal was given, my men moved forward, but were met with such a severe fire that, with the exception of the Fourth Georgia and Malone's battalion, they gave way. As we fell back, I noticed the garrison from our side of the fort rush across to the other side to take part against General Forrest's attack; and as his command caught the fire of the entire garrison, he must have suffered severely."

Forrest spoke up in an excited and angry tone, "I have no fault to find with my men. In both charges they done their duty as they've always done."

"General Forrest," Wheeler said, "my report does ample justice to yourself and to your men."

Forrest replied, "General Wheeler, I advised ag'inst this attack an' said all a subordinate officer should've said ag'inst it, an' nothin' you can now say or do will bring back my brave men lyin' dead or wounded an' freezin' around that fort tonight. I mean no disrespect; you know my feelings of personal friendship for you, an' you can have my sword if you demand it; but there is one thing I do want in that report to General Bragg—tell 'im that I will be in my coffin before I will fight ag'in under your command!"[4]

The man who so deservedly earned the name "Fighting Joe Wheeler" never showed greater restraint or class. He knew Forrest and admired his many good qualities; but he realized that, justified or not, a tempest was raging in him which had to be met with gentle words and manner rather than by strict military discipline. Quietly he said, "Forrest, I cannot take your saber, and I exceedingly regret your determination. As the commanding officer, I take all the blame and responsibility for this failure."

The next morning, the disheartened Confederates began the return march to their former positions, which took them in the direction of Charlotte. The weather continued extremely cold; and all of the men suffered intensely, especially the wounded. Covering only fourteen miles the first day, the march was halted by the severity of the worsening weather. Intelligence was received that a Federal column under General J. C. Davis was moving on Charlotte to intercept them, necessitating a change of route. The Confederates moved slowly along the valley of Yellow Creek, obliged to leave the slippery, icy road and travel through the adjacent fields and woods. Their subsistence and forage exhausted, commissaries with detachments were thrown out on each flank to collect rations for the men and feed for the horses. On February 16, to avoid collision with General Davis, the Confederate column was deflected farther to the right. The following morning, the suffering men and animals reached the bank of the Duck River opposite Centreville and found the river had risen from the recent rains to the point the local people said it was unfordable. Drawing his troopers to a halt by the freezing stream, Forrest announced, "I need a volunteer to see if it's true we can't cross here."

Without a word, Randy put spurs to his horse and rode into the river. He moved steadily out into the cold, swiftly flowing stream, breaking the ice which had formed near the bank. The water deepened steadily and was soon up to the saddle skirts of his horse. He was almost to the middle of the stream when the bottom dropped off so quickly that Chessy appeared to have stepped off a ledge as she plunged suddenly into deep water. Thrown off balance by the unexpected and awkward movement of his horse as she stumbled and sank beneath the icy water, Randy was swept from the saddle; and he also went under. When he came to the surface, his first thought was to get to Chessy. The frightened horse was about ten feet away, struggling in the freezing water and headed for the bank opposite the one from which they had come. As the current carried them downstream, he tried to whistle to her but could not purse his numb lips properly to do it. He knew that he must keep active, or numbness would take over his whole body and immobilize him. Striking out with strong strokes, he tried to swim to the horse; but Chessy was moving away from him at about the same speed he was able to make. The weight of his heavy clothing and boots was slowing him down, and they were getting heavier as the clothes absorbed water and more water seeped into his boots. He was making no headway, and the freezing temperature was beginning to have its effect. The last few days of bitter cold, fighting, marching, and lack of proper nourishment were also taking their toll; his strength was going fast, and the heavy clothing and boots were dragging him down.

"Chessy," he called, his voice barely above a faint whisper. "Chessy."

Buck had not been there when Randy rode into the river, having been sent on an errand by the ordnance officer. He returned at this time; and as he rode up to Forrest and his staff, who were watching the struggle in the water, he thought he recognized Chessy and quickly looked around for Randy. Not seeing him close by, he asked anxiously, "Is that Randy?"

"Yes," Forrest replied.

Buck turned his horse and headed downstream, trying to get through the troopers crowded along the bank. "Let me pass! Let me pass!" he cried as he pushed his way in the direction the current was carrying Randy. The troopers gave way and opened a narrow lane for him. He was so intent upon getting down the stream that he was unaware Forrest was following closely behind him. When he reached a point below Randy and Chessy, he turned his horse to enter the river; but Forrest spurred his own horse and moved up and grabbed Skin's bridle. "You can't git to 'im in time, an' I don't aim to lose another man in that river."

"Let me go, dammit! I gotta try! I gotta try!" Buck cried.

"Stay where you be!" Forrest commanded sharply. 'He's closer to the other side, an' help's there if he makes it. He'll make it on his own, or he won't make it atall. It's in his an' God's hands now."

Randy went under again but once more fought his way to the surface. As his head came above the water, he gulped fresh air into his heaving lungs; and then he saw Chessy's head in front of him. He reached toward her and managed to grasp the nose band of her bridle. Pulling himself close to the horse, he moved along her neck until he reached the pommel of her saddle. He was able to get his right foot into the stirrup; but when he tried to climb into the saddle he lacked the strength to do it and slid back into the water. It was well he did, for the water was warmer than the air above it. He managed to hang onto the saddle as the horse struggled to reach the opposite bank. Numbness began to come over him, and he almost blacked out; but he held onto both the saddle and consciousness with grim determination. He could sense a change in his mare's movements but was too dazed to realize she was now walking instead of swimming. His feet soon touched the river bottom, and maintaining his grasp of the saddle became more difficult as his body gradually emerged from the water. He held on as long as he could; and when his hands slipped loose, he fell into water about two feet deep. The effort to get up seemed too much, but he made it; and as he stumbled and crawled toward the bank, there were suddenly mounted men on each side of him, lifting and helping him. By the time they reached dry land, ice was already forming on the upper part of his clothing.

"My horse," he said in a barely audible voice. "Please look after my horse." Then darkness mercifully came over him.[5]

Buck sat rigidly on his horse watching his friend struggle for his life.

Never had he felt so helpless; all he could do was watch and pray—and pray he did, as he had never prayed before. He knew Forrest had been right to stop him. There was no way he could have gotten to Randy in time, but he wanted to try—he still wanted to try—anything but just sit here and watch. It was with great relief he saw Randy grasp Chessy's bridle; but it was with even greater relief that he saw the two men, who had followed the struggling pair down the river, ride into the water and bring the exhausted trooper to the bank. He was brought out of his deep concentration on what was going on across the river by a gentle voice filled with tenderness and understanding.

"He'll be all right now, Buck," Forrest said.

"I hope so," Buck replied, not at all convinced.

Going several miles upstream, the Confederate cavalry found a ford and crossed the river, removing the danger of further pursuit by General Davis. Buck crossed with Forrest; and they had hardly reached the other side when he said, "I'd like permission now to see about Randy."

"Would it do any good if I refused?" Forrest asked with the trace of a smile.

"Not a damned bit."

"Then I guess I'll have to give it. If you wait for the baggage wagons, you can git 'im some dry clothes."

"I'll borrow a couple of blankets and make do with them."

"I wish you both luck. If he's in a warm place, stay there till tomorrow at least. We're headed for Columbia, an'll make camp there. Join us when you can."

Buck had no difficulty locating Randy. He learned in Centreville that the man pulled from the river had been taken to the nearest house, the home of a local farmer named Joseph Carter.

The Carters had a nice but unpretentious home, much like that of Buck's parents in Perry County. They lived alone as both sons were in the Confederate army and their three daughters were all married with homes of their own. Mrs. Carter, a motherly type, had taken charge immediately when Randy was brought half frozen to her door. She and her husband quickly stripped him of his icy clothing and wrapped him in warm blankets. They placed him on a bed and rubbed his whole body, covered by the rough, woolen blankets, to restore the circulation. This revived him, and they plied him with hot herbal tea which had been strongly laced with Tennessee sour mash whiskey. By the time Buck arrived, Randy was sleeping soundly. After he assured himself that his friend was all right, he left the room without awakening him and returned to the living room with Mr. and Mrs. Carter.

"You look like you could use a drink yourself," Mr. Carter said. "Sit down while I get it."

"I don't usually drink," Buck replied, "but today I can use one."

Both Mr. and Mrs. Carter left the room and soon returned with a bottle and two glasses for the men and a cup of tea for the lady. Mr. Carter poured a large drink for Buck and a moderate one for himself.

"Here's to your friend's health and quick recovery," Mr. Carter said, raising his glass.

"I'll drink to that," Buck replied also lifting his glass. After taking a sip of the fiery liquid, he continued. "Thank you for taking care of him. He wouldn't have lasted long in the cold after what he had been through."

"We were glad to do it," Mrs. Carter replied. "We got two boys of our own in the Confederate army. I like to think somebody'd do the same for one of mine."

"I hope they never need it," Buck replied.

"If you're wonderin' about his horse, I had Jesse, one of our darkies, dry her off and rub her down," Mr. Carter said. "She's been watered and fed and now she's covered in a blanket in a good clean stall. I think she'll be all right."

"I'm glad to hear that," Buck replied. "Randy puts a lot of store in that mare."

"And well he should. She's not only a fine horse, but the men who pulled him out of the river said she was headed for the bank, but turned and swam back to him when he called her. They don't believe he would have made it if she hadn't. You might like to know, your horse is getting the same treatment as his."

"I appreciate that. He can use a good feed; he hasn't eaten too well these past few days. About Randy, can he stay the night here with you?"

"We wouldn't have it no other way," Mrs. Carter said; "and you, too, if you don't have to go back to your army tonight."

"I don't have to return, but I don't want to impose. I can find a place in town."

"Impose, my foot!" Mrs. Carter exclaimed. "You don't know how good it is to have company like y'all. This house's been quiet as a tomb since the boys left. Besides, I think your horse ain't the only one that ain't et well lately."

"You're very hospitable, Mrs. Carter; but before getting into one of your beds, I'd like to take a bath."

"I've already got water heating for that," she replied matter-of-factly. Buck laughed to himself. He thought of his mother's doing the same thing when she thought Cally would be sleeping in one of her clean beds. He took a close look at himself—this had been a hard campaign—and he couldn't blame his hostess at all.

As he lay in the warm bed that night trying to go to sleep, Buck dwelt upon the events of the day. As he recalled his friend's fight for his life in the river, he remembered Forrest's kind, gentle words as the two men carried Randy from the water; and he realized that, for the first time, Forrest had called him by his nickname.

In the latter part of February, much to Forrest's regret, Russell's Fourth Alabama, which he highly regarded as a veteran fighting unit, was detached from his brigade; and its place was taken by Holman's and Douglas' battalions, which were consolidated into the Eleventh Tennessee cavalry regiment. The remnants of Cox's and Napier's battalions were consolidated into the Tenth Tennessee cavalry and placed in the brigade. The necessity of discipline and drill had not appeared at first so important to Forrest as it did now with his widening military experience; and although very busy at the front, those troops not on reconnaissance or scouting details were drilled daily, and dress parades were scheduled regularly.

Still stewing from the defeat and his own poor showing at Dover, Forrest was ready for action. With his usual ability to get information about the enemy, he advised General Wheeler that there were 2,000 mules, lightly guarded, near Nashville which could be taken by a few hundred men; but Wheeler refused his request to make the expedition to capture them.

On February 19, he notified Wheeler to be prepared for a strong movement by the Federals from Franklin. He had received information that two regiments of cavalry had reached Franklin, making about 2,000 cavalry and 4,000 infantry there; and they were evidently preparing to move southward against the Confederates as they were repairing bridges and putting the telegraph in order. He suggested that, if the enemy did move toward them, a coordinated effort by his, Van Dorn's, Roddy's, and Wharton's commands could capture the advancing troops or cut them to pieces.

In early March, Major General Rosecrans, in order to obtain more definite information of the positions and purposes of the Confederates, ordered reconnaissances in force from Murfreesboro in the direction of Unionville and the Duck River and from Franklin toward Chapel Hill and Spring Hill. It was this latter movement which Forrest's scouts had detected, and the Southern cavalry intercepted them at Thompson's

Station. The Confederates won a complete victory in which many of the Federal troops surrendered to Forrest.[6]

Late on March 5, Van Dorn retired south with his prisoners and captured property, leaving a strong line of pickets in the area of Franklin. On the 11th, Forrest was intrusted with a division of cavalry made up of his and Armstrong's brigades. He was assigned to independent outpost duty in the area of Spring Hill, Tennessee, his picket line extending from Thompson's Station to College Grove on the Harpeth River. He had his scouts swarming in the area to the north of this line; and from them learned there were two Yankee detachments, about 800 in all, at Brentwood and at a stockade about a mile and a half from that town. These troops were not far north of Franklin and separated from each other a sufficient distance to be attacked in detail. He requested, and received from Van Dorn, permission to move against them.

On March 24, Starnes, in command of the old Forrest Brigade, was ordered to cross the Harpeth River six miles east of Franklin, which lay between Forrest and his objectives and was occupied by a large Federal force under Major General Gordon Granger, and to move in the direction of Brentwood, where 531 men of the Twenty-second Wisconsin were guarding the station on the Nashville and Franklin Railroad and a supply depot. Starnes was to send a force along the turnpike between Brentwood and Franklin to cut the telegraph line and tear up the railroad track, to send two regiments to attack the stockade, and to post the Fourth Tennessee so as to prevent the escape of the enemy garrison in the direction of Nashville or Triune. Starnes was to be on the grounds and ready to attack at daylight on the 25th, with the understanding that Forrest, with Armstrong's brigade and artillery, would join him in the assault.

Starnes moved out with Biffle's regiment, his own Fourth Tennessee under Captain W. S. McLemore, and a part of Edmondson's regiment; and at midnight he crossed the Harpeth at Davis' Mill. Fifteen men were sent forward to capture the enemy's pickets, but they were unsuccessful in doing this. The sentries wounded two of the detachment and alarmed the garrison at Brentwood. One of the sentries rode rapidly south into Franklin and notified General Granger of the attack.

Before three o'clock, Starnes reached the Wilson turnpike near Brentwood, cut the telegraph wires, and destroyed the track near Mallory Station. A strong picket force was then established on the Franklin Turnpike at Holly-Tree Gap. He positioned the remainder of his troops for the assualt and waited the arrival of his commander with additional troops and artillery. Daylight came, but Forrest with Armstrong and the artillery did not appear. Deeming himself too weak to attack so strong a position without cannon, and having waited until half past seven for his commander, Starnes thought Forrest had been compelled to abandon the undertaking; and he withdrew rapidly eastward to the Hillsborough pike. Here he learned to his great chagrin that his commander had passed by another road toward Brentwood early that morning.

Forrest had met with an unexpected delay in getting across the Harpeth River with his two guns; and when he reached Brentwood, Starnes had left. Not daunted by this miscarriage of plans, he proceeded with the business at hand. Two companies of the Tenth Tennessee, under explicit instructions, were hurried down the Hillsborough pike to guard his rear from that direction. Two other companies were sent to the pike in rear of the enemy to prevent their escape and to warn of the approach of relief from that direction. The remaining six companies and his escort were led in person to the right of the road running from Brentwood to the Hillsborough pike. To the left of this road he ordered Armstrong to move with his brigade and two of Freeman's guns and to attack at once the enemy in the stronghold.

By this time Union skirmishers were encountered; and Forrest directed Randy, with a white handkerchief on the end of his rifle, to advance and demand the usual immediate and unconditional surrender, with the Murfreesboro attachment of no quarter if resistance was made.[7] Not fully convinced of the vulnerability of his position, Colonel E. Bloodgood, commanding the Federal forces, politely invited the Confederate general to come and take him if he could. Forrest accepted the invitation. The six companies of Cox's Tenth Tennessee were dismounted and ordered to attack the Federal position in front; and Armstrong was directed to move up his men on foot, along with Freeman's artillery, and attack from the other side.

Meanwhile, Colonel Bloodgood was not idle. Early that morning, after Starnes had so rudely awakened him, he had loaded and hitched up his wagon train in the hope of escaping to the north in the direction of Nashville. Several companies of his command were formed as the advance guard of his retreating column. Thinking to make a run for it and break through before the cordon was completed, he started for Nashville. As the advance companies moved off, they had not gone over 400 yards before Forrest attacked them with his escort; and they rushed back to the fortified camp.

At this juncture, Major DeMoss, with the six companies of the Tenth Tennessee, drove in the Union skirmishers and was closing in on the

Federal position from the front. The escort had followed the flying train guard to within short range of their stronghold; and with equal eagerness, Armstrong came up from the opposite quarter, and Freeman ran his guns into battery. With no hope for aid from any source, Bloodgood deemed it best to surrender. Taken by the Rebels were 521 men of the Twenty-second Wisconsin, a number of Teamsters, and a large supply of stores in the depot which included rations, camp equipage, tents, and other military materiel.

Fully aware that his position this far within the enemy lines, and between two large bodies of troops stationed at Nashville to the north and Franklin to the south, was a dangerous one, Forrest, before rushing to attack the stockade guarding the bridge over the Harpeth, ordered Armstrong to hurry the prisoners, army wagons, and all portable captured property toward the Hillsborough pike and thence to the rear. He was then to destroy the depot, tents, and everything which could not be carried away. Colonel J. H. Lewis of the Sixth Tennessee cavalry was directed to dash down the highway toward Nashville, drive in the enemy pickets in front of that city, and create the impression that an attack was impending.

Forrest, with the Fourth Mississippi, the Tenth Tennessee, his escort, and Freeman's two guns, hurried to the stockade and bridge a mile and a half away. He surrounded the position and, without any preliminary parley, unlimbered one of the guns and fired a salute which sent the echoes reverberating through the hills and splinters flying among the astonished troops of the Nineteenth Michigan infantry.

Turning to Randy, Forrest said, "Lieutenant, take in a flag of truce an' tell 'em I have 'em completely surrounded; an' if they don't surrender, I'll blow hell out of 'em in five minutes; an' I won't take one of 'em alive if I have to sacrifice my men in stormin' the stockade."

Randy searched in vain for the white handkerchief used at Brentwood, but it had been lost; and it seemed to be the only one in the command. "Strip off your shirt," Forrest commanded, smiling in appreciation of the humor of the situation.

Randy took off the garment, tied it to the end of his rifle and rode off as the messenger of peace.[8] Captain Bassett, who commanded the garrison, realized the hopelessness of his situation and surrendered himself and the 274 men under his command. The railroad bridge and all supplies which could not be brought off were destroyed. The prisoners, along with eleven captured wagons and three ambulances, were hurried away as Forrest moved toward Spring Hill on the Hillsborough pike.

When Starnes struck the two Federal outposts, five and seven miles from Franklin, between three and four o'clock on the morning of the 25th, the picket who escaped and rode into Franklin had roused the sleeping garrison there. General Granger tried to warn Colonel Bloodgood at Brentwood, but the telegraph wire had been cut. He sent the balance of his cavalry, four regiments, under Brigadier General Green C. Smith, to reinforce the Brentwood garrison. When Smith reached there, he found that the Confederates had completed their work at that place and had left with the captured prisoners, wagons, and guns. Part of his force was sent rapidly after the raiders, and the balance went in the same direction by another route after the captured train. Three and a half miles from Brentwood, the tail of the train procession was struck.

The companies of the Tenth Tennessee and the Fourth Mississippi (about 400 men left after the detail to guard prisoners had been made) were, under General Armstrong, directed to follow and protect the captured train. The Tenth Tennessee was in the rear, but was destined not long to occupy that position. A dozen stragglers from one of Armstrong's regiments, seeking what they might devour or carry away, lingered too long about the burning storehouse at Brentwood and were leisurely following in the wake of the rear guard. They suddenly found themselves run into by the Sixth Kentucky (Union) and the Second Michigan cavalry, charging with drawn sabers at full speed. Without firing a shot or making resistance enough to give Major DeMoss warning that the Union troopers were so close upon him in force, these stragglers stampeded and dashed into the rear company of the Tennessee detachment, throwing them into panic, which spread through the command like a prairie fire. In utter confusion these troopers, accustomed to better conduct before the enemy, broke and converted the organization into a helpless mob in which each man was trying to outrun the others. Some kept to the road, while others took to the woods and byways to escape. Those on slow horses had a bad time of it, and some of them were sabered and captured.

Colonel Gordon, with only three companies of his Fourth Mississippi, was in front and heard the stampede in time to throw one company into line; and about 200 yards farther back the other two companies were formed. The Union advance was in this way temporarily checked; but the Seventh Pennsylvania, lining up behind the Kentuckians, and swinging around Gordon's flank, soon sent him and his Mississippians in wild retreat in wake of the remnant of the Tenth Tennessee.

The Federals had now retaken many of the wagons loaded with the captured property and promptly turned them toward Franklin.

Forrest had just reached the head of his retiring column with his escort when he heard of the disaster in his rear. "Come on, men!" he yelled to his escort and led them back toward the point of confusion.

When he came in sight of the retreating troopers, he threw his escort in front of them. "Halt! Halt, dammit, an' fight the enemy!" he yelled, waving his saber over his head.

Seeing some were paying no heed to his commands, he seized a shotgun from one of the escort and emptied both barrels into a squad of fleeing Rebels. The drastic measure was effective; the panic-stricken troopers stopped and formed into line of battle.

Fortunately, Starnes, who earlier in the morning had gone in pursuit of a foraging train some two miles distant from his position on the Hillsborough pike, heard that the captured train had been followed by Smith's brigade, hurried back, and came on the scene just as Forrest was rallying the disordered troops of Armstrong's brigade. With Forrest and Starnes at hand, General Smith was hit hard and forced to fall back to Brentwood. The Federal general had succeeded in getting possession of several wagons captured at the stockade and cut the mules loose and stampeded them. Lacking teams, Forrest was compelled to burn some of the wagons. He brought away three ambulances, nine six-horse wagons, two two-horse wagons, sixty mules, and six horses. Many of the soldiers who had inferior weapons exchanged them on the field, placing their old guns in the wagons.[9]

The people of the South and the army, while not detracting from the courage and ability of Van Dorn, gave Forrest the chief credit for the successes at Thompson's Station and Brentwood. Of the 2,000 prisoners captured, 1,800 surrendered directly to Forrest. The affair at Brentwood, following so closely the one at Thompson's Station, came very nearly to being the cause of a personal encounter between Generals Van Dorn and Forrest. Both men were of unquestionable courage and high spirit, quick to resent an apparent indignity, but equally quick to make amends when convinced of error. The fact that neither lacked personal ambition did not help the situation.

The confrontation took place at Van Dorn's headquarters in Spring Hill. Other than the two generals, Major J. Minnick Williams, a member of Van Dorn's staff, was the only person present. Van Dorn was obviously in a foul mood. He said to Forrest, "My quartermaster informs me that you have not turned over to him all of the arms and property you have captured."

"I directed it to be turned over. Some of my men had inferior arms such as shotguns an' flintlocks. They were allowed to swap 'em for better guns before the equipment was turned over.''

"That's not the way it's done. Materiel captured from the enemy is the property of the Confederate government—not of the individuals or units capturing it.''

His anger beginning to rise, Forrest replied, "Well, that's the way I been doin' it. The Confederate government hasn't properly equipped any of my commands, an' I've had to do it from what we captured from the enemy.''

"That's not the way it shall be in the future," Van Dorn stated firmly; and before Forrest could reply, he continued, "and there is another matter which concerns me. I am informed that several articles published in the Chattanooga Rebel, in which the honors at Thompson's Station and Brentwood were claimed for yourself, were written by one of your staff.''

The color which had been rapidly rising in Forrest's face and neck became intense with his rage, and he replied in heated anger, "I don't know nothin' about them articles you refer to, an' I demand from you your authority for this assertion! I'll hold him responsible an' make 'im eat his words, or I'll run my saber through 'im; an' I say to you as well, that I will hold you personally responsible if you don't produce the author!''

Van Dorn turned to Williams, "Major, do you know the author of these publications?''

"I do not; and I think, General, that you have done General Forrest an injustice in the suspicion that the articles originated from his headquarters.''

Van Dorn replied quickly, "I do not assert, nor do I believe that General Forrest inspired those articles or had any knowledge of them.''

Mollified by Van Dorn's statement, Forrest said, "General Van Dorn and I have enough to do fightin' the enemies of our country without fightin' each other.'' He did not press his disagreement with Van Dorn over the disposition of captured enemy arms and equipment; he had no intention of complying with his commanding general's oral directive which would leave his men in the field with inadequate weapons while he transported captured arms of better quality back to his base.[10]

From March 25 until April 10, Forrest and his command were engaged on picket, scouting, and outpost duties between Spring Hill and Franklin. They then moved with Major General Van Dorn in a reconnaissance in force and diversion to attack Franklin. When Starnes approached Franklin with his brigade, he was riding with Biffle's regiment, which was moving in front; then at considerable interval came four pieces of artillery under Freeman, followed by the remainder of the brigade strung out along the pike on which they were marching. Union cavalry under Brigadier General Stanley unexpectedly, to both forces, collided with Starnes' column at the point of the artillery. Freeman, his guns, and twenty-six artillerymen were captured.

Starnes counterattacked; the guns were retaken, and Stanley was forced back across the Harpeth river. It was asserted that Freeman, a heavy man who was not in the best physical condition, was shot dead by a member of the United States Fourth Regular cavalry because he did not move rapidly enough as the Federals retreated.

Forrest was overwhelmed with grief at the death of his chief artilleryman. He had arrived on the field and joined in the assault which drove Stanley's troopers across the Harpeth. As he came to the spot where Freeman's body lay, on the route of the federal retreat, he was deeply upset. He dismounted and took Freeman's hand in his own to see if he was really dead. With tears in his eyes and a voice trembling with emotion, he said, "Brave man; none braver."[11]

The retreat of Stanley ended the fighting; and at dark, the Confederates retired to their old campground at Spring Hill.

Chapter XII

Straight After Streight

The enlisted man on duty outside the office of Brigadier General Thomas J. Wood, at the headquarters of the Federal Army of the Cumberland in Murfreesborough, Tennessee, came to attention at the approach of Colonel Abel D. Streight, commander of the Fifty-first Indiana infantry regiment. "Is General Wood available?" the colonel asked.

"Yes sir; go right on in, Colonel," the soldier responded as he opened the door.

Colonel Streight, who was holding in his left hand several maps rolled up together, went in; and the general officer sitting behind a table at the far side of the room looked up. "Come in, Abel," he said affably.

"Thank you, General. I've been giving some thought to what you mentioned the other day about General Rosecrans' wanting to cut Bragg's supply route south of Chattanooga. I've come up with a rough plan which I believe will not only accomplish that, but it will also make possible the destruction of many of the munitions and manufacturing plants in northern Georgia."

"Have a seat, Abel; and let's see what you've got in mind. I know General Rosecrans is anxious to do this, but we don't want another fiasco like that of the Andrews Raiders and the locomotive chase. Attaining the objectives you mentioned would be of great importance to the general's strategic plans. He thinks that when he moves against the Confederate army, Bragg will fall back to Chattanooga, a naturally defensible stronghold. If the railroad south to Atlanta can be destroyed, Bragg would probably be forced to withdraw into Georgia, possibly as far as Atlanta."

Ignoring the invitation to sit down, Colonel Streight went to the table and unrolled the maps, exposing one of Tennessee and the northern parts of Mississippi, Alabama, and western Georgia. With a finger, he traced a route across a portion of northern Alabama. "In the

210

mountainous and hilly section of this state are a lot of local people who are loyal to the Union,'' he said. ''In fact, we have two companies of cavalry who came from that area. They have relatives there and are familiar with the country's topography. First, we select for the mission a special force of infantry veterans who have already demonstrated their mettle. They will be mounted and moved to Eastport, Mississippi, by river transport so both men and animals can start from that point free of fatigue. Behind a diversionary attack up the Tennessee Valley toward Tuscumbia, Alabama, they will break off and make a dash across the sparsely settled hills and mountains, where communication facilities such as telegraph and railroad are almost nonexistent, to Rome, Georgia. They will be well on their way before pursuit can be organized to go after them. Surprise, speed, and the enemy's lack of communications should insure complete success of the foray. After destroying the factories and plants around Rome, the force would then destroy a long stretch of the railroad line between Atlanta and Chattanooga.''

''You would use infantry rather than cavalry?''

''Yes, but I'd rather not say why. We would pick men who have already displayed their bravery and endurance in battle. They would be supplied with the best arms and equipment available for the mission. The two companies of Alabama cavalry would, of course, have to be included.''

''The route marked on the map is the one you propose to be taken?''

''Yes, General. It goes through some pretty rough territory; but that should be an advantage, for it will be hard for the enemy to get information about our movement.''

''I think you've got something here, Abel. Leave the map with me; I want to take this up with General Garfield. I'll be in touch with you.''

Brigadier General James A. Garfield, chief of staff to General Rosecrans, was enthusiastic over the proposal and favorably recommended it to his commanding general. After several meetings, the details of the plan were worked out. Most of Colonel Streight's proposals were adopted, and the diversionary force was to come from Grant's army at Corinth. Because of the rugged terrain, it was decided the men would be mounted on mules rather than horses as the former were surer of foot and able to stand greater hardship with less forage.

To distract attention from Streight's raid, and at the same time to fight off any pursuing column, the body of infantry and cavalry from Corinth, under the command of Brigadier General Granville M. Dodge, was to precede the expedition, drive all Confederate forces up the valley of the

Tennessee River in northern Alabama, attack Tuscumbia, and there hold them engaged until the flying column got a running start.

The highly intelligent and capable Streight was given the honor of leading the raid and, on April 7, 1863, received an order to proceed to Nashville to outfit his command as speedily as possible, "for an expedition into Alabama and Georgia for the purpose of destroying railroads in that country." He selected for the venture his own regiment, the Fifty-first Indiana; the Seventy-third Indiana. Colonel Gilbert Hathaway commanding; the Third Ohio, Colonel Orris A. Lawson commanding; and the Eighteenth Illinois, Lieutenant Colonel Andrew F. Rogers commanding. Supporting these infantry units were the two companies of Alabama (Union) cavalry and a section of twelve-pounder mountain howitzers, making a total of 2,000 men. On the transports disembarking them at Eastport would be a brigade of marines which, with the escorting gunboats, were to support the forces driving eastward along the Tennessee River.

General Dodge was sent from Corinth with a force of 5,500 infantry and cavalry to create the diversionary drive on Tuscumbia. He was made aware that his role was solely to support Streight's raid by a communication from Rosecrans which read: "Colonel Streight, with near two thousand picked men, will probably reach Eastport by Thursday. Dodge with the marine brigade and the gunboats, can occupy or whip the Tuscumbia forces and let my force go directly to its main object—the destruction of the railroads. This great enterprise, fraught with great consequences, is commended to Dodge's care, enjoining on him to despatch Streight by every means to his destination. Nothing should for a moment arrest his progress."

Streight was delayed. He embarked his troops aboard transports and moved them to Palmyra on the Cumberland. Here he landed on April 11 and crossed overland to the Tennessee River at Fort Henry. The transports moved down the Cumberland, down the Ohio, and up the Tennessee to Fort Henry where the raiders were to be loaded aboard them again. Streight discovered that many of the mules were young colts and unbroken, and time was lost in breaking them to the saddle. He did not reembark his troops on the transports until Friday, April 17.

Upon arrival at Eastport on April 19, Streight left immediately for a conference with Dodge, who was encamped at Bear Creek twelve miles to the east, and did not return until midnight.[1] While he was gone, the cargo of mules was unloaded; and these noisy animals, one and all, began to bray, the sound of their combined voices carrying up and down the river valley. The braying of mules was nothing new to some of Colonel Roddy's Confederate cavalrymen, who were hovering around the Yankees' encampment ready to pounce upon any loot or target of opportunity.[2] That night they slipped into the corral and with kicks, yells, and the firing of guns, stampeded the mules. Daylight revealed 400 were missing. All that day and part of the next were spent by Streight's men scouring the nearby country searching for them. About 200 were recovered, the others falling into the hands of the enemy.[3]

Streight marched out of Eastport on the afternoon of April 21 and brought up the rear of Dodge's troops, which were continually skirmishing with Roddy's brigade. Roddy did such a fine job of delaying them that Dodge did not reach Tuscumbia until almost dark on the 24th; and Streight, held up in replacing his mules, was not able to start his dash for Rome until one o'clock on the morning of the 27th.

At Spring Hill, on April 23, a message arrived from General Braxton Bragg directing Forrest to make a forced march with his old brigade to Decatur, Alabama, where he was to unite with Roddy, take command of the Confederate troops, and check the Federal advance up the Tennessee Valley. Upon receipt of this order, Colonel Edmondson's Eleventh Tennessee cavalry was dispatched immediately to cross the Tennessee at Bainbridge, Alabama, and effect a junction with Roddy as soon as possible. Readying his men and horses rapidly, Forrest followed with the remainder of his brigade.

Upon reaching the Tennessee at Brown's Ferry near Courtland, Alabama, on April 26, Forrest summoned Colonel Dibrell, commanding the Eighth Tennessee, and said to him, "Take your regiment an' one gun. Move along the north side of the river makin' as big a show as possible. Start collectin' boats as if to cross a large force in the rear of the Federals near Florence. Put out word that Van Dorn is comin' with his command. I want Dodge to think he's got more to contend with than what's in front of 'im.''

Forrest crossed the river with the remainder of his brigade and joined Roddy to dispute the further progress of the Federals. Although it was intended that Dodge move only as far as Tuscumbia, Streight insisted, after learning that Forrest was coming, that he push on beyond there; and Dodge did so, forcing the Confederates back to Courtland. It was here on the evening of the 28th that a man showed up at Forrest's headquarters and asked to see the Confederate commander. Randy took him to Forrest.

"General, this is Mr. James Moon, who has just arrived from Tuscumbia; and he claims to have some valuable information for you,'' Randy said.

"What kind of information?'' Forrest inquired.

"General, a large force of men mounted on mules left Tuscumbia yesterday morning in the direction of Moulton. I don't know their purpose or destination."

"How many were there?"

"I don't know. I heard them estimated at about 2,000."

"Who is in command of 'em?"

"His name is Streight, Colonel Streight."

"How did you git here, Mr. Moon?"

"By riding around the Federals in a big circle."

"If the information you have given me is accurate, you may've done a great service for your country." Then to Randy he said, "See that Mr. Moon an' his hoss are fed an' took care of, an' git word to the staff an' regimental commanders that I want to meet with 'em as soon as possible."

By the time his key men gathered, Forrest had made his plans. He had no idea of the objective of the mounted enemy, but he knew he must move against them immediately. He gave explicit directions as to the disposition of his troops whose duty it would be to confront Dodge and hold him where he was or to retard any pursuit by him. A courier was sent to Dibrell with orders to attack at once Dodge's outposts near Florence, to use his artillery freely, and to create the impression that a large force was threatening the rear of the Union commander. He hoped this would draw Dodge back as least as far as Tuscumbia and remove him as a threat to pursue. In order to prevent the possibility of a return of the raiders to unite with Dodge's column or to prevent any reinforcements reaching them from this source, he sent Roddy with his Alabama regiment, Edmondson's Eleventh Tennessee, and Julian's battalion to interpose those troops between Dodge and Streight. Roddy was then to follow after the raiders. Forrest selected Starnes' and Biffle's regiments, two pieces of Morton's artillery, and Ferrell's six pieces, formerly with Roddy, to go with him. These units were speedily prepared for the pursuit, and this he looked after personally. He selected the best horses and harness and double-teamed his artillery and caissons. He even stood by to see the ammunition distributed carefully and directed the company commanders to tell each man that, no matter what else got wet, he should keep his cartridge box dry. He had the farriers busy shoeing horses and tightening loose shoes. Three days' rations were cooked and shelled corn issued for two days' forage.

Streight had left Tuscumbia at 1:00 a.m. on the 27th in a hard rain. The poor road, turned into slush by the deluge, made progress slow. He did not reach Moulton until the afternoon of the 28th, and here he fed and rested his tired cavalcade. At 1:00 a.m. on the 29th, he moved eastward toward Blountsville. Already a few of his mules had broken down, and they were abandoned.

At the same hour, Forrest moved out of Courtland in a cold, drizzling rain on a muddy, slippery road for Moulton, sixteen miles southward. Steadily throughout the night, and well into daylight of the 29th, the Confederates rode without halt. The mud was deep, and the night so dark the animals could scarcely find their way along the road. At eight o'clock, the column stopped for an hour to feed and rest the horses; and then they moved on to Moulton, arriving there before noon.

In the meantime, Colonel Streight had kept going at a steady gait, making seventeen miles on the 29th and reaching a defile known as Day's Gap which leads to the summit of Sand Mountain. The pace was telling on his animals, and he lost more mules along the way; so he began to pick up all mules and horses he could find in his line of march, stripping the area of them.

Sand Mountain is the southwestern termination of the Appalachian range. It rises 500 feet above the adjacent valleys, and the summit is a plateau which varies in width from twelve to twenty miles. In this area, the top is undulating, cut by small streams or creeks with steep banks, some like small canyons or deep ravines. The banks are heavily fringed with small trees and dense mountain laurel. Away from the streams there is fairly heavy growth of larger trees, predominantly oak, hickory, and pine. These topographical features make it well adapted for defensive warfare, much to Streight's advantage. At the foot of this mountain, Streight rested his troops for the night, near the mouth of the defile leading to the top.

At Moulton, Forrest's troopers had taken another hour to rest and feed their horses. Just as the bugle sounded to "saddle up," the sun broke through the clouds; and as Forrest mounted his horse and gave the command, "Move up, men," twelve hundred hats were lifted and the Rebel yell split the air. To Forrest it was a great and moving moment. He knew his men were ready to pitch into any enemy he faced.

Through the rest of the day, and on into the night while Streight's men were sleeping, the Rebel troopers reeled off mile after mile, not stopping until midnight, by then only four miles short of Day's Gap. Here Forrest learned the Union troops were encamped at the foot of the mountain, and he knew they were now within striking distance. He told his men to feed their horses and rest until near daylight. Rolled in their blankets and oil cloths, the weary troopers were soon asleep all along the side of the road. It took several hours for the column to close up. The trying pace had told on many of the horses, and it was almost daylight before the last of the stragglers caught up. These were allowed a short rest before following the main column.

Not all of the Confederates had been permitted to rest. Captain Bill Forrest and his scouts were sent on ahead to ascertain what the enemy was doing. Getting between Streight's vedettes and his camp, the scouts captured the vedettes without alarming the main force and moved within observation distance of the enemy campfires. Sending couriers back to General Forrest with the prisoners and information about the enemy, the captain allowed his men to rest. Their sleep turned into a short nap; for before daylight, they were awakened by the braying of nearly 2,000 mules in one mighty effort which sent echoes reverberating through the Alabama mountains.

The Federal commander had his men fed and on the march before full daylight. At the head of the column, he moved slowly up the narrow, rocky defile toward the summit of the mountain. When the advance reached the crest, the rear guard and some loiterers were still lounging about the campfires. Suddenly, from a distance of no more than 500 yards, a cannon boomed; and a whizzing shell exploded among the startled stragglers, followed by a charge of Rebels with their bloodcurdling yells. In wild disorder, the rear guard and stragglers abandoned the campfires and cooking pots as they chased after their main column.

Instead of pursuing immediately, the hungry Rebels stopped to pounce upon whatever food they could find in the abandoned campsite; and valuable time was lost before Captain Forrest could be sent after the enemy with his scouts. Among other things the Yankees had left in camp were about fifty broken-down mules.

When Forrest reached the scene, he realized the impracticability of attacking the enemy by direct assault; so he ordered Biffle's and Starnes' regiments, the latter commanded by Major McLemore, to hasten by a neighboring pass and take the enemy in flank and rear.

As Streight's column moved across the Sand Mountain plateau, his rear guard was steadily followed and pushed by Captain Forrest's scouts and the advance guard of the pursuing Confederates. General Forrest's orders were, ''Shoot at ever'thing in blue, an' keep up the scare!''

About two miles beyond the western edge of the plateau, Streight knew he had to make a stand; and here he laid his first ambush. He had the ideal spot, a ridge circling to the rear, his right resting on a precipitous ravine and his left on a marshy creek. He had skirmishers extended beyond each flank to guard against surprise, and the mules were in the rear and out of range. He had hardly gotten his men in position when his rear guard, the two companies of Alabama cavalry, came scurrying down the road with Bill Forrest leading his men on their heels. As soon as Streight's men passed through the gap in the line left open for them, the Federals from either side of the road poured a furious and effective volley into the Confederate scouts. A Minie ball crushed the captain's thighbone, and several of his men were killed or wounded by this deadly fusillade before they could check their horses and run out of range.

General Forrest now rode to the front to inspect the Federal position. He had at hand only a portion of Edmondson's and Roddy's regiments, Julian's battalion, his escort company, and the remnants of Captain Forrest's scouts. In the hard ride since leaving Courtland, a number of the horses had not been able to keep up with the advance. Those troopers who came in late to the bivouac, and had been left to rest and care for their animals, were not yet up. There were not a thousand Confederates on the Sand Mountain plateau at this time.

Dismounting Edmondson's men, Forrest threw them into line, while Roddy and Julian, mounted, were deployed to the right; and to the left his escort and the scouts were placed. The two guns of Morton's battery, having just arrived, were brought up and opened upon the Union line. Edmondson's trained veterans advanced steadily; and when they had reached a point within a hundred yards of the Federal line, the two mounted companies on the left rode into the skirmishers on that flank. At this moment Roddy's and Julian's men recklessly urged their horses well in front of the alignment of Edmondson's men and by their advanced and exposed position brought on themselves a murderous volley from the enemy. A number of men and horses were killed or wounded; and the Rebels being thrown in confusion, the alert Federal commander seized the moment to order a charge which, forcefully made, swept the mounted Confederates on the right from the field. As Edmondson was now overlapped and enfiladed and in danger of having the right troops of his regiment captured, he and the escort and Captain Forrest's scouts also fell back, yet steadily and without confusion. Reaching the two guns, they made an effort to take these away; but several of the horses had been shot and were entangled in the gearing.

Randy, who had become separated from Buck and Forrest in the fighting, saw the danger to the guns and rushed to them to give a hand. Dismounting, he drew his knife and started slashing the harness of one of the downed horses and freed it. By this time the Federals were upon them. He drew one of his pistols and emptied it effectively into the oncoming enemy at close quarters, but the blow of a rifle butt to his head knocked him unconscious. His horse moved with the Rebels as they were forced back to a ravine where they were able to make a stand.

The Yankees were jubilant over taking the guns and were rapidly getting them ready to take back into their lines. Randy slowly regained consciousness; and as he did so, he stirred and moaned. "Hey, this one ain't dead," one of the men in blue cried. "We done got us a Rebel officer."

Randy was quickly surrounded and disarmed. He had a large knot on the side of his head, but it had bled very little. As he groggily got to his feet, one of the men said, "Them ain't no artillery markings on his uniform; what are they?"

"I think it means he's a staff officer. Colonel Hathaway'll be glad to see him. We'd better get him to the colonel right now."

Randy was quickly bustled off to the Union colonel, who took one look at his uniform and asked, "Are you on General Forrest's staff?"

"Yes, sir," Randy replied.

"What is your name and staff position?"

"My name is John Randolph Rushton, Jr., but I will not disclose my position."

"How many men does Forrest have?"

"Enough to take you and more on the way."

"How many?" the colonel pressed.

"I'll not tell you that, either."

"You're not being very cooperative, Lieutenant. If you cooperate, we'll parole you under condition you take no further part in the war until properly exchanged."

Colonel Streight had come up at this moment and heard Colonel Hathaway's proposition to Randy. He listened with interest to the young officer's reply.

"I have no intention of cooperating," Randy said; "and I will accept parole only under condition that it not be binding after you surrender to Forrest."

"And what makes you think we shall surrender to General Forrest?" Colonel Streight asked testily.

"You have no choice. You've moved too fast for infantry support from your main force; you're cut off from the Tennessee River; there's no place for you to go but ahead; and Forrest is a determined man who will ride you into the ground."

"I've met determined men before, and I'm still above ground. I have no fear of Forrest."

"Then you've never met a man like him," Randy replied.

Turning to Hathaway, Colonel Streight said, his voice showing irritability, "You're wasting your time with this man. Get his word of honor that he will not escape and forget him."

"I can't make such a commitment," Randy replied; "I'll escape if I can."

"Then place him under guard with the wagons and treat him as any other prisoner," Streight snapped as he turned and walked away.

After the Federals withdrew to their original line, Buck looked around for Randy and was not long in spotting the riderless Chessy. He began searching for his friend and learned from one of the artillerymen that Randy had tried to help with the guns and may have been wounded or captured. Knowing the position of the guns before they were taken, he made his way to that area but found no sign of Randy. Feeling certain his friend had been captured, he made his way to the place where several Federal prisoners were being held. Among them he found what he was seeking, one of the Alabama cavalrymen who was about his size. He had the man's uniform removed from him and left with it to find Major Anderson.

"Randy's apparently been taken prisoner," he said to Anderson. "I've got a uniform from one of the captured cavalrymen, and I'm going into the Federal lines to see if I can find Randy."

"You can't do that," Anderson protested; "you'll be shot if they catch you in one of their uniforms."

"What in the hell do you think they've been trying to do," Buck replied impatiently.

"Well I can't give you permission to do it—only Old Bedford can, and right now he's raving mad. This is no time to talk to him."

"That's what I figured, and it's why I came to you. Since you can't give me permission, I'll not ask for it; I'll just tell you I'm going."

"I know how you feel, Buck, but don't go now. The general is going to attack again to get those guns back, and he'll want you with him. Besides, you'll have more chance after dark."

"I wasn't planning to go among them before dark. I intend to get on their flank and scout them out first."

"Wait until after the attack. We may overrun them, and it won't be necessary for you to go in alone."

"That makes sense, Charlie—I'll wait."

Streight's elation over this early success was short lived. One of his company commanders came to him with a dirty, bearded man dressed in worn civilian clothing and leading a sorry-looking mule. "This man just came up. You'll be interested in the information he has," the captain said.

Taking a close look at the disreputable appearing individual, Streight's first reaction was to have little or no confidence in anything he might have to say. "Who are you?" he asked impatiently.

"Jethro Barlow," the man replied.

"What information do you have?"

"The Rebels ain't just behind you. There's a lot more of 'em been sent th'ough another pass south of here to head you off."

"How do you know this?"

"I been watchin' 'em ever' since they camped last night fo' miles west of you."

"Are you a native of this area?"

"That I be."

"Why are you furnishing information against your people?"

"They ain't my people; 'sides, I seen a man in their camp who I want to see dead. He killed my brother, shot my pa, an' I'm carrin' a piece of his lead in me."

"Where?"

"Right here," he replied as he unbuttoned his clothing and pulled them back to expose an ugly bullet scar at the front of his left shoulder.

"What you tell me had better be the truth; if this is one of Forrest's tricks, so help me, God, I'll have you hanged as a Confederate spy!" Streight said. Then to the captain, "Send out some scouts to verify the accuracy of this information, and keep an eye on this man until we know whether he's telling the truth."

Forrest, who always lost his temper when he suffered even a temporary repulse, was in a fuming rage over the retreat before the enemy; and the loss of two of his pet guns only added fuel to the fury blazing within him. He rode among his men with his saber drawn; and deft use of the flat side of the blade, coupled with profane remarks which figuratively blistered the surrounding air, left no doubt as to what he expected of them.

"Git down, an' hitch your hoss to a saplin'," he said, his voice husky, but loud. "There'll be no hossholders today. We're gonna retake them guns, or ev'ry man'll die in the try. If we don't take 'em, we ain't gonna need them hosses, nohow."

The unit commanders were directed to get their men in line for the assault. When this was done, Forrest rode down the line and again made it plain to his men in no uncertain language what he expected of them. While he was doing this, Major Anderson rode up beside Buck and pulled a modest bundle of ham and bread from the inner pocket of his coat. Giving half of it to Buck, he said, "We had better eat this now, I reckon; from the way the 'old man' is preparing to get his guns back, it might spoil before we get another chance at it."[4]

The order to "move up" was given, and the line of dismounted troopers in a subdued but determined mood steadily moved forward, only to see the rear guard of the Union column mount their mules and scamper away in the direction of Blountsville. This was about 11:00 a.m. on April 30. Without waiting for verification of Jethro's information, Streight had resumed his march, taking Forrest's guns with him; and he had left only a thin line of skirmishers to screen his departure.

By the time the Confederate troopers could get back to their horses and resume the pursuit, their adversaries had a start of nearly an hour. The running fight had opened, and the tactics of both leaders were now apparent. Colonel Streight would move rapidly, until his rear was too hard pressed; and then, whenever a suitable position offered, he would set up an ambush and thus discourage direct assault. Forrest tactics were summed up in his usual terse language, and he kept repeating it to his men, "Whenever you see anything in blue, shoot at it, an' do all you can to keep up the scare!"

Buck lost no time after the assault in getting Forrest's permission to try to free Randy—the Confederate general realized the valuable information such an incursion into the enemy force could produce. Cally had somehow gotten wind of his intentions; and as Buck started to leave, with Randy's horse in tow, the old scout rode up beside him and said, "Thought you might need a little help."

Buck's first impulse was to say he thought it best that he go alone, but then he realized Cally could be useful. "I need a horseholder," he replied.

"You got one."

Neither man felt it necessary to say more, and they moved off at a trot ahead of their fellow troopers. Within a half an hour, the Federal rear guard came in sight. Slowing down for the enemy to move out of view, they then turned off sharply to the right to a safe distance on the enemy's flank. Resuming a trot, they caught up first with the rear guard and then the main force, passing unobserved on the right of both. They continued to a suitable position ahead of the column and dismounted. Leaving the horses with Cally, Buck cautiously made his way closer to the road where he could get a good look at the enemy as they went by.

One of the Alabama cavalry companies was the vanguard. Behind it came one of the regiments, which was followed by the wagon train. After this came two more regiments; the artillery, including Forrest's two guns; the fourth regiment; and finally, the other Alabama company of cavalry, which was serving as the rear guard. Fortunately, Streight had not put out flankers, believing he had a sufficient start on Forrest to make them unnecessary.

Buck wasn't certain, but he thought he caught a glimpse of a gray uniform in the rear opening of the last wagon. Unfortunately, one of the men guarding the train obstructed his line of vision. To his surprise, he saw Jethro Barlow on a mule following closely behind the vehicle. If Jethro had recognized Randy, he might be hanging around in the hope Buck would show up.

Seeing the last of the column pass without spotting Randy elsewhere, Buck was almost certain his friend was in the wagon. After returning to Cally, the two of them rode rapidly ahead of the column again; and Buck once more moved in for a closer look. He positioned himself for a better view inside the wagons; and when they went by, he was sure there was a man wearing Confederate gray in the last one. Jethro was still close behind it. Satisfied he had Randy located, he now had only to wait for dark.

Six miles eastward from the battleground, a byroad came in; and along this Forrest saw the Fourth and Ninth Tennessee regiments riding swiftly, following their detour around Day's Gap. The distance had been too great to accomplish the purpose of the movement; the Federals had passed before the Southerners could reach the road along which they were travelling. Forrest did not think that either Dodge or his cavalry were in pursuit of him; but he wanted to make sure he had no interference from that quarter, so he ordered Colonel Roddy with his regiment and Julian's battalion to retrace their steps and place themselves in observation in front of Dodge.[5]

To preclude the possibility of Streight's escape toward Guntersville on the Tennessee, Edmondson's regiment, accompanied by Major Anderson, was dispatched toward Somerville and Brooksville in a general direction parallel with the route upon which Streight was moving. This placed them between him and the Tennessee.

In direct pursuit of Streight, Forrest retained his escort, Captain Forrest's scouts, and the regiments of Biffle and Starnes, the latter commanded by McLemore. It was not long before they began to overhaul the raiders. Nine miles from Day's Gap, the blue coats of the Federal rear guard came in sight; and the vedettes of the Fourth Tennessee were soon crowding them up on the moving column. For a mile the skirmishing went on, increasing in briskness and gradually demanding more and more attention from the Federal colonel. He selected a strong position on a ridge called Hog Mountain, and the two forces became engaged about an hour before dark. This encounter did not cease until ten o'clock that night.

Forrest, in person, led his men again and again in the assaults with seeming desperation. The Federals stood their ground long and manfully. Much of the fighting was at close range and at times hand-to-hand, with no light to distinguish friend from foe except the flash of pistol, carbine and artillery; and only the Federals had cannon in action. Always in the thickest of the fight, Forrest had one horse killed and two others wounded under him in this bloody encounter. Streight's picked veterans did not yield until Biffle, with a strong detachment and the escort company, had under the cover of darkness made a flank movement and borne down upon the mule holders in the Union rear. Streight quickly mounted and retreated, leaving his dead and wounded to the Confederates. In the hurry of this retreat he was unable to carry off the two guns he had captured that day and left them again in the hands of the Rebels, the guns spiked and their carriages broken.

After Streight had verified the accuracy of the information furnished by Jethro Barlow, he told the latter he was free to leave at any time; however, Jethro was content to stay with the column—he had spotted Randy and believed Buck might show up.

Buck was waiting in the bushes when the fighting started late that afternoon; and while it was still light, he saw Jethro continuing to hover around the last wagon. Streight had deployed three regiments and one company of the Alabama cavalry for the fight. The remainder of his force remained in the column of march with pickets posted fifty yards out from each side of the column at intervals of twenty feet.

Buck knew he must go in on foot, as a horse would stand out like a sore thumb among all of the mules. He had no doubt that he could take out one of the sentries; but with them so close together, he was afraid he could not do it without alarming one of the others. He would have to bluff his way in. Darkness fell, and Buck made his move. He and Cally eased in quietly with the horses as close as they dared to the halted column, to a distance of about a hundred yards. He tied Chessy's reins to Skin's saddle and instructed the older man to keep the animals facing the last wagon and to start them off in that direction if he whistled. He then moved back to the west so he would approach the enemy column at a position behind the wagons.

When he turned toward the sentry line, Buck made no effort to be quiet and was challenged as he approached it.

"Who goes there?"

"Private Dankins of Company B, Alabama Union cavalry, returning from a scouting patrol."

"Advance and be recognized," the sentry ordered.

Buck moved up as close to the picket as he thought wise.

"Where's your mule and the rest of the patrol?" the sentry asked.

"We were a four-man patrol and ran into an ambush. I'm the only survivor. My mule was shot and died about a quarter of a mile from here. I was lucky to make it back."

The picket looked Buck over carefully; and satisfied with his uniform and story, he let him pass. Buck made his way to the halted column and up toward the wagons as if he were going to the company of Alabama cavalry in the vanguard. He moved slowly and cautiously, on the alert for any sign of Jethro.

As he approached the last wagon, Buck saw Jethro standing by his mule at the rear, right side of the vehicle. His back was to him so Buck drew his knife and moved quickly. Shielding the knife as well as he could from the sight of others, he jabbed the point sharply against Jethro's back and said in a low but firm voice, "One sound or false move will be your last, and I hope you make it."

Jethro stiffened in fright, for he had no doubt who was behind him; and he remained quiet. "Now move slowly between your mule and the wagon to the front and around it," Buck said.

The subdued Jethro, knowing his life was hanging by a thread, complied silently with the instructions. Buck shifted the knife to his left hand; and as they passed between the last two wagons of the train, he drew his pistol and struck Jethro over the head with it. The stocky man crumbled to the ground near the back of the wagon ahead, and Buck rolled his body under it.

He quickly climbed into the front of the rear wagon where he would be out of sight and found in it a man stretched out on some blankets. "Randy?" he whispered.

"Buck!" Randy responded, sitting up. "Where in the hell've you been? I've been expecting you all day."

"Had to wait till dark. Are you all right?"

"Just a knot on the head. Boy, am I glad to see you!"

"Don't you have a guard?"

"He went away for a few minutes and asked Jethro to keep an eye on me."

"Let's get out of here before he comes back. Here, take one of my guns and hide it under your coat. Cally's out there about a hundred yards with our horses. We've got to get through a line of twenty foot pickets.

They're about fifty yards out. We'll split up so we can get two of them at the same time and then one on each side. When I whistle, go after your two, and that will be a signal for Cally to start the horses toward us.''

''What about Jethro?''

''I've taken care of him. Let's go. Act like you're my prisoner.''

They climbed out the back of the wagon, and Buck pulled his remaining gun; and holding it on Randy, they walked off into the dark as if a prisoner were being taken to answer a call of nature. The Union soldiers who happened to observe their departure paid them no attention. Quietly they moved toward the picket line until the dim outline of two sentries came in view. Buck pointed to the one on the left, and Randy nodded. They dropped down behind a bush and took off their boots. Creeping cautiously, sometimes crouched and at times on their stomachs, it did not take long to reach a position for their attack. Giving Randy time to get ready, Buck stood up, stepped from behind a small bush, and gave a shrill whistle.

A startled picket, only ten feet away, whirled to face the direction of the sound; and Buck fired at him. As he went down, Buck turned and fired at another sentry whom he could barely see on his right; and he dropped out of sight. Randy had with equal ease dispatched the next two on the left. By this time the whole picket line and the column behind them were alerted. Buck could hear the horses coming and whistled again to guide them. They came in sight with Skin and Chessy being led by Cally. Randy and Buck wasted no time getting on their mounts and heading for the safety of the dark amid sporadic firing in their general direction. In a short time they were back within the Confederate lines and taking part in Forrest's night assaults on the Federal position.

Streight had barely resumed his march before the Rebels were once more nipping at his heels. He realized the security of his column depended upon those at its rear; he selected Colonel Hathaway's Seventy-third Indiana to take this position, and he rode with them rather than with the vanguard.

Biffle's regiment pushed the Federal column so hard that Streight was forced to give him another check. It was now late in the night; the clouds had disappeared, and the moon was shining brightly. On each side of the road was a dense thicket of pines. Streight dismounted Hathaway's men and had them lie down in the shadows of the trees. He hurried the mules on up the road out of sight.

Cally was moving as a lone vedette at a fast clip well in front of Forrest's column. As he approached the ambush among the pines, his horse stopped suddenly, lifted its head, and raised its ears. Cally turned and made his way back to the head of the Confederate column. Forrest was informed of the situation ahead, and he ordered one of Ferrell's guns to be unlimbered and shotted with double canister. It was then pushed by the men along the soft, sandy road to a position within 200 yards of the suspected ambush. Lieutenant Jones, who commanded the artillerists, pulled the lanyard; and the canister was splattered into the pines. A second gun was brought up, and several shells were hurled into the area. The raiders remounted their mules and resumed their flight. Streight set another ambush between two and three o'clock in the morning of May 1 which was practically a repetition of the earlier one that night.

Forrest knew he would be able to wear the enemy down before they could reach their goal; and with this in mind, at three o'clock in the morning of May 1, all hands were ordered to dismount, unsaddle, feed what corn they had brought their animals, and lie down for a two hours' sleep. This was a short nap, considering the fact they had had only four hours' rest out of the last forty-eight; and for eighteen of those hours, they had fought almost without cessation.

While the Confederates slept, Streight's tired and weary, yet resolute, band was winding down the eastern slope of the Sand Mountain plateau into the valley where forage would be plentiful. They reached Blountsville at 10 a.m. on May 1; and Colonel Streight did not stay longer than necessary to give his men and stock a much needed, though brief, respite and to impress all the horses and mules in the area and enough corn for feed. The persistent hammering by Forrest had shown him the urgent need of a faster pace, and he decided to rid himself of every possible encumbrance in favor of more rapid travel. A fresh supply of ammunition was distributed, rations issued, and much of the contents of the wagons transferred to pack mules. The wagons were then bunched and set on fire; but just as the smoke was rising, General Forrest, at the head of his escort and a portion of the Fourth Tennessee, charged into the village, driving Captain Smith's rear guard in a cloud of dust through and out of town to seek shelter in the raiders' main column. Taking possession of the deserted wagons, the Confederates quickly extinguished the fires and obtained some badly needed supplies.

Streight marched on in the direction of Gadsden, with Forrest pressing hard on his rear; and there was almost continual skirmishing between the two columns. Despite frequent ambushes by small parties of men from the raiders, the Confederate cavalry leader did not for a moment relax his relentless pursuit.

Forrest prided himself upon being able to get accurate information about the enemy. Not far from Blountsville, one of Captain Bill's scouts, greatly excited, rode up to the column. "General, there's a heavy force of Union cavalry movin' on a road parallel to this'un an' they're no more'n four miles away!" he reported.

"Did you see the Yankees?"

"No, sir; I didn' see 'em myself, but while I was at a blacksmith shop, a man rode up on horseback and said he seen 'em."

Forrest reached up with both hands, grabbed the man around the neck, pulled him from his horse, shoved him against a nearby tree, and proceeded to bump his head against the rough bark. "Now, damn you," he said angrily; "if you ever come to me ag'in with a pack of lies, you won't git off so easy!"

From Blountsville to the Black Warrior River, a distance of about ten miles, Streight's rear was threatened to the extent that he was compelled to turn on his pursuers once more in order to make a crossing of this swift and dangerous stream. Under cover of a heavy line of skirmishers, he hurried the main portion of the command through a rocky ford with the loss of only two pack mules, both loaded with hard bread. Stumbling over large, loose stones in the bed of the swift, mountain stream, these animals drowned. On the east bank, the two mountain howitzers covered the pell-mell withdrawal of the skirmishers from a vigorous charge of the Tennesseans, who took a number of prisoners.

With the exception of two companies which were ordered to push on after the Federals and "worry them," Forrest gave his command another respite here for three hours. Some of the Confederates were not so tired that they did not find time from sleep to wade into the Warrior to remove from the dead pack mules what had been hard tack before it got wet. The hungry Rebels didn't mind the wetness; one freckle-faced youth said as he struggled up the steep bank with a soggy box on his shoulder, "Boys, it's wet and full of mule hair, but it's a damned sight better'n anything the old man's a-givin' us now."

After the short halt at the Warrior, Forrest once more roused his men for their fourth consecutive night march and, pushing on, overtook his advance guard, which was then skirmishing with the raiders at Big Will's Creek. Sending Biffle's men to the rear for a well earned rest and, taking their place with his escort, he now took personal charge of the attack. Gaining rapidly on the Union column, he closed in upon the raiders at Black Creek bridge.

Black Creek is a crooked, deep, and sluggish stream, with precipitous clay banks and a mud bottom. Spanning the creek on the main road leading from Blountsville to Gadsden was a rude, wooden bridge. There was no other immediate means of crossing the stream, believed impassable except by bridge or boat. Colonel Streight had built his hopes of respite from his pursuers upon placing this obstacle in their path by crossing it and destroying the bridge before the Confederates could close upon him. This accomplished, he thought he could take it easy for at least half a day and allow his worn-out cavalcade to sleep and recuperate. By nine o'clock on the morning of May 2, despite Forrest's persistent rush at the rear guard for the last four miles, all of his men were over except the rear vedette. His howitzers were in position on the eastern bank; fence rails had been piled upon the structure; and the bridge was well in flames.

Close by on the roadside, and some two hundred yards from the westerly approach to the bridge, there was a single-storied farm house with two or three rooms on either side of a wide open passageway. The owner was a widow with two unmarried daughters. Their chief means of support had been her only son, and he had gone to the war in 1861 in one of the first companies that left Gadsden to join the Southern army; and the three women were struggling to make the little farm yield enough for their support. The mother and her two daughters had watched the Yankees go hurriedly by their house; and when what appeared to be the last of them had passed, they saw smoke coming from the area of the bridge.

"Come with me," the widow cried to her daughters. "Let's pull our rails away so they won't be destroyed."

The women hurried toward the burning bridge, but stopped before reaching it when they saw it was their rails which had been used to start the fire. As they returned dejectedly toward their house, they had gone only a short distance when they saw a man in a blue uniform riding a mule toward them at full speed. Behind him were more men, dressed in Confederate uniforms, pursuing him on horses.

"Halt, an' surrender!" the leader of the Confederates yelled. The Yankee saw the burning bridge ahead, stopped, held up his hand, and handed over his gun.

"Ladies, don't be alarmed; I am General Forrest. I and my men will protect you from harm," the Confederate leader said; and then asked, "Where are the Yankees?"

"They set the bridge on fire and are standin' in line on the other side; and if you go down that hill, they'll kill the last one of you," the mother replied.

By this time, more of Forrest's men had come up and were quickly deployed in battle line across the fields on each side of the road. They soon drew enemy fire, which was returned; and the three women ran for the house. Forrest rode up to their gate and asked, "Can you tell me how to git across that creek?"

"There's an unsafe bridge two miles down the stream, but I know a trail about 200 yards above the bridge where our cows used to cross in low water," one of the girls quickly replied. "I believe your men could cross there. If you'll saddle a horse for me, I'll show you the place."

"There's no time to saddle a hoss. Git up here behind me," Forrest said. He rode up close to the bank at the side of the road, and the girl got on behind him.

The widow ran from the house and came up to them almost out of breath, "Emma, what do you mean?" she cried.

"She's goin' to show me a ford where I can git my men over in time to ketch the Yankees before they git to Rome," Forrest replied. "Don't be uneasy; I'll bring her back safe."

With a sixteen-year-old girl directing, they rode out into a field north of the house. Through this field ran a small branch in a ravine along which there was thick brush. The branch emptied into the creek just above the ford. Using the ravine and brush as a screen, they followed it until just before they came to the creek.

"General Forrest," the girl said, "we'd better get off the horse, as we're now where we may be seen."

They got down from the horse and slipped through the brush. When they got near the ford, the girl leading the way, Forrest stepped quickly between her and the creek. "I'm glad to have you as a pilot, but I'm not goin' to make a breastwork of you," he said.

The girl pointed out the ford, showing him where to enter the stream and where to come out on the other side. By this time the skirmishing across the creek was heavier, and the artillery of both sides had now been brought into action. Forrest and the girl started back to her house; and when they reached a place in the ravine where he thought she would be safe, he asked her, "What's your name?"

"Emma; Emma Sanson."

"You're a brave young lady," he replied. "I'd be grateful for a lock of hair from someone so brave an' helpful to their country. I don't think it's safe to go back to your house just now. You'll be all right here till the fightin's over. I've got some things to 'tend to. You stay put for a spell.''

After leaving the girl, Forrest brought up one of his guns to a position facing the ford. Loading it with canister, he drove the enemy from the area. Quickly throwing a part of his force across the stream, he compelled Streight's rear guard to pull out and hurry to join their main column.

When the firing ceased, Emma Sanson crept from her natural entrenchment and cautiously headed again for home. As she approached the house, Forrest came from it toward her. He smiled and said, ''I was just goin' to fetch you. I still ain't got that lock of hair.''

''I'll get the scissors,'' she replied.

They went toward the house together, and he said, ''One of my bravest men has been killed, an' he's laid out in your house. I want you to see he's buried in some graveyard near here.''

''I'll see to it,'' she replied.

The young girl cut a lock of her hair, and Forrest thanked her for it and for the valuable help she had given; and he rode rapidly away. Emma and her sister sat up all that night with the body entrusted to their care.[6]

The crossing at Black Creek wasn't easy. The cavalry went over, many of the men carrying in their hands the artillery ammunition. The guns and empty caissons, with long ropes tied to the poles, were rolled by hand to the water's edge. One end of a rope was taken to the opposite bank where it was hitched to a double team of horses, and each piece of artillery and caisson soon made an underwater passage to the east bank.

The advance guard had already hurried on after the raiders who, to their great surprise, were hustled out of Gadsden, less than four miles distance from Black Creek bridge, before they could do much damage to the limited commissary supplies there. When Streight first reached Gadsden, he surrounded it in order to corral all the horses and mules in the town. Impressing these, he set fire to several houses containing small quantities of commissaries and then had to move onward with all the speed possible to his mules and men, all now physically exhausted and the latter mentally dispirited, yet still ready to fight.

Another all-night march became necessary for Colonel Streight, although his command was in no condition to make it. Many of his animals and men were so worn out they could not keep up and were captured along the road. It now became evident to the Federal commander that his only hope was in crossing the river at Rome and destroying the bridge. This would delay Forrest a day or two and allow the Yankee troops a little time to sleep; for without it, they could not go on.[7]

Forrest's escort, now reduced to about forty effectives, some twenty of the remnant of his brother's scouts, and not over five hundred of Starnes' and Biffle's regiments made up his entire command; and with this small force, he doggedly marched eastward from Gadsden in pursuit of the raiders, who outnumbered him three to one. He followed the Federal column closely and kept up a continuous skirmish with its rear guard. At four o'clock that afternoon, Streight reached Blount's plantation fifteen miles from Gadsden, where he procured forage for his animals; and here he decided to halt. The men, their crotches sore and chafed from the uncustomary riding, were dismounted. Some were detailed to feed the horses and mules, and the others were formed in line of battle. The rear guard became severely engaged and was driven in.

The Confederates were halted, and they also formed in line of battle about 600 yards in front of the Yankee line. Aware of the condition of his own men, Forrest let them rest while he worried the enemy by advancing his sharpshooters. He could see Colonel Hathaway moving on a mule among the dismounted Yankees as he encouraged them and made adjustments in his line.

"Rushton!" Forrest called.

"Yessir," Randy answered and rode up to him.

"There's that damned colonel commanding their rear who's given us so much trouble. Can you take 'im out?"

"I think so," Randy replied. He dismounted, took his gun from its deerskin sheath and tested the range by firing at a random target along the enemy line but not near the colonel. He set the sight at 400 yards; reloaded his gun; and finding a suitable place to rest it, he took careful aim and fired. Colonel Gilbert Hathaway fell mortally wounded and died within a few minutes.[8]

"Good shootin'!" Forrest exclaimed. "He's a brave man an' a damned good officer, but he's been a pain in my butt ever since we got to the top of Sand Mount'in."

Streight remounted his weary troops on their tired mounts and resumed the march. That night the determined remnants of Rosecrans' picked band of raiders struggled on, many of them now despondent over the loss of the respected and highly regarded Colonel Hathaway; but these men in blue were not giving up.

Forrest was at last sure of his quarry, provided he could keep the remnant of his command from destruction by ambush. It was too great a danger to risk a night fight with all the advantages to the other side, so he picked out a squadron of his best men to follow and "devil 'em all night." He gave the remainder of his men their first night's rest since leaving Courtland.

Both commanders became concerned about the bridge spanning the Coosa River near Rome at about the same time. From Gadsden, Forrest had sent Buck, because he considered his horse to be in better condition than that of any other member of his staff, on a parallel route to Rome to warn the authorities there that they must guard or destroy the bridge over the river.[9] Streight also had this bridge in mind. Near Turkeytown, eight miles east of Gadsden, he had at nightfall on May 2 picked out 200 men with the best mounts; and he sent them, under command of Captain Milton Russell, to hurry to Rome and seize and hold the bridge until the main column came up. Captain Russell pushed on, crossing the Chattooga River in a small ferryboat, and on May 3 arrived at the Coosa River to find the bridge barricaded and defended by a strong company of home-guards. Buck had gotten there first, after a hard ride. Russell decided not to attack and sent word back to Streight of the situation facing him.

Meanwhile, things were not going well for the Federal commander. With heroic persistence, he urged his weary, sleepy, and worn-out men by starlight, and by the moon when it came out, as far as the Chattooga River where Captain Russell had crossed. Unfortunately for Streight, his subordinate had not left a guard at the ferryboat; and some local people spirited the boat away and hid it. Most men would have given up in despair by this time, but not Abel D. Streight. Several miles upstream was a bridge, and he led his troops in that direction through a virtual wilderness. They had to pass over an old coal-chopping for several miles, where the timber had been cut and hauled off for charcoal, leaving innumerable wagon roads running in every direction. The command was so worn out and exhausted that many were asleep; and in spite of every effort, they became scattered and separated into several squadrons travelling in different directions; and it was not until near daylight that the last of them crossed the river. This bridge was also burned; and still onward Streight plodded with his troops past Cedar Bluff, twenty-eight miles from Gadsden, at sunup and then wearily on in the direction of Rome until 9 a.m. on May 3, when he stopped at Lawrence to rest and feed. So exhausted were his men that, as soon as they were allowed to halt, they sank down upon the ground; and many of them fell asleep at once.

It was with great difficulty that a sufficient number could be kept on their feet long enough to feed the hungry mules and horses. To add to his woes, Streight received a message from Captain Russell that the bridge at Rome was too heavily guarded for him to take it. He also learned that a second column of Confederates was moving parallel with him and were now nearer Rome than himself. This was all depressing news, and at this same time he heard the sound of rifle fire; and, as Sherman called him, "that devil Forrest" was at his heels again.

Ten hours of refreshing sleep and rest had wrought wonders in Forrest's fragment of a command, and by dawn on May 3, his less than six hundred were once more in full cry after the raiders. Reaching the burned bridge over the Chattooga, the ammunition was carried over in small boats. The horses swam or forded with the men on their backs, and the cannon and empty caissons were pulled over the river bottom. So little time was lost that by 9 a.m. they were up with the Union column, although the latter had trudged along all through the night. Forrest advanced at once, purposely making the greatest possible display of his small force; yet he was careful not to make an assault which would reveal his numerical weakness. In crescentic line, and at a good distance apart, he advanced his skirmishers until he had more than halfway surrounded the Federal position. From the noise these men made, and the orders given as to the disposition and formation of the troops and artillery, one might well have thought a brigade or two was being moved in battle array rather than a little over five hundred men.

In this apparent serious predicament, Colonel Streight gathered his officers about him and with them tried to arouse his sleeping men. Some of these, when vigorously shaken, raised up to a sitting position, stared blankly around them without realizing where they were, and fell over again to the ground in deep slumber. Others could not be roused at all. After strenuous efforts on the part of the officers, about half of the command struggled to their feet and gamely rallied to their colors. Their commander lined them up for one more valiant effort and then ordered them to lie down for better protection. They did lie down, their heads to the foe; but many were soon sound asleep in the line of battle. The exultant Rebel yell, the crack and crackle of rifle and pistol, and the tattoo of horses' feet upon the ground as the rear guard and pickets came rushing into camp, could no longer awaken them. The relentless man of iron on their tail had worn them down to the point of complete exhaustion.[10]

Forrest picked this propitious moment to ask for Streight's surrender. He looked at Randy, who had informed him of what had occurred while he was a prisoner of the Union troops, "I'm gonna send in a demand for surrender. You want to take it?"

"With pleasure," Randy replied, smiling.

"I kinda thought you would."

Randy went with a flag of truce to the Union commander demanding the latter's surrender with his command.[11] The wily Forrest, knowing the caliber of his opposing leader, and his own questionable position as well, expressed an earnest desire to avoid "the further effusion of blood"; but he left off the threat of "no quarter if he had to sacrifice his men in an assault." Colonel Streight replied that he would meet General Forrest to discuss the matter.

Forrest did not want the enemy commander to see the gaping intervals, or the lack of depth, in his skirmish line, so he met him in a wood between the two lines of battle.

"General Forrest, I see one of your guns being moved forward," Streight said. "I must ask that, until these negotiations are decided, no more troops or artillery be brought up nearer than that ridge about 300 yards behind you."

"You're right in the request, Colonel; I'll take care of it," Forrest replied. He walked over to Randy and said in a low voice, "Rushton, tell McLemore an' Biffle to hold their men in their present position, an' tell Ferrell to move them guns in a circle at that ridge so General Streight can see 'em go by an' think we've got plenty of artillery comin' up."

Returning to Streight, Forrest said, "Colonel, the movement of troops an' artillery beyond that ridge has been halted"; and he took a position where Streight, in facing him, would see the guns as they were moved up to the ridge and then behind it.

Ferrell so adroitly circled the guns into sight and behind the ridge and then in sight again, that Streight finally exclaimed, "My God, General, how many guns do you have?"

"Enough to destroy your command in thirty minutes," Forrest replied.

"Before making a decision, I would like to see your troops to be certain that I am not surrendering to a force smaller than my own."

"Colonel Streight, I'll not humiliate my men by any effort to persuade the surrender of a force they've been drivin' an' beatin' in ev'ry conflict in the past three days."

"How many men do you have?"

"Enough right here to run over you and a column of fresh troops nearer Rome than you are."

"Well, I'd like to have about twenty minutes to discuss this matter with my officers."

"That you can have, but no more."

Streight returned to his command, and soon came back with a renewal of his request to see Forrest's troops to be certain he was surrendering to a force at least equal in number to his own.

"Colonel, this discussion is useless," Forrest said. Then he continued, badly stretching the truth, "I've knowed about your movement almost from the start an' been prepared for it. Now I got you where I want you, an unfordable river on the right, a mount'in on the left, a force ahead of you which you can't handle, an' one on your heels which is gaining strength ev'ry day."

"As a matter of honor, I cannot surrender to a force that I do not know to be at least as large as mine."

"If that's your decision, you'll have to live with it or die with it."

Perplexed and uncertain as to what he should do, Streight, a proud man, turned to go. Captain Henry Pointer of Forrest's staff spoke up, "Colonel, before you go, why don't we have a drink together? It could be your last."

The offer was pleasantly made, and pleasantly accepted. The drink was taken; hands were shaken by the parting antagonists; and the Federal commander rode back to his command. Before reaching it, he was met by a group of his officers bearing a white flag; and after a brief discussion with them, he returned.

"General, although I am against it, my officers wish me to surrender," Streight said. In his concern for what might happen to the two companies of Alabama cavalry, he continued, "I will do so, however, only upon the condition that all of my men will be treated as honorable prisoners of war and that my officers may retain their sidearms and personal property."

"Do you have any negroes in your command?"[12]

"No."

"Then I'll be glad to grant those conditions to any of your men who have been properly enlisted or commissioned in the army of the United States."

Realizing the need to keep Streight deceived as to their strength until the Yankees had been separated from their arms, Randy spoke up, "General Forrest, what shall we do about Armstrong's brigade now making the flank movement, Edmondson's command up ahead, and Roddy's brigade, which should have reached Gadsden by now?"

"Send couriers with orders to Armstrong an' Roddy to bivouac in the closest favorable place till fu'ther orders, an' to Edmondson to go on to Rome.''

"Yes, sir,'' Randy replied and departed as if carrying out his commander's orders.

Forrest then turned to Streight, "Colonel, I've always thought highly of the mule to pull a plow or a wagon, but I never had much regard for 'im as a mount. How do you hold with 'em?''

"Those mules were our first mistake. They are wholly unsuited for this type of operation. I doubt that we have a score left of the original 2,000 with which we started.''

"I ain't su'prised."[13]

Forrest and his troopers were welcomed as conquering heroes by the people of Rome. Before he left their city, they presented him with a fine horse as a token of their esteem, and they set aside May 6 for a day of celebration and a barbecue for his troopers; but fate would have it otherwise. Information was received on the 5th that another column of cavalry was advancing from Tuscumbia toward Talladega. The horses that Forrest's troopers had ridden into Rome were in such bad shape that almost half could not be taken out. He managed, however, to mount his troopers, many of them on horses which Streight had picked up along his line of march. Streight's mules he left for other purposes.

The disappointed men followed their commander in a forced march to Gadsden. As they were leaving Rome, Cally rode up beside Buck. "I picked up a right s'prisin' piece of news from one of the Yankees,'' he said.

"What was that?'' Buck asked.

"Your friend, Jethro, rode into the Yankee line durin' the fust fight on San' Mount'in to tell Streight about them troops the general sent to flank 'im.''

"So that's why he was there! I wonder what happened to him; he wasn't with the Yankees when they surrendered.''

"He took off after you got Randy out. They think he done it.''

"How about that?'' They both laughed at the thought of Jethro's getting the blame.

"Colonel Streight was so mad he ordered 'im shot on sight.''

"I'm sorry they didn't see him; it couldn't happen to a better fellow,'' Buck replied.

Cally turned his horse to go back to the company of scouts; but Forrest, who was in high spirits, saw him and called, "Wait a minute, Callaghan!''

Cally rode over to the general, "Yessuh," he said.

"I hear you tell some pretty good stories about the Yankees. You got one for me?"

"Well now, Gen'ral, le'me see," Cally said, revelling in being asked by Forrest to tell one of his stories. "Did you ever hear about them two Yankees who went deer huntin'?"

"Don't believe I did," Forrest replied, smiling in anticipation of a good story.

"Well, sir, these two Yankees went a deer huntin'. They set 'em up a camp an' started out to git a deer. As luck would have it, they come up on one about two miles from camp an' danged if they didn' kill the critter. It was a big buck; you never seen a prettier set of horns—musta been at least sixteen or eighteen points. They hadn' never kilt no deer before, so one of 'em grabbed one hind leg; an' his buddy grabbed t'other. They started draggin' the deer back to camp, but they was havin' an awful time—the big rack of horns kept gittin' caught on the underbrush. They hadn' hardly gone no distance when they met another hunter. When he seen the trouble they was havin', he said, 'Why don't one of you grab one side of the horns, an' t'other grab t'other side. If you pull 'im by the head, you can guide the horns th'ough the brush 'thout hardly no trouble atall.' Well, the Yankees tried this; an' sure enough, they was able to drag the deer real good. They'd gone about a mile, when one of the Yankees said t'other, 'That was a smart man. It's a heap easier to drag the deer this way.' 'He ain't so damned smart,' t'other Yankee said; 'look how much farther we are from camp.'"

Forrest laughed heartily. "Thank you, Cally," he said. "I'll have to remember to tell Miss Mary that one. She does love a good story."

The column arrived in Gadsden on May 7, and there Forrest learned that the information about the Federal cavalry column was erroneous. Dodge had actually fallen back all the way to Corinth, taking his cavalry with him. The urgency of the march removed, Forrest stayed over in Gadsden for the night and was a guest in the home of Colonel R. B. Kyle. The host thought, because of his rapidly growing reputation as a fighter, his guest's mind would be occupied only with matters relating to the war; but the only thing in which the general appeared to be interested was the colonel's two-year-old son. He enjoyed talking to the boy, holding him in his lap, and walking with him in his arms. The child responded by showing a great attachment to the general; and when Forrest left the next day, the child rode with him, held in front of his saddle, for a distance of two or three miles. When the general handed the boy to his father, who had ridden with them to take his son back home, he said, "My God, Kyle, this is worth living for!"

Forrest was leading the column, with Randy and Buck at his side, as they rode in the direction of Guntersville. They were passing through a long, narrow defile, the right of which rose steeply into a high wooded hill. On the left was a bare cliff over a hundred feet high. The sound of a rifle rang out; and at about the same time, Buck felt a sharp tug at the left side of his coat collar near his neck as a bullet tore part of the fabric away. At the top of the cliff, about 150 yards ahead, Buck saw powder smoke from the shot rapidly dissipating in the breeze.

"What in the hell was that?" Forrest exclaimed.

Buck reached up with his left hand and lifted his torn collar for Forrest to see; and he quickly took his Whitworth from its deerskin sheath with his other hand, his eyes glued to the rim of the cliff as he searched for any sign of movement there. "It came from up there," Buck said, pointing to the spot with his gun.

Forrest turned to the captain of his escort, "Send two men ahead to git to the top of that cliff an' two more back to git up from the other direction, an' have the rest of your men fire a volley into the area of that big oak." Turning to Buck he said, "I'm sorry he almost got you. I wonder who in the hell was shootin' at me?"

"I think that one was meant for me, General."

"Why?"

"An old enemy of mine was in this area as we passed through it before. I think he'd be gunning for me, but not in the open."

Recalling the scout who had also tried to kill Buck, Forrest said bluntly, "You ain't the most pop'lar fellow I ever knowed."

The detail sent out found the place where the ambusher had been, but he was nowhere around. Their quick movement to hunt him, however, was enough to send him running without attempting another shot.

The column moved on through Guntersville to Hunstville. Arriving there, they were given a very friendly reception by the grateful residents of that city, who presented Forrest with another fine horse.

Chapter XIII

Tullahoma to Home

Upon arrival at General Bragg's headquarters in Shelbyville, Tennessee, Forrest was ordered to take command of the cavalry on the left wing of the Army of Tennessee in place of Major General Earl Van Dorn, who had been killed by a jealous husband while Forrest was absent in Alabama. Forrest arrived at Spring Hill on May 16. From then until just after Rosecrans began the movement of his Army of the Cumberland against Bragg on June 22, 1863, Forrest's command, reduced to Armstrong's and Starnes' (formerly Forrest's) brigades, served on picket and scout duty on the left of Bragg's army in the "neutral ground" between Spring Hill and Columbia on the south and Franklin and Triune on the north. The division under W. H. Jackson, which had been a part of Van Dorn's command, was sent from the area to the Department of Mississippi.

Forrest had never been satisfied with the handling of the two guns which were lost in the first fight with Streight on Sand Mountain. Although he had not reprimanded Lieutenant Gould, who commanded those guns, nor pressed charges against him, he arranged for the transfer of the young man from his command when he reorganized his artillery. Lieutenant Gould took this as an unfair imputation upon his courage and brooded over what he considered to be an unjustified wrong. Forrest was in Columbia on business with the quartermaster's department; and while he was dining with a friend, Lieutenant Gould showed up and asked to talk with him. Forrest made an appointment to meet the artillery officer at three o'clock that afternoon in the quartermaster's office. The general was already there, in a room with several other people, when the lieutenant arrived. Feeling the young man would prefer talking in private, Forrest said, "S'pose we step out in the hall, Lieutenant."

Forrest had a pocket knife which he had been holding at its center between the thumb and index finger of his right hand and had been twirling the knife by hitting it gently with the index finger of his left hand. Absent-mindedly, he retained the knife in his right hand as they went into the long hall which ran from the front to the back door of the building.

The young man was upset and highly agitated, but he lost no time in coming to the purpose of his visit. "I understand that I have been left out of the battery in the reorganization, and I'd like to know why?" he bluntly demanded.

"I don't wish to discuss the matter, Lieutenant; the decision's been made."

"Decisions can be changed."

"Not this'un, an' you needn't hope to ever serve in my command ag'in."

Suddenly and without warning, the irate lieutenant drew his pistol from beneath the duster he was wearing. Forrest reacted quickly and grasped the assailant's right hand but was unable to do so in time to prevent the discharge of the gun close to his body. The bullet, of heavy caliber, entered his left hip just above the joint, striking the pelvic bone. It was deflected outward and passed on through the body without coming in contact with the intestines. The vise-like grip on the lieutenant's hand prevented a second shot, and Forrest carried the knife to his mouth with his right hand and opened the largest blade with his teeth. He thrust the blade into the abdomen of his assailant and ripped open the peritoneal cavity, inflicting a mortal wound. Lieutenant Gould dropped the pistol and ran out the back door of the building. He leaped over a low fence and ran to a nearby shop where he lay down upon a counter.

Forrest went out the front door and along the sidewalk to the office of a physician he had noticed earlier. The doctor, seated at his desk, looked up when the general entered.

"I've just been shot by a crazy son-of-a-buck," Forrest said bluntly.

"Let's have a look," the physician replied.

Forrest lowered his trousers and drawers for the doctor to examine the wound. "Is it a mortal injury?" he asked.

After examining the wound briefly, the doctor said, "I can't be certain without probing; but from the location and apparent direction of the bullet, and taking into consideration the warm weather, it will probably prove fatal."

Without a word, Forrest rearranged his clothes. Seizing the pistol of one of the officers in the room, he started for the street. Two of the men moved quickly to bar his way and to restrain him. "Git outa my way, dammit!" he said, thrusting them aside. "That scoundrel mortally wounded me, an' I'm gonna kill 'im before I die!'' He strode through the door to the street, none of the men daring to lay a hand upon him.

Someone warned Lieutenant Gould that Forrest was coming after him, and he got up from the counter and ran down the street until he fell exhausted. A crowd so quickly gathered around him that Forrest was unable to get close enough for a shot. A well dressed man emerged from the crowd; and seeing Forrest with gun in hand trying to get through, he said, ''General, you need not trouble yourself to kill him; he is already dying.''

''All right, if you're sure of it, I won't shoot 'im; but damn 'im, he's killed me; an' he sure as hell's gonna die too,'' Forrest replied, and then added, ''somebody git a stretcher an' take the sorry booger to the hotel an' have 'im cared for.''

Buck arrived on the scene at this time and said, ''They'll take care of him, General; let's get someone to take care of you.''

Forrest, now weak from the loss of blood, had to be carried to the home of the friend with whom he had dined; and here the wound was treated. The doctor's quick prognosis was in error; there was no damage to any of the body's vital organs, and the general's recovery was rapid.

Two days after the incident, Captain John Morton, who thought very highly of the wounded artillery officer, came to see Forrest. ''Lieutenant Gould is about to die,'' he said, ''and wants to see you, but he is in no shape to be brought over here.''

''Git me a stretcher,'' Forrest demanded.

A stretcher was brought, and the general was carried to the lieutenant's bedside. The young man had developed septic peritonitis and had not long to live. ''Thank you for coming, General,'' he said. ''Will you give me your hand?''

Forrest extended his right hand; and the dying officer took it and held it in both of his, saying, ''General, I shall not be here long, and I was not willing to go away without seeing you in person and saying how thankful I am that I am the one who is to die and that you are spared to the country. What I did, I did in a moment of rashness; and I want your forgiveness.''

Forrest leaned over the young man's bed; and, in a voice filled with emotion, responded, ''I do forgive you, an' I do it freely with a heart that's full of regret that the wound I inflicted is to be the cause of your death''; and the general wept.[1]

During the first week in June, Forrest learned that Brigadier General Gordon Granger had transferred his headquarters from Franklin to

Triune, about fifteen miles east of Franklin. Forrest decided to make a reconnaissance in force to determine the strength of the enemy remaining at the former headquarters. He moved with Starnes' brigade along the Columbia and Franklin pike and dispatched Armstrong with his brigade on the road from Lewisburg to Franklin. Both columns ran into pickets about three miles from their destination and drove those not captured into the town. With his usual boldness, Forrest charged right into the heart of the village, shielding his men as much as possible by keeping the houses between them and the fort.

Colonel J. P. Baird, of the Eighty-fifth Indiana infantry, commanding the Union troops at Franklin, had retired most of his men to the fort; and from there he began a vigorous display of signal flags calling to his chief at Triune for help. Forrest mistook the white signal flag as a flag of truce, and he called a cease fire. He moved forward in the open to wait for the delegation he expected from the fort; and about eighty yards from a garden hedge, a young Federal officer stepped out from behind it and cried out, "General Forrest, I know you and don't want to see you hurt. Retire at once; there is no truce; that is a signal flag."[2]

Raising his hat in recognition of the enemy officer's generous act, Forrest quickly retraced his steps. He stopped after moving about fifty yards; and, while still within easy rifle range, he looked back. The young officer had been joined by a large detachment of men. Lifting his hat again in appreciation of their gallantry, the general moved on to a place of safety.

The Confederate commander unlimbered the guns of Morton's battery; and, moving them by hand down the principal street, he advanced his men, shelling the Union troops in the houses and in the fort. He soon had possession of the town and battered down the jail door to effect the release of a number of political prisoners held there by the enemy. He also seized the commissary stores and commandeered wagons and teams to haul them away.

About this time he could hear the sound of another battle developing to the east and knew that Armstrong was in contact with an enemy force on the road to Triune. When the noise of the fight moved southward toward the Harpeth River, he correctly surmised that Armstrong was being pushed back by a superior force. Not knowing the enemy's strength, he moved south and recrossed the Harpeth to join up with his other brigade.

When Armstrong had advanced on Franklin, he had done so with only Woodward's battalion and five companies of the First Tennessee cavalry, leaving his other troops, under the command of Colonel Hobson, south of the Harpeth. In response to Colonel Baird's frantic signals from Franklin, General Granger had rushed Colonel A. P. Campbell to the rescue with the First Brigade of cavalry, which was made up of the Second Michigan, the Fourth and Sixth Kentucky, and the Ninth Pennsylvania cavalry regiments. He hit Armstrong west of Franklin; and the latter stubbornly resisted the attacks and effected a safe withdrawal, although he was pushed all the way back to the Harpeth. South of the river, Colonel Hobson, hearing the firing, advanced hurriedly to reinforce Armstrong and covered his recrossing of the stream. Armstrong was joined by Forrest, and the Union cavalry stopped north of the Harpeth. The Confederates retired three miles farther south and went into bivouac.

In camp that night, Forrest sent for Buck; and when the lieutenant got to the headquarters tent, he found the commander stretched out on a cot. "Guess I ain't got my strength back from that last wound," the general said. "Set down, Buck," he added, pointing to a folding stool.

Buck took a seat and waited. Forrest sat up on his cot and said, "You give a good account of yourself today, as you always do. You're really somethin' with that gun."

"Thank you," Buck replied, wondering what his commander had in mind.

"You're a fighter, Buck—my kinda fighter. I'm well pleased with the job you're doin', but I been thinkin' maybe I ain't bein' fair to keep you on my staff. I know I wouldn't like to be on nobody's staff. The glory an' promotions are with the troops, an' you're a born leader. You should be commandin' at least a company; an I'll see you git it, if that's what you want."

Buck could see several ramifications coming from such a reassignment. Commanding his own unit appealed to him; but it would mean separation from Randy, and it would be impossible for him to keep his promises to Ellen and Miss Carolyn. It would also probably remove him from the close association he had with Forrest, and he valued this. "General," he replied, "I appreciate your confidence, but I didn't get into the army for promotion and glory; I did it only because I felt it was my duty after our country was invaded. I'm content with my lot."

"I'm personally pleased with your choice. There ain't a better instructor in firearms in the whole army than you; but I felt, in fairness, I had to make the offer."

"I appreciate it. Don't think me ungrateful, General; but I'd prefer to stay where I am."

"How did you git your education, Buck? Your pa sure didn' have none."

"Not from books, but Pa is a very learned man in the everyday things of life."

"I was talkin' about book learnin'."

"I was fortunate. When Randy and I became friends as boys, his parents asked me to attend classes taught in their home by a very capable teacher. There were just four of us, Randy, his sister, a neighbor's daughter, and myself."

"You're a lucky young man to've had a chance like that. A proper education is important. I fit my way outa the backwoods; but I'll always talk like a backwoodsman, an' many'll look on me as such. I don't feel at all at ease around most folks that has a education, an' that can be a big load to tote at times. I tried to see that my brothers got as much book learnin' as possible."

"You may not always be grammatically correct, General; but you can be very effective in getting your message and meaning across."

Forrest chuckled. "I 'spect I been accused of overdoin' it."

Buck smiled as he replied, "I guess there have been times when someone thought that, but I've never heard anyone dare say it."

The general laughed heartily and stood up; so did Buck, knowing the meeting had come to an end. "Thank you for comin' over, Buck. I'm glad you didn' take my offer, but I feel better now it's been made. Just keep up the good work."

"I'll do my best," he replied.

Forrest returned to his camp at Spring Hill; and on June 9, he was directed by Bragg to make a forced reconnaissance of the enemy at Triune. He encountered both cavalry and a heavy concentration of infantry in that place and reported this intelligence to Bragg.

For some time Washington had been urging Rosecrans to begin a drive against Bragg's army in order to prevent troops from the Army of Tennessee being sent against Grant's drive on, and subsequent investment of, Vicksburg. Rosecrans finally commenced his advance on June 22, and Bragg was fully informed by scouts of the impending movement. Fearing a large battle with the wide Tennessee River at his back, Bragg began a retrograde movement to Tullahoma and ordered Forrest to withdraw his picket lines and join him at that place, making his march via Shelbyville where he was to join up with Major General Wheeler.

Wheeler had been assigned the task of protecting the immense train of wagons being formed up in Shelbyville to move south the valuable supplies which had been accumulated there. He had been furiously attacked about two miles north of the town at two o'clock on the afternoon of June 27. At that time, many wagons were still crossing the Duck River at Shelbyville; and others were stretched out for miles beyond the bridge on the muddy road to Tullahoma. Wheeler did his work well and checked the advance of the Federal forces until all wagons had crossed the river, although he had been pushed all the way back into the town itself.

He then moved his troopers across the river and was on the south bank ready to set fire to the bridge when Major Rambaut, of Forrest's staff, rode up and reported that the latter was near Shelbyville and moving rapidly to cross the river. Although the Federals were advancing into the town in force, Wheeler and General Martin, with 500 men from the latter's division, bravely recrossed the river with two guns to hold the bridge for Forrest's passage. They had hardly reached the northern end of the bridge, and had no time to form a line of defense, before the Union cavalry in columns of fours came charging down upon them. The two cannon, loaded with canister, were fired into the mounted Yankees; but they still came on, running through and over Martin's men who had lined up as well as possible under the circumstances. The Union troopers now had the guns and controlled the bridge, which was blocked by an overturned caisson. The Confederates were trapped on the wrong side of the river.

Realizing his dangerous situation, Wheeler, with saber in hand, shouted to his men that they must cut their way through and swim the river. He and General Martin led the charge. The Federals, cut right and left, were forced to let them through; and the Rebels leaped at full speed into the flooded stream fifteen feet below. Horses and men sank beneath the surface of the fast running river, then swollen by heavy rains, some never to resurface alive. As they were swept rapidly downstream, the enemy troopers rained a heavy fire upon them from the bank. Generals Wheeler and Martin managed to cling to their horses and reached the south bank of the river, as did most of the men; but forty or fifty perished in the water.

General Gordon Granger missed the opportunity of a lifetime. Just a few miles south of him was Bragg's vast wagon train floundering along the muddy road to Tullahoma, part of its protective cavalry scattered and in a state of confusion. He did not go after it but stopped on the north bank of the river.

As he approached Shelbyville, Forrest learned that the Federals controlled the bridge there; so he skirted the town to the north and crossed at a bridge four miles to the east. This caused an eight-mile detour before he could get between the Union forces and the wagon train to guard it.

On the 28th, Forrest reached the main army at Tullahoma and was assigned to observation on the road to Manchester. Colonel Starnes, with his brigade, was posted on the route to Manchester; and Dibrell was moved with his regiment toward Hillsborough. On June 30, Starnes encountered the advance of Rosecrans' army moving south. With his usual daring, he assailed the enemy to develop their strength, "giving them a dare," as Forrest liked to call it. Throwing out a strong skirmish line, he advanced with it.

Captain W. A. Hubbard of Starnes' old Fourth Tennessee regiment, seeing Starnes approach his position where the firing was brisk and at close range, cried out to him, "Get back, Colonel; you're making too good a target! We have things under control here!"

"Thank you for your consideration, Captain; but my place is where the fighting is heaviest."

A few minutes later, a sharpshooter's bullet caught him; and he fell mortally wounded. His loss was a bitter blow to Forrest, under whom the aggressive fighter, a physician before the war, had risen from command of a small company of independents to command of a brigade.[3]

At Hillsborough, Colonel Dibrell learned that Colonel Wilder with the Seventeenth Indiana mounted infantry and his brigade were marching on Dechard; and he hastened to the relief of the one company which was guarding the stockade there. The Federals had destroyed only a small part of the railroad when Dibrell struck them and drove them off.

Forrest moved toward Pelham to intercept Wilder and was riding with his escort of sixty men well in advance of his main column. It was a rainy night, and their identity was concealed by the oilcloth coats they were wearing. Suddenly, from around a bend in the road, came a detachment of mounted troops, about their equal in number, similarly clad in noncommittal waterproofs. Forrest asked their identity and learned they were a company of Wilder's men. When asked his identity, he replied that he was Company C of another Federal regiment which was under a different commander. The two units passed, and Forrest proceeded on. He expected the other unit to run into his main column soon, and he planned to form his escort in line to intercept them when they retreated. Unfortunately, he encountered Wilder's main column a short distance ahead. He immediately turned back and ran into and through the advance unit he had just passed, killing and capturing a number of them and stampeding the rest. Before he could join up with his command and return to attack Wilder, that wily leader had disappeared.

Bragg's army was now in full retreat to Chattanooga, and Forrest's division was assigned the duty of guarding the pass through the Cumberland Mountains near Cowan, Tennessee. After the Confederate infantry had passed through Cowan, the Federal cavalry, hovering in their rear, came in contact with the rear guard under Forrest. Firing and falling back rapidly, the badly outnumbered Confederate troopers went through the village toward the pass. As Forrest, among the last in retreat, was passing a house, he saw a woman who was berating his men for not turning on the Yankees and "whuppin' 'em back."

Not noticing Forrest's rank, or being unaware of what his uniform markings meant, she shook her fist at him and yelled out, "You great big cowardly rascal, why don't you turn an' fight like a man, instead of runnin' like a cur? I wish ol' Forrest was here; he'd make you fight!"

Forrest, unable to control himself, burst into laughter and, putting spurs to his horse, fled the scene.[4]

A few days later, the Confederate army crossed to the south bank of the Tennessee, and in July the cavalry was ordered for rest and relaxation into various districts in which forage could be obtained.

This was a low period in the life of the Confederacy. Vicksburg had fallen to Grant, and Lee had been repulsed with great loss in his three days' attack against General Meade at Gettysburg and was fortunate to be able to get his army back across the Potomac River without being completely routed. Bragg had retreated all the way to Chattanooga; and the Federal forces now controlled all of Kentucky, most of Tennessee, and the northwestern portion of Mississippi.

Forrest had lost respect for Bragg both as a man and as a commander. He could not forget the latter's having forced him to move into West Tennessee with a brigade made up mostly of raw recruits who were inadequately armed, equipped, and supplied. It still rankled him that, after they had been turned into seasoned fighting men, well equipped and armed with captures from the enemy, General Bragg had unceremoniously taken them from him and given them to the command of another. The retreat to Chattanooga without a fight had lowered Forrest's opinion of Bragg as a military commander and leader. This disaffection with Bragg probably had much to do with formation of an idea which he placed in a letter dated August 9, 1863, at Kingston, Tennessee, addressed through Bragg's headquarters to General S. Cooper, Adjutant General of the Confederate army at Richmond. In this letter, Forrest requested that he be given an independent command between Vicksburg and Cairo—in territory occupied by Federal forces—to raise troops and to obstruct navigation on the Mississippi River. He asked for only about 400 men and four pieces of artillery, all to be well mounted and equipped, to accompany him.[5]

Ten days later Forrest sent a copy of the letter directly to President Davis, to whom he wrote:

"Having understood that it was likely it not be forwarded by the general commanding the department, and believing the matter of sufficient importance to merit the consideration of your Excellency, I have taken the liberty of sending a copy direct. While I believe that the general commanding is unwilling for me to leave his department, still I hope to be permitted to go where (as I believe) I can serve my country best, especially so as an experienced and competent officer, Brigadier-General Armstrong, would be left in command of my division."

Despite the calamities which had fallen upon the Confederacy, Forrest was in high spirits. He did not see how the Southern authorities could do other than accept his bold offer to operate behind the enemy's forward lines at such a modest cost to the government. It was in such a frame of mind that he ran into Cally. "You ain't got another one of them good Yankee stories, have you?" he asked the scout.

"Well, General, I might at that," Cally replied. "You remember them two Yankees who killed the deer? They took it in their heads to go quail huntin'. They talked a fellow who had a real good bird dog into takin' 'em; but the day they was to go, he come down in the back an' couldn' make it. Like I said, he had a real fine dog, one of them English dogs called a setter. The fellow what owned the dog didn' much cotton to loanin' it to them two; but they begged 'im so that he done it, anyhow. When they brought the dog back, the owner asked 'em how they done; and they said they hadn' had no luck atall, 'cause the dog wasn t no good. What d'you mean?' the owner said. 'That's the best dog in the whole county!' 'Well, I don't think much of 'im,' one of the Yankees said. 'He kept freezin' up on us; but we kicked 'is butt good ever time he done it, an' broke 'im of that!'"

Forrest laughed loudly. "Where do you git all these stories, Cally?" he asked.

"Just from Yankees I've knowed," the scout replied.

There was little justification for Forrest's optimistic feeling about his letter. It was favorably received by the War Department in Richmond;

but when the matter was referred to President Davis, he felt "The propriety of detaching him, with a portion of his brigade, could be better decided after a report from the commanding general." The commanding general did not want to lose Forrest at this time; he thought they were on good terms and valued the contribution he was making to the army. His endorsement of Forrest's letter read: "I know no officer to whom I would sooner assign the duty ´preferred, than which none is more important, but it would deprive this army of one of its greatest elements of strength to remove General Forrest."

Bragg had his way this time with the President. Davis, on August 28 wrote: "The endorsement of General Bragg indicated the propriety of a postponement. Subsequent events have served to render the proposition more objectionable. Whenever a change of circumstances will permit, the measure may be adopted."

Rosecrans, with great boldness, was steadily pushing ahead; and Bragg was still on the defensive. On the 27th of August, the Federal Army of the Cumberland began crossing the Tennessee at Caperton's Ferry; and by September 4, most of it was south of the river. Fearing a flanking movement, Bragg abandoned Chattanooga, retiring to Dalton and Lafayette, Georgia.

The Federal commanders were much concerned over the vulnerability of their supply lines, and their prior experience with Forrest gave them reason to fear any movement on his part. Their official communications were filled with reports and rumors of his plans and with inquiries regarding his position and strength. Their information was sometimes distorted by that furnished by so-called deserters from his escort who showed up at their command posts. Forrest's escorts were selected for their devotion and loyalty to their leader as well as for their daring and capabilities. They were at times sent out to pose as deserters in order to provide misinformation to the enemy. After doing so, they usually managed to escape and returned with all intelligence they had been able to gather.

Rosecrans had not given up on his desire to break the rail communications between Bragg's army and Atlanta. After maneuvering Bragg completely out of Tennessee without a major engagement, he thought he could force the Confederate commander even farther into Georgia by breaking the railroad behind him. This task was assigned to the cavalry leader, Brigadier General Stanley, who lacked the enthusiasm for it which Streight had brought to his earlier attempt; and he gave it up when he found the Confederate cavalry concentrated in front of him.[6]

Forrest made a reconnaissance in force against the Yankee cavalryman and learned that Stanley had given up all idea of the raid against the railroad. He returned to Ringgold to reunite with Pegram's division, which had been placed under his command on September 3. Upon his return to Ringgold on the 10th, Forrest found that two divisions of Crittenden's Union corps had crossed the Chickamauga Creek at Red House Bridge and were practically isolated from the other portions of Rosecrans' army. Seeing the opportunity to capture or destroy these divisions, he informed General Bragg immediately of the vulnerability of the enemy's position and proposed that he throw his cavalry force at once in Crittenden's rear. Before any reply or orders could be received from Bragg, Crittenden, who did not appear to see the danger of his situation, was observed on the 11th to be moving farther in the direction of Tunnel Hill. Forrest threw his cavalry, dismounted, across their line of march and resisted stubbornly, from every vantage point, in an effort to retard the enemy's progress until help arrived.

There was no help. As usual, the slowly acting Bragg had missed the opportunity to administer a crushing blow on the enemy. Crittenden's heavy column of infantry pushed Forrest back until he finally found a strong position at Tunnel Hill; and here, after a hard struggle, the Union troops gave up and withdrew toward Chickamauga. Forrest received another wound in this affair, but it was not serious enough for him to relinquish his command. He was highly pleased with the leadership of Pegram and the desperate fighting of the latter's division, but he was thoroughly disgusted with Bragg's lack of action and having missed a golden opportunity to mangle one of Rosecrans' isolated units in detail.[7]

The battle of Chickamauga opened on Friday, September 18, 1863, and lasted for three days. The name came from the creek around which it was fought; and the name of the creek came from the ancient Cherokee language and meant "River of Death," a fitting site for one of the bloodiest battles of the war. Rosecrans' army was routed on the 20th; and it was saved from destruction by the determined stand of the Federal forces under Major General George H. Thomas, who was timely reinforced by Major General Gordon Granger without orders to do so.[8]

On Monday morning, September 21, Forrest and Armstrong, with a strong advance guard from the latter's brigade, moved forward on the Lafayette road toward Chattanooga and the retreating Federal army. When nearing Rossville, they came upon a rear guard of enemy cavalry.

"Let's give 'em a dare, Armstrong," Forrest said.

A charge was ordered; and the two generals, at the head of some four hundred Confederate cavalry, at full speed rode down upon the Union troopers who fired a volley and fled in the direction of Chattanooga. Forrest's horse was fatally wounded by this volley, a Minie ball passing through its neck and severing one of the large arteries. The blood spurted from the divided vessel; and Forrest leaned forward from the saddle, inserted the index finger of his hand into the wound and staunched the hemorrhaging. The animal was able to carry its rider onward with the pursuing troopers. As soon as the field was cleared, Forrest removed his finger from the wound and dismounted. His horse soon sank to the earth lifeless.

Armstrong and Forrest found themselves on the point of a knoll or spur of Missionary Ridge; and looking up in a clump of oak trees, they saw three or four Federals perched in the timber upon little platforms where they had been placed with field glasses for observation. So rapid had been Forrest's advance that these men of the signal corps had no time to get down from their perches and escape. He called to them to climb down, which they did. Taking a pair of field glasses from one of the prisoners, he then climbed the tree, from the top of which he had a full sweep of the Chattanooga valley, of the town, Lookout Mountain, the Tennessee River, and Walden's Ridge to the far north. From his perch in the tree top he dictated to Major Charles W. Anderson the following dispatch to General Polk:

"Rossville Road
"September 21, 1863

"General

"We are in a mile of Rossville—Have been on Point of Missionary Ridge Can see Chattanooga and everything around. The Enemy's trains are leaving going around the point of Lookout Mountain-

"The prisoners captured report two pontoons thrown across for the purpose of retreating.

"I think they are evacuating as hard as they can go-

"They are cutting down timber to obstruct poor passage

"ı think we ought to press forward as rapidly as possible-

"Respectfully to

"Lt Gen L Polk

"/s/ N. B. Forrest
"Brig Gen

"Please furnish to Gen Bragg"[9]

When Forrest saw the trees being cut down in the gap at Rossville to obstruct passage, he dismounted Dibrell's old regiment, now commanded by Captain McGinnis, and made a strong reconnaissance, only to discover that Thomas was fortifying himself here to hold back pursuit. Though he brought up his guns and shelled the enemy for several hours, Forrest could not move them. That night he camped on the ridge while the Federals stole away under cover of darkness and safely retreated to the protection of the heavy earthworks around Chattanooga.

As his message to General Polk had brought no action by his superiors, Forrest rode back that night to discuss the situation with them. He found Bragg asleep. He had the commander aroused and urged that they move in pursuit of the routed enemy at once as their capture was certain.

"How can I move an army without supplies? My men have exhausted ours," Bragg replied.

"General Bragg, we can git all the supplies the army needs in Chattanooga."

Bragg made no reply, and Forrest rode away in disgust.

From the moment that Rosecrans reached Chattanooga about four o'clock on Sunday, after his rapid journey from the field, he expected Bragg to come right after him. With energy born of despair, he immediately put every man and beast to work upon the defenses. If Bragg could be kept away for twenty-four hours, he might be safe. He gave orders for all troops to prepare for the attack; but no attack was made that day, nor the next; and by the morning of the 24th the Herculean labors of the army had the place well fortified.

On the 22nd, the cavalry under Forrest had moved into the suburbs of Chattanooga. During that night his troops were kept in line of battle, his left, under Dibrell, resting on the base of Lookout Mountain, his right on the Tennessee River. On Monday, the 23rd, he occupied the point or peak of Lookout Mountain, where his troops were relieved by the infantry. The cavalry was then ordered to Byrd's Mill to rest and forage, shoe the horses, and cook rations.

By September 25th the forces of Burnside were reported as being at Harrison, Tennessee, and Forrest was directed to proceed there. Marching at once, he had moved as far as Chickamauga Station, when a courier overtook him with orders to hasten via Cleveland to Charleston, drive off any of the enemy in that vicinity, and, if necessary, to cross the Hiawassee River. On the morning of the 26th, at Charleston, he discovered the Union troops on the opposite side of the river. He opened on them with his artillery, under cover of which he crossed his command and drove the enemy away. Pressing this detachment to Philadelphia, his advance under Dibrell came upon the Union cavalry under Colonel Wolford; and the Federals were badly beaten and driven in full flight from the field. One hundred and twenty prisoners were captured and sent to Dalton. It was while in pursuit of the retreating enemy on September 30 that Forrest received from General Bragg the following order:

> "Missionary Ridge,
> "September 28, 1863
>
> "Brigadier General Forrest, near Athens:
> "GENERAL,—The general commanding desires that you will without delay turn over the troops of your command, previously ordered, to Major-General Wheeler."

Upon receipt of this message, Forrest flew into a rage, at the height of which he dictated a letter to Randy for Bragg, resenting the manner in which he had been treated. He charged the commander of the army in plain, straight language with duplicity and lying and informed him that he would call at his headquarters in a few days to say to him in person just what he had written. He concluded by saying he desired to shirk no responsibility incurred by the contents of his letter. When Forrest read the letter and signed it, it was sealed and handed to a courier; and as the messenger rode away, the general remarked to Randy, "Bragg never got no such letter as that before from a brigadier."[10]

He kept the promise made in his wrathful letter and called upon the commanding general at his headquarters on Missionary Ridge to give him a piece of his mind. He took Randy with him, and they rode to Ringgold, where they took the train as far as the Chickamauga Creek bridge.[11] They proceeded from there to Bragg's headquarters by horse. Forrest was in a sullen mood, and Randy was sure a storm was brewing. He knew his general well enough not to speak at such times unless spoken to, so the trip was made mostly in silence. When they got to Bragg's tent Forrest brushed aside the sentry on duty and went inside with Randy reluctantly following him.

Bragg was alone, seated at his field desk. He rose and extended his hand, but Forrest paid no attention to it. "I ain't here to pass civilities or compliments with you but on more serious business," he said.

Bragg returned to his seat without speaking; and Forrest continued, his anger rising and his face becoming more florid as he spoke.

"You commenced your cowardly an' contemptible persecution of me soon after the battle of Shiloh, an' you have kept it up ever since. You done it because I reported to Richmond facts, while you reported damned lies. You robbed me of my command in Kentucky an' give it to one of your favorites—men that I armed an' equipped from the enemy. In a spirit of revenge an' spite, because I wouldn' fawn upon you like others done, you drove me into West Tennessee in the winter of '62 with the second brigade I organized, with improper arms an' without enough ammunition, although I asked you repeatedly for them. You done it to ruin me an' my career. When, in spite of all of this, I returned with my command well equipped by captures from the enemy, you started ag'in your spite and persecution, an' have kept it up; an' now this second brigade, organized an' equipped with no thanks to you or the gov'ment, a brigade that's won a reputation for fightin' second to none in the army, you've taken from me. You have used your position as commandin' general to further humiliate me, an' you have separated these brave men from me. I've stood your meanness as long as I intend to. You've played the part of a damned scoundrel an' a coward; an' if you was any part of a man, I would slap your jaws an' force you to resent it. You may as well not issue no more orders to me, for I'll not obey 'em; an' I'll hold you personally responsible for any futher indignities you try to impose on me. I hear you've threatened to arrest me for not obeyin' your orders promptly. I dare you to do it; an' I say to you; if you ever ag'in try to interfere with me or cross my path, it will be at the peril of your life!"

Bragg sat in stunned silence, at a loss as what to do or say in face of this furious outburst of rage from a man who was so obviously resentful of what he considered to be a systematic persecution of himself. Bragg was a brave man; but he realized that Forrest, in his present mood, acknowledged no accountability to law, civil or military, human or divine, as he stood towering over his commanding general, sometimes shaking a finger in his face to emphasize a point; and Bragg did not move a muscle or utter a word during his subordinate's invective tirade. The angry brigadier did not wait for any response from his commander; once he had had his say, he turned his back on him and stalked out of the tent. Randy, who had been ill at ease for being present during the episode, eagerly followed his commanding officer.

Outside the tent, they mounted their horses and rode away in silence. Having had his say, the fury within Forrest abated rapidly; and, after several minutes, he said in almost a normal tone of voice, "Well, what do you think of that?"

"I don't know, General. I'm afraid you have let yourself in for it."

"That son-of-a-buck'll never say a word about it; he'll be the last man on earth to mention it; an' take it from me, he'll take no official action either. I'll ask to be transferred to another field, an' he'll not oppose it."[12]

Forrest's military future was now hanging in air. Having no definite command of any consequence, and not knowing what lay ahead for him, he called his staff together. "Gentlemen," he said; "I think it's only fair to tell you that there's been a serious breach between me an' General Bragg. I got an appointment to see President Davis in Montgomery in the near future, but I don't know what's ahead for me; an' maybe you oughta be thinking about your own future. You've served me well an' faithful; an' if I git another command, I'd like to have all of you go with me. That's kinda uncertain right now, so if there's any place any of you'd like to go, I'll be more'n glad to recommend you for it."

The announcement fell like a thunderbolt upon those present. Major Anderson broke the silence, "Until we know definitely that you will not have a command, General, I'd like to stay with you."

One after the other, the staff members echoed the same feeling. Visibly touched by their personal loyalty, Forrest said, "Since we ain't got nothin' much to do right now, I'm goin' to meet my wife in La Grange for a few days. I'm grantin' a furlough of three weeks to all of you except Major Anderson. Leave your address where you can be reached with him. The furloughs may be shortened or extended." He then added with a grin, "If any of you need money to git home, Major Anderson'll take care of that, too."

The meeting broke up, and the officers quickly dispersed to get ready for the trip home. Randy said to Buck, "'Tis an ill wind that blows no good."

"I hope you're ready for a double wedding, Randy; I know I am. I've waited a long time for this furlough."

"No more than I. Let's find out about the train and see if we can get a message through to Marion."

At the railroad station they found they could take a train that afternoon which would put them in Selma the following morning at about eleven o'clock. There was space available on it for their horses, and they were able to get a message through to Marion for delivery to Prairie's Edge.

When they returned to their camp, made up of the small force, including the scouts, still under Forrest's command, Buck sought out Cally, "Are the scouts getting a furlough?" he asked.

"That's what they tell me," Cally replied.

"What do you plan to do?"

"Don't rightly know, yet. The Yankees got control of Tennessee, an' I don't think gittin' back to see my kin'd be worth dodgin' 'em."

"Come home with me, Cally. The folks would like to see you again; besides, I'm getting married to Randy's sister and want you at the wedding."

"So you're gittin' married, are you? Well, I'll be danged!" He took Buck's hand and pumped it vigorously. "'Gratulations, Buck; some gal's gittin' a good man."

"Thanks, Cally; and I'm getting a wonderful lady. You've been a good friend, and I want you at the wedding. It would mean a lot to me."

"I don' know how I'd fit in with them kinda doin's, but I would like to see Cory an' Sadie ag'in. Do you think it'll be all right?"

"If you're talking about the sheriff, I'm sure it will. The way he talked, he doesn't have a case against you; and if he has, he doesn't have to know you are there."

"Hell, I ain't worried about no sheriff; he ain't good enough to take me if I don't wanta be took. I was wonderin' if it'd be all right with your folks."

"There isn't a man in the country they would welcome more than you."

Cally replied, "You make an ol' man feel mighty proud, Buck; don't see how I can turn down a invite like this."

When they got ready to board the train that afternoon, Cally declined to sit with them in the passenger car, preferring to ride in the car with their horses. "I'd feel more to home with them," he said; "an', 'sides, they need som'uns to look after 'em."

Randy started to argue with him about it; but Buck shook his head, knowing Cally wanted it this way. Cally stayed with the horses, and Buck and Randy went into one of the cars for passengers. They had no trouble finding seats as there were several vacant ones. They selected two empty double benches facing each other and had hardly settled in them before word came down the aisle that the train would be slightly delayed in its departure as it was waiting for a general. It came as no surprise that the late-arriving passenger was Forrest. He boarded their car and sat with them. The general was in rare good humor and quite talkative, brought about by the expectation of seeing his wife again.

When the conversation lagged, Forrest looked at Buck and asked, "You plannin' to use them rings you had made in Chattanooga?"

Surprised at the question, Buck replied, "I intend to, but how did you know about them?"

"Ain't much goes on in my command I don't know about."

"Is that right?" Buck responded. "Would you like to see your horse, General?"

"My hoss?"

"Yessir, your horse," Buck said as he brought from his inner coat pocket a small pouch made from deerskin. Forrest watched with interest as Buck opened the bag and poured two rings from it into the palm of his left hand.

Forrest picked up the larger one with the stone and examined it carefully. "It's mighty purty," he said; "but I've seen finer hosses. Why'd you call it my hoss?"

"On the last night of my previous furlough, I got engaged; but I didn't have time to get a ring for Ellen. I was bringing one of our horses to you, and I met a fellow named Rice in Coffeville who had a man's diamond ring. He needed a horse, and I needed a ring; so I traded your horse for the ring."

"What kind of hoss was it?"

"A mare—one from our breeding stock. She was a half sister to Randy's mare, Chessy; and the sire of both the mares is a full brother to my gelding."

"Damm!" Forrest exclaimed. "What I wouldn't give for a hoss like that; an' you swapped it for a piddlin' ring!" He replaced the ring beside the wedding band in Buck's hand. "I see she's foaled already," he said.

This brought a laugh from the two young officers; and as Buck replaced the rings in the bag, Forrest asked, "Them wouldn't be for one of the young ladies in your school class, would they?"

"They surely are; Randy's sister, Ellen. Randy's going to marry the other one, Sally Beaumont."

"Don't tell me I'm gonna have two lovesick newlyweds on my hands."

"I'm afraid so," Randy replied.

"God help the Confederate army!" Forrest said, and then asked Buck, "That fellow Rice, did he live in Coffeeville?"

"He said he was from Coahoma County, Mississippi."

"I thought so. I believe I know some of his folks; they raise purty good hosses themselves."

"He seemed to know horses, all right."

"I'm sure he did to give you a diamond that size for the mare. If y'all got another'n like her, I'd be pleased to buy it."

"If they don't, I'm sure we have, unless the army has taken ours since I last heard from home," Randy said.

"I ain't particular where it comes from as long as it's the same blood."

The conversation died for a while, and the men rode along in silence. Forrest was the first to reopen it by saying, "Them rings took me back to my own courtin' an' marryin' Miss Mary. I didn't know her as long as y'all knowed the young ladies you're gonna marry, but that wasn't necessary. I knowed from the fust time I seen her that she was the one for me. Y'all've met her, an' know she's a lot different from me—she's from a good family, well educated, an' refined. The best day's work I ever done was when I married her."

"How did you meet Mrs. Forrest?" Randy asked.

"It was while I was livin' in Hernando. One Sunday mornin', I was ridin' on a country road an' come upon a carriage stuck in the ford of a wide creek. There was two ladies in the carriage, Miss Mary an' her mother. There was also two men close by on hossback watchin' the carriage hosses tryin' to pull the stuck vehicle loose. I asked the ladies if I could help 'em to dry land, an' they said they'd appreciate it. I got down from my hoss, waded out to the carriage, an' toted 'em ashore. I then pushed the carriage while the driver handled the team, an' we got it out of the creek. I give them two fellows settin' on their dead butts a piece of my mind for not helpin' the ladies an' run 'em off. The ladies was real grateful for what I'd done, an' I knowed right then and there that Miss Mary was the one for me. I asked for permission to call on 'em, an' it was agreeable to them. The fust time I called at their house, I found them same two sorry fellows there. I let 'em know they wasn't welcome, an' they took off. I didn't waste no time to try to convince Miss Mary that she ought to marry me an' told her she needed somebody who'd look after her, not some sorry no-good who'd set by an' not offer to help a lady in trouble. She finally said 'yes,' an' just a few weeks after we met, we was married."

"She's a gracious lady," Randy said, recalling the general's wife, whom he and Buck had met briefly in Tupelo. "You are a fortunate man, General."

"I am that," Forrest replied. "I wonder sometimes, though, how she puts up with me."

Forrest left the train at La Grange, and the two cavalrymen proceeded on to Montgomery and then to Selma.[13] As the train pulled into the station, they peered eagerly from the window in hope of seeing a familiar carriage. They soon spotted it and could see the two young lady occupants anxiously scanning each car as it approached. Ellen saw them first and started waving and trying to point them out to Sally at the same time. The girls got down quickly from the carriage and tried to keep up with the car in which Randy and Buck were riding as it moved slowly down the track. They didn't have far to go as the train was coming to a stop, and both young men dropped to the ground with their bags while it was still moving. Buck left the train first and had hardly recovered his balance when Ellen, who was running ahead of the shorter Sally, was in his arms. He held her tightly as she buried her head in the hollow of his shoulder, and he could feel her upper body, pressed closely to his own, tremble as she clung to him. Only after this stopped did she turn her tear-streaked face up to his; and he kissed her gently on the mouth, holding the kiss for a long time. When their lips parted, he said to her with the trace of a smile, "Aren't you afraid you'll ruin your reputation kissing a man in public like this?"

"Who cares about a reputation; we're going to be married tomorrow, and then I'll have you to defend it. After that, you'll be mine to kiss as I please."

She reached up and pulled his face down to hers again, and as he bowed his head toward her, he saw Randy release Sally from a similar embrace. Sally reached up and gently touched the welted scar along Randy's cheek, and she said, before she stood on tiptoe to kiss it, "I was afraid it might be gone."

As their lips met again, Buck kissed Ellen more firmly this time; and he silently thanked God for being home again—home again with Ellen, and all thoughts of war and of fighting and killing were forgotten.

Chapter XIV

Wedding Bells

The railroad station in Selma was a busy place. The line running north to connect with the Atlanta-Chattanooga Railroad just south of Dalton, Georgia, had been completed only as far as Blue Mountain, Alabama; but to the west, the Alabama and Mississippi Railroad ran all the way to Vicksburg through Demopolis, Meridian, and Jackson. Vicksburg, however, was now in the hands of Federal troops. At Meridian the latter line connected with the Mobile and Ohio Railroad running from Mobile to the Ohio River via Columbus, Kentucky. All of that line north of Mississippi was in Federal hands; but it was of no value to them as that portion of it from south of Jackson, Tennessee, to the Kentucky border had been destroyed by Forrest. The railroad from Selma to Meridian and on northward was a vital and active line of supply for Confederate forces in Mississippi.

The two young couples brazenly embracing beside the railroad track in Selma were brought back to reality by hoots and cat-calls from soldiers who were watching them from train windows. When he released Ellen, Buck reached into his inner pocket and brought out a small deerskin pouch from which he carefully extracted a diamond solitaire ring and placed it on the ring finger of her left hand.

"Oh, Buck, it's so beautiful!" exclaimed Ellen, who had been silently watching him in eager anticipation. "Where in the world did you get it?"

"Horse trading," he replied with a grin. Buck looked at the hand of Sally Beaumont who was standing nearby and was glad to see that Ellen's ring was slightly larger than the one she was wearing. He was pleased, but he felt a little ashamed that this should be important to him. "I hope we can get married right away," he added.

"Like when?" Ellen asked teasingly.

"Like today."

She laughed. "It would suit me, but Mother insisted that it not be until tomorrow. It'll be a double wedding with Randy and Sally. Oh, my goodness!'' she exclaimed. ''I haven't even spoken to Randy!'' She went quickly to her brother, embraced him, and gently kissed him on the cheek. ''I'm so sorry, Randy. How could I?''

''I guess we were both kinda wrapped up in something else,'' Randy replied with a grin. ''You're looking great, Ellen. How are the folks?''

''Just fine. Mother wanted to come with us, but Daddy talked her out of it.''

Buck, who had been standing by as Ellen greeted her brother, spoke to Sally, ''Hello, I didn't mean to ignore you.''

''I'll overlook being overlooked this time, but don't make a habit of it,'' she replied gayly.

''That I'll never do.''

The negro driver of the carriage came up at this time, picked up the two canvas bags and started to the carriage with them. ''Hello, Ben,'' Randy said. ''Are you in too big of a hurry to speak?''

''Naw, suh, Massa Randy,'' the negro replied with a broad smile, pleased with the attention from his young master. ''I ain't never too busy to speak to you.'' He laughed. ''You jes' seemed pow'ful busy, an' I didn' wanta botha you none. It's good to have you home again.''

''It's good to be home.'' Then to Buck, ''We'd better see about the horses before the train leaves with them.''

Looking down the track, Buck saw Cally unloading the last of the three animals. ''They're being taken care of,'' he said. ''Come on, Ellen, there's someone here I want you to meet.'' Taking her arm, he guided her down the track.

Seeing the man in buckskin with the horses, two of which she recognized, Ellen asked excitedly, ''It's Cally, isn't it?''

''None other.''

''I'm so glad; I didn't know he was coming with y'all. I was afraid I'd never get to meet him,'' she said.

Cally was busy with the horses and had his back to them. With the commotion around the train, he was unaware of the young couple's presence until Buck spoke, ''Cally, I'd like you to meet the future Mrs. Buck McCord.'' As the old man turned to face them, Buck proudly added, ''Miss Ellen Rushton. Ellen, this is Cally. A man could never ask for a better friend.''

''I know, and I hope you'll be my friend, too,'' she replied as she extended her hand to the lean and now completely gray Cally.

The old story teller, the man who loved to talk, was so touched by Buck's introduction and the beautiful young lady's warm gesture of friendship that he found himself at a loss for words. Taking the small hand in his own rough one, he pumped it vigorously, saying over and over, "It's my pleasure, ma'am; it's my pleasure."

The trip from Selma was pleasant. Randy and Buck rode in the carriage with the girls, while Cally followed with the horses. Sally and Ellen eagerly related the wedding plans. It was to be at eleven o'clock the following morning at Prairie's Edge, with only immediate family members and a few close friends present. The ceremony would be performed by Dr. Noah K. Davis, the president of Judson, who was also a Baptist minister. Afterward there would be a barbecue dinner served outside if the weather permitted, otherwise, inside.

"Well, you've got things pretty well settled for the wedding," Randy said; "But where do we go for the honeymoon?"

Ellen blushed, but not Sally, who responded, "We decided to leave that up to y'all. We didn't know how much time you have as you didn't mention it in your wire."

"Three weeks," Buck replied; "but it could be shortened or extended. I don't think we had better plan on going anywhere for more than a week, and it will have to be some place we can be contacted by telegraph and get back home quickly."

"I thought it might be that way," Ellen responded. "We can go to Selma, Montgomery, Cahawba or Meridian."

"Let's make it Cahawba," Randy proposed. "Aicardie's Hotel there was the former Dallas Hall and a very fine place before the war."

"It still is," Ellen replied. "Miss Rhoda King[1] said she had a very pleasant stay there recently. Does this suit you, Buck?"

Buck took her left hand in his right and replied, "Anywhere you are is just fine with me."

"Then it's settled," Randy said. "We'll send Ben to Marion to get a wire off letting the hotel know to expect us. Does the afternoon train still go down from Marion at five?"

"No," Ellen replied. "It leaves at four o'clock, but we'll have plenty of time to catch it if Sally and Buck come to Prairie's Edge prepared to travel. We can leave from there right after dinner."

The ride from Selma ended far too quickly for Buck. He would have preferred to stay on for a while at Prairie's Edge with Ellen, despite his eagerness to see his parents. Cally's being with him made this impractical; so after a warm welcome from his future in-laws, he excused himself, reluctantly said good-bye to Ellen, and left for home on horseback. The sun was low in the west as he and Cally came around the last bend and saw the McCord house in the late afternoon shadows of the shade trees. Buck could make out his parents sitting on the porch, and he knew they were watching for him. Putting spurs to Skin, he raced for home. Cally, appreciating the moment, slackened his own pace to give the young soldier a chance to greet Sadie and Cory alone. By the time Buck reached the gate, his parents were waiting by the road.

Bringing Skin to a quick stop, he leaped easily from the saddle and was quickly engulfed in his mother's arms. "Praise the Lord!" she cried. "Praise the Lord for bringing you back home safe!"

Sadie held her son tightly for a moment and then released him so he could greet his father. Cory offered his hand, but Buck brushed it aside and embraced his father instead. Touched by this demonstration of affection from his grown son, Cory returned the embrace as well as he could with his single arm. Sniffing once before he spoke, Cory said in a husky voice, "It's good to have you home, Son; it's good to have you back."

"There's no place like home," Buck replied.

Just then, Cally rode up; and Sadie, who noticed him for the first time, exclaimed, "Glory be! It's Cally! Get down, Cally, get down!"

Cally dismounted rather stiffly and had hardly gotten both feet on the ground before Sadie had him by the hand and was giving him a warm welcome. "Nobody told us you was comin'; but aside from Buck, there ain't nobody we'd ruther see."

"Thank you kindly, Sadie. It means a lot to this ol' man to hear that."

"I don't see no old man," Cory said as he extended his hand to Cally, "but you're welcome, anyhow."

"Come on, y'all," Sadie said, "let's get in the house where it'll be more comf'table."

"You go on in," Buck replied. "I'd like to feed and water the horses first."

"I'll give you a hand," Cory offered. "Hope you don't need two."

"If he does, I got 'em," Cally said; and the three of them started for the wide gate leading to the back yard as Sadie turned toward the house.

"Skin looks kinda bad, Son. Hope you ain't been neglectin' 'im," Cory said.

"No, sir. He's had some tough going, and feed isn't always plentiful. He's taken several wounds, but none of them has been serious. I'd like to leave him here with you if you have a good replacement. He's kinda jaded and has earned a rest."

"The army's been grabbin' ever'thing I raise, an' I've had trouble holdin' onto my breeding stock. They've let me keep that so far, because I let 'em have all the increase; but I've got a couple of good ones stashed away."

"General Forrest wants to buy one if you have it. I wrote y'all about trading the mare for a ring. When I told the general what I had done, he was real disappointed."

"You take your pick of the two, an' he can have the other'n; but tell 'im it's a gift, because his money don't spend here." Buck smiled. He recalled Cory's previous attitude about payment for the mare, but he wasn't surprised at the change.

They soon had the horses watered, unsaddled, rubbed down, and in stalls with troughs amply, but not overly, supplied with grain. Cory had examined Skin carefully. "Ain't nothin' wrong with 'im that a few good feedin's an' a little rest won't fix," he said as they started for the house.

They found Sadie in the kitchen as usual; and when they got to the doorway, she said, "Y'all wash up; an' by the time you're th'ough, coffee'll be ready."

At the washstand, Buck motioned to Cally to go first; but the old scout would not have it that way, so Buck washed up ahead of him. When he finished, he went to the kitchen to join his mother. She was in front of the stove and turned toward him as he entered. She looked him over carefully before she spoke. "You're nothin' but skin an' bones," she said. "You been eatin' reg'lar?"

"Not always, but I get along."

"None too well, I see. I want to put some meat on them bones before you go back. How long you got?"

"Three weeks, but it could be extended or cut short; I'm not sure. I guess y'all know the wedding's set for tomorrow morning."

"Ellen rode over yestiddy an' told us. Most mas ain't too happy over the gals their boys marry, but I'm real pleased with the one you picked. Ain't a week gone by since y'all decided to git married that she ain't been over at least once when she wasn't at school; an' she don't come just to set an' visit. Whatever I'm doin' she pitches in to help. I never seen nobody so anxious to learn to work."

"You mean she's been coming over and working with you?"

"Usually twice a week, but she didn' want me to write you about it. Maybe I shouln'a told. She probably wanted to s'prise you. She may've been raised like a gilded lily, but she ain't one now."

"Well, I'll be damned."

"I wish you wouldn' talk thataway, Son; it ain't our way, an' it don't become you."

"I'm sorry, Ma. Guess I've picked up some bad habits in the army."

"I hope that's the worst one."

Cory and Cally came in, and the three men sat down at the table. Sadie poured coffee from a pot now boiling on the stove and brought it to them. "This really hits the spot. Haven't been getting much real coffee lately," Buck said. "We try to make it out of parched peanuts and corn, but it isn't the same."

"I know; ain't it awful! I can't drink the stuff. I drink herb tea. We don't git much real coffee neither," Sadie said. "This's some I been holdin' back for a special occasion, an' this one's very special."

While the men sipped their coffee, Sadie returned to her work at the stove. "You're takin' a big step tomorrow," Cory said, looking at his son.

"I know, but it's the right step; and I waited a long time for it."

"You're lucky, Buck. Ellen's a fine lady who'll make you a good wife. I guess you learnt to pick 'em from your pa," he said with a smile.

"He was a master at it," Buck replied.

"The way y'all talk, a body'd think you meant it," Sadie said trying to hide her pleasure at their remarks.

The two men looked at each other and smiled. They both knew she expected them to say they really did mean it, but by tacit agreement neither would give her the satisfaction. Finally, with her nose slightly out of joint, Sadie spoke, "Ellen said Randy's marryin' that pretty Miss Sally Beaumont."

"I'm glad that boy finally come to his senses," Cory said. "I was afraid he was gonna marry that puny gal from Marion Junction."

"So was I," Buck replied.

Looking over her shoulder, Sadie said, "Cally, you ain't said a word. You ain't feelin' porely, are you?"

"Naw, Sadie, I'm fine. I'm just happy bein' here with y'all an' list'nin' to you."

Sadie left the stove and went into the pantry. She returned in a moment with a bottle about three-fourths filled with whiskey and placed it on the table in front of their guest. "I keep this for use as medicine; maybe it'll cure what's ailin' you."

"If it don't," Cally said with a big grin as he reached for the bottle, "it won't be 'cause I didn' give it a chance."

"Buck, the water's hot now; an' you can take a bath before supper."

Buck looked at his uniform which was much the worse for wear. Both he and the uniform were dirty from the trip on the train. His thoughts turned to Mrs. Carter up near Centreville, Tennessee; and he laughed. "I guess I do need one," he said.

"I'll heat some more, an' Cally can take his'n after we eat. I found some store-boughten, gray wool over't Marion last month, an' me an' Ellen made you two new uniforms. Try 'em on after you bathe; I may hafta take 'em up some tonight."

"Boy, am I glad to get them!" Buck said; and he got up, went to his mother, and embraced her. "I really need 'em. My other uniform isn't much better than this one, and it's been rolled up in my bag. I was afraid I'd make a pretty sorry appearance tomorrow."

He took the large pot of water from the stove and started for his room with it. "The tub's in your room, but you'll hafta draw more water from the well to cool that off," Sadie said as he went out the door.

Buck returned shortly with the pot refilled with cold water. After he placed it on the stove, he looked at Cally and grinned, "It'll be hot by the time you're ready for it."

"It'll be hot before I'm ready for it," Cally replied, resigned to taking the bath. As much as he disliked the idea, he wasn't about to cross Sadie over it.

"Buck's got a nice suit from before he got in the army. It'll be a little full on you, but I think I can fix that. It'll be better'n them buckskins for the weddin'. I got some nice soft deerskin an'll make you another suit from it before you go back."

"I don't wanta be no bother, Sadie."

"It ain't no bother. What's a friend for if you can't do a little som'thin for 'im ever' now an' then?"

Cally poured another drink into his empty cup and took a slow sip from it. He put the cup down on the table and sat back contentedly in his chair. How good it was to be with friends and a family like this. All misgivings about coming home with Buck were gone. He had planned to make some excuse to avoid going to the wedding tomorrow; but with a decent suit, he might go after all.

It was rather cool that night but not cold enough for a fire. The three men sat in the front hall talking after Cally had his bath, and Sadie busied herself altering the suit for Cally and Buck's two uniforms.

"I didn't see any cotton on the place as we came home," Buck said to his father.

"There ain't none. We're plantin' mainly grains—corn, wheat, an' oats. The Confed'racy needs 'em, an' there ain't much need for cotton with the blockade."

"What is Mr. John doing?"

"Same as me. We're sellin' some of the grain, but we're using a lot of it to feed cattle an' hogs which the gov'ment needs. We're also plantin' more cane for molasses."

"How's he doing with his sharecropping?"

"Real good. Some of his folks have bought their freedom—not many, but a few."

"Did he have any trouble getting the state legislature to approve freeing them?"

"None atall. Might have a few years ago, but not now—not with the war an' all."

"What effect has Mr. Lincoln's Emancipation Proclamation had on this part of the country?"

"None that I can see. Nobody's paid no attention to it."

"Has it had any effect on the slaves?"

"Not as I know. They still work like they always have. I know John ain't had no trouble with his, but he's not the usual master. I hear occasionally about a slave runnin' away; but no more'n usual, which is quite a s'prise with so many men away in the army. The slaves seem to be workin' like they always have."

"How are you making out here with the farm?"

"Doin' all right. The James darkies work hard, an' make good crops. I've got four of the younger ones workin' for me now with the stock. I've bought another 160 acres that join us on the south an' John on the east. Most of it's good preher land. There's a half section south of it which'll prob'ly come up for sale soon, an' I'll buy it if the price is right. I like the prehers for pasture. It grows good grass an' don't take much clearin'."

"Are you getting gold when you sell your crops and stock?" Buck asked.

"Not now. Ain't much of it around these days, an' what there is, is higher'n a cat's back. I'm satisfied with the gov'ment's money. I figure I can do my part by growin' an' raisin' things the country needs an' takin' its paper for it. I'll use that to buy land. I'm worried about John, though; he's sold most of the bonds an' stocks he had before the war an' put ever'thing into gov'ment bonds. It's his way of doin' his part for the war."

"I hope we can hold out long enough for the Yankees to get so fed up with the war that they'll give it up and let us exist in peace. The losses at Vicksburg and Gettysburg really hurt us, and we failed to capitalize on the victory we won at Chickamauga. I don't think we can ever hope to defeat the North. I believe it will end, though, if Mr. Lincoln is beaten next year."

"Well, let us pray for that," Sadie said as she appeared at the door with one of Buck's uniforms and the suit she had altered for Cally. "I've took these up. You an' Cally try 'em on to see how they fit. If yours is all right, Buck, I'll fix the other'n the same way."

The wedding on the morning of October 4, 1863, at Prairie's Edge was a small but happy affair. The Rushtons and the Beaumonts had invited only a few of their very closest friends, but none of Buck's relatives or friends of the family from the hill country were present. Because of the shortness of time, Cory and Sadie were able to get verbal invitations to only two of their relatives and a small number of friends from their church. They were not surprised at the declinations, knowing those invited would not feel comfortable at the home of the Rushtons and in the company of wealthy planters.

The ceremony, although a double one, performed in the Rushtons' front parlor by Dr. Davis, was short as there were no attendants. When it was over, the newlyweds received congratulations and best wishes from the guests; and the brides went upstairs to change into travel clothes. The remainder of the wedding party repaired to the pecan grove just north of the house where Golan had spent the night and morning barbecuing the meat and cooking a huge pot of gumbo. Although neither John nor Carolyn drank spirits, a small bar had been set up for those who did.

Well dressed in Buck's suit, Cally made a good appearance with his hair and beard neatly trimmed; nevertheless, he felt quite ill at ease among the surroundings and people at Prairie's Edge. He was quick to spot the small bar in the pecan grove and lost no time in making his way to it. He finished one drink which he gulped down and was just beginning to sip a second when others interested in quenching their thirsts arrived. Edmond Beaumont was among this group; and when he saw Cally, whom he had met in a brief introduction earlier, asked, "Are you with Forrest, too, Mr. Callaghan?" The name Forrest drew the attention of the other men present.

"Well, yes an' no," Cally replied, "I ain't in the army, but I serve with Cap'n Bill Forrest's scouts, an' wherever the general goes, we usually been there already."

His reply brought on a barrage of questions which Cally gladly answered, and he soon found himself with an avid audience eager to hear anything he could tell them about the cavalry leader who was beginning to be greatly admired and respected in the deep South. Cally lost his audience shortly before noon when the brides reappeared and it was announced that dinner was to be served.

The trip from Prairie's Edge by carriage to Marion and from there to Cahawba on the train was uneventful. Upon arrival at the river port, the newlyweds found a carriage from Aicardie's Hotel waiting for them. As they rode the short distance to the hotel, Buck saw for the first time the town which had been so important to the planters in the area. No longer a thriving port, Cahawba still retained much of its charm; and Buck knew they had made a good choice of this place for their honeymoon.[2] They were received as honored guests by the hotel personnel, who recognized them as being newly married and did everything possible to make their stay in Cahawba a pleasant one. They were given adjoining rooms on the second floor of the sparsely filled hotel, where they were much to themselves.

They had arrived in Cahawba late Sunday afternoon; and shortly before twelve on the third night, both couples were awakened by the noisy arrival of someone in the room across the hall from the one occupied by Randy and Sally. At breakfast the following morning, the late arrival of the guests was mentioned; but they saw no new people in the dining room. Nothing was thought of it at the time, nor did it seem unusual when no new faces showed up for dinner at noon. From sounds coming from across the hall, it was apparent that the room was occupied; and when the new guests did not appear for supper, the young couples began to wonder what was going on.

"Perhaps they aren't hungry," Ellen said.

"I doubt that," Buck replied. "Missing one meal I can understand, but three?"

"Oh well, it's their affair, not ours," Sally said. With that, the matter was dropped. After supper they took a short stroll about the town and then returned to the hotel. As they started down the second floor hall to their rooms, they saw the negro maid who took care of them come out of the room across from theirs. She was carrying a large tray of dishes and the remains of a meal.

"Maybe they're newlyweds like us," Ellen whispered.

"Probably are," Buck replied.

Again the matter was forgotten, but that night they could hear what seemed to be the loud voice of an intoxicated man and the muffled sound of a female voice coming from the room, but neither was loud enough to be understood. The following day, Thursday, still no new people showed up in the dining room, nor did anyone make an appearance all day Friday. Sounds continued to come from the room, and several times the maid was seen taking in a tray of food or bringing dirty dishes out. They could not help being curious about what was going on in this part of the hotel.

Saturday morning after breakfast, Ellen went upstairs to get her gloves and found the maid cleaning their room. She said to the girl, "I can't help being curious about the people across from us. They have been here several days, but I don't believe they've been out of their room. They aren't ill, I hope?"

"No'm; they ain't sick," she replied with a giggle.

"I'm glad to hear that. I thought I might be of some help if they were."

The negro smiled, "Dey don' need no he'p."

"Who are they?" Ellen innocently asked; "and why are they staying so close to their room?"

The negro's smile was quickly replaced by what Ellen took to be an expression of stark fear, "We ain't never 'lowed to talk about dem."

"I'm sorry. I didn't mean to pry," Ellen said. "I guess everything is all right if they are regular guests at the hotel."

"I didn' say dat!" the maid exclaimed, now clearly frightened. "I didn' say nothin', Missy; I didn' say nothin'—nothin' atall."

"No, you really didn't," Ellen reassured her. "Don't worry about it; I'll not say anything that might get you in trouble."

"Thank you, Missy, God'll bless you for it; he'll bless you."

"Are you a slave girl?"

"Yes'm, I belong to Massa Steen at Mar'on Junction. I don't seem to be able to have no babies, so he hired me out to the hotel."[3]

"What is your name?"

"Vira."

"How old are you?"

"Almost nineteen."

"I think I'm beginning to understand why Buck's family feels the way they do about slavery."

"What you say?"

"Nothing. Nothing, Vira. I guess I was talking to myself."

"Yes'm, I does dat sometime."

Ellen put on her gloves and started to leave to meet Buck downstairs. She reassured the slave girl, "Don't worry about anything that was said here today—everything will be all right."

"Yes'm," the negro replied with a smile. "I won't if you say so."

At dinner Ellen told the others of her conversation with the maid. Randy said, "Sounds like there's hanky-panky going on up there."

"Randy!" Ellen exclaimed. "You shouldn't think such things."

"Well, I don't know what else it could be."

When they had finished eating and went from the dining room into the hotel lobby, they saw a young man who appeared to be in his middle twenties come down the stairs. He was resplendently dressed in a garish uniform bearing the markings of a captain. As he haughtily approached the desk with an envelope in his hand, the clerk on duty in a very ingratiating voice said to him, "Good afternoon, Captain, I hope you are again finding everything to your satisfaction?"

"Just fine, as usual," the captain replied in a condescending tone. "I have a message here for my father. Have someone take it to him in Selma as soon as possible."

"Yes sir. I'll see that it gets to him right away. Will there be anything else?"

"Not now. I've got a little business to attend to down the street. I'll be back in about an hour."

By this time, the two couples had reached the foot of the stairs. "Y'all go on up. I'll be with you in a minute," Buck said.

As the other three continued upstairs, Buck went to the desk clerk and asked, "What kind of a uniform was that?"

"Militia. He's a captain in the militia at Selma."

"Is that uniform regulation? I thought for a minute he must be a part of the personal guard of the Czar of Russia."

The clerk started to smile, but quickly suppressed it. "The captain is from a very wealthy family. He does pretty well as he pleases."

"Well, I'm glad that outfit he's wearing pleases someone," Buck said, and he started for the stairs. Before he reached them, he turned toward the clerk again. "By the way, this will be our last night here. We'll leave for Marion on the morning train."

"We'll have the carriage ready to take you to the depot."

Supper that night was one with mixed emotions for all of them. They were saddened by the week's coming to an end but determined to make a gala evening of their last night in Cahawba. They lingered a long time at the table, and it was later than usual when they returned to their rooms. That of Buck and Ellen was beyond the one occupied by Randy and Sally. The group stopped at the door of the first room and were saying goodnight when the door of the room opposite opened wide for the maid to bring out a large tray of dishes. All four of them turned when attracted by the opening of the door; and beyond it, across the dimly lighted room, they saw a girl dressed in a thin negligee pouring wine into a glass. The light-reddish hair left no doubt in the mind of any one of them as to her identity.

The maid quickly closed the door and sped off down the hall as rapidly as she could. "Dear God," Ellen said in a hushed voice. "That was Beverly."

"Well, I declare!" Sally replied, mimicking her former rival. Randy stood speechless.

The train arrived at the Marion depot about noon Sunday. The Rushton carriage was waiting, and Mrs. Rushton had sent along a basket packed with a cold lunch which they enjoyed during the drive to Prairie's Edge. As they passed the gate, Ellen said to Buck, "I'll have to take my baggage in for a few minutes; I have some repacking to do."

"No problem. We have plenty of time."

When they drove up in front of the house, John Rushton, who was sitting on the veranda, waved and called to them, "Welcome back. It's been kinda lonesome around this place."

"We'll liven things up," Randy replied. Before they got out of the carriage, Ellen said to the driver, "Ben, we'll be going on to the McCords in a little while, but I'd like for you to take my bags up to my room; I need to repack them before I go."

"Yes'm. I won't unhitch duh hosses, but I'll drive 'em 'roun' back an' give 'em some water."

By the time they reached the veranda, Carolyn had joined her husband, and after greetings were over, they all went inside where coffee and cake were waiting. Ellen had hardly finished hers before she said, "Y'all excuse me, please; I've got some packing to do."

Carolyn looked at her in surprise; and soon after her daughter left the room, she made an excuse and followed her. She found Ellen in her room busily taking soiled clothes from her bags and replacing them with fresh things. "You are not staying here tonight?" she asked.

"No, Mother. I'm taking a few things with me now; and I'll be back in a few days for the rest."

"The rest of your things? I thought you and Buck would stay here."

"No; we are going to his house."

"Well, maybe you should stay there while Buck's home on leave; but I had counted so much on having all of you together at Prairie's Edge."

"Not just while he's here, Mother. I'm a McCord now; and my place is in his home, not mine."

"You can't mean that! You weren't brought up for the life they lead there."

"I know, but I'll learn to be the kind of wife he needs."

"But we thought you and Buck would make your home with us. We want you here; and when the war is over, we'll need Buck to help run the plantation. Mr. Beaumont isn't well, and Randy will have to take over there. You can't do this, Ellen, you can't!" Carolyn said plaintively, and she sank down in a nearby chair.

Ellen walked over and put her arm affectionately around her mother's shoulder, "I know how you feel. You know how much I love you and Daddy and how much Prairie's Edge means to me, but I'm a McCord now; and I must take my place with my husband, just as you took your place with Daddy after you married. Maybe we shall live here at

Prairie's Edge after the war, but that will not be my decision—it'll be Buck's.''

"I can't bear to think of your becoming a drudge. You aren't used to that kind of thing."

"I'm more used to it than you think. I always helped Mrs. McCord with her work when I visited her. Believe me, Mother, there is something rewarding about hard work; and a person can take pride in what is accomplished. There can be a lot of pleasure in making a jar of jelly or in weaving a piece of cloth and making a shirt from it. I know— I've done those things."

Carolyn shuddered. "Take one of our people with you—take Priscilla; she's practically grown up with you. Let her do the hard work for both you and Mrs. McCord."

"You know that a slave would not be accepted in their home."

"Yes, I know. I guess I was doing some wishful hoping. I'll just have to pray that everything turns out for the best."

"It will; I'm sure it will. Did you notice Buck's uniform?"

"Yes, it looks nice on him."

"He has two new ones. I helped Mrs. McCord make the other one; but the one he is wearing today I made myself with her watching and advising me. I didn't weave the cloth, but I wove the cloth and made the shirt he is wearing."

Carolyn looked at her daughter in astonishment. "Did you, really? I can't believe it."

"I did, and there are a lot of things I can do now that I couldn't before," Ellen said. "I remember Daddy saying when I was a little girl that the McCords know more about the everyday things necessary for survival than we'll ever know. I'm a McCord now, and I'm going to learn those things. I'll tell you something else, Mother, we may not win this war; and if we don't, the life we know here at Prairie's Edge could be a thing of the past. Whatever is ahead for us, I intend to be ready for it and to survive."

Carolyn looked at her daughter in disbelief. Could this determined young woman be her gentle Ellen? It was a frightening thought, but perhaps her daughter was right—maybe the life they had today would come to an end; but right or wrong, she knew Ellen was wise to prepare to meet whatever the future held for her. "I thought I was gaining another son—not losing my only daughter," she said with sad resignation.

Ellen laughed. "You have, Mother. Buck loves you dearly, and you haven't lost me—I'll be only a few miles away. It's not like it was with your mother when you left South Carolina to come to Prairie's Edge."

Carolyn hadn't considered that; perhaps she was fortunate, but she couldn't bear the thought of the life of hard work which Ellen would now have in a slaveless household. Only time could determine whether Ellen's decision was for the best. Yes, time; as always, time, the inevitable decider.

Ellen quickly settled into life at the McCord home. She tried to enter fully into the everyday woman's work, and Sadie was patient and kind to her but insisted that she limit the time she devoted to this work while Buck was with them. The weather was cooler now, and she enjoyed the evenings with the family and Cally around the fire in Sadie's and Cory's bedroom. She said little, but she learned much by listening.

Cally was a different person. The hot bath, trimming his hair and beard, and dressing up in Buck's suit had brought about a change in him. Sadie had gotten busy right after the wedding and made him a new buckskin suit; and when she gave it to him, she could hardly believe it when Cally shyly asked if she would mind heating some water for him to take another bath. He had found a new way of life, to everyone's relief; and he liked it.

Sadie's bottle of medicinal whiskey had disappeared within a few days; and soon after Buck and Ellen returned from their honeymoon, Cally asked Cory where he could buy more. Cory told him about a man who operated a still a few miles beyond the Barlow place, and Cally lost no time in heading that way. He found Cory at the stables when he returned.

"I stopped at the Barlow place on my way back," he said, "an' somebody's been there recently."

"How recent?"

"About two days—three at the most since they left."

"I'll git my gun, an' we'll take a look."

They approached the Barlow place with caution. Before reaching the clearing in which the cabin sat, the two men dismounted, tied their horses out of sight of the road, and moved on foot through the wood toward the house. Circling the dwelling and outbuildings, they found no fresh sign. Cory elected to go into the barn first, where it was evident that a mule had been recently stabled for several days. There were no tracks in the adjacent lot except those where the animal had been taken into and out of the barn, so it was clear that the visitor didn't want the mule to be seen.

The abandoned house was in poor repair, and pilferers had taken away everything of value. A fire had been built in the crude fireplace, and food had been cooked there; but the ashes were cold. "Let's see if we can pick up his trail where he left," Cory said.

"He went southwest toward your place," Cally said. "There's been too much traffic on the road since the last rain to track 'im."

"You take the left side, an' I'll take the right; an' we'll see if he left the road." Cory wanted to get a good look at the tracks, so he carefully examined the trail from the lot to the road which Cally had picked up on his earlier visit. They rode slowly back toward home, searching for tracks leading from the road, but saw no suspicious ones.

When they put up the horses and went in the house, they found Buck sitting in the kitchen talking with Sadie and Ellen as the women prepared supper. "I was beginnin' to wonder what happened to you two," Sadie said.

"We was takin' a look at the Barlow place," Cory replied. "Cally come by an' seen where somebody'd been there a few days ago." Looking at his son, he continued, "Keep your eyes open an' a gun handy, Buck. Jethro could be back."

Remembering Sheriff West's admonition, Buck asked, "Think we ought to notify the sheriff?"

"Not with Cally here. Wouldn' wanta put neither of 'em in a awkward spot. We'll take another look tomorrow."

Fear gripped Ellen as she listened to this conversation—not for herself but for Buck. She knew that, although Jethro would like a shot at either Cory or Cally, Buck would be his preferred target. In their room that night as she prepared for bed, she said to him, "There's something I want you to do tomorrow."

"You name it, and it shall be done!" Buck said lightly.

"I want you to teach me to to shoot a gun."

"Do you mean that?"

"I never meant anything more."

Buck had difficulty picturing Ellen with a gun, and his first inclination was to talk her out of it; but it dawned upon him that when he and Cally left, Cory, with his one arm, would be the sole man at the house. He knew Ellen would feel safer if she could handle a gun; and he would feel better about it, too. "Rifle or pistol?" he asked.

"Both."

"Each packs quite a wallop from the recoil."

"I'll manage; I'll hold the pistol with both hands."

That night a hard rain came down as a cold front moved through, and the temperature dropped sharply. The following morning was a bright, clear, sunshiny day, but the heavy rain had erased all hope Cory had of picking up the trail of the person who had been at the Barlow place.

Buck saddled the two horses from which he was to choose his replacement for Skin, and he and Ellen set out for the Cahawba River gravel bar with one of his Navy Colts and his Mississippi rifle. He was riding a chestnut stallion; and Ellen was on a mottled, dark gray mare. He liked the gait of the stallion, but that of the mare was equally as good.

When they reached the far side of the river bridge and turned off the causeway down to the bottom land, Buck noticed that the mare picked her way down the trail better than the stallion—she seemed much more sure-footed. At the gravel bar, he set up targets and began instructing Ellen the same way he taught the raw recruits in Forrest's command. He spent most of the practice time in dry firing; but Ellen, like Randy had been, was anxious to fire the weapons.

He let her shoot the rifle only in the prone position this time, wanting her to get used to the recoil of the gun before firing it while standing. Although she had been reasonably relaxed while dry firing the pistol, once it was loaded, Ellen became stiff and tense. She gripped the pistol grimly with both hands and held it as far from her body as she could reach. Buck worked carefully and very gently with her before each shot; and by the time they were ready to leave for home, she was more at ease with the weapon.

"You're doing real well," he said. "We'll practice dry firing every day, with occasional target practice. You should be good with both weapons by the time I leave."

"I intend to be."

As he was helping Ellen on her horse, Buck said, "I'll leave one of my pistols with you."

"But you may need it."

Buck grinned. "I'll get another one—I've got a good source."

"I'll bet."

Buck watched the horses carefully as they climbed the incline to the top of the causeway; and there was no doubt that the mare was not only the more nimble of the two horses, she responded much better to the rein. After they crossed the bridge, he said, "Want to race to the junction?"

"You're on!" Ellen cried and put her heels to the mare.

She got the jump on Buck; and try as he might, he was unable to catch her before she drew rein just before reaching the road leading to Plantersville. This almost decided it for him. Although the stallion would probably have more staying power, he liked the mare better. He had watched both horses when the guns were fired at the gravel bar, and neither had reacted with any alarm from them; but he wanted to see what the mare would do when a gun was fired from her back. After they reached the small road leading home, Buck said to Ellen, "Do you think you can handle the stallion?"

"Of course I can," Ellen said, slightly indignant.

"Let's swap horses. I want to test the mare." They drew rein, and exchanged mounts.

"Follow at a trot," Buck said. He pulled the pistol and put spurs to the mare. She responded instantaneously and raced up the road at a full gallop. He began firing at trees as he flew by them and continued until the gun was empty. The only reaction he could see or feel from the mare was that she seemed to try to run harder with each shot. Bringing the horse to a stop, he waited for Ellen to join him.

"What was that all about?" she asked.

"I wanted to see how she reacted to gunfire."

"How did she do?"

"Like an old warhorse. I'm going to replace Skin, and she's the one."

"Randy's going to replace Chessy, too, with a mare named Troja."

"He is?"

"That's what he told Daddy."

Before they reached the house, they saw Cory standing on the front porch staring down the road in their direction. As soon as they were within earshot he asked, "What was goin' on?"

"I was shooting from the mare's back," Buck replied. "I wanted to see how she would do under fire."

"I coulda told you that," Cory said, somewhat piqued. "Don't think I'd give you a gun-shy horse, do you?"

"Sorry, I didn't know. I think I'll take the mare."

"You made a good choice; she's the best horse."

"What's her name?"

Cory looked at the porch floor, embarrassed by the question. "Miss Elly," he said barely above a whisper.

Ellen was pleased. "Did you name her for me?" she asked eagerly.

"I guess as how I did," Cory replied, happy to see that his daughter-in-law was not offended by having a horse named for her. "She was just a young filly when Buck an' you decided to git married, an' she was such a purty an' graceful thing that I just started callin' 'er 'Miss Elly.' It seemed right for her."

"I feel complimented, and I'm glad you did." Then she said teasingly to Buck, "Now you'll not be able to forget me when you go back to fight for your beloved general."

"That's next to the last thing I'd ever do."

"And what, may I ask, is the last thing?"

"Not come back to you."

Ellen started to smile and make a light response, but the smile quickly faded with the sobering realization of what could prevent his coming back to her.

Nothing was seen nor heard of Jethro Barlow. All of the James negroes were alerted to be on the lookout for him or any suspicious person in the area. Cally and Cory rode over the farm, especially the wooded areas, frequently; but they found no indication that Jethro was, or had been, on the place. Whoever had stopped at the Barlow cabin seemed to have disappeared completely.

The days went by far too quickly for Buck. His furlough was until the 21st of October, and he and Randy would have to leave on the 20th to get back in time. It was now the 18th, and he and Ellen could see their days together rapidly coming to an end. Late that afternoon, Randy and Sally rode over, Sally on Chessy and Randy on his new horse, Troja.

"It isn't Christmas, but I bring glad tidings," Randy announced. "Our furloughs have been extended for thirty days more, unless terminated earlier."

"Great! How did you hear?"

"A wire from Major Anderson. Forrest is getting a new command, and we'll be notified when and where to join him. Here's the message."

Buck read the telegram carefully. "He didn't say what the command will be."

"I don't care as long as we're with the general."

As the days passed, the weather became much colder. By the first week of November, the temperature was low enough for killing hogs; and everyone joined in this operation. It was a new experience for Ellen, but one she enjoyed, especially making and stuffing sausages. She also took part with equal interest in starting the curing processes for hams and bacon. The work had been completed; and on Friday the 13th of November, Ellen and Buck were at Prairie's Edge, where they had been invited for dinner.

It was a cold day; and they were all gathered around a large, blazing fire in the front parlor. At about eleven o'clock, Simon came in and announced, "A gen'leman who says he's Gen'ral Forrest is here with a lady."

"General Forrest!" Randy exclaimed, getting quickly to his feet and rushing out to the hall.

He returned shortly escorting General and Mrs. Forrest into the parlor. Before introductions could be made, Carolyn, who had gotten to her feet, said, "Come in; come up by the fire. You must be nearly frozen." She went quickly to Mrs. Forrest to assist her and said, "I'm Carolyn Rushton; this is my husband, John; my son, Randy, and his wife, Sally; and my daughter, Ellen, and her husband, Buck McCord. Let me help you with your things, and do come over by the fire."

"Thank you, Mrs. Rushton; I am Mary Forrest, and this is my husband, Bedford."

The general bowed to Carolyn "My pleasure, ma'am; my pleasure, indeed." He went to John's chair and shook hands with him. "An' it's a pleasure to meet you, sir."

"The pleasure is all mine, General. Welcome to Prairie's Edge; we are honored to have you."

"Thank you," Forrest replied and then looked at his two young officers, each standing politely at attention by the the the chair of his wife. "Well, I see you both jumped the broom; but I can't see how two such beautiful young ladies can see anything in a coupla hoss soldiers who are out of uniform."

Randy and Buck looked at each other. Randy said, "I don't understand what you mean, sir."

"I believe you both have on the wrong markin's for a captain."

"We don't know that we're captains," Randy replied.

"Since November the fust," Forrest said. "Congratulations on your promotions; but more important, congratulations on your marriage to such fine-lookin' ladies."

"Thank you, General. Let me take your coat," Randy said and helped Forrest out of his heavy overcoat. "It's awfully cold outside today," he added.

"Yes," Forrest replied with a smile; "but not like Duck River."

"No, sir, I don't think anything is as cold as that."

After the visitors were comfortably settled before the fire, Forrest said to John, "Mr. Rushton, I know you're int'rested in the reason for our visit. I'm on my way to a new command in Mississippi an' Tennessee an' come by Selma to place an order for some cannon. I can't proceed on my trip till tomorrow afternoon; so, on the spur of the moment, I decided to come to Prairie's Edge in hope I might buy one of your fine hosses."

Buck started to tell the general he had a horse for him; but before he could do so, John Rushton replied, "General, it just happens that I have

a very fine stallion Randy was to take to you as a gift when he returned
to duty—a small token of our appreciation for the outstanding job you
are doing for the country.''

"Yours are fine an' valu'ble horses, Mr. Rushton. I didn' come here
lookin' for a gift; I expect to pay the goin' price.''

"Our government is taking my horses as fast as I raise them; in fact,
I'm having difficulty holding onto my breeding stock. They're paying
nothing like the real value for mounts of this quality, so don't look upon
this as any great gift on my part, but consider it as a modest contribution
to the cause to which we are both devoted.''

"You're a gen'rous man, Mr. Rushton.''

"Not so. I offer only the product of my pastures and my fields;
gentlemen such as you offer their time, their comforts, and even their
lives.''

"You offered your son.''

"No, he did that himself, I'm proud to say. I understand you are
going to a new command, General. Would I be amiss in asking what it
will be?''

"Not atall. Several months ago, friends in north'n Mississippi and
west'n Tennessee appealed to me to come to that area to gather their
scattered resources for defense an' offense. I made a request to our
President to give me independent command in that part of the country
along the Mississippi River from Vicksburg to Cairo, all of which is
unfortunately in the hands of the enemy. I asked for only a small force to
go with me, believing I can raise from five to ten thousand men in that
area to attack an' harass the enemy, especially their traffic on the
Mississippi. I am bein' given only a part of what I asked for. I will not
be independent, but under the command of the departmental
commander, General Joseph E. Johnston; an' other restrictions have
been placed upon me which I'd rather not have. I didn't git the men I
asked for, either; but who ever has ever'thing he wants? I'll do my best
with the cards I been dealt.''

"This is a bold and monumental task you've taken on, General. I
wish you the best.''

"We shall all be praying for your success and for the safety of you
and your men,'' Carolyn said.

"Your good wishes an' prayers'll be appreciated.''

At that moment, Samuel came in and said, "Dinner's ready to be
served.''

As they were leaving for the dining room, Forrest said to Buck and
Randy, "I know this's short notice, but the train leaves Selma for
Meridian at two tomorrow afternoon. I'd like for y'all to be on it with

me.''

The honeymoon was over.

After dinner, John took the general in his cart to show him the horses and to get the stallion he would take with him. As they drove away from the house, Forrest said, ''You've got a mighty fine son, Mr. Rushton; you can be proud of 'im.''

''I am, General Forrest; but I must admit I had misgivings about his going into the army. All of his life Randy had an aversion to the sight of blood. It did something to him, even to the point of making him ill. I was afraid of what might happen when he faced the bloody scenes of battle.''

Forrest laughed. ''He did have a little problem along that line in our fust fight; but his friend, McCord, brought 'im back to the action, an' he more'n made up for his failin'. In fact, if it hadn' been for your son, I prob'bly wouldn' be here today; he throwed himself between me an' a enemy saber. We had a good heart-to-heart talk after that fight; an' if he ever had another problem about the sight of blood, I never knowed about it.''

''I guess he was fortunate that Buck was there.''

''He was that.'' Forrest laughed again. ''McCord's a pretty cool customer. I had a talk with him, too, about leavin' the fight to go after Randy. When I asked 'im what he woulda done if Randy hadn' come back, he looked me right in the eye an' said, 'I guess you woulda lost two men today!'''

''That's like Buck. He and Randy have been friends for years. They are closer than most brothers.''

''You don't see many frien'ships like that, Mr. Rushton. Them who find it are indeed fortunate. I never did. My pa died when I was no more'n a boy, an' I had the responsibility of raisin' a large family. I never knowed much but work as a young man.''

''From what I've heard, you deserve a great deal of credit for what you have accomplished. You are living proof that hard work and industry have their rewards.''

''As I said before, Mr. Rushton, you are a gen'rous man.''

The Forrests did not linger after John and the general returned to the house. They set out immediately on the long drive to Selma with John's three year old stallion tied to the rear of the buggy. Buck and Ellen left soon afterward for the McCord home. Cory and Sadie received glumly the news of Buck's having to return to duty, and Buck then told Cory about John's gift of the stallion to Forrest. ''I didn't say anything about the horse you planned to give him, Pa; I didn't want to detract from what

Mr. John had done.''

"I understan','' Cory said. "You done right. Maybe I'll have one to give 'im next time. Right now, I can put the horse to good use.''

Early the following morning, Buck took a sad farewell of his parents, and he and Ellen rode in the buggy to Prairie's Edge with Cally following on horseback and leading Buck's mottled mare. Buck was wearing a new gray overcoat which Ellen and Sadie had made for him. They weren't aware of it at the time, but Cory left soon afterward on his horse and was leading the stallion he had intended to give Forrest.

At Prairie's Edge, they took the Rushton carriage so Sally and Ellen could accompany them as far as Selma. They got there before noon and ate the lunch Carolyn had placed in the carriage. Buck and Ellen then walked a short distance down the track. "I hope you won't regret your decision to stay with the folks," Buck said.

"I won't.''

"You've seen enough to know they lead a far different life from that at Prairie's Edge.''

"I know, but I've got to learn that life; and I couldn't do it with two better people. Don't worry about me; I'm adaptable.''

"It's a way of hard work, and you aren't used to that.''

"I'm getting used to it, and I like it.''

"Promise me this; if it gets too rough, go back to Prairie's Edge. Ma and Pa would understand.''

"I know; they're that kind. I've been intending to ask; after we got engaged, I started calling them Miss Sadie and Mr. Cory. Do you think they would mind if I called them Ma and Pa like you?''

"Mind? That would be the greatest compliment you could pay them.''

"I'm glad; I feel so close to both of them.''

Buck looked at the sun. "I don't want you to go, but you had better leave now to get home before dark.''

They rejoined Randy and Sally; and after sad farewells, the carriage pulled off up the street, leaving two disconsolate husbands silently watching it go.

It had been a long, cold trip; and Cory was glad to see the first half of it end as he rode up in front of the plantation home of Herndon Steen two miles north of Marion Junction. He got down stiffly from his horse and tied the two stallions to a hitching post. He had started up the steps to the porch when the front door opened and a negro man appeared. "Is Mr. Steen in?" Cory asked.

"Yassah, he's here. Come in." The negro led the way down the hall to a room on the right where he knocked on the door and said, "Dey's a gen'lman to see you, Massa."

"Tell 'im to come in," a voice from behind the door replied. The negro opened the door, and Cory went inside. Seated near the fire was a fat man of sixty or more years who was smoking a long-stemmed pipe. He recognized Cory and said, "Well, Mr. McCord, come have a seat. It's good to see you. I hope you're here because you finally have a horse for me. I've waited a long time for one of yours."

"Maybe I have," Cory said, taking a seat without offering to shake hands. "Are you the owner of a runaway slave gal called Vira?"

"Yes. Have you found her?"

"I'd like to buy 'er."

"Well, I don't know that she's for sale, Mr. McCord. She's young and very valuable."

"Not all that val'able—she's barren; an' barren women don't bring much."

"You seem knowledgeable about her, Mr. McCord," Steen said with a smirk. "You must know where she is, and I would like to know, too; I want my property back."

Cory ignored the statement and insinuation and said, "I have a fine stallion out front I'll trade for the gal."

"I'm afraid that wouldn't be adequate payment for her."

"That's up to you, but maybe you oughta take a look at the hoss before you make up your mind."

"If you're harboring a runaway slave, Mr. McCord, you are violating the law."

"That I know; but I ain't harb'ring 'er—I just know about 'er. If you ain't int'rested in the trade, I'll be on my way. I've got a long way to go," Cory said as he got to his feet.

"Just a minute, Mr. McCord, I didn't say I wasn't interested. Let's take a look at the stallion."

They went outside; and when Steen saw the horse, he could hardly believe his good fortune. In an effort to hide his pleasure over the deal, he tried to appear to be reluctant as he signed the papers transferring ownership of the slave. After the transaction was completed, he asked Cory to stay for dinner; but the invitation was declined. Before McCord mounted his horse, Steen offered him his hand; and Cory tried to hide his reluctance as he shook it.

It was dusk when Ellen drove into the back yard of the McCord home. Cory came out to close the gate for her and to take care of the horse and buggy. "We was beginnin' to worry about you," he said.

"It was a long, tiresome trip. I'm nearly frozen."

"Go on inside; the kitchen's nice an' warm."

Upon entering the kitchen, Ellen was surprised to see a negro girl helping Sadie prepare supper. The girl turned toward the sound of the door opening, and Ellen recognized her. "Vira! What in the world are you doing here?"

"I belongs here, Missy; I belongs to Massa McCord now."

"I don't like the sound of that," Sadie said firmly. "He won't like it neither; you call 'im Mr. McCord."

Ellen went over by the kitchen stove to get warm. She looked at Sadie and asked, "How did this come about?"

"They was gonna whup her, because she opened the door an' let y'all see who was inside; so she runned away. She went to Preher's Edge lookin' for you, an' the slave folks sent 'er over here. When she come here, she found Artie James fust. He was 'fraid you might git in trouble by helpin' 'er, so he kept 'er hid. Them two's been livin' together all this time an' not married one bit. Cory found 'er when he was lookin' for Jethro, but he never told me nothin' about it till he swapped a hoss for 'er today. Artie wants to marry 'er, but things gotta be worked out fust. I ain't havin' no outa-wed carrin' on here, so I told Cory to go git 'er an' bring 'er to the house till ever'thing's straightened out." Sadie made no effort to conceal her unhappiness with the situation.

"Where will she stay?"

"We've fixed 'er a warm pallet in the storeroom. It's as good as that darkie's house where she was livin'."

Ellen looked at Vira. The negro girl smiled, showing two rows of beautiful, white teeth. "I be all right, Missy. I likes it here. Ever'body been real good to me."

Especially Artie, Ellen thought.

Chapter XV

A New Command

It was shortly before two o'clock, and Randy and Buck were seated about the middle of a passenger car with Major J. P. Strange waiting for the train to pull out. Cally had again elected to ride with the horses. The reunion with the major had been a pleasant surprise, for this was the first time they had seen him since he had been exchanged, following his capture at Parker's Crossroad. Through the window they saw a carriage arrive with General and Mrs. Forrest and a young man dressed in a Confederate uniform.

"Who is that with the Forrests?" Randy asked.

"That's their son, Willie. He's going to be a member of the staff," Strange replied.

"He looks to be no more than a boy," Buck commented.

"He isn't, but he wanted to serve; and the general thought it best that he go with him. He may be a boy; but if he's half the man his father is, he'll be all right."

"Where's the rest of the brigade?" Buck asked.

"You didn't know? Forrest had to leave them with Bragg. They submitted a written petition to go with him, as did some others; but Bragg couldn't afford to lose them."

"You mean that none of them are going with us?"

"Only the staff and 271 men," Strange replied. "Eight staff, 65 in the escort company, 139 in McDonald's battalion, and 67 in John Morton's battery. Woodward's battalion was supposed to be with us; but when Bragg issued the order, they were not included."

"That Bragg! He does like to endear himself with Forrest. Where are the men? They're not on the train."

"They left before we did on a march to Okolona, Mississippi. Major Anderson is with them, and they may have arrived there by now. That's where we will meet them."

"How about the scouts?"

"They'll be there—what's left of them. Being irregulars, they didn't need orders from Bragg."

"I'm going to miss the old brigade," Buck said.

"You're not the only one. One of the saddest scenes I ever witnessed was when Old Bedford said good-bye to them. There wasn't a dry eye there—especially his."

"Where will the men for the new command come from?"

"Colonel R. V. Richardson is to join us with about 2,000 West-Tennesseans, and Forrest will try to assemble splinter groups and other small commands in western Tennessee and mold them into a fighting force."

"This doesn't sound very encouraging, but he's done it before."

"And he'll do it again," Strange said.

At Meridian, Forrest met with General Joseph E. Johnston, his departmental commander. From him he learned that three small cavalry brigades constituted the entire Confederate force in North Mississippi. These were under Major General Stephen D. Lee, chief of cavalry in the department. They provided details for a line of outposts running from Panola, Mississippi, eastward along the south bank of the Tallahatchie River and on to Baldwyn, a station on the Mobile and Ohio Railroad. They also sent out scouts to the north to watch the movements of the enemy. The largest of these brigades, under General James R. Chalmers, was divided into two semibrigades commanded by Colonels McCulloch and Slemmons. This brigade was on the left, from Panola to Rocky Ford. Brigadier General Ferguson and Colonel Ross commanded brigades to the east of Rocky Ford. Colonel R. V. Richardson's brigade had arrived at Okolona and was waiting for Forrest.

The Federals had strong forces at Memphis and Corinth; and between these, some ninety miles apart, were well defended posts on the Memphis and Charleston Railroad. They were capable of moving troops rapidly along this line between the two major strongholds. Their effective force was estimated to be about 10,000 men.

In assigning Forrest to his new command, Johnston wrote, "He will, on arriving there (western Tennessee), proceed to raise and organize as many troops for the Confederate service as he finds practicable. Colonel Richardson will report to General Forrest, of whose command his troops will form a part."

Forrest arrived in Okolona on November 15, 1863, and lost no time in meeting with Colonel Richardson to ascertain the status and condition of the latter's command. As soon as the amenities of introduction were over, the cavalry commander got at once into the purpose of his visit.

"What's the number an' condition of your men an' hosses?" the general asked.

"Not good. I'm down to about 250 men."

"Only 250!" Forrest interrupted. "I was told you'd have 2,000."

"I don't know where that figure came from. I brought from Tennessee only 800 men. We came out in warm weather, and the men had only light clothing. When cold weather came on, they began leaving without permission to go back for heavier clothes since we couldn't supply them here."

"Let's take a look at the men an' inventory their equipment."

This inspection was equally disappointing. There were only 247 horses fit for duty, and the entire command had only 271 guns and 151 pistols. The men going home had carried with them 517 Enfield and Austrian rifles.

Forrest was promised another regiment; but when it arrived, it numbered only 150 men. His luck, however, was not all bad. He had been able to enlist the energy and loyalty of Tyree H. Bell, a man of considerable reputation and influence in western Tennessee, who proved to be a leader of courage and ability. He and Bell were able to bring into the new command several capable officers, among whom were Colonels A. N. Wilson, John F. Newsom, R. M. Russell, and Lieutenant Colonel D. M. Wisdom. All of them had seen prior service and were favorably known to the people of the region in which they would operate. Forrest and Bell had become acquainted while serving in Bragg's army. Bell had been the senior colonel in General Preston Smith's brigade; and Forrest had asked Bell to go with him to his new assignment, promising a commission as brigadier general if he would raise sufficient men for such a command. He dispatched Bell with a small detachment into the counties west of the Tennessee River, in advance of his own movement into that area, to spy out the land and to spread the word that Forrest was coming for the purpose of occupying that section and holding it for the Confederacy.[1]

Forrest's plan was to break through the strongly held line along the Memphis and Charleston Railroad, go into western Tennessee to collect supplies and recruits, and to bring them back the same way. He was not deterred by the insignificant number in his command, having confidence that, once inside Tennessee, he would be able to rally the small, disorganized bands of Confederates there into an effective fighting force. General S. D. Lee was to cover the movement and assembled two brigades at New Albany, Mississippi. Forrest met him there with his own meager force on November 29. Lee's forces created a diversion and opened the way for Forrest to cross the well guarded Memphis and

Charleston Railroad. Lee reported to Johnston that Forrest had "marched into west Tennessee with four hundred and fifty men and two guns, having been compelled to leave the balance of his artillery for lack of horses to pull them."

The intruding cavalry leader pushed on rapidly with nothing to retard him except the two guns and five light ordnance wagons. He reached Bolivar on the 5th, where his men were welcomed by the people of that town, and arrived at Jackson in the afternoon of the 6th. Here he met Colonel Bell, who had done his job well. Three regiments were rapidly recruited or conscripted. They were organized under the able leaders Forrest and Bell had brought into the command, but many were not armed.

Forrest's incursion into Tennessee was watched by the Federal forces. Sherman had been unconcerned about it at first, saying, "I have made the junction at which I was aiming, and am rather indifferent to Forrest's reported expedition. He may cavort about the country as much as he pleases." When Forrest established recruiting stations in nearly every county of western Tennessee and in parts of Kentucky, vigorous measures were taken by Grant and Sherman to kill, capture, or expel the intruders. Expeditions were sent out against them from Columbus, Kentucky, and Fort Pillow in Tennessee. These did not bother him, but he was concerned that others might come out from Memphis or some other point on the railroad in his rear. He requested that General Lee, with all the cavalry that could be spared, be brought up to West Tennessee with the arms and ammunition he had been promised and which were now needed for the new troops. He believed that if this were done the Memphis and Charleston Railroad could be destroyed, and five or six thousand head of beef cattle could be driven out for use of the army. He added in his dispatch to Johnston, "If I hear that he is coming to help me, I will build a pontoon bridge across the Hatchie and will have the cattle gathered up by the time he can reach me. I am in great need of money and have had to advance my quartermaster and commissary $20,000 of my private funds to subsist the command thus far."

The Federal forces began to close in on the intruders from several directions. General William Sooy Smith, who had been selected by Grant to command the cavalry for the military division of Mississippi, was reported to be coming from the direction of Nashville and Columbia, Tennessee; General A. J. Smith from Columbus, Kentucky; General Grierson from Memphis; and General Crook from Huntsville, Alabama. Those from the northward were as far south as Trenton and McLemoresville by the 22nd. A column from Corinth was reported to have moved as far as Purdy and was on the road to Jack's Creek. Scouts also reported a cavalry force of 2,000 divided between Somerville and Bolivar, while the infantry was still heavily posted on the Memphis and Charleston Railroad line. General Grierson had concentrated nearly all of his cavalry command at LaGrange, a favorable point to move quickly in any direction to intercept Forrest if he attempted to withdraw to Mississippi.

Colonel Richardson, who had been stationed at Brownsville, twenty-eight miles northwest of Jackson, had recruited his force to one thousand men. On the 22nd of December, Forrest ordered him to put his small brigade in motion southward and cross the Hatchie at Estenaula, eighteen miles west of Jackson. This was accomplished on the 24th. Very few of Richardson's men had ever been under fire, and only 300 of them were armed. Soon after crossing the river, the command came in collision with the advance of the Seventh Illinois Cavalry, a part of Grierson's command, five hundred strong under Colonel Prince.

This Federal regiment had been sent north to the Hatchie River at Bolivar with orders to follow this stream from that point toward the Mississippi River and to destroy all the ferryboats and any bridges that might have been overlooked. Grierson hoped to prevent Forrest's passage over the Hatchie and force him to a long detour around the headwaters of the Hatchie and Wolf rivers above Bolivar and toward Corinth, where he would fall easy prey to the forces stationed along that line for his destruction.

Forrest had divided his command into three detachments. The first to move southward was Richardson's from Brownsville. The second and largest, under Colonel Bell, left Jackson with two pieces of artillery, some forty or fifty well laden wagons, and several hundred beef cattle being driven south. This force was made up principally of recruits, and more than half of them were unarmed; and it was also sent in the direction of Estenaula. The third, under Lieutenant Colonel D. M. Wisdom, made up of about 500 armed men, was ordered to march southeasterly from Jackson toward Mifflin and Jack's Creek to hold off an enemy column coming from that direction.

The first collision of Forrest's men with the enemy occurred at daylight on December 24, when Wisdom encountered the enemy moving toward Jackson. He handled his command quite well, maneuvering them in such a manner that he gave the impression he had a much larger force and, by doing so, held the enemy in check until the main column under Bell had made good headway toward Estenaula. Once during the day his position was seriously threatened by a Federal movement on his flank and rear. He immediately ordered eighty picked men under Lieutenants H. A. Tyler and John O. Morris to check the flankers. Tyler was given command of the squadron, which was made up of Kentuckians. He and Morris, at the head of their respective units, rode recklessly right into the Federal line. The firing was very severe and at such close quarters that the clothing of some of the killed and wounded was ignited by burning powder. It was brief but bloody work, and the Federal flankers gave way.

Lieutenant Morris was fatally wounded in this affair. While grappling with a Union trooper, their horses dashing at full speed along the highway, he and the enemy cavalryman thrust the muzzles of their pistols against each other and fired at the same time. Both fell from their horses mortally wounded.

Wisdom withdrew at nightfall and by a forced march joined the main column at daylight Christmas morning, and the Confederates were not molested further by this enemy force.

Forrest with his escort made up the rear guard for Bell's column, and they also had a sharp collision not far from Jackson with an enemy column coming from the direction of Corinth. After dashing into the enemy with his meager force, and repulsing them, Forrest moved swiftly in the wake of Bell to Estenaula, reaching there on the night of the 24th. He crossed over and joined Richardson, who was already on the south side of the river, having raised the ferryboat and crossed his men over.

No sooner had this junction been made than Forrest was informed that sharp firing had begun about five miles away in the direction of Bolivar. Prince had come up with his Seventh Illinois cavalry, met Richardson's pickets, and had driven them back upon the latter's advance guard. The Confederates were pushed back to Slough Bridge, a mile and a half east of where the Hatchie was being crossed. Here the Confederates held, and the Federals went into camp.

Forrest ordered a guard made up of ten men from his escort, under the command of Sergeant George L. Cowan, to move southwestward down the Memphis road to keep a sharp lookout for the enemy. He then marched rapidly toward the firing with the rest of his escort, followed by the remainder of Richardson's men. The men at the head of this column had orders to ride right into the enemy until they came upon something formidable. This small advance guard ran into the enemy pickets about two miles from the river and put spurs to their horses in pursuit of the flying pickets. They rode pell-mell into the picket reserves, about forty strong, who, taken by surprise and thinking the charging force was much larger than they were, also broke and ran for the main camp.

The Rebels saw ahead the enemy campfires scattered on both sides of the road. Forrest came up with the balance of the escort commanded by Lieutenant Nathan Boone. He directed the escort to go forward and reconnoiter the enemy while he brought up Richardson's men. The escort moved forward to the edge of a cornfield adjacent to the enemy's camp.

Boone could see that the Federals in the camp were in disorder and decided to take things into his own hands. He spread his force out with about ten paces between each man and instructed the officers and sergeants to give orders as if commanding a company. In a loud voice, he yelled, "Forward, Brigade! Charge!"

The small force swept across the cornfield with a tremendous racket. It was a clear, frosty night; and the horses trampled the cornstalks down with enough noise, aided by the yells of the Rebels, to make it appear that at least a regiment was charging. The Federals apparently thought the enemy was upon them in great force, for they broke and ran in disorder. The Rebels dashed through the camp and kept up the pursuit for two miles before it was broken off.

All through the bitterly cold night Bell pushed his men and supplies across the Hatchie River. The crossing was made with the loss of only one teamster and two horses, but Forrest's problems were far from over. To the south was the swollen Wolf River with all boats on it and all bridges over it destroyed; to the northwest was Fort Pillow; to the southwest was Memphis with its large garrison; just beyond the unfordable Wolf River to the south was the well guarded railroad line with Federal troops loaded on trains ready to move either east or west; and to the east, between the flooded Hatchie and Wolf rivers, lay Federal forces waiting to pounce upon him as he was forced to move in that direction.

Wily Forrest had an ace up his sleeve. A friend, Colonel Thomas H. Logan, had ventured into the section of Tennessee just north of Memphis on a recruiting mission for his regiment. He discovered that near Lafayette Station, on the Memphis and Charleston Railroad, was a bridge over the Wolf River which had been only partially destroyed. The detail setting fire to the bridge did not wait to see the results; and only the flooring of one span was destroyed, leaving the stringers partially burned but still strong. He sent this information to Forrest while the general was still in Jackson. Forrest ordered Colonel Bell ahead with 300 men to drive away any Federals in the vicinity of the bridge, to cross to the south side of the river, and to repair the bridge for the remainder of the command to cross.

Colonel Faulkner was sent with 700 men, only fifty of whom were armed, to attack the pickets within the suburbs of Memphis and, if hard pressed, to escape by the way of Hernando to Como, Mississippi.

Colonel Prince had retired toward Somerville; so Forrest, with his escort and a detachment of McDonald's battalion, took up the trail with Richardson preceding him with his command in the same direction on another road. On the 26th, near Somerville, Richardson again collided with Prince's regiment. Hearing the firing, Forrest moved to the scene quickly and took command. Throwing Richardson's unarmed men, as well as those with arms, into line of battle to make a more formidable appearance, Forrest advanced upon the enemy, who did not give way until after a hard struggle which created losses on both sides. Among the Confederates wounded was Lieutenant Nathan Boone, the commander of Forrest's escort; and the lieutenant's brother, the first sergeant of that unit, was killed.[2]

Forrest was not bothered further by Prince. He sent a detachment of 200 men east of Lafayette to create the impression a crossing would be attempted there, and he sent other detachments to tear up and obstruct the railroad two miles east and two miles west of the actual point of crossing. Bell reached the burned Wolf River bridge about daybreak on the 27th. Advancing under cover of a dense wood, his men crossed the unburned stringers and surprised and drove off a small body of Federals that had taken a position not far from the southern end of the bridge. Within the matter of a couple of hours, the bridge was repaired; and when the Confederate main column came up, it began crossing without delay at four p.m. under Forrest's personal supervision.

Crossing the Wolf River had not placed the Confederates out of danger. A strong bold dash of Federal cavalry against the tired and poorly armed men and their jaded horses might scatter the trains, stock, and troopers without weapons into the woods and swamps. With the Wolf River behind him, Forrest ordered the unarmed men with the trains and cattle to make an all-night march on the road to Holly Springs by way of Mount Pleasant. To cover them, a detachment was thrown out to the east toward Moscow with orders to fall back if hard pressed. Forrest moved in the opposite direction with his escort, three hundred men, and Morton's section of artillery. Two miles out of Lafayette he met and drove back an advance of Federal cavalry. Here his scouts came up from Lafayette and Moscow and reported the movement of cavalry and infantry from that direction in force.

The scouts were reinforced and sent back to open as hot a skirmish as possible in order to divert attention from the train escaping southward. This served the purpose; but the enemy overtook Forrest near

Colliersville (only twenty-five miles east of Memphis), and a brisk skirmish took place. Men were lost and prisoners taken on both sides. Among the Rebels captured was Forrest's chief engineer, Captain John G. Mann, who served his commander well by intimating that General Stephen D. Lee was nearby with his entire cavalry force. This seemed plausible to the Federal commander, as Lee had made a demonstration upon Saulsbury on December 4 with McCulloch's and Ross' brigades when Forrest had moved north across the railroad. The Federal commander withdrew to Lafayette and remained there for the rest of the night.

The Federal forces at Colliersville were within their fortifications and presented no problem. Rain, which had been falling for the past twelve hours, suddenly ceased; and a cold wind sprang up from the northwest. The train was now well on its way to Holly Springs, and before midnight Forrest headed his command in that direction. By daylight of the 28th he was in Mount Pleasant; and with the danger of immediate pursuit over, the command proceeded by easy marches across the country to Como.

Forrest had crossed into Tennessee with 450 men, two pieces of artillery, and five ordnance wagons. He returned with 3,500 well mounted men, at least forty heavily laden wagons, his artillery, 200 beef cattle, and 300 hogs. He was pleased with the performance of his officers and men and was especially proud of his young son, Willie, who acted as his aide and had conducted himself well. Many of the men were just from home and were not even supplied with blankets; but they endured the hardships, privation, and exposure encountered in marching 140 miles, much of it in rain and cold weather, with patience and fortitude.

The Federals could take little pride in their performance. General Hurlbut wired General Sherman on December 28, "Forrest, after having been driven from the neighborhood of Jackson, has eluded Grierson, and crossed the railroad last night." The message failed to mention that he had passed only twenty-five miles from Hurlbut's headquarters at Memphis and had sent a detachment, almost completely unarmed, to within a few miles of that place. This was not overlooked by everyone, however; for a correspondent for the *Cincinnati Commercial* wrote from Memphis on January 12, 1864: "Forrest, with less than 4,000 men, had moved right through the Sixteenth Army Corps, has passed within nine miles of Memphis, carried off over 100 wagons, 200 beef cattle, 3,000 conscripts, and innumerable stores, torn up railroad track, cut telegraph wire, burned and sacked towns, run over pickets with a single Derringer pistol...and all too in the face of 10,000 men.''³

Forrest proceeded on to Holly Springs, where he reported to General S. D. Lee. Here he learned that General Joseph E. Johnston had replaced General Bragg as commander of the Army of Tennessee and that Lieutenant General Leonidas Polk had replaced Johnston as commander of the Army of Mississippi. He reported to the latter the results of his expedition and in reply was informed that he had been promoted to the rank of major general on December 4 and would be assigned to command a district.

The men Forrest had brought out of Tennessee included the fragments of sixteen different commands. Some companies had as few as fifteen men. There were far too many officers for the number of men; but the officers, many of whom had raised their units, were ambitious and unwilling to give up their commands or ranks. The cavalry commander could see no way of making these troops effective except by an order from the War Department annulling all authority previously given to raise troops, accompanied with an order to consolidate into full companies and regiments all the troops in West Tennessee and North Mississippi, and he requested this.

On January 15, Forrest left Chalmers in command and reported to General Polk at his headquarters in Jackson, Mississippi; and there he was given command of a district designated as ''Forrest's Cavalry Department.'' This included all cavalry in West Tennessee and in North Mississippi as far south as the southern boundaries of Monroe, Chickasaw, Calhoun, Yalobusha, and Tallahatchie Counties and parts of Sunflower and Bolivar Counties lying north of a line drawn from the southern corner of Tallahatchie County and extending to Prentiss on the Mississippi River.

Forrest received from Richmond the authority he had requested to organize the men into an effective command and immediately set to work to implement a plan he already had in mind. His force, now numbering 5,100 men, was formed into four brigades.⁴ When the organization was completed, Forrest moved his headquarters to Oxford, Mississippi, a position more centrally located for watching the enemy and for offensive operations.

The newly recruited Tennesseans were, for the most part, used to operating in small bands or units with little discipline or authority over them. They were independent by nature and did not take well to military discipline. They were poorly clothed and armed, and many were discontented because of this. In Tennessee they had been prone to leave camp without permission and did not hesitate to do so in their new command. Normal attempts, such as sending out details to bring them back, did not prove effective in stopping this; and stronger measures were needed. Nineteen who marched off together were pursued, captured, and brought back in disgrace. Forrest decided to make an example of them; and after a drum-head court martial, they were ordered to be executed. Their coffins were made, their graves dug, and the culprits were advised to make their peace with their Maker. News of the affair got abroad; and the clergy, prominent citizens, and ladies met with Forrest and made urgent appeals to him to spare the lives of the men. Some of his officers of high rank advised him of their serious apprehension that there would be mutinous resistance on the part of the soldiers if an attempt were made to execute so many of their comrades.

Forrest was apparently unmoved by the intercessions and unswerved by the threat of mutiny and proceeded with the ordered executions. The men were brought before the troops, blindfolded, and made to sit upon their coffins. The firing line was drawn up before them waiting for the command, "Fire!" before he granted them a reprieve, through one of his staff officers, and remanded them to prison. This lesson was not lost on any who saw or heard of the spectacle; they were sure that the next time their commander might not be so lenient.

Except for the rigors, discomfort, and hardships of the incursion into Tennessee, both Randy and Buck had come through it without mishap. Buck was particularly pleased with the performance of Miss Elly. No horse could ever take the place Skin held in his affections, but Miss Elly had come close. She responded well to his commands and had proven to be a fine warhorse. The way she held up on the long hard march was better than he had expected. Randy was almost equally pleased with Troja, but he did not believe his mare would ever approach being as good as Chessie. Both had been working with the horses and had trained them to come to their whistle signals.

Not long after the move to Oxford, Buck and Randy received their first mail from home, and each had several letters. Buck arranged those from Ellen chronologically so he could read them in the order written. He was half way through the first one when he exclaimed, "I'll be damned! I can't believe it!"

"Believe what?" Randy asked.

"Pa bought a slave."

"You're kidding."

"That's what Ellen says—the girl who was our maid in Cahawba."

"Why did he do that?"

"I don't know yet." Buck resumed reading the letter; and when he finished, he said, "They were going to whip her for opening the door and letting us see Beverly that night, and she ran away. Ellen had been nice to the girl, so she came looking for her. Artie James was afraid Ellen would get in trouble if she helped the runaway, so he kept her hidden; and they started living together. Pa discovered her while looking for Jethro. When he learned the story, he traded a stallion he had planned to give Old Bedford for her."

"Wonder what he'll do with a slave?"

"Artie wants to marry the girl. Ma won't let her live with him until things can be worked out, so she's staying at the house and helping Ma."

Randy laughed. "That sounds interesting."

Buck laughed, too. "I'd like to see Ma with a slave. I bet you can't tell who's working for whom." Both of them returned to their letters.

"What do you know!" Buck exclaimed as he was reading Ellen's last one. "I may be a papa before long!"

"That's great! Is it definite?"

"She's not positive, but she thinks so. How about that—me a father! I can't believe it."

"You'll make a good one. Maybe it'll happen to us one of these days; I hope so. Anyway, I'll be an uncle."

Buck could see his friend's disappointment at not having received the same kind of news from Sally. "If I make you an uncle, the least you can do is make me one, too."

Randy looked at Buck, and grinned, "I'll do my level best," he replied.

At that moment the door opened, and Bill Williamson came in. From his expression they knew something was wrong. "What is it, Bill?" Randy asked.

"It's Kevin; he's dead," Bill said, his voice showing his emotion.

Buck asked, "How did it happen?"

"I got a letter from Colonel Kelley. He said Kevin was wounded and taken prisoner when Wheeler attacked Rosecrans' supply lines beyond Chattanooga. They sent him to Johnson's Island prison on Lake Erie, and Colonel Kelley just learned that he died there."

"I've heard about that prison," Buck said, "bitterly cold and inadequate shelter. A lot of our people have died there from exposure."

Bill walked over to the bed and sat down on it. Gloom fell over the room like a pall as each of the three friends went over in his mind the relationship he had enjoyed with the friendly, outgoing Kevin, who had such an impact on the course their own lives had taken.

Chapter XVI

Sooy!

When it became known to the enemy that Forrest would command the cavalry in the new department, Generals Grant and Sherman put their heads together to find a cavalry leader of sufficient ability to cope with so formidable an adversary. Grant chose Brigadier General William Sooy Smith, and on November 11 made him the chief of cavalry for the military division of Mississippi.[1]

After Grant's overwhelming victory at Missionary Ridge, near Chattanooga, on November 25, 1863, in which he drove Bragg from an almost impregnable position, Sherman, who had reinforced Thomas' Army of the Cumberland for the battle, returned to Vicksburg. In early January 1864, he and Grant planned an operation against middle Mississippi and Alabama.[2]

The plan called for Sherman to send a diversionary movement up the Yazoo River while his army moved eastward from Vicksburg to Meridian. A second diversionary force would be sent southward from Memphis toward Hernando, Mississippi; while the largest and best equipped cavalry force ever assembled in the West would move, under the command of General William Sooy Smith, from its staging area at Colliersville, Tennessee, to Okolona where it would begin destruction of the railroad to Meridian. This cavalry force of 7,000 effective men, armed with Colt repeating rifles, modern carbines, and army revolvers, was to leave Colliersville on or before February 1 and was expected to reach Meridian, a distance of about 250 miles, on the 10th. Sherman would march with his army of 20,000 men to join Smith at that place. Once this junction of forces had been effected, they could move leisurely on into Alabama for the capture of Selma with its arsenals and foundries.

For some inexplicable reason, as the telegraph lines were open between Vicksburg and Memphis, communications between Sherman and Smith broke down. Smith delayed his departure, as he was waiting for Colonel George E. Waring, Jr., to join him with a small brigade from Columbus, Kentucky; but he failed to advise Sherman of it. Sherman moved out of Vicksburg on February 3 and, pushing General Polk's small command out of Jackson and into Alabama, reached Meridian on the 14th with little opposition.

Heavy rains had so badly damaged the roads and swollen the streams that Colonel Waring found travel difficult and slow from Columbus. He did not join Smith until the 8th, and his men and horses were in such bad shape that Smith delayed his departure three more days to rest them and to reshoe the horses.

Colonel William L. McMillen, commanding a brigade of infantry, set out southward from Memphis in advance of Smith and reached Hernando on the 7th. He took Senatobia on the 9th; and on the 13th, having skirmished almost incessantly with Forrest's vedettes, he reached the Tallahatchie at Wyatt in his planned diversionary move. Smith marched from Colliersville on the 11th, accompanied by twenty pieces of artillery. He knew he would be confronted by Forrest, who he thought would have his forces scattered along the south banks of the Tallahatchie. He marched in the direction of Wyatt, where McMillen was engaged with Confederate forces across the river, giving the impression he would cross the Tallahatchie at that point. Instead, he turned suddenly east and crossed the river to the south bank at New Albany on the 16th and 17th without molestation. It was a smart move which proved to be successful.

Forrest, however, was not completely fooled. From scouts, friends, and men working under cover, he kept apprised of the enemy's intentions. He had informed Chalmers on February 6 of the impending movement from Colliersville and directed him to send twenty reliable men well to his front to watch the enemy. On the 8th he informed General Gholson, the commander of the Mississippi State militia, of McMillen's column moving on the Hernando road. In a later dispatch that day about the enemy advances, he reported, "They will move in two columns, one by Panola to Grenada, the other by New Albany and Pontotoc, towards Okolona." On the 16th he informed General Polk that the enemy had crossed at New Albany, were about 10,000 strong, and their destination was a junction with Sherman.

When Smith moved from Colliersville, Forrest withdrew all of his forces north of the Tallahatchie to the south of the river. Placing small detachments to watch the river crossings, he fell back to Grenada and ordered the remainder of his troops through Houston in the direction of West Point and Columbus. Forrest pushed rapidly east from Grenada to Starkville, where he arrived on the 18th. Jeffrey Forrest was directed to move his brigade northward to meet Smith and to oppose his advance sufficiently to develop his strength and purposes. Forrest felt that Okolona was an important point in Smith's route of march, but he did not know whether he planned to turn eastward there across the Tombigbee River to reach Columbus to the south or would turn south at Okolona to march toward Meridian. In order to safeguard against the first mentioned possibility, he sent Bell's brigade eastward across the Tombigbee to move northward to a position across the river from Smith. Bell was ill, and Colonel Barteau was in command of the brigade.

General Smith's march had been relatively uneventful. He ran into some difficulty in crossing the Tippah, a narrow, swollen stream with a treacherous bottom; and he was delayed two days in building a bridge over it. Occasionally his troopers ran into light fire from a Confederate outpost or some scouts, but he met little resistance of any consequence until his advance guard came upon a squadron of General Gholson's state militia about ten miles from Houston. The militiamen fired a volley with shotguns and squirrel rifles and then, as General Smith stated in his report, "retired precipitately." The militia was not finished, however. Smith found a larger body of them guarding the crossing of a swamp which could only be passed by a narrow, corduroy road about a mile long. Some sharp fighting took place here, but the crossing was made. Three miles north of Houston the road passed through another swampy area, and Gholson's men were gathered in force at the southern end. The road was narrow, and the adjacent areas were too miry for flanking; so Smith turned back for several miles to a road leading eastward to Okolona.

At Okolona he turned south and entered the prairie country, a section of Mississippi which was so rich in the production of corn that it was called "The land of Egypt." In outlining his plan to Smith, Sherman had written, among other things: "From Okolona south you will find abundance of forage collected along the railroad, and the farms have standing corn in the fields. Take liberally of all these, as well as horses, mules, cattle, etc. As a rule, respect dwellings and families as something too sacred to be disturbed by soldiers, but mills, barns, sheds, stables, and such like things use for the benefit and convenience of your command. If convenient send into Columbus and destroy all machinery there and the bridge across the Tombigbee, which enables the enemy to draw supplies from the east side of the valley." Smith set about a systematic destruction of the granary; and the corn cribs, gin houses, cotton, homes, and everything which could support or protect life went up in smoke or settled in ashes in the wake of the diligent detachments which shot out from the main column for miles on either side of the line of march.[3]

At Prairie Station, about fifteen miles north of West Point, General Smith concentrated his entire command; and on the 20th of February, he moved south toward the latter place. He had advanced only five miles when his advance guard was vigorously attacked and came back in confusion on the leading regiment. The assailants were Jeffrey Forrest's brigade; and they were in battle line, clearly visible across the open prairie. They were not many in number, but their commander was cut much from the same cloth as his older brother and would not be run over without a fight. The Federal commander formed to attack, and a short but sharp encounter occurred. Smith sent out flankers, and Forrest retreated to avoid being enveloped. He withdrew to, and through, West Point, offering resistance at every vantage position along the way. He cleared the town at three o'clock that afternoon, and the Federal force immediately occupied it.

Jeffrey Forrest continued his retreat to Ellis' Bridge across the Sakatonchee Creek. At the bridge was General Forrest with McCulloch's brigade and part of Richardson's. That night (the 20th), the general left Jeffrey's brigade north of the creek and stationed the rest of the men along the south bank of the Sakatonchee, and they began throwing up breastworks and placing logs for protection in anticipation of a fight the following morning.

At a late hour that night Forrest was informed that a column of Federal cavalry had crossed the Sakatonchee at a point some four miles distant from Ellis' Bridge and were destroying houses, barns, and property in that direction. He immediately ordered his escort and a picked body of men to accompany him and soon came upon the enemy. Getting between them and the bridge over which they had crossed, he captured the entire party, consisting of about thirty troopers of the Fourth United States regular cavalry.

Early on Sunday morning (the 21st), he was advised by Colonel Jeffrey Forrest that the enemy was advancing upon his position from the direction of West Point. The colonel was ordered to hold his ground stubbornly and to retire across Ellis' Bridge only when compelled to do so.

After arriving at West Point, General Smith began to worry; and the fact that he was facing Forrest probably was the main contributing factor. He had received exaggerated statements of the strength of Forrest's command, and the Confederate commander was responsible for these. Smith's reconnaissances of the Sakatonchee and the crossings of the various streams in the area disclosed they were all strongly held by the Confederates. He also received information that Forrest was to be reinforced by either a portion or all of General S. D. Lee's command. Although Smith probably had the best armed cavalry unit which ever existed, doubts began to creep into his mind as to whether he could rely upon his men. Enthusiasm he had once expressed for meeting Forrest and being ready to "pitch into wherever he found him," was rapidly fading.[4]

The attack against Colonel Forrest's small brigade north of the creek was launched on the morning of the 21st, and the Rebels stubbornly held their ground. General Chalmers, mounted on his horse, had taken a position with the remainder of his troops on the south side of the creek near the bridge. This was his first experience at fighting closely with Forrest, about whom he had heard so much; and he was anxious to observe him under battle conditions. Suddenly, out of a cloud of dust, General Forrest rode up with Buck and Randy. Forrest's face was flushed, and he seemed much more excited than Chalmers expected or thought necessary under the circumstances.

In a harsh, quick tone, Forrest asked, "What are conditions at the front?"

"I haven't been forward and have heard nothing thus far from Colonel Forrest except that skirmishing is going on. From the firing, I don't think it is a serious affair."

Forrest said quickly, with evident impatience, "Then I'll go an' find out for myself," and he headed for the bridge, with Buck and Randy trailing him.

Colonel Forrest's battle line was only 400 yards away from the bridge, and bullets were flying about the two generals where they sat on their mounts. Despite the danger, Chalmers followed as Forrest dashed across the bridge, more out of curiosity to observe Forrest than for any definite purpose. As they hurried across the bridge and toward the firing line, enemy skirmishers quickly singled them out and began firing directly at them. They had gone no more than a hundred yards beyond the bridge when they saw, running full speed in their direction, a Rebel trooper who, dismounted and hatless, had thrown away his gun and everything else that would impede his flight to the rear. Chalmers watched in astonishment as Forrest brought his horse quickly to a stop, dismounted, ran to meet the fleeing soldier, seized him by the collar, and threw him to the ground. He dragged the unfortunate trooper to the side of the road, picked up a piece of brush that was convenient, and proceeded to give him a thorough thrashing. When he had finished, he turned the frightened man toward the enemy and said, "Now, damn

you, go back to the fight! You might as well be killed there as here, for
if you ever run away ag'in you'll not git off so easy.''

The trooper marched back to take his place on the firing line, wiser if
not braver. General Chalmers looked at Buck; each struggled to
suppress a smile. Forrest returned to his horse and took the reins from
Randy. "Let's go," he said as he climbed upon his mount.[5]

The fight north of the bridge lasted only about an hour and a half
before it was broken off by the Federals who began to retire. No sooner
had Jeffrey Forrest reported that the enemy was withdrawing from his
front than General Forrest became convinced that they had begun a
retreat and that the fight this morning was only to screen it. He pushed
hard after them, driving the enemy's rear guard seven miles north of
West Point.[6]

Here, the Federals made another effort to check the pursuit. They
selected a plantation with fences, gin houses, barns, and other
outbuildings on either side of the road. Tyler rushed dangerously close
to the position; and the Yankees opened up on him with a scathing
volley, emptying several of his saddles. He immediately withdrew from
range of the weapons and was soon joined by Forrest with his escort.
McCulloch's brigade was now up, and it was ordered to the front.
McCulloch dismounted his troopers and, with about 1,000 men,
advanced upon the enemy, driving them from their position. They had
no sooner turned to run than Forrest charged them with his mounted
escort and Tyler's Kentuckians. Within about half a mile, the
Confederates on faster horses caught up with the laggards among the
Union troopers. Seeing the plight of their slower comrades, some of the
Yankees ahead turned on their pursuers; and there developed some of
the severest fighting of the day at close quarters. Forrest was riding his
horse from the Rushton stables and was ahead of everyone except the
two men from Perry County, who were matching him stride for stride.

Here, again, the Confederate general's strength, dexterity, and
horsemanship were put to good use. Slashing at the enemy with his
saber, and supported on each side by Buck and Randy with their blazing
pistols, the three of them held the Yankees off until other Rebel troopers
came up. One of the enemy forced his way close to point-blank range
and raised his pistol to fire at Forrest. The general saw him out of the
corner of his eye and whirled his horse to the left. The animal responded
instantaneously, and the bullet missed. Before the Yankee could get off
a second shot, Forrest thrust his saber through his body; and the Union
trooper fell from the saddle mortally wounded. This brief but bloody
affair seemed to convince the Federals that another stand would not be

wise, and they continued their rapid retreat. The Rebels pursued until after dark, and Forrest called a halt to rest his men and horses.

General Smith was determined to put as much distance between his rear guard and the pursuers as he could and pushed his tired troopers until almost midnight. He finally halted and went into camp three miles south of Okolona. Forrest was equally determined to see that the enemy got as little respite as possible. At four o'clock on the morning of the 22nd, he sent Jeffrey Forrest with his brigade on a road to the left which gradually converged on the one on which the enemy was moving. This was done to prevent Smith from escaping to the west. The road on which Jeffrey was moving would bring him back to the main road about one mile south of Okolona. Placing himself at the head of his escort, Forrest moved rapidly in pursuit before daybreak, closely followed by the dependable McCulloch and his brigade. Smith's outpost pickets were encountered south of Okolona, and these and the Yankee's rear guard were driven through the village.

Just beyond the limits of Okolona, Forrest discovered a considerable body of Federal troops drawn up in line of battle in the open prairie. These cavalrymen, under the command of Brigadier General Benjamin H. Grierson, were apparently ready to charge. Over to the right, the Confederate general rejoiced to see another line of battle which he recognized as Bell's brigade under Barteau. The latter had moved to Okolona pursuant to Forrest's orders of the previous morning, keeping between the enemy and the Tombigbee River. He found himself with the single brigade in the presence of an enemy sufficiently large to overwhelm him. Following Forrest's tactics of showing a bold front, he threw his men in line of battle, advanced his skirmishers, and maneuvered his force in such a fashion as to cause Grierson to defer his attack until a careful reconnaissance could be made on both of Barteau's flanks to determine what was supporting him. This delay probably saved Barteau from disaster as it gave Forrest time to come up.

When Forrest saw Bell's brigade, he left half of his escort as skirmisher to engage the attention of the enemy. With the rest, he galloped across the plain to join Barteau; and the Tennesseans burst into yells and shouts as they caught sight of their commander riding toward them. He joined Barteau, who was at the head of his troopers, a short distance behind the line of skirmishers. His eyes had been carefully scanning that line as he moved across the prairie. "You're to be congratulated on the disposition you've made of your troops, Colonel," he said.

"Thank you, General. We're pretty badly outnumbered. I've been bluffing them into thinking I'm going to attack to hold off their attacking me.''

"Let's quit bluffin'.'' Turning to the men he spoke in the loud voice which carried so well on the battlefield, "All day yesterday, we whipped their butts in fight after fight an' chased 'em till night made us stop. They're already cowed an' beaten, an' if you'll follow me with the same courage you showed in West Tennessee, we'll whip 'em ag'in! Chalmers' division an' Richardson's brigade are close by an'll join in the fun.''

Forrest looked with longing eyes in the direction of Okolona, but McCulloch's and Jeffrey's brigades were not in sight. He saw a point in Grierson's line where there was confusion; and not waiting, he rose in his stirrups, and yelled, "Charge!''; and away he went at the head of a screaming line of Rebels.[7]

As the Confederates closed on them, Grierson's front line fired a single volley and retreated to take shelter behind a second line of cavalry. Unwilling to jeopardize any further the small force at this moment, Forrest halted the charge; he threw forward his skirmishers; and, taking advantage of a stake and rail fence, he dismounted about two-thirds of the men, fighting for a short time on foot.

The United States Fourth Regulars were considered to be the elite of the Yankee cavalry force. This regiment rushed Forrest's skirmish line and forced it back within supporting distance of the battle line behind the fence. This line opened upon the Fourth Regulars and drove them back in disorder.

Forrest looked toward Okolona and saw McCulloch's column, followed by Jeffrey's brigade, coming into the village. He sent Randy to them with instructions to press forward in his rear; and mounting all troops of Barteau's command, he took advantage of the disorder into which the Fourth Regulars had been thrown and gave his well-known order, "Move up!''

Taking the lead with his escort and the Second Tennessee, he charged and broke the Fourth Regulars; and they fled the field in confusion. The Seventh Indiana rallied to their support; but they, in turn, suffered defeat. Then the Third brigade of Smith's expedition, under Colonel Lafayette McGillis, was lined up for their assistance; but Forrest would not be denied his victory and they, too, were put to rout, abandoning five guns of their six-gun battery.

The confusion in Grierson's cavalry division was complete, and the relentless pursuit and vigorous pressure brought to bear by Forrest resulted in a hopeless stampede. Officers as well as men went as best they could. Along the road and through the woods or fields on either hand, paying scant attention to commands from any source, the panic-stricken soldiers rushed and crowded until the way was choked with a surging mass of men and horses.

The Federal troops involved thus far had been the rear of General Smith's column. Little or no resistance was made by them until they reached a point about five miles westward. Colonel Waring was in advance with his brigade when he received a message from the rear of the disaster. He was ordered to form a line at the first available position and fortify it, to get together what artillery he could, to allow the fleeing troopers to pass through, and to check the enemy, if possible, until the Union cavalry could reorganize at some safe distance in the rear.

Waring realized that the situation was desperate. He formed his brigade in line with skirmishers far out on either flank and remained there until the disorganized cavalry passed through. Portions of the Third brigade were in such a state of complete demoralization that he was afraid that they would endanger the morale of his own troopers.

Upon orders to do so, Waring abandoned this line, and fell back to a new position about a mile away where another stand was made. The Second New Jersey, the Second Illinois, the Seventh Indiana, and the Fourth Missouri bore the brunt of the fighting at this position, which also had to be abandoned in face of Forrest's irresistible onslaught.

Meanwhile, General Smith was aroused to the realization of the desperate situation. Two miles behind the line which Waring had first taken to check the Rebel pursuit, he selected a position of great natural strength on a farm called Ivey's Hill, near Tallabloncla. Northward from Okolona toward Pontotoc, the road passed from the prairie into woody and hilly country. At the place he selected to make his stand, the road ran along the summit of a ridge. It made almost a right turn at Ivey's Hill; and there were houses, a gin house, stables, barns, and other buildings of a large plantation. Taking advantage of the deflection and the buildings and hastily throwing rails from fences into temporary breastworks, Smith amassed his artillery and skillfully disposed his forces to command the long, narrow road leading to his position.

As Forrest approached the stronghold, two separate lines of Federals were in plain view. He ordered the two brigades with him, Jeffrey's and McCulloch's, to form in columns of four on one side of the highway, taking advantage of the protection which the wooded land afforded. In this way they could advance without being exposed to the artillery. Bell's brigade, which had borne the brunt of the morning's fighting, was bringing up the rear at a slower pace.

Eighteen hours of hard riding had broken down some of the horses of Jeffrey's and McCulloch's brigades, but the unmounted men joined in the assault even though they could not keep up with the mounted men. The bugle sounded; and the two columns swept forward in columns of four, swinging into line of battle as they neared the enemy. Within three hundred yards of the advance Union line, a thundering volley rolled from the enemy cannon and small arms. At the first volley, Colonel Jeffrey Forrest, leading the charge at the head of his brigade, met his death. He fell, killed instantly by a Minie ball which passed through his neck, severing the spinal cord. Colonel McCulloch, at the head of his brigade, received a painful wound in his left hand.

Staggered by the terrific fire, the death of the younger Forrest, and the wounding of McCulloch, the troopers wavered and then halted. This is the moment when a counterattack by Smith might have won the day for him, but he held his men behind the protection of their works. Colonel W. L. Duckworth of the Seventh Tennessee assumed command of Jeffrey's brigade and steadied the command. He dismounted his troopers and prepared to defend the position they had gained. Colonel McCulloch had the surgeon dress his wound but refused to leave the field. He also dismounted his troopers.

General Forrest saw his brother fall and exclaimed, "My God, Jeffrey's down!" He put spurs to his horse and raced to the scene. Major Strange, Randy, and Buck, who were with him, followed, matching his pace. When they reached the spot where Jeffrey lay, the general dismounted; and kneeling, he raised his brother to a sitting position. Holding the lifeless body in his arms, he called to him in a voice choked with emotion, "Jeffy, Jeffy, talk to me! For God's sake, talk to me, Jeffy!"

The general didn't have to ask or be told; he knew Jeffrey was beyond help he or anyone else could give. He slowly bent his head, kissed his brother on the forehead, and then gently lowered the body to the ground. He stood and, with eyes filled with tears and the color drained from his face, said to Major Strange, "Please see he's took care of."

"I'll look after him, General," Strange replied solemnly.

The Confederates in the immediate area had stopped firing to watch the somber scene near them. The escort arrived, and the men were silently sitting their horses. Forrest stood with his back to the enemy; and through his tears he could see Bell's brigade coming up. He turned to face the Federals ahead and wiped the tears from his eyes to see them better. With a penetrating glare he carefully scanned their position again and again. As he did this, the color came rapidly to his face and neck until they were both a vivid red. He did not speak until after he mounted his horse.

"Colonel Duckworth!" he called, and the colonel moved to his side.

"Take half the brigade an' move to the left flank an' rear."

After the men moved off, Forrest called to the remainder of those present, "Mount your horses!"

Then he called his bugler, "Gaus!"

The bugler moved alongside his commander. "Blow the charge!" he ordered; and to his men Forrest yelled, "Let's go git 'em!"

Standing in the stirrups, with sword in his left hand raised and pointing above the enemy, the general, his face flushed and his piercing eyes now free of all tears, put the spurs viciously to his horse and rushed pell-mell toward the enemy's formidable position. The faithful escort was desperately trying to keep up.

General Smith had been frightened by the Rebels moving toward his flank and rear and had ordered his own troops to retire, which they did as rapidly as possible. They were in the process of mounting their horses when the recklessly charging Confederates hit them, and they quickly gave way under the onslaught. Forrest followed, as was his custom, and was soon far in advance of any strong support. He had immediately with him his escort of sixty men and not more than the like number of the best mounted men of the command.

The Union retreat, impeded by a piece of artillery which had met with an accident and was abandoned, along with two or three wagons and caissons of ammunition, was for the moment held up. General Smith threw into line across the road about 500 men making up his rear guard. Into these Forrest dashed, and here a bloody hand-to-hand contest took place. The badly outnumbered Confederates fought for their lives as the enemy crowded around them. Forrest was like a man possessed, taking out on the enemy the overwhelming rage and bitterness which gripped him after the loss of the favorite of his four brothers. With slashing and thrusting saber he charged time and time again at the men in blue who fell back before his fury, but some not quickly enough; for, in addition to those wounded, three fell from the wrath of his sword.

Fortunately for those Southerners engaged in this melee, Mc-Culloch's brigade came up. These men, who had proven their bravery several times that day, hesitated before going against what seemed to be impossible odds. Here McCulloch showed his mettle as both a soldier and a leader. The bandage on his wound was now saturated with blood. Raising the bloody hand high over his head, he called to his troopers, "My God, men, will you see them kill your general? I'll go to his rescue if not a man follows me!"

With that, he dashed toward the enemy, his troopers following to a man; and they hurled themselves into the thickest of the fight.

This encounter was brief, and the enemy rear guard was soon in retreat again with Forrest pressing hard after them. Inside of a mile of the last encounter, they took up another position. By this time Dr. J. B. Cowan, Forrest's surgeon, had joined him. He did this at the urging of Major Strange. The surgeon had arrived at the place of Jeffrey's death right after Forrest led his wild charge on the Federals at Ivey's Hill. As he rode up, Major Strange, who feared his commander was making a suicidal charge, said to him, "Doctor, hurry after the general; I am afraid he'll be killed."

Putting spurs to his horse, Dr. Cowan rode hard to overtake the Rebel commander; and he was riding by the general's side as they advanced toward this last stand taken by the enemy. The Federals opened up on them, and bullets were falling all around the two men. "General," the doctor said; "I think you should get out of the road; it is not right unnecessarily to expose yourself."

"Doctor, if you're worried, you can git out of the way. I'm as safe here as there."

At that moment, a piece of enemy artillery they had not seen opened up, and the general's horse fell mortally wounded. "Are you hurt?" the doctor inquired as Forrest began disentangling himself from the fallen animal.

"I don't think so," The general replied. He got to his feet and looked at the struggling horse. He knew the stallion had received a mortal wound; so he drew his pistol and put a bullet through the brain of the suffering animal. The general then turned sorrowfully toward his surgeon. "That was my Rushton hoss. I never shoulda rode 'im in battle."

"There'll be other horses."

"Not like him."

Dr. Cowan dismounted. "Take my horse, General," he offered.

"No, I'll take Long's," he said, referring to a nearby member of his escort. "He can go to the rear."

In a few moments, the whole command moved forward again, and another sharp fight occurred in which the general's second horse was killed. He had the old charger, King Philip, brought up and rode him for the remainder of the day. This horse received a slight wound in the neck before the fighting was over but was not badly hurt.

The Federals again gave way, but not before Lieutenant Colonel James A. Barksdale of the Fifth Mississippi, who had distinguished himself in the fighting that day, fell with a fatal wound. The Confederates, except for a few officers, had been dismounted for the final assault on this position. They pushed forward eagerly toward the retreating Yankees and poured out into an open field of about a hundred acres. Forrest was leading on foot this advance guard, made up of his escort and approximately 300 men from a number of different regiments, until someone offered him a horse which he quickly accepted. It was almost sunset, but there was plenty of light for the Confederates to see the enemy, in four lines, ready to charge from a ridge beyond the field. Most of the Southerners had crossed over a gully in their advance, and Forrest quickly withdrew all of them behind this natural obstruction. He formed the men in line as quickly as possible to meet the onset. At the same time he appealed to the small force to stand their ground steadily, and they responded with cheers.

The Federal bugles sounded, and the first line swept down the slope in splendid order. The Confederates waited until they were within sixty yards and opened with a scorching volley which sent the charging enemy reeling. Again the bugles sounded, and the second line charged at full gallop; and they were not stopped until they had reached within forty yards of the gully. The third line charged and was repulsed in the same manner only thirty yards from the gully. The fourth line, the largest and most menacing, was sent forward. It, too, met scathing fire; but it pushed on, some of them crossing the gully where hand-to-hand fighting took place. Both Randy and Buck had dismounted with their Whitworths to join the defense line and were giving a good account of themselves with their deadly accuracy. In the hand-to-hand fighting, though, they dropped the rifles and went for their pistols. Randy looked to his left, and he was being charged by a mounted enemy cavalryman with raised saber. He quickly turned his pistol on him and pulled the trigger, but the gun was empty. He was about to hurl the useless gun at the oncoming man when Forrest charged between them and, with a slashing blow of his saber, almost took off the head of the charging Yankee.[8]

At this time, McCulloch's brigade arrived on the scene, and these welcome reinforcements killed and wounded a number of those who had broken through Forrest's line. Among these was an aide-de-camp of General Grierson whose conspicuous bravery during the action so attracted the admiration of the Confederates that Forrest directed that special attention be given to his remains.

This was the final action of the day. Many of Forrest's men were without ammunition, and they had been fighting steadily since early morning. Both men and horses were exhausted. Camp was made, and the men had a meager but adequate supper; for many it was the first food since the previous day.

Randy could not get his mind off of the general's sorrow over the death of his brother. The scene where Jeffrey had fallen on the battlefield kept coming back to haunt him. Using Forrest's having saved his life as a pretext, he made his way to the general's tent. As he approached it, Willie, the general's son, came out. "How is the general tonight?" Randy asked.

"Not very good, Captain. He's brooding."

"Over Jeffrey?"

"Yessir."

"I'm sorry. I wish there were something I could do."

"Maybe you can. Go in and talk to him. He thinks a lot of you, Captain Rushton."

"I wouldn't want to intrude on his grief."

"Maybe it needs intruding. Please go in and talk to him; everybody else seems to be staying away."

Randy went hesitantly to the tent and gently rapped on the tentpole. A low voice which he could hardly hear asked, "Who's there?"

"Captain Rushton, sir. Would it be convenient for me to come in?"

A response was slow in coming, as though the general was having difficulty making up his mind. "Yes," he replied. "Yes, come on in."

Randy opened the flap of the tent and entered. Forrest was fully dressed and sitting on his cot. It appeared that he had been lying down. "I hope I'm not intruding," Randy said.

Again the reply was slow in coming. "No. Come on over an' have a seat," he replied, pointing to a stool near the cot.

Randy sat down. Forrest looked at him, but the young captain had the feeling his commander's mind was elsewhere. "I just wanted to thank you for saving my life today," Randy said.

"I guess I owed you," Forrest replied disinterestedly.

"I want to tell you, too, how sorry I am about Jeffrey. We all share your grief. He was a brave man who was an example to us. I feel fortunate in having had the opportunity to serve with him and to know him."

Again the general waited before he spoke, and when he did it was at first with a low, quivering voice. "I love all my brothers; they're very close to me; but Jeffy, that's what I called 'im when he was a young'n, was kinda special. My pa died before I was sixteen, an' left Ma, me, six more chillun, an' another'n on the way. That was Jeffy; he wasn't borned till four months later, an' he never got to see his pa." The general's voice grew stronger, and he was becoming more like his usual self as he talked. "He was more'n a brother to me, he was like a son. I raised 'im; I looked after 'im; I taught 'im the things a man should teach his boy; and I watched 'im grow up into as fine a gentleman as I ever knowed. By the time he got old enough for schoolin', I was doin' well enough to see he got it. He wasn't like the rest of us; he was educated an' had polish. He had a head on 'im, too. He was smart, an' a natural borned leader. He was only twenty-four years old an' a colonel. He wasn't a colonel because he was my brother; he was a colonel because he earned it, an' it was only a question of time before he'd become a general. I could see in Jeffrey ever'thing I had wanted to be.'' Here he paused.

"He was a fine man," Randy said. "We could see those qualities you mentioned."

"As I've said many times before, war means fightin', an' fightin' means killin'; but when it kills them close to you, you realize what a damned, dirty, rotten business it really is. I not only lost my brother today, I also lost that hoss your daddy gave me."

"I know. Maybe he has another one. I'll write him to find out."

Forrest's eyes lit up. "If he does, I insist on payin' for this one—no more gifts."

"We'll see," Randy said. "I've taken up enough of your time, General. You should be getting your rest." He got up to leave.

"Thank you, Randy—thank you for comin' by. I didn' want to see nobody, but I guess I needed someone to talk to; but I believe you knowed that."

Randy went to the front of the tent. Before going outside, he turned and said, "By the way, General, congratulations on the great victory today."

Forrest's eyes lit up, and the trace of a smile appeared on his face. "We whipped their butts good, didn' we?"

"We did that!"

Randy again started to leave the tent, but he was stopped momentarily by Forrest's voice, "Tell the orderly to fetch Major Strange—there's a lot of work to be done!"

General Gholson came up that night with his 700 mounted Mississippi State Militia; and the following morning, the 23rd of February, he was sent with his relatively fresh troops in pursuit of the fleeing Yankees. He kept up the chase as far as the Tallahatchie River, picking up fifty stragglers along the way. After crossing the Tallahatchie, the Federal troops made their way almost unmolested to Memphis.[9]

Forrest gathered up the wounded, Confederate and Federal, and sent them to hospitals in Okolona. Leaving details to bury the dead, he moved south to Starkville, where he established his headquarters and was joined by his entire command on the 26th. At the end of the month, he went into camp at Columbus, Mississippi. Here, on the 11th of March, he issued the following address to his troops:

"The major-general commanding desires to return his thanks and acknowledgments to the officers and men of his command for the recent gallant and meritorious conduct in defeating and routing the largest, most carefully selected, and best-equipped cavalry and mounted-infantry command ever sent into the field by the enemy. It affords him pleasure and pride to say that by your unflinching bravery and endurance a force three times your own was defeated and driven from the country. Thus by your valor and courage you have given safety and security to the homes of the defenseless, whose grateful acknowledgments are showered upon you, and whose prayers daily and nightly ascend unto heaven for your future prosperity and success. Deploring the loss of some of our bravest officers and men, he desires that you cherish their memory, emulate their example, and achieve your independence or perish in the attempt.''

Chapter XVII

Pilloried After Pillow

Forrest's defeat of Brigadier General William Sooy Smith brought him more recognition in Richmond than he had received from any of his previous accomplishments. The powers in the capitol reached the conclusion that the same thing he and Brigadier General Bell had done in western Tennessee could be accomplished in the like section of Kentucky. About March 1, 1864, Brigadier General Abe Buford, a member of one of the most influential families of Kentucky and an officer who had shown both courage and ability in the service, was ordered to Forrest with the fragments of three infantry regiments of Kentuckians. These men had served with distinction in Bragg's army, and their ranks had been decimated by the battles and hardships through which they had passed. They requested mounted service, but the Confederate government was unable to provide the necessary horses; and they were transferred to Forrest for him to supply the mounts.

Forrest's troopers were relatively inactive except Richardson's brigade, which was ordered to the area of Yazoo City, Mississippi, to join up with one of General Lee's brigades under the command of Brigadier General L. S. Ross. The purpose of this movement was to repel an enemy expedition pushing northward along the Yazoo River toward Grenada, Mississippi, its reported objective.

The cavalry leader completed the organization of four small brigades.[1] Soon after the organization was completed, the men of Forrest's staff were gathering one evening for supper. The commanding general walked over beside Buck and asked, "Captain, how's the marksmanship trainin' comin'?"

"Fine, General. I had a little trouble at first with those new recruits we picked up in Tennessee; they're a pretty independent lot who thought they knew all there was to know about shooting, but after the battle at Okolona, they're more receptive to training."

"Good," Forrest replied. "Keep after 'em. We're thinkin' about another move to the north, an' I want 'em ready. Pick out the best shots in each unit for sharpshooters and point 'em out to their commanders.''

Randy, who had been talking with Buck when Forrest came over, spoke up, ''General, I heard from Daddy today. He's got another horse for you, not a stallion but a good mare.''

Forrest's eyes lighted up. ''Rushton,'' he said ''how would you like a furlough home to pick 'er up?''

''I'd like it, but would I have time to get back before the movement north?''

Forrest thought about this before responding, ''I doubt it.''

''Then I'd rather wait until we get back.''

''That'd be better. Strange'll be needin' you here before we go, an' I want you along.''

Buck had seen very little of Cally since they returned from their furloughs. Captain Henderson, who was now commanding the scouts, was keeping his men in the field gathering information for the command. Buck went to the scouts' camp and, as usual, saw a small group of the irregulars scattered about Cally, listening to one of his stories. Buck stopped where he could hear without interrupting.

The attention of the men was glued upon Cally, who said ''There was this Yankee feller who all his life had went to church ever' Sunday. He got up one Sunday mornin', et his breakfast, 'an when he finished, he said to his wife, 'I ain't goin' to go to church today.' She looked at 'im kinda su'prised like an' asked, 'Why ain't you goin?' He replied, 'I don't like nobody down at that church, an' nobody down there likes me.' 'I know that,' she said, 'but you ought to go to church.' 'Gimme one good reason,' he replied; 'just one good reason.' 'You're the preacher,' she said.''

Buck joined in the laughter with the rest of the audience as he walked over to speak to Cally. At the sound of his voice, the old man jumped up, grabbed his hand, and began pumping it. ''It's good to see you,'' he said. ''I just got in and was aimin' to look you up; but the boys wanted to hear a Yankee story, an' I was tryin' to oblige 'em.''

''That was a good one.''

''It wasn't really a Yankee story, but they like preacher stories almost as much.''

''Hadn't seen you in so long, I was wondering what had happened to you.''

''Cap'n Henderson sent four of us to keep a eye on that feller Smith— guess he didn' want nothin' to happen to 'im. We followed im' almost all the way to Memphis. I never seen such a whupped an' skittish bunch in my whole life.'' Cally laughed. ''When they was crossin' the Tippah, we thought we'd have a little fun with 'em. We spread out, all four of us, an' popped a few shots at 'em. They musta thought Ol' Bedford had caught up with 'em. They stampeded like a bunch of light'nin' skeered cows. Several of the men an' hosses drownded in the river.''

''I heard about that,'' Buck said. ''I guess they had a right to be skittish.''

''But not to treat their hosses the way they done. They broke down so many that nearly all of 'em was afoot by the time they got to Memphis.''

''I haven't had a chance to tell you; it looks like I'm going to be a papa.''

Showing his surprise and pleasure at the news, Cally exclaimed, ''You don't say! I declare I can't believe it. You an' Miss Ellen—I can't believe it!'' He grabbed Buck's hand and started pumping it again.

With his entire force, Forrest marched northward on the 15th of March. Buford's division, with the Seventh Tennessee (from Neely's brigade) and McDonald's battalion (from McCulloch's brigade), took the advance. Buford's unmounted Kentuckians were happy to be headed in the direction of home and over the prospect of obtaining mounts and replenishing their clothes. On the 18th, General Stephan A. Hurlbut at Memphis dispatched: ''It is reported that Forrest, with about seven thousand men, was at Tupelo last night, bound for west Tennessee. I think he means Columbus and Paducah.''

The mounted troops reached Jackson, Tennessee, on the 20th. Colonel Crews was sent with his battalion in the direction of Memphis to watch for the advance of any Federal force from that direction. Colonel Wilson was left with his regiment to garrison Jackson and to prepare for the reception of Buford's unmounted men, who would arrive within two or three days.[2]

On the 22nd of March, Forrest, with his escort and the Seventh Tennessee and Twelfth Kentucky regiments, proceeded to Trenton, where he took possession of the town and set up a bureau for recruiting. The following day, Colonel Duckworth, with his own regiment, the Seventh Tennessee, and Faulkner's regiment, was sent to capture Union City. McDonald's battalion, which was marching toward Memphis under the command of Colonel Crews, was ordered to report to Duckworth for this operation. The Confederates arrived before Union City on the morning of the 24th and immediately invested the town. As they closed in upon the Federal garrison of about 500 men under Colonel Hawkins of the Second (Union) West Tennessee cavalry, some lively skirmishing took place.[3] Several Confederates were wounded, but the Unionists were driven back into a strong redoubt near the railroad station. Duckworth was without artillery; and he knew the position was too strong to be taken without severe loss, so he decided to try a bluff. He sent in a message demanding surrender. It was written in Forrest's bloodcurdling style, and he affixed the general's name to it.

Colonel Hawkins was aware that reinforcements were enroute to him and pleaded for time to consider the proposition. General Brayman was moving to his relief with 2,000 men, an ample force to overwhelm Duckworth. Hawkins declined to surrender unless he could first have a personal interview with Forrest, but Duckworth was equal to the occasion. Turning on his heels, he said, "I don't care whether you surrender or not. General Forrest is not in the habit of holding interviews with officers not of his own rank; and if you don't surrender in five minutes, he will charge the place and not spare a single member of your command!"

Hawkins had surrendered to Forrest once before, when the latter made his first incursion into West Tennessee in 1862; and he had been treated well by the Confederate cavalry leader. This, coupled with Duckworth's dire threat, induced him to surrender, much to the chagrin of General Brayman, who was only six miles away at the time. Brayman said: "The force of the enemy does not appear to be more than a quarter of the number represented, and without artillery. The number of men surrendered is probably five hundred; all well armed and equipped— about three hundred mounted; a few mules and wagons and a considerable amount of public property were lost and destroyed. Colonel Hawkins and his command had been recently paid for over a year's service, and the aggregate of individual loss on the part of the officers and soldiers will reach some $60,000."

Duckworth removed the supplies that were needed and portable and burned the rest. He sent the prisoners south with a detachment and released McDonald's battalion to move toward Memphis as originally ordered.

While this action at Union City was taking place, Forrest left Trenton with a portion of Buford's division from near Jackson and pushed northward to attack the garrison at Paducah, Kentucky, where he captured a few prisoners and considerable stores and horses.[4]

On his return toward Jackson from Paducah, a portion of Buford's division was sent in the direction of Mayfield in southwestern Kentucky, and there they were temporarily disbanded to visit their homes, replenish their clothing, improve their mounts, and report at Trenton on the 3rd of April. Not a man failed to return from furlough as directed.

Lieutenant Colonel Crews, commanding McDonald's battalion, was sent to the western part of Fayette County with directions to keep twenty men in each company and to furlough the rest to go home and refit themselves. With about sixty men, Crews was encamped several miles west of Somerville on the night of April 2 when he received information that a strong cavalry force was enroute from Raleigh on the Somerville road. He moved out early the next morning to observe the movement; and at one o'clock that afternoon, within twelve or fifteen miles of Raleigh, he encountered and was fired upon by the enemy's advance guard. Exposing his colors and a few men upon the crest of a hill as ostentatiously as possible, he concealed from the enemy the smallness of his force as he conducted a personal reconnaissance. He discovered that the enemy was evidently apprehensive about the situation and had stopped and drawn up in line of battle behind a fence on a high ridge with a company detached on each flank for protection from surprise. Crews sent Lieutenant Steinkuhl with twelve men to the right and Lieutenant T. H. Mayer with ten men to the left with orders to approach under cover and dislodge the flank detachments. He dismounted a small squad to engage the Federal sharpshooters who were firing at his exposed men. When Lieutenants Steinkuhl and Mayer attacked the flanks as directed, Colonel Crews charged down the main road with fewer than forty mounted men. It was a rash venture; but it was done with such daring and confidence that the enemy was misled so badly that two Federal regiments gave way for several hundred yards and took a defensive position, reinforced by two more regiments, among some houses and in a wood.

Crews now moved boldly around to his right, as if seeking to take his adversaries in reverse in that quarter where Lieutenant Steinkuhl was already creating a disturbance. As soon as he was out of view, Colonel Crews turned and reappeared in front of the enemy again. Disturbed by these movements, the whole Federal force immediately fell back in haste to Raleigh. General Grierson, moving on another road with a force equally as large, apparently had the same apprehension; and a rapid retreat to Memphis was made, destroying all bridges behind them.[5]

General Chalmers did not move immediately with Forrest into western Tennessee. He first had to gather the scattered remnants of his command which had been on various duties in northern Mississippi. As they marched north, one of his detachments, under Colonel J. J. Neely, came in contact with a battalion of West Tennessee Union troops commanded by a bitter partisan, Colonel Fielding Hurst.[6] Neely made short work of the encounter, killing and wounding quite a number of the enemy and capturing some prisoners, their wagon train, and a supply of ammunition which the Southerners badly needed. Chalmers had moved up by the way of LaGrange, Tennessee; and there he furnished a strong guard for 600 prisoners Forrest had captured and sent south.

Buford reported promptly at Trenton in the first week of April with his troops which had been furloughed, and Forrest sent him again in the direction of Columbus and Paducah to obtain additional horses and supplies and to create a diversion for the movement he was contemplating against Fort Pillow.[7]

About forty miles up the Mississippi River from Memphis, a bar of sand and mud stretches out from the western side of the stream well over toward the opposite Tennessee shore. When the river is at its lower stage, much of this obstruction is many feet above water for several months each year. It forms a natural dam which has turned the current and channel of the river in close to the Tennessee side. Opposite the point of this bar is a small stream known as Coal Creek which empties into the Mississippi from the east. Along the south shore of the creek and the east bank of the river is a high clay bluff which slants sharply but not precipitately seventy-five to a hundred feet to the water line below. Guns mounted strategically on this bluff could easily control traffic on the Mississippi.

When Brigadier General Gideon J. Pillow commanded the Confederate troops in Tennessee during the early part of the war, he recognized the importance of the position and began construction of the fortifications which bore his name when completed. Three separate lines of works were constructed at Fort Pillow. The most exterior line extended from the south bank of Coal Creek, in an arc curving outward slightly toward the east, to a point on the river bluff, the farthest distance from the river being about 600 yards. There was the usual ditch in front with dirt thrown up along the inner edge. About half way to the river behind this line was a second defense, covering about two acres, which was built along the crest of a hill. The third and strongest defense was a small fort built south of the junction of the creek with the river. It extended in an irregular semicircular outline from the river bluff to another point on this bluff about seventy yards to the south. This line consisted of a ditch twelve feet wide and eight feet deep, behind which had been thrown up an earth wall, or parapet, flat on top, six feet high and six feet thick. Behind this parapet was a bench upon which the defenders could stand and fire over the wall without exposing more than heads and shoulders. They could step down from the bench and be completely concealed while reloading their guns. At six places along the parapet, which was about 120 yards in length, were openings through which a cannon had been mounted to command approaches from as many directions. On the slope of the river bluff, above and below the parapet, had been constructed rifle pits to defend the approaches from either side near the water's edge and to provide protection for sharpshooters firing at boats on the river.

This would have been a relatively strong position except for the configuration of the land. Eastward of the ditch of this inner defense, for a distance of about fifty yards, the surface descended gradually and then sharply down into a crescent-shaped ravine which encircled the fort for about one-half its length. This hollow, known as Coal Creek Ravine, opened into Coal Creek near the mouth of the stream. At the south of the inner ditch was another depression, well marked but not so precipitate as the other. Here the ground sloped gradually from the ditch for about 50 yards. Along the deeper portion of this depression, or ravine as it has been called, were two rows of log cabins or shanties, extending from the mouth of the ravine at the river bank to a point in front of the center of the fort. These buildings housed the white troops of the garrison, and some were used for government and private storehouses. Within the fort proper, near the river bank, were tents with straw-covered wooden floors. These were quarters for negro troops.

At the rear of the fort, the river bluff was covered with trees and brush. Most of the trees and some of the brush had been cut down, leaving logs, stumps, brush, and an occasional tree. Just below the fort, near the log houses, the bank had been cleared for steamboats to land. To the north and east, beyond Coal Creek Ravine and in front of the fort for two-thirds of its length, the ground was broken into a series of irregular hillocks or knolls with intervening depressions or gullies. Many of these elevations were as high as that upon which the inner fort was erected and varied from 100 to 400 yards from the parapet. For 400 yards from the inner stronghold, the trees had been felled and the undergrowth cleared away so that an enemy could not approach without exposure. This had been done in 1861 and 1862; and the logs and stumps were still on the ground, while considerable undergrowth had been reproduced in the elapsed period.[8]

Even though no guns were mounted to face the river, General Hurlbut, who commanded the Federal military district, with headquarters at Memphis, deemed Fort Pillow sufficiently important to keep it well garrisoned. He used it as a recruiting post and as a refuge for fugitive slaves and residents of the nearby area who might desire protection of the United States. It was garrisoned with the First

Battalion, Sixth United States heavy artillery (colored), eight commissioned officers and 213 men; one section of Company D, Second United States light artillery (colored), one commissioned officer and forty men; and the First Battalion, Thirteenth Tennessee (Union) cavalry, Major W. F. Bradford commanding, ten commissioned officers and 285 men. There was a total of 557 in the garrison. In addition, there were about twenty white civilians in the fort, some of whom took part in its defense.

Although General Hurlbut did not believe Forrest would attack Fort Pillow after not taking Paducah, he nevertheless placed Major L. F. Booth in command of the fort by an order dated March 28. Next in rank was Major W. F. Bradford, a native of Tennessee whom General Hurlbut described as, "a good officer, though not of much experience." Hurlbut advised Booth to "confer freely with Bradford." Hurlbut proved wrong in his conclusion that Forrest would not move against the fort. In his report of April 4, 1864, the Confederate general stated, "There is a Federal force of five or six hundred at Fort Pillow which I shall attend to in a day or two, as they have horses and supplies which we need."[9]

On the 10th of the month, Forrest placed Brigadier General Chalmers in charge of the movement against Fort Pillow; and the latter made the following disposition of his troops: the First brigade, commanded by Colonel Neely, marched rapidly from Whiteville toward Memphis with orders to spread the report so that it would get to Hurlbut's ears that Forrest's whole command was coming to attack Memphis. At the same time, Colonel John McQuirk, with the Third Mississippi State cavalry and the First Mississippi Partisans, was ordered to advance on Memphis from the south and to let it be known that General S. D. Lee was also advancing with all of his troops to join in the attack. Neely moved swiftly to Wolf River, almost in sight of Memphis, and made a great show of building pontoon bridges and other structures necessary for throwing a large force across the stream. This diversion had its desired effect—General Hurlbut ordered four regiments to his aid from Vicksburg and held his forces in Memphis for its defense.

While the Confederate troops were creating the diversion around Memphis, General Chalmers moved on the 11th with portions of McCulloch's and Bell's brigades from Sharon's Ferry on Forked Deer Creek toward Brownsville and on to Fort Pillow by a rapid all-night march of about forty miles. He was fortunate to have as a guide Mr. J. W. Shaw, a civilian living in the area, who had been arrested by Major Bradford and confined within the fort. Two days before the fight, he had been permitted to visit his home and was available to provide valuable information about the topography of the fortifications and about the troops defending them.

Colonel McCulloch had been given the advance with his brigade and arrived before the fort just as day was breaking on the 12th. He sent the Second Missouri cavalry under Lieutenant Colonel R. A. McCulloch to drive in the pickets and to feel their way to the vicinity of the stronghold. At the first sound of rifle fire, the entire regiment charged so suddenly that the Federals abandoned the entire outer line of defense without serious resistance.

Forrest was following in the rear with his escort and part of Wisdom's regiment, and he had directed Chalmers to invest the fort to prevent escape of the garrison. Chalmers sent McCulloch's brigade rapidly down the Fulton road to Gaines' farm and then north toward the fort on a road paralleling the Mississippi. This brought him in sight of the inner stronghold on the side where the barracks and storehouses were located. Wilson's regiment moved on the direct road from Brownsville. Bell, with Barteau's and Russell's regiments, marched west along the bank of Coal Creek and came into position from the north side. While these movements were being made, skirmishers of the garrison, consisting of Companies D and E of the Thirteenth Tennessee (Union) cavalry, supported by artillery from the fort firing over their heads, were briskly engaged with the advance line of the Confederates; but they were forced to retire to the inner stronghold about eight o'clock that morning. Lieutenant Barr of Company D was killed in this action.

McCulloch advanced with his brigade from the south to within 300 yards of the inner fort. He did this cautiously, his dismounted men taking advantage of logs, stumps, and knolls as they moved along and across gullies and ravines which protected them from the fort's artillery and from the guns of the Federal Gunboat *New Era*, which was well out in the river and, on directions from the fort, was shelling the entire Confederate line. On the side nearest Coal Creek, Bell had with like caution, but with considerable skirmishing, advanced to a position about 250 yards from the parapet. Colonel Wilson, advancing from the front, had already made a bold dash against the Federals in the middle redoubt and now held that position, about 300 yards from the main fort. Having the fort securely invested on land, Chalmers made no further effort to advance as he waited for Forrest; but he placed sharpshooters on the high ground in front of the fort to pick off anyone showing above the parapet or within the fort. Several of the Yankee commissioned officers were lost, including the commander, Major L. F. Booth, who was killed almost instantly by a musket ball through the breast at about nine o'clock. Command of the fort fell upon Major Bradford.

This was the situation when Forrest arrived at about eleven o'clock that morning with his escort and the detachment from Wisdom's regiment. After making a personal reconnaissance of the area, he said to Colonel McCulloch, "What do you think about takin' them houses in front of the fort?"

"If I can get possession of the houses, I can silence their artillery."

"Go ahead an' take 'em."

McCulloch made the assault and took the log cabins. The fort commander had ordered the buildings destroyed, and the Federals managed to burn the front row of houses before they were compelled to retire with serious loss. From these structures, McCulloch's men kept up a deadly fire on the fort. Their position was so low and close to the fort that the enemy's artillery could not be depressed sufficiently to fire upon them.

After watching McCulloch's assault upon the buildings, Forrest said to Buck, "Did you git the best marksmen in each unit identified?"

"Yessir."

"Then pass the word to all unit commanders to post some of 'em on high ground an' have the others crawl up behind logs an' stumps to git as close as they can. Tell 'em to shoot at anybody that shows inside the fort."

"Yes, sir," he replied, and left to carry out the order.

Forrest made another careful reconnaissance of the area. As he did, the rifles from the fort began to single him out. His horse was mortally wounded; and in its panic from fear or pain, it reared and fell over on him. Badly bruised and shaken up, he called for another horse.

"General, why don't you make the rest of your survey on foot; you are too good a target mounted," Major Anderson said.

"I'm just as apt to be hit one way as t'other, an' I can see better from a hoss." The general may have been wrong in this; for before the day was over, a second horse had been killed under him and a third wounded.

It was one o'clock before the ammunition wagon arrived and the men were resupplied and ready to attack. Forrest had seen the advantage Coal Creek Ravine provided for cover and assault if he could get his men into it. It was so low that he believed the enemy could not lower their cannon enough to fire into the area, and the men could rush the stronghold from a relatively short distance. He ordered Colonels Bell and Wilson to move their men forward at least as close to the fort as McCulloch's brigade. Using the several gullies and low places, the troops were moved to the face of the Coal Creek bluff and along that to the mouth of Coal Creek Ravine. They advanced to a position not more than seventy-five yards from the fort, not without some loss when they would pass through an open area and expose themselves to fire from the parapet. Meanwhile, the gunboat *New Era* was shelling the Confederate lines incessantly as they were skirmishing and moving to their new positions; and from this they also suffered casualties as they advanced almost into the very teeth of their adversaries.

Feeling assured that he could take the fort with a quick rush, and hoping to convince the Federal commander of this and save further loss of life, Forrest joined Chalmers on a knoll about 400 yards from the fort and directed the latter to display a flag of truce and request a parley. This was between 3:00 and 3:30 p.m.; and firing ceased immediately, including shelling from the gunboat, which was notified of the truce by signal from the fort. Captain Walter A. Goodman of Chalmers' staff, accompanied by Captain Thomas Henderson, commanding scouts, and Lieutenant Frank Rogers, were sent forward along the river bank northward toward the fort with the following message:

> "Headquarters Forrest's Cavalry,
> "Before Fort Pillow April 12, 1864.
> "Major Booth, Commanding United States Forces, Fort Pillow:
> "Major—The conduct of the officers and men garrisoning Fort Pillow has been such as to entitle them to being treated as prisoners of war. I demand the unconditional surrender of this garrison, promising you that you shall be treated as prisoners of war. My men have received a fresh supply of ammunition, and from their present position can easily assault and capture the fort. Should my demand be refused, I cannot be responsible for the fate of your command. Respectfully,
> "N. B. FORREST,
> "Major General Commanding."

The three Confederate officers halted about 150 yards from the parapet. Adjutant Leaming and Captains Bradford and Young came from the fort to meet them. As the Confederates advanced toward the fort, they saw the smoke of a steamboat approaching from above and immediately sent a messenger back to General Forrest with the information that a boat loaded with Federal troops was coming down the river toward the landing. Forrest rode as quickly as he could to the river bluff, where he saw the steamer, blue with Federal troops, coming down the stream toward the beleaguered garrison and gunboat. If she had been signalled that a truce was on, she did not respect the signal by stopping, putting about, or moving over toward the Arkansas shore. Believing these to be reinforcements for the garrison, Forrest, in order to prevent their landing, ordered Major Anderson to call off two hundred men from McCulloch's brigade and take position in the rifle pits below the fort where they could command the landing and fire into the vessel if it tried to disembark the troops. Orders were sent to Colonel Bell to man the rifle pits just south of Coal Creek for the same purpose, and a detail from Barteau's regiment was soon in place. The flag of truce was flying at the time, but the officers in the fort must have understood why the movements were made as they did not protest them. The steamer was in full view, and it was their responsibility to inform the vessel of the truce and ask it to stand clear. In addition, two other steamships appeared, coming up the river from the direction of Memphis. Forrest had no intention of being denied his prey, and the commander of the fort had equally strong reason to secure a delay in the hope of being reinforced.

One of the steamboats approaching from the south was the *Olive Branch*, on which was Federal Brigadier General George F. Shepley, who had just resigned the position of military governor of Louisiana and was enroute to St. Louis. Before they reached the site of Fort Pillow, the boat captain saw on the Tennessee bank a small group of women waving excitedly and motioning for the vessel to come in closer to them. He said to the pilot, "Take her in near the shore, and let's see what they want."

The pilot gave the appropriate orders to the helmsman, and the boat moved in closer to the river's east bank. As it approached the women, the captain called, "What do you want?"

"The Rebels have attacked Fort Pillow and captured two boats on the river. They'll take you if you go on," one of the women answered.

"Are you certain of that?"

"As sure as day!"

About this time General Shepley, who had started for the pilot house when the boat moved in close to the bank, appeared at the door and inquired, "What do you propose to do, Captain?"

"I'm putting about and returning to Memphis," he replied.

"You can't do that. You've got aboard two full batteries of artillery and a detachment of artillerists. These guns and men can probably be used by the garrison of the fort."

"The guns can also be used by the enemy. If they've captured two boats on the river, they can take this one too; this is no armed gunboat, General. I'm responsible for the safety of my vessel and have no intention of letting it fall into the hands of the enemy." Then to the pilot, "Turn her about; we're going back to Memphis."

As the boat was swinging around in the stream, the general said,

"Captain, I can't order you to endanger your boat, but I can order you to stop; and I ask you to do that. I want to see if one of the other boats coming up will carry me and some of these guns to the beleaguered fort."

"Slow the engines, and hold her steady in the stream," the Captain said to the pilot.

The first boat up was towing barges. General Shepley ordered it to cast them off and to take him and a section of artillery to the fort. While the vessel was trying to free itself from the barges, another vessel, the *Cheek*, came into sight. Seeing that she was better suited for the purpose, the general had the vessel brought alongside and went aboard her with Captain Thornton, the ranking officer of the batteries, to transfer the guns. Before they could get the guns aboard, the steamer *Liberty*, loaded with Federal troops, came into sight from the north. When she reached hailing distance, the general asked, "Did you come past Fort Pillow?"

"Yes," came the reply from the *Liberty*. "Everything's all right up there; you can go by. The gunboat is lying off the fort."

"Will you go upstream now?" the general called to the captain of the *Olive Branch*.

"Yes," the captain responded.

"Then Captain Thornton and I will come back aboard."

The two officers returned to the *Olive Branch*, and the vessel proceeded on up the river. When they came within sight of the fort, they could see the United States flag flying over it; and there was no firing taking place. As they approached the gunboat *New Era*, a small boat put out from that vessel and headed for them. When it was within hailing distance, an officer in the bow called, "We do not want any boats to stop. Proceed to Cairo and have the ordnance officer there send us immediately 400 rounds of ammunition."

The *Olive Branch* increased her speed and moved as rapidly as possible upstream. After she had passed the fort, the captain and the general could see flags of truce flying outside the fortifications.

"I wonder why that naval officer didn't mention that a truce is in effect?" the general asked.

"I don't know. There's been no signal from the fort, either. Truce or not, I'm glad to get past that fort."[10]

While these things were taking place on the river and Forrest was moving troops into the rifle pits along the bluff, the Federal commander of the fort was considering General Forrest's demand for surrender and directed Adjutant Leaming to make the following response:

"General Forrest, Commanding C. S. Forces:

"Sir,—I respectfully ask one hour for consultation with my officers and the officers of the gunboat. In the meantime no preparations to be made on either side. Very respectfully,

"L. F. BOOTH, Major Commanding"[11]

In about fifteen minutes Captain Goodman returned with the following reply from Forrest:

"Major L. F. Booth, commanding U. S. Forces, Fort Pillow:

"Sir,—I have the honor to acknowledge the receipt of your note, asking one hour to consider my demand for your surrender. Your request cannot be granted. I will allow you twenty minutes from the receipt of this note for consideration; if at the expiration of that time the fort is not surrendered, I shall assault it. I do not demand the surrender of the gunboat.

"Very respectfully, N. B. FORREST, Major-General."

Upon receipt of this message, the officers within the fort held a meeting and unanimously voted not to surrender. Adjutant Leaming then wrote, as directed, and delivered the following note to General Forrest in person:

"GENERAL,—I will not surrender.

"Very respectfully, your obedient servant

"L. F. BOOTH, Major Commanding."

The Union officers apparently believed themselves secure within the confines of their fort, and this feeling was apparently transmitted to their troops. During the exchange of these messages under the flag of truce, the garrison soldiers, especially the colored ones, had mounted the parapet in considerable numbers; and they shouted to McCulloch's men, many of whom had come out from behind the barracks and houses where they had been concealed and protected, and dared them to try to take the fort. They hurled at the Rebels abusive and obscene epithets which were accompanied by vulgar gestures. These provoked similar responses from the men in gray as to what they would do to them when they took the stronghold.

Captain Marshall of the Gunboat *New Era* and Major Bradford agreed upon a signal to be used if the Union troops had to leave the fort. They were to drop down under the bank, and the gunboat would rain canister upon the Rebels above. Six cases of ammunition were taken down the bank near the water and opened for rapid distribution, if needed. Also, Major Bradford evidently made the fatal error of giving his men free access to the liquor with which the commissary was supplied.[12]

The flags of truce came down. Inside the fort, the garrison, believing themselves secure behind the six-foot parapet fronted by the ditch twelve feet wide and eight feet deep, prepared for the defense. The cannons were loaded with grape, and the men took their positions on the bench behind the parapet. A number of civilians within the fort were given arms and stood with the Union troops. The *New Era* was on station to do her part.

Outside the fort the Rebels were also getting ready. Forrest instructed the men in the rifle pits along the bluff to watch the gunboat; and when that vessel opened its gunports, they were to cut down the gunners. "Shoot ever'thing blue 'twixt wind and water till their flag comes down," he said.

His orders to his commanders and troops were explicit, "You must take that fort by storm. Ev'ry gun an' pistol is to be fully loaded, but not a shot's to be fired until you're inside the works an' fightin' hand-to-hand. You must make it quick work. The enemy can't lower their cannon enough to make much use of 'em, an' our sharpshooters behind you'll be zeroin' in on any head showin' above the parapet until you cross the ditch an' climb the embankment."

For one of the few times in his military career, Forrest did not personally lead the assault; but he took a position on a high point about 400 yards in front of the fort's center. "Anderson!" he called, and the major rode over to his side.

"Go to Colonel Bell commandin' the right, an' tell 'im when he hears the bugler sound the charge, to go over them works if he gits killed an' ev'ry man in his command; an' tell 'im I don't want to hear of Tennessee bein' left behind!"

"Yes, sir," Anderson replied and rode off.

"Rushton!"

"Yes, sir," Randy responded and rode over for his orders.

"Go tell Colonel McCulloch commandin' our left that when he hears the bugler sound the charge to go over the works if he is killed an ev'ry man in his command, an' tell 'im I don't want to hear of Missouri bein' left behind."

"Yes, sir," Randy replied as he put spurs to his mount.

"McCord!"

Buck rode up by Forrest's side. "Go check your sharpshooters on high ground. See they got plenty of ammunition, an' keep 'em firing at anything in blue above or behind the parapet. Pin 'em down till our men can git to 'em. I'll go forward then, 'an you join me.''

"Yes, sir," Buck replied, and he moved off.

Forrest sat on his horse for five minutes watching his staff officers as they travelled their different directions to carry out his orders. Then he called, "Gaus!"

The German bugler rode up by his commander's side with his battered bugle. "See that big gully about half way between here an' the fort?"

"Yah, sar," the bugler answered.

"You can git into it safely over to the south. Move up it till you're about half way between the troops on both sides, an' blow the charge like you never blowed it before."

"Yah, sar!" Gaus replied as he rode off, proud of the honor of being the one to begin the assault.

Forrest watched the bugler as he picked his way to the designated position and knew when he reached it that his commanders would have had time to speak to their men and urge them on to a valiant effort this day. When the old German reached the selected spot, he turned and looked back at his commander. Forrest half raised his right arm; and the bugler faced the fort, took a deep breath, and blew the charge with all his might. He then turned toward the southwest and blew it again, and he turned to the northwest and blew it still again. By this time, it was hardly audible above the din of the cavalrymen screaming the Rebel yell as they charged the fort on foot.

Forrest watched as the Confederate lines surged forward toward the ditch in front of the parapet, the men well bent over to make the smallest targets possible. Forrest's face, neck, and eyes were flushed with excitement; but the usual savageness of his countenance at such a time was replaced with a faint smile of pride as he watched his men move rapidly forward, unflinching and unwavering as they faced the blasts of cannon grape and the exploding rifle volleys from the enemy behind the parapet, yet not one of the charging men lifted his gun to fire a shot. Forrest was pleased to see he was right about the enemy being unable to lower their cannon enough to be effective, for the showers of grape thrown at the attackers were carrying harmlessly above their heads.

Neither was the fire of the men from the parapets very effective, for they had to raise one-fourth of their bodies above the protecting earthwork to get a shot at the oncoming Rebels. The accuracy of the Confederate sharpshooters was quick to take its toll as the enemy exposed themselves, and the defenders were firing rapidly and inaccurately in their eagerness to get down behind their cover again.

The cavalrymen quickly reached the ditch and hurled themselves into it. Here they were safe from the enemy fire; but in their eagerness to take the fort, they did not tarry. Some bent over; and the others, using their backs for steps, clambered out of the ditch to a small ledge in front of the parapet. Those who reached the ledge then helped their comrades up to it. Bell, the two McCullochs, Barteau, Alexander Chalmers, Wilson, Russell, and Wisdom were all there with them. Firing from behind the parapet had ceased; and the Confederates knew the enemy was waiting with loaded guns for them to show above the face of the earthwork, but up the embankment they went together.

Those first reaching the top met the blasts of the enemy rifles. Many fell, rolling down the incline into the ditch; but others came on, leaping from the top of the parapet for close hand-to-hand fighting with the defenders. They had no bayonets, but they carried six-shooter pistols which they thrust into the bellies of the blue-clad soldiers and pulled the triggers. The Union troops gave way under the onslaught and fell back toward the supposed safety of the river bank, but now the second line of the Confederates were at the top of the parapet firing into the retreating soldiers. As these pressed into the narrow passages between the tents, they became jammed in the area, creating easy targets; and few of them were able to raise and fire their guns in their defense.

As Major Bradford and the other survivors scampered down the bank toward the water and the ammunition waiting there for them, they expected the gunboat to open with grape upon the Rebels in the fort; but no such support came. The *New Era* was there, but not a gunport was open. Running southward along the face of the bluff to escape from the fire being rained upon them from above, the Federals encountered Major Anderson with his 200 men in the south rifle pits. Anderson gave the order for a volley which sent them reeling. They turned and ran in the opposite direction, only to meet a similar fusillade from the detachment Colonel Bell had placed in the north rifle pits.

Forrest stayed at his observation position until his men went over the parapet into the inner confines of the stronghold. He then moved as rapidly as possible, delayed somewhat by the gullies, to the fort. When he came into it, evidence of the bloody fight which had taken place was all around him; and there was no sign of organized resistance in the immediate area, only some from beneath the bluff. The United States flag was still flying, but Private John Doak Carr of Barteau's Second Tennessee regiment cut the halyards; and when the flag fell, he gathered it up and carried it to Forrest. Although many of the men on both sides who saw the flag lowered from its mast took this as a sign of surrender and ceased firing, others did not. Forrest ordered the firing to be stopped, and Lieutenant Colonel D. M. Wisdom of the Nineteenth Tennessee cavalry was sent down the line of the bluff to convey the order. Generals Chalmers and Bell; Colonels McCulloch, Barteau, and Wisdom; and Major Anderson were with their troops to enforce the order. Chalmers placed under arrest on the spot one soldier who failed to comply with it.

As Bradford and his men scampered down the bank, and then along it, first in one direction and then in the other, many of them realized the hopelessness of their situation; and they threw down their guns and raised their arms in surrender. Some, frantic with fright or frenzied by liquor or the pains of their wounds, rushed into the river and drowned or were shot to death as they tried to swim away. A large number of the white soldiers, probably because they were better trained and could see the futility of further resistance or did not fear capture as much, threw themselves behind logs and stumps and in depressions; and they escaped the high mortality of the negro troops. Many of the latter continued to fire on their assailants, probably convinced from the slaughter that had taken place that no quarter would be given. Some even managed to break through the investing lines and were pursued and killed when they refused to halt. It was a bloody affair of short duration, taking no more than fifteen minutes from the sound of the charge to the firing of the last shots.[13]

The *New Era* was still lying off the port with steam up, either at anchor or under "slow wheel" to hold her steady in the current. One of the captured Parrot guns was brought to the bluff and opened upon her. The vessel steamed up stream out of range, but hovered in the area.

As soon as the firing ceased, Forrest ordered Colonel McCulloch to take charge of the enemy's camp, prisoners, and captured property. The enlisted prisoners were herded together in an open compound, and the officers were sequestered in one of the buildings. The wounded were moved into some of the tents at the back of the fort and also into a few of the buildings south of it. Details of Federal prisoners under their own officers were sent to bury their dead.

Buck was inventorying the equipment and ammunition at each gun emplacement. As he was moving from one gun position to another he passed close to the compound where the prisoners were being held. His mind was occupied by the details of his task, and he was paying no attention to the prisoners until he heard a voice say, "The Rebs must be gittin' hard up to make off'cers outa white trash."

Buck turned in time to see a Confederate sergeant crash a rifle butt along the side of Jason's head, and the legs of the blue-clad negro buckled as he crumbled to the ground. "Keep a civil tongue in your mouth when you talk to one of our officers, you black..."

"That'll be enough, Sergeant," Buck said, stepping between the two men to prevent a second blow which the sergeant was getting ready to deliver.

"If that's the way you want it, Cap'n," the sergeant replied. He did not understand the officer's actions; nevertheless, he lowered his rifle.

Jason got to his feet somewhat unsteadily. Blood was coming from a gash on the side of his head, and a large knot was beginning to form. Buck took a folded handkerchief from his pocket and offered it to the black man. "I got my own," Jason said as he pulled a handkerchief out and pressed it against the bleeding wound.

"Maybe you should have the surgeon take a look at that," Buck said.

"I'm all right," Jason snarled.

"Is David with you?"

"Over there," the negro replied, pointing in the direction of an unconscious black man sprawled on the ground with his head and right shoulder resting against one of several bales of straw in the vicinity.

"Is he wounded?"

"Naw, jus' drunk." Buck wasn't surprised at the answer, for he had smelled liquor on Jason's breath; and he had seen open casks of whiskey scattered about the fort. Each of these now had a guard placed over it to prevent the Confederate soldiers from getting drunk on the contents.

"Captain Rushton is here," Buck said.

"I know. I seen 'im from the parapet durin' the truce."

"I'll tell him you're here."

"Don't bother; I don't want none of his pity."

Buck had to continue with his assigned task; but before leaving, he said to the sergeant, "If his head doesn't stop bleeding, send him to the surgeon."

"He'll be all right; he's got a hard head."

Buck had finished the inventory at the last gun when he ran into Randy. "I've been looking for you," he said.

"I went up river with the Yankee provost-marshal, Captain Young. We had a white flag, and he tried to signal to the *New Era* for a conference. Forrest wanted the vessel to take the Yankee wounded aboard."

"Did you have any luck?"

"No. Captain Young waved the flag; but if the boat saw it, they paid no attention, for they took off up the river."

"Jason's here."

"He is? Where?"

"He was in the prisoner compound, but he may have been sent to the surgeon."

"Is he wounded?"

"Not badly; just a blow to the head."

"Are you busy?"

"Not now."

"Let's go see him."

They found Jason in the same area of the compound but closer to David, who was still sprawled out in the same position. As they came up, Buck saw the drunken negro open his bleary eyes for a moment and then close them again. Randy went to Jason and said, "I just heard you're here. Are you all right?"

The bleeding had stopped, and Jason had tied the bloody handkerchief around his head for a makeshift bandage. "I'm all right," he replied sullenly.

"I'm glad you made it; there were a lot who didn't. Why didn't y'all surrender?"

"We didn' think y'all could take the fort, an' none of us aimed to surrender or ask for quarter."

"The Federal officers should know General Forrest better than that by now."

The name Forrest roused David out of his drunken stupor. From beneath his coat, he pulled a pistol which was hidden in the waist of his trousers. Raising and pointing it toward Randy, he said, "I gonna kill dat damned Forrest!"

"No, David, no!" Jason cried. "It's Massa Randy—it's Massa Randy!" He threw himself between Randy and the raised pistol just as David fired, and the bullet struck him in the right front side of the chest, passing through both lungs and puncturing the aorta. Buck's pistol was quickly in his hand, and he was firing rapidly at the figure on the ground. David grabbed his stomach as the first bullet caught him in the abdominal area; and his body jerked, and then again, as the second and third shots hit him in the chest. The hand clutching the gun on top of his stomach relaxed, and the weapon fell to the ground. By this time, he was dead.

The impact of the bullet hitting Jason had thrown him against Randy, who caught the former slave and gently lowered him to a sitting position. The negro was trying to speak, but with great difficulty through foamy blood coming from his mouth. "Don't talk," Randy said. "We'll get you to the surgeon."

"'Sno use," Jason muttered. "Gotta talk now or never. Tell Maw an' Paw how I die, maybe it'll he'p." His voice grew weaker. "Mass'

Randy, I wants you to know I allus..." That was as far as his trailing voice could go.

Randy was on his knees as he held Jason. He could feel him go limp and knew that his childhood friend was dead. He pulled the lifeless body close and lowered his own head until his cheeks were against the negro's short, stiff hair. Randy fought back his tears as he lowered Jason's body to the ground.

The incident quickly drew a crowd, and Buck found by his side the sergeant who had struck Jason on the head. The noncommissioned officer had seen what had happened and was looking with surprise and disbelief at the drama before him; never had he seen a white man show such affection for a negro. Buck sensed the sergeant's lack of understanding and said to him in a quiet voice, "They grew up together master and slave; but they were more than that—they were close friends."

The sergeant nodded; but, despite his sympathy for the young captain, this was beyond his comprehension. When Randy stood up, the sergeant said, "I'll see he's proper buried."

"Thank you," Randy replied. "Please get his things to me; I'd like to send them to his folks. My name's Rushton—I'm on Forrest's staff."

"I know who you are, Cap'n. I'll find out where he was quartered and git ev'rything together for you."

"I'd appreciate that," Randy replied and moved off with Buck. They walked a short way in silence before Randy spoke, "I wonder what he was trying to say when he died."

"I don't know, but you would have liked it."

"He really was my friend as I always thought, wasn't he, Buck?"

"Always. I never doubted it, and he proved it today."

"But why did he act the way he did?"

"I'm not sure, but I think I know. Y'all grew up so close together that he never felt like a slave when he was a child; and when the time came that he had to face the reality of what he was and the difference between you, he couldn't accept it. He resented the station he had to take in life, but he showed today how much you meant to him."

"I think you hit the nail on the head. You always seemed to understand him better than any of us."

"Maybe it was because I knew the way I would have felt in his place."

Randy looked at his friend. "Did anyone ever tell you what a truly fine person you are?"

"I don't believe so."

"Then consider it done," Randy said with a smile.

"I've got a friend who is even better," Buck replied.

At five o'clock General Forrest and a portion of the troops moved away from Fort Pillow. Bell, with his brigade, followed with all the unwounded prisoners and those whose injuries did not prevent their marching. Forrest, feeling the injuries incurred when his horse fell on him, travelled only five miles before stopping for the night. Bell camped ten miles from the battlefield. McCulloch, with Chalmers, followed after dark, leaving the fort abandoned except for the Federal wounded and their surgeon. The rear guard encamped two miles from the river.

As the prisoners were being moved away from the fort, Major Bradford was placed in the charge of Colonel Robert McCulloch. Many of Forrest's men held a personal grudge against Bradford for the way he and his men had treated Southern sympathizers in the area. Bradford was probably aware of this, and it may have influenced his decision not to surrender. It was a miracle that he came out of the fight alive; however, his brother did not. His body was found near the flagpole where it is believed he sent the signal to the *New Era* that they were falling back below the crest of the bluff. Bradford asked permission to superintend the burial of his brother, and his request was granted after he gave his word of honor that he would return to the Confederate camp that night after the brother was interred. Instead of returning, he used his knowledge of the area to escape.

The Confederate losses in the engagement were fourteen killed and eighty-six wounded. Of the 557 Federal enlisted troops at Fort Pillow, 221 were killed and 130 wounded, most of the casualties being negro troops. Those not wounded, or not wounded seriously enough to prevent their marching, totalling 226, were subsequently moved south into Mississippi as prisoners. Forrest sent Major Anderson back to Fort Pillow the following day to secure the landing of some passing steamer to take on the Federal wounded left behind. As he passed General Chalmers' camp, Anderson requested, and received, permission to take with him Captain Young, a Federal prisoner. Forrest also instructed Anderson, in the event he was unable to place the wounded aboard a boat: "Burn all the houses at the fort, except the one used as a hospital. Leave the Federal surgeon, and such of the wounded that cannot travel or be moved, and parole them; also the prisoners; and leave with them a nurse or two, or slightly wounded men, sufficient to wait on them. Leave with the wounded five or six days' supply of provisions and any medicine they need."[14]

Upon arrival near the fort, the two officers found a Union gunboat shelling the woods about it. Anderson went to the bluff and raised a white flag, and the shelling stopped. The gunboat, the *Silver Cloud*, sent a small boat ashore to ascertain what was wanted; and Anderson informed Acting Master William Ferguson, U.S.N., that General Forrest desired to place the Union wounded aboard the boat. A truce until five o'clock that afternoon was agreed upon.

The captain of the gunboat hailed a passing steamer, the *Platte Valley*, and the wounded were placed aboard the two vessels, a detail of Confederates assisting in this work. The task of loading the wounded and burying the remainder of the dead was completed by four o'clock, and the boats proceeded up the river. Captain Anderson lowered the flag of truce, burned the buildings and tents, and rode away with the few Confederates in the area.

On the 14th Forrest reestablished his headquarters at Jackson. The next afternoon, a serious-faced General Chalmers came to see him and said, "I understand you are aware that Major Bradford violated his word of honor and escaped."

"That scum has no honor. He'll rue the day I git my hands on 'im ag'in."

"We did get our hands on him. He was recaptured, in civilian clothes; and tried to conceal his identity, but the men knew him too well. He was brought to Colonel Duckworth, and this morning I sent him under guard with several prisoners to Jackson. A few miles out of Brownsville, some of the guards took him a short distance from the road and shot him."

Forrest smiled, showing no dismay, "You don't say?"

"Yes, I do, General. This is serious business. I think we should have a full inquiry and bring to trial those who are guilty of misconduct."

"You say he was in civilian clothes an' not in uniform?"

"Yes."

"Then that makes 'im a spy, don't it?"

"Well, yes; I guess you could say that."

"What gen'rally happens to spies?"

"They're hung."

"I guess he was kinda lucky, at that; for I sure as hell woulda hung the son-of-a-buck".

"What about the men who shot him?"

"Forgit it." Forrest smiled again. "For all we know, he mighta been tryin' to escape. Let's give 'em the benefit of the doubt. I started to kill 'im m'self. He asked to see me after he surrendered an' had the gall to protest the large number of men we killed an' wounded when we took the fort. I told 'im that war means fightin' an' fightin' means killin' an' that I'd lost a hundred men killed an' wounded in takin' a fort any bird-brain woulda knowed couldn' be defended. I asked 'im if he had ever surrendered the fort to my men, an' of course he hadn'. I also asked 'im who lowered the United States flag as a sign the place had been taken, an' he didn' know. I told 'im that if we hadn' lowered that flag, his losses would have still been goin' on an' that the negroes fit a damned sight better an' a whole lot longer than that sorry bunch of yellow-livered Homemade Yankees he was commandin'. I was tempted to run my saber through the damned fool an' told 'im to git out of my sight before I did.''

''If that's the way you want it, General; but you may be setting a dangerous precedent. I hope you never regret it.''

''I'll take my chances. After what him an his men done to the good Southerners in this area, I was su'prised he was took prisoner.''

''So was I,'' Chalmers replied. [15]

Chapter XVIII

Brice's Cross Roads

Just before arriving at Jackson from Fort Pillow, Forrest received instructions to detach a part of his command to repel a raid understood to be impending from the direction of Decatur, Alabama, through the interior of the northwestern part of that state. Chalmers was sent with his division to the threatened area via Okolona. The men of Buford's command were assembled at Jackson. Here Forrest remained until May 2, collecting all possible military resources in men, horses, draft animals, and subsistence to be gleaned from the area to the north.

Chalmers left Brownsville on the 15th of April with his command for Okolona. Riding with him was Randy, with a furlough of three weeks to get Forrest another horse from the Rushton stables. When he reached Somerville on the 16th, Chalmers divided his command. Bell, with the prisoners and artillery, took the road through LaGrange; while Chalmers, with McCulloch's and Neely's brigades, moved toward Holly Springs. Randy went with Bell. On the 18th a message was received from General Polk that the presence of Forrest's troops to repel the raid would not be needed. Barteau, with the Second Tennessee, was detached and sent on to Demopolis with the prisoners; and Randy continued on his way home with this unit. The rest of Bell's Brigade and Neely's were sent back to Forrest in West Tennessee; McCulloch resumed his position behind the Tallahatchie at Panola, and Chalmers established his headquarters at Oxford. Then, on orders from Forrest, Chalmers set out for Tupelo with McCulloch's brigade, except the Eighteenth Mississippi battalion, and swept the area eastward to the Mobile and Ohio railroad for conscripts, absentees, and deserters.

Upon arrival in western Tennessee, Bell's and Neely's brigades were distributed at points favorable for recruiting and for granting furloughs to the officers and men to visit their families, renovate their clothing, and obtain remounts. By the 28th, Buford had assembled his whole division at Jackson, including Bell's brigade, and on the 30th was ordered to move with it and Neely's Brigade on May 2 to Tupelo, convoying a large ox-train laden with subsistence, whiskey (for hospital purposes), and leather. He also moved another 300 prisoners south. The Kentucky brigade of this division, which had entered on the campaign with 1,004 men, now numbered 1,717; and Bell's Tennesseans, who took the field with 1,254, now mustered over 1,700 well-mounted horsemen.

Buford moved rapidly, despite the slow ox-train, and reached Rienzi on the Mobile and Ohio railroad on May 4. Here he transferred the supplies and prisoners to be taken farther south on the railroad, and he moved on to Tupelo, which he reached on the 6th.

Forrest also left Jackson for Tupelo on May 2 with his staff and escort, taking the route through Bolivar, Tennessee, and Ripley, Mississippi. That afternoon in the vicinity of Bolivar, he was met by scouts with information that a Federal cavalry force about 2,000 strong, under General Sturgis, was engaged in a sharp skirmish with McDonald's battalion under Lieutenant Colonel Crews on the Somerville road about two miles west of Bolivar. As he pressed forward to Crews' relief, he came upon several hundred unarmed recruits in Bolivar whom he ordered to move with his headquarters baggage train and ambulances five miles southward on the road to Ripley and encamp for the night.

He found Crews with his small force holding the Federal horse at bay and immediately assumed command. With his escort, he had a total of about 300 men. He boldly charged the enemy's front and drove back their skirmish line about three-fourths of a mile upon the main Union force, inflicting a loss of forty killed and wounded. Unable to attack further against odds of more than six to one, he withdrew into a line of fortifications which the Federals had earlier built in the western suburbs of Bolivar. The enemy, taking heart at this show of weakness, advanced vigorously upon his position; but they were beaten back by a hot fire at close range from the rifles and pistols of the dismounted and entrenched Rebels. The Federals broke in disorder and quit the field. Forrest resumed his march and caught up with his train at the encampment. Major Strange had his right arm broken by a Minie ball in this affair.

For the remainder of the month, Forrest perfected the organization of his command and devoted his time to increasing the efficiency of his force. He now had four field batteries, each with four guns: Morton's, Thrall's, Rice's, and Walton's. He had two divisions: Chalmers' with McCulloch's, Neely's, and Rucker's brigades; and Buford's with Bell's and Lyon's brigades.

The command was dispersed for reasons of forage, subsistence, and observation of the enemy. Buford's division, for the most part, was in Tupelo, from which it was engaged from the 16th to the 24th in reconnaissance as far as Corinth. About the 26th, Chalmers was sent with McCulloch's and Neely's brigades and Walton's battery on an expedition into Alabama, penetrating as far as Montevallo, for the purpose of meeting a hostile raid anticipated against the iron works in that region from the direction of Huntsville and Decatur, Alabama.

Forrest met with an unfortunate decision from the War Department. About 700 of the new recruits from Tennessee who had joined up with him were runaways from infantry regiments of Johnston's army. He was directed to return these deserters to their original commands. While most of these men had volunteered to serve in Forrest's cavalry, they did not hesitate to desert again at the prospect of being forced to fight as infantry.

Randy's furlough did not begin until he left Barteau's command at Demopolis on April 22; so he did not rejoin Forrest, who was at Tupelo, until May 13. As soon as he arrived there, he sought out the commanding general at his headquarters and found him busy with members of his staff. When he saw Randy, he quickly asked, "Did you git the hoss?"

"Yessir. She's out front."

"That's good. Let's go take a look at 'er."

When they went outside most of the other officers at the meeting followed to see the new mount. Tied to a hitching rail was a bay mare with white stockings on all four legs and a blazed face. The general looked with obvious pleasure at her. "She's a beautiful animal; how old is she?"

"Three years."

"What's 'er name?"

"Edgy."

"Edgy?" Forrest asked in surprise.

"She's a spirited animal and was high strung and nervous. She's gotten over that, but she's still got a lot of spirit."

"Wouldn' want 'er no other way," Forrest replied. He walked over to the animal and examined her carefully and could find nothing he didn't like. "Let me know how much, an' I'll send your father a draft on my bank."

"Daddy said he wouldn't accept your money for the horse, and I'm not about to get caught in the middle of this—it's between you and him."

"I'll square it someway. I sent Buck down to Meridian to check on some artillery shells; he should be back today. Y'all got a room in this house. Soon's you get settled, come in to the meetin'; we need you—Major Strange was wounded near Bolivar."

"Not seriously, I hope."

"Naw—just a Minie in the arm, but it broke the bone. He's here, but his activities are limited."

Buck got back from Meridian late that afternoon. Both he and Randy were so busy that they had little time to talk until supper. As they took places next to each other, Randy said, "I saw your folks; everybody at home is fine, except Ellen—she's having morning sickness. Guess you're going to be a papa after all."

"I know. We finally got our mail. Yours is in the room."

"It's not as bad as it was; she's getting better. Miss Sadie's doctoring her and says she should be over it completely in a couple of weeks."

"Damn! I'd like to see her. Maybe if I shot that horse, the general would let me go get one of Pa's."

"Not if he knew you shot it. I heard him tell Major Anderson that he isn't going to ride this one in battle if he can help it. Maybe you should offer to get him a stallion that could be bred to the bay."

"That's a good idea, but the time isn't right for it." Then he asked, "How are the new slaveholders doing?"

Randy laughed. "Mister Cory is trying to give Vira her freedom—it's before the state legislature now. In return, she is to work for Miss Sadie for three years. Now that she knows Vira will be a slave no longer, I think your mother likes the idea of having someone to help her. She keeps her busy."

"Well, it's time Ma began to take things a little easier; she's worked hard all her life, and Pa can afford to pay someone to give her a hand."

In the spring and summer of 1864, two great strategists were playing a memorable game of war among the pine-clad hills of Georgia. Sherman, with his usual aggression and an army much larger and better equipped than that of General Joseph E. Johnston, was slowly, by movements around the latter's flanks, forcing him back toward Atlanta. The Confederate general, a master at defensive warfare, was contesting every foot and inflicting heavy losses upon Sherman when the Union general came at him head-on. With his superior numbers, Sherman had the Confederate army at his mercy if he could keep his troops well supplied from the north and west. "That devil Forrest," as he called him, was one of the chief sources of his anxiety, for he feared the Confederate cavalryman would go into middle Tennessee and break the railroads in his rear. From the time of his Meridian expedition, much of his correspondence dealt with the necessity of killing or wounding Forrest. If he could not be killed, he must be kept busy where he was so that he could not strike the Federal lines of communication.

Now that Forrest was back in Mississippi, it became the prime object of Sherman to keep him occupied there. General Sooy Smith had failed to get him. Major General Stephan A. Hurlbut, the head of the Federal department, had grown in disfavor for failing to defeat the wily general and was replaced by General Cadwallader C. Washburne. In their search for a field commander to go against Forrest, Brigadier General Samuel D. Sturgis, who had achieved success in East Tennessee, was selected. When Forrest withdrew from Tennessee in April and May 1864, Sturgis had been ordered by General Washburne to pursue him into Mississippi and punish him. He followed him as far as Ripley, but turned back when he found that the Rebel cavalry was two days ahead of him. In a communication to Sherman of May 13, Sturgis wrote, "I regret very much that I could not have the pleasure of bringing you his hair; but he is too great a plunderer to fight anything like an equal force, and we have to be satisfied with driving him from the state. He may turn on your communications—I rather think he will, but I see no way to prevent it from this point with this force."

Sturgis was partially right in his assumption about Forrest, for in the latter part of the month, upon orders from Major General S. D. Lee, he began preparations for an incursion into middle Tennessee in which Brigadier General Roddy, operating in North Alabama, was placed temporarily under his command. He marched from Tupelo on June 1 for the proposed raid.

Sherman feared such a move and urged General Washburne to send at once a formidable expedition against Forrest. Sturgis left Memphis and Lafayette on June 1, 1864, with 3,300 cavalry, 4,800 infantry, 400 artillerists, 22 guns, and 250 wagons and ambulances.[1]

Not only were these men carefully selected, they were armed with Colt repeating rifles and breech-loading carbines, the most formidable and effective weapons known to warfare at this time. The cavalry was divided into two brigades, the first, 1,500 strong with six guns, under the command of Colonel George E. Waring, Jr., who had already proved himself as a fighter and able leader at Okolona. The second 1,800 strong with four guns, was commanded by Colonel E. F. Winslow, who had won the commendation of General Sherman when he commanded the cavalry in the expedition from Vicksburg to Meridian. These brigades formed a division under the command of Brigadier General B. H. Grierson.

The infantry was divided into three brigades, the first, 2,000 men and six guns, under the command of Colonel A. Wilkins. The second, 1,600 men and four guns, was under Colonel G. B. Hoge; and the third, 1,200 colored troops with two guns, was under Colonel Edward Bouton. These brigades were temporarily organized as a division and placed under the command of Colonel W. L. McMillen.

General Sturgis' orders were to strike the Mobile and Ohio railroad near Corinth, Mississippi, to capture any force there, and to proceed south, destroying the railroad to Tupelo and Okolona, and as far as possible toward Macon and Columbus. He was also to disperse and destroy Forrest's cavalry and to destroy everything that would support life in that rich section called the "granary of the South." He was to return to Memphis via Grenada. It was a large order, but he had the men and means to accomplish the mission.

On the third day out, Sturgis learned that the Confederates had evacuated Corinth and moved south; so he changed his direction to strike the Mobile and Ohio Railroad below Corinth. Grierson sent Colonel Joseph Kargé with 400 men to Rienzi, about ten miles south of Corinth. He destroyed the depot buildings there; but before he could do much damage to the railroad, Forrest's troopers were on him and drove him away precipitately. General Sturgis was bearing farther southward through mud and rain over bad roads, crossing a section of country which had been stripped of supplies and almost deserted by its inhabitants. He did not reach the town of Ripley until June 7. On this day, Winslow's brigade, which Grierson had ordered to advance on the New Albany road, came in collision with two regiments of Confederates under Colonel Edward W. Rucker, who had been sent to "feel the enemy" and to retire when he met them, without bringing on an engagement. Holding Winslow at arm's length, Rucker reported to Forrest at Booneville on the night of June 9.

After leaving Tupelo on June 1 with 2,000 men, Forrest had reached Russellville, Alabama, by June 3, where he was overtaken by a messenger with a dispatch from General Lee advising that an expedition had left Memphis for what he believed to be an invasion of Mississippi. Lee directed him to retrace his steps as rapidly as possible, and Forrest arrived at Tupelo on June 6 in advance of his command. Here he learned of the general direction of Sturgis' march and of that of the detachment under Colonel Winslow. He ordered Rucker to move to Rienzi and then to reconnoiter in the direction of New Albany. Bell followed Rucker as far as Rienzi, and Forrest went to Booneville, on the Mobile and Ohio Railroad, where Rucker joined him on the 9th. At this time Sturgis concentrated his entire command at Stubbs' farm where he made camp on the same day, nine miles northwest of Brice's Cross Roads.

Forrest met with General Lee, who wanted to draw Sturgis farther from his base in Memphis and then hit and destroy him in a coordinated attack. He ordered Forrest to march on the following morning from Booneville in the direction of Brice's Cross Roads and thence toward Prairie Mound to Okolona. Two batteries of artillery, Thrall's and Ferrill's, and all supplies not needed, were moved south by train; and General Lee left with them.

The road from Ripley to Fulton, Mississippi, runs in a southeasterly direction and crosses the Mobile and Ohio railroad at Guntown. On the railroad five miles north of Guntown is the village of Baldwyn, and from that place runs a road in a southwesterly direction to Pontotoc. These two roads cross each other at right angles by the home and store of a Mr. Brice, and the intersection is known as Brice's Cross Roads. Forrest would be moving on the road to Pontotoc, and Sturgis was already on the road to Guntown. Forrest felt they might collide at or near that intersection, and he made his plans accordingly.

At this time, on the 9th, the Confederate cavalry was scattered. Bell, with 1,700 men, was at Rienzi, twenty-five miles north of the crossroad. Forrest was at Booneville, only seven miles closer to the place of impending battle, with his escort of eighty-five men reinforced with a company of Georgians under Captain Gartrell, about fifty strong. Rucker's brigade, approximately 700 men, was also at Booneville; while Johnson's and Lyon's brigades, 500 and 800 men respectively, were at Baldwyn, six miles northeast of Brice's Cross Roads. The artillery, twelve pieces under the command of Captain John Morton, was at Booneville. Chalmers' division was not close enough to take part in any immediate engagement.

A courier was sent to Bell with a message to have rations issued and everything in readiness to move rapidly before daylight in the direction of Brice's Cross Roads. Similar orders were given to Colonels Rucker, Lyon, and Johnson, and to Captain Morton of the artillery. Lyon's brigade was ordered in the advance; Rucker was to follow; behind him would come Johnson, who had just arrived with a portion of his brigade, jaded and worn after a forced march from Alabama; and Bell would bring up the rear. The artillery had eighteen miles to move over roads which were muddy and miry. A heavy rain had fallen on the 8th of June; and on the afternoon and evening of the 9th, it came down in torrents, not stopping until midnight.

By the time it was light enough to see the roadway, the Confederates were in motion. About daybreak, the clouds broke away; and the sun came up to usher in a hot, humid, depressing day. Forrest had made up his mind to engage the Federals. He rode up beside Rucker as they moved southward, and said, "I'm gonna strike the Yankees at Brice's Cross Roads. I know they greatly outnumber what I have at hand, but the road along which they are marchin' is narrow an' muddy; they won't make much time. The country's so thickly wooded an' heavy with underbrush that they'll not know how few we have. Their cavalry will move out ahead of the infantry an' ought to reach the crossroads three hours ahead of 'em. We can whip the cavalry in that time. As soon as the fight opens, they'll send back to have the infantry move up. It's gonna be hot as hell; an' comin' on a run for five or six miles over these roads, their infantry'll be so wore out we can run right over 'em. I want ever'thing to move up as fast as possible. I'm goin' ahead with Lyon and the escort to open the fight."

While Forrest had all of his forces on the move by four o'clock on the morning of the 10th, the Federals were still in camp. Sturgis was not in a happy frame of mind. The white people in the country through which he was moving would give him no information, and the blacks who flocked to him told such conflicting stories that he could put little credence in them. He was almost completely ignorant as to the number of the enemy; but he had learned Forrest was somewhere close by, either in his front or on his flank. He knew he could not move much farther south without meeting him. Weighed down by the responsibility of his position, he had "a sad foreboding of the consequences." He would have liked to turn back, but he felt he could not after the boastful apology to Sherman about not being able to catch the "scoundrel" and "to bring you his hair." Reluctantly he continued his advance, and the stage was set for the confrontation.

At 5:30 on the morning of the 10th, the Union cavalry under Grierson mounted their horses and moved out in the direction of Brice's Cross Roads with Waring's brigade in the advance. The infantry leisurely cooked their breakfast and did not march until about seven o'clock. Less than a mile northeast of the crossroad is a narrow bridge across the Tishomingo Creek; and it was at this bridge that the Union advance guard encountered a Confederate outpost, drove them away, and reached the crossroad at 9:45. The Confederates retreated northeastward on the road to Baldwyn, and Waring followed them for about a mile until he came to the edge of a field through which the road passed. Here he encountered the advance of Lyon's brigade which had just arrived upon the opposite side of the clearing, a distance of about four hundred yards.

Two companies of Faulkner's Kentuckians, under Captain A. H. Tyler, formed Lyon's advance; and they made a daring charge which not only developed Waring's entire brigade but a battery of artillery which, already in position, opened up on them. The Kentuckians fell back rapidly upon their main column.

Lyon threw out his skirmishers and had formed the remainder of his 800 men in line of battle at about ten o'clock when Forrest arrived on the scene with his reinforced escort, took personal command, and opened the battle of Brice's Cross Roads.

With the exception of two or three cleared patches of land not exceeding six acres in extent immediately around Brice's house, the country, which is only slightly undulating for a mile in every direction, was not only heavily timbered, but there was an undergrowth of black-jack and scrub oaks so dense that in places the troops could force their way through them only with great difficulty. The trees and undergrowth were now in full leaf, and it was possible for either force to approach within a few yards of the other without being seen. The road to Ripley from the crossroad, before reaching the Tishomingo bridge, descended about twenty feet into the creek bottom; and along the stream there was a large cornfield in cultivation.

The field across which the two forces were now facing each other was encircled by a fence, and additional worm fences were along each side of the road passing through it. All around the field was dense growth. Grierson was satisfied that he had met the Confederates in considerable strength. He dismounted Waring's brigade (1,450 strong), which he posted behind the fence in the edge of the dense timber and divided them about equally on each side of the road. Two rifled guns and two howitzers were thrown into position on a slight elevation just behind his line, and 100 picked men were sent forward about a hundred yards, armed with revolving rifles, to conceal themselves in the corners of the fences alongside the road. To the right of Waring, Grierson dismounted his other brigade under Winslow; and this line at the right was bent back slightly toward the crossroad. He held his other six pieces of artillery in reserve.

Forrest, with about 935 men, was facing 3,200 enemy cavalry. When he realized the strength of his opponent, his chief anxiety was that they might charge and run over his small command. Rucker was still two miles in his rear; Johnson was behind him; and both Bell's brigade and Morton's artillery were farther to the rear. Forrest sent Randy toward Booneville with instructions to, "Tell Bell to move up fast, an' fetch all he's got. When he's about five miles from the crossroad, send Barteau's regiment to the right th'ough the woods an' byways across the country to slip up on the Yankee rear an' attack 'em in cooperation with us on the front. Tell Morton to bring his guns on at a gallop.''

He immediately dismounted Lyon's men and positioned them behind the fence at the northeastern side of the field and strengthened the line with brush and logs. To prevent Grierson from attacking, he knew he had to make a showing of force. By characteristic effrontery, he had alternate sections of the fence thrown down and ordered Lyon to make a demonstration by advancing from the edge of the wood into the open field.

Lyon threw out a double line of skirmishers and advanced boldly toward the enemy. Grierson should have recognized this as a pure bluff; for his left reached well beyond Lyon's right, and Lyon's left extended only a little beyond the junction of Waring's and Winslow's brigades. The artillery and small arms of the Federals opened upon Lyon's men, who kept up their feigned attack for about an hour before they retired without confusion to the edge of the wood from which they had started. By this time Rucker had arrived on the scene with his 700 mounted men, having advanced rapidly upon hearing the cannonade from the enemy.

Forrest dismounted the Seventh Tennessee regiment and Chalmers' Eighteenth Mississippi battalion of Rucker's command, placing them in line to the left of Lyon and opposing the center of Winslow's brigade. The Eighth Mississippi, under Duff, was kept mounted and thrown well over to the left toward the Guntown road to protect that flank from being turned. The enemy now had only about two-to-one odds over Forrest, but the latter was still without artillery support.

Forrest again ordered his lines forward with the same purpose for which he had made his initial attack; and after some sharp firing at long range, the Confederates once more retired. Chalmers' battalion, mistaking the intent of the movement, advanced too far and received an enfilading fire from the right of Winslow's line. His battalion withdrew in confusion, but they rallied on the main Confederate line. As the Southerners withdrew the second time to the edge of the wood, Colonel W. A. Johnson came up with his 500 Alabamians. Forrest ordered these to dismount, take position on Lyon's right, and move forward to engage the attention of the enemy's left. After some desultory fighting lasting about five minutes, the Alabamians retired.

It was now about eleven o'clock; and although Bell's brigade and the artillery were not yet within supporting distance, Forrest determined to close with Grierson before the Federal infantry could come up. He rode hurriedly along his line with words of encouragement to his troops, telling them that this would not be a feint and that he expected every man to move forward when the signal was given. He concentrated many of his men in front of the center of the Federal line; and at the sound of the bugle, the entire line sprang forward from the timber, leaped through the fence, and, screaming the Rebel yell, rushed toward the enemy. They were so eager that the units seemed to be vying with each other to see which could first reach the opposing line. The men of Waring's and Winslow's brigades were equally determined to hold their ground as their repeating rifles crackled away in a deafening roar.

It fell to Rucker to make the first impression upon the Union line. At the head of the Seventh Tennessee and Chalmers' battalion, he swept forward with such impetuosity that he carried his line fully a hundred yards in front of Lyon and Johnson. Waring hoped to check the charge by concentrating his rifles on this part of the Confederate line. When it wavered for a moment under the heavy fire, Waring sprang forward with two of his regiments to drive it from the field, bringing up the Second New Jersey and Seventh Indiana to fill the gap made in the Federal line by the countercharge.

As the Union troops advanced, the stubborn Rucker rushed forward to shout to his men, ''Draw your six-shooters, and close with them hand to hand!''; and in one of the most fiercely contested short encounters of the war, the Federals gave ground. The Confederates swept forward and, with pistols and clubbed guns, broke the center of the enemy line. Rucker, leading the assault mounted, was a fair target for the enemy. Several bullets passed through his clothing; and his horse, wounded five times, fell at last from a mortal shot. Rucker took a bullet in his abdomen; but although it was painful, it was not fatal. Despite the serious wound, he did not give up the lead of his troops until the field was won.

Johnson and Lyon had closed in with equal vigor on the Union left; while Duff's Mississippi regiment, mounted, on the extreme Confederate left, was actively engaged in holding the attention of Grierson's right. As Waring's center gave way, Johnson advanced so rapidly with his Alabamians on the Federal left that he gained a point halfway between his original position and Brice's Cross Roads. The Union cavalry was now defeated at all points along the original line.

When the Confederates were first encountered by Grierson, he sent a courier to General Sturgis, who was then some six miles back, for reinforcements. The request was repeated with greater urgency when Rucker and Johnson came on the field and joined Lyon in their desperate attack. It was, however, not until twelve o'clock that the Union commander arrived in person upon the scene; and the head of his infantry column did not appear until an hour later. These men had been urged forward as fast as the condition of the road and the extreme heat would permit. They made the last three-quarters of a mile at double-quick time.

The first Union infantry to arrive at the scene of battle was the brigade under Colonel Hoge, made up of the 113th, the 108th, the 95th, and 81st Illinois regiments, supported by Battery B of the Second Illinois artillery (four guns). This brigade was formed in line of battle behind the cavalry. Before they had fully taken position, the brigade under Colonel A. Wilkins also arrived; and it was thrown into the line at points most needed. With it was Mueller's section of the Sixth Indiana battery, reinforced by Chapman's full battery. This artillery and that supporting Hoge were positioned at Brice's house. Battery E of the First Illinois light artillery and the Nineteenth Minnesota artillery were held in reserve at the crossroads. Thirty-six hundred Union infantry were now in position facing Forrest's 2,000 men. The Federal cavalry, tired, defeated, and almost without ammunition, mounted their horses and took refuge behind the infantry, some even quitting the field without orders.

Behind the Federal battle line, in reserve, was another brigade made up of colored troops, under Colonel Bouton, positioned across the road leading northwestward to Ripley. This brigade was also supported by artillery.

In crescentic line, and this in some portion of double depth, the Federal army now extended from well north of the Baldwyn road across to, and some two hundred yards beyond, the road from the crossroads to Guntown. As the Federals were swinging into line, Captain Morton arrived with his artillery; and at his heels were Generals Buford and Tyree H. Bell with the latter's brigade. Morton had travelled for eighteen miles since daylight over roads so muddy the horses could drag the pieces only with the greatest difficulty, and for the last six miles it required the most vigorous urging with whip and spur to push them forward in a trot. Bell's men had marched twenty-five miles to reach the battle scene.

Johnson was on the extreme Confederate right; to his left was Lyon; left of him was Rucker; then came Bell and Duff. Still farther to the left, mounted and guarding that wing and ready to swoop around and upon the Union flank and rear, were two companies of mounted Kentuckians under Captain H. A. Tyler. Forrest kept his escort and Gartrell's Georgians, also mounted, with him. General Buford was placed in command of the Confederate right wing.

The two armies now opposed each other for the supreme effort. The Federal force was about 8,000 men supported by twenty-two pieces of artillery; the Confederates, not counting their horseholders, had no more than 3,300 cavalrymen to engage in the battle, plus twelve pieces of artillery. With his usual audacity, born of confidence in his men and in himself, Forrest determined to attack, notwithstanding the odds.

For about thirty minutes the sounds of war had ceased except for the occasional crack of a rifle as some sharpshooter fired upon a target of opportunity, but this was the quiet before the storm. The atmosphere was heavy with humidity, and the day depressing and intensely hot. Not a cloud was in the sky to shield friend or foe from the blazing sun. Forrest had been right in his forecast, for it was "hot as hell." The troops and animals of both forces had already suffered extremely, and a goodly number had fallen from exhaustion and sunstroke.

Forrest had no intention of letting the enemy catch their wind and motioned for Randy to come to him; and the Captain from Perry County rode up alongside his commander, who said, "Go tell Buford we're ready on the left an' to start the ball on the right an' engage as much as possible the attention of the enemy in that direction. Have Johnson crowd in as close as possible on the road leadin' from Ripley to Brice's."

The two brigades of Federal infantry under Hoge and Wilkins had scarcely effected their alignment when to their left the rifles of Johnson and Rucker told them the fight had reopened; and at this time, everything in the Confederate line of battle pressed forward. The advance by Bell's and Rucker's men was a quiet one; this was no time for the heroics of the Rebel yell. Through the almost impenetrable undergrowth, the Confederates advanced slowly, bent over and with guns trailing, as they picked their way toward Hoge's double line of men lying prone upon the ground for concealment and protection. The Federals listened to the rustling sound of a moving body of men through the foliage as the Rebels approached. Bell's men were within a few paces of the front Federal line when the rifles of Hoge's men burst forth a withering flash and murderous roar into their very faces. Under this fierce and sudden fire, which inflicted serious loss, Bell's men gave way. Quickly taking advantage of the Southerners' confusion, Hoge, believing the entire line of the enemy would yield, ordered his whole force forward in a counterattack, directed principally at the right of Bell's and the left of Rucker's positions.

Forrest realized the heavy fighting would occur in this area and remained with these troops. When he saw the disaster facing them, he dismounted himself and both companies of his escort and with them rushed into the thickest of the fray, pistol in hand, to take his place in the front rank with his men. With equal dash, Bell did the same; and with such examples by their leaders, the Tennesseans quickly rallied. Reinforced by Colonel D. M. Wisdom with 280 men of Newsome's regiment, they checked the Yankee advance. Arrested in front of Bell, the Federal infantry pushed on in gallant style against the thinner line of Rucker; but that determined officer was not about to yield the ground for which he and his men had fought so valiantly. As the Federal infantry came on with bayonets, he shouted to his men, "Kneel on the ground, draw your six-shooters, and don't run!"

Against this thin but determined wall, the Federal infantry struck hard, but rebounded. They could not break through it; in the bloody hand-to-hand combat, their bayonets were no match for six-shooters fired by men who knew how to use them with deadly accuracy at short range. Slowly the Union troops gave way, and the whole Confederate line surged forward with irresistible force.

As the center of Hoge's line crumbled away before this terrific onslaught, Johnson, with Lyon's prompt aid, pushed back the extreme left of McMillen's line until it was now doubled back upon the Ripley road. From an open position on the right, General Buford observed a sudden movement of the Federal cavalry from near Brice's house to the rear, and then he heard the distinctive sound of rifles off to his right in the direction of Tishomingo Creek. He knew Barteau was there with the Second Tennessee and quickly sent this information to Forrest. Ordering this flanking movement by Barteau had been a stroke of genius, for it not only withdrew most of the Federal cavalry from the Confederate immediate front, it had thrown the reserve brigade of infantry and the train guard into commotion. It drastically affected the outcome of the battle.

It was now past four o'clock, and Forrest knew the crisis had come—the battle must now be won or lost. For more than two hours after the arrival of Bell and Buford, the men of both armies had been in murderous strife. Forrest's men had fought with savage fierceness against heavy odds, and it seemed that the point of human endurance had been reached. The Confederate general rode along the rear of the line, encouraging his troops by telling them the enemy was giving way, that Barteau was attacking their rear, and only one supreme effort was needed to sweep them from the field. As he rode up to Morton, whose guns were in action at a position in close range of the enemy, the artillery Captain said, "General, this is too dangerous a place for you. You should go to the rear a short distance where it is safer."

Morton could see that his commander was exhausted; but he was still surprised when Forrest retired, without protest, about thirty or forty yards to the rear, dismounted, and lay upon the ground at the foot of a big tree. A few moments later, the cavalry leader called, "John, come here a minute!"

Morton walked over to the tired man stretched out on the ground. Forrest said "I believe we got the Yankees beat. They're holdin' on pretty stubbornly near the crossroads; but I think one more vig'rous charge, with the artillery takin' part, will get the job done. I'm gonna order a charge in ten minutes. As soon as the bugler sounds it, I want you to hitch the horses to your guns an' gallop forward as close as possible to the enemy an' open on 'em at close range with canister."

Forrest got up and mounted his horse. Before leaving, he said, "I'm goin' over to the right to git Buford to start the charge from his end. When you hear the firin' you'll know what to do."

Morton returned to his guns with serious misgivings about exposing them, but he had too much respect for his commander and too much faith in his tactical ability to question the order. He readied his guns for the advance.

When Forrest told Buford of his plan for the attack, the Kentuckian asked, "General, don't you think it will be awfully dangerous to expose Morton's guns like this without proper protection?"

"Buford, all the Yankees in front of us can't git to Morton's guns."

Forrest then hurried back to Bell and informed him of his plans for the proposed assault. He ordered Tyler to take his two companies of mounted Kentuckians and the escort, with Gartrell's Georgian, and, when the firing became general, to charge around the Federal right flank and into their rear, engaging at pistol range any Federal troops between their right and the Tishomingo Creek bridge.

As Gaus' bugle sounded the charge, Buford with Lyon and Johnson went forward with the right of the Confederate line in face of a tremendous discharge of small arms and artillery. Amid the wild yells and vigorous attack of the Rebels, the Federal line gave way stubbornly for a little space and then yielded in disorder.

Morton, with horses hitched to his guns, swept forward along the country road so narrow that only four pieces could be placed in action. He moved with such boldness that the Federal commander at this point must have thought he was well supported by troops in the undergrowth. When within short range of the enemy line, he unlimbered the guns quickly and had them in action, firing double canister at short range with frightful effect. Rucker's charge on the center and Bell's quick rush on the left carried away the last vestige of organization on the part of the Federals, and their line was at last irreparably broken.

As the enemy retired, Lieutenants Haller and Mayson, under Morton's orders, pushed their guns still farther by hand along the narrow road to the front, firing as they advanced. Coincident with this, Buford, Lyon, and Rucker closed in from all directions upon the Union forces, now in great confusion, crowding them to the crossroads at Brice's house where three pieces of artillery were captured and turned upon the fleeing enemy.[2]

About a quarter of a mile northeast of the crossroad, the Fourth Iowa cavalry of Winslow's brigade had dismounted, sent their horses across Tishomingo Creek, and deployed to make a desperate stand. In an endeavor to stem the disaster, Colonel McMillen threw the Fifty-fifth Colored infantry across the line of retreat behind them. The Fifty-ninth Colored infantry and Lamberg's section of artillery were placed somewhat in their rear for the same purpose. The on-sweeping tide of Confederates was not to be withstood. General Buford had boldly pushed Johnson's Alabamians so far forward on the extreme Confederate right that they struck Bouton's negro troops from the northeast on their rear and flank. At the same moment, Tyler, with his two companies of Kentuckians and the troopers of Forrest's escort and Gartrell's Georgians, all mounted, swept around the right of the Federal line with daredevil recklessness, and rode squarely into the negro infantry, their six-shooters blazing. To add to the discomfiture of the negro soldiers and the Fourth Iowa cavalry, Morton and Rice, pushing their guns by hand, were crowding along the main road from Brice's to the creek and now, within gunshot range, rattled away with charges double-shotted with canister.[3]

McMillen's forlorn attempt to stop the Confederates was demolished so quickly that he scarcely slowed the onward rush of Forrest's men. Rearward of the Federal position, across the sluggish Tishomingo Creek, was a narrow, wooden bridge which became hopelessly blocked by the overturning of a wagon and the impaction behind this of several other vehicles. To this bridge, clambering over the wreckage of wagons and fallen horses struggling to free themselves, came the fleeing Federal troops in panic, pushing each other off into the stream on either side in their wild efforts to escape. Others, seeing the hopelessness of trying to cross the bridge, threw themselves into the creek and waded or swam across. Many attempting this were drowned or shot as they floundered in the water.

In the meantime, a detachment of Forrest's escort under Lieutenant George L. Cowan had effected a crossing about a quarter of a mile below the bridge and, sweeping around upon the flank of the enemy, charged boldly in among the panic-stricken crowd of retreating Union troops and cut off or captured a large number of prisoners and some wagons. Cowan had advanced so far into the Federal lines that he came in range of Morton's relentless guns and it was only when the battle flag of the escort was waved that firing in his direction ceased.

The sun was now just above the western horizon, but Forrest had no intention of calling off the pursuit. The men who had been detailed as horseholders, and were comparatively fresh, were hurried to the front and sent upon the heels of the beaten Federal army. Two miles northwest of the battlefield, McMillen succeeded in rallying a portion of the first and second brigades under Colonel Wilkins. This line, however, could not stand longer than to permit Bouton to pass through with his negro troops. Morton came on the scene with two of his pieces; and after a single round, the Federals vanished. From this point on, resistance practically ceased to exist.

All through the night, the beaten army kept on their way. Forrest's men who had done the fighting were allowed to rest until one o'clock, and the pursuit was resumed. At 3 o'clock on the morning of the 11th, Buford came in force upon the enemy's rear in the Tallahatchie River bottoms; and here, the balance of the wagon train and fourteen pieces of artillery fell into the hands of the Kentuckian. Four miles from Ripley, Grierson rallied and made a hopeless attempt to delay the pursuit. Forrest personally led a charge of his escort and the Tennessee Seventh cavalry and, encountering only a feeble resistance, scattered them.

Sturgis' command reached Ripley on the morning of the 11th but did not tarry, for the pursuit was continued without let-up all through the day until about nightfall that evening. It was brought to a sudden halt near Salem, almost within sight of the home of Forrest's youth, when the Confederate commander, from complete exhaustion, fainted and fell from his horse. Buck, who was riding to the general's right and rear, saw him suddenly crumble in the saddle and topple from his mount, falling to the left side of the horse. Buck spurred Miss Elly to the cavalry leader; but by the time he leaped to the ground, Major Anderson, who had been riding to Forrest's left and abreast of him, was already kneeling beside the still form. He rolled Forrest over on his back, and Buck straightened out his legs. "Did he hit his head when he fell?" Buck asked.

"I don't think so," the major replied after hurriedly examining Forrest's head.

"I'm going to elevate his legs," Buck said as he spread the general's legs, grasped the heels of his boots, and raised his feet about three feet above the ground.

A somber group of Confederates had silently gathered around their fallen leader. One of them stepped forward with a canteen. "Someone go get a surgeon, Dr. Cowan, if you can find him. The rest of you stand back and give him air."

Three of the escort quickly mounted their horses and started at a gallop back down the road in the direction from which they had advanced. The remainder of the men slowly backed away, more than doubling the diameter of the circle they had created. Major Anderson lifted Forrest's head and tried unsuccessfully to get him to drink from the canteen. He then lowered his head to the ground again, poured some of the water into a cupped hand, and laved the general's face with it. Getting no response from this, he slapped Forrest's face gently and then firmly. The color was beginning to return to the general's ashen face, but he showed no signs of regaining consciousness. Looking plaintively at Buck, Anderson asked, "What do we do now?"

"I don't know. Try rubbing his hands and face to bring back the circulation until the surgeon gets here."

Anderson took off his coat to place it under Forrest's head for a pillow. When Buck saw what he was doing, he said, "Don't do that. We need to keep his head down."

"You're right about that, Buck. Keep his feet elevated," said Dr. Cowan who had just ridden up and was getting down from his horse. He came quickly to the stricken general, and Major Anderson got out of his way as the doctor knelt beside him. The surgeon carefully examined Forrest's head, his neck, and each of his limbs individually. Satisfied that there had been no damaging injury or broken bones, he stood up and said, "I can find no injury. He has probably fainted from lack of food and water and from complete exhaustion. When did he last eat?"

"Not since we left Booneville," Anderson replied. "The rest of us had a little something last night, but he was too busy to eat with us."

"Dammit, I've told him he's got to take care of himself! He probably hasn't had any rest, either. I've got an ambulance on the way, which should be here any minute. There's a house about a quarter of a mile down the road, and we'll move him there. With some food and rest, he should be all right."

The ambulance arrived a few minutes later, and the unconscious general was gently laid in it. Dr. Cowan got in with him; and the vehicle pulled off toward the farmhouse to the southeast, the glum members of the staff following. By the time they reached the house, the jostling of the ambulance had brought Forrest back to consciousness; but he was so weak that he made no protest when he was placed upon a stretcher and carried into the dwelling. It turned out that the home was that of Orrin Beck, a maternal uncle of Forrest. The general was not only welcomed into their home, but his uncle and aunt did everything possible to meet the demands Dr. Cowan made upon them. Once Forrest was comfortably in bed, the surgeon said to those staff members who had gone into the house with him, "Get out now; I'll take care of him. He'll be all right. I'd suggest you bring up the headquarters' baggage wagons and camp here tonight."

Following the surgeon's advice, camp was made; and the staff, escort, and exhausted troopers were able to be fed and get a good night's rest. The next morning, a revived but somewhat sheepish Forrest came out of the house and joined his staff and General Buford, who was with them. Chagrined by what he considered a show of physical weakness, he said to General Buford and the other, "I guess my men'll think they got a puny commander who faints like some fine lady with the vapors."

"They'll think nothing of the kind, General," Buford replied. "The men know your fortitude and strength. They also know your determination and will understand that you extended yourself beyond the capacity of your body to take it. Any man who dares to make disparaging remarks about what happened last evening shall have to answer to me personally for it."

Forrest was relieved by Buford's support. "Thank you for the gen'rous statement, General. I hope it'll never become necessary for you to take up my defense. Now, how do we stand with the Yankees?"

"They are beaten and demoralized and are trudging back toward Memphis," Buford replied.[4] "Our own men were worn out and had not had a decent meal in two days, so I called off the pursuit for them to enjoy the bounty our enemy has provided. We captured all of their wagons, seventeen of their guns, and many prisoners. I do not yet have a count of the prisoners nor an estimate of their wounded and killed, but they will be high. Our own losses were heavy, but nothing like theirs."

"Did the scouts git a rest an' have a good meal last night?" Forrest asked Anderson.

The major looked toward Buck for a reply. "Yessir. They should be in good shape today," Buck responded.

"Major, send about forty of 'em to dog the Yankee heels. We wouldn' want General Sturgis to think we forgot 'im; besides, they might git lost between here an' Memphis."

The Confederates moved slowly toward Brice's Cross Roads. Forrest spent the night in Ripley and did not reach the battlefield until the morning of June 13. His first order was for all wounded, his own and that of the enemy, to be collected and removed to hospitals along the Mobile and Ohio Railroad and for the dead to be buried. He also directed his division and brigade commanders to make detailed reports to his headquarters of all captured property. These matters taken care of, he went to Guntown where he established headquarters and began to prepare his command for future service.[5]

On June 14, the general saw Morton coming in with his guns and rode up beside the young artillery leader. "Well, John, I think your guns won the battle for us."

Flushing with pride at the praise from his commander, Morton said, "General, I am glad you think so much of our work, but you scared me pretty badly when you pushed me up so close to their infantry and left me without protection. I was afraid they might take my guns."

Forrest replied as he turned his horse and rode away, "Well, artillery is made to be captured, an' I wanted to see 'em take yours."

Morton watched his commander move off, not enjoying his sense of humor.

When the general returned to the house where he had established his headquarters, he found Major Anderson and Randy waiting for him. Anderson had in his hand some small patches with, "Remember Fort Pillow" written on them. The major handed them to Forrest and said, "These were taken off of the uniforms of some of the dead negro troops. The negroes taken prisoner had all torn them off of their uniforms."

The general slowly turned the patches in his hand as he examined them. "I heard about these; can't say I'm much s'prised."

"There's more to it than this. Captain Rushton has gathered some interesting information from the prisoners and from a few of our scouts."

Forrest looked at Randy, who reported, "A number of the white troops said that before they left Memphis, the negro troops took an oath, on their knees, to avenge Fort Pillow and to show no quarter to us. Some of their officers, including General Hurlbut, were present when this was done. As they marched from Memphis to Brice's, they made similar boasts to show no quarter. These were publicly made all along the line of march. In questioning the negro prisoners, a large majority of them stated that their officers led them to believe they would be murdered if they surrendered. That was the reason so few of them surrendered before they were run down and exhausted. They also said that on the 10th, as they moved into battle, their officers told them that they must remember Fort Pillow."

Forrest's face and neck began turning scarlet as the anger welled up in him. "You got this from a good source?" he asked.

"I talked with the prisoners myself, both white and black, also to several of the scouts. I've got no doubts whatsoever of the accuracy."

"I ain't taking this layin' down."[6]

Chapter XIX

A Different Smith

On June 15 Forrest left for Tupelo with his staff and escort and established his headquarters there. Soon afterward, General Roddy, with his entire force in northern Alabama, was placed under his command, as was Mabry's brigade, which had previously been under General S. D. Lee. The commands were scattered about the country at points believed to be advantageous for subsistence and rapid concentration. Scouting parties were sent out to keep watch on the enemy.

Efforts were made to restore the condition of the horses of both the cavalry and artillery and to replace those that had been lost. An infantry battalion was organized of the men in Roddy's, Buford's, and Chalmers' divisions who did not have serviceable mounts.

After arrival in Tupelo, Buck and Randy got the first mail from home they had received in some time. As they were reading it, Randy exclaimed, "Well, what do you know; Beverly's married!"

Buck looked up from his letter and replied, "You don't say. To whom?"

"To a fellow in Selma named Gothrow. His folks own foundries, arsenals, and other businesses there. He's a captain in the local militia."

"That must be the dandy she was with in Cahawba—he was from Selma and a member of the local militia."

"I guess it was. Sally says that Beverly is pregnant and looks as far along as Ellen. She thinks it must have been a shotgun wedding. I'm glad he was man enough to do the right thing by her."

Buck replied skeptically, "It may not have taken much of a man to do it while looking down the wrong end of a shotgun barrel."

"However he got her, he's welcome. Every time I think about her, I wonder how I could have been so stupid."

Buck laughed. "Pa could answer that for you; he has a saying that love is like a fly, just as soon light on manure as molasses."

"Yeah, I guess so," Randy replied, not fully appreciating Cory's philosophy.

Finishing their mail, the two young officers returned to Forrest's headquarters; but upon reaching the house, they found Cally waiting outside. Buck was glad to see his old friend, for it had been about two weeks since they had last gotten together. "How are you doing?" he asked as he took the scout's rough hand.

"Tol'able, just tol'able. How you two gittin' along?"

"Fine," Randy replied.

"All right," Buck answered. "I just heard from home. The folks and Ellen are all doing well. They send you their regards."

Cally made no effort to hide his pleasure at being remembered by Buck's family. "Thankee. Give 'em mine when you write."

General Forrest came out of the house and walked over to them. His first words revealed his affable mood, "How are you, Cally? I just got your report from Cap'n Henderson. Good work."

"Thankee, Gen'ral."

"You don't happen to have a good story for me, do you?"

Cally thought for a moment and replied, "Did I ever tell you about the time I was sent to find Cap'n McLemore after the battle at Parker's Crossroad?"

"I don't believe so," Forrest replied. Then, with a twinkle in his eye, he added, "As I recall, though, you never did find 'im."

"Naw. I picked up his trail; but he got back across the Tennessee before I could ketch up with 'im. I had m'self a bundle of trouble that time. There was Yankee patrols ever'where scourin' the country; they had the notion that your men had been broke up an' scattered. It was cold as blue blazes, an' I didn' have nothin' to eat for three days. All I had was five dried red peppers in my saddlebags that I was plannin' to use in stew. The fust night I was so hungry that I et them peppers by themselves. Talkin' about hot, they was hot! I've et a lot of Mex'can food in my day, but none of it was as hot as them peppers. They was bad enough when I et 'em; but when I ans'ered nature's call the nex' mornin', they plumb ne'lly set me afire."

Forrest smiled, recalling his own experiences with Mexican food. Cally continued, "But I really didn' know how hot it was at the time. I run into a Yankee patrol later that mornin' an' had to double back that way. You wouldn' believe it, Gen'ral; but when I come back, there was three Yankees squattin' around it warmin' their hands!"

Forrest roared with laughter. The general then asked, "When you were out in Texas, what did you think of the Mexican people?"

"I never took much to them grandies, you know, them rich Mex'can landowners; but I kinda liked them they call pee-ons. But even they had some p'culiar ways. I remember one time seein' this Mex'can man comin' down the road ridin' one of them little donkeys they call a burro. His wife was walkin' along with 'im, an' I never seen nobody loaded down like her. She had a big bundle balanced on her head, some stuff strapped to her back, an' both arms full. I can talk a little Mex'can, so I asked the man why he was ridin' an' his wife was walkin' with that heavy load; an' he said, 'She ain't got no donkey!'"

Forrest laughed again. "Cally, you won't do! But keep me on your heartstring when you git another good story," he said as he started for his horse tied nearby.

Cally called after him, "I'll do that, Gen'ral; sometime I'll hafta tell you about the best fight I ever seen!"

Forrest turned quickly and looked at Cally. He started to say something but changed his mind and went on his way. He had taken no pleasure in Cally's remark.

Forrest, his staff, and his unit commanders were working hard to equip his men and bring them up to first class fighting condition. To boost their morale, he issued a written address which lauded them for their recent victories.[1]

Buck was at the firing range giving instructions to some new recruits when Randy rode up and excitedly announced, "I've done it! I've done it! You're going to be an uncle!"

"That's great. How did you hear about it?"

"We just got some mail. I intended to bring yours to you, but forgot it."

"No problem, I'll get it when I come in. How is Sally—is she all right?"

"She didn't say, so I guess she is. She's really happy about it, though. She had some kind of a fool notion that I was disappointed because you and Ellen were having a baby and we weren't."

"Don't know how she could have thought anything like that," Buck said facetiously.

"Nor I," Randy replied seriously. "She said that Ellen looks like she's going to have hers any time now."

"She thinks it will be about the middle of the month."

"What do you want, Buck, a son?"

"That would be fine but so would a girl, especially if she's like Ellen."

"I want a son. I can see him now, John Randolph Rushton III. If we both have sons, maybe they'll grow up to be friends as we did."

"I couldn't ask for anything better."

General Sherman continued to fret for fear Forrest would attack his long supply line to the north. On June 16 he wired the Secretary of War: "I have made necessary orders, through General McPherson, to inquire well into the Sturgis matter; and also to send as large a force again as he can get on Forrest's trail, and harass him and the country through which he passes. We must destroy him if possible."

Sturgis' defeat had for the second time thwarted Sherman's designs on Mobile. In a dispatch to General McPherson, also on June 16, he said: "We will not attempt the Mobile trip now, but I wish to organize as large a force as possible at Memphis, with General A. J. Smith or Mower in command, to pursue Forrest on foot, devastating the land over which he has passed, or may pass, and to make the people of Tennessee and Mississippi feel that although a bold, daring, and successful leader, he will bring ruin and misery on any country where he may pass or tarry. If we do not punish Forrest and the people now, the whole effect of our vast conquest will be lost."

The expedition under Smith was not the only one designed to keep Forrest busy in his own area of responsibility. On June 28 Major General Edward R. S. Canby, commanding the Federal Military Division of West-Mississippi, telegraphed Major General H. W. Slocum at Vicksburg that "Smith's expedition would move from Memphis in early July, that a large cavalry force would leave the Mississippi River near Baton Rouge, to operate against the Mobile and Ohio Railroad, while another invasion in the direction of Mobile will start about the 6th of July." He reported to Sherman "I had previously written to General Washburne that he should employ A. J. Smith's troops, and any other that he could reach, to pursue and if possible destroy all of Forrest's command. I have placed under his control all the militia of the Northwestern states that were ordered to report to me, and several regiments of old troops from Missouri. This will give Smith an effective force of 12,000 or 15,000 men, and leave a reserve of 5,000 for other operations. I will start the expedition against Mobile four days later. A cavalry expedition will start at the same time from Vicksburg for the purpose of distracting the attention of the enemy from Smith's operations."

Sherman impressed upon Brigadier General Mower that his rapid promotion depended upon his destruction of Forrest's command and the death of its leader. From near Kennesaw, Georgia, he sent the following message on June 24:

"To Abraham Lincoln, President of the United States:

"Sir,—I have ordered General A. J. Smith and General Mower from Memphis to pursue and kill Forrest, promising the latter, in case of success, my influence to promote him to a major-general. He is one of the gamest men in our service. Should accident befall me, I ask you to favor Mower, if he succeeds in disposing of Forrest.

"WILLIAM T. SHERMAN, Major-General."

While Sherman was doing everything in his power to prevent Forrest from striking his line of supply, several of the more farsighted men of the Confederacy were pleading in vain with the government in Richmond to give up Mississippi for the time being, if necessary, and to place General Forrest in command of all cavalry in the Department of the Army of Tennessee, for the purpose of conducting operations for the destruction of the railroads supplying Sherman's army. Principals among these were General Joseph E. Johnston, who was opposing Sherman in the latter's drive toward Atlanta; Georgia Governor Joseph E. Brown; and General Howell Cobb.[2]

Unaware of the contest being waged for his services, Forrest found plenty to occupy him in Mississippi. He knew that another move was being planned against him and this time by the ablest soldier he had yet faced. General A. J. Smith had made a careful study of his adversary and was seconded by the competent Brigadier General Joseph A. Mower. There was to be no repetition of the Sooy Smith or the Sturgis disasters. The Federal generals moved southward resolved not to be surprised and determined to fight.

In a dispatch Sherman sent to Thomas on July 2, there was a ring of satisfaction over Forrest's not being on his line of supplies. He said, "I see Forrest is at Tupelo."

To Grant on the 12th of July, Sherman reported: "I have now fulfilled the first part of the grand plan. Our lines are up to the Chattahoochee. Morgan failed in his Kentucky raid, and we have kept Forrest employed in Mississippi. The defeat of Sturgis was unfortunate; still, he kept Forrest away from us, and now A. J. Smith is out with a force amply sufficient to whip him."

Major General Andrew J. Smith marched from LaGrange, near Memphis, on the 5th of July, with 3,200 cavalry under General Grierson, 11,000 infantry, and 500 artillerists with 24 guns, all well equipped and supplied. The infantry was made up of the First Division of the Sixteenth Army Corps under Brigadier General Joseph A. Mower, the Third Division of that corps commanded by Colonel D.

Moore, and the First Brigade of the United States Colored Troops under Colonel E. Bouton.

The destination of Smith's expedition was the prairie country in the region of Okolona and West Point, Mississippi. Its chief objective was the destruction of Forrest and his command, but its mission was also to devastate the land as they went. True to his instructions, Smith laid waste the beautiful country through which he passed, burning towns, private residences, granaries, gin houses, and plantations. He left an area of desolation behind him.

His command went through Ripley on the 8th of July, meeting little resistance except slight skirmishing with the outposts and vedettes which Forrest always kept in front of his main force for observation. From Ripley he turned southward toward New Albany and Pontotoc, crossing the Tallahatchie on the 9th. After crossing the river, he moved with the greatest caution. His main column was preceded by a line of battle fully a mile in length, while the cavalry was kept in heavy columns as flankers and in front. He protected his rear with a double guard of infantry, and the wagons were kept closed up between the infantry in front and rear.

On the 10th Forrest ordered Buford to send 100 picked men to the rear of the enemy to cut off his communications and to make as much of a diversion as possible between him and his base of supplies.

Smith met his first serious resistance as he approached Pontotoc on the morning of July 11. He found Chalmers and Buford, fairly well concentrated, in front of him. They looked so formidable that he did not advance more than two miles beyond Pontotoc in the direction of Okolona this day. Chalmers placed Barteau's regiment on the Tupelo road and Rucker's brigade on the Cotton Gin road. Rucker was ordered to watch the Tupelo road and to reinforce Barteau if necessary. Buford, with Lyon's and Mabry's brigades, was placed on the Okolona stage road; and McCulloch's brigade was stationed on the Harrisburg road. Forrest was informed of these dispositions.

On Tuesday, July 12, General Stephen D. Lee, commander-in-chief of the Confederate department, arrived on the scene with Forrest; and Buford reported to them the cautious advance of their formidable foe. That same morning, the Federal commander moved forward in the hope of being able to force his way to Okolona. He found the Confederates on the opposite side of a low, swampy bottom, through which ran two creeks. This bottom was about a mile and a half in width, densely timbered, and had been made almost impassable by trees which had been felled across the road.

Smith did not think it prudent to attack across this bottom and on the morning of the 13th turned eastward from Pontotoc toward Tupelo, the cavalry leading, followed by the infantry and train, with the colored brigade and the Seventh Kansas bringing up the rear. He ordered in his skirmish line on the Okolona road; and as he advanced toward Tupelo, there was almost continual skirmishing from both the front and rear of his column.

The senior Confederate officer on the field, Major General Lee, assumed command of the Rebel forces. He sent Forrest with his escort, Mabry's brigade, and Jeffrey Forrest's old regiment, to attack and press upon the rear of the enemy. At the same time General Lee moved with Chalmers' and Buford's division on the right, with a view to attacking Smith in motion at every vulnerable point.

As Forrest advanced he found the enemy about a mile from Pontotoc, on the Okolona road and, after a short, brisk skirmish, drove him into the town and then eastward on the Tupelo road. Taking advantage of every favorable position in his line of march, General Smith, with his rear guard, resisted the advance of the Confederates; and about ten miles east of Pontotoc, he made a formidable stand, holding Forrest in check until the Confederate general brought up artillery and forced the Union rear guard to fall back quickly upon their main column.

It was evident from Smith's rapid movement that he did not intend to stop and fight short of Tupelo. His object was to gain the railroad there and destroy as much of it as possible and to find a favorable position where he could give battle. Forrest had driven the enemy ten miles and, as Lee had not attacked his flanks, was fearful that he was driving the Federals too rapidly. He halted his command and waited for Lee's attack upon the enemy. After about an hour, he heard the Confederate guns open up on the foe about three miles ahead. He moved forward to close with the rear guard and, upon reaching the scene, found that Chalmers had dashed into the road, surprised the enemy, and had taken possession of the wagon train. Smith threw back a large force upon Chalmers and forced him to retire, but not before the Rebels killed and wounded many men and horses. Smith was forced to abandon and burn several wagons, caissons, and ambulances; but the Confederates paid dearly in casualties for this bold assault.

Immediately after this attack, Smith received information from General Grierson that he had possession of Tupelo. The Federal commander moved the wagon train eastward through the First Division and parked it about two miles west of Tupelo. He then formed a battle line facing toward Pontotoc, with the Third Division on the left of the road. Forrest heard firing up ahead where General Buford was attacking the enemy's flank. As night came on, the enemy became more obstinate in his resistance; but Forrest continued his attack until he reached a point two miles from Harrisburg. Here he was joined by his entire command and halted for the night.

After his men had gone into camp and the scouts had reported that the Federals were bivouacking in line of battle about a mile in front, Forrest, greatly tired from the heavy work and intense heat of the day, had dismounted and was talking with General Lee at some distance from their staffs. Lee was sitting on the ground, leaning against the trunk of a tree. Forrest had taken off his coat, spread it on the ground, and was lying at full length upon it. Suddenly he got up and called, "Buck! Git your hoss, an' come with me."[3]

By the time Buck mounted his horse, Forrest had ridden up by him, "Come on, we're gonna have a look at the enemy's position."

They took a wide swing through the wood to come up well in the rear of the Federal battle line. They had travelled quietly for about a half an hour when Forrest said, "I left my pistol."

"Here, take one of mine," Buck said, offering one of his six-shooters.

"It don't matter," Forrest said; "I don't think we'll have any use for 'em."

Not long afterward they found themselves among the enemy wagons where the teamsters were busy feeding their animals. In the dark, the color of their uniforms could not be seen; and no notice was taken of the two horsemen as they deliberately passed along the rear of the Union encampment. Having satisfied himself of the enemy's position, Forrest then turned in the direction from which they had approached the train. He and Buck had gone about 200 yards when they were challenged by two enemy pickets. Riding directly up to them, Forrest, in a tone of indignation, said, "What do you mean by haltin' your commandin' officer?"

Without further words, they passed the sentries, who did not realize the ruse until it was too late. After the two officers had gone by them, one of the sentries asked the other, "Didn't he talk like a Rebel?"

"He sure did, and those uniforms looked awfully light to me," came the reply. Turning toward the men riding off into the dark, he called out, "Stop! Stop, or we'll shoot!"

By this time the two Southerners were almost far enough away for the darkness to hide them. "Let's go!" Forrest said as he put spurs to his horse.

Buck reacted quickly, and he put himself and Miss Elly behind Forrest and between his commander and the sentries. Both men, bending low over the necks of their horses, broke into a full run down the narrow roadway through the wood. The pickets fired blindly into the dark in the direction of the fleeing Rebels, but the bullets went whizzing by without doing any harm.

By daylight the following morning, the 14th, the Confederates were in motion in the direction of Tupelo along the road from Pontotoc. Almost immediately they became engaged with the skirmishers of the wary Union commander, but these were gradually beaten back to their main fortified line. The position selected by General Smith was well adapted for defense. His line of battle, running nearly north and south, extended along the crest of a low ridge which formed the center of a large open field. From the summit of this elevation, looking west toward the direction from which the Confederates would advance, the surface of the ground gradually descended to the level of a small valley or swale, beyond which the country was an undulating woodland with scant undergrowth and fairly heavy timber. From the Federal line, which was over a mile and half in length, the distance to the timber varied with the meanderings of a shallow ravine which marked the limit of the clearing on the west side. Just opposite the center, it was about 300 yards; but the wood opposite was so open that an enemy would be visible for a distance of 500 yards. In other portions of the line, the assailants would be exposed for distances varying from 400 to 1,000 yards.

As Generals Lee and Forrest came in sight of the formidable array upon the heights beyond the clear area, they were fully impressed with the strength of the position. "That'll be hard to take, an' we'll have heavy losses crossin' the open area." Forrest said. "He can't stay put forever. It would be better to wait an' hit 'im on the march."

"We don't have time to wait; we don't know how long he will stay there," Lee replied. "There is an expedition threatening Mobile from the direction of Vicksburg, and I've got to return the infantry the commander at Mobile let me have to meet this threat. If we wait, I'll have to pull off some of our men, who are already in position and ready for battle."

"I reckon we ain't got much choice."

"Not that I see," Lee replied. "General Forrest, since most of these troops belong to your command, have served under you in successful campaigns, and have just won the splendid victory at Brice's Cross Roads, they will have more confidence in your leadership. I'll relinquish command to you for the assault today."

"Thank you, General, for your confidence; but you're the senior officer, an' it wouldn' be right for me to accept your gen'rous offer. I will, however, give you my full support in the undertakin'."⁴

"Which part of the line would you like to direct personally during the assault?"

"The right with Roddy."

"Then I'll give Buford the left, and I'll take position near the center where I can observe both wings."

The Confederates numbered 9,460 effectives with twenty pieces of artillery.⁵ Deducting the horseholders from the 7,000 cavalry, they had only about 7,500 men to attack just under 15,000 Federals in a favored position.

It was nearly seven o'clock before most of the Southern troops were in position for the assault. They made an uncoordinated attack in which the right wing, under Forrest, never got into action; and they were repulsed with great loss in a very bloody affair. By the time Forrest was ready to move with Roddy's brigade, he saw the hopelessness of the situation and formed Roddy's men to repulse an expected counterattack. It never came, for Smith failed to capitalize on his enemy's confusion.⁶

When the Yankees did not immediately take advantage of the situation, Forrest sent Roddy's division with four guns to the road leading southward from Tupelo to Verona to make a demonstration on the left of General Smith's position; but no further assaults were made by the Confederates. They withdrew to the wood, and Forrest quickly threw up breastworks behind which the troops formed in line of battle. About one o'clock Lieutenant General S. D. Lee ordered Forrest to fall back to the residence of a Mrs. Sample and to form a new line fronting on a large open field. The position selected was a strong one, and he immediately constructed temporary fortifications behind which his men took cover and anxiously waited for the counterattack which never came.

As darkness approached, Forrest ordered Rucker's brigade to report to him mounted. Cautiously he moved with them to the right, approaching the enemy's left to determine his position and strength in that quarter. By meandering through the woods, he was able to approach very near the enemy's camp before his presence was discovered. Forrest ordered his men to open fire on the Yankees, and the Union first line fell back to the main body. The enemy then opened up on him with what he described as "one of the heaviest fires I have heard during the war." He withdrew and, upon returning to camp, ordered General Buford to move to the right with his division and reinforce Roddy to resist any advance by Smith toward the prairie country to the south.

That night Smith began burning the houses in Harrisburg. General Chalmers advanced with one of his batteries and McCulloch's brigade. With the enemy made visible by the light of the burning town, the artillery shelled them very effectively.

On the morning of the 15th, Buford advanced northward on the Verona road, forced in the Federal skirmishers, and drove their main line back for about a mile. The heat was so oppressive that in this advance eighty of Buford's men fell unconscious on the field from sunstroke.

Smith still did not attack but, instead, abandoned his campaign and began a retrograde movement to his base in LaGrange by way of Ellistown.[7] By two p.m. the Union troops were in full movement back to Memphis. Bell's brigade, with Rice's battery, was placed in front of the Confederate troops and ordered to press the enemy hard. He came up with the rear guard at Old Town Creek, four miles from Tupelo, and attacked them forcefully. Mower, commanding the rear guard, turned and attacked Bell and Crossland with equal vigor; and he handled his troops with such skill and courage that the Confederates were repulsed. Colonel Sherrill of the Seventh Kentucky was killed, and Colonel Crossland was seriously wounded in this affair. McCulloch came up to the relief of Bell and Crossland and succeeded in holding his ground but, in doing so, was badly wounded.

During this engagement, Forrest was riding with Rice's battery to an advanced position to open upon Mower. They had hardly reached the place Forrest had selected for the battery when the general exclaimed, "Damn! They got me in the foot!"

Buck looked at his commander's right foot and could see that the leather of his boot was badly torn at the toe, and blood was beginning to run from it. Forrest started to dismount but stopped when Buck said, "Stay on your horse—let me take care of it."

Not bothering to take the boot off over the wounded foot, Buck drew his Bowie knife and quickly slit the leather so it could be removed easily. He looked up at Forrest who was grimacing and grinding his teeth from the pain. "From the way it's bleeding, it looks like an artery's been hit. I'll put a tourniquet on the leg, and we'll get you to the rear. Dr. Cowan is back there attending to Colonel McCulloch. Can you ride, or do you want me to hold you on?"

"I'll make it," Forrest responded grimly.

When they reached McCulloch's main body, they were told that the colonel was at a log house about a quarter of a mile to the rear and that Dr. Cowan was with him. They proceeded to the house, so small that Smith's forces had not bothered to set a torch to it. The surgeon quickly took charge; and after giving Forrest a dose of laudanum to ease the pain, he cleansed and bandaged the wound.

"How bad is it, doctor?" Forrest asked.

"Probably not nearly as bad as it hurts. There doesn't appear to be any serious bone damage; but you are going to have a very painful foot, and you've got to stay off of it until it heals."

"I've got a war to fight, Dr. Cowan."

"Not now you don't. You must turn your command over to someone else. You have pushed yourself beyond human endurance. You should seriously consider resigning from the army and looking after your health."

"That would be more painful than the foot."

"Perhaps, but that's what you should do."

Forrest turned to Randy, who was standing just outside the door of the small cabin and said, "Rushton, go find Gen'ral Chalmers, an' tell 'im to take command of the troops till I git back on my feet."

Randy left and returned about forty minutes later. When he appeared again at the door, Forrest asked, "Did you find Gen'ral Chalmers?"

"Yes, sir, but we've got a problem. A rumor has gotten out among the troops that you have been killed, and they're badly demoralized."

"Me killed? Who in the hell started that?"

"I don't know, but it has already swept like wildfire through the troops."

"Help me on my hoss," the general said.

"You can't go anywhere with that foot!" Dr. Cowan protested. "Besides, you're weak; you've lost a lot of blood."

"I'm not too weak to show my boys I'm still alive." He sat up. "Major Anderson, you an' Buck help me on my hoss."

The two officers carried their commander to his mount; and he rode to the line of battle and along it, encouraging his men and assuring them that he was only slightly wounded.[8]

General Lee continued to harass the rear of the Union column for the next three days; but Smith kept up his march northwestward, reaching LaGrange on the 21st of July.

Both the Federal and Confederate forces considered Harrisburg a victory. Although the Confederates suffered severe losses, greater than their foe, in the unsuccessful assaults upon the Union forces, especially on the 14th of July, the battlefield was given up by Smith who failed in his mission. Neither Forrest nor his command was destroyed; only four miles of the railroad (near Tupelo) were broken; and the Union commander abandoned his further purpose of reaching and desolating the rich prairie country to the south. His retrograde movement, with the Confederates nipping at his heels, was more that of a beaten than a victorious army.

Chapter XX

Raid On Memphis

The wound Forrest received at Harrisburg was the most painful of the many injuries he incurred during the war. The bullet entered the foot near the base of his big toe and came out at the most sensitive part of the sole. To the great concern of Dr. Cowan, the general spent the day after receiving his injury in visiting the houses in Tupelo where the wounded soldiers were being cared for. This was a task that was always very hard on Forrest emotionally, but one which he never shirked. It was appreciated by the men and lifted their spirits as nothing else could; and this was a time when their confidence needed to be restored, after the recent bloody repulse they had suffered.

Forrest was unable to ride, so he was transported from house to house by buggy. As he was being carried to the vehicle from the last house, he said to Dr. Cowan, who was accompanying him, ''That was the last one, wasn't it?''

''It was. I don't think you could have made another.''

''You're right, Doctor. This foot is killin' me.''

''When we get back to your quarters, you're going to bed. I'll give you something to ease the pain and make you sleep. General, you should consider again what I said yesterday about retiring from active duty and taking care of your health. You are no good to yourself or your country as a dead man.''

''I'm a long way from bein' dead, Dr. Cowan. What would my men think if I up an' quit on 'em just because of a shot in the foot. Look at Gen'ral Hood—he's lost an arm an' a leg, an' he's still leadin' his men. They have to strap 'im on his hoss. He may not be the smartest gen'ral in this army, but he's damned sure one of the gamest.''

They got the general seated in an old, rickety buggy; and Dr. Cowan looked at the bandaged, foot which was now showing signs of fresh blood. ''You've reopened the wound again, General. It's never going to heal this way. You should be in bed with the foot elevated.''

"Buck," Forrest said, "you're good at improvisin' things; do you think you could have somethin' built above the dashboard I could rest my foot on?"

"No problem. It'll be ready when you want it."

As the dilapidated buggy pulled away, Forrest looked at the spiritless nag pulling it and said, "That's the sorriest-lookin' critter I ever seen. I'm glad I never owned 'er when I was a hoss trader—I wouldn'a had the heart to sell 'er to nobody."

During the next three weeks "Ol' Bedford" was a familiar sight to his men and the local people as he moved about the country in the sorry-looking buggy, drawn by the even sorrier-looking horse, with his foot propped up on a rack above the dashboard, carefully avoiding holes, rocks, and roots which might jar the aching and tender foot.

Forrest moved south to Okolona on the 17th of July, and from there he submitted the following to General S. D. Lee: "In the event the enemy does not threaten any immediate movement against us, I respectfully suggest that Roddy's command remain or be encamped at Tupelo, Mabry's at or near Camargo, and Buford's and Chalmers' division and Neely's brigade be sent into the neighborhood of Pikeville, on Chuckatouchee Creek, to be fitted up, rested and reorganized. With this disposition of the command, at least one hundred captured negroes, now cutting forage, can be placed at work on the railroad, and in a short time have it open and running to Corinth. Mabry's brigade can be supplied with forage in the neighborhood of Camargo, and there is plenty of forage (tax in kind) on the Chuckatouchee for the other commands, and the men can also eat vegetables, which they very much need. I could establish my office and headquarters at this place, remaining nominally in command, and have to a great extent the direction of affairs in reorganizing and fitting the troops for active service in the field, and in gathering up the absentees. With the horses now being recruited in pasture, and those of dead and permanently disabled officers and men, I think the battalion of dismounted men can be remounted and sent to their respective regiments. I am also of the opinion that it would be a good plan to send home one officer from every company to get absentees, and to bring horses to those who have them at home but have not been granted the privilege of going after them, limiting the absence of the officers to fifteen days."

While at Okolona Buck received a letter from Ellen which began:

"My Dearest Buck:

"At last I have grand news for you—you are the father of a fine, six-

and-a-half pound son! He is perfect in every way and looks just like you. Ma says he is too young for anyone to really tell, but I see you every time I look at him—I do miss you so much and wish you could be here to see our wonderful child and enjoy him with me—God has truly blessed us! We never discussed names, so I have taken it upon myself to name him Cory Callaghan McCord. Isn't it a beautiful name! You may have wanted to name him for Randy, but Sally said that if they have a son they plan to name him for Daddy and Randy. It wouldn't be good to have too many around with the same name. I know how much your father and Cally mean to you, so I hope you are not unhappy with what I have done. We can call him C. C.; in fact, I'm doing it already.

"As for me, I'm just fine, thanks to the Good Lord, your wonderful mother, and Vira—I don't know how we could get along without Vira. The doctor was unable to get here from Marion in time, but they took good care of me. Since the army took over Howard College for a hospital, and as so many of our doctors had already left to serve their country, we have only one in Marion now to take care of the local people. Did I tell you that folks are now calling it 'The Forrest Hospital'?[1] I am so proud that you and Randy are serving with such an able and popular leader."

This was as far as he read. Buck folded the letter and placed it back in the envelope to finish it later; he had to find Randy and tell him the news. He was glad Ellen had named the boy after Pa and Cally. Cory Callaghan McCord—it was a name with a good, sound ring to it. He certainly didn't want his son to be named for him; he had never cared much for the name Francis—it was too much like that of a girl. He was glad he had once mentioned this to Ellen, or she might have named the boy for him.

As he neared headquarters, he met Bill Forrest outside about to mount his horse, "It's good to have you back, Bill. We missed you."

"I was beginning to think I'd never make it. That wound took a long time healing."

"Have you seen Randy?"

"The general sent him to Tupelo on the train with some instructions to Roddy. He'll be back later today."

"Is Cally in camp?"

"He just got back. You'll probably find him telling some tall tale about his last scouting detail."

Cally was finishing up a meal, the first good one he had had in several days. The old man got up eagerly to greet his young friend. "Was plannin' to git over to see you," he said as they shook hands.

"Thought I'd bring you the good news," Buck responded with a smile. "Ellen wrote that we have a fine six-and-a-half-pound boy!"

Cally grabbed Buck's hand and shook it again. "That is good news! I'm proud for you an' for Miss Ellen, too. Is she all right?"

"She's fine. Thought you'd like to know—she named him Cory Callaghan McCord."

The old man looked at Buck in disbelief. As the realization came to him of what she had done, tears welled up in his eyes as he reached out with his right hand and gripped Buck's upper left arm; and the muscles tightened in his jaws as he tried to stop the trembling of his chin. Several seconds passed before the old scout spoke, "You mean she named him for me?"

"She did that, and it was her idea."

"I don't know what to say, Buck. Nobody never done nothin' like this for me before." He sniffed and rubbed his eyes with his left hand. "Y'all make me a proud man, mighty proud. I'da been s'prised if you'd done it, but Miss Ellen—I never expected nothin' like this. Tell 'er I'm grateful, really grateful, for what she done."

"I'll tell her. She'll be glad to know you're so pleased about it."

Although General Joseph E. Johnston had waged a successful defense against Sherman, inflicting serious loss when the Yankee general came at him head-on and managing to reach the outskirts of Atlanta with his army intact and strong, President Davis, who never particularly liked Johnston, nor cared for his type of warfare, relieved him from command of the Confederate Army of Tennessee on July 17, replacing him with General John B. Hood. Three days later, Lieutenant General S. D. Lee was transferred from his department to Hood's army at Atlanta; and pending the arrival of his replacement, Lieutenant General Richard Taylor, General Dabney H. Maury was temporarily placed in command of the Department of East Louisiana, Mississippi, and Alabama.

General Maury showed his confidence in his cavalry commander in the following communication to Forrest: "The prairie country appears to me to be the first object of your care. I know how disproportionate the forces at present under your command are to those which we understand the enemy has, but it will be difficult for him to advance far into the country while you are before him. I would not, if I could, undertake to prescribe to you any plan of operations. I wish you to understand that I intrust to you the conduct of affairs, and desire only to be able to aid you effectively with the means of executing your views."

The infantry which was present at the Harrisburg battle had been returned to Mobile, and Roddy's division was sent to northern Alabama to guard against a possible raid from Nashville. A remnant of Mabry's brigade had been dispatched to the area of Canton, Mississippi, to repel a raid moving eastward from the Mississippi River. The remaining cavalry and dismounted men were dispersed throughout the prairie region where sustenance could be obtained.

Although General A. J. Smith had reported his "defeat of Forrest at Tupelo" (Lee actually commanded the Confederate forces in that engagement) and the Northern press was filling columns with the great exploit, it became apparent that General Sherman was not satisfied with the result of the campaign. With his characteristic discernment, he knew Smith had not killed Forrest nor destroyed his command; and neither had he destroyed the railroad, nor laid waste to the rich prairie country. The commanding general did not hesitate to show his dissatisfaction with Smith's return to Memphis; and he ordered General Washburne to send him back at once with a larger command, if necessary, to keep Forrest occupied.

Sherman dispatched to Washburne: "Order Smith to keep after Forrest all the time. I think a few more days will bring matters to a crisis. Johnston is relieved and Hood succeeds to the command."

General Washburne wired Sherman in defense of his subordinate: "General Smith thinks you have a wrong impression in regard to his fight. He has returned for lack of supplies. I have ordered him to move again against Forrest. He will move as soon as he can get ready, unless you think that he had better go to Mobile."

Upon urgent instructions from Sherman, Washburne and Smith brought all their energies to preparations for a return invasion of Forrest's territory. They received a rumor, however, which gladdened their hearts. Washburne gave it so much credence that he wired Sherman on August 2: "I have a report that Forrest died some days ago of lockjaw."

Sherman relayed this to Grant and then queried Smith: "Is Forrest surely dead? If so, tell General Mower I am pledged to him for his promotion, and if 'Old Abe' don't make good my promise, then General Mower can have my place."

Even though Mower had not killed Forrest, "Old Abe" came through with his promotion; and on August 12 Sherman wired Secretary of War Stanton: "Please convey to the President my thanks for the commission of General Mower whose task was to kill Forrest. He only crippled him; he is a young and game officer."

General Smith had learned by experience; this time he did not mean to get so far from his supply base, and he rebuilt the railroad from Memphis to Holly Springs, Mississippi. Neither did he intend to advance far from that point, being content to hold Forrest's attention until the railroad was extended farther. Early in August, a heavy force consisting, according to Sherman's dispatch of August 11, "of 10,000 infantry, 4000 cavalry, with 3000 colored troops from Memphis, and in addition three Minnesota regiments sent from St. Louis," had been concentrated for the expedition. Moving the cavalry over land and the infantry by rail, Smith reached the Tallahatchie between Holly Springs and Oxford by August 9, 1864.

In a communication to General Maury, made with Forrest's concurrence, General Chalmers, who was commanding the Confederate forces north of Oxford, reported that they were aware of Smith's concentration and the proposed movements of two other columns, one from Vicksburg toward Selma and the other from Decatur, Alabama. Forrest had only 5,357 effective troops and was short in experienced officers; but he proposed to meet the larger column and, if able to defeat it, to then go after the other two in detail.

Upon receipt of information that the Federal column had started south from Memphis, Forrest took the field in his buggy; and he ordered ten days' rations prepared for the troops, one hundred rounds of small arm ammunition per man and two hundred rounds for each artillery piece. He started at once in the direction of Oxford.

General Chalmers was ordered to destroy any remaining trestles or bridges on the railroad south of Holly Springs, to fall back to the Tallahatchie, cross to the south side of the stream, and to offer as much resistance as possible. Chalmers, fighting persistently, was beaten back to Oxford by August 10, where he was joined by Forrest with Bell's and Neely's brigades and Morton's artillery. Chalmers' division, which now comprised McCulloch's, Neely's, and Mabry's brigades, was reinforced by Bell's brigade and placed at Hurricane Creek, about eight miles north of the town. Here the Confederates stubbornly resisted for three days until nightfall on the 13th, when Smith succeeded in throwing a heavy force around their flank which threatened their rear. Chalmers withdrew the entire force to Oxford. The enemy confronting the Confederates were estimated by Chalmers to be 18,000 infantry and 7,000 cavalry, both figures high.

Forrest realized that his badly outnumbered force could not cope successfully with the enemy, so he conceived a brilliant but extremely daring and dangerous plan to force the enemy back to Memphis. On August 18, he left Oxford under the cover of darkness with 2,000 men selected as having the best mounts, taking a course due west. Chalmers was left in command of the immediate front at Oxford with instructions to make the greatest possible demonstrations of force by attacking the enemy vigorously at various points.

Clearing the enemy's right wing, Forrest was miles away to the rear of Smith's position by daylight despite bad roads and swollen streams; and the Federal commander had not a suspicion of the movement. By seven o'clock on the 20th, he had bridged and was crossing the Hickahala a few miles north of Senatobia and so informed Chalmers, urging him to "hold the enemy hard and press them up so as to engage their full attention." This Chalmers was doing so effectively that the Federal general did not know the force in front of him had been diminished until after Forrest reached his destination.

Crossing the Hickahala was no easy task. The creek was up, and there was only one small boat available. Forrest sent ahead a detail of men to pick out a suitable place for crossing, to fell four trees and leave their stumps, and to twist together wild grape and muscadine vines into two long, heavy cables. When Forrest arrived ahead of his troops, these were ready and waiting. They were wrapped around the stumps on each side of the stream and secured there. The heavy cables sagged to about three feet above the water. The small ferryboat was placed under the center and anchored there. Cypress logs were floated into place and secured to give extra support where the cables would lower from the weight placed upon them. As the troopers arrived, those in advance carried over their shoulders planks which had been stripped from gin houses, cabins and other buildings. A floor was laid and the entire force passed over in about an hour.

Seven miles to the north it was necessary to build a similar bridge over the Coldwater River. This was twice as wide as the Hickahala, and it took three hours to cross it. Notwithstanding these difficulties, at dark on the 20th, Forrest reached Hernando, Mississippi, only twenty-five miles from Memphis. He had been forced to leave two of his four guns at Panola, because the terrible condition of the roads had broken down some of his horses. Each gun required ten horses to keep up with the cavalry.

At Hernando Forrest stopped a few hours to feed and rest his men and horses and then pushed on toward Memphis, arriving at the outskirts of the city at three o'clock on the morning of the 21st with 1,500 men. The horses of the other 500 had given out, and their riders were allowed to drop out and return to Chalmers.

Forrest had carefully planned an assault on Memphis. His scouts had given him detailed information on the location of the three generals in the city. His objective was to capture them and the troops in their

immediate vicinity. He had no intention of assailing the strong Fort
Pickering, which was heavily garrisoned. His troops were divided into
five detachments. Each detail was to move directly to the spot indicated
for its mission. Captain William H. Forrest and his "forty thieves"
were to take the advance; capture the pickets without firing; and, as soon
as this was done, to ride at full speed to the Gayoso House and guard all
outlets to prevent the escape of General Hurlbut or any other Federals
quartered there.

Colonel Neely was placed in command of a second detachment with
orders to attack and engage the attention of a regiment of Illinois
infantry which was encamped in the suburbs of Memphis near the road
over which the Confederates would travel.

Colonel Logwood was in command of another force which was to
follow immediately behind Captain Bill Forrest. He was to station a
portion of his troops at Main and Shelby Streets as a reserve and send
the remainder of his squadron to the wharf to capture any transports
there.

Lieutenant Colonel Jesse Forrest, with his picked detachment, was to
move straight to the house of General Washburne on Union Street and
capture the commander of the Union department.

General Forrest, with Colonel T. H. Bell and detachments of
Newsom's, Russell's, and Barteau's regiments, and two pieces of
artillery under Lieutenant Sale, would remain in the suburbs to cover the
withdrawal of the details making the dash into the city.

The troops moved forward quietly. Captain Forrest, well in advance
with ten men, was challenged as he approached a small bridge spanning
Cane Creek.

"Who goes there?"

"A detachment of the Twelfth Missouri Cavalry with Rebel
prisoners," he responded.

"Dismount and come forward alone on foot."

"All right," he replied but moved forward on his horse with his ten
men following closely.

As soon as he could make out the dim outline of the Federal
cavalrymen, Captain Forrest, sticking spurs to his horse, rushed forward
and with his pistol knocked the picket senseless to the ground. He then
charged ahead with his men to surprise the reserve pickets who were
thirty or forty yards farther up the road. Unfortunately, one of these was
quick enough to discharge his gun, and this alerted the second reserves,
which were still farther ahead.

Knowing the alarm would spread rapidly, General Forrest ordered the details to go in, and the whole Confederate force moved forward at a run. The men had been instructed to be quiet; but in the excitement of the moment and their eagerness, they began yelling and shouting like ungovernable Indians.

As Captain Forrest swept forward in the direction of the Gayoso House, he came suddenly upon a Federal battery of six pieces which was posted in an open space at the side of the street on which he was travelling. Several of his men rushed in among the surprised and demoralized artillerists, who deserted their guns and took to their heels, seeking shelter among the nearby houses. The Rebels did not pursue, nor did they take any action to spike the guns or otherwise disable them. Upon arrival at the Gayoso House, Captain Bill did not bother to dismount, but he rode his horse into the hotel lobby, where he gave instructions to his men to bar all egress and to search the hotel for their prey. Major General Hurlbut had the good fortune to be sleeping elsewhere that night and escaped capture.

Lieutenant Colonel Jesse Forrest arrived at Major General Washburne's headquarters on Union Street to find that the general had been warned and had fled, in his nightshirt, to Fort Pickering, which was about a half mile away. He had left in such a hurry that he did not bother to take his uniform or personal effects. Two or three members of his staff were captured before they could follow their commander, and Lieutenant Colonel Jesse Forrest gathered up the Union general's uniform and personal effects and later delivered them to General Forrest.

A detachment which had been sent to capture General Buckland was also too late. The yells of the Confederates and the cracks of rifles here and there attracted the attention of the sentry guarding his residence, who immediately awakened the general. Buckland found safety by changing his place of residence.

The detail led by Colonel Neely came in contact with a regiment of Federal infantry which, aroused by the picket firing at Cane Creek Bridge, had sprung to their arms and were in battle array when the Confederates came in sight. As soon as they began firing at Neely's command, General Forrest, who was nearby with Bell's brigade, moved forward promptly upon the flank of the infantry. In doing so, he came upon a detachment of encamped Union cavalry and charged among them, capturing a number of their horses and some prisoners. The rest were put to flight. As Forrest moved forward on the flank, Neely also advanced upon the infantry and drove them from their camp. These, with the cavalry which had been driven from their horses, took refuge in a large brick building, a seminary, and opened fire upon the Confederates with considerable annoyance.

Failing to capture the general officers who were their goals, Colonel Logwood and the two Forrests, Bill and Jesse, combined their forces within the city and started to rejoin the main column. They were confronted by the battery of six pieces which had been previously captured but not spiked. It was now manned and the pieces ready to be turned on them. Without hesitation the Confederates rode at the guns and drove the gunners away; but the garrison in Memphis was now thoroughly aroused, and the men were running in large detachments to plant themselves across the streets on the route the Rebels had to take. The Southerners did not have time to carry off the captured guns and pushed on rapidly to rejoin their main body.

Greatly disappointed at having failed to capture any of the general officers in Memphis, General Forrest withdrew his entire command in the direction of Hernando. As they were leaving the city, a detachment of the Sixth Illinois cavalry, under Colonel Starr, made a vigorous assault upon the Confederate rear guard with whom General Forrest was riding. The Confederate general made a countercharge with his escort in which a sharp hand-to-hand contest took place. In a personal encounter with Forrest, Colonel Starr was seriously wounded and taken out of the fight.

After the repulse of this attack, no further pressure was exerted upon the rear of the Confederates as they withdrew. From Cane Creek Bridge, Forrest sent Major Anderson and Randy into Memphis under a flag of truce with General Washburne's uniform and personal effects and a message to the Federal general proposing an exchange of prisoners.[2] He also informed Washburne that a number of officers and men had been captured and hurried away before they could be properly clad, and he requested that their clothing be sent to them. He proposed to wait at Nonoonnah Creek for a reply. After reaching the creek, he received the reply in which Washburne declined the exchange of prisoners, claiming he had no authority; but he did send the clothing for his men.

In the afternoon of the 21st, Forrest reached Hernando with his prisoners; and from there he sent the following message to General Maury: "I attacked Memphis at four o'clock this morning, driving the enemy to his fortifications. We killed and captured four hundred, taking their entire camp, with about three hundred horses and mules. Washburn and staff escaped in the darkness of the early morning, Washburn leaving his clothes behind."

At Hernando he paroled the prisoners and directed them to return to Memphis. He continued on to Panola, reaching there on the 22nd, and sent Buck and Randy to Chalmers with the following orders: "If the enemy is falling back, pursue them hard. Send Buford to capture their foraging-parties. Keep close to their camp. Order Captain Henderson to scout this way." He closed the communication by saying he would rest his troops at Grenada for three or four days, if possible.

As soon as he was able on the morning of the attack, General Washburne tried to get a dispatch through to LaGrange for forwarding on to General Smith in the vicinity of Oxford, but the telegraph line had been cut. It was not repaired until about noon, and the following message was sent on from LaGrange with an escort of 100 men at one o'clock that day, the 21st: "We were attacked at three o'clock this morning by a force said to be led by Forrest in person. The fight is still going on. They left Oxford two days ago, crossed the Tallahatchie at Panola. You will at once order all your cavalry to move to intercept them. You will move one-half across at Panola, and the rest at Abbeville. They must be cut off and caught. Move rapidly and spare not horse-flesh. Their horses must be jaded, and they can be caught."

This was followed up with a second order:

"Major-General A. J. Smith:

"The enemy has retired on the Hernando road. He has five hundred prisoners, but failed to take the battery. I am at a loss to know whether he means to cross at Panola or go via Holly Springs. With a force to dispute the Panola crossing, and another force crossing at Abbeville and moving towards him until they strike his trail, and then following him until overtaken, he may be captured. His men and horses will be so much worn down that they will be an easy prey...

"You had better send fifteen hundred cavalry to hold the crossing at and above Panola, and send the rest of your cavalry across at Abbeville. If vigorously pressed they can be caught."

These two messages were received by General Smith at Oxford between ten and eleven o'clock in the morning of the 22nd. As soon as it became absolutely certain where Forrest would cross on his way out, Washburne informed Smith by a message the latter received at Oxford on the 23rd that Forrest had left Hernando that morning intending to cross the Tallahatchie at Panola, that his horses were jaded, and that he would probably cross during the night. In case Smith did not intercept him at Panola he should catch him between Yocona and Tallahatchie.

Smith did not move a portion of his cavalry to Panola as directed. He sent the following dispatch to Washburne:

"From Abbeville, Mississippi, August 24th.
"Major-General C. C. Washburn:
"On arriving at Oxford yesterday morning Brigadier-General Hatch was detailed to proceed to Panola and destroy the railroad from that point south along the line. Then we heard of Forrest's raid to Memphis, but could not believe it. I soon received your despatches of the 21st, and was induced to believe from your last telegram and information received at Oxford that Forrest would retreat through Holly Springs. I at once ordered the second division of cavalry to this point, with instructions to Hatch to return to Abbeville and join the second division and proceed at once towards new Albany and intercept Forrest. I arrived with the infantry command about 10 A.M. today, and find the river booming and our bridge broken down. Recent rains in this region have made the roads almost impassable. I hope to communicate by telegraph by 12 M."[3]

Also on the 24th, General Sherman telegraphed to Washburne: "If you get a chance send word to Forrest that I admire his dash but not his judgment. The oftener he runs his head against Memphis the better. This case illustrates the importance of converting those armories into regular citadels with loop-holes and flanks. See to it."[4]

As Buck and Randy were preparing to leave on the 22nd for Oxford with Forrest's dispatch to General Chalmers, "Old Bedford" rode over to them and said, "Your hosses have had a rough trip; don't push 'em too hard. Find a good place to camp at dark, an' rest em for the night."

"We can use a little of that ourselves," Buck said.

"Can't we all," the general replied as he turned his horse and rode away.

It was in the late afternoon when they left Panola, so they had travelled only about fifteen miles when the sun went down. They were moving across country, and had come to a small branch which had a spring just a few feet away that was flowing cool, clear water. They watered their horses in the stream, and each drank thirstily from the spring before filling his canteen. To the right was a gradual slope upward to a hill at the top of which was a grove of large oaks. "That looks like a good place to camp up there in the trees," Buck said.

"It looks all right to me. It has good cover. There may be Yankee patrols in this area."

They moved deeply into the trees before stopping, unsaddling, and rubbing down their horses. They fed the animals the last of their grain and then looked to their own needs. Knowing that a fire might be risky, they ate a meager and unpalatable meal of cold cornbread and baked sweet potatoes, both several days old. As he finished the food with an appetite still unsated, Buck thought of his mother's heavily laden table. "Do you remember your mother telling you to clean your plate?" he asked.

"She'd have no trouble with me now," Randy replied as he recalled the four and five-course dinners that were a ritual at Prairie's Edge. "What I wouldn't give for one of those meals."

"Think we'll ever see them again?"

"If I didn't, I'd think we're wasting our time in this war."

"Maybe we are," Buck replied.

The conversation died, each man content with his own thoughts. Eventually Randy asked, "Do you think one of us should stand guard tonight?"

"I don't think so. We are well hidden in these trees, and nobody's apt to slip up on us."

"Your word's good enough for me."

They spread their waterproofs and blankets, and the tired officers were soon asleep. They were awake and up before sunrise. The first faint glimmer of light was beginning to show on the eastern horizon, but it was not visible from where they were in the trees. With no more food for man or beast, they saddled their horses to continue the trip. As they were about to mount them, Buck said, "I've got to see a man about a dog," and he walked off into the trees.

"I'll take the horses down to the branch and water them," Randy said.

He mounted his horse and made his way to the spring and branch, leading Miss Elly. He dismounted and hardly had both feet on the ground before a voice came to him from across the stream, "Don't make no sudden or stupid moves, Johnny Reb; or you'll be one dead Rebel."

Randy froze, and the reins of Miss Elly slipped from his hand to the ground. He could make out the dim figure of a man across the creek about twenty feet from him. In his hands was a rifle pointed at Randy. The man was standing between two bushes about waist high, and Randy surmised that he must have heard him coming and had hidden behind one of them. "Looks like you got me cold," he said.

"And you'll be a lot colder if you don't do what I say."

Randy saw three other men loom up out of the darkness behind the man with the gun. One of them asked, "What you got, Vick?"

"A Johnny Reb. He looks like an officer. Hold up on making that fire till we know how many there are." Then to Randy, "Where's the man that horse belongs to?"

"Dead. I'm returning him to camp."

"That's a crock. How many men are with you?"

"Enough that you'd be a damned fool to fire that gun."

"And you'd be a damned fool to give me cause to. Now you move over to this side of the stream real careful and cautious like."

Buck decided to meet Randy rather than wait for him to come back. As he reached the edge of the grove, he heard the voices of the men below him but could not understand what was being said until Randy was ordered to cross the stream. He had two of his pistols, but the Whitworth was in the sheath attached to his saddle. He knew that if Randy had been taken prisoner, he would have little chance to free him without a horse and the rifle.

Pursing his lips, he whistled shrilly for his mare, repeating it several times. Miss Elly was very nervous and tense; she sensed that something was wrong. At the first sound of Buck's whistle, she whirled and raced up the hill in his direction.

"What in the hell's going on?" the Yankee named Vick exclaimed. He recovered from his surprise and fired quickly at the fleeing mare, but the bullet went harmlessly by her. He was using a Spencer repeating rifle; but before he could fire again, Randy had his pistol in his hand and was firing rapidly. Vick's body spun around as the first bullet caught him in the chest, and the rifle fell harmlessly from his grasp. A second Yankee went down; and the other two dived behind the bushes, one to the left and the other to the right.

Randy leaped on his horse; and putting spurs to the mare, he raced along the stream to take advantage of the cover afforded by the small trees and bushes growing by it. He heard shots from the direction of the spring, but none seemed to come near him. He slowed his horse and circled to the right to get back to the top of the hill. He had not moved very far when he thought he heard a noise ahead. He pulled the mare to a halt and listened. He could hear the steady, rhythmic sound of a horse approaching; and out of the gloom emerged a man on a horse. He recognized the horse before he did the rider. "Buck?" he questioned.

"Randy, is that you?"

"Yeah."

"What did you run into down there?"

"Yankees."

"How many?"

"Four."

"Is that all? I thought you needed help."

"I did. One of them got the drop on me."

"How many of them did you get?"

"Two, but I don't know how badly they're hurt."

"I'd like to go back and try for the other two, but there may be more. We've got to get 'Old Bedford's' orders delivered."

"We sure have and had better get the hell out of here."

They put spurs to their horses and moved off at a canter. About fifteen minutes later they slowed to a less telling pace. Buck asked, "Randy, do you remember that first night after we left home—when we camped near Montevallo?"

"Sure. Why?"

"I just wondered," Buck said. "Did it bother you to shoot those men back there?"

"No," Randy replied with a grin. "They needed killing."

"You've come a long way, Ol' Buddy—a long way."

Chapter XXI

Too Little And Too Late

The battle for Atlanta had come to an end. General John B. Hood evacuated the city on September 1, 1864; and Sherman's first troops, Major General Henry Slocum's XX corps, moved in the following day to occupy the Southern stronghold and major transportation and supply center. Forrest contacted President Davis and proposed a move against Sherman's lines of supply. Lieutenant General Richard Taylor, the son of Zachary Taylor and the brother-in-law of President Davis, had taken over from General Maury the command of the Confederate Department of East Louisiana, Mississippi, and Alabama. President Davis wired him on September 6: "General Forrest telegraphed me, on the 5th instant, that, if permitted to select from his present command four thousand men and six pieces of artillery, he thought he could, in middle and west Tennessee, disturb the enemy's communications and recruit his command. If circumstances permit it, I think it would be well to employ him in operations on the enemy's lines of communications, as well as to interfere with the transportation of supplies and reinforcements to General Sherman's army. Of this you must fully inform yourself and freely exercise your judgment."[1]

Forrest had ordered General Chalmers' division to Mobile in answer to an urgent call from General Maury for assistance in defending that port. He was enroute to Mobile to take personal command of the cavalry and stopped in Meridian, pursuant to orders, to meet with Lieutenant General Taylor, the new departmental commander. General Taylor informed him that he considered Mobile safe for the time being and that all their energies should be directed toward the relief of Hood's army, then west of Atlanta, by worrying Sherman's communications north of the Tennessee River; and to do this, Forrest must move his cavalry in that direction at the earliest moment.

To General Taylor's surprise, his cavalry leader had so many questions about how he would cross the river, how he would be supplied, what he was to do with prisoners, what should be his line of retreat in certain contingencies, how he would recross the river, and similar matters, that he thought that this man, about whom he had heard so much, had no stomach for the expedition. Once the cavalry leader had isolated the chances of success from the causes of failure, he rose and asked for Fleming, the superintendent of the railway who was on the train by which he had arrived. When Fleming appeared, Forrest inquired of him what he could do about moving supplies. Once these matters were settled, the cavalryman in a dozen sharp sentences told his wants, said he would leave a staff officer to bring up his supplies, asked for an engine to take him back to his troops twenty miles to the north, and told the new departmental commander that he would be moving soon into Tennessee and hoped to give a good account of himself there.

Forrest began immediate preparations for the raid. He had the railroad repaired to Cherokee Station in Alabama, and Chalmers was left in command of the troops not going on the expedition. Forrest's command arrived at Cherokee Station on September 18, 1864. Among his troops were 400 dismounted men who had been formed as an infantry battalion under Lieutenant Colonel Barnett. He planned to mount them with captures from the enemy.

Forrest moved on the 21st to Ross' Ford at Colbert's Shoals, where he forded the river, which was about a mile wide at this point, and made camp for the night five miles west of Florence, Alabama, since dawn having marched twenty-five miles and crossed a formidable river with artillery, trains, and dismounted men.

At daylight on the 22nd the Rebels marched; and at Shoal Creek, six miles east of Florence, they were joined by Colonel William A. Johnson, with 900 men from Roddy's division, who had been ordered to cross at Bainbridge for this purpose. This brought his force up to about 4,500 including those dismounted. Halting only to supply the Alabamians with ammunition, the column continued toward Athens, Alabama, now a Federal stronghold. At ten o'clock on the night of the 22nd, the Twentieth Tennessee, under Lieutenant Colonel Jesse A. Forrest, and the Fourteenth Tennessee, under Lieutenant White of Kelley's brigade, were sent to McDonald's Station, a point between Athens and Decatur on the Alabama and Tennessee Railroad, which ran between Decatur and Nashville. Their mission was to cut the telegraph wires, destroy the railroad, and capture some horses and mules the Federals had corralled there.

On the morning of the 23rd, the main column moved forward and arrived near Athens late that afternoon. The stronghold was invested and

Forrest convinced the commanding officer to surrender by misleading him into believing that his force was much larger than it was.[2]

Forrest reported to General Taylor by courier: "My force captured this place this morning, with thirteen hundred officers and men, fifty wagons and ambulances, five hundred horses, two trains of cars loaded with quartermaster's and commissary stores with a large quantity of small arms and two pieces of artillery. My troops in fine spirit. My loss, five killed and twenty-five wounded."

He also reported to Taylor that he had received information which led him to believe that another move toward the prairie country from Memphis was contemplated and that he had ordered Chalmers to destroy all the trestles and bridges along the line of the Memphis and Charleston Railroad from LaGrange to a point as near Memphis as he could reach.

With his prisoners and booty headed in the direction of Corinth under a guard commanded by Colonel Nixon, Forrest moved north with his main column. On the 25th he came upon a strong stockade consisting of two blockhouses and a fort guarding the Sulphur Springs trestle, one of the most important bridges on the Alabama and Tennessee Railroad. The stockade surrendered after being attacked with artillery and rifle fire.[3]

Colonel George Spalding, with 800 Federal cavalry, had been ordered to support the troops at the Sulphur Spring (or Sulphur Branch) stronghold. He arrived near the trestle from the north at about eleven o'clock in the morning of September 25 and engaged the Confederates. After fighting for about twenty minutes, he learned that the fort had surrendered, so he "deemed it prudent to withdraw to Elk River."

As expected, the appearance of Forrest in northern Alabama and middle Tennessee caused considerable concern in the headquarters of various Federal commands. On September 25, Major General Rousseau at Franklin, Tennessee, reported to his superior, Major General George Thomas: "Despatches just received indicate that this afternoon the forces at Sulphur Branch trestle, consisting principally of dismounted men from the Ninth and Tenth Indiana cavalry, eight hundred strong, with two pieces of artillery, and in a fort surrendered to Forrest, who appears to be tearing up the track and capturing block-houses and forts as he goes. General Croxton left Franklin with brigade of cavalry at daylight this morning. I have sent by train to Pulaski thirteen hundred cavalry and a battery, and will follow in an hour with all the other force that can be spared from here. Troops sent to reinforce the Nashville and Chattanooga road should report to General Milroy at Tullahoma, as he has full instructions where to place the men."

Forrest's invasion had evidently interfered with the grand strategy of Grant and Sherman; on the 26th of September, from City point,

Virginia, Grant telegraphed Sherman: "It will be better to drive Forrest from middle Tennessee as a first step, and do anything else that you feel your force sufficient for."

Sherman replied: "I have your despatch today. Have already sent one division (General Newton's) to Chattanooga and another (Corse's) to Rome. Our armies are reduced, and if I send back more I will not be able to threaten Georgia much. There are men enough to whip Forrest, but they are necessarily scattered to defend the road. Can't you expedite the sending to Nashville of the recruits that are in Indiana and Ohio? They could occupy the forts. Forrest is now lieutenant-general and commands all the enemy's cavalry."

With horses captured from the enemy, Forrest had mounted all of his men who started out on foot and had supplied remounts to others whose horses had given out. He continued his raid northward. General Buford was ordered to follow the railroad with his command as far as Elk River, and he found here an abandoned blockhouse, which he burned. He then destroyed the bridge over the river and the long trestle approaching it.

Colonel Spalding had withdrawn to the Elk River stockade; but as Buford approached, he withdrew toward Pulaski after his pickets were driven in. He thought it best to move his cavalry out of the position as soon as possible. Sending for the officers commanding the colored troops garrisoning the stockade, he advised them that he would have to withdraw his cavalry or Forrest would have him surrounded by daylight and ordered them to hold the blockhouses at all hazards. They promised to hold them until they were knocked to pieces. He then moved off slowly in the direction of Pulaski. He stopped at daylight "to learn the location of the country" and, to his surprise, learned instead that the officers and negro troops left to hold the bridge had abandoned the stockade without firing a shot and were actually ahead of his cavalry.

Colonel Spalding arrested the colored troops, and sent them under guard to the blockhouse at the Richland Creek bridge. Upon learning that the captain in command at Richland Creek had ordered the colored soldiers to pack their knapsacks preparatory to moving to Pulaski, he sent direction to him to make a stubborn resistance. He also advised him that his cavalry would support the defenders of the stockade and that he would shoot any officer and soldier he found deserting his post. His orders and threats did little good, for the garrison of fifty men surrendered after a short resistance; and the Confederates crossed the creek and camped that night ten miles from Pulaski.

On the 27th, Forrest advanced toward Pulaski; and six miles from that place, Buford's division collided with a heavy force of Federals, who made a determined stand. Resisting stubbornly every inch of ground, the Yankees were pushed back to within three miles of the town. Additional Confederate forces arrived, and the engagement became general. The Union commander attempted to flank the Confederate left, but Forrest broke up the movement with his artillery. The Confederate general ordered a charge, and the Federals retreated hastily to their breastworks at Pulaski. In this affair, Colonel Johnson received a severe wound through the knee joint from which he suffered greatly for the rest of his life.

Forrest made a personal reconnaissance and found that the enemy was too numerous and too well entrenched to justify an assault. He remained in front of the town until nightfall, maneuvering his troops as though he would make another assault. He then ordered large campfires to be built for the purpose of deceiving the enemy; and, leaving pickets to notify him if the Federals advanced, he withdrew, encamping eight miles east of Pulaski. Before leaving, however, he sent Colonel Wheeler with 300 men north of the town to destroy the railroad and telegraph lines toward Columbia. Wheeler did this work well and also burned a large stockpile of wood intended for use of the locomotives.

That night Forrest sent the following message to General Taylor: "I have driven the enemy, after fighting all day, into his fortifications at this place and find General Rousseau with a heavy force well fortified. I will move to the Nashville and Chattanooga railroad. My loss today about one hundred; enemy's much heavier, having contested ground for several miles. Enemy concentrating heavily against me."

The cavalry leader was right, for General Thomas reported: "As Forrest changed the scene of his operations from the Decatur railroad over to the one leading to Chattanooga, General Rousseau moved rapidly by rail around through Nashville to Tullahoma, and prepared for his reception. On the same day, 5,000 men under General Steedman crossed north of the Tennessee River from the direction of Chattanooga. Newton's division was ordered from Atlanta on the 26th of September, and Morgan's corps started on the 29th of September to reinforce the troops operating against Forrest." In this report he speaks of Forrest and his command, "an enthusiastic cavalry command led by one of the boldest and most successful commanders of the rebel army."

The Confederates reached Fayetteville on the 28th. Captain Boone was sent with twenty picked men from the escort to the Nashville and Chattanooga railroad north of Tullahoma to cut the telegraph wires and to tear up rails. Captain Kelleher was detailed with thirty men of the Twelfth Tennessee for the same work south of Tullahoma. On the 29th, Forrest moved toward that place with his main column; but upon arrival at Mulberry, he learned from his scouts that the enemy was in heavy force in Tullahoma and that heavy reinforcements were coming by rail from both Nashville and Chattanooga.

That same day Sherman had telegraphed Grant: "Forrest is in middle Tennessee, and will get on my main road tonight or tomorrow."

To General Webster in Nashville, he wired: "General Grant telegraphs me that he has ordered many troops to Nashville. I want you to recall General Burbridge and concentrate all the troops possible to push Forrest. I send General Thomas up to Stevenson to work from this direction. I can hold Atlanta and my communications back to Chattanooga."

He followed this with another wire to Webster: "I will send up the road tonight another division, and want you to call forward from the rear all you can get, to operate in Forrest's rear."

To General Granger Sherman telegraphed that he should drive any squads of Forrest's men across the Elk and threaten the fords at Lamb's and Elkton and act in concert with Rousseau. "Keep your surplus men so as to move quick and to strike Forrest's line of retreat or communication."

Sherman telegraphed Halleck on the 29th: "I take it for granted that Forrest will cut our road, but I think we can prevent his making a serious lodgment. His cavalry will travel one hundred miles in less time than ours will ten. I have sent two divisions up to Chattanooga and one to Rome, and Thomas started to-day to clear out Tennessee, but our road should be watched from the rear, and I am glad General Grant has ordered reserves for me to Nashville. I can whip his infantry, but his cavalry is to be feared."

To General Elliot, chief of cavalry, Department of the Cumberland, he also telegraphed that day: "Our cavalry must do more, for it is strange Forrest and Wheeler should circle around us thus. We should at least make ten miles to his hundred."

He sent a second warning to Granger: "A strong division has gone up the road, and will act against Forrest. Don't scatter too much or try to hold too many points. We will have some heavy reinforcements from the north."

General Rousseau wired General Thomas: "Forrest struck the road, and destroyed it thoroughly from Athens to within a few miles of Pulaski. He will not leave until he has thoroughly destroyed the railroad, unless killed or captured. His force is an effective one, and amounts to six or seven thousand men, with artillery."

Learning of this message stirred Secretary of War Stanton on the 29th to telegraph the Governor of Michigan: "There is urgent need that every enlisted man be hurried forward to Nashville, to guard General Sherman's communications, without delay.''

On September 30, Sherman telegraphed Thomas to ''push right at Forrest with as heavy a force as you can get and as soon as possible. If you can turn him towards Lamb's ferry Granger should hold him in check until the infantry can get up. We will never have a better chance at him than now. I will watch Hood here.''

General Rousseau summed the situation to Sherman as follows: ''Forrest struck the road at Athens, and destroyed it to within a few miles of Pulaski, where I had repulsed him on the 27th instant. He is here to stay, unless driven back and routed by a superior cavalry force. Infantry can cause him to change camp, but cannot drive him out of the State. Forrest's movements are much more cautious than formerly. He has attacked no place held by white men, but every post held by colored troops has been taken, and his destruction of railroad was most thorough. I have here about three thousand cavalry, not enough to fight him without support. This is much more than a raid; I regard it as a formidable invasion, the object of which is to destroy our lines, and he will surely do it unless met by a large cavalry force, and killed, captured, or routed. The cavalry, supported by infantry, can fight and defeat him, but he must be caught. He will not give battle unless he chooses to do so.''

With all the concentration against him, particularly along the Nashville and Chattanooga Railroad, Forrest wisely called a halt. He had expended most of his artillery ammunition, and his force had been depleted considerably by large details sent back to guard prisoners and take care of seized property being sent south. He was forced to abandon for the present his intention of destroying Sherman's main railroad line. He did what few military leaders like to do; he divided his force. General Buford, with a portion of his division, the artillery, and Kelley's and Johnson's brigades, was sent toward Huntsville with instructions to tear up the Memphis and Charleston Railroad between there and Decatur and, if possible, to cross the Tennessee at the latter place.

With the remainder of his troops, consisting of Bell's and Lyon's brigades, the Seventh Tennessee, and his old regiment, Forrest moved, by an obscure and circuitous route, to the right of Shelbyville. He reached Lewisburg about noon on the 30th and continued on to the Duck River where he bivouacked for the night. He reached Spring Hill on October 1, captured there some Federal horses and wagons, and continued on in the direction of Columbia. While at Spring Hill, he tapped the telegraph line and picked up some valuable information concerning the movements of the various bodies of troops trying to intercept him. To confuse the enemy, he sent some messages to General Rousseau, the Federal departmental commander, giving him false reports which stated that Forrest was still destroying the railroad from Nashville to Decatur.

Twelve miles from Columbia, he captured four blockhouses and their garrisons of 120 men. The blockhouses, a large government sawmill, and three railroad bridges were burned. A fifth blockhouse, guarding a bridge, was encountered; but the commander refused to surrender. Having no artillery, Forrest called for volunteers to destroy the bridge, which was well protected by the blockhouse garrison; and both Randy and Buck were among those who stepped forward.

"Not you, Buck," the general said; "I want you to take charge of the sharpshooters who'll cover 'em." Then to Randy, "We'll soak some rich pine in turpentine, an' you pick out ten men to go with you. Y'all git down below the bank an' move along the edge of the stream to the bridge. Buck'll place some sharpshooters to cover you."

Randy selected his men, and rich, pine knots were gathered, which were made more flammable by soaking them in turpentine. Each man was given two of the large knots, and the detail dropped down the bank to the stream's edge at a point where they could not be hit by gunfire from the stockade. Buck divided his sharpshooters—half were placed where they could fire at anyone in the structure who came in sight on the north and east sides of it; the other half were placed where they could cover the area between the stockade and the bridge to prevent any of the garrison from extinguishing the fire after it was ignited.

Randy and his men moved slowly along the stream, usually at a crouch but sometimes crawling to prevent exposure to the enemy. They stopped upon reaching the bridge, and Randy said, "We want to place about half of these pine knots where they will burn the wooden supports of the bridge, putting some of them as far out as possible. Once in place, we'll light them, the farthest out first. Be careful and fast—as we climb out on the supports, we'll be open to fire from the blockhouse. Does everybody have dry matches?"

"I don't," one man said. "I got mine wet when I slipped and fell in the stream back there."

The man was given matches, and Randy said, "We'll all move as fast as possible, half on each side of the bridge. We want to get out as far as the fourth uprights. We'll be climbing on the supports, so we'll each take just one knot. Are there any questions?"

"How about the other knots?" one man asked, "Do we have to climb out twice?"

"No; after we get back to the protection of the bank, we'll light them and toss them up on the bridge. One more thing, the men who go out on the trestle the farthest will do all the lighting, so they won't have to climb back by burning timbers. As soon as the rest of you get the knots in place, get off the trestle."

The trooper seemed satisfied. "I was skeered we'd have to climb back on a burnin' bridge."

"All right, men, let's go."

Randy started to climb out first on the trestlework, but one of the men said, "It'd be best if you went last Cap'n; then you can see what the rest of us are doin'. You ain't got nothin' to prove to us."

"I guess you're right," he replied and stepped aside to let the troopers go ahead of him.

The men moved quickly and worked fast. A few shots came their way, but these had been fired rapidly without careful aim—Buck's sharpshooters were doing their job. They soon had the rich pine blazing on the under supports of the bridge, and the last two men scrambled back to the protection of the bank. Here they took their time as they lighted the remaining knots and tossed them upward onto the floor of the structure.

Satisfied that the fires were properly set and would do the damage intended, the detail returned the way they had come. The south end of the bridge was now in flames.

A door on the east side of the blockhouse was partially opened as if some of the men in it would attempt to put out the flames; but Buck's sharpshooters opened up on the door and put any such thought out of the minds of the blockhouse occupants. The Federals and Confederates both stood by and watched the bridge as it was consumed by flames.

On the morning of the 2nd, Forrest continued his march on Columbia. About six miles from that place, Colonel Wheeler was sent ahead to drive in the enemy's pickets. The town was invested; but after a personal reconnaissance, Forrest decided that it was too strong to be taken without artillery. He withdrew westward to Mount Pleasant, where he camped for the night.

Forrest knew that the Federal forces, estimated to be 30,000 men pursuing him, were concentrating to prevent his escape. He decided to move as fast as possible to the Tennessee River. Word was received from Buford that he had been unable to cross the Tennessee in the vicinity of Decatur and was enroute to Florence. Forrest was also headed there. He stopped at Lawrenceburg on the night of the 3rd and, by travelling all day on the 4th and 5th, reached Florence, where he found the Tennessee so swollen by recent rains that it was not fordable.

There were only three small ferryboats available; and Buford, who had arrived thirty-six hours ahead of his commander, had already ferried the artillery, wagons, and a large part of his command to the south side of the river.

The ferries were kept going, transporting men, ammunition, guns, saddles, and the weaker horses which would not be able to swim the river. On the 6th, Forrest received a report from his scouts that the enemy was at Athens in force and was advancing toward his point of crossing in two columns. He sent Colonel Windes of Roddy's division to Shoal Creek to contest the Union advance, with orders to hold them as long as possible, and, when forced to retreat, to withdraw to the west in the hope of decoying the Federal forces in that direction. Two regiments of Bell's troops were sent to reinforce Windes, who was then directed to attack the flank and rear of the enemy column in order to create a diversion in that direction. He did his job so well that it was not until the 8th that his force was driven back and the advance of the Union column entered Florence.

As the Federals approached Florence, Forrest had, in addition to those men with Windes, about a thousand troopers still on the north side of the Tennessee.

A few miles down river, there was a long island covered with an almost impenetrable growth of cane and, in addition, large oaks and hickories. He had the ferryboats drifted down the stream to this island. The saddles and equipment were stripped from the horses and piled into the boats; and these and the men were ferried across to the island, which was about 200 yards from the north shore. The horses were led to the high river bank; and they were pushed into the stream and swam the river, being guided by pilot horses led by men in skiffs, the same way the crossing had been made after the battle at Parker's Crossroad. Men and horses quickly disappeared from sight in the thick cane as they moved to the south side of the island. The ferryboats were brought to this side, where the troopers and their horses were leisurely ferried the remainder of the distance across the river, completely hidden from the Federals who were lining the northern bank of the Tennessee. The men aboard the ferries took their turn at the oars and poles. Forrest was worried and exhausted, and his temper was evident by the profanity he was using. The general, as tired as he was, had a pole in his hand with which he was helping the boat across. There was a young lieutenant in the boat who was making no effort to assist in propelling the vessel. Irritated by this, Forrest asked him, ''Why don't you take ahold of a pole or oar an' help this boat across?''

"As an officer, I don't believe that I am required to do that kind of work as long as there are enough private soldiers to do it," the lieutenant replied.

The general flew into a rage. He was holding the pole in one hand; and with the other, he slapped the young officer so hard that he fell across the gunwale and into the river. Forrest held out the pole to the unfortunate lieutenant who grasped it and was helped back into the boat. "Now, damn you, git hold of an oar an' go to work! If I knock you out of the boat ag'in, I'll let you drown."

As soon as the troops under Windes, who were retarding the advance of the Federals, learned that Forrest was on the island, they retreated down the Tennessee River and on October 13 safely crossed it, with a loss of but two men killed and four wounded.

Forrest returned with his troopers to Cherokee Station, and here learned of the approach of a flotilla up the river with reinforcements for General Rousseau. These troops, under the command of Colonel George B. Hoge, consisted of the 113th and 120th Illinois and the Sixty-first Colored infantry, and Company G of the Second Missouri light artillery. They formed part of the 3,000 troops under Major General C. C. Washburne who had sailed from Cairo on October 1 for Florence. They were ordered on October 8 to proceed up the river to Eastport, Mississippi, move rapidly out to Iuka, break the railroad, destroy the bridges, and then to hold Eastport until further orders from Washburne. They were turned back by a force under Colonel D. C. Kelley.[4]

Concerning the raid into northern Alabama and middle Tennessee, Forrest reported: "During the expedition, I captured 86 commissioned officers, 67 government employees, 1,274 non-commissioned officers and privates, 933 negroes, beside killing and wounding in the various engagements about 1,000 more, making an aggregate of 3,360, being an average of one to each man I had in the engagements. In addition to these, I captured about 800 horses, seven pieces of artillery, 2,000 stands of small arms, several hundred saddles, fifty wagons and ambulances, with a large amount of medical, commissary and quartermaster's stores, all of which have been distributed to the different commands. The greatest damage done to the enemy was in the complete destruction of the railroad from Decatur to Spring Hill, with the exception of the Duck River bridge. It will require months to repair the injury done to the road, and may possibly be the means of forcing the evacuation of Pulaski and Columbia, and thus relieve the people of further oppression." His losses were 47 killed, and 293 wounded.

Forrest moved his troops from Cherokee station to Corinth, arriving there on the 12th of October.

Among the commissary stores captured were quantities of coffee and sugar; and for the first time in many months, Forrest's men were enjoying real coffee. After reaching Corinth, the general called in Major G. V. Rambaut, his chief of commissary, and instructed him to have a bag of it charged to his personal account and to ship it to John R. Rushton at Prairie's Edge.

Sherman began to despair of keeping intact his communications from Nashville to Atlanta. On October 9, he telegraphed Grant: "It will be a physical impossibility to protect the roads, now that Hood, Forrest, and Wheeler, and the whole bunch of devils are turned loose without home or habitation."

A little later, he said to Grant: "I propose we break up the railroad from Chattanooga and strike out with wagons for Savannah."

The indomitable will by which Forrest was driven was taking its toll on him physically. Before leaving Cherokee for Corinth, he wrote General Taylor and requested leave.[5]

While he was in middle Tennessee, Forrest had picked up information that there were immense quantities of stores collected at Johnsonville, Tennessee, where Sherman had established a base for his commissariat. This information had been passed on to General Taylor; and Forrest had no sooner dismounted from his saddle in Cherokee than he received orders from General Taylor to destroy those stores. This contemplated expedition was mentioned in his request for leave, and the much-needed rest was promised him upon his return; but events over which neither he nor General Taylor had control would make this impossible. General John B. Hood, commanding the Confederate Army of Tennessee was in northern Alabama preparing for a campaign into Tennessee.

On October 12, Forrest informed General Taylor: "I will move into west Tennessee in a few days, and you may rely on my doing all I can towards accomplishing your desires and in facilitating your suggestions. I am satisfied that the amount of supplies reported as being in west Tennessee have been greatly exaggerated. I can subsist my command there and will be able to gather up some wheat and hogs, but not in amounts as large as has been suggested. Our currency cannot be used in that region, and the people, instead of collecting their surplus supply of hogs, will scatter them in the woods to prevent them falling into our hands. To hunt up and press the needed supplies will require much time, and will take all my command to accomplish much. If you can furnish salt, or anything the people could use at home, they would interest themselves in hunting up and furnishing the government with every article of supply that they could possibly spare. It is my present design to take possession of Fort Heiman on the Tennessee River, below Johnsonville, and thus prevent all communications with Johnsonville by transports. It is highly important that this line be interrupted, if not entirely destroyed, as I learned during my recent operations in middle Tennessee that it was by this route that the enemy received most of his supplies at Atlanta. I shall exercise diligence in gathering up the large number of deserters and absentees in Tennessee. As fast as these are gathered up I would suggest that they be sent to you and placed at once in the infantry service. The facilities of these men for running away is much greater in the cavalry service, and they should be placed in positions remote from their country[6]... My men and horses are greatly jaded by the labors of the recent raid. It will require a month to recuperate and place my command in proper condition. In the recent engagement I lost in killed and wounded about 400 men. I still have on the other side of the river about 500 men unable to cross. These losses, with those ordered back to Georgia by General Hood, have greatly reduced my command. General Chalmers' brigade of 500 men will probably swell my command to 3,400 troops... I have commenced repairing the telegraph-line from Grand Junction to this place (Corinth), and from here to Jackson. Both lines will be in operation in a few days."

Chalmers, who was in the neighborhood of Memphis, had been directed to move, if affairs permitted, to unite with Forrest at Jackson and to leave troops enough under an efficient officer in the neighborhood of Memphis to worry the commander there and to give the impression that Forrest was moving to attack that place. General Chalmers was sent an urgent order, also on the 12th, which read: "Fetch your wagons and the two batteries with you.[7] I will supply you with the artillery ammunition at Jackson."

Preparations completed, Bell was ordered to take post with his brigade at Lavinia, Tennessee.

Two days later, Buford took up a line of march for Lexington, Tennessee, between Jackson and the Tennessee River. It had been reported that the Federal cavalry leader, General Hatch, was crossing the Tennessee River into West Tennessee.

With the escort and Rucker's brigade, which was under the command of Colonel D. C. Kelley in the absence of the wounded Rucker, Forrest left Corinth on the 19th; and he established headquarters at Jackson, Tennessee, on the 21st. From here he reported to General Taylor the unserviceable condition of his command, stating that a large number of his horses had died as the result of the great exposure and fatigue to which they had been subjected, that many of his men were sick and worn out, and that he had been compelled to permit a large number of men to go to their homes in West Tennessee to procure horses and clothing.

Chalmers reported with 250 men of McCulloch's brigade and 300 of Mabry's. These, with Rucker's brigade, now made up his division. Buford had advanced toward the Tennessee, thrown his scouts across the river, and found that there was no indication of the enemy in the neighborhood of Clifton. Upon receipt of this information, Forrest ordered him to move northward, via Huntington and Paris, to the mouth of the Big Sandy River.

Chalmers was sent forward to cooperate with Buford and took positions at Fort Heiman and Paris Landing on the Tennessee. Forrest arrived on the scene on the 29th, as did Colonel Rucker, who had sufficiently recovered from his wounds to resume command of his brigade. Bell, with his Tennesseans and one section of the old Morton battery, was stationed near Paris Landing, the guns commanding a stretch of the river for about a mile up and down the stream. Approximately five miles below, at Fort Heiman, General Buford, with his division and two twenty-pounder Parrot guns, was thoroughly guarding the river at that point.

The Confederates did not have long to wait for their prey. They had moved so fast and had covered their approach so well that the Federals were completely unaware of their being in the area. On the morning of the 29th, the Union transport *Mazeppa* came around the bend from the north towing two barges. Heavily laden with freight destined for Johnsonville, she was a rich prize. The first battery let her get well past their position before opening up on her. The fire was deadly accurate, each shot passing through her. At the third round, she was so crippled that the pilot headed her for the opposite shore, where the crew, except the captain, abandoned the boat and fled to the wood.

The Confederates did not have even a skiff or a canoe to reach their booty across the river. "Who's a good swimmer?" General Forrest asked.

A number of men responded, including Buck and Randy. Wanting to send an officer, Forrest said, "All right, one of you two go; decide between you."

"I'll take this one; you had the last job at the bridge," Buck said.

"Noway. This is one thing I do better than you," Randy replied as he began undressing.[8]

"The water's pretty cold, and it's a long swim. Let's see if we can't find something to help."

Searching the shore, they located a large piece of driftwood and a small plank which could be used as a paddle. Hanging one of his six-shooters around his neck to keep the powder dry, Randy shoved off for the eastern shore amid catcalls of the men along the bank.

"Cap'n, your rudder's missin'!"

"Watch out for splinters!"

"Hey, Cap'n, how'd you git that shot in the back? I didn' know you was a Yankee!"

"Is that what you call bareback ridin'?"

The troopers thoroughly enjoyed watching one of their officers, naked, struggling in the Tennessee current with the makeshift craft. Randy had started across well upstream of the transport, and he managed to come alongside the *Mazeppa*, whose captain promptly surrendered to him and offered a hand to help him aboard. The captain even found some clothes left by one of the crew members for the shivering conqueror to put on. The two of them then launched the boat's yawl and rowed to the west bank of the river. A hawser was made fast to the steamer, and it was warped to the western shore. It was indeed a rich prize, and the cavalrymen found themselves amply supplied with blankets, shoes, clothing, and all the necessities, along with a few luxuries.

While the cargo of the transport was being carried ashore, three gunboats appeared and began shelling the men unloading the vessel. The Confederate batteries returned the fire and forced them to retire. Fearing that the gunboats might return in force, Forrest ordered the captured steamer burned after the cargo had been removed.

The following morning, the steamer *Anna* came down the stream from the direction of Johnsonville and successfully ran the gauntlet of the Confederate guns. She was hit several times but not in a vital place. Her success tempted a similar try by the *Venus*, which was being convoyed by the *Undine*. They were permitted to pass the guns of the first battery into the trap. That battery opened on them and struck both vessels repeatedly without material damage. When they came within range of the next battery, these guns fired upon the two boats with more telling effect. The steamers put about and tried to run past the first battery; but this time they received serious hits and backed off down the river, stopping out of range of both batteries.

Colonel Rucker asked for, and received, two guns to move to the river bank close enough to sink or capture the steamboats. Before he could get into position, the *J. W. Cheeseman*, another transport, approached the upper battery, and was allowed to pass it. The batteries opened upon her, and she was disabled. By this time Rucker was in position with the two guns, the Fifteenth Tennessee regiment, and the Twenty-sixth Tennessee battalion; and became engaged with the *Undine,* attacking with such vigor and success that the gunboat was disabled. She was driven to the opposite bank, where all of her officers and crew who were able to do so abandoned the vessel and escaped.

Lieutenant Colonel Kelley, commanding the Twenty-sixth Tennessee battalion, attacked the *Venus,* which was defended by a small detachment of Union infantry. So effective was their rifle fire that the vessel surrendered to him; and going aboard with two companies of his battalion, he crossed to the other side of the river, took possession of the gunboat, and brought both vessels to the west side of the stream.

While this fight was going on, another gunboat, No. 29, appeared from the south, anchored about a mile and a half away from Rice's battery, and opened upon him. Rice returned the fire, but the range was too long for his guns to be effective. Forrest ordered him to move nearer the vessel; and when he did so, the gunboat retired up river.

The *J. W. Cheeseman* was so badly damaged that she was of no use to the Confederates. All property was removed from the steamer, and she was set afire. The transport *Venus* and the gunboat *Undine* were only slightly damaged. The latter was one of the largest gunboats on the river, carrying eight twenty-four pounder brass howitzers. Her crew had made an attempt to spike two guns and to disable another by jamming a shell in the muzzle, but these obstacles were quickly removed.

Forrest decided to make use of the captured boats. To Colonel W. A. Dawson he said, "I want you to git them boats in op'ratin' condition, an' help in the attack on Johnsonville an' the Federal boats there."

"General, I don't know anything about boats and fighting them."

"Don't worry about that; do the best you can. I'll put Cap'n Gracey on the Venus with two of the big Parrots, an' that'll give you a lot of firepower."

The boats were readied, and as Colonel Dawson went aboard the gunboat, he said to Forrest, "General, I will go with these boats wherever you order, but I tell you candidly I know very little about managing gunboats. You must promise me that if I lose the fleet you won't give me a cursing when I wade ashore and come back on foot."

"No, Colonel; you do the best you can; that's all I want. I promise not to haul you over the coals if you come home wet; but I want you an' Gracey, if you see you're goin' to be caught, to run the boats into the bank. Let the men save themselves as best they can an' then set the steamers on fire. Now let's make a trial run with them boats."

The trial was not a big success; the boats behaved awkwardly. The crews were able to get up enough steam to make headway against the current, and they didn't run the boats into the banks. They performed well enough for Forrest to try to use them in his assault.

On November 1, the "horse marines" steamed slowly and cautiously up the river, keeping in close contact with the troopers along the shore. Forrest's sailors were enjoying themselves, occasionally offering words of sympathy to their fellow troopers who were having to ride horses or drive artillery teams. For two days things were uneventful for the steamers; but on November 2nd, having gained courage and experience, but not judgment, they ventured too far ahead of their comrades on land. At three o'clock that day, Lieutenant Commander King, U. S. N., with gunboats No. 32 and No. 29, started from Johnsonville and, five miles down river, rounded a bend and came suddenly in range of the *Venus*, which was well in advance of the *Undine*. The trained Federal sailors made short work of Forrest's navy. The *Venus* was badly damaged; and seeing that he was about to be captured, Gracey ran the nose of the vessel into the bank, and he and his men jumped off without setting fire to the boat. The *Undine* witnessed the disaster, turned about, and sought shelter under the protection of the field artillery.

Lieutenant Commander King picked up the *Venus*, which still had aboard the two twenty-pounder Parrot guns and 200 rounds of ammunition, a great loss to Forrest. Also left aboard the vessel were 200 boxes of shoes, two bales of blankets, 575 boxes of hard bread, and other freight taken from the *Mazeppa* which had been placed aboard the *Venus* for transportation and convenience.

On November 3, the *Undine* again moved up the river, this time more cautiously; and when the enemy gunboats came in sight, she made a show of fight in an attempt to lure the Federal boats into an ambuscade by the Confederate batteries. The *Key West*, the advance gunboat, received nineteen shots but managed to get away. The remainder of the flotilla closed in upon the *Undine*, and Colonel Dawson was compelled to abandon her, but not before she was set afire and subsequently destroyed.

On the afternoon of November 3, Forrest, accompanied by Captain Morton, reached the bank of the Tennessee opposite Johnsonville, which lies on the east side of the river. They carefully selected the most favorable positions for the artillery, and that night the guns were moved into position and masked. Thrall's guns, which had arrived the day before with Mabry's fragment of a brigade, were placed slightly above, or south of, Johnsonville; Morton's old battery and Hudson's pieces were placed opposite and just below the town. The movements had been so carefully made that the enemy was unaware of the presence of the Confederates.

The river landing at Johnsonville was lined with transports, barges, and gunboats. On the bank were large warehouses filled with valuable supplies, while several areas of the shore were covered with every description of army stores. Military and navy forces there comprised the following: Forty-third Wisconsin, 700 men; detachment of the Twelfth, Thirteenth, and 100th United States Colored infantry (number not given); quartermaster employees numbering 800; six ten-pounder Parrot guns, four twelve-pounder Napoleons, and two twenty-pounder Parrots (captured on the *Venus*); and the gunboats *Key West*, *Elphin*, and *Tawah* with their naval guns.

About two o'clock in the afternoon of the 4th, an enemy gunboat approached the western shore; but the vessel retired hastily when a Confederate gun sent a shell through her side. The cannonading was commenced by a section of Morton's batteries commanded by Lieutenant Brown, and the other Confederate guns joined in. From across the river, the enemy artillery and gunboats returned the fire with spirit. The Confederate artillerists soon had the range; and by cutting the time fuses with precision, spots of smoke and flame soon began to appear among the boats lining the waterfront, in the warehouses, and among the piles of goods along the wharf. The conflagration spread rapidly; and by nightfall, the wharf for nearly a mile up and down the river was a solid sheet of flame.

Forrest received a dispatch from General Beauregard, who had been given command of the Confederate army of the West, directing him, as soon as he had accomplished his mission, to move with his entire command to middle Tennessee and cooperate with General Hood in the advance of the main body of the Confederate army toward Franklin and Nashville. Pursuant to these orders, he moved his command six miles that night, by the light of the enemy's burning property, in the direction of Perryville, Tennessee.[9]

There were so many reports flying around as to Forrest's whereabouts that Sherman, with evident humor, had wired Grant on November 1: "Forrest seems to be scattered from Eastport to Jackson, Paris, and the lower Tennessee; General Thomas reports a capture by him of a gunboat and four transports."

On November 6, omitting the humor, Sherman reported to Grant;

"That devil Forrest was down about Johnsonville, making havoc among the gunboats and transports."

General Thomas telegraphed Halleck in Washington; "I have determined to send the Twenty-third Corps to Johnsonville, and have telegraphed Colonel Thompson, who has a force of 4000 men, not to abandon Johnsonville."

To the commander at Columbus, Kentucky, Sherman wired, "If enemy approaches Columbus, the guns of large caliber must be defended to the death, and the town should be burned by you rather than Forrest should get a pound of provisions or forage."

General James H. Wilson, in a dispatch to Grant, said: "Sherman estimates that Forrest has 26,000 men mounted and menacing his communications."

While these dispatches, and many others, were flying about, Forrest was trying to get back across the Tennessee. He reached Perryville on the 6th, and found no boats or ferries available. He had only two yawls, taken from the transport, which he had hauled on wagons. He undertook to build rafts; but there had been heavy rains, the river was up, and a great quantity of heavy driftwood in the stream made crossing dangerous in the fast current. By nightfall on the 7th he had gotten Rucker's small brigade across before giving it up as a bad job. He directed Rucker to proceed down the east side of the river to Florence, and he took the rest of the command to Iuka, Mississippi, via Corinth, arriving there on the 15th. It had been a hard trip. In order to move his artillery over the muddy roads, he impressed local oxen, which were used in relays. Each relay of steers would be driven for fifteen or twenty miles, and would then be turned back to their owners, who drove them home. These were replaced by a new relay.

Forrest reached Cherokee Station on the 16th, and here he placed his command on cars and moved them to Florence. He arrived there on November 18, 1864, and reported to General John B. Hood.

Chapter XXII

The Beginning Of The End At Nashville

Upon arrival at Florence, Alabama, Forrest was placed in command of all the cavalry of the Army of Tennessee. In addition to the troops which had been serving with him in Mississippi and West Tennessee, this gave him a division under General W. H. Jackson and a fragment of Dibrell's brigade, some of whom had served under him in the old brigade.

After attempting with little success to break Sherman's lines of communication in northwestern Georgia, General Hood had decided on a bold and dangerous stroke to get Sherman out of Atlanta. He moved his entire army into northern Alabama and began preparations to march into Tennessee, thinking that this would draw Sherman in pursuit. He left Lieutenant General Joe Wheeler with his cavalry to watch Sherman and to harass him as much as possible. Even if he failed to draw Sherman out of Georgia, Hood thought that he might be able to defeat Major General George Thomas and his Army of the Cumberland. Accomplishing this, the door to Kentucky, and even southern Ohio, could be open to him. This was an optimistic and dangerous undertaking for an army which has been estimated by historians to be anywhere from only 30,000 to 40,000 men.

When Hood began his march northward, General Thomas was in Nashville busily assembling an army of 50,000 men, some of his reinforcements coming from Missouri. In Hood's more immediate front at Pulaski was Major General John M. Schofield with two corps of approximately 22,000 men.

Forrest, commanding the entire cavalry force with Hood's army, numbering only about 5,000 effectives, moved out from Florence in advance of the infantry and encamped at Shoal Creek on November 18. Buford and Jackson were ordered to advance farther northward over the military road. On the following day, the 19th, at Butler's Creek, a foraging party of Kentuckians came in collision with a brigade of Union cavalry under Colonel Datus Coon, of Hatch's Union division, which pounced upon the Confederates so vigorously that the latter gave way, abandoning to the Federals one or two wagons from Buford's headquarters train.

Brigadier General Frank C. Armstrong was near enough to hear the fighting and, with his usual judgment and speed, marched toward it. Buford's men had rallied promptly after the first flurry of surprise, and the Federals were caught between the two Confederate forces. Coon's men were handled so roughly that they sought safety in flight, leaving several prisoners in the hands of the Rebels. In this affair, Colonel Edward Crossland, who had scarcely recovered from the painful injuries received at the Battle of Harrisburg in July, again was wounded severely.

In spite of the exceedingly inclement weather—rain, sleet, snow, and ice—Forrest set out on the march toward Nashville with the remaining division, under Chalmers, on December 21. They took the road by West Point to reach Henryville on the 22nd. Meanwhile, Buford and Jackson arrived at Lawrenceburg on the 22nd, where they again encountered a portion of Wilson's cavalry, which offered but slight resistance and retreated toward Pulaski.

Although these first encounters with the Union cavalry were to do little to improve the poor opinion the Confederates, especially Forrest, had of the Union horse, the Southerners were to learn before this campaign was over that they were dealing with an entirely different brand of mounted Federals. In a telegram, dated September 23, 1864, to Sherman from Grant, the latter had asked: "Do you require a good cavalry leader? It seemed to me that you have during your campaign suffered for the want of an officer in command of cavalry..."

In Sherman's reply on the 23rd, he said: "I do want very much a good cavalry officer to command, and have been maneuvering three months to get Mower here, but Canby has him up White River. My present cavalry need infantry guards and pickets, and it is hard to get them within ten miles of the front..." Sherman's disdain for the fighting qualities of his cavalry was shared by his infantrymen and artillerymen who openly treated them with contempt.

On the 25th, Grant said in a wire to Major General Meade: "I will have to send a cavalry commander to Sherman and think of sending Gregg. At present, and to this time, there has not been an officer with cavalry in the west whom it was safe to trust, without infantry to guard them from danger..."

Gregg, however, was not chosen; instead, a young West Point graduate, James Harrison Wilson, who had attained the rank of brigadier general at the age of twenty-seven years and was commanding the Third Cavalry division under Major General Phil Sheridan in the Shenandoah Valley, was selected. He was breveted a major general and reported to Sherman at Gaylesville, Georgia, in the early part of October. Sherman had given up in disgust his attempts to catch and bring to bay the elusive General John B. Hood and had decided on a march to the sea instead, leaving Hood to be taken care of by Major General George Thomas, commanding the Army of the Cumberland.[1]

Wilson's first move was to call in all details and detachments and to permit none to be made thereafter without his personal authorization. These men were returned to their units, which were organized into brigades, the brigades into divisions, and the divisions into a corps. He had only about 5,000 of the men mounted and began the difficult task of remounting the others. He was able to complete this only after receiving permission to impress all horses south of the Ohio River. With this authority, he procured 7,000 mounts in a period of seven days. So thorough was this impressment that Vice President-elect Andrew Johnson, who lived in Nashville, lost his two carriage horses. A circus in that city lost everything except its ponies.

Wilson was occupied with these duties in Nashville; and well before the tasks were completed, he left on November 21, while they were still in progress, to join the Federal forces contesting Hood's advance toward Nashville and to take personal command of the cavalry in the field. These numbered about 4,500 at this time, but the number would rapidly increase to 12,000 within a very short period as remounts were acquired and the men were equipped.[2]

With Hood's army moving well to the west of Pulaski, toward Columbia, Tennessee, Schofield's position at the former place became untenable; and General Thomas on November 22 ordered him to fall back with two divisions to Columbia and for General Stanley to follow with the other two divisions on the 23rd.

On November 23, Chalmers' division came in contact with a column of Union cavalry at Henryville and drove them after slight resistance through and beyond the town for several miles. Finally, at Fouché Springs, the Federals were found drawn up in line of battle in considerable force. Forrest came up with his escort and took command. Rucker was directed to go forward to skirmish lightly with the enemy and hold them where they were. Colonel D. C. Kelley was sent with a battalion around the left flank, and Forrest went around their right with his escort of eighty men to gain the enemy's flanks and rear. The Confederate general soon found himself in the rear of the Federal line. The Union commander did not believe that the Southerners were in force nor that he would be seriously attacked at the late hour of the day. In any event, while it was still light, Forrest saw a considerable number of the enemy cavalry who had dismounted, unsaddled their horses, and were building fires in preparation for making camp. He had not been joined by the forces under Colonel Kelley; and despite his numerically inferior number, he dashed into the enemy, his men firing right and left with their six-shooters into the surprised and disorganized Yankees, who were thrown into such confusion that they scattered in all directions. About fifty prisoners, twenty horses, and an ambulance were captured.

Rucker, hearing the firing of Forrest's attack, charged the enemy with determination from the front and drove them from the field. The Federals, giving away before Rucker, bore down upon Forrest in such number that he was compelled to turn off into a byroad to escape them. Riding at the head of his escort with Buck and Randy slightly to his rear, he came suddenly upon a squadron of Federals commanded by an officer who ordered them to halt. Not knowing the identity of the men in front of him, he continued to advance; and it was not until they were almost upon them in the dark that he realized that they were Yankees. The Union officer quickly levelled his pistol at Forrest, the muzzle of which was almost in touch with the general's body, and was in the act of firing when Buck, by a quick movement of his hand, knocked the weapon upward.[3] It discharged, but the bullet missed the Southern cavalry leader. By this time, the escort was upon them, and the Federal detachment, seeing that they were badly outnumbered, surrendered.

Early the following morning, Rucker continued his march to Mount Pleasant, where he captured 35,000 rounds of small-arm ammunition and the guard left with it. From here, the stubborn enemy was pursued to the suburbs of Columbia where, in a desperate hand-to-hand fight with a small but determined detachment of Union cavalry, Colonel W. A. Dawson was killed after he had emptied his pistol and was trying to wrest one of the enemy's colors from its bearer. Buford and Jackson had steadily driven the Federals toward Pulaski and at Campbellsville engaged Edward Hatch's division, which was driven from the field.

Hood pressed hard after Schofield, forcing him northward until he reached the entrenchments of Franklin in the morning of November 30, 1864.[4]

Franklin lies just south of the Harpeth River which flows northwesterly into the Cumberland. As was his custom, General Forrest made a personal reconnaissance of the enemy's position. When General Hood arrived on the scene, he reported to him, ''Gen'ral, the enemy's mighty strongly entrenched. A direct assault on him will be powerful costly, an' a lot of men'll be killed an' wounded.''

"I don't think the Federals will stand strong pressure from the front. The show of force they are making is a feint in order to hold me back from a more vigorous pursuit.''

"That stronghold ain't no feint. Gen'ral Hood, if you'll give me one strong infantry division with my cavalry, I'll flank the Federals from them works in two hours' time.''

"The battle has already been ordered, and the units are being brought into position for it. I want you to divide your cavalry and post them on both flanks. If the assault proves successful, I want you to complete the ruin of the enemy by capturing those who attempt to escape in the direction of Nashville.''

"There's no way we can take them works without a high loss; but if that's the way you want it, that's what it'll be.''

"It won't be all that bad; you'll see, General.''

By three o'clock two corps of Confederates were being formed for the attack, Cheatham's on the left and Stewart's on the right. General S. D. Lee's corps was held in reserve. Following Hood's orders, Forrest placed Chalmers' division, with a fragment of a brigade under Biffle, on the extreme left of Cheatham's corps along the Carter's Creek pike. He placed Jackson's and Buford's divisions immediately on the right of Stewart's corps.

Buford's men were at first deployed in immediate contact with Stewart's right wing, and on the south side of the Harpeth River. Somewhat eastward of Franklin and along the Lewisburg pike, and between this highway and the Harpeth, Jackson's command was thrown boldly across the river, where they were immediately confronted by Wilson's cavalry in superior numbers.

As Hood's initial assault went forward, the cavalry moved with them. On the left, Chalmers became heavily engaged with an infantry force posted behind a formidable stone wall which had been strengthened by hastily constructed breastworks of earth, and he was unable to dislodge them. Advancing as closely as he could to the enemy line, he ordered his men to protect themselves in every way possible and to maintain a constant fire in order to hold employed the enemy in front of them. On the right, Buford encountered some of Wilson's cavalry in an advanced position; and pitching into them with his usual determination, he soon drove them to the north bank of the Harpeth. His dismounted troopers, disregarding the freezing temperature of the water, waded the stream in pursuit and joined Jackson and Forrest, who were already across. At this time the total strength of the two cavalry forces was about equal; but Forrest had been forced to divide his, and those across the river were outnumbered almost two to one.

Realizing that he had to hold his position, General Wilson ordered Hatch and Croxton to attack the Confederates with vigor while Harrison, with Capron's old brigade, looked to the left and rear. The battle raged between the two cavalry forces, both dismounted, with great fury until nightfall; and despite their superior numbers, the Federals were unable to drive the Confederates south of the river until dark. Forrest learned of Hood's failure to dislodge the Union forces in Franklin and withdrew his men across the Harpeth.

Hood's assault on the stronghold at Franklin was a bloody affair and has been compared with that of Pickett at Gettysburg. Eleven times his men went forward to the slaughter. They did not succeed in carrying all points of the Federal defenses, but they did manage to effect entrance at one or two points which they maintained until late in the night, when the Federals left the field and withdrew toward Nashville. Hood reported capturing 1,000 prisoners, but he also reported losing 4,500 men killed, wounded, and taken prisoner. Among these were five generals killed, Major General P. R. Cleburne, and Brigadier Generals Gist, John Adams, Strahl, and Granbury. Among the wounded were Major General Brown and Brigadier Generals Carter, Manigault, Quarles, Cockrell, and Scott. Brigadier General Gordon was taken prisoner. These general officers were irreplaceable, but the greatest injury to Hood and his army was the loss of confidence in him by his officers and his men.[5]

As Schofield's army moved toward Nashville to join up with General Thomas, it was pursued by Forrest. At daylight on December 1, with Buford and Jackson, he struck the enemy at Wilson's Crossroads. Morton opened fire upon them with one of his batteries; and Buford charged, dislodging them and taking several prisoners. Without further resistance, a portion of Forrest's command continued its march toward Nashville.

Chalmers moved across to the Hillsborough Pike and then along it to a point opposite Brentwood. Here he crossed over to the Franklin pike and encamped for the night. The following day, the troops under Chalmers were thrown out along the Hillsborough and Hardin pikes, while Forrest directed Buford to take his division to Mill Creek and form in line of battle across the Murfreesborough highway. Jackson's division was ordered to take a position so as to cover the Nashville and

Mill Creek pike. When the infantry arrived late in the afternoon, Forrest began doing what he did best—raid, plunder, and harass the enemy.[6]

On December 5, Major General Bate arrived with his infantry division, having been ordered to report to Forrest and to cooperate under his directions for action against the enemy forces in and about Murfreesborough.[7] Forrest's cavalry and Bate's infantry joined near Lavergne. They advanced on Murfreesborough and drove the Federals into their works. Buford was ordered to picket from the Nashville and Murfreesborough pike to the Lebanon pike on the left and Jackson to picket on the right to the Salem pike. The Confederates then went into camp for the night.

On December 6, Forrest made a forced reconnaissance on the enemy at Murfreesborough, his troops consisting of Bate's division, two additional infantry brigades under Sears and Palmer, and Buford's and Jackson's divisions. He advanced in line of battle; and after two hours of light skirmishing, the enemy pickets and skirmishers were driven in. The Union troops ceased firing after retiring into their entrenchments and showed no disposition to give further battle. Holding his men in line of battle, Forrest made a personal reconnaissance with a regiment and decided that the position was too strong to justify a direct assault. This was good judgment, for Major General Lovell H. Rousseau, commanding the forces there, had about 7,000 infantry, cavalry, and artillery and had strongly fortified this position. Forrest decided that he would do no more than hold the enemy in place to prevent their union with Thomas in Nashville.

General Rousseau, however, decided to take the offensive; and about ten o'clock on the morning of the 7th, two brigades of infantry and 1,326 cavalry, all under Major General R. H. Milroy, moved out of Murfreesborough on the Salem pike. Observing the movement, Forrest withdrew about a mile to a new and better position on the Wilkinson pike. He did this in order to be able to throw Jackson's and Buford's divisions between the advancing Federals and their stronghold and capture them when the infantry, upon whom he felt he could completely rely, had beaten them in front.

The infantry was ordered to throw up temporary protection, and a satisfactory breastwork of rails, logs, and stones was hastily constructed; and Forrest calmly waited for the Federal attack. Milroy moved forward, with his cavalry in advance, to within half a mile of the Wilkinson turnpike; and after a spirited artillery duel lasting about thirty minutes, he fell back into a thick wood out of sight of the Confederate line. Milroy found the Confederates too strong for a frontal assault, so he moved in the cover of the wood in a northeasterly direction until his line of battle was astride the Wilkinson turnpike. Here he formed his men in a double line for the assault.

To meet this movement, Forrest was compelled to change his front by withdrawing a portion of his line and placing it directly across the Wilkinson pike in front of the advancing Federals. Riding along the line, he addressed the infantry, "Men, you're ever' bit as strong as the enemy and you got protection. All I ask is for you to hold 'em back for fifteen minutes. That'll give me enough time to gain their rear with my cavalry, an' I'll capture the last one of 'em."

The Federals advanced boldly, stopping only to deliver their volleys. When they came in short range of the Confederate infantry, to the surprise and dismay of Forrest and Bate, the troops of these units, who had fought so well on other fields, broke in disorder and fled in panic. Forrest realized the peril of the situation and sent Major Strange to Brigadier Generals Armstrong and Ross to tell them that everything depended on the cavalry. He was wild with fury and, with General Bate, dashed in among the retreating men. He rode up and down the line yelling, "Rally, men—for God's sake rally!"

Bate was also exhorting his men to stand and fight, but the panic-stricken troops paid no heed. Rushing toward a color bearer who was running for dear life, Forrest ordered him to halt. When the retreating man refused to obey the command, the general drew his pistol and shot him down. Dismounting, he seized the colors, remounted, and rode in front of the soldiers waving their fighting emblem. The men responded to his urging and halted their retreat. With the assistance of the cavalry charges under Armstrong and Ross, the assault of the Federals was checked.

The Yankees then immediately retired within their fortifications. Their rapid withdrawal into Murfreesborough was due in a great part to Buford, who had been ordered to operate to the left of Forrest's line. He saw the opportunity to attack Murfreesborough from his position on the field and made a bold assault by which he succeeded in penetrating well into the heart of the city. This created considerable anxiety in the mind of General Rousseau, who ordered Milroy to return at once to the fortifications.

Disappointed with the performance of the infantry in this engagement, General Hood ordered them withdrawn; and they were replaced by two other brigades. Forrest remained in front of Murfreesborough, but his command was active. On December 11, Buford was directed to picket the Cumberland River in direction of the Hermitage. On the 12th, the infantry was engaged in destroying the railroad from Lavergne to Murfreesborough. On the 13th, Jackson, operating south of Murfreesborough, captured a train of seventeen cars and the Sixty-first Illinois infantry regiment of about 200 men. The train, which was loaded with supplies, was destroyed.

On the morning of the 14th, Forrest moved with his two brigades of infantry across Stone River and east of Murfreesborough looking toward capturing the enemy's forage trains. While on this expedition, he received a dispatch from Hood that a general engagement was in progress in front of Nashville and directing him to hold himself in readiness to move to the army's assistance at any moment. He retired from Murfreesborough with his entire command to the Wilkinson Cross-Roads, six miles from Murfreesborough, on December 16. At nightfall, a courier brought word of the disaster which had befallen the Confederates at Nashville. He also brought urgent orders from his commanding general to fall back toward Duck River and to concentrate the cavalry to protect the rear of the beaten army.

The battle of Nashville and the subsequent retreat were the beginning of the end for Forrest's cavalry, although most of his troops were not actually involved in the battle itself. The sleet had stopped; the ice had melted; and on December 15, 1864, "Slow Trot" Thomas was ready to fight. He moved out of his fortifications at Nashville with an army almost twice the size of that of Hood, who was entrenched on a five-mile front atop some high ground south of the city. Biffle's brigade had been positioned by Hood on his extreme right; and Chalmers, with only Rucker's small brigade, was in charge of the extreme left of the Confederate line. On the 14th, Chalmers had informed Hood of the weakness of his force and its inability to cover the ground allotted to it. The commanding general reinforced this portion of his alignment with Ector's infantry brigade.

When the battle opened, Wilson's cavalry corps formed the extreme right of Thomas' army. They were over 12,000 strong, and many fought as dismounted infantry. They struck Ector's infantry brigade so hard that the Confederate general was forced to withdraw his command back and to the east on the main infantry line so precipitately that he was unable to inform Chalmers, who was even farther to the left, of his retreat. This left the Hardin pike wide open, and Wilson took advantage of it, throwing forward a strong body of mounted troopers. The only opposition facing them was the Seventh Alabama cavalry which, though fighting stubbornly, was unable to give effective resistance. Advancing two miles along this highway, General Wilson captured Chalmers' headquarters wagons and ordnance train. Chalmers, backed up along the Cumberland River and cut off from the rest of the Confederates, was in a perilous position; however, he skillfully extricated himself and effected a junction with the left wing of Hood's army late that afternoon. The remainder of the Southern army had fared little better that day, having been driven back to the Harpeth Hills by nightfall when the fighting ceased.

General Thomas thought that the battle was won and over that day, but General Schofield did not agree, "You don't know Hood," he said. "He'll be right there ready to fight in the morning."

Schofield was right; Hood was there, with his army stretching across both the Franklin and the Granny White pikes, but he did not have the force to withstand Thomas' juggernaut. His left gave way first and then his center; but his men continued to fight on. As a heavy rain began to fall, Hood gave the order to retreat down the Franklin road; and this they did precipitately in confusion.

That second morning of the battle, Chalmers was again attacked ferociously by a heavy column under Wilson, who was moving heaven and earth to turn the left flank and get in the rear of the Confederate infantry. Realizing how disastrous this could be, Chalmers concentrated all of his available forces and moved rapidly to the Granny White turnpike where he secured a strong defensive position. He got there none too soon, for he received a courier from Hood informing him of the defeat of the Confederate army. The message said in substance, "For God's sake drive the Yankee cavalry from our left and rear, or all is lost."

Chalmers, Rucker, and Kelley strengthened their position by obstructing the road with trees and building a barricade of rails and brush. After dark on the 16th, the Federal cavalry, flushed with their success, bore down on them with courage and confidence. Rucker's brigade took the brunt of the fierce onslaught, but there was vicious hand-to-hand combat all along the line. The weather was bitterly cold; and the falling rain had turned into sleet which covered the earth with ice and made footing treacherous for both man and horse. In addition, the hands of the troopers were so cold that it was difficult for them to cock their pistols or to hold the weapons in their hands.

Colonel Rucker became engaged in a bitter saber duel with the Federal Colonel Spalding. Slashing and thrusting at each other, they were both handicapped by the dark. Each was strong, skillful, and an excellent horseman; and the issue was doubtful until a stray bullet broke Rucker's sword arm, and he was compelled to surrender. He was taken to the rear as a prisoner and was questioned by General Hatch, to whom he remarked: "Forrest has just arrived with all of his cavalry and will give you hell tonight. Mark what I tell you."[8]

Rucker was questioned as to the coming of Forrest and repeated the statement in such a manner that the Federal cavalry leaders apparently believed that the Confederate general was now on the field. About this time, Randolph, who commanded one of Rucker's regiments, opened a side volley upon the Federals which threw them in confusion, and they retreated several hundred yards. Rucker was greatly gratified to hear someone say, "General Wilson has ordered everything in camp." Hood's army was able to continue its retreat southward without being further harassed that night by Wilson's revitalized cavalry.[9]

Forrest knew that the battle at Nashville could not go well for Hood. Not only was the Southern general badly outnumbered, the battle at Franklin had done much to break the spirit of his men. Expecting a retrograde movement by Hood, he hastened Buford's division in the direction of Franklin; and he moved with the wagon trains, the sick and wounded, several hundred infantry who were unfit for duty for lack of shoes, and a considerable drove of beef cattle and hogs which had been gathered up for use of the army.

At daylight on the morning of the 17th, the troops of both armies were astir. The Confederate cavalry, under Chalmers, had had little respite from the desperate work of the previous day. When the Union cavalry ceased their attack, Chalmers left a thin line of skirmishers to offer such resistance as they could, and these men built fires to impress the enemy that the entire cavalry had gone into camp. With the remainder of his command, which had become considerably scattered and not a little disorganized, Chalmers hurried toward Franklin and arrived there on the morning of the 17th. In the absence of Forrest, he was given command of all the cavalry at that point and was to act with General S. D. Lee in protecting the rear of the army. Fortunately General Buford arrived at this time with his division and reported to Chalmers.

General Lee still held his immediate command together in good fighting shape; and he selected two brigades, Pettus' Alabama and Stovall's Georgia, which he organized, with the cavalry, into a temporary rear guard and waited for the onslaught by the Union cavalry. It was not long in coming.

Major General Wilson was in the saddle early on the 17th and pressed forward vigorously with the brigades of Hammond, Croxton, and Knipe. At Brentwood he ran into the Confederate cavalry outposts and drove them with little difficulty to Hollow-Tree Gap, four miles north of

Franklin. Pursuing the Confederates with a boldness bordering on rashness, the Union troopers ran into a stronger detachment of Forrest's cavalry and the two brigades of infantry under Stephen D. Lee, and suffered a temporary check.

Unable to dislodge the Confederates, Wilson threw his forces around them on each side of the pike, compelling their rapid withdrawal to Franklin. This flanking movement was checked by Brigadier General Gibson with his brigade and a regiment of Buford's cavalry under Colonel Shacklett. These checks permitted the Confederates to reach Franklin with little difficulty.

By four o'clock that afternoon, Wilson had crossed a considerable part of his cavalry over the Harpeth River and began a bold and vigorous attack, charging with his troopers and pushing forward his lines to the front of the rear guard. These desperate attacks were kept up until long after dark; but Pettus' Alabama and Cummings' Georgia brigades, the latter commanded by Colonel Watkins, repulsed every attack while Chalmers covered their flanks with his division. The Federal cavalry did succeed in getting in Stevenson's rear and attacked Major General Clayton's division about dark; but they were repulsed, Gibson's and Stovall's brigades being principally engaged.

This was bloody work on the 17th, the fighting often at close quarters, the men slashing and thrusting with sabers, and firing six-shooters at point blank range. Even the cavalry generals emptied their "Navies" several times that day. Lieutenant General S. D. Lee was wounded near nightfall but he refused to relinquish command until the safety of the troops was assured. He was succeeded in command by Major General C. L. Stevenson.

Language is inadequate to describe the suffering of the soldiers and animals on each side. It was now midwinter, and for several days after the battle at Nashville, it rained and froze, alternately. The roads were deep in mud and covered with ice which broke underfoot, adding difficulty to the marching of both infantry and cavalry. The weather was intensely cold, the troops wet and hungry, and the horses and men worn out. With unsurpassed heroism the soldiers of both armies stood uncomplaining to their desperate work. Food was scarce for the horses; and many of them, famished with hunger, or crippled with hoofs fallen off from frost and mud, fell by the wayside never to rise again. Many of the unmounted Southerners had their shoes disintegrate completely as they struggled on the muddy and icy road.

Early on the 18th, the Southerners continued their retreat toward Columbia. Except for a little skirmishing between the advance of Wilson's corps and the extreme rear guard of the Confederates, little action took place. Rutherford Creek, a few miles north of Columbia, was the first formidable obstacle in the path of the retreating army and its pursuers. While Forrest's cavalry was holding Wilson's corps at bay, Cheatham arrived near the stream, and threw up defenses in order to protect the passage of the wagon train. This safely over, he crossed to the south bank; and was immediately followed by the cavalry, which destroyed the bridge over which they crossed.

Wilson's delay at this creek, and in waiting for his supply train to catch up, gave the Confederates two days of much needed respite. This permitted the Rebels to cross Duck River and gave Forrest time to destroy the bridges after them. It had been Hood's plan, if defeated at Nashville, to retire across this river to Columbia and stay there for the remainder of the winter; but his army was in such a deplorable condition that he deemed it best to recross the Tennessee River without delay.

Forrest had arrived at Columbia on the 18th, and agreed with Hood's decision to continue the retreat. He volunteered to take command of the rear guard, requesting, in addition to his cavalry, 4,000 serviceable infantry to be commanded by the able Major General E. C. Walthall. Hood accepted his proposal, and gave him the fragments of the following commands: the brigades of General W. S. Featherston, Colonel J. B. Palmer, Colonel C. W. Heiskell (who had succeeded General Strahl), Colonel C. H. Olmstead (who had succeeded General Smith), General J. B. Johnson (who had succeeded General Quarles), Colonel H. R. Field (who had succeeded General Maney), and General D. Coleman (who had succeeded General Ector). These remnants were consolidated by placing Palmer's and Smith's brigades under Colonel Palmer, Field's and Heiskell's under Colonel Fields, Reynolds' and Coleman's under General Reynolds, and Featherston's and Johnson's under General Featherston. [10]

Forrest's first action after taking command of the rear guard was to charge Major Anderson with the task of impressing all oxen and other draft animals and to have the wagons double teamed in order to pull half the wagons and guns more rapidly over the quagmire roads to Tennessee. He personally looked after effecting the safe passage of the Confederates across Duck River and the destruction of the bridges. The bedraggled Rebel army was soon on its way south again.

Wilson reached the Duck River, and here he stalled—Forrest's destruction of the bridges had been for many miles in each direction from Columbia and very thorough. Generals Thomas and Wilson had anticipated the latter's pursuing and harassing a retreating army and had provided a train of pontoons and adequate supply trains. These, however, moved so slowly that the train with rations did not reach

Wilson at Rutherford Creek until the 20th of December. The pontoon train was not only slower, it got on the wrong road and did not reach him on the bank of the Duck River until late on December 23. Wilson was too wise to attempt to swim the swollen and icy stream with Forrest's men behind cover on the other side, and he was compelled to wait until the morning of the 24th to cross it. This delay gave Forrest time to return the teams from the first trip to the Tennessee and to save the remaining half of the wagons and artillery.

It had not been possible to remove all of the supplies, and Buck had been given the responsibility of seeing to the destruction of the ammunition that could not be taken out, and Randy had to do the same for the other supplies. All able-bodied men had marched out, and to help them in this work the two officers had civilian volunteers who were loyal to the South. Buck finished disposing of the ammunition and then assisted Randy with his task. They had no sooner set fire to the last of the supplies when a resident of the town rushed up to them and said, "Y'all better get out of here. The Yankees just finished laying their pontoon bridge."

Leaping on their horses, whose condition was somewhat improved with the few days' rest, they galloped southward out of town. They soon slowed to an easier pace and had travelled but a few miles when they saw ahead General Forrest riding with Majors Strange and Anderson. They increased their speed and joined them. Buck rode up beside Major Anderson and asked in a low voice. "What are y'all doing way back here, and where's the escort?"

"They're up ahead with the rear guard. You know the general—he said he wanted to ride back to be sure the supplies and ammunition were destroyed. We waited at the top of a hill back there until he saw y'all leave—I think he just wanted to be sure you got out all right."

"Why didn't he bring the escort with him?"

"He didn't think it necessary with the enemy across the river, and he wanted to save their horses."

"We'd better get on down the road." Then he called to General Forrest who was riding ahead of him, "General, Wilson has completed his bridge."

"When?" Forrest inquired.

"Just before we left."

They were travelling up a hill; and when the top was reached, Buck turned and saw a detachment of Federal cavalry cresting the top of the hill where Forrest had waited. They were coming at a full gallop. Buck said to Forrest, "There's a squadron of cavalry on our tail coming on hard. Y'all strike out; Randy and I'll see if we can't slow 'em down at long range with the Whitworths.''

Buck rode quickly into the trees on the side of the road, and Randy went into some on the opposite side. The other men spurred their horses and ran at full gallop down the road. Buck and Randy dismounted, grabbed their rifles, found a rest for the guns, and adjusted the sights. "What range you setting?" Randy called.

"Five hundred," Buck replied.

The enemy charging down the road in column of fours made an easy target. The two Southerners fired almost simultaneously—one of the Yankees fell from his mount, and the horse of another went down. Those moving rapidly behind the fallen horse and wounded man piled into them; and their horses, too, went down, causing others coming behind them to fall. There was a wild pile-up of a dozen or more animals with their riders, many of whom were seriously injured in the melee. Those troopers who had not fallen brought their mounts quickly to a halt. By this time, Buck and Randy had reloaded and fired again into the teeming mass of men and animals. Without regard to the number of men they might be facing, those Federals who were able rapidly sought safety behind the crest of the hill to their rear.

After firing another round, Buck called, "Let's get out of here. That ought to slow them down for a while!"

They mounted their horses and galloped off after Forrest and the others.

They had travelled no more than a mile when they came upon a lone Confederate infantryman who was valiantly struggling down the pike. His shoes were gone, and his feet were torn and bleeding. They saw him stagger and fall and then get up and move on in the direction the retreating army had taken. As they came up behind him, the soldier fell again. He struggled to get up but could not make it. The two mounted men stopped their horses, and Randy got down and assisted the soldier to his feet. "I'll help you in the saddle and ride behind you," he said.

"Thank you, Captain. I thought I could make it, but I guess the wound in my shoulder made me weaker than I thought. There weren't enough ambulances, and I had my choice of walking or being left to be taken prisoner.''

With Buck's aid, the wounded man was helped in the saddle, and Randy got up behind him. "Guess I shoulda stayed behind," he said. "I thought of it; I don't live too far from Columbia and might have made it home; but that woulda been deserting, and I didn't want to do that."

"Where do you live?" Randy asked.

"Near Centreville."

"You don't happen to know a Carter family who lives on a farm just the other side of Centreville, do you?"

"I sure do—they're my folks. Do you know them?"

"I wouldn't be here today if it weren't for them. They took care of me when I almost drowned in the freezing duck River a couple of years ago."

"Your name must be Rushton. Mama wrote me about that." He looked over at Buck and asked, "Yours wouldn't happen to be McCord?"

"It is; it's a small world, isn't it?"

"It ain't been for the last nine days."

They caught up with the rear guard and arranged for the wounded man to ride in one of the supply wagons which had been partially emptied since leaving Columbia. As they left him, he said to Randy, "I'll write Mama about this. She'll be pleased to know it was you who saved my life back there."

"I'm not sure I saved your life, but I'm glad I was able to repay the kindness your folks showed me."

Forrest fell back and took a strong position at Richland Creek south of Columbia and prepared to meet the pursuing Federal cavalry. Six pieces of artillery were placed in a well selected position on the main pike, and these were supported by Buford's and Chalmers' divisions and Ross' brigade of Jackson's division. General Wilson, after a careful reconnaissance, was so well convinced of the inadvisability of trying to cross the creek here that he took immediate steps to throw his men across above and below the Southerners. He finally succeeded in crossing well up the flank of the Confederate position, and Forrest was forced to abandon the strong defensive position and fall back in the direction of Pulaski. In the fight, which at times was hand-to-hand, Brigadier General Buford was badly wounded and was compelled to relinquish his command which, for the time being, was combined with that of Chalmers.

Of the infantry which had volunteered to cover the Confederate retreat, fully 300 of them were without shoes; and their feet were so badly cut by the ice and the rough marching that they could scarcely hobble along on foot. These men, however, had not lost heart; and they were willing to fight to the death if necessary. They wrapped pieces of blankets around their raw and bleeding feet, tied them on with thongs, and still trudged on, staining the snow and slush with their blood. Forrest could not stand the sight of this and ordered some of the wagons to be emptied of their precious contents to give transportation to the brave and determined men. When it became necessary to fight, they left the wagons, took their places in line of battle, and performed effective service; and private Josiah Carter was always foremost among them.

On the retreat southward, Forrest took advantage of every favorable place to check Wilson's persistent cavalry, which was dogging him much in the manner he had pursued Colonel Streight. Many of these clashes were no more than skirmishes by small detachments of the Rebels while the main rear guard was continuing its movement toward the Tennessee, but they delayed Wilson by forcing him to stop and form a line of battle or flank them. Fearing the wiles of Forrest, the Union general could treat none of these brushes lightly.

About seven miles south of Pulaski, the Confederate general found a place to his liking at King's Hill (also known as Anthony's Hill). The approach to the hill from the north was through a narrow valley, shut off on each side by ridges of considerable height. Morton's artillery was placed on the crest of the ridge and masked in position to sweep the valley along which the enemy would approach. Armstrong's and Ross' brigades were dismounted and thrown into line with Featherston's and Palmer's infantry in close support and to one side of the artillery. From the opposite side of this crescentic formation, Jackson's division, mounted, was lined up with Reynolds' and Field's infantry. Breastworks of logs and stones were thrown up, and Chalmers was placed upon the right flank for observation in order to prevent any flanking movement. Skirmishers were thrown out in front. A half mile ahead of these, toward Pulaski, a small force of mounted Confederates was left at the mouth of the gorge with orders to fire and to retreat rapidly in order to draw the Yankees into the trap.

As soon as the Federals came in sight, the detachment of mounted men fired and retreated as ordered. The Northerners charged this rear guard; but when Wilson entered the narrow valley, he suspected a trap, knowing that Forrest would not likely pass up such a favorable position. He ordered one of his regiments to dismount, and he carefully pushed them forward with one piece of artillery loaded with canister. The Confederates remained concealed until the enemy was within close range. At a given signal, Morton opened upon them with canister, and each side of the horseshoe delivered a volley of musketry. The Federals broke in great disorder; and the Rebels, leaving their breastworks, charged them. Jackson's mounted detachment led the charge, capturing the gun, a number of prisoners, and several hundred horses of the dismounted men.

That night, the 25th, Forrest camped at a small stream called Sugar Creek and again strengthened his position with rails and logs. The following morning, one heavy with fog, the advancing Federals drove in his pickets. As they came on, the Yankees could not see the Confederates until at very close musket range. The Southerners opened upon them with a volley which threw them into confusion, and they retreated in disorder. Two mounted regiments of Ross' brigade and two infantry regiments were ordered to charge at this opportune time, and the Federals were thrown into a complete rout. The pursuit lasted for two miles until the Rebels ran into a stronger force. Forrest then withdrew his troops to Sugar Creek, where he waited in battle line for two hours. When the enemy did not appear, he resumed the retreat toward the Tennessee River. The Federal cavalry made no further attack, and he crossed the river on December 27. Wilson's advance guard, under Spalding, reached the north bank of the river just as the bridge had been swung to the south side and the last of the Rebels were disappearing in the distance.[11]

Chapter XXIII

The End At Selma

The Confederate and Union forces had the wide Tennessee between them, and they were mutually content with it that way. Wilson's force was jaded, and he said his troops were "nearly on foot when his advance guard reached the Tennessee River..." Forrest's were even worse off, for they had joined the Nashville campaign without a day of rest after the arduous expedition against Johnsville. Many of their horses had died on the march and in battle, and others were in such deplorable condition that they had to be abandoned. Replacements for all of them were unobtainable. Not so with Wilson; he had authority to impress anything he could find, and he did a thorough job of it. At last Sherman had found a cavalry leader who could, as he put it, "beat Forrest stealing horses."

After the Tennessee had been crossed on December 17, Forrest received permission from General Hood to leave Roddy's brigade to guard the crossing of the river and to protect against incursions of the Federal cavalry; and he took the remainder of the troops to Corinth, where he was better able to obtain food for his men and forage for his horses. With the exception of Ross' brigade, which was made up of Texans, the other brigades, on January 5, 1865, were furloughed for twenty days to return to their homes to procure new clothing and, if possible, get fresh mounts.

The furloughed troopers travelled in units with their officers and were ordered to round up stragglers and deserters and to raid and harass the enemy as much as possible in the occupied territory. Under the direction of General T. H. Bell and other officers, numerous minor raids and expeditions were made against the enemy, capturing supplies and horses and greatly disturbing navigation on the Cumberland, Tennessee, and Mississippi Rivers. Acting Rear Admiral Lee of the Union navy, in January 1865, wrote to General Thomas: "I respectfully suggest that, if consistent with your plans and views, Forrest and his gang be entirely cleaned out of western Kentucky and Tennessee."

In a dispatch to Thomas about this time, Sherman said: "I suppose Forrest is again scattered to get horses and men and to divert attention. I would like to have Forrest hunted down and killed, but doubt if we can do that yet."

Desertions were becoming a major problem in Hood's demoralized army. On January 14, the commanding general directed Forrest to "keep picked bodies of cavalry near at hand, that they may be ready to pursue and capture any men that may desert from the army. If the first party of deserters can be caught and promptly punished, it will perhaps deter others from doing the same." This task fell to Ross' brigade of Texans who were on picket duty while the rest of the command was furloughed.

During the period that Forrest was at Corinth, Roddy's brigade was caught off guard by a detachment of General Wilson's cavalry under Colonel Palmer. Roddy had apparently furloughed too many of his men to go to their nearby homes for the same purposes that Forrest had granted leave to those under his immediate command. Colonel Palmer boldly crossed the Tennessee River with his Union cavalry force, defeated Roddy's Southern troopers, and captured and destroyed General Hood's pontoon bridge and wagon train. A communication from General Beauregard to General Cooper at Richmond, dated January 22, 1865, advised: "General Hood reports the loss of his pontoon-train, eighty-three boats, one hundred and fifty wagons, and four hundred mules, due to inability of General Roddy to bring his troops from their homes. I wish to substitute another brigade in its place, and put all cavalry of this department under one commanding officer, Forrest."

The Confederate cavalry leader was given command of all Confederate cavalry in the Department of Alabama, Mississippi, and East Louisiana. He moved his quarters to Verona, Mississippi, and issued the following communication from there:

"(Circular)
"HEADQUARTERS CAVALRY DEPARTMENT OF
ALABAMA, MISSISSIPPI, and EAST LOUISIANA.
"Verona, Mississippi, January 28, 1865.
"In obedience to orders from the department headquarters I hereby assume command of the District of Mississippi, east Louisiana, and west Tennessee. In doing so it is due to myself and the troops thus placed under my command, to see that every effort will be made to render them thoroughly effective. To do this, strict obedience to all orders must be rigidly enforced by subordinate commanders, and

prompt punishment inflicted for all violations of law and of orders. The rights and property of citizens must be respected and protected, and the illegal organizations of cavalry, prowling through the country, must be placed regularly and properly in the service or driven from the country. They are in many instances nothing more or less than roving bands of deserters, absentees, stragglers, horse-thieves, and robbers, who consume the substance and appropriate the property of citizens without remuneration, and whose acts of lawlessness and crime demand a remedy, which I shall not hesitate to apply, even to extermination. The maxim that 'kindness to bad men is cruelty to the good' is peculiarly applicable to soldiers; for all agree, without obedience and strict discipline troops cannot be made effective, and kindness to a bad soldier does great injustice to those who are faithful and true; and it is but justice to those who discharge their duties with promptness and fidelity that others who are disobedient, turbulent, and mutinous, or who desert or straggle from their commands, should be promptly and effectively dealt with, as the law directs. I sincerely hope, therefore, while in the discharge of the arduous duties devolving upon me, and in all the efforts necessary to render the troops of this command available and effective to suppress lawlessness and defend the country, I shall have the hearty co-operation of all subordinate commanders and unqualified support of every brave and faithful soldier.

"N. B. FORREST."[1]

One of Forrest's first acts after taking command of the cavalry was to reorganize his troops. All Mississippians were placed in Chalmers' division, the Alabamians and Kentuckians in a single brigade under Buford, the Tennessee troops under Brigadier General T. H. Bell, while Ross' Texans were placed under Brigadier General W. H. Jackson. Colonel Robert McCulloch, with his aggressive and effective regiment, the Second Missouri, was made an independent command directly under Forrest.

Randy was not included in the furloughs that had been granted most of the command on January 5, for he was needed by Forrest in the mass of staff work confronting him; but Buck was among those given leave. He left his horse, rifle, and other personal property in his friend's care, telegraphed Ellen, and set out for Marion by train. He arrived there the following morning and found her holding their son as she waited anxiously by the track. Buck was off the train and had them both in his arms before the cars came to a stop; but he did not hold them long, for the six-month-old baby loudly voiced his objections to this unexpected development.

"Hey, what's the matter, Fellow?" Buck asked as he released Ellen and the child and reached for his son.

C. C. wanted no part of this stranger who had tried to smother him and turned to his mother for protection. "You frightened him," Ellen said. "He'll have to get used to you."

"I hope it doesn't take too long; I've got only eighteen days."

Ellen laughed, "He'll be over it by the time we get home. He has his father's friendly personality."

Cory came over to them and greeted his son warmly. "How's Ma?" Buck asked.

"Doin' just fine," his father replied. "She can't hardly wait for you to git home."

They reached the buggy, to which Cory had tied his horse; and Cory held the baby while Buck helped Ellen into the vehicle. Buck made no effort to take his son; he didn't want to risk frightening him again. It was a nice trip home, and Ellen brought him up to date on the latest family news. They were getting along well, but were now having to make do with only the things they could provide for themselves. The government was taking almost everything they could produce in the way of grains, hay, cured and salted meats, horses, and mules, but had backed off on taking their breeding stock. Her father suspected that General Forrest may have been responsible for this. Sally was doing well, although she had put on quite a bit of weight with her pregnancy; but Mr. Beaumont was having problems with his heart and was in very poor health. Vira had just gotten her freedom, but did not seem particularly excited about it; she and Artie had married, and she was continuing to work at the McCord house. The pleasant trip was over before they were aware that so much time had passed. Buck had taken it easy with C. C., making no further attempt to hold him; but he would say something to the baby occasionally and affectionately pat him on the arm or leg.

Cory had ridden on ahead and reached the McCord farm before them. As they came around the bend and in sight of the house, they could see him and Sadie waiting on the porch. They were by the road when the buggy pulled up in front of the house. Buck quickly tied the reins around the buggy whip and jumped down into Sadie's arms. When he released his mother and turned to help Ellen down, he first held out his arms for C. C. who willingly came to him. Buck smiled with satisfaction as he held his son for the first time.

It was a happy day, the kind that is long remembered, as Buck and his family were again united. The house was filled with lively conversation and rang with laughter as they turned this into a truly festive occasion. Buck and Ellen, with C. C., visited the Rushtons and Sally for a short time that afternoon, but they were home well before dark; and supper in lamplight was another pleasant affair.

As they lay together in bed that night, the house was quiet; and Buck held Ellen close to him, "Oh, Buck, I miss you so much," she said softly. "Isn't this war ever going to end?"

"I think it will soon, but not the way we want it."

"You mean we'll be defeated?"

"I don't see how we can hope for anything else. General Forrest seems to be of the same opinion. Before I left for home, I stopped by to thank him for the furlough; and he said that it probably wouldn't be long until we all have a permanent one. He thinks that with Hood's army broken, Sherman in Savannah and Beaufort where he can be supplied adequately by sea, and no one in front of him with the strength to contest a move to the north, we can't make much resistance in the deep South. He believes it is only a question of time until General Lee's lines at Petersburg will be broken, for Grant is wearing him out. With unlimited resources of men and money, he will ultimately force Lee to leave Virginia or surrender. The general doesn't believe the army will follow Lee out of Virginia, and that will end the war."[2]

"If he thinks it is hopeless, why does he go on fighting?"

"He's a good soldier and devoted to the cause. He will continue to do his duty and fight until those above him bring it to an end—just as I, and thousands more like me, shall do."

"Surely our leaders can see the futility of further resistance?"

"They ought to; but either they don't, or they are afraid to face the consequences of surrender."

"What will happen then?"

"I guess we'll be part of the United States again—they say they're fighting to preserve the union. We will be at their mercy, though; and we can only hope they'll be merciful. The slaves will be freed; but we shall be better off than most Southerners, because we don't depend upon them. So will your folks, as many of their people are now sharecropping. Those who will really be hurt are planters like the Beaumonts who depend entirely upon slave labor. Whatever is ahead, it can't be much worse than what we have now."

Ellen snuggled closer. "It'll be better. We'll be together; and together, we can face whatever comes. I've learned a lot from Ma and Pa. We'll make it."

Buck returned from furlough and found little had happened during his absence as far as operations were concerned. Randy was anxious to get the latest report on Sally's condition, and it was not until almost the middle of February that he received a letter telling him of the birth of a beautiful girl weighing just a little over five pounds and that she was doing well. Randy was elated, and quickly sought out Buck to share the good news.

"That's great," his friend said. "I hope you aren't too disappointed over its not being a boy."

"What do you mean? Why should I be disappointed—who could ask for anything more than a pretty little girl? She's apparently going to be small like Sally. I can hardly wait to see her."

"Have y'all named her yet?"

"Sally wants to name her Sarah Ellen, and I'm all for it."

"I like that—the names go together."

"They really do. I'll suggest that we call her by both names."

"That will please Ellen. Are there any operations coming up in the near future you know about?"

"There are none planned for the rest of the month."

"Has the reorganization been completed?"

"The plan was completed before y'all got back from furlough, and it's now in effect."

"Then all the staff work on it is done?"

"Completed."

"Why don't you hit Old Bedford for a furlough? He ought to be able to spare you for a couple of weeks. He's family minded and will understand your wanting to go home."

As Buck had surmised, Forrest was sympathetic to Randy's request; and the new father left for Marion the next morning on a furlough of two weeks.

On February 28, Forrest was promoted to Lieutenant General, and the following day he moved his headquarters to West Point.

The scouts had reported in January the concentration near Waterloo, Alabama, on the Tennessee, of a large Union cavalry force under Major General James H. Wilson. Very close watch was kept on this, and the buildup continued all during January and February. Other expeditions for the invasion of the territory were being organized in the areas of Memphis, Vicksburg, and Baton Rouge. In addition, a heavy concentration of Federal forces under General Canby was being collected in the area of Mobile, and still another army of invasion was being formed in Pensacola. By March 1 Union forces, numbering fully 75,000 men, were ready to march into Forrest's department as soon as weather conditions permitted.

Wilson's cavalry on the Tennessee River were Forrest's chief concern. He foresaw that their objective was an invasion of middle Alabama and in all probability the destruction of the arsenals at Selma. This was the primary reason for the transfer of his headquarters to West Point, and he began concentrating his forces in that area. He not only gathered in all absentees he could find but conscripted all men who were fit for service, going so far as to use fifteen-year-old boys and old men as horseholders in order to free able-bodied men for the fighting line. The roads to Tuscaloosa and to Eutaw were marked and blazed so that his troops would have no trouble following the right roads. He directed that a pontoon bridge be built across the Black Warrior River at Finch's Ferry near Eutaw, and it was further ordered that five days' rations be kept on hand ready to be cooked as soon as the troops received orders to march.

Forrest now had a formidable adversary commanding the Federal horse, Major General Wilson, who had busied himself in massing his cavalry and bringing it to top fighting efficiency; and he had the full backing in this of Major General George Thomas, commanding the Union Army of the Cumberland. By the middle of March, Wilson, with remarkable zeal, had completed the organization of the most magnificent body of mounted troops ever gathered under one commander in the western hemisphere. He called to his assistance young men of experience who had already won reputations for courage, ability, and energy; and he had one of the best cavalry staffs ever organized. He gathered in his camps along the Tennessee 27,000 cavalrymen, of whom 17,000 were mounted; they were now poised and ready to strike.

Generals Thomas and Wilson had decided to invade central Alabama for the purpose of destroying the arsenals and foundries in Selma along with the Confederate stores there. This accomplished, circumstances would then decide the further objectives of the expedition. They were going contrary to a directive of General Grant simply to make a demonstration with 5,000 men on Tuscaloosa and Selma, because they felt that so small a force would be at the mercy of Forrest. They intended a strike in full force.

Knipe's division of Wilson's cavalry was sent by steamer to General Canby in the vicinity of Mobile. Leaving Hatch's division, about 7,500 dismounted men, in camp, Wilson marched on March 22 for Selma with his first, second, and fourth divisions, 14,000 effectives made up of 12,500 mounted and 1,500 dismounted men. The latter were used as escort to the train until such time as they could be mounted, and each division was supported by an artillery battery of four guns. The Union troopers were armed with Spencer magazine repeating rifles, the most formidable small arm known to warfare at this time. Each trooper carried five days' rations, one pair of extra horseshoes, and one hundred rounds of ammunition. Five days' rations of hard bread and ten of sugar and salt were taken on pack animals. The supply train consisted of two hundred and fifty wagons, which were sent back to the Tennessee as fast as the contents of each was consumed. In addition, there was a pontoon train of thirty canvas boats, hauled by fifty six-mule teams.

Starting on diverging roads, the command moved southward in three columns, with directions to rendezvous near Jasper, Alabama. They arrived there without opposition and proceeded on to Elyton, in Jefferson County, reaching that place on the 29th and 30th of March.

While at Jasper on the 27th, Wilson learned of the advance of a portion of Forrest's command, believed to be under Chalmers, which was moving toward Tuscaloosa, Alabama, by way of Bridgeville. He had great respect for Forrest and knew he must move rapidly to beat him. He decided to strip himself for the race to Selma. He ordered his division commanders to replenish their haversacks, pack on mules everything they must take, leave the wagons, haul nothing but the artillery, and march with the greatest possible speed toward Elyton and on to Montevallo.

Forrest had kept himself informed as well as possible as to Wilson's movements. His position was one of great difficulty because of the expected advance of a second expedition toward Montgomery from Pensacola, compelling him to divide his command, which in its entirety was still far smaller than that of Wilson. Buford was sent on the 23rd to Selma to complete a pontoon bridge there and to send a portion of his brigade to look out for the Federal invasion from the direction of Pensacola.

Chalmers' division had been thrown forward on the 17th as far as Pickensville, Alabama; and on the 25th, one of his brigades, Armstrong's, with Hudson's battery, was ordered toward Selma via Finch's Ferry, where the pontoon bridge had already been laid. They were directed to take eighty rounds of ammunition per man, and 200 rounds of artillery ammunition for each gun. Starke's brigade of Chalmers' division was ordered to follow the next day on the same route with a similar issue of ammunition. On the same date General W. H. Jackson's division was directed to follow without delay via Tuscaloosa.

Leaving as many troops as could be spared from the command to meet the expedition threatening from Memphis and to protect the country in the direction of the Mississippi River, Forrest moved in person toward Selma, reaching the bridge over the Sipsey River on the 29th.[3]

By the afternoon of March 30, Wilson had concentrated his Federal cavalry in or near the village of Elyton. He had left his wagon train between the two forks of the Black Warrior, guarded by his dismounted men. At Elyton he detached Croxton with 1,800 men to proceed toward Tuscaloosa; capture that place; and destroy the bridge, the factories, and other public property, including the Alabama Military Academy. Accomplishing this, he was to rejoin the main column by way of Centreville, where the road from Tuscaloosa to Selma crosses the Cahaba River. Croxton camped eight miles from Elyton that night and pushed on in the direction of Tuscaloosa the following day. At four o'clock in the afternoon of the 31st, he came into the road in the rear of the main column of Jackson's division, which had just passed the intersection as it moved toward Centreville.

Croxton did not know it, but he missed the opportunity to do Jackson great harm—he had come into the road between the Confederate general and his artillery and train, which were trailing several miles behind his main column. Had he turned to the right, Croxton could have captured the guns and train; but he elected to trail Jackson's main column. At the same time he sent a courier to inform his division commander, General McCook, and General Wilson of his change of direction.

That night Croxton changed his mind and reversed his march in the direction of Tuscaloosa, to which he had been ordered. He had proceeded only a short distance when one of his rear companies was vigorously attacked by Jackson, who had learned of the enemy cavalry on his tail. The company commander, Captain Parrish, was wounded and his unit captured. Instead of continuing in the direction of Tuscaloosa, which would have brought him upon Jackson's artillery and train, Croxton headed rapidly due west and then north, bypassing Tuscaloosa and reaching Johnson's Ferry on the Black Warrior forty miles north of the city.[4]

On March 30, Upton's division, on orders from Wilson, advanced toward Montevallo, drove in the Confederate pickets, and arrived there about dark. He was followed by General Long's division and LaGrange's brigade of McCook's division. General Wilson reached Montevallo at one o'clock on March 31st; and a sharp engagement took place between the Federals and a small force of Confederates, Roddy's division and a detachment of infantry militia under General Dan Adams. The Confederates were forced back to Six Mile Creek south of

Montevallo, and Wilson's troops destroyed the iron and steel works in the evacuated town.

Here the Confederates were reinforced by 300 Kentuckians of Crossland's brigade and made a gallant stand, especially the Kentuckians who were defending the bridge across the creek; but they had to withdraw again when they were being outflanked by greatly superior numbers. Upton's Federal division camped fourteen miles south of Montevallo that night.

During this time Forrest had been riding rapidly across the country from Centreville toward Montevallo with his staff and escort, some seventy-five in number. He came within sight of this road just as the conflict at Six Mile Creek ended and saw the road filled with Federal cavalry moving south. Not liking to miss an opportunity to hit the enemy, he formed his small force of dependable men into a column of fours and approached within fifty yards of the Yankees. He charged their column and broke through. Turning, he now dashed upon the fragment north of him and drove it rearward for half a mile, but there his adversary stood drawn up in a heavy line of battle to receive him. Changing direction southward at a charging pace, he found the road strewn with signs of the recent battle. He had taken a few prisoners and learned from them that General Wilson was already south of him, pressing Roddy and Crossland back toward Selma. Being in the midst of the main cavalry force with less than seventy-five men, Forrest thought it best to withdraw. Making a detour from the line of the road, he succeeded in finding Roddy and Crossland about ten o'clock that night confronting the enemy near Randolph.

As Forrest had marched from Centreville toward Montevallo, nine miles beyond the former place, at two o'clock in the afternoon of the 31st, he sent Lieutenant Glass, of the First Mississippi cavalry, to General Jackson, directing him to move straightway to the plantation of Mr. James A. Hill, "where General Jackson will find orders for his movement. Should Brigadier-Generals Bell or Campbell be in the advance of General Jackson, they will turn back as above directed."[5]

At six o'clock that night, after finding Wilson in force south of Montevallo, he changed his orders to Jackson, directing him to get behind and follow Wilson on the road from Montevallo to Selma. The courier carrying this message was intercepted by Wilson's troopers, and he had two other dispatches on him. These messages gave Wilson the valuable information that Forrest's forces were scattered and that those directly in his front under the Confederate general were of little strength. He deduced from the message that Chalmers was also west of the

Cahaba and knew that if he forced the marching and fighting toward Selma with sufficient vigor he had control of the situation.[6]

Wilson thought that Croxton was harassing Jackson's rear and felt that the greatest danger to his own forces would be for Jackson to overwhelm Croxton and then fall on the rear of the main column as it moved toward Selma on the Montevallo road. The Federal commanding general was at Randolph, only fourteen miles from Centreville. He ordered McCook with the other brigade of his division, LaGrange's, to march as rapidly as possible to Centreville, capture the bridge over the Cahaba, and open communications with Croxton. This done, McCook was to attack Jackson with his united division; scatter his forces; confuse him as much as possible; and then fall back, burn the bridge at Centreville, and take the direct road to Selma.

McCook was successful in capturing the Centreville bridge but was unable to contact Croxton. He found Jackson but decided not to risk an engagement and retreated across the Cahaba. He burned the bridge, leaving Jackson upon the west side of a swollen and unfordable stream, thus preventing his joining Forrest in the fighting which occurred during the next forty-eight hours. McCook then moved toward Selma on the direct road, a route which served as a screen for Wilson's right flank.

On March 31, Forrest had sent a courier to Chalmers urging him to push forward across the Cahaba with all possible celerity to Ebenezer Church and place his men in position where he would be joined by his commanding general. With Crossland's brigade, a detail of two hundred men from Armstrong's brigade, Roddy's brigade, and the militia under General Don Adams, he had a force of less than 2,000 men facing Wilson's 9,000 in Upton's and Long's divisions at Randolph. Planning on being joined by Chalmers' division at Ebenezer Church, he believed he could offer sufficient resistance to the Federal cavalry until Jackson's division could strike the enemy in the rear and flank.

Taking advantage of his knowledge of the small number of men facing him, Wilson, on the morning of April 1, hurled Long's and Upton's divisions against the small Confederate force in his front. They encountered small detachments of Confederates and drove them back with slight effort until they reached a point about five miles north of Plantersville known as Ebenezer Church. At this place Forrest had selected a strong position along Bogler's Creek and had fortified it with logs and rails. His artillery was placed to command the roads approaching the bridges over the stream on the main road from Montevallo to Selma and on the old Maplesville road, which were not far apart at this point. To the left, Crossland's three hundred men were posted, while on the extreme right a detachment of state troops under General Adams was placed. Forrest received the first information of the disintegration of his plans—a message from Chalmers that he had met with such obstacles in his route that he would not be able to unite with him that day.

Forrest was in a rage after reading the dispatch. He sent an urgent message to Chalmers that Wilson was pressing down on him with great vigor and an overwhelming force and that he would accept no excuse for Chalmers to fail to join him at Plantersville or before he was driven into the works at Selma. Chalmers was moving with Starke's brigade along one road, and Armstrong was moving with the remainder of his brigade along another route about five miles northward.

Forrest's courier with the message to Chalmers passed through Armstrong's brigade, and that general read the dispatch and forwarded it on immediately to his division commander and advised him that he would not wait for orders but would move rapidly to join up with Forrest. He urged General Chalmers also to press forward to Plantersville to the rescue of their chief. Armstrong advanced with all possible haste; but he was unable to reach Forrest until that night at Plantersville, after the action which took place farther north along Bogler's Creek.

The Confederates were in position at the creek, waiting for the Federal cavalry. Forrest was about a hundred yards south of the bridge with a few members of his staff and several of his escort when a one-armed man in civilian clothes rode up on a fine horse from the direction of Plantersville. Forrest did not see him until he was less than twenty yards away, and he watched in silence as the rider approached. The man got down easily from his horse, and the general saw a six-shooter pistol in a holster strapped around his waist. The newcomer drew a Mississippi rifle from a deerskin sheath attached to his saddle and turned to face the General. "Howdy, Bedford," he said.

"Hello, McCord; it's good to see you. It's been a long time." He walked over and shook Cory's hand.

"Where can a one-armed man be the most help?"

"Sure you want to git in this?"

"When the fightin' starts takin' place at my front door, it's time I got into it."

"All right. Those men over there are my escort. They go where I go. You can be one of them, if you want."

"That'll be fine. I won't git in nobody's way."

"Have you seen Buck?"

"Naw, I just got here."

"He carried a message to the artillery over on the other road. He should be back soon."

Cory left to join the men of the escort. After he was out of earshot, Major Strange asked, "Is that Buck's father?"

"It is."

"He's just got one arm; he won't be much help."

"You may be su'prised when the fightin' starts. He's a lotta man."

A few minutes later, the Federals appeared, Long's division on the main road and Upton's not far behind on the old Maplesville road. As soon as the skirmishers opened fire, Long reinforced his advance guard, which was composed of a battalion of the Seventy-second Indiana, by the remainder of that regiment. They were dismounted and advanced with their Spencer repeating rifles pumping out a sheet of lead. They broke through and drove back the Confederate line. Long then threw Lieutenant Colonel White with the saber battalion of the Seventeenth Indiana Mounted infantry into the assault.

Forrest moved into the flashing sabers with his escort and the detachment from Armstrong's brigade.[7] There occurred one of the severest hand-to-hand conflicts between cavalry units during the war. It was a test of Confederate six-shooters against Yankee sabers. Forrest himself was recognized and viciously attacked by the enemy. Among his assailants was a brave young officer, Captain J. D. Taylor of the Seventeenth Indiana, who assaulted him vigorously but not wisely. He and five or six others had the general surrounded and were slashing at him with their sabers. One blow knocked the general's pistol from his hand, and he was struck several more times before he managed to free his other pistol from the scabbard and shoot Captain Taylor from the saddle with a mortal wound. Cory saw Forrest's perilous situation and spurred his horse into the melee, guiding the stallion with knee signals, while the pistol in his hand was spurting flames. One man fell from his onslaught, and another left the fight clutching his side where he had been hit.[8] Captain John Eaton also came to his commander's relief and shot another of those crowding Forrest.

As this fight at close quarters was going on, Brigadier General Upton arrived on the Old Maplesville road with his division, Alexander's brigade in the lead, and assaulted the Confederate militia on the right flank. These men gave way and left the field in great disorder, compelling the entire Confederate line to retreat precipitately, losing three guns and 200 dismounted men as prisoners. A desperate running fight was continued to Plantersville, where approaching darkness brought it to a halt. In this retreat the fighting was fierce, the Federal cavalry often riding stride to stride alongside the racing Southern cavalrymen.

Buck had just left the battery on the Old Maplesville road when he heard the noise of the original Federal assault. He hurried toward the fighting and ran into several mounted enemy before reaching the main road. With his six-shooter firing as rapidly as he could with one hand, he emptied first one gun and then the other from his belt holsters before reaching the main road. As he came up to it, the whole Confederate line gave way into the rapid retreat toward Plantersville. Buck pulled one of his pistols from a saddle holster and rode in among the Union and Rebel cavalry, who were now thoroughly intermingled. As his faster horse moved up on those ahead of him he made good work with this gun until it too, was empty. He drew his last loaded pistol, and the race southward continued. To his great surprise, he saw his father ahead of him on the easily recognizable stallion.

Cory had emptied his pistol in the fight around Forrest. He drew his rifle, which was also empty, from the sheath; gripping it at the small of the stock with his hand—grown even stronger after the loss of his left arm—he was using it as a club. As he caught up with one of the racing Yankees, a sweeping, crushing blow of the rifle barrel against the side of the head or body would knock the adversary from his horse. Ahead he saw Forrest, again surrounded by several Federal cavalrymen against whom he was desperately defending himself. Urging his horse on to an even faster pace, Cory caught up with them. Forrest dismounted one of his attackers, but there were four more pressing him hard. As Cory came up to the trailing Yankee, he unhorsed him with a quick blow of the rifle barrel against the side of his head, which brought the sickening sound of crushing bone. He moved up to the next man and knocked him from his horse with a vicious blow to the side of his body. The two remaining Yankees were on the opposite side of Forrest; and when they realized that they were now alone, they wheeled their horses from the road toward an adjacent wooded area. One of them stopped short of the trees, drew his Spencer rifle, and emptied it rapidly in the direction of Forrest and Cory. Buck, who was riding behind his father, thought he saw Cory's body react as from the impact of a bullet; but he showed no other signs of having been hit.

Buck put the spurs to the tired Miss Ellie, and the mare responded as always. He soon caught up with his father; and as he drew even with him he asked, "What are you doing here, Pa?"

"Just thought I'd give a hand," Cory replied.

Buck laughed. "That was a pretty good hand you were giving back there. You weren't hit were you?"

"Just a mite."

They reached Plantersville shortly after this, and it was apparent that the Federal pursuit had been called off. Forrest halted the movement of his own troops for a well-earned rest—they had been driven twenty-four miles that day and were now only nineteen miles from Selma.

Cory started to get down from the saddle; but as he did, he suddenly went limp and fell to the ground. Buck was quickly off his horse and knelt beside the body which was lying face down on the ground. He turned his father over, opened his coat, and saw the blood which had been slowly but steadily coming from a wound just below the rib cage on the left side. "I thought you said you weren't badly hurt."

"I'm gut shot. I knowed there wasn't nothin' you could do."

Dr. Cowan broke through the circle of men who had formed around the man on the ground and said, "Let me take a look, Buck."

Buck stood up and backed out of the way. The doctor knelt beside Cory and opened his coat fully. Buck could see where the bullet had come out on the opposite side of the body at about the same level at which it had entered. "He's badly hurt. His intestines and body organs are probably torn up. My guess is that he's bleeding inside very badly."

"What can you do for him?" Buck asked anxiously.

Dr. Cowan looked at the man on the ground and did not reply.

"Tell 'im, Doctor; I'm a growed man," Cory said.

"Nothing, really, except to make him easy and hope that his body will heal itself. I've seen it done."

"But not this..." and that was as far as Cory got. His body went limp, and his head rolled to the side.

Buck looked in disbelief, "Is he dead?" he anxiously asked.

Dr. Cowan felt for a pulse and after a moment said, "I'm afraid so." He stood up and looked at Buck, "Who is he?"

"He's my father—my father, Cory McCord. Isn't there anything you can do for him?" Buck pleaded.

"I'm sorry, Son; it's too late, but there wasn't anything I could have done, anyway, not with a wound like that. Just be thankful that he went fast; those wounds can be extremely painful. I saw him back there on the road; he's a demon in a fight."

At this time Randy broke through the circle and saw Cory on the ground. There was no need to ask; he knew Cory was dead. He went to Buck and put his hand on his friend's shoulder, "I'm sorry," he said. "Is there anything I can do?"

"Help me get him across his horse."

They lifted Cory and placed his body, face down, over the saddle. Someone brought leather thongs and Buck tied his father's arm and legs together so he would not fall off. As Randy watched him, his mind went back to the time Buck had similarly tied a deer when they first met. He thought of the years they had had together and how Cory had been such an important part of those times, treating him like a second son and teaching him all the things he taught his own boy. Grief welled up in him; but he was aware that his own sorrow was nothing compared with that of his friend, for he knew how close had been the relationship between the man lying across the horse and his son.

Buck got on his horse and Randy handed him the reins of Cory's stallion. "I'll go with you," he said as he started toward his own mount."

"I'd like that, but you better not. Tell the general I'll be back by dawn."

"Back from where?" Forrest asked as he shoved his way between two men of the group silently watching the scene before them.

"I'm taking Pa home."

"You ain't goin' nowhere. I need ever' man I got."

"I live less than fifteen miles from here, and I'm taking Pa home. I'm an officer now, General; and you can have my commission if you want, but I'm taking him home," Buck replied; and he slowly brushed his right hand against the thong of his right gun to free it, hoping this would not be noticed.[9]

Randy saw Buck's action and moved close to him. "Our commissions came in pairs, and they'll go as a pair," he said. "Mine goes with his; we stand together."

Forrest was tired and suffering from his wounds. He had just learned that Chalmers was nowhere near Plantersville, and he had heard nothing from Jackson. The frustration of being unable to concentrate his command, and the anger over the beatings his men had taken for the past two days were almost enough to drive him to a serious mistake; but, as always under adverse conditions, Forrest's judgment was sound. The dead man had twice that day come to his aid and had probably saved his life both times, and he also considered the great value he placed upon the loyalty and support the two young captains had always given him. "All right, go ahead if it ain't no fu'ther'n that; but git your butt back here by daylight. If you see Chalmers, tell 'im I'm goin' on to Selma an' to join me as fast as he can. I'll leave a rear guard here, an' you can join up with them in the mornin'."

Without saying anything more, Buck moved off leading Cory's horse. It was a long and sorrowful ride which finally came to an end. The house was dark as he approached it; and not wanting to frighten the women inside, he stopped in front rather than going to the rear. After tying the horses to the fence, he went to the door. As he knocked on it, he called, "Ellen! Ma! It's me—Buck!"

He heard movement in the front bedroom, and his mother called, "Just a minute—I'll be right there."

A lamp was lit in her room, and he heard the sound of bare feet running across the floor. The door was unlatched and flung open, and there stood Ellen in her nightgown. "Buck!" she cried. "What a wonderful surprise!" She threw her arms around him, and he was holding her tightly when his mother appeared at her bedroom door with the lamp. He let Ellen go; she sensed something was wrong and moved to one side.

"Ma," he said, but got no further—he didn't have to; his voice and expression told the story.

"Where's he at?" Sadie asked.

"Outside on the horse."

"Le's git 'im in."

"I'll get him."

"You'll need help."

"I'll manage. You get the bed ready." He turned and went outside, leaving the door open.

"We'll put 'im in the company room," Sadie said as she crossed the hall. Ellen followed to help with the preparation.

In a few minutes Buck came through the door with Cory in his arms. Ellen knew her husband was strong, but she was surprised at how well he carried his father's large body. The bed was ready, and he laid Cory on it. "I'll heat some water," Sadie said and started out of the room.

"Let me do it, please," Ellen pleaded. Sadie stopped, and Ellen left for the kitchen.

Sadie went to the bed and looked at Cory's wound. "How'd it happen?" she asked.

"We were in a running retreat. There were five Yankees around General Forrest trying to kill him. Pa went to his aid and took down two of them. The general put down another. The other two skedaddled, but one of them stopped and emptied a repeating rifle toward Pa and the general. One of the shots got Pa."

"I'm glad he done good; he woulda felt bad if he hadn'."

"What in the hell was he doing there, Ma?" Buck asked in exasperation and grief.

"He never talked about it none," Sadie said; "but I knowed 'im too well not to know it galled 'im no end that he couldn't fight for his country. When we heard y'all was bein' pushed down the road to Selma by all them Yankees, he said it was time he done somethin'."

"It was a crazy thing to do."

"Don't never talk about your Pa that way! He done it 'cause he had the same sense of duty an' love for his country as you. He wouldna been the kind of a man you'd want for a Pa if he hadn'."

"I'm sorry, Ma—it's just that I loved him so much."

Sadie looked her son squarely in the eye and said, "You think you loved 'im more'n I did?"

Buck realized that, in his own grief, he had lost sight of his mother's. "Of course not," he replied contritely.

He went to Sadie and held her. Only then did the strong Sadie break down and cry convulsively. A few minutes later, a gentle rap came at the back door. She had calmed down by this time, and Buck asked gently, "You all right, now?"

"I'm all right; see who's there."

It was Artie and Vira, who lived in a cabin built for them in the back yard. They knew from the lights and voices that something out of the ordinary was taking place. "Howdy, Mista Buck. I'se glad to see you home. I thought somethin' might be wrong," Artie said.

"There is, Artie. Pa's been killed. Y'all come in. We'll need you."

Vira went to the kitchen to see how she could be of help, and Buck said to Artie, "First, take care of the horses out front. Mine is kinda jaded. Swap her for Skin, and saddle him up—I've got to go back tonight. There's a mess of Yankee cavalrymen in the area, a lot of them. They're going to be grabbing every horse and mule they can lay their hands on—and cattle, too. I want you to run everything we've got into the deep woods, including the hogs; and cover their tracks. Put a couple of men with them, and keep them hidden until it's safe to bring them out. Take in enough feed to take care of them for at least six weeks. We've got that much, haven't we?"

"Yassah. We's got plenty of grain."

"You may not have it very long. Maybe you'd better take in most of it. I'm going to write a note to Mr. Rushton telling him to do the same thing. I'll ask him to prepare two impressment receipts, one for him and one for us, showing that the Confederate government seized all of our stock and most of our grain. You give him the numbers of ours. If the Yankees come around and wonder why stock farms have no stock and grain, we can tell them our government impressed everything ahead of them; and we'll have the receipts to back us up. Do you understand?"

Artie grinned. "Yassah, I un'erstan'. That stock'll be in the woods 'fore daylight. I'll put two men in there to take keer of 'em, an' there'll be somebody here in a few minutes to take the note to Mista Rushton."

After Artie left, Buck took a lamp and went in to see his sleeping son.

He wanted badly to pick up the boy and hold him, but this was no time to awaken a sleeping baby. He then went to the kitchen and wrote the note to John Rushton. By the time he finished, one of the younger James boys was there to deliver it. He went back to the room where Sadie was undressing her husband. He gave her a hand; and while they were busy at the task, he told her what he had ordered Artie to do with the stock and grain. As they finished undressing Cory, Ellen came in with the warm water. Buck shaved his father, and Sadie gave him a bath. They then dressed him in his Sunday clothes and best shoes. The unpleasant but necessary job finished, they went into the kitchen, where Vira had made coffee from some given them by the Rushtons and had warmed up some food for Buck. He didn't think he was hungry; but when he sat down at the kitchen table, he remembered that he hadn't eaten since early that morning; and it was now almost midnight. He ate rapidly and heartily, without realizing what he was consuming. When he finished, he got up; it was time he started back to Plantersville.

"Ma," he said, "I hate to leave you at a time like this, but I've got to be back before daylight. I'm sorry I won't be with you at the funeral service."

"Do you really have to go?" Sadie said.

"Yes'm, I promised General Forrest; he needs every man he can get."

"Now you un'erstan' why Cory had to go?"

Buck appreciated the way his mother had set him up. He replied, "Yes'm. I knew all the time. I was just upset about everything. It seemed so unnecessary."

"What woulda happened to Gen'ral Forrest if your pa hadn' been there?"

"He probably would have been killed."

"Then it was necessary," Sadie said in a tone of voice ending the discussion.

Ellen got up and went to her room to get a shawl. Sadie said, "You go talk to Ellen while I fix some food to take with you. Y'all ain't had a chance to say two words since you got here."

"What would I ever do without you?" he asked.

Sadie had risen to her feet. She turned away from him and said, "I ain't a wife no more, but I'm still a ma."

Buck left her with her sorrow, knowing she wanted to be alone, and went out to join Ellen. They were in the sitting room when Sadie came out and handed him a large package of food. "I put in some for Randy," she said.

"He'll appreciate that; he's always been partial to your cooking. Goodbye, Ma; God be with you."

"An' with you, too. He'll see us th'ough." She took her son into her arms and held him for a long time. When she released him, he and Ellen went outside to the waiting horse.

Sadie came to the door and called to him, "Thank you for bringing 'im home to me."

"It was the least I could do," he replied.

He kissed Ellen goodbye and climbed on Skin. As he looked down at her before leaving, she raised her hand, put it on his, and said, "She'll be all right. I'll look after her."

Buck smiled wanly; he knew she would.

Buck reached Plantersville well before daylight. He had to dodge a Federal cavalry patrol, but his trip was otherwise uneventful. He found Major Anderson in charge of the rear guard of a hundred men. The two of them decided to divide the small force into two squadrons, Anderson commanding one and Buck the other. One squadron would form in line of battle to hold off the Federal cavalrymen while the other moved down the road to take up a new position. When the first squadron became hard pressed, it would retreat hastily through the second squadron to take up another strong position beyond it. They did not hold the mass of Federal troopers in check, but they were able to delay their progress to give Forrest time to reach Selma and prepare to defend that place.

Forrest had arrived in Selma early on the morning of April 2. He immediately reported to General Taylor, his departmental commander, and then went about preparing for defense of the city. A courier was sent to Buford, whose division was south and southeast of Selma, to join him as soon as possible.

Selma, a city of 8,000 people, was situated on a bluff well above the highwater mark on the north side of the Alabama River. The land sloped gently upward to the north, and the area surrounding it was mostly cultivated land. The outer line of earthworks and stockades extended in a semicircle of about three miles in length from the river bank east of the town to the river bank at the west. There was an inner, but not yet completed, line covering the principal roads into the city.

The most intense excitement prevailed in Selma. Everyone who could escape had fled to the country; and although Forrest in such emergencies was merciless in forcing all able-bodied male citizens into the ranks, he could not muster enough of them to man the defenses, despite an order issued on the morning of April 2 that every male citizen, no matter what his calling or position, "must go into the works or into the river."

Relying chiefly upon Armstrong's brigade which numbered 1,432 men, they were stationed to hold the left of the Confederate position. Roddy's men were placed on the extreme Confederate right, while the militia and new conscripts filled the center between the two commands. Rearward of the militia, Forrest was stationed with his escort and the Kentuckians of Crossland's brigade. So sparse were the 3,100 defenders that many of them were from six to ten feet apart in the defenses.

Forrest moved along the line talking to his men and encouraging them. When he came to the area defended by the militia, he saw a pompous young officer in the most resplendent uniform he had ever seen. "Who in the hell is that popinjay?" he asked General Dan Adams.

"That, General Forrest, is Captain Cornelius Gothrow of a local militia company he organized and equipped."

"He's struttin' around like a peacock showin' its tail feathers. I hope I don't have to depend on many like him to hold this place."

"You won't find many like him anywhere," General Adams replied.

Forrest completed the inspection of his lines and went to meet with General Taylor. The departmental commander asked, "Well, General, what do you think of the chances to hold Selma?"

"I don't think much of 'em. We're facin' the best armed troops I ever met—them repeatin' rifles they got fire six times as fast as those of my men. Besides, we got practically no grape or canister to repel an attack, an' I don't have much faith in the militia an' the men I conscripted— most of 'em are just boys an' old men who wouldn' be accepted for regular service. I've placed 'em between Armstrong an' Roddy, an' I've positioned my escort and Crossland's Kentuckians behind em' to support 'em an' hold 'em in place. I think, General Taylor, that you've got a greater responsibility than the defense of Selma; an' you ought to take a train out of here before this place is surrounded."

"It's that bad?"

"If you want to escape capture, you better leave now." General Taylor took Forrest's advice and left by the last train hauling ordnance, stores, and supplies out of the city.

Lady luck had smiled on Major General James Harrison Wilson more than once in this campaign. First, an apparently inept movement by Croxton turned out to be most effective by delaying Jackson to the point that he was unable to cross the Cahaba before the bridge at Centreville was destroyed. Then a courier was intercepted with messages which revealed that Forrest's troops were scattered, and this information proved extremely valuable to the Federal general in the disposition and movement of his own troops. On the afternoon of April 1, a British engineer named Millington, who had worked on the defenses at Selma, gave himself up to General Upton. He let his knowledge be known and drew a detailed sketch of the defenses, gun emplacements, and topography of the area. With this data, Wilson was able to make an effective plan of attack.

Wilson had his troopers on the march at an early hour on April 2. All wagons, camp-followers, animals, and surplus impedimenta were left in the rear so as not to delay or interfere with the fighting men. His subordinate commanders had been fully briefed on the importance of taking this city of arsenals and foundries, and the details of the defenses were thoroughly explained to them.

As the Federals approached Selma, General Long turned to his right and crossed over to the Summerfield road with his division, while Upton continued on the direct route. At three o'clock in the afternoon, the Federals arrived at a point where, from the higher ground, they caught sight of the city. Here they developed their battle line with the assaulting regiments and their supports dismounted, and the horses were taken to the rear.

In order to be safe from an advance by Chalmers or Jackson upon his right or rear, Long posted one regiment in this direction to protect his horses and the pack train. The rest of his division, about 4,500 strong, was posted across the Summerfield road. His front line contained about 1,500 men, and the remainder of his assaulting troops followed in close column and in supporting distance.

Upton's division was also moved rapidly into position, all dismounted except Alexander's brigade. He was on Long's left and was concealed from view of the Confederates by a small wood. Wilson placed one of his batteries on the Summerfield road and the other on the Plantersville road. Everything was in readiness for the assault, but Wilson decided to wait until dark to make it. Before it began, a part of Chalmers' division arrived and attacked the regiment which Long had placed to protect his flank and rear. General Long reinforced the regiment by another one and concluded that they could hold off the Confederates until the battle in front was won. Without reporting the attack on his rear to Wilson, or waiting for the prearranged signal to begin the assault, Long dashed forward and ordered his dismounted line to advance. The time was just after five o'clock.

It was a bold and courageous attack made by General Long and his men across an open area with approximately twenty artillery pieces opened upon them. A they approached the entrenchments, they met effective rifle fire from the Confederates behind the parapets. Thirty-eight men and four officers were killed and 270 more wounded, but Long's men kept coming with their Spencer repeating rifles and carbines spitting out their deadly fire. General Long was himself a casualty, falling with a bullet through his scalp within a few yards of the Confederate works, but his men could not be stopped. They climbed over each other's shoulders as they clambered up the works and over the parapets where they were bravely met in hand-to-hand fighting by the Southerners.

General Upton was not idle. When he heard the sound of fighting, he moved forward rapidly with his division against that portion of the line defended by the militia. These troops, made up principally of old men and boys with little training and no previous battle experience, gave way, leaving a gap through which the Union soldiers swarmed. Forrest rushed into the break and endeavored to stem the tide of disaster until Roddy could be moved over to unite with Armstrong. He saw the militia captain in the gaudy uniform running in wild panic to the rear. He leaped from his horse into the frightened man, and both went down. The general was quickly on his feet and grabbed Captain Gothrow by the lapels of his coat, "Git back in line you damn coward, or I'll kill you!" he yelled.

The terrified officer started to speak, but Forrest turned him around and, with a well-placed foot in the rear, propelled him back toward the fighting line.

The breach could not be closed; and the Federals swept through, forcing the defenders back and necessitating the withdrawal of Armstrong and Roddy to the second or interior line. Here they were again vigorously assailed. Forrest saw the officer in the bright uniform once more fleeing in fright to the rear; and without hesitation, he lifted his pistol and shot him. The bullet caught Captain Gothrow on the right side of the chin, taking off part of his lower jaw. He went down, but he was up again in a flash and running pell mell to the rear. The general started to take another shot at him, but his attention was needed elsewhere; the second line was now breaking.

Randy had been a witness to both incidents involving the general and Captain Gothrow. When he saw this second episode, he said to himself in a low voice, "Poor Bev."

Unable to stem the Federal onslaught, Forrest knew that further resistance was hopeless; but he had no intention of surrendering. He ordered his dismounted men to secure their horses and to escape the best way they could and to meet him west of the Cahaba river. Armstrong was still holding his men together and covered the stampede into and through Selma. Fortunately night came on; and many of the defenders, especially the militia, knew their way about the city. Forrest, with his escort and a considerable number of men from various detachments who rallied around him, escaped on the road toward Burnsville. Others got out by this same route before Upton discovered it. Armstrong, with a portion of his men, started out this way; but they took the wrong road and found the Federals across their path. He placed himself at the head of his men and cut his way through the enemy. Some even escaped across the Alabama River, General Dan Adams among them; but all who tried did not make it this way, for the river took its toll.[10]

After proceeding along the Burnsville road until he felt it was safe to do so, Forrest cut over to the Plantersville road on which the Federals had moved. Turning northward, he collided with the enemy and was compelled to fight his way through. A Federal cavalryman tried to cut him down; and the general killed him, the thirtieth opponent he had taken out of combat in close quarters fighting. This was his last personal encounter with the enemy, having had twenty-nine horses shot from under him in the "fightin' an' killin'" since his first engagement at Sacramento, Kentucky, in 1861.

On the same day that Selma fell, April 2, 1865, General Lee began his evacuation of Richmond and Petersburg. For all practical purposes, the Civil War was coming to an end.

Chapter XXIV

The Finale

As the advance guard of Forrest's escort moved along the narrow road in the darkness north of Selma, they came unexpectedly upon a Federal outpost near the residence of Mr. M. Godwin. The pickets, supposing that any troops approaching from that direction would be their own, did not realize that Forrest's men were upon them until they were made prisoners. Lieutenant George L. Cowan, commanding the escort in the absence of Captain Boone, who had been wounded the previous day in the fighting near Plantersville, learned from the captured troopers that they belonged to a small squadron of the Fourth United States Regulars who were camped near Mr. Godwin's home. He also learned that there was close by a small scouting party from the squadron. He decided to try to capture both groups.

When the remainder of the escort came up with Forrest and his staff, a detail was sent out to locate the scouting party and found them a little distance from the road, burdened with articles of jewelry, plate, and the like from nearby houses. The entire party was taken prisoner. It was now the turn of the men in the camp.

The pressure of the past three days' fighting, the wounds which were painful but not serious, the lack of sleep and rest, and the severe defeat at Selma were all showing their effects upon Forrest's strength and vitality. He seemed subdued and had little to say. As the troopers began dismounting to approach the Federal cavalry camp on foot, Forrest started, rather stiffly, to get down from his horse. "We have plenty of men without you and your staff, General; there are only about fifty of them," Lieutenant Cowan said. "I see no need for you to expose yourself unnecessarily—y'all stay here with the horses."

"We've got plenty of men to handle them," echoed Acting Lieutenant John Eaton; and several of the troopers chimed in to back him up.

Forrest stopped in his effort to dismount and settled back in the saddle, saying nothing.

The Confederates cautiously approached the Godwin home. A number of Federals were seen about campfires in the horse lot a short distance from the house. Cowan sent several men to surround the house and ordered another detachment to approach the horse lot from a different direction. Waiting until his men had time to get to their positions, he charged upon the regulars. They did not reach the fence around the lot before the aroused Federals began firing at them, and Lieutenant Cowan was wounded. It was a brief but bloody affair, with the regulars, veterans of many conflicts, bravely standing their ground. When the second group of Confederates opened upon them from a different direction, the surviving Union troopers leaped over the fence and made good their escape. Hearing the firing at the lot, two officers and an orderly, who were in the house, ran out and were shot. One of the officers was killed, and the other died the following day from his wound. A total of thirty-five men were killed or wounded, and five were captured. [1]

Rapidly resuming the march northward, the Confederates met and captured more plundering "bummers," and the results of that night's work were at least sixty killed, wounded, or captured. They reached Plantersville early on the morning of the 3rd and captured a Federal hospital and a considerable number of wounded in charge of Dr. McGraw of General Wilson's staff. Forrest halted here until four o'clock in the afternoon to give his men and their jaded horses food and rest.

The period of rest and refreshment seemed to revive the cavalry leader, for he was in a much better frame of mind. He had decided to go to Marion to reassemble his troops; and before mounting his men to resume the retreat, he called Buck and Randy over to him. "How far did you say your house is from here?" he asked Buck.

"About fifteen miles," he replied.

"An' yours would be about the same," he said to Randy. "How would you two like to go home an' git a belly full of sweet milk for a change?"

"I couldn't leave before right now," Buck replied with the trace of a smile.

"Nor I," Randy said.

"We should git to Marion sometime tomorrow mornin'. Y'all be there by the followin' mornin'."

The two friends started off, but Forrest called Buck back. The general seemed ill at ease as he said, "This ain't easy for me to say because it goes ag'in my nature to apologize, but I'm sorry about Saturday, specially for what happened to your pa. He give a good account of hisself, an' I prob'bly owe my life to 'im. I wasn't thinkin' straight when I acted the way I done."

"I understand, General. You've been going through a rough time the past few days."

"Your pa was quite a man. You may not know it, but he was the only man who ever beat me in a pers'nal fight."

"I knew it."

"You did? Who told you, Cally?"

"No one. He's the only man I've ever known who could have done it."

"I'm not so sure of that. I wouldna wanted to take on my brother Bill before he was wounded up around Sand Mountain, an' I sure don't feel up to takin' 'im on today; but that's enough of that—I know you're anxious to go home, so git goin'."

Buck needed no further encouragement and quickly rode over to where Randy was waiting. The two of them started westward down the road at a trot.

Right after they moved off, a skinny youngster, no more than a boy, turned off the Selma road onto the one they were taking. They did not see him, but General Forrest did; and his eyes lit up, for the youngster was leading Edgy, his mare from the Rushton stables. The general had given up all hope of ever seeing the animal again. As the boy rode up to him, he asked, "Where'd you git the hoss?"

"I'm a horseholder," the lad replied. "I know how much stock you place in this mare, so when they said to get out of Selma, I grabbed 'er and took off."

Forrest took the reins of the mare and anxiously began checking over the animal. Satisfied that she was all right, he asked, "What's your name, Young Fellow?"

"Patterson, sir; Ezra Jackson Patterson."[2]

The general looked at the youthful face and asked, "How old are you?"

"Sixteen."

"Sixteen?" he questioned.

"Well, I'm goin' on sixteen."

"An' I'm goin' on a hundred. Where you from?"

"Tullahoma."

"When's the last time you et?"

"Yesterday morning."

Forrest turned to his son, who was nearby. "Willy, see that this boy gets somethin' t'eat."

As they went off together, Forrest's orderly took the mare's reins. "She could use some feed herself," he said.

"Feed the boy's hoss, too." the general ordered.

The night before, six deserters, four Confederates from Hood's army and two Yankees from Wilson's cavalry were camped well off the road just south of Randolph. A slight noise coming from the direction of the road made all six of them grab quickly for their guns. "Take it easy, Fellas—I been watchin' you for twenty minutes an' don't mean no harm," a man said from the darkness of the nearby trees.

"Come out where we can see you," one of the Yankees commanded.

Jethro Barlow stepped out into the light of the campfire, both arms half raised and a rifle in his right hand. "I come peaceable," he said and walked over by the fire.

"Who be you, an' whatta you up to?" a tall, slim man in dirty and worn butternut asked.

"My name's Jethro Barlow, an' I'm just a bummer like y'all. Pickin's ain't been very good; an' from what I heared back there, y'all ain't doin' so good, neither. That smells like real coffee," he said looking at the pot on the fire.

"You got a cup?"

"I'll git it," Jethro said, turning to go back the way from which he had come."

"Leave the gun," one of the men in blue ordered.

Jethro reluctantly put down his rifle and walked off into the dark. He returned in about five minutes leading a mule and carrying a metal cup in his hand. Without asking, he helped himself to a cup of coffee. Sitting down in the circle of men, he took a sip of coffee and asked, "How'd y'all like to go after somethin' valu'ble—somethin' real valu'ble?"

"Like what?" asked the tall man in butternut, who appeared to be the leader.

"Gold," Jethro replied.

"Who's got gold in this pore-butt country?"

"A one-armed man who lives on a farm with just two womenfolks."

"Where?"

"'Bout thirty-five miles from here. We can time it to git there at dark tomorrow."

"How much gold you talkin' about?"

"Don't know exactly, but it oughta be consid'able. Folks say him an' his pa wanted ever'thing in gold, an' they're mighty thrifty folks who don't spend much. They been hoardin' it for years.''

''How long you knowed about this?''

''Some time now.''

''Why ain't you gone after it before?''

''With only one arm, he's still more'n one man can handle.''

A stocky man dressed in butternut laughed. ''I guess the seven of us can take 'im.''

''If nothin' don't happen,'' Jethro replied.

As Randy and Buck travelled the road westward from Plantersville, they had no idea of what was ahead for them. Jethro and the six deserters had moved south until they came to the road which would take them past the Barlow place to the McCord home. As planned, they reached it just after dark. Jethro was unaware that Cory had been killed, and he was taking no chances. The seven cutthroats stopped a quarter of a mile short of the house, hid their mounts in a wooded area, and proceeded the rest of the way on foot.

Those inside the McCord home had finished supper, Sadie and Ellen eating in the dining room and Artie and Vira in the kitchen. Artie had left and returned to the cabin, and Sadie was telling Vira which of the leftover food was to go in the slop for the hogs. Ellen had gone to her room and was putting the baby down for the night.

Since Jethro was reasonably familiar with the McCord place, the others were letting him call the shots. He sent the tall man with two others through the large gate to the rear of the house and posted one of the band at each side of the front porch. He and the seventh man planned to knock on the front door, and when it was opened, to charge into the house.

Artie was seated at the table in the cabin with the door open. He thought he heard a noise in the back yard and went to the door, ''Anybody dere?'' he called.

From off to his left, a voice responded in a low voice, ''Stay right where you're at if you wanta stay alive.''

Artie had a hand on each of the door jambs, and he froze in this position; but he called in a voice loud enough to be heard inside the house, ''Don't shoot, Mista—I ain't got no gun!''

''Damn you, shut up,'' the man off to the left hissed, his voice still low.

The women in the kitchen heard Artie's deliberately loud plea, and Sadie said to Vira, ''Latch the door''; and as the negro woman moved to close it and fasten the latch, Sadie went quickly to the dining room to check the door there. Finding it already latched, she pulled up a chair and got Buck's Mississippi rifle from the rack above it. She had no sooner gotten down than she heard a firm knock at the front door. As she went toward the sitting area, she rapped gently on Ellen's door and said in a hushed voice, "There's somethin' queer goin' on. Somebody at the back, an' now somebody's knockin' on the front door."

Sadie went to the middle of the sitting room and called, "Who's there an' what do you want?"

"We want to talk to Mr. McCord," a voice replied.

"What do you want to talk to 'im about?"

"That's between us an' him," came the response.

"You'll have to come back later—Mr. McCord ain't here."

The sound of muffled voices outside the door could be heard. Ellen, who had come out of her room, went back inside and got the pistol Buck had left with her. The voice from the porch was again heard. "Open this door, or we'll tear it down—we're comin' in."

"You come th'ough that door, an' one of you ain't goin' back out," Sadie replied.

On a signal, two of the men hurled their bodies against the door from the outside at the same time that two more thrust porch chairs through the windows of the front bedrooms. The wooden latch splintered, and two of the men stumbled into the room. Sadie fired at one of them, and he went down clutching his chest. Ellen raised her pistol and fired at the other, but the shot only creased the side of his arm; and he ran into the kitchen, which the frightened Vira had left, having sought safety in the pantry.

A man in a gray uniform appeared at the door of the company room, and Ellen turned the pistol on him. Holding it with both hands this time, she fired more deliberately; and the man went down. She cocked the gun and waited, watching the kitchen door across the room from her. The sound of the shots had awakened C. C., who was now crying loudly. The noise drowned out the sound of a man emerging cautiously and quietly from the closet connecting the two bedrooms on this side of the house. He slipped up behind Ellen and grabbed her, pinning both arms to her sides. It was Jethro, "That'll be enough of that!" he said.

The man in butternut now emerged from the kitchen with his gun pointed at Sadie, "Don't make no moves," he said and removed the empty rifle from her hands.

Jethro took the pistol from Ellen and said to the Confederate deserter, "Open the back door an' let 'em in."

The tall man in butternut and the other two came through the opened door. One of the latter was pushing Artie ahead of him with a rifle at his back. The tall man looked at the bodies on the floor and asked, "Are they dead?"

"I think Jenkins is—I don't know about Frank." The Confederate walked over to the man Ellen had shot and rolled him over with his foot far enough to see his face. "If he ain't dead, he soon will be," he commented.

Jethro looked at Sadie. "Where's your husband?"

"He ain't here."

"I know he ain't here, Lady. Now tell me where he's at, or you'll git the butt of this gun on the side of your dumb head."

Sadie did not reply; she glared at Jethro, determined to tell him nothing. Barlow raised the gun and was about to strike her. Ellen cried out, "Wait, don't hit her! He's dead."

"He wasn't dead last week—I seen 'im."

"We buried him yesterday afternoon in the family cemetery on the hill."

"Up by them oaks?"

"Yes."

"Go take a look," he said to the man whom Ellen had nicked on the arm.

The man left and returned shortly, "There's a fresh grave up there."

"All right," Jethro said to Sadie. "You tell us—where's the gold?"

"I don't know what you're talkin' about—I don't know nothin' about no gold."

"You know Lady, an' you're gonna tell." He went into the bedroom to the crib and picked up the crying baby. Ellen started toward him, but the tall man grabbed and held her. She struggled but was unable to break free.

Jethro returned to the dining room with the crying C. C. He grasped the baby by the ankles with his right hand, and said to Sadie, "Now you start talkin' if you don't wanta clean this brat's brains off of your wall."

"Put the baby down—I'll tell you. Mr. McCord didn' tell me about his bus'ness, but if he had any gold, it'd be in the safety place."

"An' where's that?"

"In the chimly," she said. "I'll show you." Jethro put the baby down on the floor and followed Sadie into the bedroom. The man holding Ellen released her and went in after them, as did the rest of them except the one holding the rifle on Artie. Ellen went quickly to her child and picked him up.

Sadie pointed out the removable brick, and Jethro was so eager to get it out that his hands were shaking. When he finally managed to remove the brick, he reached in and brought out the box. His disappointment at its size and weight were clearly mirrored in his face, and he reached into the hole and felt around to be certain that he had not missed anything. Finding nothing more, he opened the box and emptied its contents on the bed. There were a five dollar gold piece and several silver coins. The rest was paper, Confederate bank notes and government bonds. Holding up the banknotes and bonds, he said, "These ain't hardly worth the paper they're on!" he exclaimed. Then to Sadie, "Where's the gold?"

"If he had any, he musta bought the bonds with it or used it to buy the last land," she replied.

"Not Cory McCord. It's hid somewhere. Bring me that baby ag'in," he said to one of the men.

Vira had slipped out of the pantry with a large butcher knife in her hand and had eased over by the door to the dining area. The man guarding Artie had his back to her as he was watching what was going on in Sadie's bedroom. Vira rushed at him with the knife upraised and brought it down with all her might into the left side of his back. "Run, Missy, run with the baby!" she screamed.

Ellen fled toward the back door. Two of the men rushed out of the bedroom to stop her, but Artie and Vira pitched into them, holding them up. Jethro and the tall man came to their help, but they were assailed from the back by the strong Sadie who had picked up a poker from beside the fireplace. They disposed of Artie and Vira with blows of rifle barrels to the head, but it took a bullet to stop Sadie, who was giving Jethro more than he could handle.

The delay wasn't long, but it was enough for Ellen to run into the barn, open the back door which led into the small pasture, and close it before she raced over to the rail fence which ran along the road. It was a bright, starry night, but the moon was not up. She knew that Roana was in the pasture somewhere; for all the other horses had been run into the woods, and the roan mare had been left to pull the buggy. She could not see the horse; and she could tell from the noise that the men were searching for her in the barn, cabin, and other outbuildings.

She went as quickly as she could to the far end of the pasture. She knew that she would probably give her position away if she whistled for the mare and thought about escaping into the wood across the road; but she believed it would be better to try to get to Prairie's Edge for help, if possible. She whistled shrilly and could hear the mare whinny over by the creek and then start moving, but the animal was not getting closer. Ellen whistled again, and she could now hear the horse coming toward her. She found a large stump near the fence where she could mount with the child; and putting C. C. down on the ground for a moment, she tore down a section of the rails so she could get out of the pasture without jumping the fence.

She had barely finished this task when Roana trotted up. She led the animal by the mane to the stump, gathered up C. C. from the ground, and climbed on the horse. As she went through the gap in the fence, guiding the mare by the mane, she could hear the cutthroats rapidly approaching from the direction of the house. She turned down the road, and put her heels to Roana's sides. She recognized the voice of the tall man saying, "You would leave the hosses a quarter of a mile on the other side of the house!"

At this time, Buck and Randy were on the Plantersville road at a cutoff which would lead to the McCord home about two miles away. When they parted, Buck wanted to put the spurs to Skin and race for home; but he knew his horse had been pressed hard for the past forty hours, and he could not bring himself to do it. When he came within sight of the house, he knew something was wrong; for several of the James negroes were around it. He hurried to the front gate; and Artie came out, "Mista Buck?" he asked.

Dropping off the horse, he replied, "Yes, Artie, what's wrong?"

"Thank God you're here. It was dat Mista Jethro Barlow; him and six mo' fellas come lookin' for Mista Cory's gold..."

"Ellen, the baby, and Ma—are they all right?"

"Miss Ellen got away wif the baby, but they done kilt your ma."

"Where did Ellen go?"

"Down the road toward Prehur's Edge. They followed her, but they had to git their hosses fust. We's just gittin' ready to go after 'em."

As Buck leaped on Skin, Vira came to the door. "Take care of Ma," he called to her and put the spurs viciously to Skin's sides—there was no thought now of saving the horse.

Buck reached the Plantersville road and had gone only a short distance toward the junction with the Selma road before he caught up with Randy. Barely slowing, he called to him, "Come on! Jethro and some cutthroats have been to the house, and they followed Ellen to Prairie's Edge!"

As they raced down the road, the white board fence soon came into view. "Come on, Skin," Buck pleaded. "I never jumped you much, but don't fail me now." He swung the horse as far to the right on the road as he could and then turned him sharply toward the fence. Skin did not let him down; the horse cleared the fence, and he was in the pecan grove. Randy was following closely; and he, too, made the jump. As they came into the open area of the back yard from between two cabins of the house servants, they heard a woman's piercing scream. Both men hit the ground running before their horses came to a stop, and their pistols were quickly in their hands.

As they ran up to the back door, Buck, who was in the lead, saw a tall man in a Confederate uniform scamper out of the butler's pantry with a bag which appeared to be full of loot. Without hesitation he fired, catching the man in the upper right arm near the shoulder. The man dropped the bag and turned to run down the hall, but Buck's second shot caught him; and he went down. The sound of one of the women crying came to them from upstairs. Together, he and Randy ran past the downed man and saw John Rushton's wheeled chair at the bottom of the stairs; and beyond that, Samuel was lying in the hall near the front door. When they reached the chair, they could see the crippled man was about half way up the stairs, struggling to pull himself and two rifles to the second floor.

"Hurry! For God's sake, hurry!" John pleaded.

Buck's two shots had alerted the men upstairs, and one of them, with a ready rifle in his hands, appeared in the hallway above. Before he could get a shot off, the two men rushing up the stairs fired almost in unison; and the shots sent him reeling backward. When they reached the top of the steps, they could see him on the floor at the far end of the hall. Carolyn, her dress torn and her hair disheveled, came out of a guest room on the right. "Thank God you got here in time! Ellen's in her room and Sally's in yours," she cried.

Randy ran down the hall to his room. A man in blue was trying to climb out the window onto the roof of the back porch; and Randy shot him twice, the force of the bullets carrying him onto the sloping surface. Randy hurried to the window and got there in time to see the man roll off the edge of the roof to the ground below.

He looked for Sally and could see one of her feet, from which she had lost a shoe, sticking out from under the bed. Getting down on his hands and knees, he looked under the bed and saw Sally turn loose the bedropes which she had been holding onto for dear life. It was obvious that she had taken refuge under the bed and that the man had been trying to pull her out. The fear of what might have happened over, Randy could not help laughing nervously. "Did you lose something under there?" he asked.

"Randy! Is that you?" Sally cried, as she scrambled out from under the bed.

He lifted her to her feet; and she looked around for the man who had tried to assault her but did not see him. "Where is that damned Yankee? I hope you killed him. Do you know what he was trying to do to me?"

"I've got a pretty good idea; I think he's dead now."

All at once the starch went out of her, and she wilted. As she fell against him, her arms went around him for support; and she said, "Oh, Randy; I was so frightened," and she began to cry.

He held her tightly. "It's all right now," he said. "It's all right. Go ahead and cry it out, but it's over."

Buck did not have as far to go as Randy; Ellen's room was opposite the one from which Carolyn had emerged. He rushed through the door with his pistol in hand; but he came to a quick stop, for across the room Jethro Barlow was holding Ellen as a shield. He had one arm tightly around her waist, and in the other he had a Bowie knife with the point at her throat. "One wrong move, an' I'll slit 'er gullet."

Buck stood motionless. His eyes rapidly scanned the room, and he saw a rifle leaning against the foot of the bed. He noticed that Jethro had a bloody face and head as though he had taken a terrible beating. "Looks like we've got a standoff," he said.

"You've got a standoff; I've got your wife," Jethro replied boldly, but inside he was a frightened man. He had lost all interest in gold— now he wanted only to get out of this alive.

"Be careful of that knife," Buck said slowly in a voice that was cold and menacing. "If anything happens to her, there's no place this side of hell you can hide that I won't find you; and when I do, you'll wish you were there already."

Jethro knew enough about the McCords to know this was no idle threat; he wanted no part of Buck now or ever on his trail. There was no way he could get to his rifle and stand a chance against the man if he harmed his wife; she, alone, was his only security. "Do as I tell you, an' nothin'll happen," he said. "Fust, put up that gun, an' then take off the gunbelt."

Buck returned the gun to the holster, unbuckled the belt, and placed the belt and guns in a nearby chair. Then he said to Ellen, "Be careful, Honey, and do as he says."

"Back out into the hall an' to the head of the steps, but keep in my sight." Jethro commanded.

As Buck painstakingly followed these directions, Jethro moved at the same pace until he was at the doorway, still holding Ellen in front of him. "Now you back real slow-like down the steps, an' I'll come after you. Where's your hoss?"

"Out back."

"We'll go to the hoss when we git down the steps."

At this time, Randy and Sally came into the hall behind Jethro.

"Don't do anything foolish, Randy," Buck cautioned. "He's got a knife at Ellen's throat."

The stairs were clear; Samuel had recovered, and he and Carolyn had gotten John into his chair. Buck backed slowly down the steps to the first floor, taking care to keep in sight of Jethro who was following awkwardly with Ellen. They moved through the first floor hall, across the back porch, and down the steps in the same manner. As they neared the two horses, standing together unhitched in the yard, Jethro ordered Buck to move over to the side. Keeping Ellen between him and her husband, he made his way first to the rear of Randy's horse where he took the knife away from Ellen's throat long enough to jab the horse quickly in the rear with it. The animal ran off into the pecan grove.

Jethro was not sure how he would be able to mount the other horse and make his getaway, but the sight of the pistols in saddle holsters and the Whitworth in its sheath seemed to be the answer to his problem. He reasoned that he could take the rifle out of the sheath faster than he could open a holster and get a pistol. One thing was certain; he had to kill Buck. After what had happened to Sadie McCord, he knew that his own life wouldn't be worth a wooden nickel as long as Buck lived.

Buck was aware that once Jethro had his hands on a gun, he would use it, but he also knew there would be a short time between the release of Ellen and getting the gun; and this was the moment for which he was waiting. Fortunately the rifle was on the side of the horse toward Buck, and Jethro didn't think to order him around to the other side.

Jethro backed slowly until he was close to the horse and by the rifle. He was certain that he would be able to get the rifle out and shoot Buck before the latter could get to him. With a quick movement, he threw Ellen out of the way to the left and whirled to get the rifle from the sheath, but he was not fast enough. Buck's Bowie knife was in a sheath attached to the back of his trousers belt. With a fast movement of his left hand, he raised the tail of his coat; and with an equally quick movement with his right, he pulled out the knife and threw it. As Jethro turned toward Buck with the rifle in his hands, the knife caught him at the base of the throat. About the same time, he was thrown against the horse by the impact of a heavy bullet fired from the back porch roof where Randy was standing in the shadows with the rifle of the man he had killed. Jethro made a strange gurgling sound, and his knee slowly buckled as he went to the ground.

Buck knew he had made a lucky throw—he had aimed for a lower and wider part of the body. Striking a vital part of the throat at that distance was more by chance than skill. He went quickly to Ellen and helped her to her feet, but he kept a wary eye on Jethro, who was now on the ground writhing in pain from the mortal wounds. As he watched, Jethro stopped struggling and lay still. "Are you all right?" he asked Ellen anxiously.

"Yes, I'm fine," she replied as she brushed dirt from her dress.

He held out his arms, and she came to him. "You're trembling," she said in surprise.

"I know," he replied. "I've never been so damned scared in my life. They killed Ma, and I knew Jethro would just as quickly kill you."

Ellen drew back in surprise and horror. "They killed Ma? I should never have left her, but everything happened so fast."

"What did happen?"

Ellen related the events as far as she knew them, and Buck said in disbelief, "She let them kill her for the stinking gold? Why didn't she tell them where it was? It wasn't worth her life."

"I don't think it was a question of equating the gold with her life—it was a matter of principle with her. The gold was something that belonged to Pa which he valued, and she wasn't going to give it up to them."

"There may not have been any—maybe Pa did buy bonds or the land with it."

"No. It's still there in its hiding place. We had a long talk this afternoon, and she said she wanted me to know about it in case anything happened. She was going to show me tomorrow where it's hidden."

"I can't see it. Her life for the gold—it doesn't make sense."

"There's something else you ought to know. She said she knew when Pa left to join up with y'all that he wouldn't come back alive and that the biggest part of her life went out when Pa died. She knew where he is, and she was just biding her time until she could join him. She felt that the Lord left her here without him for some purpose, and she wanted to fulfill that purpose and join Pa."

"I don't know what it could have been—she wasn't here long after Pa died. Ma could get some peculiar ideas at times, especially where her faith was concerned. We'd better go in and see if the folks in the house are all right. Then I want to go home and see about Ma."

"*We'll* go home to see about Ma."[3]

Then they saw them, the Rushton people, men and women. Led by Golan, they had the house surrounded. In their hands they carried every conceivable weapon available to them, knives, axes, hatchets, scythes, pitchforks, hoes, handles of all descriptions, and even hammers. They had come to defend the home and family of their master and landlord.

Buck and Ellen left C. C. at Prairie's Edge and went home. On arrival, they found that some of the James women had cleaned up the house and the men had disposed of the three dead men. Vira and one of the women had taken care of Sadie and prepared her body. They had laid her out on the freshly made bed in her best dress. It was not until Buck saw her this way that the realization of his great loss struck him. He knelt by his mother's bed, placed his face down on a quilt she had made; and all the pent up sorrow for her and Cory poured out. Ellen knelt beside him and gently placed her arm around his shoulders. The negro women quietly slipped out of the room to leave them alone with their grief.

Fifteen minutes later, Buck and Ellen, both now fully composed, came out of the room and went to the back porch where the negroes had gathered. Vira and Artie were both there. Buck said to all of them, "I want you to know that I appreciate everything you have done for us tonight. Your friendship to my family through the years has always been something we valued, but there are two among you who deserve our special thanks. Tonight Vira and Artie did a very brave thing at the risk of their lives; and because of it, my wife was able to escape and save our son. We shall always be grateful to them for this."

"It wasn't just us," protested Artie. "It was mos'ly Miss Sadie. Me and Vira couldna stopped 'em, but Miss Sadie grabbed that big poker an' lit into 'em like Samson lit into the Philistines with the jawbone of un ass. She was somethin' to behold! She'da kilt that Barlow man if'n the tall skinny one hadn' shot 'er."

"An' that's the truth, Mista Buck—the whole blessed truth!" Vira said emphatically.

Buck and Ellen looked at each other. Now they understood the blood and abrasions on Jethro. "Maybe that was the purpose," Ellen said softly.

He thought of Ellen here with him and of C. C. safe and sound at Prairie's Edge, mainly because of his mother. Did she really have this purpose in being there? "It could have been; and if it was, she fulfilled it with a vengeance," he replied.

Somehow, knowing this and that it wasn't for the gold, made the pain of her loss easier to bear. They went back inside the house arm in arm, and he said to Ellen, "Don't ever feel guilty about leaving with the baby. That's what they all were fighting for and what Ma died for. You did your part, and it was the thing to do; their efforts and sacrifice would have been for nothing if you hadn't done what you did. You deserve as much credit as they for saving the baby."

Ellen did not reply, but she tightened her arm around his waist—she felt better about it, too.

Early on the morning of the 5th, Buck said goodbye to Ellen and C. C. and rode to Prairie's Edge to meet Randy. His mother's funeral the day before had been a sad one for him, and he was reluctant to leave Ellen again with the danger of deserters and bummers about. They had decided that she would spend her nights at Prairie's Edge and go to the farm each day to see about things there. Buck had talked with Artie and was convinced that the young man was capable of taking care of the stock. With most of the animals in the woods, there wasn't much to be done at this time except to see that they were properly fed. Randy joined up with him at Prairie's Edge, and they continued on to Marion. Buck had a lot of things on his mind and would have preferred to ride in silence; but Randy was bubbling with pride and excitement over his baby daughter, and Buck knew it would not be possible to shut up his friend without offending him.

They arrived at Marion to find that General Forrest had established his headquarters in the James P. Tarry home on West Lafayette Street. The general's wounds had been treated at the Confederate hospital on the Howard College campus, now commonly known as the Forrest Hospital; and he was carrying his right arm in a sling. There were no serious injuries; but the arm, which he had used to ward off saber blows, was badly bruised and painful. When he had arrived at Marion at ten a.m. on the 4th, he found General Jackson there with his division, Chalmers with Starke's brigade of his division, and the entire train and most of the artillery brought from Mississippi still intact. Stragglers from the battle at Selma were drifting in. One of Forrest's first acts was to establish a strong picket line along the Cahaba River. He set his staff to work getting his command in condition for service and in recruiting and in replacing his worn out horses and mules.

On the 6th, two of the pickets brought in an officer from General Wilson's staff who was travelling under a flag of truce. Wilson asked for a meeting to discuss the exchange of prisoners and other matters of interest, and Forrest agreed to meet him the following day at Cahawba. After the meeting with the Federal emissary was over, the general asked Randy and Buck, "You two fellows familiar with Cahawba?"

"Yes sir," each replied.

"Where could I make my headquarters there?"

"Aicardi's Hotel would be a good place," Randy said.

"I'll want you to go with me to the meetin' with General Wilson tomorrow."

They went to Cahawba the following morning by train, but General Wilson did not show up. He tried to make the trip, but swollen streams and swept-away bridges made him give it up. He managed, however, to get word to Forrest through the pickets that he would try again the following morning. His second attempt was successful; and, upon arrival, he went to the home of Colonel Matthews, who lived in the Crocheron home at the intersection of Cahawba Street and 2nd Street North.

Although Colonel Matthews was a wealthy planter and slaveholder, he did not give up his allegiance to the Union. He sent an invitation to Forrest for him and his staff to have midday dinner with them. The Confederate general appeared at one p.m. with his two staff members. The Southerners were ill at ease, and Forrest was very reserved; and he seemed to be relieved when Colonel Matthews interrupted to say, "Gentlemen, I've been told that dinner is ready. In order to enjoy it while it's still hot, may I suggest that we eat now and you continue your discussion afterward."

The entire group sat down to a bountiful Southern dinner; and with the good food and good cheer, the reserved Confederates soon relaxed in the pleasant atmosphere. When it was over, the two generals retired to the parlor to talk privately. Wilson tried to discuss other military operations and their possible consequences; but Forrest had little to say, although he was unable to conceal his unhappiness over the way things were going for the Confederacy.

General Wilson had requested the meeting because of his concern over what may have happened to General Croxton, whom he had sent in the direction of Tuscaloosa, having heard nothing from him since the latter part of March. He feared his division commander may have suffered a severe defeat, and said, "General, I should like to discuss with you the exchange of prisoners. I have 2,700 of your men."

"I'm afraid you're bringing up a matter in which I have no authority. You are holdin' consid'ably more of my men than I have of yours, an' the diff'rence would have to come from our military prisons. I will, however, git in touch with my superiors an' see if anything can be worked out. I'll let you know later."[4]

"I thought you might have taken some of General Croxton's men prisoner."

"Not many. He seems to be wand'rin around like Moses in the wilderness."

Having learned what he wanted to know, General Wilson ended the meeting with the statement that he had to get back to Selma. Forrest and the two members of his staff returned to Marion. It was here that the first unconfirmed reports were received that General Robert E. Lee had withdrawn from Richmond and Petersburg and was in retreat, but these were not accepted as factual.

Wilson left Selma and moved on to Montgomery, which fell to him with no resistance. He notified General Thomas from the first Confederate capitol that there was no force to oppose him and that supplies were sufficient to subsist his command. He thought Forrest would follow him as he moved toward Columbus, Georgia.

Forrest had no such intention. He knew that he could do little more than harass Wilson's rear and that this would serve little military purpose. Moreover, the Federal cavalry was on its way out of his department into that of another command. He remained in Marion until he moved to Gainesville, Alabama, arriving there on April 15. It was here that rumors reached his command that Lee had surrendered at Appomattox Court House on April 9. These created consternation among his soldiers, and on the 25th he issued an address to his troops in which he said that he did not believe that General Lee had surrendered, and he urged every man to "stand firm at his post and true to his colors."

Five days later Forrest was notified by General Richard Taylor that he had entered into an agreement with General Canby, of the United States Army, for the cessation of hostilities. He immediately called a meeting of his staff and announced this latest development to them.

"What do you propose to do?" Major Anderson asked.

"Comply with Gen'ral Taylor's orders."

"General, most of the men will go wherever you lead them. We can cross the Mississippi and join up with General Kirby Smith," Major G. V. Rambaut suggested.

"The war's been lost. The Yankees now control most ever'thing this side of the Mississippi—who would support an army in the West? I see no hope in continuin' the fight. I never believed in sacrificin' men for no purpose; that's why I didn' go after Wilson. Enough of 'em's died as it is."

Major Strange then spoke up. "General, I agree wholeheartedly with everything you say. I think further resistance would be absolutely useless. What I am concerned about is your personal safety. You have gotten some very bad publicity in the Northern press. I'm afraid you may be singled out for special punishment. You should consider going to Mexico, Cuba, or England."

"How many of the men could I take with me?"

Surprised at the question, Major Strange said, "Why, none, I suppose; at the most, very few."

"Major, I never asked my men to do nothin' I wouldn' do myself. I can't ask 'em to sign surrender an' loyalty statements while I run off. I've shot men for less. I'll take my chances along with them."

"You're right, General. Please accept my apology for thinking you would do otherwise. My interest in your future safety got the better of my judgment."

"Your apology is accepted, Major; an' I do appreciate your concern."[5]

On May 6 an official circular was issued to the troops announcing the surrender of Lee's army on the 9th of April and later that of General Joseph E. Johnston in North Carolina.

About this time it was reported to General Thomas that Forrest did not intend to surrender and that he would lead his command across the Mississippi to Texas and Mexico, marching by the way of Memphis, which he proposed to capture. Thomas placed so much credence in the rumor that he telegraphed General Hatch at Eastport, Mississippi: "Send under a flag of truce a summons to Forrest to surrender upon the terms given by General Grant to Generals Lee and Johnston. Inform him of the rumors which have reached you, and that you are prepared for him, and if he attempts such a reckless and bloodthirsty adventure, he will be treated thereafter as an outlaw, and the States of Mississippi and Alabama will be so destroyed that they will not recover for fifty years."

It required all of Forrest's tact and influence with his troops to persuade some of them to surrender. Many were overwhelmed with disbelief and grief, and they gathered in groups to discuss the situation. Some openly wept like children, and others said they would never surrender as long as they had horses and guns; and these latter proposed to Forrest that he lead them to the Trans-Mississippi Department to continue the struggle. To this he replied, "No, what could not be accomplished here could never be done in the thinly settled West."

The men eventually accepted the wisdom of their commander's decision and disconsolately consented to the surrender. On May 9, Brigadier General E. S. Dennis arrived at Gainesville as the Federal Commissioner to execute their paroles. The night before, many of the units, like the Seventh Tennessee regiment, solemnly gathered around their bullet-torn battle colors and reverently cut the flag into fragments so that each could carry away with him a bit of the beloved emblem of their unit and its heroic conduct.

Major General W. H. Jackson was appointed as the Commissioner on the part of the Confederates to authenticate muster rolls, in duplicate, of each general and his staff; of each regimental staff; of each quartermaster and commissary, and their employees; and of each company. To each noncommssioned officer and private was then issued a certificate of parole, bearing the number opposite their names, respectively, on the muster rolls. Each of these was signed by the two Commissioners.

The officers were required to sign the following obligation in duplicate:

"I, the undersigned, prisoner of war, belonging to the Army of the Department of Alabama, Mississippi, and East-Louisiana, having been surrendered by Lieutenant-General R. Taylor, Confederate States Army, commanding said department, to Major-General E. R. S. Canby, United States Army, commanding Army and Division of West-Mississippi, do hereby give my solemn parole of honor that I will not hereafter serve in the armies of the Confederate States, or in any military capacity whatever against the United States of America, or render aid to the enemies of the latter, until properly exchanged in such manner as shall be mutually approved by the respective authorities."

This was approved by both Commissioners, and General Dennis added his endorsement that the officer in question would "not be disturbed by the United States authorities as long as he observed his parole and the laws in force where he resides."

On the day of Brigadier Dennis' arrival, Forrest issued the following farewell to his men:

(Circular)
"HEADQUARTERS FORREST'S CAVALRY CORPS,
"Gainesville, Alabama, May 9, 1865.
"SOLDIERS,—By an agreement made between Lieutenant-General Taylor, commanding the Department of Alabama, Mississippi, and East Louisiana, and Major-General Canby, commanding United States forces, the troops of this department have been surrendered. I do not think it proper or necessary at this time to refer to the causes which have reduced us to this extremity, nor is it now a matter of material consequence as to how such results were brought about. That we are beaten is a self-evident fact, and any further resistance on our part would be justly regarded as the very height of folly and rashness. The armies of Generals Lee and Johnston having surrendered, you are the last of all the troops of the Confederate States Army east of the Mississippi River to lay down your arms. The cause for which you have so long and manfully struggled, and for which you have braved dangers, endured privations and sufferings, and made so many sacrifices, is to-day hopeless. The government which we sought to establish and perpetuate

is at an end. Reason dictates and humanity demands that no more blood be shed. Fully realizing and feeling that such is the case, it is your duty and mine to lay down our arms, submit to the 'powers that be', and to aid in restoring peace and establishing law and order throughout the land. The terms upon which you were surrendered are favorable, and should be satisfactory and acceptable to all. They manifest a spirit of magnanimity and liberality on the part of the Federal authorities which should be met on our part by a faithful compliance with all the stipulations and conditions therein expressed. As your commander, I sincerely hope that every officer and soldier of my command will cheerfully obey the orders given, and carry out in good faith all the terms of the cartel.

"Those who neglect the terms and refuse to be paroled may assuredly expect when arrested to be sent North and imprisoned. Let those who are absent from their command, from whatever cause, report at once to this place, or to Jackson, Mississippi, or, if too remote from either, to the nearest United States post or garrison, for parole. Civil war, such as you have just passed through, naturally engenders feelings of animosity, hatred, and revenge. It is our duty to divest ourselves of all such feelings, and, so far as it is in our power to do so, to cultivate friendly feelings towards those with whom we have so long contested and heretofore so widely but honestly differed. Neighborhood feuds, personal animosities, and private differences should be blotted out, and when you return home a manly, straightforward course of conduct will secure you the respect even of your enemies. Whatever your responsibilities may be to government, to society, or to individuals, meet them like men. The attempt made to establish a separate and independent confederation has failed, but the consciousness of having done your duty faithfully and to the end will in some measure repay for the hardships you have undergone. In bidding you farewell, rest assured that you carry with you my best wishes for your future welfare and happiness. Without in any way referring to the merits of the cause in which we have been engaged, your courage and determination, as exhibited on many hard-fought fields, has elicited the respect and admiration of friend and foe. And I now cheerfully and gratefully acknowledge my indebtedness to the officers and men of my command, whose zeal, fidelity, and unflinching bravery have been the great source of my past success in arms. I have never on the field of battle sent you where I was unwilling to go myself, nor would I now advise you to a course which I felt myself unwilling to pursue. You have been good soldiers, and you can be be good citizens. Obey the laws, preserve your honor, and the government to which you have surrendered can afford to be and will be magnanimous.

"N. B. FORREST Lieutenant-General"

Word went out to those on picket, scouting, and other duties to come to headquarters to surrender. As these and stragglers came in, the muster rolls grew until about 8,000 officers and men had been paroled and allowed to return to their homes by May 16. Among the last to come in was Cally, who had been scouting in northern Mississippi and Tennessee and did not take part in the defense of Selma.

Buck and Randy had been asked by Forrest to help in the parole process and were still in Gainesville when Cally arrived. He was not sure that he needed to be paroled, but wisely decided he should leave the decision to someone else. He lost no time in looking up Buck and took hard the news of the deaths of Cory and Sadie.

"What are your plans now that it's over?" Buck asked the old Tennessean.

"I been givin' it some thought, but I ain't sure yet," he replied.

"Come home with me, Cally. Like Ma once told you, there will always be room for your plate at our table. Besides, you know a lot about horses and cows, and I need you."

"I don't know, Buck. It won't be the same 'thout Cory an' Sadie. Miss Ellen is too elegant a lady to set at the same table with the likes of me day after day."

"I guess she showed how she felt about that when she named her first child for you."

Cally smiled with pleasure. "She did do that, didn' she?" he said. "Let me think on it, Buck. Whatever I do, I 'preciate bein' asked."

The work was done, and the time to go home had finally come. Buck had seen Cally again, but the old scout had not yet made up his mind about what he would do. Buck and Randy said their goodbyes to their friends, and they went in to see for the last time their commanding general, who was leaving the same day for his plantation home in northwestern Mississippi. It was a difficult time for men who were trying to hide their emotions. The hardships and experiences during the war years together had created mutual feelings of respect, loyalty, and affection between the general and his two staff officers which each would carry with him and cherish for the rest of his life. They had been strong men together, and they wanted to be equally as strong in parting.

The last few days had not been easy for Forrest, and he looked tired and haggard. "I guess you are ready to leave," he said. "Thank you for stayin' to help with the paroles; I know you were anxious to git back to those pretty wives of yours.''

"We were,'' Randy said, "but leaving the command isn't all that easy.''

"I know,'' Forrest replied sadly. Then trying to get the conversation on a more pleasant note, he said to Randy, "Tell your father that I still owe 'im for the mare, an' I'll be in position to settle up with 'im soon.''

"Daddy doesn't expect payment for the horse. Besides, that sack of coffee you sent him was far more than he would have gotten from the government.''

"The coffee was a gift. I'll be in touch with 'im. Guess you want to be on your way, so goodbye an' best of luck to you both. I feel fortunate to've had you serve with me.''

Forrest offered his hand; and Randy, who was closer than Buck, took it. He held it for a moment, and the sadness of each of the two men was registered on his face. When he released Forrest's hand, Randy impulsively embraced him. He felt the general stiffen and then relax as he clumsily returned the embrace. When they parted, Forrest said in a voice husky with emotion, "That was the fust time I ever hugged a man.''

"Get ready to hug another one,'' Buck said as he, too, embraced his commander.

By this time the eyes of all of them were filling with tears, and the two young officers turned to make a hasty departure. When they reached the door, Forrest called, "Just a minute!''

They stopped and faced the general. "Tell me, Buck,'' he said; "I seen you loosen the thong on your gun that day in Plantersville; you really wouldn' have shot me would you?''

"It depended on you, General.''

"How's that?''

"I was taking Pa home, and I would have shot anyone who tried to stop me.''

Forrest roared with laughter. Then he said, "You ain't changed a damned bit! As for you, Randy, don't think I didn' see you move to his side when you thought there might be trouble. You've changed a helluva lot from the young dandy who couldn' stand the sight of blood. You made the kind of soldier your folks can be real proud of. If I'm ever in another war, I want you two with me.''

"You know where to find us, but don't come for that reason—come as a guest. You'll always be welcome at either of our places,'' Randy replied.

With copies of the paroles in their pockets, the two officers set out for home. They reached Greensboro late that night and stopped at an inn. It was almost noon the following day when they parted at the road junction by Prairie's Edge, and each headed for his own home. As Randy rode up to the circle in front of the house, Sally came running out to meet him, "Where have you been?" she cried. "Didn't anybody tell you the war is over?"

Randy jumped off his horse and caught her, "It is now!" he said jubilantly as he lifted her off the ground and swung her around and around. When he stopped, Sally reached up with her right hand and gently caressed the scar on his cheek.

Buck rode up to his home and stopped at the front gate. He went inside the house but saw no sign of Ellen. Vira stuck her head out of the kitchen door to see who had come in and exclaimed, "Lawdy me, if it ain't Mista Buck. She's out back talkin' to Artie."

He heard C. C., whom he had awakened from a nap, and went in and picked him up. With the baby, who had immediately stopped crying, on his arm, he walked out the back door; and over by the barn he saw Ellen talking with Artie. The sound of his boots and spurs on the steps attracted her attention, and she turned around.

"I thought you'd never get here!" she exclaimed, and ran to him. He took her in his arms as well as he could while holding the baby, and she clung to him for a long time. When they parted, she said, "I was hoping Cally would be with you."

"I asked him to come, and he may yet. I think he was afraid he wouldn't fit in."

"He should know better than that! Maybe he'll come if I ask him. We'll have to get in touch with him."

Buck leaned down and kissed her gently on the forehead. When he raised his head, he said, "You are truly a wonderful person."

Ellen seemed a little embarrassed by the praise, and changed the subject by saying, "Let's walk up to the cemetery—I want you to see what I've done to Ma's and Pa's graves. It's just been finished."

They went slowly up the hill to the small grove of oaks. The two new graves, side by side, had been outlined together with a border of smooth river rocks and each had a small granite headstone showing the name, date of birth, date of death, and, as an emblem of their faith, a small cross. "That's real good, Ellen; simple and symbolic—the kind of thing they would want, especially Ma."

They stood there in respectful silence for a few moments, and then Ellen said. "Now that Pa's gone, I'd like to call the baby Cory."

"So would I," Buck replied. "I never cared much for the initials."

They turned to go back to the house; and from their vantage point the bend in the road to the southwest could be seen, and around it rode an old man in a buckskin suit. Buck smiled with pleasure; Cally was coming with his plate.

"There's Cally!" Ellen exclaimed. "I'm so glad."

"So am I; I didn't know how I'd be able to get in touch with him."

Buck was holding Cory in his left arm; and as they started down the hill to meet Cally, Ellen possessively clung to his right arm with both hands. "I can't believe the war is really over," she said. "It seems too good to be true."

"It's over, thank God," he replied. "The fighting and killing is finally over!"

THE END

NOTES AND COMMENTS

Chapter I

1. I digress from facts—the northern edge of the Black Belt lies a few miles farther south than I have placed it.
2. The Whitworth rifle was not perfected until 1857. In this story, performance of the gun is based upon what I have read of it; however, Ralph Walker, a Selma, Alabama, gunsmith who is knowledgeable about muzzleloaders, insists that it is not nearly as accurate as claimed.

Chapter II

1. Andrew Russell was my great-great grandfather. According to articles published in the *Greensboro Watchman* of January 27 and February 3, 1898, he and his two brothers were the first white settlers (in 1816) in the area of Greensboro, Alabama, which was originally known as Russell's Ridge. He was bothered by marauding Indians; and after having to hide in the wood and swamp from them, he moved into the northern part of Perry County. There he prospered in both worldly goods and children, having at one time sixteen offspring at his table. It was a common saying among the early settlers when a young married couple was without children, or was not increasing their family fast enough, "Indians ought to skeer 'em." His prosperity was attributed, "not so much to his own energy, but his wife was one of the most thorough going business women of all the pioneer class of that day...Their home was noted for its hospitality and the excellent food supplied to its numerous guests." I never knew my great-great grandmother, of course; but I believe that I have unintentionally patterned Buck's mother after the person I thought she might have been.

Chapter III

1. John Yeager was my paternal grandfather.

Chapter IV

1. It was customary in the South when I grew up for people to address their older friends by their first names, preceded by Miss for ladies and Mister for men. I regret that this custom is rapidly disappearing. For years I had not observed it being done until my daughter and her family moved to Fort Valley, a small town in central Georgia. It brought back pleasant memories to hear my granddaughters' friends address my daughter as "Miss Nancy" and my son-in-law as "Mister Russell," his given name. There is an elderly lady here in Leesburg, Florida, where I now live, who is still affectionately called "Miss Lucie K." by her younger friends; but this practice is not commonplace throughout the South today.

Chapter V

1. There has been controversy over who actually designed the first Confederate flag. In September 1919, forty-nine years after the first flag was raised over the Confederate capitol in Montgomery, Major Orren Randolph Smith of Henderson, North Carolina, claimed to have designed it. The United Daughters of the Confederacy, the United Sons of the Confederacy, and the United Confederate Veterans have all recognized Major Smith as the designer. This incident of the flag having been designed by Nicola Marschall is based upon a treatise presented to the College of Arts and Sciences at the University of Louisville on January 3, 1949, by Owsley C. Costlow, entitled "The Life of Nicola Marschall". On the campus of Judson College in Marion, Alabama, stands the "Marschall Oak," under which Nicola Marschall presented a Confederate flag of his design to a company of soldiers raised in that area.

Chapter VI

1. I have found D. C. Kelley's name in some references to be spelled Kelly and Hambrick's to be spelled Hamrick.
2. Despite slavery being accepted and legal in the South, slave trading was not looked upon as an honorable profession.
3. A departure from fact to bring in a fictional character. Kevin seemed a likely choice since none of my references showed who took Hambrick's place.
4. Leonidas Polk had been a classmate of Jefferson Davis at West Point but had left the army six months after graduation to enter the ministry. He was active in the founding of the University of the South at Sewanee, Tennessee, and was a bishop in the Episcopal Church when Davis appointed him as a major general.
5. Another variation of fact. The *Conestoga* departed but not because an officer and the pilot were shot. Some of Forrest's men did fire effectively into the vessel's gunports using Maynard rifles. They were: Sergeant Thomas B. Sheridan, later a major; Private R. H. Balch, afterward a lieutenant colonel; Private Aaron Burrows; and Surgeon S. M. Van Wick.
6. It was Private W. H. Terry who threw himself between Davis and Forrest, and he received a mortal wound in this heroic action to save his commander's life.

Chapter VII

1. Johnston has been criticized for not sending sufficient forces to Fort Donelson to defend it and to crush Grant; but in fairness to him, it must be remembered that, in addition to Grant's army, there was a mass of Federal troops under Buell facing what was left of the Confederate line in central and eastern Kentucky.
2. Forrest killed this sharpshooter with a Maynard rifle which he borrowed from one of his men. Berge sharpshooters were expert marksmen who worked as individuals rather than as a unit, dispersing in the morning with each man finding his own spot of concealment and vantage to snipe at the enemy.
3. I have used Wyeth's account of the battle of February 15. It differs

considerably from that of the Federal Major General Lew Wallace as recounted in *Battles and Leaders of the Civil War*. Wallace had a very low opinion of Brigadier General Gideon Pillow, both as a soldier and as an individual. Wallace said that as a result of their success attained in the morning, the Confederates had captured the road necessary for their escape, but "Pillow's vanity whistled itself into ludicrous exaltation. Imagining General Grant's whole army defeated and fleeing in rout for Fort Henry and the transports on the river, he deported himself accordingly...Without deigning even to consult his chief, he ordered Buckner to move out and attack the Federals...There was nothing to do but obey; and when Buckner had begun the movement, the wise program decided upon the evening before was wiped from the slate." Wallace is probably right in this, for the road to Nashville and the southeast had been opened for escape of the Confederates as planned; and Wyeth makes no mention of this, nor does he give any reason for the failure of the Confederates to make an effort to escape at that time, even though the Rebel soldiers made the attack carrying their knapsacks, indicating that they expected to keep moving. Wallace also claimed that his troops pushed back the Confederates into their entrenchments and reoccupied the battlefield at 3:30 o'clock that afternoon. Wyeth indicated that the Confederates were ordered by Pillow to retire within their entrenchments; that the ones on the left did so slowly and were followed a short distance by McClernand's division, which had been heavily reinforced; and that the Federal line occupied only a portion of the battlefield area. Wyeth's version is supported by Forrest's official report, made immediately following the battle, in which he stated that after the fight ended about 2:30 p.m., his troops were employed in gathering up arms and in assisting in getting off the wounded; that he was over the battlefield three times taking off the wounded and taking into the Confederate lines nine pieces of artillery he had captured and 4,000 stands of arms; and that he was two miles up the river on the road to the forge, and no enemy was in sight when dark came on. His report disputes a further claim by Wallace that Forrest made a reconnaissance that night and found not only that the ground had been reoccupied but also that the enemy had extended farther around the Confederate left. Forrest did not find it that way. The men he sent out saw only fires but no enemy. Forrest was of the opinion that these were old fires which had been fanned into flame by the high winds and fed by the wounded.

4. Forrest's and Pillow's men had not been engaged with the enemy since two o'clock that afternoon and Buckner's since six. A steamboat with ammunition was coming from Clarksville, and it did arrive on the

night of the 15th in time for the ammunition to be distributed, had the fight been continued on the 16th. As for rations, there were ample; for Grant reported having captured considerable provisions when the fort surrendered.

5. After Forrest left the conference with the generals, there occurred at Floyd's headquarters what has been described as a comic opera. The question arose as to what the Federal authorities would do with the prisoners. Floyd had been President Buchanan's Secretary of War and was under indictment in Washington. He announced that it was his intention to leave on the two steamers arriving from Clarksville and take as many of his men as the vessels would accommodate. Pillow insisted that he would also leave. Floyd tried to pass the command to Pillow, the next in line; but Pillow, who said that he would die before surrendering, refused to accept it. The command fell to Buckner, who held the same view about leaving, but he felt it was his duty to stay and surrender with his men.

Floyd left with most of his command on the two steamboats, and Pillow escaped across the Cumberland with some of his men. Approximately 1,500 men got out with the two of them.

In the early morning of the 16th, Buckner offered to capitulate and asked to discuss terms. Grant was in no mood for such a discussion and replied: "No terms other than immediate and unconditional surrender can be accepted. I propose to move immediately upon your works."

With no reasonable option, Buckner surrendered before an attack was mounted. Historians differ as to the number of men surrendered. Unfortunately, Grant made no record at the time; years later, he estimated the number to be 15,000. The historian Benson J. Lossing puts it at 13,500. John Allen Wyeth, by deducting from the total force the number killed, the wounded evacuated up river before the surrender, and those who escaped, calculated the number of prisoners to be 10,271. Regardless of the number, the loss of Fort Henry and Fort Donelson was a disaster for the Confederacy in more ways than one.

General Johnston, who had already withdrawn his forces from Bowling Green, now found the position of those in Columbus, Kentucky, untenable and ordered the river port evacuated. Abandonment of that citadel, with its guns commanding the Mississippi River, made possible the taking in March by the Federal forces of Island Number Ten, which had been fortified by the Confederates. The loss of that bastion resulted in the evacuation of New Madrid, thus opening the Mississippi as far south as Memphis. Nashville, endangered by the threat of attack by both Buell and Grant, the latter now less than a hundred miles away, was abandoned by General Johnston, who moved his headquarters to Murfreesborough. He later followed this with a retrograde movement which massed his troops at Corinth, Mississippi, not far south of the Tennessee border. Thus Kentucky was abandoned by the Confederates and much of Tennessee temporarily so. With Forts Henry and Donelson in their hands, river communications for the North were opened on both the Tennessee and Cumberland Rivers into the very heartland of the South. Gloom descended upon the new nation, and in some places panic ensued.

How the troops lost at Donelson might have affected the outcome of the battle at Shiloh, had they been available to Johnston and Beauregard, is a matter for historians and military strategists to ponder. What is known, however, is that the loss of the two river forts definitely played a very important part in the Confederates' failure to get England and France to recognize their new government, and that it came at the time when the North needed a victory to reverse the waning support of the war by its people.

Because of the surrender at Fort Donelson, a bright new star rose on the Northern military horizon. This success, together with the phrase "unconditional surrender," so conveniently fitting the initials of Grant's given names, caught the imagination of his fellow countrymen; and he became a national hero overnight. With his history of drinking, he was by no means in good favor with Major General Halleck, his immediate superior, nor with Major General George B. McClelland, the latter then serving as general-in-chief. In fact, he was held in such low esteem by both of them that serious consideration was given to placing him under arrest for his conduct following the victory. As it was, he was replaced in command by Brigadier General C. F. Smith. After being forced from the field in an earlier attempt to take Belmont, Missouri, and later allowing the garrison at Fort Henry to escape, his military career might well have come to an end at Fort Donelson had he failed to take the fort or had the garrison there eluded him.

Fort Donelson was a small battle with great consequences.

Neither the Confederate government nor history dealt kindly with Floyd or Pillow. President Davis relieved Floyd of all command in the Confederate army; however, he did later serve with the Virginia state forces. Pillow was reprimanded, suspended, and never thereafter given a command of any importance; however, Wyeth had a good opinion of him as did Forrest, who later requested that Pillow be assigned to serve under him. Buckner was exchanged in August 1862, and subsequently served the Confederacy with distinction in several major battles in the Western area.

Chapter VIII

1. In *The Blue and the Gray*, Henry Steele Commager furnished a description of the Rebel yell by Harvey Drew, a member of the Ninth Virginia Cavalry attached to General J. E. B. Stuart. According to Drew, it was: "Woh-who-ey! Who-ey! Who-ey!" The first syllable, "Woh," is sounded short and low; and the second, "who," with a very high and prolonged note deflecting upon the third syllable, "ey."

2. Wyeth's account indicated that Forrest contacted Beauregard. The Eastern Acorn Press publication *The Battle of Shiloh* reflects that he reported the information to General Hardee and to General Breckenridge and was directed to find Beauregard. Unable to locate the commanding general, who was sleeping in General Sherman's captured tent, he went back to Hardee and was told by that general to return to his regiment.

3. In his report dated April 8, 1862, to General Grant, Sherman stated: "The check sustained by us at the fallen timber delayed our advance, so that night came upon us before the wounded were provided for and the dead buried, and our troops being fagged out by three days' hard fighting, exposure, and privation, I ordered them back to their camps, where they now are."

4. *The Battle of Shiloh*, published by Acorn Press, contains a quote from the Confederate Private Henry Morgan Stanley (who later located Dr. Livingston in Africa) that the Rebel yell drove all sanity and order from the men and inspired them with the wildest enthusiasm.

5. The John C. Caraguey home is today the residence of Mr. and Mrs. Russell Bailey. When my wife and I were visiting a friend, Mrs. William H. Peeples, in Coffeeville a few years ago, we were invited to the Baileys' home for morning coffee. As we sat in the front parlor of this beautiful antebellum house, Mr. Bailey told us some of its history. He said it had been used as a hospital after the Battle of Shiloh, and on a window pane behind where I was seated were the initials of a Confederate soldier who had scratched them there with a diamond ring. I saw the letters "GPR" on the pane. Mr. Bailey said the initials were believed to be those of a Confederate soldier from Virginia named Greek P. Rice. I digressed in the story by having the wounded soldier to be from Coahoma County, Mississippi. I had a good friend of the same name, the late Judge Greek P. Rice of Clarksdale, Mississippi, in Coahoma County, whose forebears came to Mississippi from Virginia. The coincidence of the unusual names makes a family connection almost a certainty. I'm sorry Greek never knew about this window.

Chapter IX

1. Terry's Rangers derived the name from its first colonel, who fell in a skirmish near Green River, Kentucky, in 1861.
2. Forrest's adjutant, Major J. P. Strange, is usually given credit for writing Forrest's communications and putting them in grammatically acceptable language during this period, and later Major Anderson did this; however, Forrest, although uneducated, expressed himself well and was quick to detect an unclear statement or an awkward phrase; the wording may not have been his, but the thoughts were.
3. At this time, Federal forces under Grant were in control of northern Mississippi; and those under Buell had occupied the middle and western portions of northern Alabama. Grant had established his headquarters at Corinth, Mississippi; and Buell had his at Hunstville, Alabama. Both Grant and Buell had long lines of supply extending from the Ohio River across Kentucky and Tennessee by railroad and by the Tennessee and Cumberland Rivers. The raid on Murfreesborough created consternation among the Federal forces. Buell ordered Major General McCook to move with his division to Columbia, Tennessee, as the Rebel cavalry was threatening the Franklin and Columbia bridges of the railroad connecting Hunstville to Nashville via Decatur, Alabama. Colonel Miller, commanding at Nashville, withdrew his troops temporarily from Lebanon and placed strong pickets and patrols on all roads leading to Nashville. Buell ordered reinforcements to him and ordered General Nelson at Athens, Alabama, to move into Tennessee. He also ordered General George H. Thomas at Tuscumbia, Alabama, to march with all rapidity to Murfreesborough. Grant also sent troops into Tennessee from northern Mississippi. An all-out effort was being made by the Federal commanders to protect their supply lines and to corral Forrest.
4. On July 18, Forrest moved out at the head of his column toward Lebanon, Tenessee, about thirty miles east of Nashville. Arriving near Lebanon on the 20th, he found that the Yankee troops there had learned of his advance and that they had retired to Nashville. He followed them; and four miles from that city, he came upon a strong stockade manned by twenty men guarding a bridge. He now had cannon; and he quickly convinced them that their stockade could not stand an artillery attack. They surrendered, and he burned the bridge. Moving farther around the city, his advance guard, the Eighth Texas, had a lively encounter with a detachment of Federal troops at Antioch Station and captured them. The depot there, filled with government supplies, was destroyed; and all

rolling stock was burned. He moved in close to Nashville, skirted the city and turned southward toward Murfreesborough. On the road to that place, he captured another contingent of men guarding a bridge and burned the bridge. He camped twelve miles south of Nashville on the 21st, and here he paroled his prisoners. He moved again toward Murfreesborough and captured a wagon train with 360 of the Thirty-Sixth Indiana regiment which had left Nashville on the 20th.

Chapter X

1. Grant reinforced General Sullivan at Jackson, Tennessee, with troops from his army at Oxford; and forces from Corinth and Forts Heiman, Henry, and Donelson were sent to cooperate with him. Colonel Robert G. Ingersoll (the famous lawyer and lecturer) who commanded the Eleventh Illinois cavalry, reported on the 18th that Forrest had crossed the Tennessee the previous day 3,000 infantry, 800 cavalry, and six pieces of artillery and was still crossing the river at Wright's Island. Also, General Grant wired Admiral Porter that Forrest and Napier were on the west side of the Tennessee with between 5,000 ad 10,000 men. On the same day Brigadier General J. C. Sullivan reported that his cavalry was whipped at Lexington and that Colonel Ingersoll had been taken prisoner by the enemy, reported to be between 10,000 and 20,000 men. He also reported that Cheatham's brigade (infantry) and Napier's command were west of the river. On the 19th, Grant reported to his superior that he had reinforced Sullivan to the full extent of the capacity of the roads to carry them. He thought the enemy must be annihilated, but it could be trouble and could require additional forces from Oxford. At Columbus, Kentucky, Brigadier General Thomas A. Davies, acting on what he believed to be reliable information that Forrest had 7,000 troopers and ten pieces of artillery backed by a large infantry force, ordered General Fisk's brigade to reinforce him at Columbus. Forrest had the pot boiling, and he would keep the fire under it.
2. Ingersoll was subsequently exchanged; but he returned to civilian life soon afterward, feeling that the army wasn't for him.
3. Dibrell was sent with his regiment and a section of artillery under Lieutenant Morton to attack the stockade at Forked Deer Creek and to destroy the bridge the garrison was guarding. Starnes and his Fourth Tennessee were ordered to capture Humboldt. When he arrived there, Starnes wasted no time with parley or flags of truce but charged in

among the Yankees, who surrendered immediately. He took more than 100 prisoners, burned the supplies he could not carry off, and destroyed the railroad depot and the nearby trestle bridge. Forrest moved on Trenton with the rest of his force and was equally successful. He arrived there and immediately charged the Federal position. His skirmishers were stopped by sharpshooters positioned in brick buildings, with a loss of two killed and seven wounded. Rather than risk his men, Forrest invested the place and opened with artillery upon the stockade and the buildings in which the sharpshooters were located. At the third round, a white flag went up; and the entire command surrendered. Here he captured 20,000 artillery rounds and 400,000 rounds of small ammunition. Everything that could not be carried away was burned, including 600 bales of cotton, 2,000 barrels of pork, and a large lot of tobacco. During the same day, the 20th, Russell, acting as rear guard at Spring Creek, was attacked by an infantry column moving out of Jackson in pursuit of Forrest. The Fourth Alabama charged them on horseback; and the enemy became panic stricken and retreated across the creek, burning the bridge after them. Nothing further was heard from this column. On the 21st, Forrest moved farther north toward Union City and was joined by Starnes and Dibrell, the latter having failed to take the stockade at Forked Deer Creek or to destroy the bridge. Two companies of the 106th Illinois valiantly held the stockade until 400 Yankees under Colonel G. P. Ihrie came up and drove off the Confederates. At Rutherford Station, two companies of Federals were captured by Forrest; and the trestles, bridges and rails were destroyed from Trenton to Kenton Station. At Kenton, Colonel Thomas J. Kenney and his 119th Illinois were captured, and 22 men left in a hospital were paroled. The destruction of an extensive trestle and the crossing of the Obion River delayed the Confederates here until noon of the 22nd. Still pushing northward, Forrest reached Union City at 4:00 p.m. on the 23rd and charged into the town, capturing 106 Federal troops. Later in the day, he crossed into Kentucky. Until the 25th, Forrest was engaged in destroying railroad bridges over the bayou near Moscow, other bridges over the North and South Forks of the Obion, and several miles of trestles in the bottom lands of that area. With one exception, there was not a bridge left on the railroad between Jackson and Moscow. Neither were any trestles standing, and the rails over much of the distance were ruined from buckling caused by fires built on top of them.

4. Bucked and gagged was a form of punishment used in both armies. The punished soldier was made to sit down with his knees drawn up to his chin. His hands were tied together in front of his legs, and a stick was inserted above his arms and under his knees. To add to his

discomfort, a stick, or sometimes a bayonet, was placed across his mouth and tied there with a cord fastened to each end and run behind his head. The man was usually left in this position until he showed some signs of repentance or subordination.

5. Sullivan may have thought the blow administered to Forrest was greater than it actually was; or, perhaps, he wanted to bask in his own glory. He telegraphed Grant that he had achieved a great victory, meeting Forrest, 7,000 strong, and routing him with great slaughter. Later he reported that Forrest's losses were estimated at 1,500 killed, wounded, and missing and that Forrest's force was completely broken up and scattered over the country without ammunition. Grant wired his superiors that Sullivan had given Forrest a tremendous thrashing. They were greatly overestimating the facts in their reports about the Confederate cavalry leader. His losses were twenty-five killed, about seventy-five wounded, and approximately 250 captured by the enemy. The captured included Major Cox and Forrest's adjutant, Major Strange. He had also lost three pieces of artillery, four caissons, two ambulances, and five wagons with their contents—seventy-five thousand rounds of ammunition. The Federal casualties were at least fifty killed, 150 wounded, and about 100 taken prisoner. They had three guns knocked out and lost three caissons, fifteen wagons, and two ambulances. All except the three guns were carried off the field, along with 1,800 badly needed blankets and the same number of knapsacks. Sullivan's greatest error, however, was in believing that Forrest's troops were scattered and without ammunition.

6. Lieutenant Colonel W. K. M. Breckenridge, who commanded the Sixth Tennessee cavalry (Union) on this occasion, reported to Brigadier General Dodge, to whose command he belonged: "On the morning of January 1st, near Clifton, a very short time after sunrise, our pickets were driven in by Forrest's advance. We first made an effort to form on a hill and then fell back to the foot of the hill. I then changed position, and would have been all right had it not been that one of the companies in the rear did not receive the order to fall back until they were very much exposed to the enemy fire. In the meantime the enemy made an attempt to surround the company. We lost about six men as prisoners. We made our retreat and got in the rear of the enemy to annoy him all we could. We found that his rear was moving at a very rapid rate and followed them within a short distance of the river, and found that they had been advised that their rear was followed. I did not deem it prudent to follow farther."

7. A fictional character has been substituted for Lieutenant Edwin H. Douglas, who commanded this section of artillery.

8. Company after company was made to unsaddle their horses and pile saddles, blankets, guns, and other equipment in the boats; and these were carried immediately over with as many as the vessels would hold. Others of the troops rapidly constructed rafts of fence rails and logs that would hold from five to ten men each; and on these frail floats, they paddled across. There was no time to ferry the horses. Two men would man a canoe or skiff, while a third held the bridle of a horse. They would strike out for the other side with the animal swimming by the side of the boat. When the pilot horse was a short distance from shore, the other animals, stripped for the plunge, were led to where the bank was perpendicular to the edge of the water. The bridles were taken off, and one after the other they were pushed into the stream. They could do nothing but swim, and naturally took out after the horse already in the river. At least one thousand of these animals were struggling in the river at the same time.

This campaign into middle Tennessee had lasted only two weeks. During this time, they had averaged marching twenty miles a day in cold, wet, disagreeable weather on roads which were almost impassable. The troops were engaged with the enemy almost every day; and when not so engaged, they were destroying stockades (approximately nineteen), bridges (about fifty), trestles, rails, and supply depots. The railroads were so badly damaged that Grant abandoned them as a line of supply; and they were never rebuilt for that purpose. Grant was so hampered by the loss of supplies that he was forced to give up his "campaign into the interior and return to La Grange and Grand Junction, making the Mississippi River the line over which to draw supplies." On December 27, General-in-Chief H. W. Halleck telegraphed Grant, "I think no more troops at present should be sent against Vicksburg. I feel that you have already too much weakened your own force. Concentrate and hold only the more important points." It was probably the success of this campaign which instilled in Sherman the respect and fear of Forrest which became apparent when he later commanded the troops pushing into Georgia.

Chapter XI

1. The name of the rebuked artilleryman is not known, but it was Lieutenant Edwin H. Douglas who gave Forrest the demonstration of how artillery was unlimbered and placed in battery.
2. Other biographers, namely Jordan and Pryor and J. Harvey Mathes,

give a different version than the one I have used of Wyeth as to how the move on Fort Donelson began. According to them, Bragg called Forrest to his headquarters and ordered him to join Wheeler, who was already enroute to attack Fort Donelson. They relieved Wheeler from making the decision to initiate the attack against the fort.

3. Wheeler thought that the garrison of the fort would have surrendered if the position of Forrest's men had not been abandoned; however, this opinion is difficult to understand in view of the circumstances prevailing.

4. Forrest's anger at Wheeler seems unjustified. He was probably upset over his own blunders in moving his men impulsively before the scheduled attack and again when he thought his horses were threatened, so he was overly sensitive to anything which cast even a shadow of criticism over his men or himself; also, the heavy losses he had suffered with no resulting military gain would have greatly upset him. Here we have an example of the second of Forrest's major faults (the first being his violent temper), his propensity for serious conflict with his superiors in command. He was such a natural leader that he may have found it difficult to take second place to anyone. It is likely that his driving ambition could not tolerate any failure of a superior which might reflect adversely upon his own performance or reputation. This latter theory is borne out by the conversation he had with Major Anderson and Dr. Ben Woods before the assault on the fort began.

5. The officer who entered the freezing Duck River to test its fordability was Major J. M. Crews, acting inspector general on Forrest's staff. He was pulled half-dead from the river by men on the opposite bank.

6. Major General Earl Van Dorn, who then commanded the left wing of Bragg's army and had concentrated the cavalry in his department, had five brigades commanded by Brigadier Generals Forrest, F. C. Armstrong, G. B. Cosby, and W. T. Martin, and Colonel J. W. Whitfield. In all, there were about 6,000 effective troopers; and with these there were Captain S. L. Freeman's six guns of Forrest's command and Captain Houston King's Second Missouri battery of six pieces belonging to Whitfield's brigade. With this force he moved out to meet the Federal troops.

General W. H. Jackson, commanding a division composed of Armstrong's and Whitfield's brigades and King's battery, was given the advance and proceeded at a considerable distance ahead of the other troops. Arriving within four miles of Franklin, they collided with a body of Federal soldiers who were bound for Spring Hill, their mission being to find out what Bragg's men there were up to. In this Federal column were 2,837 troops, and in addition, the Eighteenth Ohio battery of six long-range Rodman rifled cannon. Six hundred of the Union force were cavalry, the remainder infantry.

When Jackson came in sight of the enemy, he concluded there were too many for him to attack without help. He decided not to advance upon them; and seeing that, the Federal commander deployed to attack him. At long range the artillery opened on both sides, and for about two hours both commanders seemed satisfied with this duel at a distance, which made a great deal of noise but did little damage. At last, Colonel John Coburn, of the Thirty-third Indiana infantry, who commanded the Union forces, advanced his cavalry; and there was a lively skirmish with small arms. The result was that the Confederates retired in the direction from which they had come, reaching the vicinity of Thompson's Station, on the Alabama and Tennessee railroad, about nightfall. Here they were joined by the balance of Van Dorn's cavalry; and almost in sight of each other, the Federal and Confederate columns bivouacked for the night. The casualties of the day were small for either side.

During the night, Forrest's scouts reported the enemy to be a brigade of infantry, two regiments of cavalry, and a body of artillery. His own force much larger, Van Dorn was more than willing to give battle.

Colonel Coburn, commanding the Federal forces, had no such accurate information. He learned from two negro boys that Van Dorn's army was north of Spring Hill, moving to take Franklin. From other reports, Coburn estimated that Van Dorn's army numbered 15,000. He was undecided whether to run or fight. His written orders from Brigadier General James A. Garfield were to proceed to Spring Hill. He sent a message back to Brigadier General C. C. Gilbert at Franklin informing him that he believed there were more of the enemy confronting him than his superior had anticipated and requested instructions. Receiving none, Coburn bravely decided to go on as ordered; and this game commander prepared to attack.

Early on the 5th of March, Van Dorn had his men stretched out in line of battle ready and, although in superior force, waiting for the Union troops to attack him. He had selected an excellent position in the neighborhood of Thompson's Station; had lined up Armstrong's and Whitfield's brigades on either side of the turnpike; and away off to the right of his line, and somewhat to himself, had placed Forrest with his brigade and his six pet guns of Freeman's battery. Forrest was never more anxious for a fight than at this moment, for he and his men were all smarting from the whipping received at Dover.

Feeling his way along, Coburn came on, determined to do his best with his smaller force. He advanced slowly and cautiously, so much so that it was not until ten o'clock in the morning that his troops were well engaged. As the Federal troops advanced, the Thirty-third and Eighty-fifth Indiana, with two guns, formed their right; the Twenty-second Wisconsin and the Nineteenth Michigan, with three guns, was the left wing. To the left of this line several companies of dismounted cavalry occupied a strong position in a dense thicket of cedars crowning a knoll, and just behind this point the remainder of the cavalry was formed under the command of Colonel Thomas J. Jordan. The One Hundred and Twenty-fourth Ohio was held in reserve with the train. With these, Coburn advanced by a demonstration of his cavalry on his left and a charge by the two Indiana regiments of his right wing. As this attack began, the artillery of both sides opened with great spirit and with rapid fire. The Federals came on gallantly under orders to charge King's battery, which was in their immediate front. Behind a stone fence, and in excellent position for defending these guns, was Whitfield's brigade which had been strengthened by Colonel S. G. Earle's Third Arkansas regiment from Armstrong's brigade.

The charge of the Union cavalry was of short duration. Forrest, who had the Confederate extreme right, anticipated their move; and he ordered Starnes' and Edmondson's regiments to drive the dismounted enemy troopers from the cedar knoll, and this they did in short order. At the same time, he advanced the remainder of his line against Jordan's mounted force, compelling them to take refuge behind their infantry. Seeing the opportunity afforded by the retirement of the Union cavalry, Forrest hurried Freeman's battery far to the front and posted it so favorably that it not only swept the advancing Federal infantry in flank, it enfiladed their battery, causing it to limber up and leave its position and, with the cavalry, quit the field. Forrest's entire line was now half a mile in front of the main Confederate line of battle.

At this time, the charging Federal infantry had reached within 200 yards of Whitfield's men crouching behind the stone wall. These now rose with a well-directed volley; and immediately afterward, they leaped the fence and charged the Union line. With this destructive fire and the countercharge from the front, and Forrest's battery playing on their flank and his troopers pushing Jordan's cavalry from their position, the Indianians broke and fled back across the swale and on behind the hill on which they had been first aligned.

Here, although their artillery and cavalry had fled the field, the men on foot were rallied. The Confederates under Whitfield and Earle dashed up the hill, behind which the regrouped enemy had halted to contest their advance; and the game Indianians turned upon their pursuers, driving them back down the hill and into the valley to their former position, where the thwarted Rebels held their own.

Van Dorn again ordered his troops to drive the Federals from the hill they still held so stubbornly. Whitfield and Earle for the second time went at them, and Armstrong's entire brigade joined in the charge. The Nineteenth Michigan and the Twenty-second Wisconsin rushed to reinforce their comrades, and a fierce combat at close quarters took place, in which the Rebels again failed to drive the enemy from the coveted position. Armstrong was badly handled in this affray and left his battle colors in the possession of the Michiganders. In this dilemma, Forrest, who had already, without orders, pushed his men and artillery far in advance of the Confederate line, now charged on the flank and rear of the enemy and thus closed their avenue of escape. As his troops swept down the Union flank, the Twenty-second Wisconsin broke; about one-half of this regiment scattered in the wood, and many of them avoided capture.

Coburn began to retire from the battlefield with most of his troops in compact order. When he met Forrest's division, posted behind fences, trees, and other favorable cover, barring his way, he formed his brigade with fixed bayonets. It was a cardinal point of Forrest's military make-up never to stand and take a charge but, as he expressed it, to "charge too."

Seeing Coburn's maneuver, he ordered a charge which was led by Colonel Biffle and Lieutenant Colonel Trezevant, the latter commanding Cox's regiment. The enemy opened a heavy fire upon them; and Trezevant was killed, as was Captain Montgomery Little of Forrest's escort. Forrest's horse was also killed, and the cavalry leader continued the charge on foot. When the Confederates were within twenty feet of Coburn's line, the enemy threw down their guns and surrendered, between twelve and fifteen hundred of them.

As soon as the Federal commander surrendered, Forrest directed a strong detachment to mount their horses and pursue the flying cavalry, artillery, and the One Hundred and Twenty-fourth Ohio infantry. The latter, being in reserve, had gone to the rear with the wagons. These troops, however, had such a running start that only about seventy-five captures were made, chiefly from the regiments which had borne the brunt of the fighting. The Ohio regiment did not lose a man. The Union cavalry lost twenty-seven in all, and their artillery had only one man wounded.

Forrest's losses were ten killed, fifty-seven wounded, and two missing.

7. It was Major Charles W. Anderson who carried the message.

8. Again, it was Major Charles W. Anderson who carried the message, having taken off his shirt and tied it to the end of his saber.

9. In his report on this affair, General Smith claimed that, in the judgment of his officers and himself, no less than 400 to 500 of Forrest's men were killed, wounded, and taken prisoner and that, but for the overwhelming force, numbering no less than 5,000, the success of his troops would have been unquestioned. Smith exaggerated Forrest's losses even more than he did the size of the latter's forces. The Confederate loss for the entire expedition was one officer and three men killed, three officers and thirteen men wounded, and thirty-nine men captured or missing; total, fifty-nine. The Union losses were four killed, nineteen wounded, and four missing in Smith's pursuing cavalry, and 750 officers and men captured at Brentwood and Harpeth bridge, all of whom were brought away in safety. Total loss 758—not including teamsters and other employees.

10. It is to Major J. Minnick Williams that we are indebted for the details of this encounter, and I have embellished them slightly.

11. It was said of Freeman, "His favorite pieces were his twelve-pounder howitzers, his preferred ammunition two-thirds canister, and his distance as close as his general would let him go."

Chapter XII

1. Dodge arrived at Eastport ahead of Streight and did not wait. He had run into a small Confederate cavalry force at Glendale before he reached Bear Creek, and they retired before him. He crossed the creek with little difficulty and pushed on another thirteen miles toward Tuscumbia. Colonel P. F. Roddy, with a small brigade of Confederate cavalry, attacked one of Dodge's columns with such vigor that it was thrown into confusion. Roddy captured two pieces of artillery, twenty-two artillerists, and a company of mounted infantry. Although Dodge retook one of the guns, he was so troubled over the results of the day and Streight's failure to appear as scheduled that he fell back to Bear Creek to wait for the latter and to send for more help. He asked for Fulton's brigade of 2,000 men and another section of artillery. These arrived in due time, bringing his force to about 7,500 men.

2. In some references his name was spelled Roddey.

3. The lost time proved to be a critical factor in the outcome of Streight's mission, and this was not the only problem contributed by the mules. The individual who selected these animals over horses for the mission knew something about them but not much. The mule is primarily a draft animal and usually performs poorly as a mount. It is both slow and stubborn. In addition, it lacks strength in the proper

places to carry a rider and is prone to break down when ridden for an extended period or faster than a walk.

4. It was Captain Henry Pointer of Forrest's staff who made this remark as he offered part of his small bit of ham and bread to Major Anderson.

5. This was an unnecessary precaution; Dibrell with his lone gun had done his job so well behind Dodge that the latter not only failed to pursue, he drew back to Tuscumbia.

6. The story of the assistance given Forrest by Emma Sanson is taken from her written account of the incident with slight embellishment on my part, but much of the language is her own.

7. If the state of the Hoosier colonel's men and horses was so bad from fatigue and loss of sleep, what was the condition of those pursuing him? Forrest's men had had no opportunities for obtaining fresh horses or mules when theirs succumbed to the terrible strain to which they were being subjected. The Federals had swept the country clear of livestock as they marched; and in this, as in the tremendous tactical advantage of the ambuscade, they had the Confederate leader at a great disadvantage. Many of Forrest's men had not tasted food in twenty-four hours, and a number fell from their horses from sheer exhaustion and slept by the roadside as their commands rode past their seemingly lifeless bodies. Despite the example of their leader—who did more work and fighting than any subordinate—and notwithstanding the details, whose duty it was to keep the men awake, rouse up the sleepers, and put them on their horses, Forrest's command had now crumbled away to a mere remnant. From 1 a.m. on April 29 to noon of May 2, they had marched 119 miles and fought almost without cessation the last 52 hours; and still the strongest of them pushed on, determined to stay with their leader. Edmondson and Anderson were not up yet—and did not get up until after the surrender. Their duty was to keep Streight from escaping northward, and they were preventing this.

8. Colonel Hathaway was mortally wounded by Private Joseph Martin, a sharpshooter.

9. Colonel John H. Wisdom of Forrest's staff was the officer who made this ride to Rome.

10. In his official report, Colonel Streight said, "Nature was exhausted. A large portion of my best troops actually went asleep while lying in line of battle under a severe skirmish fire."

11. It was Captain Henry Pointer of Forrest's staff who was actually dispatched on this mission.

12. Forrest refused to treat runaway slaves as prisoners of war. He regarded them as lawful property of their previous owners and returned them to their former masters whenever possible.

13. Streight surrendered 1,466 men at this time. The officers were separated from their men and taken into Rome, about twenty miles away. The others followed later. Enroute there, Federal Captain Milton Russell and his command, which had been sent to seize the bridge at Rome, were met on their return from that mission. He was deeply upset over his commander's surrender but now had no alternative but to do the same. This brought the prisoner total to about 1,700.

In the pursuit of Streight, Forrest marched his men the last forty-eight hours, jaded as they and their animals were, ninety miles; and they averaged forty-one miles over bad roads each day of the total march, encumbered with artillery. They fought for hours, several times daily, for three days prior to Streight's surrender. Forrest led men whose acts of individual heroism make no figure in battle reports; men whose endurance of fatigue and long abstinence from food, combined with their unbroken morale, were things of which to be proud; men to whom he appeared to have given his own indomitable strength and spirit.

Chapter XIII

1. A witness to this scene said, "Forrest wept like a child." He was speaking figuratively, but I could not bring myself to use the statement in its entirety and left out "like a child"; it did not seem descriptive of the way Forrest would have shown his emotion.
2. Forrest was of the opinion the young officer must have been one of those he had captured at Murfreesborough who had been later exchanged, for they had been very grateful for the manner in which they had been treated.
3. If Starnes had a fault, it was the daring recklessness with which he always threw himself and his command at the enemy; fear seemed to be a word lacking in his vocabulary. Forrest knew that any task assigned him would be done well, with all his energy, and without question. He trusted him implicitly and had great affection for him as a friend. If Lee lost his right arm ("Stonewall" Jackson) at Chancellorsville, then Forrest lost his left this day in front of Tullahoma.
4. In recounting this story later, Forrest said, "I would rather have faced a battery than that fiery dame."
5. The letter read as follows:

"GENERAL,—Prompted by the repeated solicitations of numerous friends and acquaintances residing in west Tennessee and northern Mississippi, also by a desire to serve my country to the best of my ability, and wherever those services can be rendered most available and effective, I respectfully lay before you a proposition which, if approved, will seriously, if not entirely obstruct the navigation of the Mississippi River, and in sixty days procure a large force now inside the enemy's lines, which without this, or a similar move cannot be obtained.

"The proposition is this: Give me the command of the forces from Vicksburg to Cairo, or, in other words, all the forces I may collect together and organize between those points—say in northern Mississippi, west Tennessee, and those that may join me from Arkansas, Mississippi and southern Kentucky. I desire to take with me only about four hundred men from my present command—viz., my escort, sixty; McDonald's battalion, one hundred and fifty; the second Kentucky cavalry, two hundred and fifty—selected entirely on account of their knowledge of the country in which I propose to operate. In all, say, men and outfit, four hundred men, with long range guns (Enfield), four three-inch Dahlgren or Parrot guns, with eight number one horses to each gun and caisson, two wagons for the battery, one pack-mule to every ten men, and two hundred rounds of ammunition for small arms and artillery.

"I would like to have Captain (W. W.) Carnes, now in Chattanooga, in some portion of General Bragg's army, to command the battery, and, in case he was detached for the expedition, that he be allowed to select his cannoneers, etc. I have resided on the Mississippi for over twenty years, was for many years engaged in buying and selling negroes, and know the country perfectly well between Memphis and Vicksburg, and also am well acquainted with all the prominent planters in that region, as well as above Memphis. I also have officers in my command and on my staff who have rafted timber out of the bottoms, and know every foot of the ground between Commerce and Vicksburg. With the force proposed, and my knowledge of the river-bottoms, as well as the knowledge my men have of the country from Vicksburg up, I am confident we could so move and harass and destroy boats on the river that only boats heavily protected by gunboats would be able to make the passage.

"I ask also authority to organize all troops that can be obtained, and that I be promised long-range guns for them as soon as organizations are reported. There are many half-organized regiments, battalions, and companies in northern Mississippi and west Tennessee, but they are without arms and have no way of getting out, and it only requires a little time and a nucleus around which they can form, to organize and put them in the field. I believe that in sixty days I can raise from five to ten thousand men between Vicksburg and Cairo, well mounted and ready for service as soon as provided with guns and ammunition.

"In making this proposition, I desire to state that I do so entirely for the good of the service. I believe that I can accomplish all that I propose to do. I have never asked for position, have taken position and performed the duties assigned me, and have never yet suffered my command to be surprised or defeated. I should leave this department with many regrets, as I am well pleased with the officers in my command and with the division serving under me. I shall especially regret parting with my old brigade. It was organized by me, and a record of its past services and present condition will compare favorably with any cavalry command in the service, and nothing but a desire to destroy the enemy's transports and property, and increase the strength of our army, could for a moment induce me voluntarily to part with them. There are thousands of men where I propose to go that I am satisfied will join me, and that rapidly (otherwise they will remain where they are), until all the country bordering on the Mississippi from Cairo down is taken and permanently occupied by our forces.

"I am, general, very respectfully, your obedient servant,

"N. B. Forrest, Brigadier-General."

6. With thirteen regiments of cavalry, supported by General McCook's infantry following behind him, Stanley moved down Wills Valley between Sand Mountain and Lookout Mountain, crossed the latter, and reached Alpine and Summerville. General Wilder was to create a diversion on Bragg's right near Ringgold and Tunnel Hill to hold Forrest in that area. The Federal commanders believed Forrest to be in Philadelphia, Tennessee, on September 6, based upon false information furnished by one of the cavalry leader's "deserting" scouts.

The farther Stanley pulled away from McCook's infantry, which was to hold the pass for his return, the smaller his thirteen regiments looked, especially when he found in front of him the cavalry of Wheeler, Martin, Wharton, and Forrest, the latter having moved rapidly from Ringgold on September 6 to arrive at Alpine on the 8th. Stanley wisely abandoned the mission and retraced his steps back up the mountain.

7. By September 11, it began to dawn on Rosecrans that the Confederates were tired of running and ready to turn on him for a fight. The chase after Bragg from Tullahoma across the Tennessee had been little more than a summer excursion. He had so little respect for the Southern general that he scattered his troops all over the country, with slight regard to any possible necessity for rapid concentration. Generals Negly and Baird, who had crossed Lookout Mountain and descended the eastern slope through Steven's Gap into McLemore's Cove, found

themselves on the 11th confronted by a strong force of Confederates, which advanced upon them in such threatening fashion that they rapidly reclimbed Lookout Mountain and retired. The effort to cut them off and capture them was badly bungled. On the same day, Forrest, at Tunnel Hill, had hammered away at Crittenden so vigorously that the latter also discovered that "the better part of valor was discretion" and retired toward Chattanooga. The Federal general began at last to display considerable anxiety and to concentrate his scattered legions. As the hot and dusty days slipped by his concern increased, for he heard that Longstreet was coming with additional troops from Virginia and, indeed, was near at hand. On the 16th he dispatched to Burnside, who was in the vicinity of Knoxville: "The enemy intends us all the mischief in their power. It is of the utmost importance that you close down this way to cover our left flank. We have not the force to cover our flank against Forrest now. He could cross the river above us before we could discover it. I want all the help we can get promptly."

8. General Joseph Wheeler commanded all the mounted Confederate forces on the left wing and confined his operations exclusively to this portion of the field, leaving Forrest in full sway on the right flank. Practically all the cavalry on the Southern side fought at Chickamauga on foot and in line with the infantry. On the left, Wheeler defeated the Union cavalry at Glass' Mill, driving them for nearly two miles to Crawfish Spring; and finally, on Sunday afternoon, September 20, he formed the extreme left of the Confederate infantry line of battle, sweeping the field from Lee and Gordon's Mill back to the rear of Federal General George Thomas' position, until darkness put an end to the pursuit.

On the right it may be said that Forrest struck the first and last blow— firing the opening and the final shots in this engagement. On the 18th, Brigadier General Bushrod R. Johnson, commanding a division composed of his own, McNair's, Gregg's, and Robertson's brigades, was directed to advance from Ringgold to the Chickamauga Creek, cross it at Reed's Bridge, and march prepared for a collision with the enemy from that point up the creek in the direction of Lee and Gordon's Mill. Johnson's force at this moment was the right flank of the Confederate infantry line; and with it on the right, and nearest to Rosecrans' base at Chattanooga, Forrest's cavalry was moving. In touch with Johnson and to his left, a division of the Confederate reserve corps, under Major General William H. T. Walker, was directed to proceed by a parallel route and cross the creek at Alexander's Bridge or, if too strongly resisted there, to wade the stream at Nyram's Ford about one mile farther up the creek. Next in order was the division of Major

General S. B. Buckner, which in like manner had orders to advance and effect a crossing at Thedford's Ford, still farther away in the direction of Lee and Gordon's Mill.

On September 9, when Forrest reached Dalton, Georgia, he had dispatched the brigade, under Colonel Hodge, to watch the Cleveland and Dalton road. Colonel Scott's brigade was stationed on the route from Ringgold to Chattanooga. Pegram's division was at Pea-Vine Church. Armstrong, with his division, was in front of Cheatham's infantry, along the Lafayette and Chattanooga road; while Forrest, with his escort and about two hundred and forty men (a remnant of General John H. Morgan's cavalry which had not been swallowed up in the wild Ohio raid), was positioned at Dalton.

As Johnson approached Reed's Bridge about noon Friday, September 18, Forrest went to the front, having with him his escort and Morgan's remnant—three hundred men in all. Off to the right, as Johnson advanced, Pegram's division was moving, to keep an eye on the Union forces which might be near enough to interfere with the Southern infantry. When General Johnson arrived within one mile of the enemy's position, near Reed's Bridge, over which the Federals had already crossed, he threw his troops in line of battle.

General Forrest, with his escort, proceeded to the front to develop the position of the enemy and was soon skirmishing with them. From Pea-Vine Creek, where the skirmishing commenced, the Federals were driven back by Johnson and Forrest but not without creditable resistance. At Reed's Bridge they made a final and more stubborn stand. Here the Confederates crowded them with artillery and then charged with infantry and cavalry, driving them away so precipitately that they did not take time to burn the bridge. The entire attacking force moved across the Chickamauga; and being joined by Pegram's division, they marched up the creek toward Alexander's bridge.

About 4 p.m. Major General John B. Hood arrived and took command of all the troops on this part of the field. The infantry slept in line of battle that night, about 800 yards from the Vineyard House, and near the log schoolhouse on the highway from Lee and Gordon's Mill to Chattanooga. Forrest scouted and picketed the country a mile to the right of this position and went into bivouac with the main body of his troops in rear of Hood's line, near Alexander's Bridge. The Federal forces encountered here were a brigade of cavalry under Colonel Minty.

Very early on the 19th, General Forrest was ordered to move with his command to the Confederate right, in the direction of Reed's Bridge and Chattanooga, and to develop the enemy. Advancing promptly with Pegram's division near the bridge, he was soon engaged with Union troops in such strength that help was needed. Forrest sent a courier to the infantry with the message that he had raised a hornet's nest and could not hold on long without reinforcements. It was evident to him now that the Federal commander had outwitted Bragg. While the latter was marching his troops from the neighborhood of Reed's Bridge up the Chickamauga, all the same night Rosecrans was sliding his long line of battle in the opposite direction to get nearer to Chattanooga, so that in case of disaster, his antagonist would not get in between him and refuge there. Wise Rosecrans, for here now, a mile at least to the right of this flank of the Southern infantry, was a large force and a long line of Union troops. Major General D. H. Hill, who passed up this way, said, "I found that while our troops had been moving up the Chickamauga, the Yankees had been moving down, and thus outflanked us."

As no reinforcements came, General Forrest sent Major Anderson to General Polk, asking him to give him Armstrong's division. Polk, needing half of this cavalry for his portion of the line, answered with the other half, sending Dibrell's brigade, which double-quicked and was in short order dismounted and in the thickest of the fight. As no satisfactory answer had come to Forrest's repeated messages for the infantry line to be moved in his direction, he now instructed Pegram to hold what he had, "no matter what might happen," until he could go for help and return with it. Pegram promised to do it and held to his promise, but at terrific cost. From behind trees and logs, and every possible point of vantage, these cavalrymen on foot fought with the stubbornness and precision of infantry. They held on like grim death, and grim death held on to many of them. One-fourth of them went down, although Forrest hurried back and brought the infantry with him.

It was Colonel Claudius C. Wilson's brigade which came to the rescue; and at Forrest's request, the Georgians swung into line immediately on his left and never waited a moment. These veterans of other bloody fields moved forward rapidly to close range before delivering their well aimed volleys into the Union line, which yielded under the pressure, and the retreating Yankees were pursued by all. Forrest was elated over the conduct of Wilson's men. He later reported, "They advanced in gallant style, driving the enemy back and capturing a battery of artillery, my dismounted cavalry advancing with them."

Forrest was now in command of all troops at this end of the line. He pushed forward, and with Wilson drove back the second Federal line of battle, following this until a third line, behind well constructed defenses, was developed. Colonel Wilson was now ordered by General Forrest not to attempt to carry this position until more troops could be brought up. At this moment the brigade of General Matthew D. Ector appeared on the field, having orders to report to Forrest, who placed it on the right of Wilson, the dismounted cavalry being pushed still farther over on Ector's right flank.

Meanwhile, the Union lines had been reinforced and now felt themselves strong enough to take their turn as the aggressors. Before Forrest could get Ector's men in place and ready for a general assault, a heavy column of Federals advanced. Ector's men fought valiantly to hold their ground; but Ector became worried about his right flank, and sent his adjutant, C. B. Kilgore, to Forrest to advise him of the concern.

"Tell General Ector not to bother about his right flank; I'll take care of it," Forrest replied. The Federals advanced well beyond General Wilson's left flank, overlapping him and opening an enfilade fire along his line which forced him to retire his brigade. In doing so, Forrest's entire line was carried back. Ector, who was on Wilson's right, again sent Kilgore to Forrest. Kilgore found him in the thickest of the fight near a battery where every man was blazing away like mad.

"General Ector wishes to advise you that he is now concerned about his left flank," Kilgore said.

Forrest was furious. He turned around and shouted to Kilgore above the din of the battle, "Tell General Ector that, by God, I'm here an'll take care of his left flank as well as his right!"

Morton's and Higgins' batteries had done excellent work; and as was Forrest's practice, their pieces were shoved to the front almost up to shotgun range. As they retired, the thick wood and, in places, the heavy undergrowth made it no easy matter to bring away their artillery as the game Federals were coming on in steady lines and with fixed bayonets. The general held his troops steadily at work as they gave back. There was no break to the rear, but from tree to tree and from behind every point of shelter, these men, making a determined resistance, loaded and fired their guns with deadly effect. The horses of one of Captain Huggins' pieces, in charge of Lieutenant Edwin H. Douglas, were all killed or wounded. Douglas told Forrest he would have to leave the gun unless he could get help to pull it out. The general called to four of his escort who were mounted and nearby; and quickly throwing the collars and hames over the troopers' saddled horses, the traces were attached; and the cavalrymen dragged Forrest's precious gun to safety.

The men fell back in good order, the Federals not following beyond their original position. Just at this minute, Major General W. H. T. Walker came up and took command of his infantry. The fighting here had lasted from early morning to 1:30 p.m. Cheatham's division came on the field to relieve them and, with Cleburne, succeeded after a terrific struggle in driving the Federals from their entire line. They slept on their arms that night, masters of the bloody field. General Walker paid a high and well earned compliment to the fighting qualities of the men under Forrest in this hot, vicious, and deadly fighting that morning and early afternoon. "The unequal contest of four brigades against such overwhelming odds is unparalleled in this revolution, and the troops deserve immortal honor for the part borne in the action."

In the hottest of the fight, General Forrest's horse, presented to him by the citizens of Rome, was mortally wounded. As the troops were retiring, Major Anderson was with the general in the rear of the line, up and down which he was galloping, encouraging his men to stand to their work, and ready to threaten, or do more than threaten, any who dared to give back too rapidly. During this trying time, a private soldier cut loose from his place in front and broke for the rear. He unfortunately ran near to the general and his aide. Forrest whipped out his six-shooter, ordered the man to halt, and was in the act of making an example of him when Major Anderson exclaimed, "Oh, General, think!"

Forrest hesitated for a moment; and then lowered his pistol, letting the frightened man go in peace. (Anderson later said: "I knew him and his moods so well that I had learned just how to take him. I am confident that, in the excitement of the moment, knowing the supreme disregard he felt for life—even his own, when the fate of a battle hung in the balance—had I said, 'General Forrest, don't do that!' he would have killed the man without a doubt, and I might have gotten a turn, too.")

Saturday night (the 19th) General Frank C. Armstrong arrived with his second brigade, and took command of his division which, with Pegram's, was thrown to the extreme right, guarding that flank, contiguous to the Reed's Bridge road. During the night, a general readjustment of the opposing lines of battle was made. The struggle of the 19th, severe and bloody as it was, had never become general. The firing had at no time swept continuously down the lines. When the fighting ended that day, the advantage was decidedly with the Confederates, who held all the ground upon which the contest had opened, and more.

Rosecrans' anxiety about his left wing and the path to the rear and Chattanooga had greatly increased. Thomas' corps, heavily reinforced, was on the Federal left; and all through the night and during the early morning the axes were ringing along the five or six miles of battlefront, trees were crashing to the ground, and busy picks were playing tattoo on the earth as the Federals labored to strengthen their positions. They had been beaten on Saturday; and they knew the morrow would require all that art, skill, and courage could do to hold the Rebels back.

At daybreak on Sunday morning General Forrest and his cavalry found themselves in line with the division of Major General J. C. Breckenridge, which, a little after daylight, reached Cleburne's right and now became the extreme right of the Confederate infantry. Still to the right of these, in line of battle at dawn, were Forrest's troopers. They all were a part of Bragg's right wing, commanded by Lieutenant General Polk. The left wing was under the command of Lieutenant General James Longstreet, who had just arrived by train with two divisions from the Army of Northern Virginia. Bragg's plan of battle was for Polk to begin the assault at daybreak on the morning of the 20th (Sunday) at the extreme right; and units would continue the attack, in succession, down the line to the left.

Daylight came; the troops were there; but the attack was not made. Polk's order to General Hill was not delivered; the courier could not find him in time. The whole Confederate army was waiting for the sound of cannon and musketry on the right; it did not come until 9:30, and these three hours of priceless daylight were gone forever.

Breckenridge, advancing at 9:30, soon came in contact with the Federals and was fully engaged by ten o'clock. As his troops moved forward, Forrest also moved, a continuation of the infantry line. Armstrong's division, with the exception of the First Tennessee regiment and McDonald's battalion, was dismounted and sent in well on the right. Pegram's division, having already suffered extremely, was at this time held in reserve; while the two mounted detachments were kept out on the flank. Breckenridge met with determined resistance; the enemy were strongly entrenched, and it seemed almost impossible to dislodge them. Time and again his troops assailed the works, only to be driven back with terrific slaughter. In those two desperate hours, men perished by the hundreds. The Kentuckians gave up their lives in reckless fashion, and among them was General Ben Hardin Helm. (Brigadier General Benjamin Hardin Helm, described by Longstreet as "one of the most promising brigadiers," was President Abraham Lincoln's brother-in-law, having married Mary Todd Lincoln's sister, Emilie.)

As the attack by the Confederates moved down the line to the left, the Federal troops under General Thomas were severely pressed; but beyond him, a vague or erroneous order issued by Rosecrans to General Wood "to close up on Reynolds as fast as possible, and support him" created a gap in the Union line. Reynolds was not on Wood's immediate left, and the latter had to pull his troops out of the Federal line to comply with the order. About the same time, Stewart's division, on the right of the left wing commanded by Longstreet, on orders directly from Bragg, had moved forward against the Union center and had become heavily engaged. Longstreet followed this with attacks by the divisions commanded by Hood, Bushrod Johnson, and Hindman. Johnson found in front of him the position Wood had held and vacated. With no one facing him, he moved aggressively forward and cut the Federal line in two. Seizing this golden opportunity, Longstreet pushed his other troops forward vigorously; and on this part of the field, he knocked the right wing and center of Rosecrans' line of battle to pieces. Two Federal corps melted away, a disorganized and beaten mass; and within a few minutes, most of them were in wild flight in the direction of Chattanooga. Carried away with this flying mob were the commanding general of the army, two corps commanders (McCook and Crittenden), and Assistant Secretary of War Dana (the last mentioned present as an observer), all in the ruck and never halting until they reached Chattanooga, ten miles from the battlefield.

Major General Gordon Granger, commanding the Federal reserves near Rossville, realized the dangerous situation facing the Union army; and, without orders, he moved to the relief of Thomas, who had taken personal command of the remnants of Rosecrans' right and center in the vicinity of Snodgrass Hill. Thomas now commanded all the Union forces remaining on the field, and they were concentrated roughly in the shape of a horseshoe.

On the Confederate right flank the fighting had also been severe. Well may General Breckenridge have reported that "this was one of the bloodiest encounters of the day." Armstrong and Forrest moved over to the right; and reaching a little beyond the Union entrenchments, found open going and pushed well beyond the alignment of the infantry. It was glorious work for the cavalry. The threatening position of Forrest's men, reinforced by Adams' and Stovall's brigades of Breckenridge's division, and the determined assaults by the Confederate infantry under Breckenridge and Cleburne, gave Thomas so much concern that he called for help time and time again. When Granger moved to his aid from the direction of Rossville without orders from Rosecrans, after Longstreet had broken through the center and right of the Union line, Forrest's scouts had wind of their coming and reported the movement to him. He quickly sent to Breckenridge for more artillery, and Gracey with his two Napoleons was added to the artillery of Morton and Huggins. As Granger's troops came in sight, Forrest's three batteries opened on the head of his column with such vigor and precision that Granger's rapid march toward Thomas was arrested; and he was compelled to throw himself into line of battle and fight his way through. For more than an hour Granger's march was retarded. With his numerically superior force, he compelled this portion of the Confederate line to retire, but not more than two hundred yards. Here Forrest held on stubbornly, forcing Granger to make a considerable detour to reach Thomas' right in the area of Snodgrass Hill. (In his memoirs, *From Manassas to Appomattox*, General James W. Longstreet complained that Granger had marched in front of Forrest and the right wing of the Confederate army and no one warned him of this movement.)

It was during this engagement that Major General D. H. Hill, just from the major battlefields of the Army of Northern Virginia, riding with his staff to this quarter, saw the Confederate line sweeping in steady line around the Union left. "What infantry is that?" he asked Major Anderson, who happened to be nearby.

"That is Forrest's cavalry," Anderson replied.

"Can I see General Forrest?"

"Yes, he is there with his men. I'll take you to him."

Forrest saw them approaching and rode to meet them. His artillery had just moved forward to the open field in front of Cloud's Spring and were hurrying into battery at this advanced position. As Forrest came near, General Hill, raising his hat in salutation, said, "General Forrest, I wish to congratulate you and those brave men moving across that field like veteran infantry upon their magnificent behavior. In Virginia I made myself extremely unpopular with the cavalry because I said that so far I had not seen a dead man with spurs on. No one can speak disparagingly of such troops as yours."

Concealing whatever pride or elation he felt at this high compliment to himself and his troops and anxious to get back to the business at hand, Forrest simply said, "Thank you, General," waved his hand, and galloped away to his favorite battle position, by Morton's battery.

General Daniel H. Hill, who was on the right wing of the Confederate army with Forrest, said in mentioning the advance of Granger: "That ever-watchful officer, General Forrest, reported to me soon after that a heavy Yankee column was coming from the direction of Chattanooga. His active scouts soon brought in some prisoners. His artillery opened upon it, and a portion of it went to the left of the corps, and, in advancing upon Cleburne, was met with a storm of shot and shell and driven back in confusion. General Forrest agreed to move forward and seize the Chattanooga road. The left wing was driving the Yankees everywhere. Forrest was thundering on the right." He closed by saying: "No eulogy of mine could add to the reputation of General Forrest and his soldiers, who, though not under my command, most heartily cooperated and rendered the most valuable service. I would ask no better fortune, if again placed on a flank, than to have such a vigilant, gallant and accomplished officer guarding its approaches.''

The whole Federal army now on the field withdrew inside of Thomas' horseshoe defenses on Snodgrass Hill, beaten but still under the leadership of this indomitable soldier and still presenting a fighting front. On the right side of Thomas' horseshoe, Longstreet hurled attack after attack against him in the area of Snodgrass Hill; but with the timely arrival of Granger's troops on the field, Thomas stubbornly held his position and prevented a complete rout of the entire Federal army. He was justly given the name, ''The Rock of Chickamauga,'' for his heroic stand. Night brought an end to the Confederate assault, and the tired and hungry Rebels sank to the ground for rest and sleep. Not so the Federals, who were retreating for the greater part of the night in the direction of Chattanooga.

On no field of battle in the war did cavalry do more efficient and persistent fighting than did that of Forrest's at Chickamauga. His men were kept on the field during the night of the 20th, and troopers and horses suffered greatly for the want of water. During the last two days' engagement, his men were without rations, and the horses had received only a partial feeding.

9. When General James W. Longstreet was asked in 1896 to comment on this message, he replied; ''It was that despatch which fixed the fate of the Confederacy. General Bragg had decided to march around Rosecrans, leaving him in Chattanooga, when the despatch was received which caused Bragg to think that the place would be abandoned on the night of the 22nd, when he decided to turn back and march through Chattanooga.'' General Longstreet had advocated this immediate movement across the Tennessee, throwing the army, flushed with victory and full of confidence, between Burnside and Rosecrans, and cooping the latter up in Chattanooga, where it was believed he would soon have been starved into surrender or forced to retreat over Walden's Ridge and the Cumberland Mountain with all the loss of morale and prestige this would have induced. The army of Rosecrans at this crisis was not in good fighting trim. The corps of Thomas alone was solid and fully effective. Dissension, not to the point of mutiny but serious enough to impair their effectiveness, had crept into the corps of McCook and Crittenden. The subordinate officers in those corps had complained to Rosecrans about their commanders' fleeing from the field of battle and threatened to resign unless they were removed. Rosecrans was not disposed to be severe with them for quitting Thomas and the field, for he was in the same boat. Taking it all in all, the Federals in Chattanooga were not a happy family. If anything sealed the fate of the Confederacy

after the battle of Chickamauga, however, it was Bragg's failure to move rapidly anywhere. This gave Rosecrans the opportunity to strengthen the defenses of Chattanooga and to get his demoralized army organized. When Bragg found the enemy too strongly entrenched by the time he belatedly arrived before Chattanooga, he still could have moved around the city as Longstreet said he had first intended to do.

10. It was to Major Charles W. Anderson that Forrest dictated this strong letter to Bragg. I have been unable to locate Bragg's original order to Forrest to turn over his troopers to Wheeler, and Wyeth does not indicate the reason for the transfer or the number of men involved. Shelby Foote, in *The Civil War, A Narrative,* makes it clear that it was because of a raid Wheeler was to make on Rosecrans' supply line in Tennessee. Captain J. Harvey Mathes in *General Forrest* states that Forrest turned over all his men except Dibrell's brigade and Huggins' battery, "which he was allowed to retain for the time being."

Wheeler left on September 30, two days after Bragg issued his second order to Forrest. He was successful on his mission but at a very high cost to himself. He captured and destroyed a heavily laden, 400-wagon supply train at Anderson's Crossroads in the Sequatchie Valley; and he then moved north to McMinnville and on west to Shelbyville, capturing both towns and destroying supply depots in each of them. He became engaged in a running fight with greatly superior Union forces and, after being repulsed at Murfreesborough, turned southward again. Before escaping back across the Tennessee River, he lost more than 1,000 men and four of his guns; but the damage done to Rosecrans was almost irreparable.

11. Dr. J. B. Cowan of Tullahoma, Tennessee, Forrest's chief surgeon, is the officer who accompanied him to the meeting with Bragg, and we are indebted to that gentleman for the details of what transpired between the two men. Wyeth's account of this affair leads one to believe it occurred in Forrest's next meeting with Bragg. According to Foote's narrative, a couple of days after Forrest wrote his angry letter, he met with Bragg, who assured him that his men would be returned to him after Wheeler's raid; and Forrest was given a ten-day leave to meet his wife in La Grange, Georgia. During his stay there, he received a copy of an order by Bragg placing Wheeler in command of all cavalry in the Army of Tennessee. Forrest had vowed, after the fiasco at Dover (Fort Donelson), never to fight under Wheeler again; and such an order would probably have angered him sufficiently to bring on the confrontation with Bragg. Foote indicated that it was subsequent to this order that Forrest had his meeting with his commanding general, and he may have been right about this.

Although Wyeth professes that Forrest and Wheeler respected each other and remained friends for life, I find it difficult to believe that such feeling, at least on Forrest's part, existed at this time. Wheeler was a West Point graduate, and Forrest looked almost with disdain upon most officers coming from that academy. In addition, Wheeler was a small man and very young, then only twenty-six years of age. He was senior to Forrest, and I am sure that being outranked by the small, young West Pointer must have rankled the much older Forrest who, despite all his claims to the contrary, was, indeed, an ambitious man. Forrest may very well have been riled by Wheeler's having been selected to lead the raid across the Tennessee, but I have no doubt that he would have been extremely angry over the selection of Wheeler to command the cavalry of the Army of Tennessee, as this would have placed him under Wheeler's command.

12. Forrest was right; the incident never found its way into the official records. The cavalry leader did not offer to resign his commission, as he did not want Bragg to think he was doing so in order to avoid the consequences of any official action the latter might take against him. He was fortunate in one respect, though; President Davis visited Bragg's headquarters about this time (in connection with complaints from some of Bragg's subordinate generals about the way the battle of Chickamauga had been handled), and he made an appointment to see Forrest in Montgomery upon his return from a visit he was about to make to Mississippi. He was unfortunate in another respect, however; Bragg later became military advisor to President Davis and carried into that position a very strong animosity toward the explosive cavalry leader.

13. I had to lay fifty miles of track—there was no railroad connecting Montgomery directly with Selma at this time, the Alabama River being the means of shipping and travel between the two river ports.

Chapter XIV

1. Mrs. Rhoda King was the widow of Edwin W. King, the owner of several plantations in the Black Belt and another near Centreville. After the death of her husband and her son-in-law, she personally took over the management of these extensive operations.

2. This first capitol of Alabama had in 1825 received and royally entertained General Lafayette as an honored visitor. The building of the railroad between Marion and Cahawba connected it with railroads

serving most of the Black Belt, and it became the most important port on the Alabama River. With the coming of the war and the resulting blockade of the port of Mobile, shipping decreased; and the small busy city of 5,000 began to decline rapidly, although it was still a cultural and social center for the area.

3. It was a common practice for masters to hire out slaves whose services they did not need.

Chapter XV

1. Forrest's transfer to Mississippi did not go unheralded by the Federal forces. The day before he arrived at Okolona, Sherman, who was at Vicksburg, was informed that Forrest was organizing a force to operate on the river south of Memphis and that he had as many as six pieces of artillery. Two days later, General Stephan A. Hurlbut, the Federal district commander with headquarters at Memphis, was notified that Forrest would attack Colliersville on the Memphis and Charleston Railroad before the 18th of November.

2. The results of the battle are summed up in Colonel Prince's official report: "The enemy having gained our rear, we were compelled to retire, and, owing to the broken character of the ground, in considerable disorder. The loss the enemy sustained in killed and wounded must have exceeded our entire loss, which will not exceed forty killed, wounded, and missing."

3. The correspondent's report was surprisingly accurate, except for the allegation that Forrest had burned and sacked towns during this incursion.

4. The first brigade was constituted of the Twelfth (Lieutenant Colonel J. U. Green), Fourteenth (Colonel J. J. Neely), Fifteenth (Colonel Thomas H. Logwood), and Seventeenth (Major Marshall) regiments and Street's and Bennett's battalions, all West-Tennessee troops. Brigadier General R. V. Richardson commanded this brigade—1,500 men, rank and file.

The second brigade, 1,600 strong, commanded by Colonel Robert McCulloch, was made up of the Second Missouri under Lieutenant Colonel R. A. McCulloch, Colonel W. W. Faulkner's Kentucky regiment, Lieutenant Colonel Leo Willis' Texas battalion, Keizer's Tennessee battalion, Franklin's Tennessee ba'; alion, Lieutenant Colonel Alexander H. Chalmers' Mississippi battalion, and the fragment of the Second Arkansas regiment commanded by Captain F. M. Cochran.

The third brigade, 2,000 strong, Colonel Tyree H. Bell commanding, was composed of Russell's, Greer's, Newsom's, Wilson's, and Barteau's (Second) Tennessee regiments.

The fourth brigade, 1,000 strong, commanded by Colonel Jeffrey E. Forrest, included McDonald's battalion, the Seventh Tennessee, McGuirk's Third Mississippi State Troops regiment, the Fifth Mississippi (Lieutenant Colonel Barksdale), and Duff's Nineteenth Mississippi battalion.

The brigades commanded by McCulloch and Jeffrey Forrest (the second and fourth) were organized into a division commanded by Brigadier General J. R. Chalmers.

Chapter XVI

1. Smith was not Sherman's choice, and the plain-spoken general wrote his superior on December 19, "I deem General William Sooy Smith too mistrustful of himself for a leader against Forrest. Mower is a better man for the duty." Grant's decision was made, and it prevailed.

2. Although Sherman indicated both in his official report and in his later published memoirs that their goal was only to reach Meridian, Mississippi, official correspondence and dispatches clearly show that they intended to move against Selma and possibly, if feasible, on to Mobile. One of the main objectives of the campaign was to destroy railroad communications from Meridian to Okolona and from Meridian to Selma.

3. This may well have been the beginning of the North's "scorched earth" policy, which was practiced by Sherman in his march from Atlanta to Savannah and then northward and by Major General Philip H. Sheridan in the Shenandoah Valley.

4. To further complicate his situation, Smith was burdened with about 3,000 slaves whom he had encouraged to run away from their masters. These contraband and their mounts were serious impediments to travel as well as creating other problems.

5. News of this incident spread rapidly, reaching Northern periodicals. One enterprising artist drew a cartoon of it which he entitled, "Forrest Breaking in a New Conscript."

6. Forrest began this push by ordering Captain H. A. Tyler, who had distinguished himself in defeating the Federal flanking movement at Jack's Creek, to take his company and another company from Faulkner's Twelfth Kentucky, about 150 men in all, and to go hard after

the retreating Federals. The purpose of the enemy now developed, Forrest began a fast concentration of his troops in order to close in upon them. Dispatches were sent to General Richardson, who was about twelve miles to the west, to move at once to the bridge across Line Creek and onward in the direction of Okolona. The State troops under Gholson were to move in the same direction, bearing a little westward toward Houston. Chalmers was to follow with his division, while Forrest, with his escort, would press forward to keep up with Tyler. Barteau, commanding Bell's brigade, was ordered to keep between the enemy and the river and to move with all possible speed and endeavor to intercept the retreating column at Okolona.

Tyler pushed vigorously after the enemy and came up on their rear guard as it was passing through West Point. With his small force, Forrest and his escort having not yet joined him, he drove them without serious resistance through the village, killing and capturing several. At West Point, he learned that the entire Federal column had moved, apparently in rapid retreat, northward on the road to Okolona. He reported this to Forrest by courier and pressed hard after them. Slight skirmishing continued along the route, but no strong opposition was encountered until reaching a point about six miles north of West Point. Here Tyler encountered what he estimated to be about 1,500 mounted troops and several pieces of artillery in well selected positions. The enemy line faced the Rebels in open country, but just behind that line was some heavy timber which offered good protection and could hide additional troops. Tyler wisely dismounted his column, threw it into line on one side of the road out of reach of the enemy's artillery, and waited for help.

Forrest soon arrived with his escort and took personal command. He advanced in the direction of the Federals, but their battery opened up with such precision as to convince him of the rashness of moving toward them through the open field. He told Tyler that Chalmers' division (Jeffrey Forrest's and McCulloch's brigades) was immediately in the rear and coming up; and he directed him to remain where he was but, if the enemy gave way, to charge them and press the pursuit vigorously.

With his escort, the general moved out to pass the flank and rear of the enemy in order to reconnoiter their position. This movement was detected by the Federals, who immediately limbered up their artillery and retreated in haste. Tyler followed, moving directly down the road, and was soon in contact with the Union rear guard. Forrest was disappointed that his main column had not yet come up.

7. Colonel Barteau, who was in many battles with Forrest, said of him: "One of his many peculiarities was that in battle he never seemed to

touch his saddle, but 'stood up' in his stirrups, an attitude which gave
him the appearance of being a foot taller than he really was. As he was
over six feet in stature and of large proportions, and of necessity rode a
large horse, it was not difficult to recognize his imposing presence at
any ordinary distance along the line.''

8. Randy has been substituted for Major Thomas S. Tate, a member of
Forrest's staff, whose life was saved by Forrest; and it was a carbine
rather than a pistol that Major Tate was in the act of hurling at his
adversary.

9. Colonel George E. Waring, who commanded the First Brigade of the
Federal force, said of the retrograde movement: ''The retreat to
Memphis was a weary, disheartening, and almost panic-stricken flight,
in the greatest disorder and confusion, and through a most difficult
country. The First Brigade reached its camping-ground five days after
the engagement, with the loss of all its heart and spirit, and nearly
fifteen hundred fine cavalry horses. The expedition filled every man
connected with it with burning shame, and it gave Forrest the most
glorious achievement of his career.''

Colonel Joseph Kargé, of the Second New Jersey Cavalry, confirms
the dilapidated condition of the Federal horse: ''The regiment lost by
death on the march and in camp the majority of its horses, and of the
remaining one hundred and sixty-one, only fifty-five can be called
serviceable.''

The commander of the expedition, General Smith, reported as to his
losses: ''Our total loss, killed and wounded, will reach about four
hundred, and of stragglers they must have picked up two or three
hundred, possibly more, but this is immaterial.''

This victory was won by Forrest with no more than 2,500 effective
troops, against 7,000 of the best armed cavalry the world had ever seen.
The failure of Smith to join Sherman in Meridian aborted the plan to
move on to Selma and, possibly, Mobile. After Sherman's arrival at
Meridian on the 14th, his command, while waiting for Smith, busied
itself until the 20th with the destruction of railroads and other public
property in the area. Hearing nothing from Smith, he abandoned
Meridian and returned slowly to Vicksburg, moving slightly north of the
direct line in ''feeling'' for his delinquent cavalry leader.

Sherman never forgave Smith for failing to join him in Meridian. In
his memoirs he says: ''General Smith was ordered to move from
Memphis straight for Meridian, Mississippi, and to start from there on
the 1st of February. I explained to him personally the nature of Forrest
as a man, and his peculiar force; told him that in his route he was sure to
encounter him; that he always attacked with vehemence, for which he

must be prepared, and that were he repelled at a first attack, he must in turn assume a most determined offensive, overwhelm him, and utterly destroy his whole force. He knew that Forrest could not have more than four thousand cavalry, and my own movements would give employment to every other man in the rebel army not immediately present with him, so that General Smith might safely act on this hypothesis. I wanted to destroy General Forrest, who was constantly threatening Memphis and the river above, as well as our route to supplies in middle Tennessee. In this we failed utterly, because General Smith, when he did start, allowed General Forrest to head him off and to defeat him with an inferior force near West Point, below Okolona." He adds: "Of course I did not, and could not, approve of his conduct. I had set so much store on his part of the project that I was disappointed, and so reported officially to General Grant. General Smith never regained my confidence as a soldier, though I still regard him as a most accomplished gentleman and a skillful engineer. Since the close of the war he has appealed to me to relieve him of that censure, but I could not do it, because it would falsify history."

Chapter XVII

1. The First brigade was commanded by Colonel J. J. Neely and was composed of the Seventh (Colonel W. L. Duckworth), the Twelfth (Lieutenant Colonel J. U. Green), the Fourteenth (Colonel J. J. Neely), and the Fifteenth (Colonel F. M. Stewart) Tennessee regiments.

The Second brigade, commanded by Colonel Robert McCulloch, was made up of the Second Missouri (Lieutenant Colonel R. A. McCulloch), Willis' Texas battalion (Lieutenant Colonel Leo Willis), First Mississippi Partisans (Major J. M. Parks), Fifth Mississippi cavalry (Major W. B. Peery), Nineteenth Mississippi battalion (Lieutenant Colonel W. L. Duff), Eighteenth Mississippi battalion (Lieutenant Colonel A. H. Chalmers), and McDonald's battalion from Forrest's old regiment (Lieutenant Colonel J. M. Crews).

The Third brigade, commanded by Colonel A. P. Thompson, consisted of the Third (Lieutenant Colonel G. A. C. Holt), Seventh (Colonel Edward Crossland), Eighth (Colonel H. B. Lyon), and Twelfth (Faulkner's) Kentucky regiments, and Jeffrey Forrest's regiment (Lieutenant Colonel D. M. Wisdom).

The Fourth brigade, commanded by General T. H. Bell, was made up of the Second (Colonel C. R. Barteau), Sixteenth (Colonel A. N.

Wilson), and Twentieth (R. M. Russell) Tennessee regiments.

Neely and McCulloch's brigades were formed into one division, which was placed under Brigadier General James R. Chalmers, and Thompson's and Bell's were organized into another division under General Abe Buford.

2. This section of Tennessee was not as strongly garrisoned with Union troops as it had been before. Many of the Federals in western Tennessee and northwestern Mississippi, as well as some of those at Vicksburg, had been pulled out to support Sherman's advance toward Atlanta. The area had not been abandoned by the Federals, however; they still held major strong points along the Mississippi and the Tennessee Rivers. Memphis alone had 6,700 men, under the command of General Hurlbut, including Grierson's 2,200 cavalrymen.

3. Here we have a Southern force made up principally of Tennesseans facing a Union force also composed of natives of that state. Such units usually felt bitter animosity toward each other, especially the Confederates who disdainfully referred to the Tennessee Federal troops as "Tories" or "Homemade Yankees." These Union loyalists were often deserters from the Confederate army who were not eager to fight for either side.

4. On the 26th of March, Captain H. A. Tyler, with his company and two other detachments of Rebels, was sent in advance to dash into Paducah along several separate roads to drive the enemy into the fort and their gunboats. This fort was a strong earthwork situated in the western part of the town near the Tennessee River. It was surrounded by a deep ditch, in front of which fallen timber had been formed into an abatis. It was garrisoned by 665 men who were commanded by a resolute officer, Colonel S. G. Hicks of the Fortieth Illinois infantry. Tyler's troops were followed by other detachments; and using the houses for protection, they moved in close to open a brisk fire on the enemy. After an hour of this, Forrest sent in a demand for surrender, worded almost identically with others he had used, and ended with, "If you surrender you shall be treated as prisoners of war, but if I have to storm your works you may expect no quarter." Colonel Hicks would not give up without a fight. Forrest had no intention of storming such a strong position, wanting only to hold the men in the fort and on the gunboats while he removed all supplies and horses he could obtain in the city. His casualties had been light until one of his brigade commanders, A. P. Thompson, decided on his own to storm the redoubt. This charge brought a terrific volley from the fort, and a number of the Confederates were killed or wounded before they retreated. Among those killed was Colonel Thompson.

In his official report Forrest said: "I drove the enemy to the gunboats and the fort, and held the town for ten hours; captured many stores and horses; burned sixty bales of cotton, one steamer, and a dry-dock, bringing out fifty prisoners. My loss, as far as known, is twenty-five killed and wounded, among them Colonel A. P. Thompson."

5. Forrest briefly mentioned this incredible encounter in a report dated April 4, 1864, but the details came primarily from Lieutenant Colonel Crews. They are confirmed to some extent by Federal Major General Stephan A. Hurlbut's testimony before the Congressional sub-committee investigating what took place at Fort Pillow. Hurlbut stated, in part: "Forrest moved up and crossed the line of the Charleston and Memphis Railroad to Jackson, Tennessee, and occupied it. General Grierson was directed to go out with his cavalry, feel him, attack him, and cripple him as much as possible. He went out, and reported that he was a little too strong for him, and he could not touch him."

6. Colonel Hurst was one of the "Homemade Yankees" who was accused of many atrocities against Tennesseans loyal to the South. General William Sooy Smith, the chief of cavalry of the military division of Mississippi, no later than January 17, 1864, had in writing to General Grant said: "We have given Colonel Hurst a roving commission with his regiment (the Sixth Tennessee Union cavalry), and directed him to 'grub up' west Tennessee. I think he will reduce the district to order." "Grub up" he did, so much so that the Federal authorities forced his command to repay a very considerable sum of money extorted from civilians. Among other crimes attributed to him were: killed Lieutenant Joseph Stewart and Privates John Wilson and Samuel Osborn, of Newsom's regiment (Forrest's cavalry) after they were taken prisoner; shot to death and forbade sepulcher to Private Martin of Wilson's regiment (Forrest's cavalry) after Martin's capture; put to death by torture Lieutenant Willis Dodds of Newsom's regiment after capturing him at the residence of his father in Henderson County, Tennessee; shot to death Private Alexander Vale of Newsom's regiment after capturing him in Madison County, Tennessee.

7. Buford arrived in the neighborhood of Columbus on the 12th of April, the same day Fort Pillow fell. He sent Captain Tyler with a picked detachment of about 150 men to make a demonstration on Columbus, while he moved on Paducah with his main force. General Buford had learned from one of his scouts that a number of mules and horses were at the latter place, and these became his principal objective. He arrived at Paducah on the morning of the 14th and advanced with a great show of force, driving the Federals again to the gunboats and fort, and held them there until he gathered up the horses, 150 fine animals.

As part of his strategy, as soon as the pickets had been driven in, he sent a note under a flag of truce to the Federal commander, to which Forrest's name was signed, demanding the surrender of the garrison and threatening to give no quarter if compelled to carry the place by assault. Like Forrest, he had no intention of attacking the stronghold and withdrew as soon as he had completed his mission.

Meanwhile, Captain Tyler was carrying on a similar game of bluff with the commander of the post at Columbus. Arriving in sight of the place, he marched his men across an open space on a hill in full view of the garrison, repeating the circuit several times and changing the position of the horses in order to create the impression that he had a large number of men with him. He also sent in a note under a flag of truce, signing General Buford's name to it, demanding surrender. It was almost identical with the one Buford had sent to Colonel Hicks at Paducah and to other notes which Forrest had himself dictated:

"HEADQUARTERS CONFEDERATE FORCES
"Before Columbus Kentucky, April 13, 1864.
"The Commanding Officer, United States Forces, Columbus, Kentucky.

"Fully capable of taking Columbus and its garrison by force, I desire to avoid the shedding of blood, and therefore demand the unconditional surrender of the forces under your command. Should you surrender, the negroes now in arms will be returned to their masters. Should I, however, be compelled to take the place, no quarter will be shown to the negro troops whatsoever; the white troops will be treated as prisoners of war.

"I am sir, yours,
"A. BUFORD, Brigadier General."

Although the Federal commander at Columbus thought he was faced by Buford's entire brigade, made up mostly of mounted infantry, he replied, "Surrender is out of the question."

Captain Tyler rattled his sword for a while and then joined Buford in his withdrawal to the south.

8. I have gone into detail as to the construction and layout of Fort Pillow so that the reader can better understand the events which follow.

9. Although Forrest officially gave the capture of horses and supplies as his reason for moving against Fort Pillow, Jordan and Pryor in *The Campaigns of Lieutenant General Forrest and of Forrest's Cavalry* and Mathes in *General Forrest* both give a further reason which may have been the primary one. These writers claimed that Forrest moved against

the fort at the request of residents in the area loyal to the South and of some of his officers and men, because small detachments of both white and black troops from Fort Pillow in foraging raids had subjected defenseless women and children and old men to "robbery, insult, and greatest humiliation." It was the desire to relieve the Southern sympathizers from this abuse and persecution that induced Forrest to attack the fort as much as the attraction of the needed horses and supplies.

10. This account of the three vessels, embellished with dialogue, is taken from the testimony of General Shepley before the Congressional sub-committee investigating the Fort Pillow affair.

11. Major Booth had been killed earlier that morning, but Major Bradford was able to conceal this from the enemy by signing Booth's name to the response.

12. Several of Forrest's officers, men of reputation and standing, stated that there were in the fort open vessels of whiskey to which cups were attached. Perhaps Major Bradford felt that liquor would bolster the courage of his troops.

13. Major General Hurlbut testified before the Congressional sub-committee: "It is unquestionably true that the colored troops fought desperately and nearly all of them are now killed or wounded."

14. I have not used Forrest's normal vocabulary in this instruction because it is a quotation from *Official Records*.

15. There is no evidence whatsoever that such a conversation between Generals Forrest and Chalmers took place. The latter was the kind of man who would not have let the men who killed Major Bradford go free, but there is no official record of their having been brought to trial for the unwarrantable murder. The only person who could have overruled any action by Chalmers would have been General Forrest. Also, the meeting between Major Bradford and Forrest is pure fiction, as there is no record of any such protest by the commander of the Federal fort.

On April 18, a sub-committee was appointed by the United States Congressional Committee on The Conduct of The War to take "testimony in regard to the massacre at Fort Pillow." They left Washington the following morning to carry out their assignment. They went beyond their instructions, and took testimony in reference to the operations of Forrest and his command immediately preceding and subsequent to the events at Fort Pillow. The committee reported in substance:

"1. That Forrest, in violation of the rules governing civilized warfare, had taken advantage of the existence of a truce to place a portion of his command in a position favorable for assault, which position he could not have obtained but for the prevalence of the truce.''

''2. That after the fort had been carried by storm, an indiscriminate slaughter, which spared 'neither age nor sex, white nor black, soldier nor civilian,' was carried on.

''3. That after the fighting had ceased, several of the wounded of the garrison were intentionally burned to death in the barracks and tents which were destroyed by fire.

''4. That the 'rebels buried some of the living with the dead.''''

The report by this sub-committee created a furor in the North, and Forrest was branded as a bloody, ruthless killer. The people in the South defended their popular cavalry leader, and the incident further increased the hatred and ill feeling between the peoples of the two nations. John Allen Wyeth went to great pains to refute the findings of the sub-committee. I shall not go into detail as to how he reached his conclusions; however, I shall give a brief resume of them, much of which is based upon the testimony of responsible Confederate officers, official reports, and reliable witnesses before the sub-committee:

1. The only troops moved during the flag of truce were those placed in the rifle pits at the north and south ends of the fort, and this was done to prevent the landing of reinforcements from the vessels carrying Federal troops.

2. There were no women and children in the main fort at the time of the assault; they had all been moved by barges to a place of safety. There was no indiscriminate slaughter after the fort was carried by storm since there was no formal surrender, the flag of the United States was still flying over the fort, and most of the garrison, especially the negroes, continued to fight or attempted to escape. The large number of survivors out of the force of 557, 226 taken prisoner and about 100 wounded and others taken aboard the *Silver Cloud*, attest to the fact that there was no wholesale slaughter of troops who surrendered.

3. The burning of the buildings and tents did not take place until the day after the assault. Some of the wounded testified before the sub-committee that they were moved out of the buildings before they were set afire. It is possible that there may have been some dead bodies in the buildings which were overlooked, for both the defenders and attackers had used them for cover the previous day.

4. The dead Yankees were buried by details made up of the prisoners who were under the direction of their own officers. If any Federals were buried alive, it was done by their comrades in arms.

In view of the animosity existing between the Rebel soldiers and the negro troops and between the two factions of Tennesseans, there had to be instances where Federals who tried to surrender were unwarrantably shot. This usually happens when a defended position is taken; in fact, some military commanders have put all defenders to the sword. A prime example of wanton killing, and this against civilians, is shown in the communication from General Sherman to one of his subordinates: "Cannot you send over about Fairmouth and Adairsville, burn ten or twelve houses of known Secessionists, kill a few at random, and let them know it will be repeated every time a train is fired upon from Resaca to Kingston."

The fact that so many of the defenders survived is a credit to the Confederate officers for stopping the carnage within the unsurrendered fort before it was complete; for once the Rebels had gained the inside and top of the parapet, the badly outnumbered defenders were massed together to make easy targets for them. So were those who tried to escape down the bluff and in the river.

Chapter XVIII

1. In an official report, Washburne stated: "The number of troops deemed necessary by General Sherman was six thousand, but I sent eight thousand. Everything was in complete order, and the force consisted of some of our best troops. I saw to it personally that they lacked nothing to insure a successful campaign."

2. Later, in referring to this period of the battle General Sturgis said: "I now endeavored to get hold of the colored brigade which formed the guard of the wagon-train. While traversing the short distance to where the head of that brigade should be found, the main line began to give way at various points. Order soon gave way to confusion, and confusion to panic...The army drifted towards the rear and was beyond control. The road became crowded and jammed with troops, wagons, and artillery sank into the deep mud and became inextricable. No power could check the panic-stricken mass as it swept towards the rear."

3. Few performances during the war can equal that of Morton and his artillerymen. They travelled with their guns eighteen miles, the last eight at an attempted gallop, on wet, muddy roads that were almost impassable, to reach the battlefield. Once on the scene, they stood to their work constantly during this hot, humid day, much of the time pushing their guns forward by hand along roads on which General Sturgis said his artillery, "sank into the deep mud and became

inextricable.'' Suffering intensely from thirst, they drank the blackened powder-stained water from the sponge-buckets which were being used to clean and cool the guns rather than send one needed man away to fetch water. Some of the wounded even refused to go to the rear. James Moran, a mere lad, who was badly wounded, when told by Captain Morton to go to the hospital, replied, "Captain, I don't want to go; I can stand it until we run 'em away.''

4. Captain James Dinkins in *Personal Recollections and Experiences in the Confederate Army by an Old Johnnie* relates an amusing story about General Sturgis. On his way to Brice's Cross Roads, the Federal general spent the night in a home near Salem, and he stated to the lady of the house that he was after Forrest and that, if the Confederate general would stand up and give him the chance, he would bring Forrest back as a prisoner. The lady replied, "Look out, he may send you back running.'' The general laughed and said, "No danger, and do not be surprised if I stop on my return with Forrest as a prisoner.''

The news of the Union defeat and retreat reached Salem before Sturgis did, and the lady was waiting at the gate to see if he had Forrest. When he had left Salem, his uniform was bright and new; but the general returned covered with mud. Both he and his horse were exhausted and presented the appearance of defeat and disaster. The lady facetiously asked, "General, did you find Forrest?''

"No,'' Sturgis replied, "but he found me!''

5. When the final reports came in, Dr. J. B. Cowan listed 493 Confederates killed and wounded. Casualties in Rucker's brigade were twenty-three percent, and in Lyon's command they were over twenty percent. These two commands had taken the brunt of the fighting. Forrest's men captured 250 wagons and ambulances containing all of the enemy's baggage and supplies, seventeen pieces of artillery, 5,000 stands of modern small arms, and 500,000 rounds of small-arm ammunition.

The detailed reports of Sturgis' command show his loss to have been heavy. Colonel Hoge reported 748 killed, wounded, and missing out of 1,674. Of the 926 who escaped, only 267 had not thrown away their guns. Wilkins' regimental commanders reported 1,003 lost in the second brigade (the Ninth Minnesota lost 287 out of 665). Bouton's colored regiments lost 528 out of a total of 1,200; Waring's cavalry brigade lost 207; and Winslow's cavalry brigade lost 126. Federal losses totaled 2,612.

With a force of about 4,000 Forrest had overwhelmingly defeated an enemy numbering 8,000 men well equipped with modern weapons and numerically superior artillery. In his official report Sturgis stated: ''I need hardly add that it was with feelings of the most profound pain and regret that I found myself called upon to record a defeat and the loss and suffering incident to a reverse. Yet there is some consolation in knowing that the army fought nobly while it did fight, and only yielded to overwhelming numbers. The strength of the enemy is estimated at twenty thousand men.'' He adds, ''A very intelligent sergeant who was captured says that the enemy had actually engaged 12,000 men, and had two divisions of infantry in reserve.''

The Yankee defeat caused considerable anxiety in the headquarters of General Washburne in Memphis, General Grant in Virginia, and General Sherman in Georgia, and also in the Federal capitol. Stanton, the Secretary of War, on June 14 telegraphed General Sherman that he had received the report of battle between Sturgis and Forrest, ''in which our forces were defeated with great loss. Washburne estimates our loss at not less than three thousand. Forrest in pursuit.'' Sherman replied that he had just received the same news of the defeat of Sturgis, ''whose chief object was to hold Forrest there to keep him off our road. Of course it is to be deplored, but we must prepare for all contingencies. I have ordered A. J. Smith not to go to Mobile, but to go to Memphis and to defeat Forrest at all cost. Forrest has only cavalry; I cannot understand how he could defeat Sturgis with eight thousand men.'' On the 15th, Sherman adds to Stanton: ''I will have the matter of Sturgis critically examined, and if he should be at fault he shall have no mercy at my hands. I cannot but believe he had troops enough. I know I would have been willing to attempt the same task with that force; but Forrest is the devil, and I think he has got some of our troops under cower. I have two officers at Memphis who will fight all the time—A. J. Smith and Mower. The latter is a young brigadier of fine promise, and I commend him to your notice. I will order them to make up a force and go out to follow Forrest to the death, if it costs ten thousand lives and breaks the Treasury. There never will be peace in Tennessee until Forrest is dead!'' With an evident air of satisfaction, this bloody-minded warrior closed this dispatch by saying: ''We killed Bishop Polk yesterday and have made good progress to-day.'' (Lieutenant General Leonidas Polk had been sent with his small army from Mississippi to reinforce General Joseph E. Johnston, who was contesting Sherman's drive toward Atlanta. During a conference of Johnston's staff on June 14 near Marietta, Georgia, he was hit by a shell and killed instantly.)

On the 16th of June, Sherman advised Stanton that he would send as large a force as he could muster to get on Forrest's trail and harass him and the counties through which he passed. ''We must destroy him if possible.''

6. Forrest's first letter to General Washburne, dated June 14, 1864, read in part as follows:

''It has been reported to me that all your colored troops stationed in Memphis took, on their knees, in the presence of Major-General Hurlbut and other officers of your army, an oath to avenge Fort Pillow, and that they would show my troops no quarter. Again, I have it from indisputable authority, that the troops under Brigadier-General Sturgis, on their recent march from Memphis, publicly and in many places proclaimed that no quarter would be shown my men. As they were moved into action on the 10th, they were exhorted by their officers to remember Fort Pillow. The prisoners we have captured from that command, or a large majority of them, have voluntarily stated that they expected us to murder them, otherwise they would have surrendered in a body rather than taken to the bushes after being run down and exhausted. The recent battle of Tishomingo creek was far more bloody than it would have been but for the fact that your men evidently expected to be slaughtered when captured, and both sides acted as though neither felt safe in surrendering, even when further resistance was useless. The prisoners captured by us say they felt condemned by the announcements, etc. of their own commanders, and expected no quarter.

''In all my operations since it began, I have conducted the war on civilized principles, and desire still to do so; but it is due my command that they should know the position they occupy and the policy you intend to pursue. I therefore respectfully ask whether my men now in your hands are treated as other Confederate prisoners of war, also the course intended to be pursued in regard to those who may hereafter fall into your hands.

''I have in my possession quite a number of wounded officers and men of General Sturgis' command, all of whom have been treated as well as we were able to treat them, and are mostly in charge of a surgeon left at Ripley by General Sturgis to look after the wounded. Some of them are too severely wounded to be removed at present. I am willing to exchange them for any men of my command you have, and, as soon as able to be removed, will give them safe escort through our lines in charge of the surgeon left with them. I made such an arrangement once with Major-General Hurlbut, and am willing to renew it, provided it is desired, as it would be better than to subject them to the long and fatiguing trip necessary to a regular exchange at City Point, Va.

"I am, General, etc.

"N. B. Forrest,

"Major-General"

The communication was sent with a flag of truce by Lieutenant Colonel R. W. Pittman. It drew from General Washburne the following response:

"Headquarters District of West-Tennessee
"Memphis, Tennessee, June 19, 1864.

"Major-General N. B. Forrest, Commanding Confederate Forces:

"General: Your communication of the 14th instant received. The letter to Brigadier-General Buford will be forwarded to him.

"In regard to that part of your letter which relates to colored troops, I beg to say that I have already sent a communication on the same subject to the officers in command of the Confederate forces at Tupelo. Having understood that Major-General S. D. Lee was in command there, I directed my letter to him. A copy of it I inclose.

"You say in your letter that it has been reported to you 'that all the negro troops stationed in Memphis took an oath, on their knees, in the presence of Major-General Hurlbut and other officers of our army, to avenge Fort Pillow, and that they would show your troops no quarter.' I believe it is true that the colored troops did take such an oath, but not in the presence of General Hurlbut. From what I can learn, this act of theirs was not influenced by any white officer, but was the result of their own sense of what was due to themselves and their fellows who had been mercilessly slaughtered. I have no doubt that they went into the field, as you allege, in the full belief that they would be murdered in case they fell into your hands. The affair of Fort Pillow fully justifies that belief. I am not aware as to what they proclaimed on their late march, and it may be, as you say, that they declared that no quarter would be given to any of your men that might fall into their hands.

"Your declaration that you have conducted the war on all occasions on civilized principles can not be accepted; but I receive with satisfaction the intimation in your letter that the recent slaughter of colored troops at the battle of Tishomingo creek resulted rather from the desperation with which they fought than a predetermined intention to give them no quarter. You must have learned by this time that the attempt to intimidate the colored troops by indiscriminate slaughter has signally failed, and that, instead of a feeling of terror, you have aroused a spirit of courage and desperation that will not down at your bidding.

"I am left in doubt by your letter, as to the course you and the Confederate Government intend to pursue hereafter in regard to colored troops, and I beg you to advise me, with as little delay as possible, as to your intentions. If you intend to treat such of them as fall into your hands as prisoners of war, please so state. If you do not so intend, but contemplate either their slaughter or their return to slavery, please state *that*, so that we may have no misunderstanding hereafter. If the former is your intention, I shall receive the announcement with pleasure, and shall explain the fact to the colored troops at once, and desire that they recall the oath that they have taken. If the latter is the case, then let the oath stand, and upon those who have aroused this spirit by their atrocities, and upon the Government and people who sanction it, be the consequences.

"In regard to your inquiry relating to prisoners of your command in our hands, I state that they have always received the treatment which a great and humane government extends to its prisoners. What course will be pursued hereafter toward them must, of course, depend on circumstances that may arise. If your command, hereafter, do nothing which should properly exclude them from being treated as prisoners of war, they will be so treated.

"I thank you for your offer to exchange wounded officers and men in your hands. If you will send them in, I will exchange man for man, so far as I have the ability to do so.

"Before closing this letter, I wish to call your attention to one case of unparalleled outrage and murder, that has been brought to my notice, and in regard to which the evidence is overwhelming.

"Among the prisoners captured at Fort Pillow, was Major Bradford, who had charge of the Fort after the fall of Major Booth. After being taken a prisoner, he was started with other prisoners, in charge of Colonel Duckworth, for Jackson. At Brownsville they rested over night. The following morning, two companies were detailed by Colonel Duckworth to proceed to Jackson with the prisoners. After they had started, and proceeded a very short distance, five soldiers were recalled by Colonel Duckworth, and were conferred with by him. They then rejoined the column, and after proceeding about five miles from Brownsville, the column was halted, and Major Bradford taken about fifty yards from the roadside and deliberately shot by the five men who had been recalled by Colonel Duckworth, and his body left unburied upon the ground where he fell. He now lies buried near the spot, and, if you desire, you can easily satisfy yourself to the truth of what I assert.

"I beg leave to say to you, that this transaction hardly justifies your remark, that your operations have been conducted on civilized principles; and until you take some steps to bring the perpetrators of this outrage to justice, the world will not fail to believe that it has your sanction.

"I am, General, respectfully, your obedient servant,

"C. C. Washburne,

"Major-General."

With this response General Washburne furnished Forrest with a copy of the following letter which he had written to Major-General S. D. Lee:

"Headquarters District of West-Tennessee,

"Memphis, Tennessee, June 17, 1864.

"Major-General S. D. Lee, Commanding Confederate Forces, near Tupelo, Mississippi.

"General: When I heard that the forces of Brigadier-General Sturgis had been driven back, and a portion of them probably captured, I felt considerable solicitude for the fate of the two colored regiments that formed a part of the command, until I was informed that the Confederate forces were commanded by you. When I heard that, I became satisfied that no atrocities would be committed upon those troops, but that they would receive the treatment which humanity, as well as their gallant conduct, demanded. I regret to say, that the hope that I entertained has been dispelled by facts which have recently come to my knowledge.

"From statements that have been made to me by colored soldiers, who were eye-witnesses, it would seem that the massacre of Fort Pillow had been reproduced at the late affair at Brice's Cross-Roads. The details of the atrocities there committed I will not trouble you with. If true, and not disavowed, they must lead to consequences, hereafter, fearful to contemplate. It is best that we should now have a fair understanding upon the question of treatment of this class of soldiers.

"If it is contemplated by the Confederate Government to murder all colored troops that may by the chances of war fall into their hands, as was the case at Fort Pillow, it is but fair that it should be truly and openly avowed. Within the last six weeks, I have, on two occasions, sent colored troops into the field from this point. In the expectation that the Confederate Government would disavow the action of their commanding general at the Fort Pillow massacre, I have forborne to issue any instructions to the colored troops as the course they should pursue toward Confederate soldiers that might fall into their hands; but seeing no disavowal on part of the Confederate Government, but, on the contrary, laudations from the Southern press of the perpetrators of the massacre, I may safely presume that indiscriminate slaughter is to be the fate of colored troops falling in your hands. But I am not willing to leave a matter of such grave import, and involving consequences so fearful, to inference, and I have, therefore, thought it proper to address you this, believing that you would be able to indicate the policy that the Confederate Government intended to pursue hereafter in this question. If it is intended to raise the black flag against that unfortunate race, they will cheerfully accept the issue. Up to this time, no troops have fought more gallantly, and none have conducted themselves with greater propriety. They have fully vindicated their right (so long denied) to be treated as men. I hope that I have been misinformed in regard to the treatment they have received at the battle of Brice's Cross-Roads, and that the accounts received result rather from the excited imaginations of the fugitives, rather than from actual facts.

"For the government of the colored troops under my command, I would thank you to inform me, with as little delay as possible, if it is your intention, or the intention of the Confederate Government, to murder colored soldiers that may fall into your hands, or treat them as prisoners of war, and subject to be exchanged as other prisoners.

"I am, General, respectfully, etc.,
"C. C. Washburne,
"Major-General"

Washburne shows an extremely weak position in dealing with his negro troops; he writes as though he has no control over them. He as good as admits that he was aware of their oath of no quarter and that he took no steps to prevent their taking this course.

Forrest had moved his headquarters to Tupelo by the time General Washburne's letter of June 17, intended for Major General S. D. Lee, reached that place; and it was delivered to him. The anger he felt upon first learning of the negro troops having taken the oath in the presence of their officers was nothing compared with that brought on by this communication from Washburne. He immediately dictated his second letter to the Federal general:

"Headquarters Forrest's Cavalry, Tupelo,
"June 23, 1864.
"Major-General C. C. Washburne, Commanding U. S. Forces, Memphis:

"General: I have the honor to acknowledge the receipt (per flag of truce) of your letter of the 17th instant, addressed to Major-General S. D. Lee, or officer commanding Confederate forces near Tupelo. I have forwarded it to General Lee, with a copy of this letter.

"I regard your letter as discourteous to the commanding officer of this department, and grossly insulting to myself. You seek, by implied threats to intimidate him, and assume the privilege of denouncing me as a murderer, and as guilty of the wholesale slaughter of the garrison at Fort Pillow, and found your assertions upon the *ex parte* testimony of (your friends) the enemies of myself and country.

"I shall not enter into the discussion, therefore, of any of the questions involved, nor undertake any refutation of the charges made by you against myself. Nevertheless, as a matter of personal privilege alone, I unhesitatingly say, that they are unfounded, and unwarranted by the facts. But whether these charges are true or false, they, with the question you ask, as to whether negro troops, when captured, will be recognized and treated as prisoners of war, subject to exchange, etc., are matters which the Governments of the United States and the Confederate States are to decide and adjust, not their subordinate officers. I regard captured negroes as I do other captured property, and not as captured soldiers; but as to how regarded by my Government, and the disposition which has been, and will hereafter be made of them, I respectfully refer you, through the proper channel, to the authorities at Richmond.

"It is not the policy or the interest of the South to destroy the negro; on the contrary, to preserve and protect him; and all who have surrendered to us have received kind and humane treatment.

"Since the war began, I have captured many thousand Federal prisoners, and they, including the survivors of the 'Fort Pillow Massacre,' black and white, are living witnesses of the fact, that, with my knowledge or consent, or by my orders, not one of them has ever been insulted or maltreated in any way.

"You speak of your forbearance, in 'not giving to your negro troops instructions and orders, as to the course they should pursue in regard to Confederate soldiers that might fall into (your) their hands,' which clearly conveys to my mind two very distinct impressions. The first is, that, in not giving them instructions and orders, you have left the matter entirely to the discretion of the negroes as to how they should dispose of prisoners; second, an implied threat, to give such orders as will lead to 'consequences too fearful' for contemplation. In confirmation of the correctness of the first impression, (which your language now fully develops,) I refer you most respectfully to my letter from the battlefield of Tishomingo creek, and forwarded to you by flag of truce, on the 14th instant. As to the second impression, you seem disposed to take into your own hands the settlement which belongs to, and can only be settled by, your Government. But if you are prepared to take upon yourself the responsibility of inaugurating a system of warfare contrary to civilized usages, the onus, as well as the consequences, will be chargeable to yourself.

"Deprecating, as I should do, such a state of affairs; determined, as I am, not to be instrumental in bringing it about; feeling and knowing, as I do, that I have the approval of my Government, my people, and my own conscience, as to the past; and with the firm belief that I will be sustained by them in my future policy, it is left with you to determine what that policy shall be—whether in accordance with the laws of civilized nations, or in violation of them.

"Very respectfully, etc.,

"N. B. FORREST,

"Major-General."

The above communications are taken from *The Campaigns of Lieut. General Forrest and of Forrest's Cavalry* by Jordan and Pryor. They do not go further into this controversial matter, and I have not found other references to it or located subsequent correspondence between the commanders dealing with the subject. Forrest may have been too busy with military operations to go into it again; and Washburne must have realized, after Forrest's second letter, that he was treading on extremely dangerous ground. Even if his military superiors should take no action against him, which is unlikely, it is believed his civilian government would have been outraged over his not stopping, and apparently condoning, his negro troops initiating and continuing a war of "no quarter." Once started, something like this can spread rapidly and get out of hand. It can also seriously affect world opinion of a nation. Washburne was probably wise enough to discontinue further correspondence and to hope the matter would go away. He must have taken steps to halt the "no quarter" practice, for it does not seem to have surfaced again.

Chapter XIX

1. Quoted below is the address, written in the flowery language of that time (June 28, 1864):

"SOLDIERS,—After a long and laborious campaign, the major-general commanding deems it an appropriate occasion to address you a few words of recapitulation, acknowledgment, and congratulation.

About the 15th of February last the campaign which so gloriously terminated at Tishomingo Creek was inaugurated. Major-General Sherman, with a large and well appointed army, undertook to penetrate the central counties of Alabama and Mississippi. His object was avowedly to capture Selma and Mobile, and to desolate that productive region of country from which the granaries of a large section of the Confederacy were supplied. Generals Smith and Grierson had their duties assigned them, and were to act a conspicuous part in the work of spoliation and piracy. With a large co-operating cavalry force thoroughly armed and equipped, they were to descend through northern Mississippi, carrying fire and sword with them. On they came like a blighting sirocco. At West Point you met them. There you threw yourselves across the rich prairies, a living bulwark, to stay the desolating tide. Compared with the enemy, you were but few in numbers, but every man became a hero, for all seemed impressed with the importance of the momentous struggle. You proved yourselves equal to the expectations of the country. You met the proud and exultant enemy. The result is known to the world; you drove him howling back in ignominy and shame, broken and demoralized. Sherman's campaign was thus brought to an abrupt conclusion, and Mississippi and Alabama saved. The victory was a glorious one, and with heartfelt pride, the general commanding acknowledges your unexampled gallantry. This great work was accomplished by Colonel Bell's brigade, commanded by Colonel Barteau, Colonel McCulloch's and Colonel Forrest's brigades. But great as was this victory, it is not without its alloy. The laurel is closely entwined with the cypress, and the luster of a brilliant triumph is darkened by the blood with which it was purchased. It was here that Colonel Barksdale gave up his life, a willing sacrifice, upon the altar of his country. He fell in front of the battle, gallantly discharging his duty. He sleeps, but his name is imperishable. Here, too, fell the noble brother of the general commanding, Colonel Jeffrey E. Forrest. He was a brave and chivalrous spirit, ever foremost in the fight. He fell in the flower of his youth and usefulness, but his dying face was proudly turned upon the victorious field which his own valor had aided in winning. Peace to the ashes of these gallant young heroes.

"After a short repose you were called to a new theatre of action. By long and rapid marches, which you endured without murmur or complaint, you found yourselves upon the waters of the Ohio, sweeping the enemy before you wherever you met him, capturing hundreds of prisoners, valuable and needed stores in the quartermaster's and ordnance departments, while securing for yourselves a character of endurance, valor, and efficiency which might well excite the envy of the most famous legions in military history. At Fort Pillow you exhibited the same conspicuous gallantry. In the face of a murderous fire from two gunboats and six pieces of artillery on the fort, you stormed the works and either killed or captured the entire garrison, a motley herd of negroes, traitors, and Yankees. This noble work was accomplished by parts of Chalmers' and Buford's divisions, composed of Bell's and McCulloch's brigades, commanded by Brigadier-General Chalmers; and for his gallantry on this and other occasions General Chalmers deserves the enduring gratitude of his countrymen. For the exhibitions of high soldiery bearing on these fields you have earned from your country and its government the most grateful and well-deserved plaudits. Congress has voted you complimentary resolutions of thanks and tendered you a nation's homage.

"But the crowning glory of your great deeds has yet to be named. Tishomingo Creek is the brightest leaf in your chaplet of laurel. General Grierson, not satisfied with his test of your prowess, united with General Sturgis, at the head of one of the best-appointed forces ever equipped by the Yankee nation—complete in infantry, cavalry, artillery, and supply-trains. They came forth with threats of vengeance towards you and your commander for the bloody victory of Fort Pillow, made a massacre only by dastardly Yankee reporters. Again you responded bravely to your general's call. You met the enemy and defeated him. Victory was never more glorious, disaster never more crushing and signal. From a proud and defiant foe, enroute to the heart of your country, with declarations both by negro and white troops of 'no quarter to Forrest or his men,' he became an enemy beaten, defeated, routed, destroyed. You drove the boasted minions of despotism in confused flight from the battle-field. Seventeen guns, 250 wagons, 3000 stands of arms, 2000 prisoners, and killed and wounded 2000 more are the proud trophies which adorn your triumphant banners. The remainder is still wandering in the bushes and bottoms, forever lost to the enemy. There were not over three thousand of you who achieved this victory over ten thousand of the enemy. Had you never before raised an arm in your country's cause, this terrible overthrow of her brutal foe would entitle you to her deepest gratitude. Again your general expresses his pride and admiration of your gallantry and wonderful achievements. You stand before the world an unconquerable band of heroes. Whether dismounted, and fighting shoulder to shoulder like infantry veterans, or hurling your irresistible squadrons on the flying foe, you evince the same courageous bravery.

"Soldiers! amid your rejoicing do not forget the gallant dead upon these fields of glory. Many a noble comrade has fallen, a costly sacrifice to his country's independence. The most you can do is to cherish their memory and strive to make the future as glorious as you and they have made it in the past.

"To Brigadier-General Buford, commanding division, my obligations are especially due. His gallantry and activity on the field were ever conspicuous, and for the energy displayed in pursuing the enemy he deserves much of his government. He has abundant cause to be proud of his brigade commanders, Colonels Lyon and Bell who displayed great gallantry during the day. Colonel E. W. Rucker was prompt in the discharge of every duty. His brigade displayed conspicuous steadiness during the fight. Colonel W. A. Johnson, commanding brigade from General Roddey's command, merits notice for his coolness and bravery on this occasion, and for the valuable services rendered by his troops. Nor can the general commanding forget to mention the efficient aid rendered by the artillery, commanded by Captain John W. Morton. He moved rapidly over the roughest ground and was always in action at the right time, and his well-directed fire dealt destruction in the masses of the enemy. The general commanding also takes pleasure in noticing the intelligent alacrity with which Major C. W. Anderson, Captain W. H. Brand, and Lieutenants Otey, Donelson, Titus and Galloway of my staff conveyed orders to all parts of the field. They were ever near my person, and were prompt in the discharge of every duty. Soldiers! you have done much, but there is still work for you to do. By prompt obedience to orders and patient endurance you will be enabled to repeat these great achievements. The enemy is again preparing to break through the living wall erected by your noble bosoms and big hearts. In the name and recollections of ruined homes, desolated fields, and the bleaching bones of your martyred comrades, you are appealed to again. The smoke of your burning homesteads, the screams of your insulted women, and the cries of starving children will again nerve your strong arms with strength. Your fathers of '76 had much to fight for, but how little and unimportant was their cause compared with yours. They fought not against annihilation, but simply to be independent of a foreign yet a constitutional and free government. You are struggling against the most odious of all tyranny, for existence itself, for your property, your homes, your wives and children, against your own enslavement, against emancipation, confiscation, and subjugation, with all their attendant horrors.

"In conclusion, your commanding general congratulates you on the brilliant prospects which everywhere pervade our cause. The independence of the Confederate States is a fixed, accomplished, immutable fact. The ray of peace is glimmering like bright sunshine around the dark clouds. Be true to yourselves and your country a little while longer and you will soon be enabled to return to your desolate homes, there to collect together once more your scattered household goods.

"By order of Major-General N. B. Forrest.

"C. W. ANDERSON, Assistant Adjutant-General."

2. General Joseph E. Johnston said that on June 13 and July 16, 1864, he suggested to the President of the Confederacy directly, and on four occasions through General Bragg to Mr. Davis that "an adequate force under the most competent officer in America for such service, General N. B. Forrest, be sent to operate against Sherman's communications. I did so in the confidence that this cavalry would serve the Confederacy far better by insuring the defeat of a great invasion than repelling a mere raid." (Lieutenant General Joseph E. Wheeler, commander of Johnston's cavalry, claimed that he suggested to his commanding general that Forrest be brought in for this purpose; and, although senior to Forrest, he offered to relinquish command and serve under him.)

Another urging this was Joseph E. Brown of Georgia, one of the ablest governors during the Civil War. In a formal document addressed to President Davis he requested that Forrest be placed in command of all cavalry, with a special view of operating with the army of General Johnston. When this was refused, he sent the following telegram to Mr. Davis on June 5, 1864:

"I regret that you cannot grant my request. I am satisfied that Sherman's escape with his army would be impossible if ten thousand good cavalry under Forrest were thrown in his rear this side of Chattanooga, and his supplies cut off. The whole country expects this, although points of less importance should be for a time overrun in the destruction of Sherman's supplies. Destroy these, and Atlanta is not only safe, but the destruction of the army under Sherman opens Kentucky and Tennessee to us. Your information as to the relative strength of the armies in northern Georgia cannot be from reliable sources. If your mistake should result in the loss of Atlanta, and the capture of other strong points by the enemy in this State, the blow may be fatal to our cause, and remote posterity may have reason to mourn over the error."

President Davis was angered by Governor Brown's message, and he lost no time in showing his indignation at the Georgia governor by replying:

"Your telegram received. Your dicta cannot control the distribution of troops in different parts of the Confederate States. Most men in your position would not assume to decide on the value of the services to be rendered by troops in distant positions. I would be glad to know the source of your information as to what the whole country will expect and posterity will judge.''

In July 1864, General Howell Cobb, of Georgia, made a similar plea for Forrest's services in a letter addressed to Mr. James A. Seddon, the Confederate Secretary of War:

''Allow me to express to you an opinion that the defence of Atlanta, Georgia, and the certain defeat and destruction of Sherman's army are involved in some movement to be made by Forrest, if possible, on Sherman's lines of communication. Unless it is done, I see no end to the slow process of Sherman's advance through Georgia. If his communications were cut for ten days, his army would be destroyed. To effect such a result, could we not afford to uncover for a short time the country protected by Forrest?''

It is not understood how President Davis, a former military man who had once served as the United States Secretary of War, could have been so blind to the wisdom of these requests. I can only conjecture that he may have been reluctant to bring Forrest out of Mississippi and leave his home state unprotected against the desolation the Union forces could wreak upon it; or he may have been influenced in his decision by General Braxton Bragg, his military advisor, who bore a deep resentment toward Forrest for the verbal castigation and insults he had suffered from the cavalry leader.

3. It was Lieutenant Samuel Donelson, a member of Forrest's staff, who accompanied the general on this reconnaissance, and it is to him that we are indebted for the details of the ride.

4. One reason Forrest may have declined the offer to command the troops in the fight was his physical condition. It was not the best. For some time he had been badly plagued by boils, and on June 28th he had written General Lee from Tupelo, ''I am suffering from boils. If the enemy should move out, I desire you to take command of the forces. Our force is insufficient to meet this command. Can't you procure some assistance?''

5. Chalmers' division, composed of McCulloch's and Rucker's brigades, 2,300; Buford's division, made up of Bell's, Lyon's, and Mabry's brigades, 3,200; Roddy's division, composed of Patterson's and Johnson's brigades, 1,500; Beltzhoover's infantry and the dismounted troopers of Gholson's and Neely's brigades, 2,100; and 360 artillerists with the twenty guns.

6. The Confederates formed under the protection of the timber, nearly a mile distant from the Federals. Mabry's brigade made up the extreme left; touching his right was Bell's brigade. Both of these commands

were to the left, or north, of the road leading from Pontotoc to Tupelo. Crossland's brigade of Kentuckians came next; and to his right, and somewhat drawn back, was Roddy's division. Hudson's battery was assigned to move with Roddy, while the batteries of Morton and Rice were in line with Mabry and Bell. Thrall's guns were held in reserve with Chalmers near the center of the Confederate line where two brigades, McCulloch's and Rucker's, formed a reserve, being deployed about 400 yards behind Crossland. Still farther to the rear, a quarter of a mile, the 2,100 dismounted cavalry and infantry formed a second reserve of the Confederate line under General H. B. Lyon.

As the Confederates moved forward under protection of the timber in which they had been deployed, General Lee tried to draw the enemy out of their entrenchments and induce them to assume the offensive. At the edge of the clearing the Rebels halted, and they opened a brisk fire at long range. In this preliminary action artillery on both sides took an active part. Fully an hour was spent in this attempt to draw the Federal commander from his stronghold with no effect other than to bring his attention to the Confederate right, where Roddy, back in the timber, a mile away, was deploying his division. Taking the movement of these troops as a threat to his left, General Smith hurried reinforcements to that quarter.

By now it was eight o'clock, and the heat of the sun in a cloudless sky was intense. For thirty days the rainfall in this section had been so little that the earth was parched. The highways were filled with dust, and the wet-weather streams and branches were dry. Water was so scarce that both armies found it difficult to fill their canteens. The Confederates were facing directly east toward the blazing sun, giving the enemy a decided advantage with the light at their backs. Lee told Forrest that it was now time for him to go to his portion of the field for the attack, and the two generals synchronized their watches. Forrest left, and at the appointed time, Lee ordered his left wing to advance; but he had failed to allow sufficient time for Forrest to get to his portion of the field and ready the troops under him for the attack.

General Lee had a good plan for the assault, once it had been decided to make the desperate attempt. The left and right wings were to move together, but the right was not ready. The eagerness of the Confederates to charge threw the attack further out of sync.

Crossland, in the center, ordered his men to move surely and steadily, but it was impossible to restrain the ardor of the men. Believing that they were strongly supported on the left and right, the men charged forward screaming the Rebel yell across the open area, exposed the whole time to a most terrific fire of artillery and small arms. Without any protection whatsoever, they ran forward, swept by two full batteries discharging grape and canister. Not seven hundred strong, they pressed up within a hundred yards of the Federal breastworks; and then from their place of safety, with guns at rest, fully 4,000 rifles of the Union infantry opened upon this forlorn group with a murderous volley. They fell by the scores, and for a moment the line staggered as if it were about to yield. Realizing that retreat would be more dangerous than advancing, Crossland and Faulkner both mounted, rode out in front of their men, shouting "Forward, men! Forward!"

The men quickly rallied and pressed on toward the enemy. Within a few yards of the foe's breastworks, Faulkner's horse went down; and he, twice wounded, was left on the field. About ten men penetrated the enemy stronghold, and these were quickly killed or taken prisoner. At this critical time, the Federals to the right of the assaulting line rushed forward from their position; and from the flank, they poured an enfilading fire on the unfortunate Kentuckians. Flesh and blood could not stand such a withering storm of lead, and those who had not fallen broke for the shelter of the wood from which they had launched their attack. They were aided in this retreat by Rice's and Thrall's batteries. Rice's battery had moved forward with them in the advance, and Thrall's battery was moved up to support Rice during the withdrawal.

Seeing the desperate situation of Crossland's brigade, Buford hurried forward Mabry and Bell to strike the right of the Union position in order to divert a portion of the fire which was being concentrated upon the Kentuckians. Mabry's command reached the open area a hundred yards in front of Bell's Tennesseans, who had not yet cleared the timber. In the emergency created by Crossland's precarious situation, Mabry did not wait for alignment with Bell but charged forward with great daring, only to meet a fate scarcely less tragic than that of Crossland's brigade. In face of a furious cannonade his brigade advanced steadily; and within 300 yards of the enemy works, a terrific fire of small arms was opened upon them. Mabry immediately ordered a charge, but the heat was so intense and the distance so great that some of his officers and men fell fainting along the line. The fire of the enemy artillery and small arms was very effective; and many were killed and wounded, leaving his line almost as thin as a line of skirmishers. When they reached within sixty yards of the enemy's works, Mabry knew that his line was too much weakened to drive their foe, so he halted and directed his command to take cover in a hollow behind a low fence in front of them.

Bell's brigade rushed forward into the breach between Mabry's halted brigade and the retreating Kentuckians of Crossland's command.

Despite the concentration of fire against them, they did not relinquish their effort until the surviving remnant of Mabry's Mississippians had withdrawn under their protection. The Tennesseans paid dearly for their valor—Colonels R. M. Russell, C. R. Barteau, A. N. Wilson, J. F. Newsom, Lieutenant Colonel D. H. Wisdom, and Major W. T. Parham—in fact, the commander of every regiment—were shot down.

McCulloch's brigade was thrown forward to relieve Crossland; but fortunately did not advance farther, for General Lee halted the attack.

The Confederate artillery did its part in this assault. Morton's old battery, under the command of Lieutenant Sale, moved forward in the open behind Mabry and Bell to within 400 yards of the enemy works, throwing its shot and shell with deadly accuracy. It drew the fire of the Illinois and Indiana batteries, so concentrated that five of seven gunners and six of eight horses of one piece alone were disabled. Sergeant Brown, who commanded the piece, although wounded three times, refused to quit his gun; and when the Confederates retired from the field, the piece was rolled away by hand. Another gun had a wheel shattered, but it was also dragged away.

Where was Forrest, who commanded the Confederate right, while this was going on? The missing Confederate general had a mile to travel before reaching Roddy, whose troops were much farther withdrawn than the other Confederates. After giving Roddy the necessary orders to move his command up for the assault, Forrest went rapidly forward to locate a position for Roddy's troops to take. When he came to the clearing, he saw how Crossland's brigade, in its rashly precipitated charge, had been cut up by the deadly fire the Federals were able to concentrate on him. By the time Roddy's command got up, Forrest had seen the futile assaults being made by Mabry and Bell. He knew that Roddy's troops would receive the same treatment in what would now be a piecemeal attack. Unwilling to sacrifice his men in an unprofitable slaughter, he did not push forward with them, saying to Roddy, "Buford's been bad cut up. Withdraw your men to their hosses; an' move to the left behind McCulloch, an' git ready to repel a counterattack. If the enemy's ever gonna make one, now's the time."

The account of this battle is a composite of Wyeth's and that of Jordan and Pryor.

7. General Smith gave as his reason for withdrawing: "My troops were so exhausted with the heat, fatigue, and short rations that it was not possible to press them farther. Sixty prisoners were captured unwounded. During the afternoon [the 14th] the enemy attempted to attack our rear from the east side of Tupelo, and were repulsed [Roddy's demonstration, ordered by Forrest]. At sundown, as they were making

no demonstration whatever, I directed the main bodies of my command to fall back about six hundred yards toward the wagons. AT 11 P.M. the enemy attempted a night attack, drove in the skirmishers, but were promptly met and repulsed [the attack by Forrest with Rucker's brigade]. On the morning of the 15th…it became a matter of necessity to return. I am sorry to say that for the lack of transportation, and the character of their wounds, I was obliged to leave about forty of the worst wounded of my command at Tupelo. I sent out one brigade of cavalry on the Pontotoc road to bring off a gun of the enemy which had been disabled the day before, which they did after some slight skirmishing. Being now nearly noon, and no demonstration from the enemy, I directed Colonel Moore, commanding the third division, to withdraw his line and take the advance and proceed on the Ellistown road [a north-northwesterly direction], moving very slowly, the train to follow with sick and wounded, General Mower and the remainder of the cavalry covering the withdrawal. On reaching Old Town Creek we encamped for the night.'' In his official report, Smith says, ''much of the bread was spoiled when drawn from the commissary depot, and there was on hand but one day's rations left…Our ammunition was issued, and we had remaining only about one hundred rounds per gun; it therefore became a matter of necessity to return.''

The reasons General Smith gives for abandoning the mission of his expedition do not appear plausible. He left his base at LaGrange, Tennessee, on the 5th of July, supposedly well supplied and equipped, for an extended campaign with its destination the prairie country of Mississippi. It is not understood how he could have just one day's rations left only ten days later and also be short of ammunition. He still had on hand 100 rounds for each of his twenty-four guns after the battle at Harrisburg had been fought. In the prairie country to the south, wheat and barley had been harvested and were in plentiful supply; and the fields were filled with ripe and ripening corn. Wyeth is of the opinion that Smith knew he could not stay where he was; and after seeing the reckless bravery and determination of the Confederates assaulting him on the 14th, he had no desire to attack them in their fortified positions.

The losses in the fight on the 13th, 14th, and 15th were the heaviest that Forrest's troops had ever encountered. Crossland had about 600 men engaged in the assault and lost 276 killed and wounded and thirty missing. The remnant of General Morgan's Kentucky cavalry, 80 in number, under the command of Captain Campbell, lost 5 killed, 19 wounded, and 2 missing. Mabry left one-third of his 750 men upon the field in killed and wounded. Bell's brigade lost 47 killed, 353 wounded, and none missing. The losses were amplified by the fact that so many high ranking officers were killed or wounded. In addition to those already mentioned, Colonel Isham Harrison, Lieutenant Colonel John B. Gage, Lieutenant Colonel Thomas M. Nelson, and Major Robert C. McKay, all of Bell's brigade, were killed. Many other field grade officers were either killed or wounded.

Forrest's command never fully recovered from the losses at Harrisburg. The war had been going on for almost three-and-a-half years, and the shortage of manpower made it impossible for him to bring his units back to their original strength; but his greatest loss was in the large number of capable and dedicated officers who were killed or so severely wounded that they could not return to active service.

8. C. W. Robertson of Somerville said (after the war), "The effect produced upon the men by the appearance of General Forrest is indescribable. They seemed wild with joy at seeing their great leader was still with them."

Chapter XX

1. Some of the buildings used by the hospital are still standing, and they serve today as the Administration Building and the Chapel of Marion Military Institute, which is located on the campus of old Howard College.

2. In appreciation for the return of his uniform and personal effects, General Washburne had Forrest's former tailor in Memphis make the Confederate general a gray uniform, which was sent to him under a flag of truce.

3. Washburne was critical of Smith's conduct, as he later said, "There were but two lines of possible retreat for the enemy, one via Holly Springs, and the other by way of Panola. The Tallahatchie was very high and impassable, except upon the bridge at Panola. Had my orders been obeyed, Forrest would have found himself penned up between the Coldwater and the Tallahatchie, and escape would have been impossible. That Forrest should have left our immediate front at Oxford and made this move on Memphis without being discovered is somewhat strange. Forrest made a forced march in advancing and retreating."

4. Sherman's low opinion of Forrest's judgment is unjustified, for the Confederate general accomplished his purpose. On the 23rd of August, General Maury reported that Forrest's movement in the rear of General Smith had caused him to pause in his advance into Mississippi; and on the following day Forrest received from his departmental commander

the following dispatch: "You have again saved Mississippi. Come and help Mobile. Fort Morgan, after a long and fierce struggle, was captured by the enemy yesterday. The attack on the city will be made at once, I expect. Will the retreat of the enemy from North Mississippi enable you to come with any of your force? We are very weak."

On the 29th of August, Forrest telegraphed to General Maury: "Enemy left Holly Springs at two o'clock yesterday, marching rapidly in the direction of Memphis and La Grange. [I found the latter town to have been spelled LaGrange in some references.] They say they are ordered to reinforce Sherman."

In addition, such consternation had been created in Memphis by the raid that a widespread feeling of panic was created in the city two days later by a rumor that Forrest was returning in force. Colonel Thurston, inspector general at Memphis, said in his report: "On the 23rd of August the whole town was stampeded at about ten o'clock in the morning by a report that Forrest had returned in force and was again in town. It was the most disgraceful affair I have ever seen, and proves that there is demoralization and want of confidence by the people in our army, and by our army in some of its officers. On this day there were no Confederate troops nearer than Forrest's rear, which was probably not less than twenty-five or thirty miles distant, and the alarm was caused by some of the troops firing off their guns, which had been loaded since Sunday."

Chapter XXI

1. This was an excellent decision by Davis, but it came much too late. Had it been done when urged by General Johnston, Governor Brown, and General Cobb, and had Forrest been given sufficient men to carry out the mission, it probably would have insured the defeat of Sherman's plans and may have resulted in the destruction of his army; but now with Atlanta in his hands and the fields of Georgia teeming with ripening corn, Sherman had other alternatives to feeding his army rather than depending upon his long supply lines through Kentucky, Tennessee, and Georgia.

2. About two miles from Athens, on the 23rd, Union pickets were encountered and driven into the village and then into the fort, from which the Federals opened upon the Confederates with two pieces of artillery. When the outposts were first fired on, the whistle of a train coming south from the direction of Nashville was heard; and Forrest ordered Colonel C. R. Barteau, with the Second Tennessee, aided by

Major Anderson, who had been put in charge of the escort, to move rapidly to the north side of town to break the track behind the train so that it could not escape and to cut the telegraph lines. In carrying out these orders, this detachment ran into and captured about 200 horses which were being run out of Athens to prevent their falling into Confederate hands.

General Tyree H. Bell was directed to move his brigade to the right and occupy the eastern portion of the suburbs. He met resistance but forced his way through and bivouacked for the night in the position designated by his commander. Colonel Kelley was ordered to move around with his brigade and occupy the southeastern portion of the town, his left touching the railroad and his right joining Bell. General Buford, with Lyon's brigade, was stationed on the west, his left on the Florence and Athens road. Colonel Jesse A. Forrest and Lieutenant Colonel White, who had successfully performed the duty assigned to them on the previous night and were marching from the direction of Decatur, halted and deployed between the Brown's Ferry road and the railroad. Colonel W. A. Johnson, with his brigade, occupied the street leading from the courthouse toward Florence. The artillery was brought up and unlimbered strategically. Captain Morton, now the chief of artillery, placed Hudson's battery, commanded by Lieutenant E. S. Walton, northeast of the fort; one section of his old battery, commanded by Lieutenant J. M. Mayson, on the west; and another section, under Lieutenant J. W. Brown, on the north. The investment was completed.

Forrest's descent upon Athens had been made so swiftly and with such secrecy that the first indication the Federal commander, Colonel Wallace Campbell of the 110th United States Colored infantry, had of the presence of the enemy was about three o'clock in the afternoon of the 23rd when a railroad worker reported that two or three hundred Confederates were tearing up the railroad about four miles south of town. He immediately ordered 100 men to be ready to leave on the train due to arrive from Nashville. About four o'clock he boarded the train with them and moved south approximately four miles, where he ran into Colonel Forrest's line of pickets. Knowing that the train would be stopped lower down the line, the Confederates let it pass and hastily obstructed the track in its rear.

Seeing the trap into which they had fallen, the Yankees abandoned the train and started back to Athens, taking refuge in a blockhouse in the suburbs of the town. Here they were engaged by Colonel Forrest's men for an hour and fifteen minutes, losing three men killed and four wounded before they escaped to the fort in Athens. It was then that Colonel Campbell first learned of Forrest's investment of the town with a force estimated to be 12,000 troops with nine pieces of artillery, and that the commissary buildings had already been captured. After trying to destroy all government property he could, Colonel Campbell ordered the Federal troops into the fort.

At seven o'clock in the morning of the 24th, Forrest ordered a general advance upon the fort, and his artillery opened upon it. All units moved forward except that of Kelley, who was directed to remain in position, throw out flankers, and hold in check reinforcements reported to be advancing at that time from Decatur. The Confederate general knew that he could not take the stronghold without serious loss and employed bluff which had worked so well for him in the past. Ordering a cease fire, he sent Major Strange and Randy in to the Federal commander, under a flag of truce, with the following message:

"HEADQUARTERS FORREST'S CAVALRY
"In the Field, September 24, 1864
"Officer Commanding U. S. Forces, Athens, Alabama:

"I demand an immediate and unconditional surrender of the entire force and all government stores and property at this post. I have a sufficient force to storm and take your works, and if I am forced to do so the responsibility of the consequences must rest with you. Should you, however, accept the terms, all white soldiers shall be treated as prisoners of war and the negroes returned to their masters. A reply is requested immediately.

"Respectfully,
"N.B. FORREST, Major-General, C.S. Army."

Colonel Campbell replied, "I have the honor to decline your demand this date."

Upon receipt of this response, Forrest sent Major Strange and Colonel Galloway in with another flag of truce, and Colonel Campbell sent Lieutenant Colonel J. A. Dewey and Acting Assistant Adjutant-General William T. Lewis to meet them. The Confederate officers informed their Union counterparts that General Forrest was determined to take the fort; and if he were compelled to storm it, he could not be responsible for the consequences. Colonel Campbell refused to comply with this demand, and Forrest sent in the following message:

"Colonel—I desire an interview with you outside of the fort, at any place you may designate, provided it meets with your views. My only object is to stop the effusion of blood that must follow the storming of the place.

"N. B. FORREST, Major-General."

Colonel Campbell, accompanied by Lieutenant Colonel J. A. Dewey, met with Forrest, who told the Federals that he was determined to take the fort; and if he were compelled to storm the works, it might result in the death of the entire garrison. He gave the Colonel an exaggerated indication of his strength, and offered the Colonel and one other officer the privilege of reviewing his troops. Colonel Campbell returned to the fort to discuss the matter with the commanders of various detachments in the stronghold, and it was decided that if Forrest had eight or ten thousand men it would be worse than murder to try to hold the works.

Accompanied by Captain B. M. Callender, Colonel Campbell rode around Forrest's entire line and satisfied himself that there were at least 10,000 men and nine pieces of artillery confronting him. He reached this surprising estimate of the Confederate strength, because Forrest had arranged his forces so that some were dismounted and appeared to be infantry. After the Colonel passed them, they were mounted and moved quickly to another position, where they were seen as cavalry. The Federal commander had been dillydallying, expecting reinforcements would be sent from Decatur. It was now eleven o'clock; and he did not believe they could reach him in time, so he surrendered the stronghold.

Under the terms of surrender, the officers were to be sent to Meridian or some other point; and after Forrest communicated with General Washburne, they would be paroled, not to act in opposition to the Confederate forces, until exchanged. They were also permitted to retain all personal property, including horses, sidearms, and clothing. The enlisted men were to be turned over to the Confederate government as prisoners of war, to be disposed of as its War Department saw fit.

The reinforcements hoped for by Colonel Campbell were closer than he thought, but they would have been no support for him. A detachment of the Eighteenth Michigan and 102nd Ohio infantry, under Lieutenant Colonel Elliot, had been hurried forward by train from Decatur. They had been intercepted by the Rebels under Colonels Kelley and Jesse Forrest and Lieutenant Colonel Logwood. The Union troops took a strong position behind a lot of cordwood stacked along the railroad track. They were attacked on the flank and driven from their breastwork by the Fifteenth Tennessee under Logwood and two companies of Forrest's regiment, losing several killed and eight taken as prisoners. The Federals made a detour through the woods in hope of reaching Athens, but Jesse Forrest moved rapidly with his remaining eight companies and placed himself across their path. A severe hand-to-hand encounter took place in which Colonel Forrest was badly wounded through the thigh, and several other Southerners were killed or seriously wounded. Reinforcements arrived while this contest was at its height, attacking the Federals in flank and rear; and the Yankees threw down their arms and surrendered.

There remained only two small blockhouses with their garrisons. One surrendered immediately, the other after an artillery shot penetrated the wall, killing two and wounding another defender.

3. At a considerable distance from the fort, but within reach of his long-range guns, Forrest saw an elevation that would command the strongest of the enemy positions, all of which were well designed to resist assault. He placed two heavy Parrot guns of Hudson's battery here, under the command of Lieutenant E. S. Walton, and disposed the remainder of his artillery on different sides of the Federal stockade. When the guns opened, Colonel Kelley's brigade, under their cover, rushed across an open area to a position where they could use their rifles to great effect. In this advance several of Kelley's troopers fell, and the Colonel's horse was killed under him; but his men were in position where their fire was so accurate that the enemy scarcely dared to raise their heads above their works. In a short time resistance from the fort ceased, and Forrest sent in, under a flag of truce, a demand for surrender. After a short parley, Colonel J. B. Minnis, the commanding officer, surrendered.

The Federal garrison suffered heavily; the colonel commanding, Lathrop, was killed early in the fight, and the dead lay thick along the works of the fort. The captures included 973 prisoners; 700 stands of small arms, two pieces of artillery; three ambulances; sixteen wagons; 300 cavalry horses and equipment; and medical, quartermaster's and commissary stores. The fort, blockhouses, and trestle were all burned, the last mentioned being seventy-two feet high and 300 feet long. The prisoners were turned over to Colonel Logwood, who started them toward the Tennessee River.

4. Colonel Kelley was sent with 500 men and a section of artillery from Hudson's battery, under the command of Lieutenant Walton, to take position at or near Eastport in order to prevent any advance from that direction. Colonel Kelley skillfully disposed and concealed his troops, masked his artillery in a strategic position, and waited. Three transports approached, convoyed by the gunboats *Undine* and *Key West*. The *Key West* went past the landing and seemed to be satisfied that no enemy was near, so Colonel Hoge landed his troops. When their horses were put ashore, Lieutenants Lytle and Boals started out to reconnoiter the area but immediately ran into Kelley's pickets. Walton's section of artillery opened with deadly accuracy upon the gunboats. The *Undine* was disabled and drifted down the river; the *Key West* followed her.

Colonel Hoge formed his command into line of battle; but when the gunboats departed down the river, he ordered his men back aboard the transports. Before they could all be embarked, a shell hit a caisson of the battery aboard the steamboat *Kenton*, exploding it and setting fire to the boat. Immediately after this, a caisson on the *Aurora* exploded, setting fire to her and rupturing her steam pipe. Colonel Hoge had gone aboard the *Kenton*; and despite his orders and entreaties, the transports backed out, parting their lines, leaving about two-thirds of the Federal soldiers on shore. These men retreated in good order downstream, along the edge of the river; and some of them were taken aboard the transports. Colonel Hoge decided to return to the large Federal base in Johnsonville, Tennessee, and reported a loss of 18 killed, 31 wounded, and 25 missing. He also reported that they had been fired upon by a battery believed to be composed of six guns and another battery of three pieces.

5. Forrest's letter to General Taylor read, in part, as follows:

"GENERAL,—I have been constantly in the field since 1861, and I have spent half the entire time in the saddle. I have never asked for a furlough for over ten days in which to rest and recruit, and except when wounded and unable to leave my bed have had no respite from duty. My strength is failing, and it is absolutely necessary that I should have some rest. I left a large estate in Mississippi, and have never given my private affairs a day's attention at any one time since the war began. Will make the trip to west Tennessee, and hope as soon thereafter as you can do so you will relieve me from duty for twenty or thirty days to rest and recruit...I have captured since I came into this department over thirty pieces of artillery, fitting up my command with four batteries (in all sixteen guns). They are now scattered, and I desire, if possible, to get all my command together, and with General Chalmers as senior officer feel that it would be safe to leave the command for a short time, which, in my present state of health, is absolutely necessary, and which you will confer a favor on me by granting as early as consistent with the good of the service."

6. Absence without leave, straggling, skulking, and actual desertion were a serious problem for both Union and Confederate armies. The men in them were undisciplined and independent, and many thought nothing of straying or leaving their commands. Despite all efforts, some harsh to the point of execution, to stop these practices, neither side was satisfactorily able to control them.

7. "Fetch" was a favored word of Forrest. Although he was more than willing for his staff to correct and properly phrase his messages, he would not let them change this word from his early years.

8. Private W. C. West, of Company G, Barteau's Second Tennessee,

was the man who offered his services and bravely made this bareback ride across the Tennessee.

9. In his report, Forrest stated that he captured and destroyed four gunboats, fourteen transports, twenty barges, twenty-six pieces of artillery, and $6,700,000 worth of property, and captured 150 prisoners. (The Federal estimate of the losses was $2,200,000.) His own losses during the entire expedition were two killed and nine wounded. The raid created a considerable stir among the Federal commanders, several of whom were sure that Forrest was preparing to move against Memphis, which was fortifying itself for the onslaught.

Chapter XXII

1. Sherman thought that his cavalry could be organized into three divisions, but Wilson convinced him that by calling in the cavalrymen who were scattered out on various details as escorts, at depots and camps, and many other duties, there were enough men for six or seven divisions. Asking only that Wilson fully mount and equip the division under General Kilpatrick, which would accompany him on his march to the sea, Sherman gave Wilson a free hand to organize and equip the remainder to help Thomas defeat and destroy Hood.

Wilson remained at Gaylesville, or nearby, until October 29, when he left for Nashville. He felt that Generals Kenner Garrard, George Stoneman, W. L. Elliot, and Benjamin H. Grierson, all now under his command, would find it awkward serving under him, since he had previously been their junior in rank. He arranged for their transfer to other service, thus obtaining complete control of the mounted troops of the military division.

2. Had Hood not been delayed at Gadsden, Alabama, for a month waiting for ammunition, supplies, and recruits, while Forrest was making a raid toward the Cumberland River, he could have advanced with his three corps of infantry and cavalry before Wilson had reorganized and fully mounted his troopers. Major General James H. Wilson was of the opinion that without a strong Union cavalry supporting his infantry and artillery, and before the arrival of reinforcements, Thomas would probably have been overthrown and Tennessee and Kentucky overrun.

3. It was Major Strange who struck the weapon, causing the bullet to miss Forrest.

4. Arriving on the 24th at Columbia, which is located on the south side of Duck River, Forrest found Schofield firmly entrenched there with his

entire force. He invested the place from the south and waited for Hood. The Confederate infantry came up on the 27th. Schofield withdrew most of his command across the Duck River to better defend against the Rebels' crossing it. Hood did not throw his main force against Columbia but, following Forrest's cavalry, crossed the river upstream from that town and began moving toward Spring Hill, intending to cut off Schofield from any further retreat toward Thomas in Nashville.

General Wilson had massed his cavalry on the turnpike between Lewisburg and Franklin to control this highway. The pike was east of the one Schofield was taking, and the two highways converged at Franklin; but before doing so, the one Schofield was on would go through Spring Hill, while the Lewisburg pike passed about six miles east of that town. Jackson was directed to move on the Lewisburg pike toward Franklin until he developed the enemy. It was not long until Armstrong, of Jackson's division, sent back word that he had struck the enemy cavalry in force. Forrest ordered him not to press them too vigorously but to hold them where they were until he could get on their flank and rear. Moving rapidly northward with Chalmers' division, the cavalry commander ran into Union pickets and heavy skirmishing took place. Buford, with Chalmers' division, advanced upon the enemy cavalry, but they were strongly positioned and stood their ground so well that he was forced to fall back. Forrest now dismounted his entire command; and making his usual flanking movement, dislodged the enemy.

Schofield was slow in leaving Columbia on the 29th, but he did send Brigadier General Stanley with a division northward to Spring Hill. Stanley reached that place in time to take a secure position from which he was able to ward off the assaults of Hood's advance guard who reached there about noon that day. Schofield did not leave Columbia with the remainder of his force until late that afternoon.

It was Hood's wise strategy to throw his army between Schofield and Stanley, but his carefully thought out plans went awry. He ordered Cheatham to place his corps across the turnpike between the two Federal forces; but for some reason, never fully explained, Cheatham failed to carry out the order, although it was repeated to him in writing later that night. The Confederates went into camp east of the turnpike; and while they slept, Schofield marched by them into Spring Hill, uniting his army, which continued to move toward Franklin and Nashville.

On the morning of the 30th, the entire cavalry was ordered to press the enemy on the Franklin pike. This was vigorously done but with little success, as the enemy had heavily guarded his flanks. The Federals retired to Winston Hill where they held Forrest at arm's length until the

Confederate infantry arrived. They then abandoned their position, taking refuge behind the fortifications in Franklin.

5. Some sources give Hood's losses to be above 6,000 men.

6. Colonel D. C. Kelley, with a detachment of 300 men and two pieces of artillery, reached the Cumberland River about twelve miles from Nashville on December 3 and captured two transports laden with horses and other United States government property. The horses were quickly unloaded; but before he succeeded in getting all of the cargo on shore, the enemy's gunboats, coming down from Nashville, recaptured the transports and a portion of the freight. Kelley brought off fifty-six prisoners and 197 horses and mules.

On the same day, December 3rd, Forrest, with Buford's division, succeeded in capturing stockade No. 2 with eighty prisoners. Several more were killed or wounded by the opening shots from one of Morton's batteries. While this attack was in progress, a train loaded with troops came in sight a considerable distance down the track; and before the engineer could reverse his engines and escape, it was crippled by the artillerists. The Confederates were unable to reach the train in time, and the Union troops aboard it stampeded and scattered in the woods. Almost the entire command escaped capture.

On December 4, Buford's division captured blockhouse No. 3 with thirty-two prisoners. After this, on orders from General Hood, Forrest, with Buford's and Jackson's divisions, proceeded toward Murfreesboro, where he set up pickets along the line of the Nashville and Chattanooga railroad and as far north as the Cumberland River.

General W. H. Jackson on December 5 captured near Lavergne a redoubt with its garrison of eighty men, two pieces of artillery, a number of wagons, and a considerable supply of stores. Another detachment of cavalry captured a blockhouse near Smyrna station, taking thirty-five prisoners.

While Hood stayed in front of Nashville, an interesting drama was taking place between General Grant and General Thomas. Although the latter was one of the most effective and dependable fighters of the Federal armies, General Grant, for some reason, did not seem to hold him in high regard. Grant, with as much justification for it as Sherman, had a deep-seated fear of Forrest and what he might do. On December 2, he said in a dispatch to Stanton, "It looks as if Forrest would flank around Thomas until Thomas is equal to him in cavalry." On the 5th he telegraphed the Union general in command in Nashville, "Is there any danger of Forrest moving down the Cumberland to where he can cross it? It seems to me while you should be getting up your cavalry as rapidly as possible to look after Forrest, Hood should be attacked where he is.

Time strengthens him in all probability as much as it does you." To the latter message, Thomas replied, "I have no doubt Forrest will attempt to cross the river, but I am in hopes the gunboats will be able to prevent him." Grant's principal anxieties were that Forrest would cross the Cumberland, get on Thomas' line of supply and force the latter to withdraw to Louisville, or that Hood would cross that river and move toward Ohio.

Thomas was well thought of by his men, who referred to him affectionately as "Ol' Pap," but because of the deliberateness with which he operated he was called "Slow Trot" by a few others. He was being far too deliberate for the impatient Grant, who wanted him to get out of Nashville and attend to Hood. Grant thought Thomas should have gone after the Confederate general following the latter's repulse at Franklin, but "Slow Trot" had his reasons for delay. He was waiting to be reinforced by General A. J. Smith with his Sixteenth Corps and other troops from Missouri. Also, he had been convinced by the new cavalry commander, J. H. Wilson, that unmounted cavalry is useless; and he wanted to get the cavalry on horses and fully equipped—he wanted them strong enough to cope with Forrest. Smith arrived with the reinforcements, and Wilson had 12,000 of his cavalry mounted; but a terrible storm of freezing rain, lasting for several days, struck the Nashville area, and Thomas did not feel it advantageous to fight in such weather. Grant, much perplexed by what he thought was foot dragging, and although not supported by the Secretary of War or the President, prepared three separate orders to relieve Thomas from command and for Schofield to replace him. In fact, he was in Washington, on his way to Nashville to take care of the matter personally, when the War Department received a message on December 15 from Nashville of Thomas' attack and victory. It was sent on to Grant at the Willard Hotel, where he was stopping for the night.

Grant read the message and said, "I guess we will not go to Nashville."

He immediately telegraphed Thomas: "I was just on my way to Nashville, but receiving a dispatch from Van Duzer, detailing your splendid success of today, I shall go no further."

Of the many Federal generals about whom I have read, George Henry Thomas has to be my favorite. In addition to his remarkable military accomplishments, his character appeals to me. Offered command of the Army of the Cumberland, to take General Buell's place, he refused because he felt that the strategy for the army had already been set; but when General Rosecrans was given the command, Thomas objected because he was senior to the new commanding general. Lincoln solved this by antedating Rosecrans' commission; and Thomas appeared to be satisfied with this obvious manipulation, serving the new army commander faithfully, to the point of saving his army from complete rout and annihilation at the battle south of Chattanooga, where he won the well-deserved appellation, "The Rock of Chickamauga." He refused President Johnson's offer of promotion to full general because he thought it was politically motivated; and he also declined to run for President of the United States, when urged to do so, not wishing to challenge his wartime comrade and former superior, General Grant.

7. I do not understand why Hood sent Forrest off to Murfreesborough when facing an army larger than his own in Nashville, much less ordering one of his infantry divisions to him.

8. Versions of the fight between Colonel Rucker and General Spalding vary with the narrator. According to General Wilson, Captain Joseph C. Boyer also became engaged with Rucker, and it was not clear whether Spalding or Boyer actually took Rucker's sword. It did, however, come into the possession of Spalding, who retained it for twenty-five years before returning the weapon to Rucker, who was then a prominent citizen and industrialist in Birmingham.

Rucker's arm had to be amputated, and he was treated with respect, kindness, and consideration by his captors. General Hatch gave up his bed, in a room he shared with General Wilson, to the Confederate cavalry leader, and slept on the floor, rising occasionally to give the prisoner a drink of water.

9. Grant was no longer worried about "Slow Trot" Thomas, but his mind was far from being at ease concerning Forrest. From in front of Petersburg, he wired Thomas: "The armies operating against Richmond have fired two hundred guns in honor of your great victory. In all your operations we hear nothing of Forrest. Great precautions should be taken to prevent his crossing the Cumberland or Tennessee below Eastport." On the 17th the rumor spread among the Federal commanders that Forrest had been killed at Murfreesborough. The source was General Rousseau, who reported that Forrest had been killed and fifteen hundred of his men captured at that pace.

10. It is not clear why Hood did not draw Forrest back toward him on the 15th when the attack began; why Forrest did not get word of the disaster until nightfall on the 16th; why the cavalry leader was ordered to fall back toward Duck River rather than come to the immediate support of the retreating army; and why Forrest, who sent Buford with his division directly to the Nashville and Columbia turnpike, did not go with that command rather than plod along with another unit which was

slowed by driving a herd of beef cattle. This was certainly out of character for him.

Once he joined up with Hood, Forrest was primarily responsible for saving the defeated army. General Thomas stated in his report: "Forrest and his cavalry, and such other detachments as had been sent off from his main army, joined Hood at Columbia. He had formed a powerful rear-guard, numbering about four thousand infantry and all his available cavalry. With the exception of this rear-guard, his army had become a disheartened and disorganized rabble of half-armed and barefooted men, who sought every opportunity to fall out by the wayside and desert their cause, to put an end to their suffering. The rear-guard, however, was undaunted and firm, and did its work bravely to the end."

11. Hood's army was broken and to a great extent demoralized. It never again was an important fighting force for the Confederate cause. In his official report, General George H. Thomas claimed: "We captured 13,189 prisoners, including seven general officers and nearly one thousand other officers of all grades, and seventy-two pieces of serviceable artillery. During the same period over two thousand deserters were received, to whom the oath was administered." Those who survived this destruction of an army and lived to fight another day did so only because of the determined and resolute fighting of Forrest's cavalry and the dedicated infantry who formed a part of the rear guard under the cavalry leader's artful command.

Chapter XXIII

1. These bands of cavalry, which were attached to no organization of the Confederate army, were in effect no more than guerrillas, living off the land and people and contributing little or nothing to the war effort. Some were led by officers who had been commissioned to raise a troop, but these officers had never made their units a part of the army. They were a sore point with Forrest, and this is only one of his several communications dealing with this subject.

2. These views of Forrest were expressed to Major Powhatan Ellis. He mentioned only General Lee's situation, and I have embellished upon that by bringing in Hood's defeat and Sherman's completion of his march to the sea.

3. At this bridge two men were brought in as deserters. They admitted that they had been in the service and were on the way to their homes in Kentucky. They had no passes or other papers to show why they were

leaving the army, and a drum-head court-martial was called. One of the men claimed to be too old for service, and the other claimed to be too young. They were both condemned and executed. Their bodies were exposed by the road in plain view of where the troops would pass, and upon a tree was nailed a sign in large letters which read: SHOT FOR DESERTION.

It was subsequently established that the statements made by the two men were true—one was too old and the other too young for service, and Forrest was criticized by some for these executions. In fairness to him, it must be recalled that neither of those executed had any document to show proper release from the army. Also he had been directed by General Hood to make an example of the first deserters caught, but these were probably not the first. His action here may have been justified by military law, but he was certainly bending that law in the following dispatch to General W. H. Jackson: "The lieutenant-general directs that you leave one commissioned officer with twenty men here for the purpose of guarding the three crossings—this bridge, and Carter's and Colter's ferries, one above and one below. They will remain here until day after to-morrow morning, when they will bury the two men who have been shot here at the bridge to-day, then follow on and report to their commands at Marion, Alabama, or wherever they may be. Should the officer left behind catch other deserters, he will take them to the bridge and execute them."

4. Croxton later turned again toward Tuscaloosa and on the morning of April 3 captured the town, which was garrisoned by a small number of home-guards or militia. He took the town with little or no opposition and destroyed all government property there, including the state university which housed the Alabama Military Academy. He was now completely isolated from Wilson and wandered about the area. On April 6, he unexpectedly collided with the command of General Wirt Adams, was worsted in the encounter, but escaped with the loss of two officers, thirty-two men, and two ambulances. He continued in his wanderings and arrived again at Elyton on the 19th, causing one of his waggish troopers to say, "He must have been allotted one of the horses Wilson had impressed from a circus—it could not get out of the habit of moving in a circle." Here he learned that General Wilson had captured Selma, had gone on to Montgomery, and was marching eastward. Croxton headed for Georgia. He did not rejoin his commander until May 20 at Macon.

As ineffective as Croxton may have appeared, he rendered a valuable service to Wilson. The delay Jackson encountered by attacking and driving Croxton off seems to have been sufficient to cause him to be unable to reach Centreville before the bridge over the Cahaba had been destroyed.

5. Major General James H. Wilson, in *Under the Old Flag*, states that Forrest arrived at a point nine miles beyond Centreville on March 30; but in comparing the time element with other events, there is no doubt that the March 31 date is correct.

6. The three messages are quoted:

"SIX MILES FROM MONTEVALLO, March 31, 1865, 6 P.M.
"Brigadier-General W. H. Jackson, Cavalry Division:
"GENERAL,—Since the despatch of 2 P.M. of this date, per Lieutenant Glass, the lieutenant-general commanding directs me to say that the enemy are moving right on down the railroad with their wagon-train and artillery. He directs that you follow down after them, taking the road behind them from Montevallo. He further directs me to say that he does not wish you to bring on a general engagement, as he thinks their force is much stronger than yours; and an engagement should be avoided unless you find the balance of our forces in supporting distance of you."

"CENTREVILLE, April 1, 1865, 2 A.M.
"GENERAL,—I opened the enclosed despatch from General Jackson, to ascertain his position, etc. Sent couriers last night at 11:30 to Chalmers and Mason. From reports received, and from this despatch, enemy's cavalry, or a portion of it have crossed the Cahawba, and General Jackson will attack them at daylight. I shall remain here for further orders and developments, and at daylight will take one side of the river or the other. Have sent to General Jackson to know the position of his artillery. If the couriers can be relied on, the enemy is between him and the battery. Have the dismounted men intrenched on this side (east) of the river, and if the enemy are as represented, will move the battery here, cross it over, and move on the nearest road to Selma, as directed. The courier can explain General Jackson's position and that of the battery. From his statement the battery is in rear of General Jackson, on Tuscaloosa road, and the enemy is between his force and his artillery. Have heard nothing of General Armstrong, but sent orders to General Chalmers to move to or between enemy and Selma. Will despatch you all information as soon as received.
"Respectfully, CHARLES W. ANDERSON, Aide-de-Camp."

"March 31, 1865, 8:45 P.M.
"James Hill, Sr.:
"MAJOR,—I find the enemy encamped on Huntsville and

Tuscaloosa road at White's, three miles from point where Huntsville road comes into Tuscaloosa road and six miles from this place. Their strength not yet ascertained. I am closing around them with the view of attacking, or, if they move to-night, will drive into them. I am placing a force between them and Tuscaloosa. Have also directed Colonel Cox, who is in charge of artillery, and train, some fifteen miles from here, that in case I do not gain their front and they advance on Tuscaloosa, to fall back before them, impeding their progress; to notify Colonel Hardcastle, commanding post, to have everything in readiness to meet them; and to tear up planks on the bridge and remove them, nothing preventing. All appears bright, and I expect success.

"Respectfully,
"W. H. JACKSON, Brigadier-General"

7. Wyeth states that Forrest moved to the attack with his escort and two companies, under the command of Captain H. A. Tyler, of Crossland's brigade. He probably was in error about this, as a detachment of 200 men from Armstrong's brigade had been with him and his escort before this fight. Crossland's brigade had been placed on the Confederate left.

8. It was Private Phil Dodd who spurred his horse to the general's rescue and shot the Federal soldier who was pressing Forrest so closely, thus enabling the general to draw his pistol and kill another one.

9. Officers in both the Federal and Confederate armies could resign their commissions and leave the army, and many did.

10. The number of Confederates killed and wounded at Selma was never reported, but it was probably less than that of the Federals, by General Wilson's admission. The Union general claimed to have captured 2,700 prisoners, numerous pieces of cannon of several types, and large quantities of ammunition and powder. The greater blow to the Confederacy was losing this important depot of manufacture and supply, one of their last. The arsenals, foundries, iron works, and ordnance works, occupying twenty acres along the river bank, were all destroyed by fire, as were the several powder factories.

Chapter XXIV

1. In the Federal official reports of this campaign it is stated: "Forrest, retreating from Selma, came across a party of Federals asleep in a neighboring field, and charged on them, and refusing to listen to their cries for surrender, killed or wounded the entire party, numbering twenty-five men."

In the *Life of General George H. Thomas*, it is stated, in referring to this incident, "Forrest fell upon the party with the ferocity of a wild Indian and killed every man of it."

Major General James H. Wilson also mentioned this fight in *Under the Old Flag*, stating: "On the way his escort fell upon an outlying detachment of the Fourth Cavalry at a farmhouse and killed the last one of them, including Lieutenant Roys in command. Such incidents as this were far too frequent with Forrest. He appears to have had a ruthless temper which impelled him upon every occasion where he had a clear advantage to push his success to a bloody end, and yet he always seemed not only to resent but to have a plausible excuse for the cruel excesses which were charged against him."

Wyeth went to a great deal of trouble to discredit the first two allegations. (The third was made after he published his biography of Forrest.) He obtained affidavits from a number of Confederate officers and doctors who were present at the affair attesting that Forrest himself was not present at the fight; that the Union Fourth Regulars, a veteran fighting unit, had put up strong resistance; and that no one was shot or maltreated after he surrendered.

The first of the three allegations was made soon after the action took place, while the other two were made many years later.

2. Ezra Jackson Patterson is the great grandfather of my friend, Carter Perkins, of Leesburg, Florida.

3. An incident similar to this occurred on the night of April 2 after Forrest and his escort escaped from Selma. Soon after reaching the Plantersville road, their attention was attracted by women's screams coming from a residence near the highway, and Forrest sent a detachment to investigate the disturbance. They surrounded the house; and several men in blue uniforms ran out trying to escape, but they were all killed or captured.

4. Forrest's declination to exchange prisoners does not make sense. General Grant had initiated the policy of not exchanging prisoners with the Confederates knowing that the enemy could not replace their men, while he could. I cannot fathom Forrest's missing the opportunity to regain his men at the time he was having such difficulty in recruiting replacements, unless he did not believe Wilson's offer to be a serious one. Neither does it appear reasonable that Wilson would be offering to exchange prisoners in violation of Federal policy.

5. I have read different versions of Forrest's reaction to the surrender and how he reached a decision on what his own course should be. This one is mine; the dialogue is mostly fictional, but the rationale by which his decision was reached is typical of the Confederate general.

ARKANSAS

MISSISSIPPI RIVER

OBION R.
S. FORK
DRESDEN
PARIS
KENTON
RUTHERFORD
McKENZIE
B/C SAND
McLEMORESVILLE
HUNTINGTON
FORKED DEER CR.
TRENTON
CLARKSBURG
PARKER'S CROSS ROADS
COAL CR.
HUMBOLDT
LAVINIA
SHARON'S FERRY
S. FORK
CARROL STATION
FORT PILLOW
LEXINGTON
BROWNSVILLE
JACKSON
JACKS CR.
HATCHIE R.
ESTENAULA
HENDERSON
SOMERVILLE
NEW CASTLE
BETHEL SPRINGS
RALEIGH
BOLIVAR
PITTSBURG LANDING
WOLF R.
SHILOH
MEMPHIS
MOSCOW
LICK CR.
COLLIERSVILLE
LA GRANGE
GRAND JUNCTION
MONTEREY
MEMPHIS & CHARLESTON
EASTPORT
MT. PLEASANT
SALEM
CORINTH
R.R.
WAT
HERNANDO
BURNSVILLE
CANE CREEK BR.
COLDWATER RIVER
COLDWATER
HOLLY SPRINGS
RIENZI
IUKA
CHEROKEE STA.
NICKAHALA CR.
RIPLEY
BOONEVILLE
STUBBS FARM
ROSSFORD
SENATOBIA
WYATT RIVER
NEW ALBANY
TISHIMINGO CREEK
COMO
TALLAHATCHIE RIVER
ABBEYVILLE
BRICE'S CROSS ROADS
BALDWIN
SARDIS
GUNTOWN
PANOLA
OXFORD
ELLISTOWN
PRAIRIE MOUND
PONTOTOC
HARRISBURG
TUPELO
FULTON
TALLABONCLA
IVEY'S HILL PLANTATION
VERONA
COFFEEVILLE
OKOLONA
OLD TOWN CREEK
MISSISSIPPI RIVER
HOUSTON
SARTOUSA CR.
PRAIRIE STA.
YALOBUSHA RIVER
GRENADA
YAZOO RIVER
NEW ORLEANS & MEMPHIS R.R.
WEST POINT
ELLIS' BRIDGE
COLUMBUS
STARKVILLE
ARTESIA
PICKENSVILL
MISSISSIPPI
MACON
MOBILE & OHIO R.R.
TOMBIGBEE RIVER
GAINESVILL
EUTA
LOUISIANA
CANTON
GAINESVILLE JUNCTION
DEMOPOLIS
HILLSBORO
VICKSBURG
ALABAMA & MISSISSIPPI R.R.
MERIDIAN